SEASONS OF LOVE

A BEATEN TRACK ANTHOLOGY

DEVEN BALSAM • NEPTUNE FLOWERS
OFELIA GRÄND • PAUL IASEVOLI • A.M. LEIBOWITZ
DEBBIE MCGOWAN • DAWN SISTER • BOB STONE
ALEXIS WOODS • A. ZUKOWSKI

Beaten Track
www.beatentrackpublishing.com

Seasons of Love

First published 2018 by Beaten Track Publishing

ISBN: 978 1 78645 232 0

Beaten Track Publishing,
Burscough. Lancashire.
www.beatentrackpublishing.com

ABOUT SEASONS OF LOVE

Love follows no rules. Like sun in winter and rain in summer, love can blossom in the most unexpected places. This richly diverse collection of stories proves that love is as universal and as varied as the seasons.

THE STORIES:

TOURIST SEASON

DEVEN BALSAM

Sometimes the darkness becomes too familiar. Sometimes, love lights the way out.

One of Zeus's own children has a favorite office, hidden deep beneath the streets of Asheville, NC. Hades' existence, while satisfying, is due for a surprise when his path converges with that of Korey, a gifted art student.

***

Genre: fantasy LGBT dark romance

Keywords: Asheville, greekgods, mythology, dark romance, queer, trans, gay

KOREY

THE SIGHT OF it reminded him of its scent, rain and wind, the split sky of darkness and blue. Bruised thunder burling and growling at its lover from across the contrail streaks, eggshell sunshine sweating its serpentine skin, a full-bellied, feathery snake preening above an unseasonably warm November landscape. The maples held their yellow coins in gnarled fingers. The oaks shivered as the death-sweet wind teased their vintage, book-paper leaves, trying to pry them loose like a banker pulls a deposit slip from a confused, old man.

Korey held his sketchbook with light fingers as he crossed Biltmore Avenue, where the 240 ramps rose and fell. He jogged a little faster when a green Mini came too close. The day was so beautiful that pedestrians had become invisible, and he was no exception.

The whimsical neighborhood of Montford reflected the patchwork sky. Shadows crept like wind-spooked cats across ribald facades. Korey passed green gingerbread, purple craftsman, petal-pink Tudor, all garish yet pleasing beneath the half-ink sky.

A crow balanced on a streetlamp wire, tipping forward and back, calling to its kin, *graw graw graw.* Its number and its signature. Crows numbered two and five quickly answered and joined three, and they all flapped away towards the blue side.

Then he felt the sadness come, sidelong grief clipping him like the green Mini almost had. He nearly dropped his sketchbook. He knew where to go now, where the day had tried to lead him. Down Cullowhee, right at the sign, up the inclining streets to greener, quieter hills.

He stopped to watch the shadows of the trees looming overhead. The clouds above raced before the rampant wind, yet the coal-hued arms of shadow upon the asphalt remained fixed.

Korey continued on, hurrying through the black iron gates of Riverside Cemetery.

***

"Hello, Bell. Hi, Wilson. Howdy, Stern."

Something about the interconnected winding paths that encircled the hills and gatherings of graves beneath the bold sun always soothed him. Sometimes he'd sit at the edge of a set of crumbling, stone steps to sketch one of the visitors to the cemetery. Across the lawn, a woman clutched white roses to her chest before gently setting them down before a weathered headstone.

Korey followed the swirling leaves away from her, satisfied with his sketch, and came to another favorite place. Beth Ha-Tephila, the Jewish part of the cemetery. Standing away from the majority of the graves, a line of tall conifers watched like wise elders. Their shadows, too, stretched towards him, as if they wanted to reach for him.

"It's a good day for it," said someone behind him. Korey slowly glanced around, fear thrilling him like the wind stirred the leaves.

"Didn't see you come in."

"I come and go."

Korey nodded, wishing the man would go, but then he really looked at him.

The man wore a soft, black overcoat. Cashmere? Perhaps. A gray button-down shirt beneath, the first two buttons opened to show a lean but muscular, beautiful neck. His long-fingered hands were clasped together. His trousers neatly pressed, stretched taut across strong thighs.

But his face, that was the most striking feature. Deep-brown skin. Warm, twinkling eyes framed by thick lashes. A finely tipped nose, crooked at the bridge, that broadened just before it reached his full, gently smiling lips. His dark beard, neatly trimmed, matched his hair—pure black but for a few specks of silver.

Korey realized he'd been staring at the man for well over any acceptable amount of—

"It's okay," said the stranger. "You're allowed to. And call me H. Capital *h* with a dot."

"I like to come here to be alone."

"And yet, you draw portraiture."

"Well, we're all alone together, I guess. The subjects and myself."

"I guess."

"Why do you come here?"

H. shrugged. "Days like this seem to draw me out of my cave. I like the energy. Do you mind if I walk with you a while?"

A question that should have made Korey uncomfortable, strangely, did not. *File this whole day under S for strange,* he thought.

Or H for hello. Or handsome.

"I don't suppose not."

H. smiled at him, nodded his head. Korey half-expected him to extend his arm, but he didn't. "You lead the way."

Korey left the Jewish cemetery and together they followed the road as it curved closer to the highway and the French Broad River. Korey paused before a statue he liked.

"They bring their kids here," he said, pulling out his sketchbook, though he could draw this from memory he'd done it so many times. Atop two pedestals, four tiny columns surrounded a central, wider column, and atop this an angel in a nightgown held her hand to her lips. "They play tag around her. It's cool."

"It is cool. Do you have a drawing of them as well?" said H.

"Somewhere, one sec," said Korey, leafing through his sketchbook. "Here you go." He held it up for H. to see.

"You have a remarkable gift."

"Thank you."

"What should I call you?"

Korey looked at him for a moment, instantly uncomfortable.

"You simply haven't introduced yourself. I like to have a name to pair with a face."

"It's Korey."

"Nice to meet you."

Korey let the tension drop, realizing he'd been too quick to judge. "Same."

"Which way next?"

"I don't know—east?" He'd no idea which way east actually was, but it seemed just as good as any other direction. This made H. smile, and Korey was beginning to really like the look of that.

"An excellent direction." H. placed a long hand on Korey's back. Chills traveled across him—pleasurable chills.

How long was it since he'd been touched? He couldn't actually remember.

"I hope that was okay."

Korey nodded, feeling a smile bloom on his own lips. "It was."

"So what do you do, Korey?" They were following the road now down to a leaf-strewn lawn, vivid green despite it being so late in the year. Their steps crunched the brown leaves; a lovely sound, and Korey realized this too had escaped him. When did he last appreciate how beautiful sounds were? He'd been so lost in his isolation after dropping out of school.

"I'm sorry, what?" He realized H. had asked him a question.

"Besides drawing stunning portraiture."

"Oh." He stopped to read the inscription on a veteran's gravestone. "Well, I was in college. Third year. Kind of bombed the last semester. Taking some time to regroup before I go back."

"Nothing wrong with that," said H. "What were you studying?"

"Art, despite everyone cautioning me against it. I understand their point, but why study something I don't enjoy? What would be the point of living then?" He glanced at H. and saw that the man's smile had cooled. "How about you?"

The smile returned, but it was a shadow of its former, lovely self. "I spend each day trying to figure out how to enjoy it best."

Korey laughed. "Must be nice."

"It is."

Thunder interrupted the drowsy nature of the air then; the dark side of the sky had taken the advantage.

"I guess that ends the walk."

"For now. Would you like to come to a party tonight, Korey?"

"I don't know. Not really my thing."

"Well, there are different kinds of parties. Some are too loud, too crowded, with terrible beer and even worse company. But some—like the one tonight—are quiet, thoughtful. Just the right amount of lighting, very good food, and even better company. Like myself."

"I'll think about it. Where will it be?"

"Fifty-one Poplar Street."

***

He sat at the edge of his bed, looking at his hands.

The neighbor on the other side of the wall yelled for her husband, again. It had become a nightly routine.

Sirens wailed down Broadway. The rain seemed to have let up.

There was nothing to do tonight and sleep wouldn't come.

"Guess I'll check it out," he said to the cobwebs. The neighbor on the other side of the wall yelled *shut up!*

***

The streets, the limbs of the trees, the rooftops all glistened with cold rain. The moon gazed down from a ring of clouds. Korey followed the hedge wall. He'd returned nearly to the cemetery's gates before the moonlight caught the shine of a mosaic plaque, half-hidden in ivy.

51.

He looked through the hedge, up towards uneven stone steps. There was no typical *thump* of an overly loud sound system, no raucous laughter, no reek of beer. He hurried up the steps to see light glistening on the lawn to the left of the house. Following the stone path around, Korey came to another three steps, leading down to a basement door, partially opened.

"Perhaps not," he said to himself.

H. appeared in the doorway, pushing it open with one graceful hand. He smiled up at Korey. "This is my friend, Anne." A woman poked her head out of the doorway and waved to him. Three white Chihuahuas scampered past them and barreled up the steps to menace Korey's feet.

"Terrible children," said Anne, hurrying to usher the dogs back inside. "Won't you join us?"

"Okay," said Korey, following Anne into the basement.

The room was larger than he'd expected, lushly decorated with antique tables and overstuffed sofas. H. had taken a seat in a crimson wingback chair, and was listening to someone seated on an ottoman beside him with rapt attention. Middle-Eastern styled iron lamps lent a drowsy glow to the décor. There was a pungent smell of something familiar.

"What is that scent?"

"Benzoin, of course," said Anne. Korey watched her disappear into a candlelit kitchen, reemerging moments later with a tray of snacks. "Hungry?"

"I," said Korey, "just ate."

"Anne," said H. in a sonorous voice that carried through the room as if it were a theater and he in the midst of a Shakespearean tragedy. "Too soon."

Anne set the tray down and shrugged before another woman caught her attention.

Korey clutched his sketchbook. He found a velvet bench to sit on and started to draw someone leaning against an ornately carved mahogany side table.

"Mr. Korey," said H., in a quieter voice. "When you have a moment, I'd like you to join this conversation."

"Sure." Korey slipped the pencil back behind his ear. "I can come back to this." He walked over and found a spot to sit on a couch. "Once I see someone I kind of keep them, like a screenshot in my head."

"May I see what you've done so far?" asked the other person.

Korey handed them the sketchbook.

"Remarkable."

"Photographic, wouldn't you say?" said H., popping a ruby-red grape into his mouth. "Fruit?" He offered the bowl to Korey.

"No thanks."

"You've quite a gift, my friend," said the other person, handing back the sketchbook. "Photographic and generous. She's never looked better."

"Oh, no, I try not to change people. I think people are beautiful, in their own way, just the way they are," said Korey.

"I'm sorry, forgive me," said the other person. "And also forgive for not introducing myself, I'm Mac." They extended their hand, and Korey shook it once. "What I meant is—Mel's not usually that serene. She's a bit of a spitfire. You've captured her in a contemplative moment."

"Siblings," said H. "Kind of a love and hate relationship."

"Definitely," said Mac. "Do you think I could—I know it sounds weird—keep this?"

"Of course," said Korey, carefully tearing out the page and handing it to him.

"Mother's Day's coming up. You know," said Mac, staring at H.

"I'm well aware."

"Thanks, person?"

"Korey."

Mac glanced at H., and smiled, before standing up. "Pleasure to meet you Korey. Carry on the excellent work."

"I will, and um, same." *Same? You idiot.*

He looked around the room, at the people coming in and out, some from upstairs, some from the basement entrance, others from the kitchen. Someone lit a pipe, and cannabis mixed its ripe scent with the benzoin and cooking-food smells. Korey rubbed his temples, wondering if he should try to sketch again.

"Too much?" said H.

"A bit, yes."

"Come. There are more rooms—just as lovely as this one."

"Okay."

Korey followed him down a hallway, then down a flight of stairs into a room that overlooked, somehow, a moonlit garden. Two loveseats were set in a V, with a round, antique table before them.

"Anything to drink?"

"No, thank you, though. I'm sorry if I'm a terrible guest. I just don't have a massive appetite." Korey looked at H. in the strange, white light. He was wearing a thin T-shirt, silk, possibly? Impeccably tailored trousers in a lighter hue than that afternoon. When H. leaned forward to pour himself some wine, the shirt lifted slightly, allowing Korey a view of H.'s chiseled waist. His fingers twitched upon the blank page he'd somehow opened in his book.

"I give you permission, freely, to draw me," said H. "I'd be honored."

"Well I can, if you want me to. But oftentimes it's just a crutch. I'm honestly terrible at social situations."

"Do you have any idea why that is?"

"I just feel, I suppose, gross and awkward."

"Gross? As in ugly? Or too much?"

Korey laughed. It felt so good to laugh. "Both, really."

"Well, you're neither, in my eyes. You're a very handsome young man. Where does your family hail from?"

"You mean, my ethnicities?"

"If that's what they're calling it nowadays, sure."

"My dad's Chinese, my mom is Dominican. They always called her *la morena*. She's very dark-skinned. Rest of the family on her side isn't."

"Lovely combination."

"Oh. Well, thanks."

"I apologize if my compliments make you uncomfortable."

"I just don't really think about the way I look. My face, you know. I guess I'm still getting used to it."

"Truer words were never spoken. We all have this challenge."

"We...do?" Korey smiled.

"How long have you been an artist?"

"Since I can remember?"

"Where do you take inspiration from?"

"Life, really."

"Really." H. looked out the window. "The moon's exquisite tonight. I miss seeing it."

"I'm a big fan of the pre-Raphaelite period."

"Ah!" H. set down his cup and leaned forward. "Good taste. So am I. They brought back realism to an era that was heavily influenced by impressionism and abstract art."

"Yes!" said Korey. "The brothers sought to return to the intensity. The lushness of life."

"Do you paint?" asked H.

Korey stared out at the moon. "I did. I was starting to work from a little studio at school. Then I guess I blew it. So, I just sketch now."

"All the time in the world to revisit one's former practices, provided they were good practices."

"I know. I just really don't know how I got so derailed."

"Why think of it as being derailed? Think of that poem—by Robert Frost."

Korey looked at H.'s face in the candlelit gloom. Somewhere else in the house, the three dogs click-clacked slowly across a wooden floor. Suddenly, something shifted in H.'s eyes. A sadness, maybe, casting over like clouds across the moon.

"Thanks for inviting me."

"Well, I just wanted to help."

Korey got up to stretch his legs, and noticed a chess set on a high side table to H.'s left. The pieces were ornately-wrought brass, sullenly gleaming, exotic. He walked over to examine a piece, but waited, his hand poised over the king's crown. "May I?"

"Have at it. Let me ask you—quite the loaded question. What's your favorite focus, in art?"

"Interestingly worded." Korey lifted the king, the style undoubtedly Italian, not too old but old enough to capture a pleasing shape, a satisfying weight to the piece. "The symbolists were cool. Not really my style though. It's funny, because I love abstract art. Love it. I have mad respect for the pre-Raphaelites, as I mentioned. Which makes sense because of my style. But, sometimes I wonder if I should even bother."

"Why should you not?"

"Because we have cameras. Cameras take the most realistic picture of all."

"Are cameras omnipotent?"

Korey laughed. "What?"

"Can cameras see everything? All subjects?"

"The right kind of camera, yes. I imagine it could. Night vision, infrared."

"But can the camera see emotion?"

"No, people can. The eye that looks at the photograph. The photographer—"

"The photographer might see it, but all they can do is manipulate the play of light. Somehow the artist can manipulate the very lines in the subject's face, in their eyes, so that if they're lucky, they can show what's going on inside the subject's soul."

"You give the artist a lot of credit."

"Actually, I'm giving *you* the credit. Your portraits are astounding."

"I don't know what to say. Thank you."

H. stood up and retrieved the king from Korey's hand to set it back on the board. H. smelled like darkness. Comforting, delicious darkness. Like cool rain in the shadows of a late summer day. Korey felt H.'s lips press against his forehead.

Korey laughed. "You're odd."

"It's true. I am," said H. and kissed Korey's lips, gently.

"It's a good odd."

"You should visit me at my office one day. When you have time."

"All I have is time. Where's your office?"

"Take my card." H. slipped a small square into Korey's back jeans pocket and removed his hand to briefly cup the curve of his ass. He kissed him again.

Somehow the perfume of H.'s mouth went straight to some place in Korey's brain, what was it called, the amygdala—

Then he was kissing him back, his hands running up beneath H.'s shirt, feeling the velvet of him, the hard and the soft.

"I'm sorry," said H., taking a breath before pressing a series of kisses along his neck. "I'm getting away from myself." H. pressed a kiss onto Korey's throat, began to unbutton his shirt. His long, warm fingers spanned across Korey's stomach, before hooking into the waistband of his jeans.

"Stop."

"I'm sorry, I thought you were enjoying—" said H.

"You need to stop." Korey stepped back, his heart racing, mouth full of the taste of H., eyes dizzy from the dim light and sudden desire. He twisted away from H. to grab his sketchbook, stumbled toward the rectangle of light that indicated the hallway and exit. "And I need to go."

H.

THE BAFFLED KING *composing Hallelujah.*

The wind seemed torn between a chill heart and a heat that rose from the very Earth.

Their reunion would come soon; they'd both delayed it too long. But she was just as placid as he regarding their arrangements. His partner of too many years to count—he'd honestly lost count, but so had she, they'd discovered over wine one late evening at home—was content to have her own adventures. He couldn't remember when he'd had one himself, but he was free to do so. The rivalry had aged beautifully, to become something more akin to a mutual, deep-seated appreciation.

Downtown Asheville was wild with dry leaves and torn handbills, each spiraling along its steep streets and loosely set cobblestones as if in competition. H.'s grey coat flapped about his trouser legs. He squinted. The light seemed too bright, too sharply vivid for his soft eyes. He realized he'd forgotten his sun shades.

He could hear a crowd chanting in the distance.

He'd found no evidence of Korey. It was foolish to blindly try to step into this young man's world for hope that a stray bit of luck would lead H. to him. Now he followed his own curiosity. Turning a corner at a coffee shop, he strode past a chain-link fence barricading the public from venturing into a construction zone. Above him towered a dark, semi-gutted building, the outlines of the lettering *BB&T* remaining for now. Diagonally across from this stood the squat, sun-bleached, and unremarkable obelisk erected to honor a confederate named Vance.

H. stood in the shadows of the former BB&T building and watched the somber procession circling the monument. The crowd held signs, some with photographs printed upon them, others with names and dates, some with both. From atop a riser, a violinist played a sweet, sad melody, the notes echoing between the surrounding buildings, lifting to the white sky like the leaves and the handbills.

Something caught his eye.

He crossed the street, not looking at the oncoming traffic as motorists jerked to sudden stops or applied their horns to express their displeasure. Now he stood across the smaller side-street from the gathering. Three young people held signs with photographs of faces. H. shielded his sky-blind eyes with his hand.

One of the faces was Korey.

He became aware that the violin had ceased its song, and a voice announced a poem to be read, written by someone named Ava Dupre.

To know thyself,
so absolutely,
yet possess no tangible proof
leads our gaze upon a sea of faces
a crowd of bodies
in the white house
on the dance floor
or in them streets
we don't see ourselves,
though we see self-doubt exists in all.

He felt the rage welling up from his feet, up along his spine, up through all the ancient tributaries that formed his ancient being, sentiments and reactions not felt in what seemed like an entire swarm of millennia. Hornets, bees, war. Not his domain but not forbidden to him either.

"Today, November twentieth, we remember those who have fallen victim to acts of hate. May they rest in power."

The dark skies seemed to follow him like a pack of dogs as he fled the pain that choked his throat, strangled his heart, lit his fingertips with electricity. As he stormed away from the gathering, thunder clapped a single drumbeat. Cold rain struck the ground like needles.

KOREY

HE FELT RESTLESS in the darkness of his room.

He could hear the neighbor again, fussing at her husband. Hear the dog across the hall. The creak and groan of the furnace kicking on and stretching the pipes with steam because the night was filled with miserable cold and pouring rain.

The lightbulb above the sink twitched; its yellow light glowed bright hot just before it winked out.

"Damn it."

He could hear doors all along the hall opening, people's voices rising in volume.

"You got one too? What's yours say?"

Curious, he left his room to follow them down the stairwells, out to the lobby where a man spoke in loud, pseudo-comforting tones.

"You're being offered a fair price for the current market. No one's getting kicked out. You have sixty days to make your decision."

"How are you calling it a decision? These are eviction notices."

Korey watched the small crowd, most of them dressed in their pajamas, each holding opened letters. A woman rocked a crying baby. An old man in a bathrobe, sweatpants, and sandals stood at the edge of the crowd, just watching, listening. Korey realized he'd brought his sketchbook out of the room and began to draw him.

After a while, the man noticed him and walked over. "Can I see?"

Korey showed him the sketch and the man smiled, joy igniting his eyes like a long-cold hearth and its winter fire. “Remarkable.”

“Thank you.”

“It’s going to be harder for guys like you and me to stay here too, you know.” The man turned, and slowly shuffled away.

***

The rain continued for over a week. Korey thought it would never let up.

The day it stopped, he left his room for another walk. The sun burned steadily beyond a swiftly racing sky of clouds and blue. Voices echoed along the streets. Pigeons wheeled and soared from roof to roof.

“Hi,” said H., standing beside a lamppost just beyond Korey’s building’s front entrance.

Startled, Korey fumbled for the proper words. “Hi,” was all he could manage.

“I wanted to apologize to you.”

“It’s okay. You don’t have to apologize.”

“I want to?”

“All right. Apology accepted.”

“Can we walk somewhere?”

“What for?”

“Because I have some news for you.”

They walked past a sculpture of a black iron and turned the corner to head west on Battery Park, towards Page.

“What’s the news?”

H. stopped, looking across the street at more construction. “Your place. Your building. Was in peril of being purchased and demolished, correct? In order to build yet another hotel.”

“That’s right. How did you know?”

“Did some research.”

“Okay, and? So?”

“I contacted the people of The Preservation Society of Buncombe County. As well as a Mr. Nash Wyatt.”

"Who is that?"

"The man who still owns your building."

"I thought it had already been sold."

H. smiled. "Not yet. And now—not for some time. You see, I managed to convince Mr. Wyatt to sign a preservation easement."

"A what now?"

"A preservation easement. It protects a historic property from being demolished, basically."

"Wow, really? Seriously, thank you so much." Korey pressed himself against H., squeezing him in a ferocious hug. "All the residents have been losing their minds over this. So much worry."

"I can imagine."

"How did you convince the owner not to sell?"

"I was in a bad mood. I'm not proud to admit that when I'm in a bad mood, I can be very convincing."

Korey let his arms drop, ending the embrace.

"Oh, I didn't threaten the man. I don't have the heart for such things anymore. I emphasized his lack of empathy, however. To the point that he didn't very much like the direction he was going in."

"Well, thanks. Again."

"You're very welcome."

"Guess...I'd better be going."

"You don't have to if you don't want to."

"I do, want to. See you around, H."

Korey glanced over his shoulder after he'd put a block's worth of distance between them; H. was still standing there, the wind teasing the hems of his coat.

***

Thanksgiving week had come and gone. He felt guilty for not going home, but he just couldn't bring himself to travel.

In fact, he couldn't bring himself to do much at all.

He'd filled the last page of his sketchbook. And it was truly the last page; Korey had filled the front and back of every page with images of people he'd found interesting. Now he needed a new sketchbook, and he couldn't find his wallet, even after he'd searched the room for days.

At least there was still food in the fridge, but his appetite was as absent as many of the apartments in his building.

Determined to rise out of the black mood that had settled on him, Korey took the card H. had slipped into his pocket.

92 Patton Ave. Lower level. Suite H.

"Suite H, really?" Korey laughed to himself.

The neighbor on the other side of the wall yelled for him to shut up and keep it down.

***

Korey was so relieved to have something to do, he didn't even feel the bite of the wind that chased the lingering crowds of tourists about the city. Following the zigzag of the intersecting streets, he came to the odd little periwinkle building on the corner of Coxe and Patton, The Thirsty Monk.

He went around the back to see if perhaps there was a door to offices there.

"Nope," he said as he followed a couple into the bar, carefully avoiding a jostling, jovial crowd. The late-afternoon sun leaked warmly through the front windows. A chalkboard sign read:

Do I want beer?

a. yes

b. a

c. b

He found the stairs heading down to the lower level, this space called the Belgian Bar, and made his way around the room, again dodging patrons and staff until he found the hall leading to the restrooms. He passed two doors, then an open door leading to a dishwashing area, then finally came to a smaller door at the end of the hallway. He turned the tarnished, brass knob, expecting it to be locked, but then noticed someone had written "H" there with a Sharpie.

***

"This is a spectacularly weird place to have an office."

"That's a good word for me, I like it. Spectacular, I mean. Though, I suppose, weird works too." H. smiled that glorious smile, the one that made Korey feel things he'd not felt in years, possibly ever. "Have a seat. Can I get you anything?"

"Even the air smells like beer here."

"It's quite delicious. One of my favorite places to get work done. I made a dig at beer earlier when we spoke of parties, but good beer is worth more than gold."

"Where else do you have offices?"

"All over," said H., sweeping his long hand through the air. "But listen. I want to say—" H. glanced at the desk between them before looking into Korey's eyes "—it's very nice to see you."

"Same." Korey smiled at him, and slid the sketchbook across the desk. "It's full."

"May I?"

"Please."

H. lifted the book from the desk as if it were a sacred text, cradling it in a graceful hand and slowly leafing through it with the other, carefully avoiding touching anything but the very edges of the pages. He paused on one page, muttering words of praise, then returned to the first page. "This is you."

"Yes. A few years ago. Five years ago, actually."

"You're a handsome young man, that's for sure."

"That was before I… Before—"

"Before you began your journey of five years." H. closed the book and slid it back across the desk. "That you've recorded beautifully here."

"Something like that."

"I want to suggest something to you, Korey, and I hope you will hear me out."

"Okay."

"It's my feeling that your journey here in Asheville has come to an end. But that it continues, *should continue*, elsewhere."

"You think I should drop out of school?"

"It goes beyond that."

"What do you mean?"

"Korey."

H.'s eyes were full of kindness, and sadness, and suddenly Korey remembered, or knew, or, *both*. "You're right. I've been sticking around, because… Honestly I don't know why."

"It's easy to get confused when someone else changes the course of your life so suddenly."

"I guess that's it."

"And that's why I sought you out. To help you towards your next direction. I just didn't expect things to happen as they did."

"What do you mean?"

"Do you think the workers at the Belgian Bar see a door to my office?" H. stood up to walk around the desk and opened the door. Servers walked past holding trays of dishes. A woman reached for the door handle, then turned around, realizing the restroom was behind her.

"They don't even see it?"

"Well, they do, but it's a utility closet. A *locked* utility closet."

"Then it's all in my mind."

"Consciousness is where the soul takes root. Where it grows into something *spectacular*."

"How does that help me now?"

"Because the soul keeps going. Through a different level of consciousness. When one door closes—" H. walked back past his desk to open a door that Korey hadn't noticed until now "—another opens. Cliché, but that's because it's true." Beyond the door, sunlight shone upon green grass, and the smell of warm soil and fresh water blew into the room, driven by a sweet-petaled wind.

"Wow."

"I want you to come home with me."

"I, well—"

"It's a fairly vast home. You don't have to do anything other than exist in it. If you never want to talk to me again, never want to kiss me again, I'll be okay with that."

You don't look like you'd be okay with either, but whatever you say, H.

Korey got up and walked to the open door, peering outside. Rolling hills tumbled down to a shining river, upon which sailed two long-hulled boats. The three Chihuahuas tumbled about on the grass, yipping excitedly at each other. Korey closed the door and looked at H. "Actually, that's the other reason I came here."

"Oh?"

"I really want to kiss you again." He reached for H., gripping the back of his strong, graceful neck, brushing his lips against H.'s until he couldn't stand to wait any longer, and kissed him deeply, hungrily. H.'s hands moved over him, sparking fire across his skin, and he *felt* everything; it had been so long since he'd felt anything at all. Not since the park, the party. For a moment though, one last hesitation. He pulled away.

"What is it?"

"There's something you should know."

"I know, Korey."

Korey looked down at the floor, flexing his hands, feeling like his heart was a poison cup in his chest that burned as it spilled, leaching out into his bones.

"A body is a vessel of the soul. I can make love to whatever you present me with, if you choose to present me with it. I want to make love to the man that is *you*, sweet Korey."

Korey bit his lip, until H.'s hand was cupping his face and gently thumbing away the teardrop as it rolled down his cheek. The poison turned to fire, and the fire to golden sunlight, as Korey drank another kiss from H.'s full, sweet lips.

ASHEVILLE – Ghost or hoax? Patrons of downtown's Thirsty Monk have questions after three sightings of a so-called romantic couple have been reported in a utility closet in the iconic bar's downstairs hallway. A worker claims she saw two men locked in a "passionate embrace" when she opened the closet for cleaning supplies; a customer says he saw the door was open and mistook the closet for a restroom, almost stumbling onto the men as they "made out." Two months late for Halloween, the bar owners have decided to honor the ghostly couple with a brew named in their honor: Hades' Kiss.

***

***First Snow of the Year Blankets The Area** – With leaves still clinging to some trees, western North Carolina saw a record snowfall last night, including ice and hail. Amounts vary by county but suffice to say, winter is back.*

ABOUT DEVEN BALSAM

Deven Balsam is a single dad, resident DJ at Asheville North Carolina's oldest running gay bar, and new author of sci fi, fantasy, and speculative fiction. He weaves a bit of romance, horror, and spirituality into everything he writes. Originally a Yankee from the New York metropolitan area, he currently lives on a mountain at the edge of 250 acres of Pisgah National Forest, and that suits him just fine.

Website: https://devenbalsam.weebly.com

BY DEVEN BALSAM

Tourist Season

Three: A Tale of the Bookseller's Children
(Expected 2018)

MACHETE BETTY AND THE OFFICE SHARKS

NEPTUNE FLOWERS

Tim is in the A team, professionally trained to investigate allegations of the potential mass hypnosis of the nation... But Tim is bored and horny. Who wouldn't be? The office is full of idiots, and summer just keeps getting hotter and hotter. Reality starts to blur, screensavers come to life, and before he can say jiggyjig, he finds himself cavorting with a chain-smoking foul-mouthed merman.

Tim's training is forgotten as he becomes immersed in fishy hedonism and office shenanigans. Can he save the day? Or will the team be forever lost in shameful acts of bouncybounce?

Find out in this *tail* of office boredom and surreal fun.

Warning! This story does not reflect realistic relationships with mermen or sharks.

***

Genre: contemporary LGBT fiction, humour

Keywords: surrealism, British, romance, LGBTQ+, mermen, mayhem, humour

Advisory: mature content

CHAPTER ONE

MONDAY, IT WAS bloody boiling, the air stale with sun and apathy, both weighing heavy on my limbs and eyelids. Even the screensaver fishes seemed sluggish, limping past the coral reef like they couldn't be bothered. I watched the same shark for a while flirting with a dolphin, too tired to wonder about the possibility of sharkphin babies. The night before, I'd had a dream about Jaws and being chased through the ocean, both terrifying and exhilarating.

Around my desk, it was much like being inside the screensaver image. Particles of dust floated in the air like debris in water, and my colleagues' voices were muffled and booming. My head was swimming.

Eventually, I dragged myself away, determined to turn to more useful pursuits. "Bring me joy, Machete Betty," I implored my computer, so called because of her tendency to swallow important files. I was sure she sometimes read my mind, seeming to know my mood and inner desires. On cue, Betty took me instantly to my favourite dating site. Grinning faces, beards, glasses and lies offered me happiness by way of a date. After seriously considering Jack 'own house and pension' Campbell and Philip 'Rohypnol in polyester slacks pocket' Lewis, I snapped back to the duties of the day.

"Is anyone getting weird dreams?" The team was trained to spot bizarre anomalies, including physical manifestations—side effects of studying subliminal messaging online—and while a dream about Jaws wasn't anything to worry about, still I needed to check. As a highly professional team, we were constantly on the lookout for symptoms of irritation and squabbling, attraction, losing touch with reality and doing unexplained things. For anything out of the ordinary.

"Nope."

"Naw."

"Niet."

"En garde!" Tash, the manager, shouted suddenly, brandishing what looked like a cardboard sword. Fuck sake. She waved it around, making me ache to remind her that only yesterday she had sent out a frosty email about time-wasting and professionalism. "Gabbagabba!" Tash gushed and then poked me in the shoulder with the sword. "Gabbagabba, Tim."

"Not today," I said coldly, attempting to convey iron messages of hostility. "I've too much to do."

Betty flickered a message from the dating app. Immediately I clicked, expecting to see yet another smiling older chap by day, serial killer by night. Not that I wouldn't consider dating someone like that. Of course not. As long as he washed his hands. Beggars couldn't be choosers, after all, nor was 'judgemental' my middle name.

However, instead of a potential date, the front cover of a book flashed repeatedly. *In, out, in, out, shake it all about.* I watched it so long it began to look like dancing. "Is that Shakespeare? I can't quite see the title. Can you see it, Tash?"

She peered at the screen. "Yeah. That play about fairies and love. But why can't you come? I really wanted all of you to give feedback on the group T-shirts." She smiled in her 'winning' way, but all I wanted to do was pull her hair. Oh, she seemed all pally and 'come to the pub with us, Tim'; however, I couldn't get in with somebody like that. An irritating bugger who got all the office awards and pay-rise challenges. Daughter of the director. Of course, I was above such menial rubbish anyway. What did I care about pleasing the bosses? With a proven track record of work excellence and a CV to die for, there was absolutely no need to compete like these idiots did. I didn't need this job.

Not very much.

And bitter wasn't my middle name either.

"No. Too busy. I've got a lead to follow." I nodded at Betty and tapped a few random letters for extra effect. The flashing book disappeared, turning back to my screensaver. "Some of us have real work to do." Taking arse-kissing photos of a T-shirt to email to the bosses could not be considered real in any sense, obviously. "You know? What we're here for? To investigate allegations of the potential mass hypnosis of the entire nation?" I sniffed wittily, to emphasise the importance. "I think that's a bit more vital than a T-shirt, don't you? B'more vital." It's funny, but lately I'd been slurring my words a bit, or maybe it's only boredom making me sound like a drunken idiot.

Her smile wavered and something flickered in her eyes, alerting my akin-to-conscience. Maybe I'd gone a bit far, overboard with the sarcasm. I did tend to forget these young things don't have the staying power I do, no experience of life and all its knocks.

"Sorry." I smiled. "You don't need my opinion anyway. Much better off asking the lookers, eh?" I pointed down the office where all the beautiful people sat. "Tupp, that's who you need. Tuppy Tupp Tuppery."

Right on cue, the ginger-haired journalist bounded up like Bambi on acid. "What's this? Tim not playing, Tash? I should chop off his head." He laughed bashfully, and it was all I could do not to spit on his shoes. "Bad boy." It was all I could do not to get on my knees and beg.

"That's right, Tupp. Tim's got work to do," Tash barked. "Got a lead, or so he says."

"Have you, Tim? Informant come good? Mafia and spies?" He casually put an arm across Tash's shoulders, and this show of affection forced me to actually switch from the local dating app to *work*, for the first time that day. Bitter, bitter, bitter.

Not that he'd led me on when I first joined the team, almost eight months three days and twenty-eight minutes ago, or not intentionally. Nope. It was just I hadn't realised he looked at *everyone* ravenously, chin on hand. How could I have guessed he'd go round touching *their* knees and arms too, and anywhere else he fancied? That he was just that type of person, a friendly sort whose pores oozed the suggestion he wanted to go a round of physical jiggyjig?

I couldn't have known, but that hadn't stopped me making a fool of myself round the back of the pub, on my knees and shitfaced drunk. "Oh, mate," he'd said, stopping my hands on his zipper. "It's probably my fault for giving you the wrong impression. I mean you're a great guy, but…"

"Mm." I put on my glasses and shuddered slightly.

But.

Butbutbutt. Dating app serial killer, here I come.

I had no proof he'd told anyone, only the sinking truth that if I was in his position, I certainly would have. Gossip like that was much too good not to be spread.

"Got a lead, yeah." Had I fuck.

"Great!" He moved away from Tash and stood right behind me, smelling of aftershave and washed shirts, of clean living and niceness. This was a man who washed his pots and never had thoughts about poisoning the neighbours. Not him. "Be a shame you're not in the gabbagabba, though. I'd miss you."

To my horror, he started massaging my shoulders. It was the kind of horror that didn't feel like horror, much more like pleasure and sudden, screaming arousal. My disloyal body melted.

"Oh! You're tense, man."

If there was one thing I hated, it was when they said 'man' to appear cool. They all did it here—Tash, Tupp, Emma and Crack. My irritation was intense, sadly not enough to stop me from putting my head to one side to accommodate his touch. Casually, he undid the top button of my shirt and slipped his

hands inside. Ding dong! I would certainly push him away, with anger and rightly so. I would, would, certainly I would…in a few minutes. Once my stupid heart had stopped racing and my even more stupid underpants had stopped doing the Hokey Cokey. He was incorrigible, dashing and delicious.

"Yeah, you are," Tash agreed, watching the physical play. "You've been working too hard. How about this—if you come for the T-shirt, we all go to the pub after? I'll pay."

"How about that?" Tupp leaned down so his head touched mine, and his face was far too close for comfort. "Will you come?"

Oh, I'd come all right. "Well, I…" I let my head roll back so he could stroke my neck and under my chin. "Ungg."

"You will?"

I was such a pushover. "All right."

"Fantastic! You're too nice, Tim." Tash banged the desk and strode off to piss off someone else. "Ten minutes in the Bernard Cribbins room. En garde!"

***

"Thanks for coming to the gabbagabba! Team photo!" Tash flashed the camera, but it seemed to me she aimed it in my direction. I blinked against the unexpected light and rubbed my eyes, seeing fish tanks and coral reef.

"Bloody hell. You trying to blind me?"

"Sorry! New lens! T-shirts! What do you think?" Tash all but threw the pictures across the desk.

"Fantastic!"

"Woohoo!"

"Killed it dead, girl!"

"It's bollocks," I said calmly, my shoulders still stinging with the devastating loss of Tupp's hands. "It gives off the wrong impression. No. Definitely not. Nope." Bitter was not my middle name, not I.

"What do you mean?" Tash wailed. "I spent hours working on it? What?"

To be honest, I did not give a flying fuck about the T-shirt one way or another, and anyway, I hadn't bothered to look beyond the title, 'were team triumph'. I was horny, hungry, and sick of a job that was frankly beneath me. By now, I should be managing director of an international media investigative corporation, instead of stuck with this lot of sharks. And something else was beginning to clog up my brain, like missing a birthday. I knew it was there, but somehow the details evaded me.

"You've missed out the apostrophe," I said coldly. "Need I say more?" I leaned back in my chair to gloat. "Were team triumph? You mean we used to be but now we're not." I gnashed my teeth cleverly. "We are, you see?" I grinned at Tupp. "We, apostrophe, are. We're. Not were. It gives the impression that we are all incompetent twats." Sadly, my cutting comment was lost because it came out 'twass'. Unexpectedly, I gnashed my teeth.

"But it's not meant to—it's—oh!" Tash wailed. "Don't you see? It's meant to show that we're a team who doesn't stick to the rules. We crash through the grammatical structures of the media to find the truth." She deflated. "It…it was deliberate."

"No, it wasn't. You fucked up," I said calmly, desperate and incurable horniness warping my every breath. "Eh, Tupp?"

"I like it. It's a nice idea, and if we wear it, we will look like people who kick arse, instead of office slaves who spend all day looking up dating apps." Emma—best friend of Tash—glared at me. "I got it! Didn't you *get* that it was deliberate, Tim?" Her sudden and frankly scary laughter was shrill enough to break the window. I gnashed my teeth again and then watched as, one by one, the team did the same. It was great to know I still had some influence.

"Yeah, I like it too. Not that I know much about T-shirts." Crack laughed. "And I'll be honest here, shall I?" Oh, fuck off. Honest? He wouldn't know honest if it jumped down and bit him on the arse. "I didn't even notice! Hah-hah-hah. I'm not great at apostrophes and semi-thingies." If there's one thing I hate, it's people who put themselves down so that others will jump to their defence.

"Colon," I added helpfully. "Semi-colon. Or did you mean semi-detached? Or semi-erection?"

Crack frowned. "Are you trying to be funny?"

"No."

"Look, I know I don't add much to the meetings." He sighed, and that meant we were in for a long and boring rant about how worthless he was, which might be interesting if I didn't happen to know he'd already slept with both Tash and Emma.

Tash cut in swiftly. "Craig, that's not true! Your opinion is very valuable. Look at last week, when we couldn't work out the logo for the team signature. But shall we get on?"

Crack blushed. His name wasn't really Crack; I just called him that because he always had his trousers pulled up tightly into his arse and because it made me feel superior. "No, you don't need to say that."

"Good, then. Let's get on." I tapped the table. "The nation is at risk with every second that passes."

"No, but really?" Crack's voice boomed. "Is my opinion really valuable? Really, really, really?"

"Um, the nation?" I insisted, bouncing on a wave of indignation.

"It's true." Emma went on buttering his fragile ego, and then Tupp caught my eye. He winked and then rolled his—rather gorgeous—blue eyes. If there's one thing I hated, it was eye-rolling as an alternative to speaking your mind. I hated it, but still I couldn't look away, and neither could my underpants.

"So do we mind about the apostrophe? Does it work?" Tash batted her eyelashes.

"Mind? Of course we don't mind! Who would mind working with genius? Who would mind viewing a creative guru?" Tupp stood up and sat on the table, shoes and all. This was something he did rather a lot. If he'd only let me bang him, it would be much more acceptable. I'd even laugh at his jokes. If only he'd let me bang him, I'd follow him round like a puppy and stop hiding his coffee cup.

Despite being a tall guy, he crossed his legs neatly, revealing a great big bulge in the chasm of joy department. "You know what we need? A group hug." And then he crawled across the table, somewhere between a bum shuffle and a lurch. The others laughed and pointed, and it all made me bitter—more bitter—and cross, especially when he got to Tash and fell into her lap *instead of mine.* I about threw up with jealousy, but bitter was not my middle name even if deserving was.

"I don't suppose *your dad* will mind, though." I went for the kill. "Your dad, millionaire owner of the media corporation, Tash. I mean, what does it matter what I think? What any of us think? Must be nice to have connections."

For once, the team went silent, and Tupp rolled off Tash and shuffled back to his seat.

"Tim, man," Emma whispered. "No need for that."

"Think you might've gone too far there, Tim," Crack said.

***

After the pub, I walked home as usual. The afternoon had dragged on with its everyday share of bitchery and arse-kissing, but for some reason I had no glee at how many points had been scored. I suppose I was thinking again about Tupp, and how unfair the universe was, and perhaps that was why I decided to go the river route. I hadn't been that way for ages. For one thing, it's at least a mile further than the road route. For another, you never knew how many bloody dogs were there, just waiting to run at you or lick you with their slobbery tongues. If there was one thing I hated, it was slobber not belonging to Tupp.

But the biggest reason was strange and not something I thought about very often. The last time I'd attempted the pathway along the river, skirting the bluebells and rhododendrons, I'd had what I best could describe as an unexplained encounter. I don't really know what happened, only that I was feeling a little heady and dizzy, a common side effect of my job. Sometimes the whole team felt sick; often it was mainly me. One minute, I was gazing into the water, the next, I woke up sitting on a bench with a huge boner and the hazy recollection of a man. I don't know if I'd fainted and was helped by some kind stranger or what. But I'd felt unsettled and wary, terribly unsexed, and hadn't gone down there ever since.

The night of the T-shirts, I turned away from the busy road and down the steps that led to the river and the infamous path. I needed to get away from the smoke and the noise of cars and civilisation. Maybe I even needed to get away from myself?

"You're pitiful," I murmured, stepping down the stone stairs into the warm darkness of the trees and the woods. "You need to get a new job." And I did. Taking pot shots at people wasn't really my thing—or it hadn't been until I came to the media investigation unit and witnessed all the flattery and corruption that apparently fuelled what should have been a fantastic place to work. "You need to get a new life." The river was high and fast, the water rushing past like crowds of people trying to get away. For a time, I stood there, listening to the sound and immersing myself…

"You OK? Can you open your eyes? Tim?"

Colours and lights, dark and cold. I saw people from long ago as if it was yesterday, and heard voices and songs. I struggled to open my eyes. "Where am I? Is this hospital?" I could sense someone nearby and hands stroking my hair. Even half unconscious, my lonely self tried to hold the hands back. "Who are you?"

Briefly, arms held me tightly. "You know who I am. I missed you."

I opened my eyes fully at last. I was next to the river in the darkness. My head was pounding, and I couldn't altogether feel my limbs. A cloud was enveloping me from inside, like coming down with flu.

So what I saw, it could just have been a trick of a high temperature and a fall. Because that's the only explanation that makes sense. How else could I explain watching a man—half a man—swim away from the bank and into the middle of the river. He swam with perfect strokes, like an Olympic athlete. Despite the coldness of night, his arms and upper body were naked as far as I could tell, pale flesh shining from the light of the moon. "Wait," I called. He turned to face me, paused as I tried to stand up, then dived down under the water.

The last thing I saw was some kind of flipping thing like a fish, and then he was gone.

CHAPTER TWO

TUESDAY, THE OFFICE lighting really got on my nerves, making my eyes hurt and my head buzz. "Whas going on, Machete Betty?" The shark on the screensaver winked at me as he got serious about seducing the dolphin, and for some reason, the walls were plastered with 3D pictures of squid. Crack wore flippers, but then he was a dork. That day, I hated him passionately enough to miss out sugar in his coffee.

"Are—are any of you getting weird dreams?" The team was regularly trained to recognise strange symptoms, anything that could be a result of the hours we spent scrutinising the internet. Every member of the team would notice overly dramatic feelings such as hatred or admiration. While I wasn't about to admit what I thought I'd seen at the river, I knew better than to say nothing.

"Hmm? What type?" Emma rubbed her face with her hand. "I haven't been feeling so good this week. Headaches, sickies, that stuff. Not sure about dreams though. What was it about, you ugly great bastard? I hate you."

"Urgh, nothing much. I can't remember really."

"And it's so bloody hot! Summer solstice soon. Maybe it's just the heat getting to your brain."

"Mm. Could be."

It *had* been hot the last few weeks, stifling heat that seemed to gather during the day and thump you in the chest at night. I don't think any of the team was sleeping. Every day we moaned about the sun and lack of air.

"I had a dream. It was about you." Tupp crept up behind Emma and shouted suddenly in her ear. "Boo!" Fuck, but that man could be irritating.

"About me?"

Emma shot up from her chair, knocking over a glass of water and a stack of plastic hats. "Jesus Christ, Tupp! What is your fucking problem?"

...was something I'd obsessed over the last eight months, four days and twelve minutes ago, I don't mind admitting. If there was one thing I hated, it was a man who led you on, leading you like a horse to the trough with no actual intention of allowing you to drink.

"Yeah, Tupp. Cut it out." Yeah, Tupp. Let me kiss you. Let me touch your face. Let me worship the ginger hairs above your eyes and sprouting from your ears.

"Sorry," he apologised, and began crawling like a cat on the tables.

Emma and I watched him creeping carefully around the gaps. "What is it with you and tables? You know most people use the floor for worching. Walking? Fuck, I'm tired."

"Maow."

When he lay across the desk like something dragged in through a cat flap, I suppose we should have told him to get off. But the day was hot and it seemed too much effort, so we left him there, right behind our computers where all the wires and plugs congregated. I don't know, but just lately we seemed to be doing a lot of odd things. He sighed and grumbled for a while, raising his arms above his head like a little kid demanding attention, before making quiet noises like a kitten. "I had a dream too," he meowed. "It was colourful and silly, like drinking too much cider."

"*Did* you drink too much cider last night, Tuppy?" Emma tugged at his trousers. "After we left the pub?"

"Yeah."

Tuppy? "You did?" I asked, with more than a little interest. Tupp left the pub before I did—alone, as far as I could see. All

I knew about his life outside the office is that he flirted with everyone, was unfairly gorgeous and wouldn't let me blow him. I suppose he must also have been rather clever to be in our team; either that or he, too, was sleeping with someone or the kid of a rich director. "Do tell."

"Urgh." He began shifting about. "I'm so hot! I wish I was naked! Can I take my shirt off?"

"Yes!" I said, rather too loudly. "Please do. Strip yourself bare." My underpants smirked.

Emma gagged. "No, Tupp."

He peeled it off and flung it across the room, where it landed. Half-naked, he lay back down. "Well, I just felt so—hot! And out of sorts. I had all this energy stored up and no way of expelling it. You know? So I tootled off home and then found myself drinking a bottle of dynamo cider." He suddenly adopted a fake Cornish-type accent. "Ye olde cyder."

"Couldn't you just have had a wank?" Emma demanded. I noticed suddenly that she was wearing one of the turtle plastic hats that had appeared, and may well have been doing so for some hours. This place was the pits, and seemingly it was getting pittier.

"Indeed!" I said helpfully, then selected a plastic hat and also attached one to Betty. "Does it suit?"

"Shut up. I hate you," Emma replied. "Don't ever speak to me again."

Tupp ignored us and ranted on for ages about cider and the way it affected his limbs. "And then I was so terribly dry. You know? Dry like the desert, so I stood under the shower with an erection as big as the leaning tower of Pisa."

"Oh, yes? Show me."

"Yes!" His voice went round and round with the broken fan and damned if I didn't fall asleep, because the next time I took notice, the day was half gone and Tash was running round the office with her sword, shouting about the gabbagabba.

***

After work, I took the route down by the river again. I wanted to satisfy myself that the apparition—or whatever—was just my imagination. I remembered his shoulders and back as he swam away, and this savoury image reminded me of Tupp and his cider tales. "Good god!" I turned away from the pavement. I must admit my underpants formed a goodly part of that decision.

That day, the river bank burnt with heat and everything was rather pretty. Butterflies and flowers, smells and the sounds of summer. But still, my feet felt heavier than usual, and I had an odd sense that something important was missing.

By the time I reached the river, my headache had returned. There wasn't a soul about, so I sat for a while and began absently making little boats from the long reeds that floated on the current.

"Facking hell, mate. Will you stop that? Stop flinging bits of crap at my head."

An angry southern voice made me start. I looked up into the sun, its brilliance blinding me. "What? Who?" I blinked to try to clear the whiteness, and then I shat a metaphorical brick.

It sat there, just below the river bank. I say 'it', though the chap was clearly male. It was the creature of the night before. In my panic to get away, I slipped down the bank towards the thing rather than away from it, my hands grabbing at reeds and rocks. My limbs seemed to work against me, and soon I was flat out on the mud. In the end, I gave up struggling against gravity and looked.

"Awright? Stop making such a noise, you twat."

It was smoking a cigarette, and for some reason, this—rather than the scales and lack of logic—was what my brain fixated on. "They're going to kill you," I croaked, trying not to look at its tail, which started down low on its stomach, just below the belly button. "Nicotine is deadly." Did it have lungs?

The fish man blew smoke right into my face and laughed loudly. "That's if the pollution doesn't. You want one?" He flipped his tail.

Of course, I couldn't look away then, staring rudely at the greens and blues all mixed together over the bumps and mounds of his shape. "You're—you're a fish?"

"Innit. Fish without the chips. What a bastard, eh?"

"Pollution and cigarettes? Aren't you meant to be unearthly and surreal? Singing to hapless sailors and waving your breasts? And I'm pretty sure mermaids don't swear. Not usually, anyway."

"Meant to? A law, is there? Do me a favour." He ground out the cigarette into the bank. "Do I look like a mermaid?" He grinned and ran his hands up and down over his chest. This unusual show affected my underpants profoundly.

"Well...yes. And no. Your tail does." I pointed. "There's a definite similarity. Surely you can see that?"

"I can sing to you if you like," he cleared his throat, and sang to the tune of 'My Old Man's a Dustman'—

"Tim Baker is an idiot,
He wears an idiot's cap,
He thinks he's so superior,
But all he does is nap."

He stopped to laugh, and laugh, and though it wasn't funny, I couldn't help but join in. A sense of being, finally, where I was meant to be in life, slipped over my aching head. "Jesus Christ. What is going on?" I cackled. "This is a dream, isn't it? You're not real."

"Fucked if I know. But you keep on coming here, so you must like it. What do you mean, I'm not real? Don't you want me to be real?" He reached out suddenly and took my hand. His touch was warm, like that of a human man. It had been so long since anyone had touched me except Tupp's massage and the dog next door. "You're not very happy, are you?" He squeezed. "Always moaning and frowning. What's up?"

My eyes stung with the sudden intimacy. "I—I'm lonely," I confessed.

"I know you are." He shifted nearer. "No need to be, not anymore."

The tears came flooding out, and then he held me tightly, like he cared. I could say it was the fog in my head or confusion, but the truth is, sorrow exploded because he noticed me.

CHAPTER THREE

WENSDAY, WENSADY, FULL of woe. After sex I've miles to go. "Look at Crack. Why is he doing the breaststroke on his chair?" I watched him, sat there swimming.

Emma shrugged and looked at me like I was stupid. "Exercise is good for you. Swimming uses more muscles than anything else except a night in the sack."

"Well, yes. I know that." I watched Crack move from breast stroke to butterfly crawl and then the sense of Emma's words moved—really moved—into my being. I began swimming too. "Is anyone else getting headaches?" As a team, we are rigorously trained to look for any physical abnormalities, like mass hallucination, as a result of our work scrutinising the internet for subliminal messages.

"No, no. You're not quite doing that right." Emma stood up and showed me how to position my hands to achieve optimum speed or whatever. "What kind of headaches?"

"Urgh. Ones in the head?"

"Oh. Then no. I have been having a few headaches in my feet, though." She lay on the floor and sighed. "I need a holiday."

"You know, I don't like this shark, and neither does the dolphin." I began to sob suddenly, deep crying from the very pit of my ocean bottom. "Stop it, Betty! Where's Tupp? I like Tupp. I really, really like him."

"Oh, he's swimming too."

"Right."

"Don't cry, Tim. You can't help being a miserable bastard. You do realise everyone hates you?"

Things seemed to be going downhill, what with the heat and the shark. By now, I should have been director instead of having to swim with the tide. "I think…I need to find something," I tried to explain. "You know? It—it's missing."

"Yeah, man." Emma pulled at my trousers from the floor. If there's one thing I hate, it's people saying man, elongating it like it was made of mozzarella cheese. "Me too. All my life I've been looking. Is it gabbagabba?"

"Urgh. No, it's not philosophy." I slithered onto the floor next to her. "I need to…find something." But the elusive thing couldn't be found. I swam after Emma towards the gabbagabba room, evading the lecherous shark because I wasn't that kind of man. "I like your stroke," I told Tupp, who was flat out naked on the meeting table, his red hairs like lava from an earthquake, erection bobbing upwards. Seeing him like that—all vulnerable and hairy—made my underpants ache. "I say!"

"Do you? Do you really? I'm struggling, Tim, I don't mind telling you. Where is it?"

That Tupp should be in pain was unacceptable. I pulled him into me, feeling that something terribly important needed to be done. "I'll keep you safe," I assured him. "We'll find it."

Queen Tash carried a long trident. She sat at the head of the table, occasionally banging it to get our attention. "It has come to my notice that things are not going the way they should. Things are amiss!"

For a while, I could see only the Tupp of Tupp and how utterly gorgeous he was. As I held his fins and kissed the tears from his eyes, I knew that…I knew it would certainly…I knew. We talked for hours about the hidden city of Atlantis, his face turning into that of the fish man and then back to the Tupp. I knew. Man, but I knew. His words went from his usual mild-mannered to the dirty-talking jibes of the riverbank until my head was spinning. Was this Tupp or was it Neptune? Ma-aan.

"Do—did I meet you last night?" I whispered when he finally paused talking.

"Meet? No. We went to the pub and then I got on with my book, Tim." His grin once again reminded me of the fishy fellow.

"Oh. What book?"

"Something about love potions. I'm so very tired. Shall we sleep awhile and away with a slumber?"

My arse did not know my elbow. In the far corner of the room, Emma began slithering towards the queen. The next time I opened my eyes, I saw that she and Tash were rolling around together naked, and Crack was balancing the trident on his head.

***

After a rather average day's work, I once again found myself tripping down the steps to the river, hurrying through the greens and whites of the wild garlic flowers. My heart was beating wildly with anticipation and also trepidation. All day I'd thought about the foul-talking fish who'd held me so tightly, who'd seen through the follies of the day into the sad lonely spot that was Tim. I thought about him, about Tupp, and the whole mess of existence.

Summer was everywhere—in the bees and the trees rustling far above—in the hazy warmth that enveloped the world. Walking quickly, it seemed to me this was the only part of the day that had made sense, yet still the niggle that something was amiss continued to tug at my consciousness.

"Where are you?" I whispered, even though there was nobody else around. "I'm here."

"You again!" A laughing voice filtered up from the water. "You got fuck all else to do?"

"Actually, I have a very important job to do! My department is vital in the protection of the nation. We are trained to spot pattern anomalies that may be subliminal messages attempting to—"

"Yeah, yeah. Have a pew. Talk to me about something that really matters. I want to know about *you*."

About me? Nobody wanted to know about me. They wanted me to pay my bills and taxes, be a functioning member of society, fit into the routines that make it up, sure. But know about me? I tried to remember the last time anyone had asked, and I couldn't. "Well, I…" Funny, but the question made my face heat up. "What do you want to know?" I tried to study his features, but all I could focus on was the heat and the redness of his hair.

"What do you want in life, Tim?"

If anyone else had asked me that, say down the pub or in the office, I'd probably drone on about pensions and share certificates, and not worry too much until they began snoring. But in that quiet spot, I felt lost and adrift. "I don't know."

"Course you do. You wanna be loved."

"Loved?" I laughed. "I'm not a teenager and this isn't a soap opera. It's my life. *Love*?" I spat out the word like it was poison, but a lonely tear dripped down my nose.

"Yeah, love, dickhead, and right now your life consists of talking to Neptune and being sarcastic. What does that tell you?" He popped something in his mouth and began chewing.

"That I'm going crazy?"

"That you're missing the plot, yeah. Come here." He opened his arms wide. I tried to look disgusted. After all, a middle-aged man had no business snuggling with a giant fish, but instead I rushed down the banking and straight into his haddock embrace. "That's nice." He nuzzled my hair and intermittently made huge bubble gum bubbles. "So how come you aren't doing this every night with someone special?"

"Surely the question here," I began.

"Oh fuck off! You don't half talk like a knobhead sometimes. All posh and uppity, like you're the king's pizzle. You can cut that out with me 'cause I know you go on dating sites." He sniggered rather cruelly.

"I do not!" If there was one thing I hated, it was bullying. "Surely the question is who the hell are you and what are you doing here, codpiece?"

"Who am I? Oh, you know that." He kissed my head again. "I'm just waiting for you to come and get me, tiger. Then you can take me off to somewhere exotic and nibble my fins."

If there was one thing I hated, it was being called a tiger. I tried to tell him so in between snogs, but everything only grew hotter and more confusing. My underpants, frankly, did not help.

"Shall we swim? I'm so very hot," I gasped, allowing him to fiddle with my undercarriage. "I say!"

"Swim? I fucking hate water."

"But you're a fish."

"Yes, life is full of ironies," he chuckled. "Did you know my middle name is Salt?"

I fell asleep with the trickling of water and the knowledge that I was lost.

CHAPTER FOUR

THURSTY? WHO GAVE a shit what day it was. If there was one thing I hated it was fish. Machete Betty insistently flashed pictures of some bastard in tights and a drug addict with wings. I blinked for a while, trying to find Australia, but soon gave up and fell into the arms of Tuppy Tupp. "Have anybody got headaches?" We're highly trained to recognise, after all. "How about you?" I kissed Tupp's tufty ear. "How are you feeling?" Somewhere in the distance, I was aware of Betty making noisy bleeps.

"Do it to me again, Tim," he begged. "I—I just want it. Sex! Sex! Sex!" His laughing was mead. All I'd ever wanted was to lie with Tupp in a corner of the office, naked and sweaty, rolling him this way and that, having him at will. At the side of my computer, the river gushed by, and all around the sweet heady smell of wild flowers perfumed the air. At times, his legs appeared more like a fishy tail; at all times, he wanted more sex. We'd been at it for hours, or it could have been weeks. Delicious tumbling and chasing amidst the grasses and trees, rocking and thrusting into the breeze. At first, I'd been worried about covering up, because I was a highly trained professional, but now, I ran freely, limbs and bits swinging with unadulterated joy.

"Where's everyone else?" I tugged at his ear hair with my teeth. "We should be—be—looking for it."

"Oh they're having sex too. Queen Tash has tied Crack up and now they're riding his waves." Tupp licked my stomach. "You're the most beautiful tiger I ever saw. Your stripes and fangs…"

"Fangs?" I watched him through a fog of love.

"Mm! Most tigers are deadly, but not you. For ages—you know I was afraid of you? Always so clever and quick, I know you thought I was stupid."

"But…"

"But now I see you for who you really are! You're kind and caring. Not all tigers would have made sure the team eat and keep warm. You know? You could have eaten us all! It's like you kept all your goodness hidden inside in case it covered the world in… goodness." He began to grow hard again. "I want you so much. I—I love you. This time we've spent together has been the best time of my life. Do you want bubble gum?"

My breathing was losing it once again. Watching Tupp getting aroused just from talking about me was not something a person could be prepared for. "But you turned me down? That time at the pub?"

He threw his head back and laughed. The sinews and muscles of his pale body were pulled tight as I started touching him again, powerless to resist. "That's because I was scared, Tim. I'd had far too much to drink, you see. I can never get it up after a few pints. Then afterwards, you just avoided me. Every time I went near, you sneered and made jokes. I lost the nerve. We were both idiots." Fully hard now, he sat with legs apart on his knees like all my wishes come true. I ran my hands up between his thighs and then down again. "Touch me, Tim! Be my tiger!"

So I did. If there was one thing I hated, it was someone who wouldn't be a tiger.

***

After work, I ran down the steps to the river, desperate to find the missing thing. The heat had turned into storms with drenching rain and growling thunder. Shivers wracked my body. "Where are you?" I shouted. The pathway had become a slippery nightmare with tree roots barring the way. It were as if all the air had been sucked away, leaving only a heaving, deadly place. I had to stop every few minutes to rest my aching limbs and because I seemed to have no energy left. “Help me!” I screamed, my head heavy with the oppressive atmosphere and an increasing fear.

“Here! I’m here.”

I fell into an old hut at the side of the trees, but instead of meeting the fish man, Tupp was crouched inside, rocking. He spoke haltingly as if he, too, was in pain.

“Tim. You have to do it.”

I squeezed in next to his shivering body and knew he was right. Somewhere in my thudding head, I remembered. I shouted out the words, “Machete Betty! Code Shakespeare! A Midsummer Night’s Dream.”

There was a deafening crack of thunder as the world began to break apart. I hugged Tupp, and he hugged me, and then we fell into the chasm that opened.

CHAPTER FIVE

THE DIRECTOR ADJUSTED his glasses. The clock on the wall ticked and a bee buzzed over by the window. Even now, four weeks later, I kept digging my nails into my palms to check I was still in reality. "So. I'd like to remind us all why we're here." This was the first time the team had been back to the office. I'd seen Tupp a few times in the hospital as we recovered, but that was all. I hadn't seen the others since arriving a few moments ago. Everyone sat with eyes downcast, presumably thinking of the events of a month before.

Nudity.

Sex.

Nudity.

More sex.

Much, much more sex.

My underpants twitched. I risked a glance at Tupp sideways. He looked back and smiled, bushy eyebrows shooting up. Of course, by now, I was fully free of the group hallucinations that had caused the catastrophic failure of the A-team, but yet I thought for a second I saw his tail once again and smelled the riverbank.

His eyes were shining, that strange combination of brown, red, and gorgeous. The top button of his shirt had come undone and red hairs were climbing to be free.

I blinked against the sudden barrage of images of him on top of me, in my arms, kissing, running, laughing…

"Tim!" the director said sharply. "Put Tupp down!"

"Sorry, sir. It's a little difficult to focus in this heat. Perhaps it would have been better if we'd all had the opportunity to meet informally first?"

"So you could ogle?" he snapped. "The hospital got sick and tired of chasing you, preventing you breaking into each other's rooms every night so you could." He rubbed the bridge of his glasses. "It's fucking amazing nobody got pregnant."

"Well, I…" Tupp said, deliciousness pouring from his body like bright-red love hearts. "Actually, I believe…"

Underneath the desk, something nudged my foot. I sat back and looked to see what was rubbing my shoe, then up my leg. Tupp's toes wriggled up, like waving. I suppressed my smile and began slipping off one shoe so my toes could join his.

"Where do I start? You were all trained, *meticulously* trained! Yet not one of you saw the warning signs—or if you did, you chose to ignore them. Machete Betty was screaming Code Red at full blast, but still nobody raised the alarm. For one whole day, you endured hallucinations which led to orgies and—" he stopped to weep "—more orgies. Disgusting shows of affection and sexual deviance…"

"I say…" I began indignantly.

"I knew something was wrong," Queen Tash said quietly. I remembered her and Emma making Crack scream with multiple orgasms, Emma one end, she the other. "I admit, I—"

"*Why*?" the director shouted suddenly. "Why didn't anyone say the code word? Do you have any idea how this makes me look? By the time Tim initiated shutdown, you were all completely gone. When the ambulance arrived, they found the whole team locked—I say locked—in pleasure. Craig was in—" he paused to pucker his face into an ugly shape "—handcuffs and duct tape, sporting a fox-tail butt plug! If this gets out, the department is ruined. On the way to the hospital, the staff reported multiple orgasms. Shameful!" He began to sob quietly.

"Let's take five minutes." I pulled on Tupp's hand.

***

In the staffroom, the clock ticked loudly. "Tea?" The hum of the fridge seemed overpoweringly loud but not enough to squash the awkwardness. Crack, Emma and Tash had gone into the other meeting room, so it was just Tupp and me.

Gently, he took the cups from my shaking hands and led me to the plastic sofa that made noises like farts. "No, I don't want tea, and neither do you. What I want is what I've wanted for months. To talk to you, Tim, to really talk." He pushed me down, amidst atrocious noises.

"Do you really hate water?"

He laughed. "Yes! And I smoke, but don't tell my mum." He sat close, but not close enough. "What do you remember about it?"

"You were half fish, and you swore a lot."

"And you were a tiger man," he grinned wolfishly. "And when we banged, I..."

He pulled my head to his and then we kissed. This time, there were no sharks or river, only heat and longing. I found my hands in his hair and my tongue pushing against his. I climbed onto his lap like he was a rocking horse waiting to go. "But is this real?" I asked, between writhing. "What if it's just hallucinations again?"

"It's real. I admit it went too far." He spoke into my ear. "It was...it was me, you see. I planted the messages into the screensavers because I was—" I pulled back from his embrace in astonishment "—bored and horny and desperate for you. And also because I was sick and tired of all that mindless training. We are a highly skilled team programmed to spot anomalies...blah, blah." He giggled. "When all the time Emma was running an online gambling business and Craig was watching porn."

"But—"

"Oh my god I didn't think it would take over the whole team!" He scrubbed his face with his hands. "Shit, I didn't even believe all that stuff about the messages. I thought at most it might make us want to go swimming after work. I should never have done it. And then I got swept up in it—in you. I know it was false, but it felt so real, and so does this! Those times mean more to me than anything else."

I knew exactly what he meant because I'd spent the last few weeks thinking exactly the same thing. "Oh my god." I sat back on his legs. "You have to tell them. I thought you were goody two shoes!"

"I'm so sorry. I'll understand if you never talk to me again."

"Are you crazy? All I can think about is you."

***

The director mopped his forehead with tissues cut into the shapes of starfish.

"Look, the thing is I never intended… I only… I didn't realise how powerful it was!"

The director took off his glasses and glared at Tash. "How could you? My own daughter?"

"But it was me who…" Tupp stood up. I jumped up with him and put my arm across his shoulders.

"Actually, I…" Crack started.

"Oh, but surely it was me?" Emma flung.

"It was me, yes. I did it. I'm sorry! I didn't intend it to be so strong, honestly. I was doing a little research of my own by placing subliminal messages in the screensaver." Tash shook her head. "I don't understand what went wrong!"

"Wait! Did you initiate the messages in Betty?" I asked. Tash nodded. "Well, that explains it! Machete Betty strikes again. I've always said that computer is alive." The laugh began deep down, somewhere like Australia. It bubbled up, and as it escaped, I realised that I didn't care if I lost my job, because now I had something much more important. I gripped Tupp's hairy hand and knew I might never let him go. "I'm sorry," I laughed, "but can't we just put it down to the heat and the summer solstice? There's no harm done, is there? The truth is, we were all shittlessly bored and horny."

"But, Tim…" the director began.

"Anyway, Tupp and I would like to request a period of extended leave. In fact, we may never return. We've a date in The Peak District at the Three Fishes."

"No, Tim, I cannot allow it! And you still have some explaining to do!" He pointed at the others. "You mean to say you *all* fiddled with office equipment?"

If there was one thing I hated, it was an overprotective parent. I led Tupp away quietly, and in the shouting and noise, nobody seemed to notice or care.

"Let's go down to the river first, with fish and chips," I said. "We need to talk, and kiss. Let's start from the beginning."

The End

ABOUT NEPTUNE FLOWERS

Neptune Flowers is a British author, best known for short stories and pub poetry.

ONCE AROUND SEVEN

OFELIA GRÄND

Oswald Sattle is out of money and out of options. After more than eight months of sleeping in his car, when an acquaintance from his past offers him a job opportunity in the middle of nowhere, he can't turn it down. No matter how much he'd like to.

Joshua Roth moved to Nortown four years ago, and he has everything he needs—a job, friends, peace and quiet. He's not interested in a relationship, or anything else that would upset the life he's built for himself.

But sometimes fate has other plans, and a single glimpse can completely change the course of a life.

In a small town, where everyone knows everyone else's business, reaching for what you want can feel like a risk. But some risks are worth taking.

***

Genre: gay romance

Keywords: gay, Nortown, HFN, prior abusive relationship, lumberjacks, acupuncturist, romance

Advisory: mature content

ACKNOWLEDGEMENTS

There are two amazing human beings I wouldn't last without—Al and Amy, thank you for taking on yet another lumberjack! And a huge thanks to all of you who get excited when I say I'm working on another Nortown story; it shocks me every time.

CUTE GUYS & OPEN RELATIONSHIPS

Oswald Sattle gazed out the windscreen of his Toyota Camry—a sorry sight. Both the car and the view. *How fitting.*

Cracks melted into a spider web on the asphalt before him, the tenement houses to his left were a soulless grey, and the shop in the bottom floor of the last house in the row made him long to turn the key and keep on going. He should keep going. Why he'd come here, he didn't know.

The morning was damp and dull, the leaves in the process of turning orange, and Oswald had been fighting to breathe for two hundred and seventy-three days.

Two hundred and seventy-three days ago Oswald had been the happiest he'd ever been, happier than he'd ever expected to be…and now he was here. In Nortown.

In one second, everything had changed. One slow tick of the clock had been the starting shot for people to squirm in the benches, then the buzz of their whispers rose in the church. Oswald had walked into the room where Guy was getting ready before the ceremony, and there Matt Herman had been on his knees with Guy's cock buried in his throat.

Oswald's world had crumpled. His fiancé had cheated on him on their wedding day, and with Matt. Matt was sweet and kind, and Oswald had always considered him a friend. Worst of all was that Matt had smiled at him, Guy had sighed, and all the while Oswald was dying.

Humiliation painted his face as he sank into the memory. *In the church, Guy cheated on me in the church.*

He forced down another breath. As long as he could get some oxygen into his system, he could keep going. There was no need to think of hopes and wants—all that mattered was to fill his lungs with air and stay upright. He didn't need anyone to tell him things would turn out fine, that he was still young and would find someone new—he wasn't all that young and as for finding someone... There had never been anyone but Guy. No one had ever wanted him before Guy. If he'd ever wanted him.

It didn't matter much. He didn't have anyone but Guy, not that he'd ever really had him. Apparently.

He tapped his forefinger seven times against the steering wheel and looked at the clock on the dashboard. Aiden would be here soon. He glanced at the sign above the door to the massage studio next to the rundown motorway café—could he work there? He couldn't breathe.

No!

He couldn't stay here, couldn't be around people. He had to leave, had to keep on going. He cast a glance over his shoulder. The mattress he'd squeezed into the back of the car, the pile of clothes, and a few sets of untouched acupuncture needles was all he owned.

Tapping his forefinger seven times against his knee, he filled his lungs with air. Breathing. That was the only thing he had to do. Just keep on breathing.

The key dangled in the ignition, but somehow the little leather owl keychain slipped between his fingers when he tried to grab it. His hand trembled as he tapped the steering wheel seven more times, but at least the tapping calmed his heart and let some more air into his system.

The sound of a door clicking shut made him glance to the left. A man hurried out of a tenement house and crossed the street. He wore grey sweats and a black T-shirt that clung to a chiselled chest. His hair pointed in every possible direction, and he was rubbing a hand over a coppery beard as he yawned. Oswald turned away, not wanting to get caught watching anyone.

A tap on the passenger side window made him jump. *Fuck!*

Aiden waved at him through the glass, his green eyes sparkling and his dark curls peeking out from underneath a knitted cap. Oswald forced a smile onto his lips. *Fucking Aid.*

Why had Aiden called him? Why couldn't he just have forgotten about him like everyone else had?

Aiden yanked the passenger door open. "Hey, man! Come on, let me buy you a cup of coffee." He nodded towards the café, and just as Oswald looked at the entrance, the man from the tenement house slipped inside. He quickly tore his gaze away from the man's backside.

"Hi." Oswald clenched his hand into a fist as to not tap the window before reaching for the door handle. Somehow he made it out of the car, fingers still trapped in a fist and with both feet on the ground.

"It's so good to see you." Aiden wrapped his arms around Oswald before he had time to react. He already smelled of coffee, but there was also a hint of lavender.

The scent made Oswald's eyes burn; it reminded him of another time, another life. He wasn't the same person anymore, but he couldn't let Aiden see that.

He needed to leave, needed to keep going, needed to find a place where no one knew him. But he was running out of money, and the nights were turning colder. He might not take much joy in living, but he didn't want to freeze to death in his car.

"Come on." Aiden let go of him and smiled. "I'm so freaking glad you came, you have no idea."

"You are?" Oswald tried to keep the surprise out of his voice. When had someone ever been glad to see him? Guy had pretended to be, but— He tapped his finger seven times against his thigh.

"It'll be great. I'm so excited that something finally will happen around here. It took forever to get hold of you. I had no idea you'd moved."

"Yeah…" Ice filled his gut. "Guy and I…we…erm—"

"Yeah, Jason told me. I'm sorry, man." Aiden squeezed his arm, and as usual, Oswald held his breath, but thankfully he didn't continue with the speech of him being better off without Guy. He wasn't, but he couldn't have stayed with him either, not after…

"You…erm…have been in contact with Jason?"

Aiden gave him a strange look. "Of course. He's thrilled you're coming too, you know."

Oswald stumbled on empty air but managed to stay upright. "Jason?"

"Yeah, sure. I told him you were on your way."

Oswald was going to throw up. "He's here?"

"Sure. He's working today, so you'll see him in a second."

Oswald stopped. "Aiden."

"Yeah?"

"I can't."

"Can't what?"

"I can't see Jason." Hot and cold dashed around in his belly, and he was sure whatever was in it soon would climb up his throat and out onto the asphalt.

"Why not?" Aiden frowned and Oswald's gaze fastened on the crease between his eyebrows—it was much easier than to meet his stare. "He and Guy… Guy told me he and Jason had been—"

"But Jason has been with Tom for over a year now. He hasn't been with Guy in a long time."

Time stopped.

"You knew?" Oswald's gut tried to turn inside out. Aiden had known and hadn't said anything. Saliva flooded his mouth as he started tapping his thigh. *Breathe. One-two-three-four-five-six-seven.* All he had to do was breathe.

"Are you okay?" Aiden touched his arm again, and Oswald held completely still, waiting for him to move away. "I have to say, I never understood it, but you seemed happy. Weren't you happy?"

"With my fiancé fucking my friends?"

Seconds swished by—those hated seconds. So much could change in just a tick of a clock.

"Sweetie…" Oswald winced at the word, but he reminded himself it wasn't the first time Aiden had called him sweetie and he didn't mean it in a patronising way…probably. Guy only ever used endearments to belittle him, but this was Aiden.

Oswald forced down more air and counted to seven as his forefinger tapped the pad of his thumb.

"You had an open relationship. If you weren't okay with Guy being with people you knew, then you should've told him so. I'm sure you guys had rules, right?"

Oswald heard the words, but something about them didn't make sense. More seconds ticked by as he tried to sort them out. "What do you mean, open relationship?"

Aiden's eyes narrowed, the sparkle in them had died. "You weren't monogamous. Everyone knew that."

Oswald swallowed. For a second, he was certain he'd fallen asleep in his car and this whole conversation was a nightmare, but the almost painful grip Aiden had on his arm made him suspect it wasn't the case.

"Ox…"

Oswald shuddered at the nickname. An ox was robust and stable. Oswald was a scraggy excuse of a man; there was nothing strong about him—nowadays even less than before.

"You were with others too, right?"

He opened his mouth to respond, but not a sound came from his lips.

Aiden's eyes widened and he let go of his arm. "You agreed to…he was the only one who saw others?" The apprehension in his voice might have been funny if it hadn't been Oswald's life they were discussing.

"Agreed to what?" Oswald shouldn't be snapping at Aiden. He didn't think Guy had ever been with him, he hadn't thrown Aiden's name in his face, but how would Oswald ever know for sure? He tapped his thigh again.

"You didn't have an agreement?" Aiden locked his fingers around his wrist as if to force himself not to touch Oswald again.

Oswald shook his head, one quick motion as he pressed his lips together from preventing any embarrassing sounds from escaping him.

"Oh, babe, I'm so sorry. I always assumed…everyone did, you know."

Oswald nodded but turned towards his car. He had to get out of here.

"Morning, Aiden." The man from the tenement house gave Aiden a nod as he passed, then he smiled at Oswald—a quick quirk of the lips. Oswald stopped mid-step and forced himself to respond in kind, though he feared it looked more like a wince than a smile.

"Joshua! This is Oswald." Aiden gestured towards him, and the man, Joshua, stopped to look, a sparkle lit in his blue-green eyes.

"He's gonna work with me."

Oswald's no was drowned out by Joshua's "You are? Here in Nortown?"

"He is." Aiden beamed and bounced on his feet.

"You're a massage therapist, too?" Joshua's eyes swept over his face as he took a sip from his to-go cup, and Oswald wanted to hide.

"Acupuncturist."

Joshua winced. "Needles? Really?"

Oswald surprised himself by smiling. "Yeah, though I do acupressure, too."

"Oh good, that I might be able to endure." Joshua grinned and started walking again. "Nice to meet you, Oz. I'll come see you when you're up and running."

Oswald watched him go, a bit uncertain about what had just happened.

"Just like that?" Aiden threw his hands in the air. "I've tried to get him to come see me for a year, and all you have to do is show up." The smile told him Aiden was kidding, but Oswald wanted to cower anyway. "It will be great." Aiden nudged his arm. "Do you want to see the studio now?"

"I-I was…" Oswald glanced at his car. He should leave. "Yeah, sure."

***

Joshua Roth ran up the stairs into Andre's flat and over to the living room window where he could see Aiden lead Oswald towards the café.

"What are you doing?" Andre, his colleague and carpooling buddy, came out from the bedroom, dressed for work which meant sweats and a T-shirt. They'd change once they got to the sawmill—protective gear on at all times.

"Aiden brought a new guy." Joshua rubbed his neck and looked as they disappeared in through the door to the studio.

Andre came to stand next to him. "A new guy?"

"Yeah, an acupuncturist. He's gonna work here."

"Shit, needles." Andre shuddered, and Josh chuckled.

"That was what I said." Joshua grabbed his bag of clothes. He'd been staying with Andre for five days, but tonight, he'd go home. Friday, finally, and he should be able to live in his own place.

His cabin had almost burned to the ground, some electrical short circuit or other in the kitchen, and it had taken some time to restore it. Josh had known he needed to go over the electricity but as long as things worked, he kept pushing it into the future—he guessed he should be glad he had a future.

He could've died.

The last few days he'd had electricians, chimney sweepers, and plumbers stumbling over each other, so he'd fled to Andre's. But, according to the phone call he'd received yesterday, they'd be done today. Now he just needed to fix everything up inside, but he could do that. He knew his way around a paint bucket.

"But…is he really gonna work here? Is there anyone who'd pay to get needles stuck into them?"

Josh had no idea. The guy had been ready to bolt, so maybe it didn't matter. Rubbing his chest, he looked out the window again. There had been hurt in the guy's eyes, not that Joshua had any plans on doing anything about it. Same as there was a pain in Andre's eyes that he didn't have any plans to try to soothe. He was here if Andre wanted to talk, if he wanted to get drunk and sob on his shoulder, but fix it? Nah, people needed to fix their own shit. Josh had his life under control, and he expected everyone else to have theirs under control as well.

It wasn't that he didn't care about his friends, of course he did, and he was a good listener. He probably knew more about Andre than any other person on this planet, not that he had the first couple of years they'd rode together. Back then, they'd talked about work, the weather, and other boring shit, but then Zachary Fane had come to town. Joshua knew he should've told Andre that he was gay too once Andre had come out to him, but he didn't want people meddling in his business. Knowing what was going on in everyone's life kept him calm, he liked being aware of what was going down, but he never told anyone. They weren't his secrets to tell, and he didn't want anyone spreading his secrets either. So he listened, he kept quiet, and he lived a good life.

Everything was great.

He grinned and glanced at Andre. "Probably not. Cute guy, though, so perhaps you should go see him."

What Josh had been thinking when he'd said he'd come by the studio when Oswald had set it up he didn't know, because

Aiden had been on him about coming to see him more times than he could count, and he hadn't gone no matter how much his body ached. He didn't mind hanging out with Andre, not at all, he loved Andre, but people often assumed you were gay if you surrounded yourself with queer friends, and he didn't need the complication. Not that he cared what people said about him, but he liked it just fine when people assumed he was single because he hadn't found the right woman yet. Made life easier. And coming out now was just silly—like it was catching in this godforsaken town. Nope, Joshua was fine with things being just the way they were.

"You thought he was cute?" Andre raised an eyebrow.

Cute? Had he said cute? He was cute, looked like he'd slept in his car. His dishwater-blonde hair was a mess and he wore a day or two worth of stubble. Joshua turned to Andre with a blank face. "Small, a little twitchy, much like Aiden, actually. Not your type?" He knew it wasn't. There was nothing small or twitchy about Zachary Fane and apparently he was the only guy who could get Andre hot and bothered. Josh didn't see the allure, but to each their own.

Andre shook his head. "Another one?"

When Josh widened his eyes, Andre sighed. "Don't get me wrong, I like Aiden just fine, but do you remember when Nortown was calm? When there were no squealing men in the café, when we didn't have lattes, flapping hands, and bouncing curls?"

Josh chuckled. "Nope, man. Just moved here four years ago, remember?"

"But even then…" Andre shrugged.

"He didn't strike me as a squealing guy." *No, he seemed more like a run-and-hide kind of guy.*

"I meant nothing by it. I love Aiden and what he's done for the village." For a second exhaustion clouded Andre's eyes, and Joshua had to fist his hand not to reach out and touch him. Then the mask of total control slipped back into place. "Are you ready to go?"

"Sure. You don't want a cup to-go? I can run down and get one while you start the car."

Andre frowned at him. "When have I ever wanted a cup to-go?"

Joshua shrugged and looked at the door to the massage studio one last time.

LAVENDER & CANOES

OSWALD LOOKED AT the room Aiden had set up as his treatment room. It was beautiful—smaller than his last, but the energy was more relaxing.

"Looks really nice, Aid."

"But?" Aiden tilted his head to the side as he watched him.

"But… I don't know if I'm fit to work." He would have to, though. The money he'd lived on for the last two hundred and seventy-three days was the money he'd saved for a down-payment on a house. He'd wanted him and Guy to live in a house, to maybe even have a family one day…or a dog. Perhaps a dog would be better than children—Oswald didn't know what to do with children.

It had taken years to scrape together; that Guy hadn't put anything away should've been his first warning perhaps. But, there would be no house, and unless he started working soon, there would be no Oswald either.

"Are you sick? Oh, babe, you're not, are you? Please say you're not."

Oswald winced at the 'babe' but tried to hide it. "No, just not fit mentally." He tapped his thumb seven times against his thigh, then curled his toes seven times inside his shoes.

Aiden shook his head. "What happened, Ox?"

He shrugged. "It's all right, I'll…I don't have much money."

"Don't worry about it." Aiden reached out and squeezed his arm, and Oswald tried not to flinch. Aiden was touchy-feely, and it was fine. It wasn't that he didn't like touch. He wasn't a germophobe or anything, it was just… How should he react?

Should he touch back? Should he just stand there? What did the touches mean?

When Guy touched him he wanted sex, and there was safety in that—a hand on his shoulder and he could just as well drop to his knees on the spot. It was easy; he knew his role and what was expected of him.

Growing up, he could never remember anyone hugging him or having him sit on their lap or other things he saw parents do with their kids. He guessed being shuffled around guaranteed no one took the time to bond with him.

"If it doesn't work out, I can ask someone else." Aiden gave him a guarded look. "I don't know…are you still in contact with anyone from school?"

Oswald blinked at him. It had been years since they'd met at the Bodywork Institute. He remembered their names, but that was all. "No, sorry."

"You know what?" Aiden grinned, his green eyes sparkling. "I don't want anyone else. I know we haven't worked together before, and we haven't been the closest of friends, but I think we could be great. So, if you want to try it out, perhaps work a day or two a week just to see if it's possible, you can do it rent free."

"Aid, I know you dragged me here because you needed money. I can't let you pay for me."

"No, but hear me out, okay? I have this—" he gestured around "—and I'm only using one room because I can only have one client at a time so whether you use it or not, the room is still here. And yes, I need someone to split the rent with, I need to be able to take a day off now and then, and I can't afford it at the moment. But I'm willing to lend you the room for free for, say, a month or two and you can see if it works for you."

"That's very kind, Aiden, but—"

"So we'll do it like that, yes?"

Oswald breathed in, allowed the scent of lavender to loosen some of his muscles and nodded. He'd come here, hadn't he? "Okay, but I won't start next week. I need a week to…to land."

Aiden flung himself at him, arms closing around his neck. "It'll be awesome, Ox! Where are you staying? Do you need to come live with Tristan and me? You can, you know. There isn't much room, but we'll manage."

Oswald's heart was pounding in his ears. "No, that's all right. I'm…erm…I'm staying at the hotel."

Aiden frowned. "In…Northfield?"

There wasn't one in town? Oswald nodded. "Yeah, in Northfield."

***

Oswald drove and drove, and then he drove some more. Going off the main road might not have been his smartest decision, but the narrow gravel roads had begged for him to come. All around there were trees, one more colourful than the other, and for the first time since Aiden had managed to get hold of him, he could fill his lungs with ease—well, maybe not ease, but it was easier.

It would be easy to lose himself in the woods. Give up. Fade away. No one would miss him if he weren't to be anymore. He'd held on for two hundred and seventy-three days; maybe it was all right to let go. It was fitting, decomposing together with the leaves falling off the trees.

Frowning, he drummed his thumb seven times against the steering wheel. He needed out of the car. Needed to think away from the sad reality of the mattress and the pile with a few sets of clothes that were all he owned.

He'd walked out of Guy's apartment without taking a single thing of what they'd bought together, without a single souvenir. Since he was a kid, he'd learnt not to get attached to things; fewer items made it quicker to pack.

The forest cleared a little up ahead, and Oswald was surprised to see a sign. Had he perhaps found Northfield? He should probably check on a map where that was and get his sweet arse over there so he could find the hotel Aiden had mentioned.

The sign was red and white, flaking paint revealing dark-grey wood underneath. 'Canoe Rentals', it said.

Canoes? It couldn't be too hard, could it? He'd get some fresh air and exercise and wouldn't have to think about his pitiful life trapped in a rusty Toyota. Stopping by the road, he drummed his finger against the window seven times and jumped out. On the way over to the cottage, he pressed his forefinger against his thumb—he only made it to five before a man came out to meet him. After having said hello, he started over and managed seven uninterrupted taps.

***

Joshua sighed as he walked into his cabin. There was craft paper on the floor, cords and shit that the electrician had cut off and left lying around, not to mention the dirty footprints. He guessed it was his job to clean up—not that he would do much. He was painting the living room this weekend so the protective plastic and paper might as well stay where they were.

There was nothing he'd rather do than have a quick shower—the layer of sweat and sawdust clung to him—but this shit would still be here when he got back. Better get it over with now than get grimy again.

It wasn't sparkly clean, but an hour later he'd swept the living room, so there weren't any loose parts on the floor, and cleaned the kitchen and bedroom so he could be there without feeling like he was walking into a construction site. There was nothing he could do about the smell—it had that new touch to it that he hated. Maybe it would be better once he'd cooked something, though he doubted it because the stove was new too. But soon, it would feel like home again.

A quick shower and then he was out the door. Having breathed in sawdust all week, he needed some fresh air, and the river was calling him.

Throwing his fly-fishing rod in the car, he drove off into the forest. The gravel roads on his land snaked their way to the river, and then, when he couldn't drive any farther, it was about a thirty-minute walk before he was at his fishing place.

It took longer for him to get there than it normally did so he couldn't stay long. The nights were getting darker fast, but he needed the quiet, needed to breathe the fresh air, hear the water. Soon, the leaves would fall off the trees, but it only made it more beautiful. Nature was clinging onto life for as long as it could, the abundance of colour as it went out like fireworks only to wake up in a few months again. He loved autumn. All seasons had their charm, but not like autumn.

He sighed and let the week go. The knowledge that he'd go home soon, have a beer, and then sleep for as long as he wanted did wonders for his sanity.

And then an empty canoe came floating down the river.

CURSES & LATE-NIGHT SWIMS

JOSHUA STUMBLED AS he dragged the canoe up onto the riverbank. It was one of Taylor's which meant there probably was a tourist in the woods somewhere. It wouldn't be the first time someone had failed to pull the canoe out of the river before stopping to stretch their legs.

Josh had left his phone in the car, so he couldn't call Taylor and ask to whom he'd rented the canoe. Taylor's place was quite a bit from here, so chances were they'd lost it upstream and already had informed him.

For a second, he played with the idea of ignoring it. He didn't want to spend his Friday evening trekking up the river. Especially considering it would be dark soon and he hadn't managed more than a couple of casts. Growling, he disassembled the fly rod.

Someone could be hurt. *Fucker.*

Leaving his gear by a tree, he walked upstream, keeping his waders on in case he needed to get back into the water, and looking for signs of people.

Dusk was falling, and the few moments of peace Josh had managed to get in were gone. He was sweating again, but the water, while not really cold yet, was cold enough to be dangerous if someone were left in it overnight. Though, if they were still in the river, there were probably more significant problems than cold at play...like a concussion.

Unease crept into his belly. The waterfall was a good fifteen minutes' walk from here, and it wasn't a big one, but you couldn't go down it with a canoe. There was a portage. The canoer got out about 500 metres from the fall and carried the canoe past it.

Joshua increased his speed. If someone had gone down the fall there would probably have been more damage to the canoe, but had he checked? He hadn't, not closely.

If someone had gone down, fallen out, hit their head... Joshua wasn't really keen on finding a dead body this particular night. It hadn't been how he'd pictured it going.

***

The shock of hitting the water had stolen Oswald's breath, then fear had kicked in. *So fucking clumsy.* He'd steered the canoe towards the portage; there had been signs pointing to where he should go, and the man he'd rented the canoe from had talked him through it.

Wasn't standing up in a boat the first thing you learnt not to do? Oswald didn't know, but when he'd begun swaying and wobbling those were the words ringing in his head.

It had been colder than he'd thought it'd be, but the pull of the current was what had panic roaring in his ears. Funny how when he realised he might die if he went down the waterfall he wanted to live. Invisible hands had dragged him down under the surface, and he'd fought them until his muscles ached, until his lungs burned, until a numbness had all but immobilised him.

He'd hit a rock. The pain in his hip as he'd crashed into the solid shape was jarring, but he'd managed to cling to it. Frothy whitewater washed over him as he tore his hands to shreds on the stones—crawling, pulling, dragging. When he'd finally managed to haul himself onto a rock a couple of metres from the riverbank, he'd collapsed there.

Where the canoe had gone, he didn't know, and he didn't have the energy to move. He lay there panting until his eyes drifted closed. He'd just rest for a little bit, just a few minutes; then he'd go the last bit till he was up on dry land.

A few seconds later he began chuckling. *So fucking pathetic.* No wonder Guy had needed others. He couldn't even get himself down a river without fucking up.

The chills came next, his entire body shaking and shuddering and the chuckles turned into sob-like sounds.

Oswald didn't sob; he didn't cry—crying never helped anything. He'd walked in on his husband-to-be with his cock buried in the best man's throat—and he hadn't made a sound. He'd walked up to the altar and told everyone the wedding was off—and he hadn't cried. He'd gone back to the apartment he'd shared with Guy for the last five years and packed his clothes—and not a single tear had escaped his eyes. He'd stood there while Guy had been screaming at him that he was ridiculous, that none of the others meant anything, that everyone knew that, no matter how many others there were, Oswald was the one who mattered. Oswald was the one he'd chosen to marry—and he hadn't uttered one word in response.

Two hundred and seventy-three days, or was it two hundred and seventy-four now? He cracked his eyes open. It was near-full dark, so it might have turned into day number two hundred and seventy-four. With chattering teeth, he looked around.

A bird screeched not far from him; he'd always believed the forest was quiet after dark. Resting his forehead against the rock he tried to make his teeth stop chattering, but it was freaking cold.

Then a branch cracked, and the sound of muttered curses followed.

***

Joshua followed the trail up past the waterfall. It had taken longer than he'd thought it would. His sweat-soaked long-sleeved T-shirt was clinging to his body, and it didn't help that the darkness had grown thicker around him. He wasn't afraid he wouldn't find his way back; he'd walked here often enough in daylight to know where things could get dicey but also when the worst that could happen was he'd scratch himself on a twig.

He walked as close to the river as he could. It was easier to see there than among the trees. The sound of the water quieted as soon as he'd passed the fall. It still sounded louder than it did downstream, but at least he could listen again.

Glancing out over the river, he missed the branch that had fallen over the trail. His legs caught in it, the crack as he stumbled loud enough to wake the dead, and he cursed the devil and his mother while rubbing his calf—no blood.

As he looked out over the river again he thought something moved on a rock just a little bit above where the currents really sped up.

"Hey!"

The form moved again, and a moan travelled in the wind. *Fuck.* He'd hoped he'd imagined it. "Are you all right?" *Stupid question.*

"Splendid. Thanks for asking."

Josh smiled. A man judging from the voice and probably not in danger of dying on him. "Well, then, are you planning on sleeping out there tonight or could I perhaps persuade you to join me up here where it's a little dryer?"

The silence lasted too long for Joshua's liking. "You still with me?" The man groaned, and Josh's stomach knotted. Perhaps he was more hurt than he'd assumed. "Wait there. I'm coming to get you."

He ran back to the branch he'd tripped over and grabbed it. It was long enough for him to test the ground before stepping into the stream. He hoped it wouldn't be deeper than his waders. "You still with me?"

Poking with the stick, he tested the uneven ground and slipped first one then the other foot into the water. He held on to the grass on the riverbank for a few seconds while trying to determine if it was safe to let go. The current was strong, not enough to pull him down, but if he slipped…

Moving one foot, then the stick, then the other foot, and all the while the tug of the current intensified… The man on the rock was crawling towards him, still out of the water but seemingly prepared to take another dip.

"Wait for me, okay?" Joshua looked at him, blond hair clinging to his forehead and the closer he came the clearer he could hear his teeth chattering. "Oswald?"

The man narrowed his eyes, but the chatter of his teeth didn't stop. "Great, of course, it's someone who knows who I am."

Joshua chuckled. "Sorry, man. May I ask, though, why the late-night swim?"

Oswald groaned, one foot slipping in the black river. "Late night? What time is it?"

"I'm guessing around seven." Josh curled his fingers around Oswald's slim wrist, his skin almost colder than the water. "Come on, man." He tugged a little, wishing he could carry him so he wouldn't have to get back in, but not daring to.

"Shit, it's cold."

Josh nodded. "We'll get you warm in no time."

"Somehow, I doubt it."

Yeah. "Okay, but if you give me an hour I'll have you nice and toasty." Josh bit his lip as he pictured Oswald snuggled up in his bed. That was just plain stupid—he didn't have guys snuggle in his bed, ever. "Where are you staying?"

He guided Oz to take a step, then took one himself, and then tugged at Oswald's arm again. Little by little they neared the riverbank, though Oz swayed more than once and Josh clung to the stick jammed between rocks at others.

"I'm not." Oz's voice shook, and Josh could tell his entire being was shivering.

"You're not, what?"

"Staying anywhere. I told Aid I was living in the hotel. Turns out there wasn't one in the village."

Josh chuckled once more. "Okay."

The picture of his bed flashed before his eyes again.

CARS & VOODOO

OSWALD DIDN'T REMEMBER the guy's name. They'd been introduced, but that had been a lifetime ago. With one last tug, the guy managed to pull him out of the water and onto the grass-covered riverbank.

"There you go."

Oswald would've said something if it hadn't been for the trembles shaking his body.

"Do you mind if I check you over?" It wasn't until he asked that Oswald realised the man hadn't touched him any more than he needed to. Not once he'd had solid ground under his feet—or rather, body, since he'd crumbled to the ground on the first step out of the water.

"I'm fine. Only my hands hurt." And his hip, and elbow, and forearms. His entire body ached, his throat sore as if he'd been screaming for hours.

"Okay…I guess it can wait then. You didn't hit your head?"

Oswald shook his head, tapped his thumb seven times against the ground, then rasped, "No."

The silence stretched, and Oswald was distantly aware of the man pacing a couple of metres away from him, but he didn't have the energy to care.

"Oz?"

Oswald jumped. *When had he moved close?*

"I know you're tired, but we need to get moving."

"Where to?" Where the fuck should he go? His car was far away from here, and the canoe was…wherever it was. His wallet and phone were in his pockets, the phone most likely useless after a dip in the river, and maybe the contents of his wallet as well.

"If you're okay with it I'll take you home. A hot shower and you can borrow some clothes."

Oswald made a sound he hoped would be taken for a chuckle. Borrowed clothes he'd drown in sounded nice despite the embarrassment it would bring him.

"What's your name again?"

"Oh, sorry. Josh. Joshua Roth."

"And you're Aid's friend?"

Silence crept into the air again. "No, not really. Everyone knows everybody in a backwater intersection like Nortown, but I don't hang out with Aiden on my off time, no."

"Why?" Why wouldn't he hang out with Aiden? Guys usually flocked around him like bees to honey. He glanced at Joshua. Could be he wasn't gay and didn't see the allure. He didn't exactly like the relief flooding him, but it was there nonetheless.

If Joshua were straight, none of his touches would mean he expected sex—not that he was touching him now, but it took that alternative out of the equation.

Joshua chuckled. "I like peace and quiet."

Oswald smiled, and not the fake smile he'd had to plaster on from time to time during the last months. "I do too."

"Okay, then." Joshua offered him a hand. "It's a bit of a walk, not the easiest path either if you don't know your way in the dark, so I suggest we start moving."

***

Joshua wanted to keep hold of Oz as they walked, but every time he touched him Oz tensed, not shying away, but his teeth stopped chattering as if he froze up, so most often Josh let him stumble on his own. Slowing down as they neared the place where Josh had pulled up the canoe he held out his hand. "Might need some help here."

"Why?"

Oswald didn't take his hand, and Josh frowned. "It's stones, an old cairn that's plummeted into the river. Come on. We're almost at the place I left my things."

Josh swallowed a curse as Oswald swayed when his foot slipped on one of the rounded stones. He grabbed his elbow. "Here." Oswald didn't protest when Josh linked their arms together. "It's only for a few metres."

"Sorry."

"Nothing to be sorry about, I'm just happy I don't have to carry you. Imagine if you'd hit your head, if you'd been unconscious." Josh didn't add 'dead' to the list.

"I meant for being clumsy. I know it's an annoyance, that I'm an annoyance."

Josh frowned, not that Oswald would be able to see it. *Annoyance?* Shit, the poor sod could be dead or still up in the water slowly succumbing to hypothermia. "You're not. It's dark, the ground is uneven, you're cold and probably more than a little tired. Give yourself a break." Josh probably shouldn't have growled the last part, but come on! "Ready for another dip?"

"W-what?"

"My car is on the other side of the river. We'll have to cross it."

Oswald's trembling increased.

"The current isn't nearly as strong, and while it probably will reach about waist-high on you, it's not for more than a few steps." If it would have helped, Josh would've lent him his waders but he was already soaked, plus they'd be too big. He'd neatly pushed Oswald into the small-guy-category when he'd first seen him, but he'd compared him to Aiden. Aiden was small. Having Oz walking next to him now made him realise small really was small. The top of his head didn't reach Joshua's shoulder. He almost wanted to test and see if Oswald could walk under his arm without having to duck. The sound of teeth chattering made him push away all thoughts of size.

"You'll be all right." He curled his fingers around Oswald's wrist and slipped into the water.

It was chilly, but he didn't get wet. Oswald wasn't so lucky, the hitch of his breath had Josh wincing. "It'll get easier after this, I promise."

"Your car is there, on the other side?" They strode through the current.

"Ah…erm…no, it's a bit farther on, but it's a really nice trail, nice and smooth, no stones or branches."

"How…how much farther?"

Josh tugged and pulled and soon they were past the deepest spot. "Almost there."

"I-I meant…shit…" the teeth chattering reached a new level "…till we're by the car."

Josh considered lying. "It's about half an hour, sorry. Come on." Joshua took the last steps and got up on the riverbank, pulling Oz with him. "I'll pour you a nice big whisky once we get home."

"I-I'm not m-much…of a…drinker."

Joshua chuckled. "It'll warm you right up."

***

Oswald wasn't sure if he was dreaming. Perhaps he had a fever and was hallucinating.

"How are you holding up?" Joshua touched his elbow, and Oswald jerked away, stumbling as he did so. Joshua grabbed his arm, and before he could stop himself, he hissed. It hurt.

"Shit, are you hurt? You said you were fine." There were hands everywhere. Or maybe not everywhere but Joshua was gently running his hands over Oswald's arms, shoulders, and up his neck. A shiver, different from that of the cold, shot through Oswald.

"I-I'm fine." He tried to step away, but Joshua curled his fingers around his wrist again like he'd done several times since he fished him out of the water.

"I'm not sure I trust you, Mr…"

"S-Sattle."

"Sooner or later I'll check you over, just so you know. We'll have you out of those clothes, and I'll have a look."

Oswald held his breath. *What did that mean? Have a look.*

"Mind out of the gutter, Mr. Sattle. I can hear the cogs turning."

"I wasn't… It wasn't anything like… I wouldn't think… I know you're not—"

Joshua chuckled which only made Oswald more confused than before. "I'm joking, Oz. Your virtue is safe with me."

"Oh…" If he hadn't been about to freeze to death, he might have blushed, but as it was the embarrassment gave him no warmth. Even if Joshua had been gay, he wouldn't have wanted someone like Oswald so he didn't need to waste energy thinking about what it would have been like. And he hadn't. "Sorry."

"What for?"

Oswald didn't know, but there was probably something he should apologise for. He didn't want to risk infuriating Joshua further though, so he kept quiet.

"So, Oz, if you're Aiden's friend, how come you haven't visited him before?"

Oswald concentrated on putting one foot in front of the other. It was harder to see the ground now since the trail went into the forest, but it was as Joshua had said—no stones or other obstacles.

"Oswald?"

"Sorry… What did you say?"

"Why haven't you been to Nortown before? Or maybe you have, and I just haven't seen you."

"Erm…no, I've never been here." Silence settled again, and Oswald forced himself to keep moving.

Joshua ran a hand through his hair, or, at least, Oswald thought he did. He didn't look up to check, but he heard the rustling of his movements, and maybe there was a sigh too.

"How long have you known Aiden?"

Oswald wasn't sure his legs obeyed him anymore. They moved, which was good, but he wasn't sure he was the one making them do it.

"Oswald!"

He jumped at Joshua's raised voice and then, before he could stop himself, he flinched. "Sorry."

"No, it's okay. I'm just…you're sure you didn't hit your head?" Joshua reached for his head, but Oswald moved away.

"I didn't hit it. I fell into the water." He shuddered. "But it was pretty deep where I fell; then the current pulled me towards the fall, that's where the rocks came."

"Okay, good. Keep on talking." There was a growly edge to Joshua's words, and Oswald's mind blanked. *Talk? About what?* "I'm not hearing you, Oz. Keep up the chatter."

"W-why?" Oswald wasn't interesting enough for someone to want to listen to him. Guy had always said it was mind-numbing to hear him talk. His mouth was made for sucking cock, not talking.

"If you go quiet on me, I'll assume you're hurt and take you straight to the hospital, and if your speech turns slurred, I'll know you're hurt, and I'll take you straight to the hospital."

"Is there any way I can avoid the hospital?"

"Of course. All you have to do is keep talking."

Oswald's heart began hammering, and he drummed his thumb against his thigh seven times. Josh would be bored out of his mind before they reached his car. "This feels like blackmailing."

Joshua laughed softly, way closer than Oswald had believed him to be. "Then we understand each other. Now, talk."

Oswald sucked in a breath. *Talk.* What should he talk about? He pushed his forefinger against his thumb seven times. His pulse rang in his ears. He had nothing to say.

"Why did you become an acupuncturist?"

"I wanted to help people." That was easy; many people had asked him that question.

"Why not a doctor, then?" Joshua walked so close their arms almost brushed against each other.

"Not smart enough."

"I'm not sure I believe you, but okay. Why not a massage therapist like Aiden?"

Oswald slowly blew out the air. "I'm a little strange with touch." *Too honest.* He bit his lip, cursing himself for not thinking before talking.

Josh was quiet for a moment too long. Oswald went through his words in his head again. *Stupid.* He should've lied, should've said something about…about…what could he have said?

"Strange with touch? You like sticking needles into them instead? You're a Voodoo practitioner, aren't you?"

"What? No!"

Joshua chuckled again. "You're too easy, Oz." He touched his shoulder, just a quick squeeze. "Look there." He pointed through the trees and Oswald came close to tears when he saw the shape of a car.

SUNFLOWERS & SHOWERS

JOSH STARTED THE car and turned on the interior light.

"Urgh." Oz squinted and turned away, but Josh didn't care.

"Let me look at you." He touched Oz's shoulder lightly.

"I'm fine."

There was dried blood on Oz's hands, but he couldn't see any in his hair which was good. "I'll believe that when I see it."

Eyes so pale they couldn't be called anything other than grey turned his way. A small wrinkle appeared between Oz's brows as if confused. It was that confusion that worried him. Simply because there wasn't any blood in his hair didn't mean he hadn't hit his head.

"I'm fine."

"We'll see." Josh grinned and started driving. He turned the heating to the max in hopes of making Oz more comfortable. "Keep talking."

"What? I'm fine. You can see that I'm fine." Desperation shone in his eyes, and Josh debated letting him off the hook...but no. He liked hearing him talk. He had a lilt to his voice he hadn't heard before, and the slightly raspy tone might very well be from having spent too long in the water, but Josh liked it.

"There is no way I can say you're fine simply by looking at you for two seconds in crappy car lighting. How long have you known Aiden?"

Oz glared at him, and Josh bit his cheek not to grin.

"I don't know Aiden."

"You don't? I could've sworn he introduced you back in town."

"Now you're just being... Sorry."

This time, Josh did grin. "What am I being?"

"Nothing, I didn't mean... I met Aiden at the Bodywork Institute where we studied. Not together, we took different classes, but it's a pretty small school and after a while..." He shrugged. "By the time we were finished everyone knew each other."

"Okay, and then you stayed in touch?" Josh glanced at him, once again seeing that small wrinkle appear.

"On and off. I-I met Guy soon after, and Aiden...I guess he started working at the hotel."

"In Whiteport?"

"Erm...yeah, Whiteport." Oz rested his head against the backrest, his eyes only half open.

"So..." *Shit, what should I ask now?* "How come you're going to work with Aiden now?" Tension crawled into the car. Oswald sat up straighter again, and Josh almost regretted his question.

"I...erm...left Guy and..." He shrugged.

Left Guy, huh. Well, better to leave than be left. "Sorry."

"It's okay; it's been Two hundred and seventy-three days, I'm actually at the two hundred and seventy-fourth—by this time at night I had left Whiteport."

Joshua rubbed his chest. What should he do with that information? "You're...erm...on friendly terms?"

Oswald shrugged. "I don't know. He was...quite angry with me, of course."

"Of course?"

"Well, yes. I ruined our wedding."

Before Josh could do anything to stop himself, he white-knuckled the steering wheel, but with a deep breath and a lot of will, he managed to loosen his grip. "You were to be married?" Shit, that was more than just a broken relationship, it was a shattered dream.

"Yes." That one word held so much longing, so much sorrow that Josh was willing to let him off the hook about talking. "But I did the right thing. I never would've been enough, and he deserves someone who can be that for him."

The car was turning warm and toasty, and Josh was almost sad he'd soon have to drag Oz out into the cold again, but right now, he so badly wanted to escape this conversation that he was looking forward to it.

"I'm boring you."

"No! No, absolutely not." Boring wasn't the word—making him uncomfortable maybe, though Josh didn't know why. He didn't have to do anything other than listen and he'd normally have no problem with that no matter the topic, but… He couldn't pinpoint what it was. *Could be the counting of days…yeah, that's it.* Someone who knew it was two hundred and something days had not moved on. It didn't matter. Josh wasn't here to hook up; he was here to save a life, apparently.

"I know I'm boring. Mind-numbing. I'll be quiet now."

"Oh, no. You're to keep on talking. What's your favourite… colour?" Josh would've rolled his eyes at himself if he weren't afraid Oswald would take it to mean he was rolling his eyes at him.

***

Colour? Oswald tapped his toe against the floor liner seven times. What colour did he like? "I don't know."

"You don't know your favourite colour?"

He'd failed an easy question. Oswald wasn't good at conversations—Guy had that right. "I…erm…I guess it depends…"

"On?" Joshua smiled.

He's just trying to be nice. "Well, for instance, I look ill if I wear a yellow jumper, so not yellow for clothes, but that doesn't mean I don't like yellow in…say flowers. I love sunflowers, very pretty."

Joshua took a left turn into a narrow driveway and stopped by a log cabin surrounded by large trees. Oswald couldn't tell if they were oak or beech, but they surrounded the cabin like a cloak. His breath caught, so peaceful—a secret place hidden away from the world. "It's beautiful."

Josh frowned at him. "It's dark. You can't see shit."

"Yeah, no, I guess, but…" He'd said the wrong thing, again.

"Come on, let's get you out of those clothes so I can have a look at you." Joshua opened the door and hopped out. *Have a look at me?* What did that mean?

Oswald followed, his intestines turning into a messy ball of yarn. Joshua had saved him from the water without yelling at him, he'd taken time out of his schedule to make sure Oswald was okay, and he'd promised him dry clothes, but what did he expect in return? He drummed his thumb against his thigh. *One-two-three-four-five-six—*

"This is it." Joshua held the door open, and Oswald's breath stuttered. He hurried to tap his thumb again before moving forward, needing to get the seven taps in before he could move on.

Joshua tilted his head to the side and watched him. The light from the lamp next to the door lit Joshua's hair, making it appear redder than it had that morning. "You okay?"

"I'm fine."

The way Joshua's eyes narrowed made Oswald think he might not have sounded very convincing. "Of course you are, you were just out for a late night swim in the river."

"It's not that late." Oswald winced, he should shut up. But Joshua didn't shout at him, he grinned and shook his head.

"Come on. I'm beginning to think you like walking around dripping wet."

"I do not!" Oswald bit his tongue, just because Joshua hadn't yelled at him before didn't mean he had the patience of a saint.

"Come on, now." Joshua still had a smile on his lips as he ushered Oswald inside the cabin. "It's not big, and it's a little… not done, but it's liveable."

Oswald looked at the bare walls with spots of spackle, the buckets and painting materials in the corner and the sofa and TV in the middle of the floor covered by protective plastic. "You're renovating?"

"A necessary evil. There was a short circuit in the kitchen, the entire northwest corner of the cabin went up in flames."

"Shit." Oswald could only imagine seeing his home going up in flames—or no, he couldn't. He frowned. He didn't have a home, had never had one. He'd believed he and Guy would build one together, but the flat hadn't been his. They'd bought some of the things together, sure, but it was Guy's flat and despite Oswald saving as much as he could so they could buy a house together, Guy hadn't been all that willing to move.

"Yeah. Though it could've been so much worse."

Oswald nodded.

"So, a shower?"

For him alone, right? Oswald tried looking at Joshua without being caught doing so, but the shivers still keeping possession of his body made it hard to do anything subtly. He tapped his right forefinger seven times against the inside of his left wrist.

"Go take a shower. Bathroom's in there, towels on the shelf, and if you leave the door open, I'll bring some clothes for you."

"You're going to come into the bathroom while I shower?" *And do what?* What did he want Oswald to do?

"Or I can go find you some clothes now that you can take with you, no big deal."

Oswald forced himself to breathe. "No, it's okay. I'm silly."

"It's okay, Oz. I'll just go grab them."

"No, no. Take your time." Shit, he couldn't even let the man find him some clothes in peace. No wonder Guy had needed a few days away at times. "I'll be in the shower." He started walking towards the bathroom door.

"Oz." Joshua caught his arm but let go as soon as Oswald stopped. "Just wait here, and I'll get you the dry clothes. I wasn't thinking about how it might make you uncomfortable if I were to come in while—"

"No, of course not. You're straight, so why would you think twice about seeing a guy naked, right? I mean you're probably playing football on the local team and shower with thirty guys, seven days a week. I'm being stupid, more silly ideas—"

"Silly ideas?"

Oh shit. "Ah, yeah, well... Guy always said I got my knickers in a twist for the smallest things and had my head filled with silly ideas such as people taking an interest in me." *Oh God, the embarrassment.* Not only had he let Joshua know his imagination often ran away with him, but he'd also confirmed he sometimes acted like the pinhead everyone thought he was.

"Charming."

And now Joshua was annoyed. *Shit.* "Sorry."

"Guy, he sounds really charming."

Oswald frowned a little, but it was true, he was charming...or he used to be. "Most people think so." He took a deep breath, and this time, his muscles relaxed a little. He was making everything more complicated than it was—as always. Joshua was just a nice man who picked him up out of the river; he didn't want to get into Oswald's pants—silly ideas—so the small touches were probably...concern? *Yes, of course, concern.*

Joshua still suspected he might have hit his head, probably why he wanted Oswald to leave the bathroom door unlocked so he could rush in if Oswald were to topple over. He smiled at Joshua and started walking towards the bathroom, his eyes burning at the thought that someone cared if he fell and bashed his head.

BRUISES & HALLUCINATIONS

JOSH PINCHED THE bridge of his nose as he watched Oswald walk into the bathroom. Guy might just deserve to die. He couldn't be sure, of course, but… *Yeah, the fucker needs to die.*

He should talk to Aiden, see if he knew anything.

He went into the bedroom, got some sweats, a T-shirt, and socks. *Underwear or not?* It'd be weird either way—too big, borrowed underwear. He put a pair on the top of the pile and hurried to the bathroom. The water was on so he deemed it'd be safe to enter. And apparently, being straight or not mattered when coming into bathrooms. Josh shook his head and cracked the door open.

"What are you doing?"

Oswald was standing fully dressed in the shower, the shower stall door wide open, and water spraying the bathroom floor.

"Oh…hi…erm…" Fog rose from within the shower. "I…erm…my fingers hurt, and I really wanted to get warm. Don't worry, I'll clean it up and I'll—" He closed the shower door.

"Oh, for fuck's sake, Oz." Josh opened the door again and started unbuttoning the light-blue shirt that now was stained from his dip in the river, probably algae and stuff. One after the other, he undid the buttons, noticing Oz tapping his fingers together. He'd done that several times already.

The shirt came off, and then Josh reached for the hem of the once-white T-shirt Oswald was wearing.

"Okay, might as well have a look now, right?" He looked into Oswald's eyes trying to see if his pupils were dilated or of different size. They looked fine. "Head fine?"

"Yes, I told you."

Josh grinned. "You did, but you could have been trying to fool me to get out of the hospital trip."

"I never lie."

"Everyone lies, especially if they've hit their head."

Oswald was frowning again. "I didn't hit my head."

"Good, 'cause I'm not giving you any whiskey if you did." Josh took a steadying breath and looked down at the naked torso. Scrapes and bruises along the ribcage but mostly just creamy white skin. Joshua raised his hand to check the ribs when he noticed Oswald doing that breath-holding thing again. "You don't like touch." He'd said something about that, hadn't he? Josh had just chosen not to listen because more often than not he wanted to reach out and feel him there—a hand on a shoulder or an arm, innocent touches instead of holding his hand or caressing the bare skin of his neck.

"I don't mind touch when I know what it's for."

"Okay." He could work with that…maybe. *What does he mean 'what it's for'?* "So…" He breathed in deep. "I'm gonna touch your ribs to check nothing's broken."

"You can know that by touch?"

Could he? "I…no probably not, but if you scream, I'll take you to the hospital."

Oswald paled and bit his lip as if it would prevent any sounds from escaping him.

"Don't do that. I'm not gonna hurt you. Just tell me if it… hurts." Yeah, okay so maybe he was gonna hurt him after all. Josh pressed a little on the ribs on the side where there was some bruising. Oswald didn't move a muscle. "Does it hurt?"

"Yes." And yet he stood utterly still.

"Is it sharp, dull, achy?"

"It feels like I have a bruise and you're poking it."

Josh snorted. "That about covers it. Okay, let's move on." He unbuttoned Oswald's jeans, but before he could pull them down, Oswald pressed himself against the wall.

"I can do it."

"Okay, go ahead." Probably should have said he was about to pull his trousers off.

Oswald's grip on the fabric was clumsy, and Josh frowned—should've checked his hands. The scrapes were evident, and his fingertips appeared a little swollen. Could you break fingers by holding on to stuff? When the jeans didn't come off Joshua looked up at Oz. His gaze was fixed on the wall behind Joshua, his face blank.

"Oz?"

"Yes?"

"The jeans."

Oswald pressed his lips together. "Do you have to see?"

Do I? Did he want Oz to take off his clothes to check him for injuries or because he wanted him naked? No, it was injuries… the second part was a bonus he had no intention of letting Oz know he took any pleasure in whatsoever. "Let's just get it over with, buddy. It's just a precaution, I think maybe you're in shock, and if you are, you might be hurt worse than you realise." *Yep, sounds plausible.*

Oz pushed down the jeans—no underwear. It was a battle not to react, but Josh focused on the nasty-looking reddish-purple bruise on Oswald's hip. "That doesn't look too good."

"Not much to show off." Oz kept his gaze on the wall.

"On the contrary, that bruise is spectacular. You'll wear it for weeks."

Oswald glanced down. "Oh…"

"Yeah." Josh raised a hand to touch but stopped himself. "How does it feel?"

Oswald stared right into his eyes. "Embarrassing."

Oh… "I meant the bruise. And you have no reason to be embarrassed about anything." *None, whatsoever.* Oswald was nicely put together—lean, but with muscles, creamy skin all over, no body hair to speak of except a happy trail leading Josh's attention from his belly button to the blonde curls around his cock. He let out a breath and forced an impassionate expression to his face.

"Sore. It's okay."

Josh stepped away. "Okay. I'll leave you to shower then we'll have a look at your hands. I'll be in the kitchen when you're ready." He grabbed Oz's dirty clothes and went to throw them in the washer. He didn't think he'd appreciate having to walk around in Joshua's clothes until they fetched his car. Then he needed to fix some food. Oswald needed to eat.

***

Oswald wanted to sink to his knees in the shower when Joshua left, but he didn't. Instead, he washed as quickly as he could and turned off the water. The clothes Joshua had left were, of course, way too big, but at least they were dry. He drummed his thumb against the door handle seven times before he opened the bathroom door.

As he walked into the kitchen, Joshua looked up from where he stood going through the freezer and gave him a sparkling smile. "That was fast."

"I…erm…yeah." Should he have stayed in the shower longer?

"I gave Taylor a call to let him know we're bringing the canoe to the drop off place tomorrow. That okay?"

Oswald nodded. A lump formed in his throat which only proved how silly he was. Someone making a call for him shouldn't move him to almost-tears.

"Come on." Josh held out a hand as if he expected Oswald to walk into his embrace. *Does he?* No, that couldn't be it. Oswald stayed where he was, but that was apparently wrong too because Joshua frowned.

"I'm sorry."

"What for?" Joshua tipped his head to the side, and Oswald's heart began beating too fast, he tapped his fingers seven times against his thigh.

"I don't know what you want. I don't want to do anything wrong, but I don't..." Oswald was crazy, Guy had always told him no one ever would stand to live with him except him, and it was true. He could tell he frustrated Joshua, and all he wanted was to please him, but he didn't know how. It was easier with Guy; he told Oswald what he should do. Clean the flat. Make food. Do the laundry. Suck him off. Sleep on the couch tonight. And yet he did the wrong things more often than not.

"You can't do anything wrong, Oz."

"I can. I do it all the time. I always do the wrong thing."

"You haven't done anything wrong."

But he had because now Josh was growling at him, just like Guy did when he wanted something, and Oswald couldn't figure out what it was.

Joshua closed the freezer and started walking towards him. Oswald tapped his thumb and forefinger together seven times. In one swift motion, Joshua caught his hand, his fingers gentle around his wrist, then he tapped his thumb against an unscratched spot which happened to be Pericardium 6. He didn't think Joshua knew anything about acupressure points. It was funny, though, since it calmed the heart, but then Joshua tapped his finger much like Oswald did. *One-two-three-four-five-six-seven.*

Oswald wished the floor would open up and suck him down. Joshua had noticed; no wonder he was growly.

"I'm sorry. It's annoying, I know." Oswald hated the way his voice shook.

"Do you find it annoying?" Joshua still had his fingers curled around his wrist, the warmth of him making Oswald's arm tingle.

"No, it calms me, but I know it's annoying for those around me."

Joshua frowned, again. Oswald never could say the right things. An apology was lingering on his tongue, but when Joshua shook his head, he swallowed it.

"Guy said that?"

"Ah…erm…yes." *How could he know?* "And I should be pressing on that spot you tapped instead. I know acupressure, but I've done the finger thing since I was a child and…and it's hard to break a habit. I will try, though. I promise."

Joshua rubbed the spot he'd tapped. "This spot?"

"P-6. It's calming, helps against nausea and motion sickness… among other things."

Joshua smiled. "You'll have to teach me one day."

"You could…erm…come see me when… Unless I get myself drowned or something before I start working."

Chuckling, Joshua let go of his hand. "You'll be all right, Oz. I'll just fish you out of the water if you fall in again. Come, sit here." He gestured at a chair by the kitchen table and turned on the overhead light. "Show me your hands."

Oswald turned both his hands over, resting the backs of them on the table. His fingertips were torn, a little swollen, and he had a rather nasty gash across the heel of his thumb.

"Anything hurt more than the rest?" Joshua was studying his fingers without touching.

"I'm glad I said to Aiden I wouldn't start working on Monday. They don't look pretty, do they?"

Joshua held up his hand next to Oswald's. A large, steady, callused hand. When he turned it over, there were a few small cuts over his knuckles; some paint stains decorated the back of his hand and short clean nails.

"Pretty?" Joshua chuckled.

"Yes." It came out like a whisper, and Oswald flinched, afraid he'd insulted Joshua with that one little word.

Joshua snorted but didn't sound mad. Oswald must've tensed up because a second later his shoulders dropped. Joshua moved away, and shortly after, a glass appeared before him.

"The promised whiskey." Joshua grinned.

"I'm not much of a drinker."

"No?" Joshua tilted his head to the side, watching him with an expression Oswald couldn't place.

"No. It's unattractive when I get too loud."

"You get loud?" A chuckle again.

"Yes…no, not really. I guess I talk too much, maybe."

"Well, there's no one around here so you can get as loud as you want." Joshua was quiet for a few moments. "You don't have to drink it if you don't want to."

Oswald eyed the amber liquid. "No, actually, I think I do want it."

Joshua grinned and raised a glass of his own. "Cheers, then." He sipped the whiskey, and Oswald knew he should look away but couldn't, and Joshua didn't stop looking at him either so perhaps it wasn't that great of a mistake.

"You went to look at the studio with Aiden today?"

The whiskey burned his throat as he took another swallow. "Yeah. I told him I couldn't do it, but he said to try it for a little while. See if it works. He showed me the room I'd have, and it was really nice."

"Yeah, Tristan has done a good job fixing it up."

Oswald nodded, he'd never met Tristan, but Aiden had been talking about him. "I can't afford to say no to work. Two hundred and seventy-four days without an income…" He shrugged.

"Try it. You can always move back to Whiteport and work there if there aren't enough clients here." The way Joshua said Whiteport made it sound like it was worse than hell, and it was. Oswald wouldn't go back to Whiteport no matter what.

Joshua grinned. "We'll figure it out. Just sit back and enjoy, I'll fix us up something to eat." Joshua went back to the freezer, and tension crept back into Oswald. Guy never cooked, said it was Oswald's job since Guy had a more tiring job. He bet Joshua had a more tiring job than he did, too. Especially considering that Oswald wasn't working.

"I should help." He started to get up from the chair.

"Nope, you should sit there and work on getting loud."

Oswald found himself in a hallucination where Joshua winked at him. Had to be a hallucination.

WHISKEY & WILDERNESS

JOSH WAS IN trouble. The whiskey warmed his chest. The food, while not award-worthy, had tasted fine, and seeing Oswald inhale it had added to the warmth in his chest. Then there were the smiles, the shy little giggle that escaped Oswald now and then. The way he moved his hands more and more as he talked the more relaxed he got.

Joshua wanted to throw him on his bed and kiss all the bruises better. He wanted to know if Oswald would giggle if he ran his fingertips along his ribs, if he would squirm if he kissed him in the right places, if he would moan when Josh entered him.

Joshua tipped his glass back only to find it empty. Should he have another whiskey? No, probably not.

Oswald's glass was empty as well, a light flush on his cheeks, and his pale eyes tired. *Understandable.* Josh was fine just watching him sitting there in his kitchen, but when Oz—for the second time in just a couple of minutes—tried to suppress a yawn, Josh figured he should stop ogling his guest and let him get some rest.

"Come on, sunshine. Let's get you to bed." Josh pushed back his chair and got to his feet watching out of the corner of his eyes how Oz tensed.

"It's okay; I can sleep on the couch."

Josh raised an eyebrow. "You don't want to sleep in the dust in there, and the sofa is covered up. The bed is big enough for both of us."

Oz drummed his finger seven times against the tabletop. It made Josh realise he hadn't done it since before they'd eaten.

Only when he's uncomfortable, then. He pressed his lips together. "You're perfectly safe; I won't touch you."

"No, I know." The glance he got was quick, and his face blank. Josh didn't like it. "And even if things were different I know you wouldn't want— I…erm…"

Josh stopped himself from pinching the bridge of his nose, and he didn't let the groan out either. "You don't know what I'd want, Oz, not that it—"

"Oh, no, I know. I didn't mean to imply I know anything."

And that was no better. "Look, I know you're tired, you've had a long day. I'm tired. It's been a long week. Let's get some sleep, yeah?"

Oswald nodded. "I haven't slept next to anyone for two hundred and seventy-four days."

"Then it's time, don't you think?"

"I…erm…is it?" Oswald looked confused. "Maybe…I just never figured I'd ever sleep next to anyone again."

An *oh, babe* or another equally silly expression wanted to push itself past Josh's lips, but he refused to let it. He didn't need to make Oz any more confused than he already was. "Good-looking guy like you?" Josh grinned at him. "It's only a matter of time. Stop thinking and let's find you a toothbrush."

***

Oswald's heart was drumming too hard for him to be able to sleep. Joshua's bedroom was small but nice—a bed, bedside tables, a closet, and a door leading out to a porch. Oswald wanted to go out there, but he didn't dare to get up from the bed in case Joshua got annoyed with him.

Guy had often wanted him to sleep on the couch, so he didn't have to listen to Oswald if he got up in the night, and it happened more and more during the last years—that he needed to get up and move around in the middle of the night. He was constantly tired, constantly on edge, constantly looking for the right thing to do.

He wanted to turn over but didn't dare to. Guy would growl at him for not lying still when he was about to fall asleep, and Joshua could growl too. There had been times when a little growliness had crept into his voice. Oswald didn't want to ruin a lovely evening by making him growl, but he had to move. The tingles in his bones turned into prickling, and his ribcage shrank. Slowly, he shifted his weight, rolling from his back to his side, facing away from Joshua.

"Are you in pain?"

He tensed at Joshua's voice in the dark. "No…it's okay, just a little sore."

"Are you sure? Maybe I should've given you painkillers instead of whiskey."

Probably, but he didn't want Joshua to feel bad. "I liked it."

"You'll be all right, Oz."

What a strange thing to say. It *was* a strange thing to say, right? Joshua's breathing deepened, and Oswald matched it. His mind was still racing but, as he breathed with Joshua his muscles unclenched and his body grew heavy. The rhythm of Joshua's ins and outs washed over him like waves—calm and soothing.

***

Oswald opened his eyes. Something was wrong. He was balancing on the edge of a bed, not the mattress in his car, and a solid warmth was pressed against his back. He looked down at the strong arm wrapped around his waist.

The light of dawn had crept into the bedroom, which meant Oswald had slept longer than he normally did. He'd slept the entire night. Must be because he hadn't been freezing.

For a few seconds, he allowed himself to be held. It was safe when Joshua was sleeping, a few moments just to soak up the sensation of body contact and warmth. Joshua sighed, still in his sleep, but it was enough for Oswald to know it was time to move away. He didn't want Joshua to have to wake up and be embarrassed—and waking up curled around him would most definitely do that.

Oswald tried to slip out of bed, but as he moved, Joshua's arm tightened around him. He tried to gently lift it enough to roll down onto the floor without waking Joshua, but the arm refused to let up.

"Oh, sorry. Am I hurting you?" The grip around him loosened but Joshua didn't remove his arm. Oswald held his breath, waiting for Joshua to realise what he was doing and maybe get angry with Oswald for putting him in this position. One second became two, and Joshua didn't move. Oswald's heart thudded in his throat.

"Joshua?"

"Mmm."

Is he still sleeping? Oswald hovered with his hand over Joshua's arm, not knowing if he should lift it off him or…what? Touch it, touch Joshua? No, he couldn't touch Joshua like that. He wouldn't like it.

"You want to get up?"

Awake. He was awake, and he was still holding Oswald. "I… erm…yeah, I think…"

Joshua chuckled and rolled over, taking his warmth with him. Oswald didn't let himself regret it. Instead, he slipped out of bed, reached for the socks he'd taken off before crawling in last night and slipped them on. He glanced at Joshua, who had his eyes closed, and went to the porch door.

The October morning was crisp, the T-shirt and sweats he'd worn since he got out of the shower not enough to fight off the cold, but Oswald stayed out there anyway. The view was breathtaking. The trees surrounding the cabin were large—old forest—the trunks thick and moss-covered, the leaves sparkling in yellow, red, and orange. Oswald smelled the earthy air, and figured this was what it was like to step into a fairy tale. It was so quiet, he could stay there forever.

He walked up to the railing. On one side, it was like a porch, but the cabin was built at the top of a slope, so the farther end of the porch wasn't a porch; it was more like a balcony.

"Hey."

Oswald startled and turned around. Joshua was standing leaning against the doorpost, his hair tousled and his chest bare.

"Hi." Oswald's mouth went dry. Joshua matched the forest, the calm wilderness, the red of his hair—he belonged here.

"You want to go into town and grab some breakfast before fetching the canoe?"

Town? His heart jumped again. "Yeah, sure."

BOYFRIENDS & LIES

JOSH PARKED OUTSIDE Jen's café and glanced at Oz. He was nervous and twitchy, the finger-tapping and drumming had increased the closer to town they'd come, and for a moment, Josh had considered turning around simply to spare him, but if he were to work next door to the café, he needed to get used to the people there sooner or later.

"Do you…erm…know if Jason is working?" Oz kept his eyes glued on the café door.

Jason? Right, Aiden and Jason were friends from before, he hadn't thought about Oswald maybe knowing him too. "I don't know."

"I'm not sure…I want to see him."

Ah, well, living here and not seeing Jason could turn out to be tricky. "You want me to go check?"

"No-no, I'm being silly. It's just Guy… Jason and Guy… Never mind."

It was becoming harder and harder to ignore anything with Guy's name tied to it and now Jason's too. "Say the word and we're out of here, Oz." Because locking him away in his cabin would solve all problems. Josh could just feed him, get him drunk, and snuggle up with him in bed—yeah, right.

Oz looked at him with an uncertain smile. "You're not angry?

"Angry? Why would I be angry?" Josh *was* angry, but at a person he'd never met. How much of Oz's self-doubt was Guy's doing and how much had he brought with him into the relationship to begin with?

"Because I'm being silly."

"Ever thought about maybe you're not being silly, that maybe your feelings are legit?"

Oz widened his eyes a little. "I am being silly, Jason used to be a friend, not a close one, but still a friend."

Josh nodded. "Okay, so we go in there, have some breakfast, and then we go fetch the canoe."

"Right." He drummed his fingers against his leg and grabbed the handle. "Okay."

Josh went before Oz to the door and held it open for him. The café was bustling as always on Saturdays. Both Jen and Jason were working, and Josh had to force himself not to reach out and touch Oswald—in support, of course.

"Ox!" Aiden shot to his feet and waved. Marge and Monica, whom he'd been sitting with, looked curiously in their direction. Josh waved but headed for the table closest to the counter. He wanted to talk to Aiden but not with this many people around.

As he sat down Jason nodded at him. There was a question in his eyes, but Josh ignored it. "A coffee, please. Then we're having breakfast."

Jason grinned and started on the coffee. Josh watched as Oz and Aiden talked, hands flapping with increasing intensity, and Oz only tensed a little when Aiden hugged him. From what Josh could see Oz told him about the canoe ride, at least it looked like he described falling into the water if the gestures were anything to go by.

A cup of coffee appeared on the table before him and Josh nodded a thanks. "You know Oswald, right?"

Jason shrugged. "Not really, fucked his boyfriend once." Josh choked on the coffee and Jason smirked. *Fucker.* "You did what?"

"Oh, I don't recommend it. The man's an idiot and a crappy lay, I don't get how Ox endured for as long as he did."

"Why would you sleep with someone else's boyfriend?"

Jason shrugged. "I was horny, I guess. I don't remember."

"What did Oz…" Josh frowned. He could understand Oswald's reluctance to go here if Jason had been with…Guy. "Didn't Oz mind?"

Jason grimaced. "They were in an open relationship. Guy told everyone they were, but then Aiden told me yesterday Ox never got the memo."

"What?" He looked across the scarred turquoise counter top to where Oz stood. He'd grown more tense since Josh last had looked. *What had Aiden said?* For a second he considered going over there but then he turned back to Jason.

"Hi." Andre slumped down on the chair across from him.

"Oh, hi. I didn't see you."

"You were too busy looking elsewhere," Jason chipped in with another smirk—smug bastard. Andre followed his gaze to Oswald and Aiden.

"I was just about to leave. What are you up to today? Want help painting the living room?"

Josh opened his mouth to speak, but Jason beat him to it. "I'm thinking he'll be busy doing other things this weekend, isn't that so, Joshi?"

Joshua struggled to keep his face blank as Andre gave him a confused look.

"I…erm… I need to help Oz with a canoe."

"Who's Oz?" Andre's grey eyes—not pale grey like Oswald's, more gunmetal grey—narrowed.

Joshua gestured towards where he'd stood only to realise he wasn't there anymore. "The new guy, Aiden's friend."

"Joshua's future boyfriend." Jason snickered.

"Shut it, Jason." Josh's voice was sharper than he'd intended, but fuck, Jason was annoying at times.

Andre frowned. "You're not—"

"Oh, come on, Andre, the man is as queer as they get…or is it we get? How can you not see it?" Jason chuckled and left to pour Mrs. Johnson a cup of coffee.

Josh growled but heard a breath hitch next to him. Oswald stood there wide-eyed, fingers tapping so fast Josh figured there must be seven hundred taps instead of the usual seven.

"You… Why…" Andre rubbed his forehead, and Joshua's stomach turned into a knot.

"Oz, this is Andre, my *friend*." Why he emphasised the word he didn't know. It was hard to breathe, harder yet to smile. The buzz of the café grew in his ears, leaving him dizzy.

"Hi." Andre nodded towards Oz but didn't offer his hand. Oz nodded back. Josh filled his lungs again.

"Come on, Oz. Sit down and we'll eat some. Andre, want to join us?"

"I-I need…to…" Oz gestured towards the door and slipped away before Joshua could stop him.

"You lied to me." Andre glared, his forefinger drumming against the table—not seven times, though.

"I never lied. I never said one thing or another."

"I poured my heart out, and you never once… I always figured you were waiting for the right woman, that you came here because of a bad break-up or something and that you'd tell me when you were ready." Andre shook his head.

"I'm sorry. I didn't think it mattered. We're friends. Who I fuck has nothing to do with it."

"Except it's part of who you are, and now I feel like I don't know you."

"Oh, come on! You know me, this changes nothing." Joshua hoped it didn't change anything. He had to go find Oz, but how could he run away from Andre now?

Andre shook his head. "I can't believe you never told me. How could you not once have mentioned being gay?"

Joshua rubbed a hand over his face. "I didn't think it was anyone's business. It's not like I've had a boyfriend since I moved here. I wanted to be able to talk to people without having them thinking about me as another gay guy in town. Who I'm with has nothing to do with who I am."

Andre shook his head. "Whatever you say."

"Don't be like that." Joshua's chest ached. He'd never meant to hurt Andre; it was just…easier not to say anything.

"Like what? How I act has nothing to do with who I am."

Joshua groaned and pulled at his hair.

"So…are you gonna run after him?"

Josh nodded. "Yeah…yeah, I think I am."

He started to stand when Andre's sad smile made him stop.

"How come everyone is running after the small blonds?"

"Don't do that. You're gorgeous, and you know it, and someday soon, someone's gonna run after you."

Andre gave him a wry smile and took a sip of Josh's coffee.

***

Oswald took breath after breath. The air had a nip to it despite the sun shining. Looking out over the cars parked outside the café, he wondered what he should do. Where could he go?

"Oz?" Joshua came up behind him; his hands shoved in his pockets.

"You said you were straight." Oswald drummed his thumb against his hipbone. It shouldn't matter—except it did. Now Oswald wouldn't know what he'd want.

"I never said that. You did." Joshua took another step closer.

"But you didn't deny it." *Why hadn't he?*

"It seemed to calm you, so…" He shrugged.

"Of course it did." Oswald winced at his tone. He shouldn't be snappy.

"Why?"

"Why? It's obvious, isn't it?"

"Not really. I don't see how it changes anything." Joshua took another step closer, close enough to touch now.

"It changes everything." The words weren't more than a whisper, but Joshua's shake of his head told him he'd heard them.

"Explain it to me, Oz, because I don't see how it would."

Explain it? Explain it how? "I don't know what you want."

"What I want?" Joshua gave him a confused glance and Oswald sighed. This was why he needed Guy. Guy would tell him what he wanted, what he expected Oswald to do. Joshua would have him guessing, and when Oswald guessed, he made mistakes.

"Yes, what you want. When you touch me, what does it mean? When you came into the bathroom yesterday, what did it mean? When you held me this morning, what did that mean? What did you want me to do? When you were straight, I knew you touching my hand didn't mean you wanted a blow job…" Joshua spluttered; Oswald went on. "But now I don't know. Not that I think you'd want me, I know I'm nothing special, but you have to tell me because I don't know."

Joshua took his hand, gently holding his torn fingers. "Me touching your hand means I want to touch your hand, and if you don't want that, you pull your hand away or you tell me not to touch you. Me coming into the bathroom was to make sure you were all right since you're injured. There was nothing sexual about that, okay?"

Oswald nodded. Pull his hand away? He didn't think he could do that, but he understood the shower. Had Joshua been hurt he'd want to check him over too.

"As for me holding you this morning, you felt nice in my arms, but if it made you uncomfortable, it won't happen again."

If it made him uncomfortable? "I…erm…I'm stupid."

"No, you're not."

"Yes, I am. Guy was—"

"I don't give a shit about Guy, Oz. He sounds like an arse from what I've heard."

"No…or he could be a little…but he was right. No one has been able to stand me for as long as he did, and I was the one leaving, so it's my fault that I'm lonely… But he was right, people grow tired of me and send me off to the next in line. It's always been like that. I'm faulty." He tried to smile, but it was hollow. "That's why you have to tell me what to do to keep you happy because I'm not smart enough to figure it out by myself."

He was assuming he would spend more time with Joshua which was stupid. Joshua had said he'd help Oswald with the canoe, but he hadn't promised anything beyond that. Just another sign of how stupid he was.

Joshua rubbed his forehead—Oswald was apparently already driving him mad. "Do you want breakfast?"

Breakfast? Oh right, that's why they were here. "I…erm… yeah. If you want to have breakfast."

Joshua tilted his head to the side and grinned. "So if I said no, you wouldn't want breakfast?"

"Erm…" He wanted breakfast, but if Joshua didn't want to have breakfast…

"You already said yes, Oz, no need to change your answer." Joshua slung his arm over Oswald's shoulders. "I'm touching you because I want to and because I want to feed you."

Oswald nodded. "Okay."

"Do you want me to remove it?"

Remove the arm? Oswald's heart sped up, his thumb vibrating with the need to start tapping against something.

"Oz?"

"I…erm…I don't know."

The arm disappeared, and while it was a little easier to breathe the loss of the touch left him cold.

"Okay, let's go without touches when we aren't certain. Come on." Joshua started walking back towards the café.

FAMILIES & SUNSHINE

JOSH FORCED HIMSELF not to be disappointed over the fact that Oz didn't want him to touch him—stupid. Why would he want him to touch him? He was a little weird about body contact and all of a sudden Josh figured snuggling in bed and holding hands was the best idea he'd ever had. *Idiot.*

But knowing he was an idiot didn't change the fact that his hands burned with a need to slide over Oswald's body. He wanted to know what he tasted like, what sounds he would make if Josh touched him just right.

He swallowed his groan and headed back to the table where they had been sitting. Andre stood as they approached, nodding at Oz and putting his hand on Josh's shoulder.

"You could join us if you'd like." The knot in his stomach hadn't evaporated and he needed to know he and Andre were okay.

"Another day. Pick me up on Monday." Andre's fingers dug into his shoulder, one short signal that made some of the tension in his muscles slip away.

"Sure." It was his week. He and Andre took turns driving to Northfield, and next week was his. They worked in the same place, same hours, so there was no use going in two cars.

"He doesn't like me." Oz tapped his fingers together.

"It's not that. I've known him for four years, I know almost everything there is to know about him, and I let him believe I'm into women. He feels a little...betrayed." And one part of him could understand; another wanted to snarl at the entire fucking town because it wasn't their business.

Jason appeared again, smirking, and Josh gritted his teeth.

"Hi there, Ox."

Oz tensed, his face going a little pale, and turning to an expressionless mask. "Jason." He nodded, and Josh wanted to smile at the frosty greeting.

"It's good to see you, man."

Oswald opened his mouth, but no sound came out. Jason's smile slipped a little, and Josh would've enjoyed it if it hadn't been for the panic growing in Oswald's eyes. Reaching over the table, he touched Oz's hand, just a brief touch since there shouldn't be any touching.

"We'd like some breakfast, please." Josh smiled at Jason and went about listing what he wanted.

"I'll have the same," Oz whispered when Josh made his order. He wanted to protest, wanted to force Oz to make a decision, but he stopped himself. This wasn't the time to push.

When Jason moved away, a shaky breath escaped Oz.

"You okay?" Josh wanted to touch him again.

"Absolutely."

"Don't lie to me, sunshine."

Oz glared. "Don't call me that."

Oh, temper. Josh chuckled. "Then don't lie to me."

***

Oswald followed Josh through the forest. It was the same path they'd walked yesterday in the dark, but he never would've found the way by himself.

"How will we get the canoe to the drop-off place?" That was something he should've thought about earlier.

Joshua grinned at him. "We're gonna paddle down the river. The paddle is still in the handle, I checked."

They were going to paddle? Oswald held his breath as he remembered the cold water dragging him down.

"You okay?" Joshua reached out but stopped himself from touching him. Oswald forced himself not to frown. Did he want

Joshua to touch him? He did, but why? His touches so far had been gentle, there more to reassure than to guide him.

"Yes."

Joshua narrowed his eyes. "You sure, babe? If you don't want to go in the canoe, I can take it to Taylor, and you can take the car."

"Don't call me that."

Joshua's eyes widened, then he grinned. "Why not? No one's here to hear it."

"I don't like it when you're condescending." His heart leapt to his throat. Had he said something like that to Guy, there'd have been hell to pay. Joshua stopped so fast Oswald almost stumbled into him. *Shit.*

Oswald tapped his fingers together. He should've kept his mouth shut, should've accepted it as he always did when Guy called him something like that.

He closed his eyes and waited for the fingers digging into his shoulder, pushing him to his knees. Nothing soothed Guy's bad temper like a blow job; if it was really bad, he'd fuck Oswald, roughly, no matter where they were. Why had he stopped carrying lube with him? He forced some air into his lungs. For an outburst like that, a blow job should be sufficient, though.

The hand on his shoulder never came. He held his breath again, but when nothing happened, he risked opening his eyes.

Joshua was watching him, his face expressionless apart from the thin lips. "I would never hit you."

"No, of course not." What would be the point in hitting him? He couldn't see how Joshua would get any pleasure from it.

"Did Guy hit you?" His voice was calm, controlled.

"No, never."

"Okay, good...that's good." He rubbed his forehead and breathed out as if he too had held his breath. "But you know you can tell me if he did, right?"

"He never hit me." What made him think he had? Guilt swamped Oswald's mind. Had he made Guy sound that bad? He wasn't bad. He had a temper, sure, but he tolerated all of Oswald's annoyances—no one else had endured for as long as Guy had. And if it hadn't been for Oswald's unreasonable inability to share, they'd be married now. Oswald had tried, he really had tried to reason with himself before going up to the altar and telling the guests the wedding was off, but he was…selfish.

Joshua nodded. "What did you think I would do?"

"What?"

"You waited for me to do something."

"No, I didn't." He swallowed as he pictured Joshua's cock sliding between his lips.

One step brought Joshua up close. He didn't touch him but as he bent down his breath ghosted over Oswald's cheek. "Don't lie to me, sweetheart." Oswald could've sworn his lips touched the skin below his ear, but perhaps it only was the whispered words. Seconds went by, and Joshua just stood there, so close they should be touching and yet they weren't.

"And for the record—" Oswald tried not to shiver, but Joshua's voice was a little hoarse, and his lips were so close "—when I say babe it isn't an insult."

He moved away, and Oswald almost groaned. The shivers made his entire body tingle.

"So?" Joshua's eyes sparkled as if he knew something Oswald didn't. "Do you want to take the car?"

"I…erm…" He'd meant to go down the river by canoe. "No, I'll go with you."

"Great! It's a nice route this time of year. You'll see."

***

Josh tried to ignore the way Oz's breath had hitched, he tried to forget his scent, tried hard to suppress the need to taste his lips. There would be no touching, none whatsoever unless Oz wanted it—if he gave the go-ahead to touch, Josh would touch, but not until then…which might be never.

He was sure Oz came from an abusive relationship, he might not have been slapped around, but there was emotional abuse, and Josh might not be the right man to deal with that shit. Probably not. But that didn't mean he didn't want to be that man.

He wanted to be the one who erased Guy from Oz's memory.

Josh pushed the canoe into the water holding on to it while he waited for Oz. Oz, however, was busy watching the trees arching over the river.

"You want to hop in first?"

"Oh, sorry…erm…" His eyes grew wide as he watched the canoe with suspicion.

"Get in, and I'll push us out."

He did, gripping the railing hard as it wobbled a little when Josh jumped on.

"There." He reached for the paddle that was secured in a handle—only one paddle.

"You okay?"

"Sure." He didn't look okay, not at first, but as they slowly made their way down the river, Oz began to relax. "Wow." He looked up at the bright autumn leaves as the canoe glided in under a large beech.

"Yeah." Josh grinned at the look of awe and lack of finger tapping. Oz relaxed was a sight to behold. The black water was calm around them, the occasional bird sang in the trees, and serenity filled his mind. This was what life was about.

"You've been canoeing before?" He must have, or Taylor wouldn't have let him go out on his own.

"I spent a summer with my mum's cousin; they had a canoe."

Not an answer to the question, but… "Your mother's cousin? Are you close to your family?"

"No, haven't spoken to them in years." He stiffened a little after the words were out, but Josh pretended not to notice.

"No? Not even your mother?"

"No."

O-okay. "Okay. My family lives in Northfield. I think Mum was quite disappointed when I moved away, not that she said anything about it, but I think she pictured family get-togethers every week or so." And it wasn't that he was too far away to make it happen if he wanted to.

"She did?" Those pale eyes looked at him as if he'd just said something absurd.

"Sure."

"She'd have time for that?"

Time? Josh tried not to react. "Absolutely. She loves having all of us gathered, Dad too of course, but he doesn't get quite as manic about it." He grinned to show he was joking.

"All of you? Do you come from a big family?"

"Three sisters."

"Three?" His voice rose.

"Yup. All of them married, and all of them have kids."

"And your parents want you to meet…often?"

Joshua laughed. "Don't look so shocked. It's a bit overwhelming but fun." And if they could stop nagging about him having to find someone, he might have joined them more often.

"I can't imagine. I hardly saw my mum growing up and—" He clammed up.

"And?"

"I moved around a lot, lived with relatives when Mum… couldn't look after me. I don't have any siblings."

Shit. "Oh, babe, I'm sorry."

Oz glared. "Don't babe me."

"Honey?" Josh winked. "Anytime you want to experience some crazy family situation, let me know, and I'll introduce you to the chaos of the Roth family."

"I thought you said you like peace and quiet." Oz pushed a strand of blonde hair from his eyes as he watched Josh manoeuvre the canoe.

"I do. I love my family, and it's fun seeing them now and then, but I need peace and quiet."

Oz nodded.

"Why couldn't you stay with your mum when you were a kid?" Perhaps not something he should've asked.

"Oh, she tired of me."

Josh almost dropped the paddle. "What?" *For the love of…* He gritted his teeth to keep from saying anything else.

"I'm draining."

"You're not."

"So they took turns looking after me as I grew up. Mum worked on a cruise liner so she was abroad a lot and…well, who'd want a weird kid taking up their time, right?"

"Anyone with some sense." What kind of mum handed her kid over to relatives and took off? Josh's fingers curled around the handle of the paddle hard enough to make his knuckles turn white.

Oz shrugged. "When I turned eighteen I was on my own for a couple of years, studied, and then I met Guy." He watched the water. "We were together for five years. That's the longest time I've spent with anyone."

And Guy was an arse.

MATTRESSES & LAUGHS

OSWALD HAD ENJOYED the ride down the river, but talking about his childhood and then his failed relationship with Guy had melancholia nipping at his core. Joshua was silent. Maybe it was time to say goodbye. A day with Joshua had made him feel more alive than he had in a long time, but he didn't want to overstay his welcome.

When they arrived at the place where they should leave the canoe, Oswald hinted that perhaps he should go find that hotel in Northfield Aiden had been talking about. Joshua gave him a look with raised eyebrows and a shake of his head.

"I should've taken your car." Oswald looked at Joshua and then at the forest surrounding them.

"Why? Didn't you like paddling?"

"I did, but now we're stranded."

Joshua laughed, a soft chuckle that had a butterfly tearing free in Oswald's belly. "No, Taylor will be here any minute. We'll help him load the canoe on his trailer, and he'll drop us off by your car, and you'll drive me to mine, and then we'll go home and figure out what to eat for dinner."

For a second, there was a hint of uncertainty in Joshua's eyes, but then it was gone.

"Oh…" He should come up with something to say.

"It's okay to say no."

"Of course, I mean, I know."

Joshua moved closer, a hand on his elbow, sliding up his arm to stop on his shoulder. He gently massaged Oswald's muscles, stepping closer yet again. Oswald held his breath, wanting to melt against Joshua's chest, but was he allowed to? Joshua's fingers moved up his neck, and shivers skidded over Oswald's skin. He let out a shuddering breath and was about to rest his forehead against Joshua's chest when a car drew nearer.

Oswald jumped away, not wanting Joshua to get angry with him for having put him in an awkward situation by standing too close. Joshua caught his hand, squeezed it lightly, and let go of him.

"Taylor." Joshua smiled and went to shake the canoe man's hand. Heat climbed Oswald's face. Both of them were here because he fell out of the canoe. *Pathetic.*

He tried not to be in the way when Joshua and Taylor loaded the canoe, he tried to smile and respond when they talked to him, but mostly he was focused on their facial expressions and body language. He looked for tense muscles, fingers curled into fists, thinning lips, frowns, and other signs that could tell him if they were angry with him.

No one so much as glanced at him.

***

Old man Taylor, who wasn't as old as Joshua liked to think, drove them home. Something had made Oz crawl back into his shell, but Josh wasn't too worried. Once they got home, he'd get him to relax again.

"Here we go." Taylor hopped out of the car and Joshua followed, ready to help unload. It was quick work. Joshua thanked Taylor for his help and walked towards Oz's car. Oswald however lingered, walked up to Taylor and while Joshua didn't hear what he said it was obvious it was an apology. Taylor only smiled and shook his head, touching Oz's shoulder, and nodding towards Joshua. Oz tensed, Joshua saw his finger tap against his thigh, but it wasn't too bad. With a nod he came walking towards Joshua, the sun catching in his hair making it glow yellow.

"He didn't want any extra payment." Oz was frowning.

"No, why would he?"

"He had to come get us."

Joshua shrugged. "But he would have anyway. He'd have picked you up yesterday evening if I hadn't, wouldn't he?"

"I…erm…"

Joshua stilled. "Wouldn't he, Oz?"

"No, I…erm…said I had someone who'd pick me up."

Josh held his breath for a second then made sure his muscles were relaxed and his smile carefree before he turned to Oz again. "Okay, but he would've picked up the canoe, so it wasn't any extra work for him." He tried to push away the cold in his gut. *Why did Oz lie?* How would he have found his way back if Josh hadn't found him?

Oz's eyes narrowed. "Yeah, but still."

"Taylor is a good man." He grinned. "Come on now, sweetheart. I'm starting to get hungry." He winked and yanked at the car door, waiting for Oswald to unlock it.

"Don't call me that either."

He chuckled. "But honey—"

"Not that either."

"Please, sir, would you be so kind and unlock the car." Josh raised an eyebrow, still grinning, when Oz began to fidget.

"It's…erm…the car is a mess."

"I'm sure it's fine, we're just going home anyway."

Oswald nodded but didn't unlock the car.

"Come on, babe. I don't care if the car is a mess, just unlock it so we can get going." Joshua waited for the protest of being called babe to come, but Oswald only looked away. A second later, he heard the lock click. Oz opened his door, still refusing to look at Josh.

Later, he'd fix it later. He'd have Oz laughing, or at least smiling, and talking without thinking, without weighing his words first.

As Josh took his seat, he tried not to be horrified by the mattress in the back. The back seats were removed—or perhaps folded down, he wasn't sure—and a mattress took up the entire area. It had a pillow and a cover, and a small pile of clothes along the side. Two hundred and whatever days… Josh hoped he hadn't slept in the car for that long.

Oz had his gaze fixed on something far away, something that probably wasn't there at all.

"Do you know the way to where we left my car?" Josh wouldn't comment on the mattress, not now at least.

"I…erm…" Oz narrowed his eyes, looked around as if he hadn't seen their surroundings before. "I think I can find the way to where we should turn, but after that, I'm not sure."

"Go, then." Josh wanted to reach out and touch Oswald's hand, but instead, he smiled.

***

Oswald was hovering in Joshua's kitchen. He didn't know what to do. He should leave, but Joshua kept tugging him along, kept suggesting things he either couldn't or didn't want to say no to. But he couldn't stand here completely useless either. Joshua would grow tired of having to fix things.

"I can do the cooking." He had to. He had to do something to please Joshua before he got angry or bored with him.

"There's not much left to do." Joshua stirred something in a pot. "But if you want, you can set the table. Plates in the upper-left cupboard."

Setting the table wasn't enough. He did it, of course, but he needed to find something else. What would Joshua want from him? His heart began thudding. He was so useless, couldn't even come up with something that would make him happy. He couldn't clean; half the cabin was covered in plastic. Had he known how to paint, he'd have done it, but he was afraid of destroying Joshua's home. Perhaps he could hire a painter…only he didn't have much money.

"Are you okay?"

Oswald jumped. "Yes, of course."

"Are you sure? You look a little green."

Great, he couldn't even look pretty for Joshua—not that he was pretty. In the beginning, Guy had always told him he was, that he was beautiful, gorgeous. Oswald didn't know what he'd done that had changed his looks except growing a little older, but he wasn't pretty anymore. "I'm fine."

Oswald tapped his fingers together discreetly behind his back—Joshua saw far too much.

"If you say so, sunshine."

Oswald opened his mouth to protest, but then he caught Joshua's gaze, noticed the twinkle in his eyes, and huffed. Joshua burst out laughing. Before Oswald could react, Joshua's arms wrapped around him, and he nuzzled Oswald's neck, making tingles follow his touch. "You're so goddamn beautiful, I have a hard time behaving." His lips touched a spot just below Oswald's ear that had shivers erupt, and then he moved away, going back to the pots.

Maybe Oswald was making this much harder than it needed to be. It wouldn't be the first time he'd done that. Perhaps Joshua was just like Guy, and with Guy, a blow job went a long way. A few minutes on his knees and it could take away a lot of irritation, and while Joshua didn't act like he was annoyed, it was just a matter of time.

He breathed in, tapped his thumb against his thigh seven times, and walked up to Joshua. His heart drummed in his ear, but he pushed it away. Joshua wouldn't be angry because Oswald took some initiative, would he?

Reaching out, he touched Joshua's arm.

BLOW JOBS & RELATIONSHIPS

JOSH TURNED AT the touch. Oz touching when not needing to was worth turning around for. With a visible swallow and a smile that looked more like a wince than an actual smile, Oz sank to his knees right there by the stove.

"What are you doing, babe?" Josh had a pretty good idea, and one part of him was all for it, another was screaming at him to stop this and to do it smoothly.

Oz didn't respond. Instead, he reached for the button in Josh's trousers. His cock twitched as those pale eyes turned up to meet his, but something was off.

"Oz, honey?" Josh gently took Oz's hands. "The food is about done." He tugged a little, wanting Oz on his feet.

"We can be quick." The words weren't more than a whisper and Josh had no doubt whatsoever that it would be quick, but that wasn't the issue.

"I don't want quick."

"But you said..."

What had he been saying? "Come on." He tugged at Oz's hands again.

"You don't like blow jobs?" Oz pulled his hands away and got to his feet. Instantly, he began tapping his fingers. "What do you like? I can do something else... I can...if you just tell me—"

"What do you like?" Such a weird conversation to be having right now.

Oz avoided his gaze, tapping his fingers again. "I just want you to enjoy yourself."

It rang false. "And I just want *you* to enjoy *your*self." Josh reached out and ran his thumb over Oz's cheekbone. "I want you panting and moaning, and I want you wanting. And I'll probably hate myself for saying this for all eternity, but right now it didn't feel like you were dying to suck me off."

"But I like you." The desperate tone in his voice had Josh's heart breaking.

"And I like you, a lot."

"You have to tell me what you want me to do."

Josh sighed. "And you have to tell me what you want me to do." Or perhaps they could skip talking altogether.

A quick breath. "I can't do that. It's not… That's not how… With Guy—"

"We're not with Guy, are we?" God, he wished he could strangle that arsehole.

Oswald shook his head.

"So how about some food?" He should just have accepted the blow job, and they wouldn't have had this awkward situation.

"But…I haven't done my part."

His part? "You have to explain that to me."

Oz made a frustrated sound and ran a hand through his hair, fisting the blonde strands before letting go and looking at Josh. "You've done everything. You've cooked, you've taken care of the canoe, you bought breakfast, you called Taylor, you fished me out of the water, you cleaned me up, gave me dry clothes, and I've probably forgotten a dozen other things you've done. I need to do my part. I've set the table. Setting the table doesn't equal all the things you've done." The words came faster and faster until Josh feared he'd choke on them.

He reached out and touched Oz's shoulder. "Oz, I live alone. I always do all parts myself. And you're my guest, all right? There is nothing you have to do."

"But you'll grow tired of me if I don't take care of you. You'll want me to leave if I don't know what to do to please you!"

"I don't want you to leave. All you have to do is be here, that's your part, okay?" Having Oz around made his chest warm and his body tingle; it made him smile.

Oz opened his mouth, then closed it, then opened it again. "What?"

"I like spending time with you, that's all I want." *Yeah, right.* "Come on now, let's eat."

***

Likes spending time with me? No one liked spending time with him. Guy tolerated him because he came with…well, some perks, but apart from getting off, getting his food cooked, and his flat cleaned Oswald doubted he enjoyed Oswald being around. The bite he'd put in his mouth grew and grew.

Guy hadn't called him since he left, hadn't tried to find him—he didn't think, at least.

"Are you okay?" Joshua tilted his head to the side.

"Yes, sure." Oz nodded. Josh didn't look like he believed him.

"Are you upset because I— Because I really wanted to, but—"

"No! No." Heat climbed Oswald's cheeks. No one objected to a blow job, or Oswald didn't think they did. Either Joshua didn't like oral sex, or he didn't like Oswald. The latter was far more likely.

Oswald moved a few pieces of potatoes around his plate. Seconds bled into minutes, and he feared he'd suffocate on the silence. He tapped his forefinger against his knee seven times, then his thumb against his thigh—another seven. Putting a small piece of broccoli in his mouth, he bounced his foot—*one, two, three, four, five, six, seven.*

"Okay." Joshua put down his fork on his empty plate. "Let's get it over with."

"W-what?"

"If blowing me will get you to calm down, I'm willing to make a sacrifice."

Sacrifice? "No."

"No? You won't blow me?"

He would. "I don't want you to make a sacrifice."

"Ah, now we're getting somewhere." Joshua grinned. Oswald was clearly missing something.

"We are?" He looked down at his plate, still filled with food. No matter how much he wanted to finish it, he couldn't.

"Yes. Do you want to eat more?" Joshua nodded towards the plate—not scowling, growling, or sighing.

"I…erm… No? Thank you."

"You can reheat some later if you get hungry." Joshua grabbed their plates and got to his feet.

Later… Oswald glanced at the clock—ten past seven. Was he to stay the night again? He glanced at Joshua. It would be so nice to crawl into bed next to him, to feel those strong arms around him again.

Jumping to his feet, he grabbed a pot off the table. He'd never get to stay if he didn't help out.

"Put it on the stove, and we'll deal with it later."

Later.

As soon as Oswald had let go of the pot, Joshua wound his arms around him from behind. "How are you doing?" His warmth had Oswald's shoulders dropping, and he rested his head against Joshua's chest.

"I'm fine." Exhausted and confused but all right *right now.*

Joshua nuzzled his neck; he did that a lot, Oswald realised. It was nice; no one ever had done it like that before, like he needed them to. "Yeah?"

"Yeah."

"So, you're spending the night?"

Tension crawled back into his muscles. "I…erm… Do you want me to?"

"Stay. I want you to stay." Joshua's lips slid over the skin behind his ear, his beard rasping gently.

"Okay."

"Because you want to stay, right? Not because I said I wanted you to."

God, it was hard to think when Joshua touched him like that. "No. Yes."

Joshua chuckled. "What was that?"

He groaned. "Don't be annoying."

Joshua turned him around and then hefted him up onto the counter. "But, baby, I am annoying."

Oswald was still flailing when Joshua pushed in between his legs and captured his mouth in a soft kiss, swallowing the sound of surprise that escaped him. He wasn't used to kisses, but that didn't stop him opening up for Joshua.

***

Oswald melted into him as soon as the initial surprise bled away. Smart or not, Josh didn't know, but he had to taste him. The soft kiss he'd meant it to be turned more demanding when Oz's tongue came out to meet his. Blood pounded in his ears and rushed down to his groin. Oz moaned, an almost inaudible moan, and Josh forced himself to break the kiss, or he was gonna get handsy.

"Normally, I would suggest we'd move to the sofa, but it's covered in plastic." He smiled, his gaze dropping to Oz's mouth.

Oswald stiffened. "Normally? You do this often?"

Shit. "Ah, no. Haven't since I moved here, actually."

Oswald's eyebrows shot up. "You haven't been with anyone since you moved here?"

Josh's initial reaction was to tell him it wasn't any of his business, but he bit his tongue. This was Oz; he feared a response like that only would spur his imagination or, worse, have him blaming himself for doing something wrong. "I hooked up with a guy in Northfield last summer, once. So, for the last four years, there's been one guy." Sad but true.

"One? Total? Not that you have some you usually see but don't count?"

Josh laughed, then choked on it when he remembered what Jason had said. "Everyone counts, always. And I don't share." *Oh, shit that came out wrong.* "Don't freak out, I didn't mean that we're…" He gestured between them. "You know? Erm…what I'm saying is that if I'm seeing someone, I'm not seeing anyone else, and I'm not okay with that other person seeing anyone else either."

Oswald blinked at him, those pale eyes filled with confusion. “But wouldn’t you get bored?”

“No!” Joshua ran a hand through his hair. This was too heavy a conversation to have right now. “No, I wouldn’t get bored. The whole idea of being in a relationship, as I see it, is that you want to spend time with the person you’re with.”

Oswald held his breath, then he whispered, “You said you like spending time with me.”

“I do.”

“I like spending time with you, too.”

Josh blew out a breath. “Good. Then we spend some time together and see if we still like spending time together when the weekend is over, yeah?”

“You want me to stay all weekend?”

“It’s already Saturday night, honey.” Joshua grinned as he prepared for the affronted look that was bound to come, but Oswald didn’t object to the honey. “You can stay longer if you want, though.”

“Stay? Oh, no, I don’t want you to have to put up with me.” He tapped his fingers together.

“Stay with me, Oz. You have a week until you start working, right? Stay here, save your money, and we’ll see if we can find somewhere for you to live. And if I’m tired of you or you’re tired of me after a week, we’ll go separate ways, no harm done.” Josh wouldn’t be tired of him.

“I…erm…I don’t want to be in your way.”

“Oh, you won’t be. You’ll be painting my living room, starting tomorrow.” Joshua nuzzled his neck. “And then I’ll be working Monday to Friday so you’ll have the cabin to yourself, and you have your car so you can go into town and see Aiden, check out the studio some more, get the feel of things. It’ll be all right, baby. Nortown is pretty nice when you let it be.”

Joshua kissed that spot behind his ear that made Oswald shiver and wondered if there were other spots like it hidden elsewhere on his body.

MOANS & NIBBLES

OSWALD'S HEART WAS thudding so hard he feared it'd stop from exhaustion. *A week.* Even if it were the only week he'd ever get with Joshua, it would mean a week when he'd be warm, he'd have someone to talk to, and someone to share meals with. And maybe some kisses. He really liked kisses.

"Are you sure?" He didn't want Joshua to grow tired of him and a week might be too much.

"I'm sure. I've never been surer of anything." The mumbled words caressed his neck, and Oswald shivered again. Hesitantly, he reached out and touched Joshua's shoulder. *So strong.* The muscles moved underneath his hand as Joshua wrapped his arm around him, pulling him closer. "You smell so damn good, Oz. I think I might take you to bed and smell you all over."

Oswald giggled, he tried to stop the sound, but it bubbled out of him. Joshua stopped and looked at him, his eyes sparkling. A blush climbed Oswald's face as he pressed his lips together.

"Oh, no, keep on laughing at me." Joshua wasn't angry which made more bubbles want to spill out. "But before you start up again, may I take you to bed?"

"At seven o'clock?"

"Close to half past." Joshua grinned. "I'll let you get up again once I've smelled you."

Nerves filled his gut. What would Joshua want him to do?

"No?" Joshua tilted his head to the side. "That's all right. You want coffee? Or maybe some tea? I might have some cinnamon buns in the freezer." He started to move away, and panic clawed at Oswald's throat.

"Wait." It wasn't more than a whisper.

Joshua stilled, a hand lingering at Oswald's waist. "For as long as you want."

He wanted to tap his fingers to ease some tension, but he stayed as unmoving as Joshua did. "I-I didn't mean you weren't allowed to move."

"No?" Joshua raised his eyebrows and grinned; then he was nuzzling Oswald's neck again. "So I can still smell you as long as I don't take you to bed?"

Oswald dug his fingers into Joshua's shoulder. "You can take me to bed if you tell me what you want me to do." It sounded so pathetic, but if he didn't know beforehand, he'd just worry about it when they were there.

Joshua groaned, and tingles skidded down Oswald's body.

"I did tell you, baby. I want to lay you down on the bed, then I want to remove your clothes, or some of them if that's okay?" Oswald nodded. He wouldn't mind if Joshua removed some of his clothes as well. "And then I'm gonna smell you."

The giggle came again. "I wouldn't recommend it."

Joshua chuckled and kissed his neck, then lifted him off the counter. Joshua's hard length pressed against him as he slid down Josh's body and onto his feet. Heat pooled in Oswald's gut and he pushed closer.

"You might change your mind and beg me to smell you."

Oswald thought about his sweaty feet and shook his head. "Nope. Maybe I should take a shower."

"Nope, you can shower after." Joshua started walking him backwards, hands moving down his back, not groping but sliding down his arse. "I can help make sure you're clean."

The vision of Joshua in the shower with suds running down his body had Oswald moaning.

"Yes, that's it. I want more sounds."

Oswald stiffened for a second. *Sounds?* But then Joshua kissed him, and a new little sound escaped his lips. Joshua responded with a moan of his own and Oswald smiled. Who'd thought moans could make him long for more, make him want?

***

Josh pulled Oz's T-shirt over his head as soon as they entered the bedroom. "All right?"

Oswald nodded and pulled Josh down for another kiss. Oz would've laughed, but it was the first time he'd initiated a kiss, so he gladly went with it.

As they neared the bed, Joshua held on so Oz wouldn't fall when they walked into it. Following him down onto the mattress, Joshua broke the kiss and moved down Oswald's neck. He inhaled. "Smells nice here."

Oswald wiggled around as Josh trailed his neck with soft kisses, then he nipped a little and Oz jumped. "Tastes good too." Moving down, he followed the collarbone with his tongue.

"Joshua." Oz tried to squirm away, but Joshua caged him in with his arms.

"Yes, baby?" He moved down over the hairless chest, slowly making his way towards the nipple. "Smells nice here too." He scraped the skin with his teeth and then covered the taut nipple with his mouth and sucked a little.

"Joshua!"

Chuckling, he let go. "Yes?"

"W-what—"

"Smelling you." He drew in some air.

"Isn't that kind of…erm…weird?" But his fingers curled in Joshua's hair, holding him in place.

Joshua laughed again. "Of course it is, but you never said I couldn't be weird."

Sitting up on his knees, Josh pulled his shirt off, debating if taking Oswald's jeans off would be moving too fast.

"Oh god, look at you." Oz's breathless words made Josh stop and look down at himself. He looked like he did every day.

"What?" He didn't have the lithe body Oswald did, there was far more brawn to him, and perhaps he should've looked into manscaping, but no one had ever complained before.

"I've never seen..." He reached out and touched Josh's chest. "It's such a dark red, and...you have to be strong."

"Erm..." Josh scratched the hair on his chest a little self-consciously.

"You're beautiful." Oswald was still staring at his chest, and Josh began grinning.

"No, honey, you are. And that reminds me, I think we had some more smelling to do."

Oz groaned. "You're silly."

He was, but Oz was smiling, and there was no finger-tapping or trying to figure out what to do to please him. Wrapping his fingers around Oswald's wrist, he bent over him and captured his lips in a kiss. His cock screamed at being contained in his jeans, and he rubbed it against Oz in an attempt to shut it up. Oz moaned which didn't help the matter at all.

"So...erm..." Oz tilted his hips, creating more friction. "You're walking around in a chequered shirt and carrying timber all day?"

"Sure, feed that fantasy, darling." Joshua rubbed against him some more, and Oz chuckled, but it transformed into a groan as Joshua ran his thumb over Oz's nipple. God, he loved the sounds he made.

"You don't? I thought you were a lumberjack." Oswald's fingertips dug into his shoulders, his head falling back farther on the pillow, exposing his throat. Joshua sought out that spot behind his ear again.

"Sawmill. A lot of carrying going on, but it's noisy as hell, sawdust everywhere, and we're wearing vests, gloves, helmets and shit." He slid his hand down Oz's chest and stomach, skimming the waist of his jeans. His hard cock was right there, and Joshua cupped it, and rubbed.

"Oh…"

Joshua popped open the button in Oz's jeans. "Okay?"

"Yesss…"

"Want you naked." He kissed Oz's neck fully aware of the tension creeping into him.

"I…erm…yeah. Perhaps I should go shower first. We've been walking around all day and…erm…I've been sweating, and I'm not fit like you, and—"

"Hush." Joshua kissed his lips. "If you don't want to, say no, but I've been walking around all day too, and you're beautiful, so fucking hot it makes me want to…do unspeakable things to you." He grinned to show Oz he didn't mean anything creepy. "Come on, baby. Let me touch you." Josh didn't care if it sounded like he was begging—he *was* begging.

"Yeah, okay." Oz shoved his jeans down, fast—no underwear.

"Whoa, easy. Don't want you to break anything."

***

Oswald flushed. *Shit.* He was too needy, too…just too something. He couldn't think. This was the part of sex he wasn't good at.

"So hot," Joshua breathed against his neck and fisted his cock. Oswald almost yelped. He wasn't used to anyone touching him during sex. Sometimes he'd touch himself when Guy fucked him if he wasn't too rough. If he was, Oswald didn't get hard at all.

"You want t-to…erm…" He couldn't ask.

Joshua continued his kisses and nibbles, his hand pumping Oz's cock in a way that made stars go off behind his eyes.

"I want, but what it is doesn't really matter to me. What do you want?"

"Oh…erm…" Anything. Everything.

"Want me to make you come?" The grip on his cock grew a little firmer without turning painful in any way. "Want me to suck you off?" Josh sucked on his neck, then nipped a little.

"I…erm…want you inside of me." Joshua tried to hide his jerk, but Oswald noticed. Shit, he shouldn't have said that.

"Yeah?" Joshua pressed a little firmer against him, still dressed in his jeans. "You sure?"

Am I? He nodded, but he wasn't entirely sure.

"Gonna make you feel so good." There was a growl in his voice that would've made Oswald smile if it hadn't been for the nerves filling his chest. Joshua kissed him again, hot and all-consuming, then he climbed off the bed. His jeans hit the floor, and Oswald's breath caught as he watched Joshua walk naked around the bed to the bedside table. His muscles played under the skin, his cock hard and flushed, so thick Oswald feared he might have asked for too much.

A condom and a bottle of lube landed on the bed, then Joshua was back to kissing him. Oswald forgot that he didn't know what he was doing and that he was awkward in bed. Instead, he lost himself in the kisses and the touches. He ran his hands over Joshua's shoulders, arms, chest. Played with his nipples and was rewarded with some grunts. His caresses turned more and more frantic, and he sought out Joshua's every touch, squirming and wiggling to get his hands where he wanted them to go. Joshua chuckled, but it wasn't mean or condescending.

Need burned in Oswald in a way he wasn't sure was healthy. He couldn't get enough of Joshua, couldn't touch enough. He ran his hands over every part of skin he could reach.

The sound of the cap of the lube bottle opening yanked him back to reality, and his heart pounded faster.

"No, don't go all tense on me now, babe."

Easy for him to say, he wasn't the one who'd have that thick cock jammed into him. Oswald jumped as Joshua's lube-slicked fingers found his opening. He braced himself for the breaching, waited, and then waited some more. Joshua found his mouth again, nipping at his lips only to soothe the bite with his tongue.

Oswald couldn't concentrate on the kiss when Joshua's fingers slid over his entrance, circling, caressing, playing.

Panting, Oswald forgot he'd been nervous about the touch and pressed against Joshua's finger. Moaning, Joshua deepened the kiss and pushed in, holding still for a few seconds before moving his finger in and out of Oswald. The heat spreading in his limbs took him by surprise.

"Oh god."

"If you say so." Joshua was clearly amused, but Oswald wasn't in a state where he cared, especially not when Joshua found that spot that had him shuddering. It was like he knew where it was… and cared to find it.

Joshua lined up a second finger, entered slowly, and found that spot again. Oswald groaned, both at the slight burn and at the pleasure washing over him. He helplessly looked up at Joshua; how could he know how to touch him? The thought left his mind as Joshua's fingers hit home again.

Shivers raced through his body, and he started to roll his hips to meet Joshua's thrusts.

"Yes. Do that again. Fuck yourself on my fingers. Makes me so hot, Oz. I think I could come just from watching you."

On a normal day, Joshua's words would've embarrassed him, but he couldn't find it in himself to be embarrassed. "Joshua." The word was part begging, part needing reassurance.

Joshua kissed him, first on the mouth then the neck, and Oswald clung to him. His entire body tightened, and he feared he'd come too fast for Joshua's liking. "Please…" He continued to push himself onto Joshua's fingers, clawing at his shoulders.

"Anything, baby. What do you want?"

"Yes."

Joshua chuckled, but the fingers left his body, and Joshua shifted around, searching for the condom. Oswald drew in a shuddering breath, his muscles tensing. It was happening. He filled his lungs and started to turn over—wouldn't want to be too slow to get into position. Annoying Joshua now wouldn't be good.

A hand on his hip stopped him. "I'd like to see your face if that's okay?"

See my face? Why would he want that? Oswald nodded, if Joshua wanted it that way, then they'd do it that way. It couldn't be too bad, could it? Then Oswald smiled, he wanted to see Joshua too.

***

Josh didn't know what to do with the confused look, didn't want to think about what it might mean, so when the smile came he kissed Oswald long and hard. He rolled them on the bed, so Oz ended up on top. When a look of something close to panic flew over Oz's face, Josh rolled them again. "Like this?"

Oz nodded and hooked a leg around him. Josh took it as a sign.

Guiding himself to Oswald's opening, he looked down, hoping for eye contact. Oz squeezed his eyes together and held his breath. Josh frowned. Despite the need roaring in him, he didn't thrust. He added a little pressure, more to make sure he stayed in place than to breach, then he wrapped his hand around Oswald's cock.

Oz's eyes flew open, his lips parting, and a soft moan escaped as Joshua worked his length. Precum coated the silky skin and Josh slid his thumb over the head. With another sound, Oswald thrust into his hand then pushed down on Josh's cock, not hard enough to take him in but close.

Josh muttered a curse at the overwhelming urge to move, but he kept still. After another thrust, Oz looked into his eyes and moaned. Josh pushed in, slow but steady, while continuing to touch Oswald.

"Feels so good, baby." He got a whimper in response. "So fucking nice, Oz."

Once all the way in, he kept still, watching the flush on Oswald's face, the way he bit his lip, and listened to his breaths. Sliding his hand up and down Oz's length, he grinned when Oz pushed against him. The grin was replaced by a groan and then Joshua started moving.

"Joshua." It wasn't more than a whisper but the way Oswald's hands ran up his arms and his hips rolled to meet his thrusts made all Josh's doubts disappear.

He thrust a few times, then corrected his angle until he found the right one. Oswald clawed at him, met his motions in a way that had Joshua seeing stars. Heat built inside as he looked down at the way Oswald's muscles contracted. A steady flow of *oh-gods* spilt from his mouth, and Josh figured it was all right to up the tempo, skin slapping, sweat beading, and need clawing.

Then Oswald pushed at his shoulder, and Joshua withdrew and fell onto his back. A moment of surprise flitted through him when Oswald climbed on top of him, but Josh would do anything Oswald wanted. "You want me like this?" He ran his hands over Oswald's arse and up his hips.

"I want to try it, if it's okay?"

"You can try anything you want." Josh held his breath as Oswald lowered himself onto him. Oswald moaned and let his head fall backwards—so fucking beautiful Josh couldn't help but run his hands all over him.

"Be careful with your promises, I might get carried away." The words were probably meant to be teasing, but the heat in Oswald's eyes and the breathy tone made them sound serious, not that Josh minded.

"You can get as carried away as you want, babe. There are very few things I would object to."

Oswald rolled his hips, pushed himself up and down and tested different angles until he found one that worked. Josh let him play for a while, but the need tore at him.

He fisted Oswald's cock again, and as he clenched around Josh, there was no return.

"Oh God, Joshua." With flushed cheeks and closed eyes, Oswald moved with more desperation.

It wouldn't last, but Josh didn't care. Shivers washed over him and the urge to thrust harder, faster, took hold of him. Oswald's cock grew in his hand, and his body tightened. With a muffled cry, sprays of cum painted Josh's hand and torso. There was nothing he could do then. He got swept away, the intensity of his climax stealing his breath. Wave after wave of shattering explosions erupted from his body.

With a grunt, Oswald collapsed on top of him, lazily taking his mouth in a kiss before nuzzling his neck. The scent of clean sweat and sex clung to the bedroom.

Joshua sniffed his hair. "You do smell damn nice."

Oswald was quiet for a second before a giggle built. It started soft but grew louder and ended with a sigh.

"You all right?" Josh ran a hand over Oswald's back.

"Yes… That was really nice." Oswald tilted his head and gazed at Josh.

"It was." Josh kissed him. "Shower?"

"Oh god, yes."

Josh chuckled and moved them off the bed, tugging Oswald with him.

BITCHES & POSSIBILITIES

Two weeks later

OSWALD LOOKED OUT the window of the flat he and Joshua were here to see. The café was right across the street and the studio was in the same building, so it wouldn't take him more than a minute or two to get to work. The grocery shop, on this side of the road, would take no more than a few minutes' walk either. It was perfect—he hated it. He already missed the huge trees surrounding Joshua's cabin, he longed for the silence, the peace.

"It's just for six months, to begin with." The woman Joshua was talking to giggled annoyingly.

"Yes, we know."

"It might be longer, but six months I know for sure."

Oswald drummed his thumb seven times against his thigh. He should be over there talking to her, Joshua shouldn't have to, but he feared he'd throw up soon.

"We'll have a look around." He could tell by the voice that Joshua was smiling. *Bitch.* Oswald stiffened—what was wrong with him?

"What do you think?" The hand on the small of his back was warm, and Oswald slapped a smile on his face.

"It's nice."

"You don't have to go. You can stay with me."

Oswald wanted to. He wanted to cling to Joshua and never let him go, but he needed—they needed—him to stand on his own two feet for a little while. Being with Joshua was easy, he was happy when they were together—safe, but Oswald was well aware of how easy it was for him to lose himself in a relationship. Joshua was nothing like Guy, nothing at all, and it had taken him a week simply to realise Joshua didn't expect him to do everything around the house. With each day that went by, the picture he had of Guy altered, but he still needed time to sort his head out. "I think I need this."

"Need what?" Joshua's hand slipped away only to curl around his wrist.

"Six months." Six months to land, six months to see if being an acupuncturist in Nortown would work, if working with Aiden would work.

"And then you'll come home?"

Oswald smiled. *Home.* "Yes."

Joshua nuzzled his neck. "But you'll still see me, right? During these six months."

"Every day."

"Thank god. I don't know if I would stay sane knowing you're here and not getting to see you."

It was absurd to think Oswald would forbid Joshua to do anything, but his words still wrapped around him like a warm blanket. He went up on tiptoes and kissed him on the cheek. "I'll move back in the spring. It's only one hundred and eighty-one days."

"One hundred and eighty-one days till the season of love?" Joshua wiggled his eyebrows.

"Any season can be the season of love, all five hundred twenty-five thousand six hundred minutes of the year."

"You keep track of far too many numbers, baby."

"I know." He smiled, and it wasn't until the woman cleared her throat he realised he'd lost himself in Joshua's eyes. Joshua winked and turned to her.

"We'll sign a contract for six months, but if you plan on being away for longer, you'll have to find another tenant."

Oswald squeezed Joshua's hand and looked out the window again. Nortown wasn't big, and it wasn't the prettiest town he'd seen, but it sure had possibilities. And it had Joshua.

ABOUT OFELIA GRÄND

Ofelia Gränd is Swedish, which often shines through in her stories. She likes to write about everyday people ending up in not-so-everyday situations, and hopefully also getting out of them. She writes contemporary, paranormal, romance, horror, Sci-Fi and whatever else catches her fancy.

Her books are written for readers who want to take a break from their everyday life for an hour or two.

When Ofelia manages to tear herself from the screen and sneak away from husband and children, she likes to take walks in the woods…if she's lucky she finds her way back home again.

Sign up for Ofelia's Mailing List to get a free short story and updates on new releases and ongoing projects:
http://is.gd/3n1tCK

You may also find her on various social media:
Goodreads: https://www.goodreads.com/author/show/7874960.Ofelia_Gr_nd
Google+: https://plus.google.com/+OfeliaGrand/posts
Facebook 1: https://www.facebook.com/ofelia.grand
Facebook 2: https://www.facebook.com/pages/Ofelia-Grand/1405427199716172
Pinterest: https://www.pinterest.com/ofeliagrand
Website: http://ofeliagrand.com

BY OFELIA GRÄND

Knickers in at Twist

From All of Us to All of You

Silent Woods

Blood on Sand

Dazzle Me

Buried Desires (with Amy Spector)

Deadly Sugar (Deadly Sugar #1)

Deadly Secrets (Deadly Sugar #1.5)

A Christmas Princess

Once in a Snowstorm (Nortown #1)

He Melted Us

Once in a Forest (Nortown #2)

The Empty Egg (Nortown #2.5)

Falling Through

Once in May (Nortown #3)

Happy Endings (Nortown #3.5)

Buried Desires 2 (with Amy Spector)

Deadly Lies (Deadly Sugar #2)

Deadly Dates (Deadly Sugar #2.5)

The Deadly Sugar Collection

The Maddest of Men

Once in the Underworld (Nortown #4)

Just Words (Nortown #4.5)

The Lords of Lettuce

Eight Feet of Magic

Trapped

Worth His Salt

Once Around Seven (Nortown #5)

WINTER BLOSSOMS

PAUL IASEVOLI

Chris, a naïve twenty-four-year-old, breaks up with the first man he's ever lived with. In the months that follow, he travels from Queens to The Hamptons, Manhattan to Brooklyn to find love. In the process, he discovers more about himself and realizes the man he hoped to meet has been in front of him the entire time.

Winter Blossoms will take you on a ride through the streets and subways of New York City. Every stop along the way highlights the 1980s' vibrant, gay nightlife. Part nostalgic romp, part coming-of-age story, *Winter Blossoms* will delight the reader as it comes into full bloom.

***

Genre: gay/bisexual literary fiction

Keywords: love, romance, New York City, 1980s

Advisory: mature content

DEDICATION

To Bill, my life's love.

ACKNOWLEDGEMENTS

I would like to give a word of thanks to all the people who have helped me get as far as I have in my third career. First and foremost, Rick Bettencourt, who guided me along the writer's road. Debbie McGowan, who encouraged me to write this story beyond the first chapter. Thanks to Susan Yansick who has supported my writing efforts for the past six years. And to my beta readers, Sybille Bruning—*Ich danke dir*; Zach Wichter, my former student who has become his teacher's teacher—*Love you, Kiddo.* And to all the members of the FWA Bradenton group—you've shared my highs and lows, but never let me down. Lastly, to Paula Streeter, my cover designer—your insight into the story brought Samuel to life for Chris.

RISE TO FALL

I PICKED UP THE phone.

"Robby?" a woman's voice asked.

"No."

The receiver clicked and the line went dead.

It was the third time that week *the voice* had called asking for Robby. It might have been my curt "no" that put her off from explaining any further as to what she wanted with Rob, or "Robby," as she said.

When he came home at five that night, I found the courage to ask about the caller.

"A woman asking for Robby?" He stared at the wall. "Nobody calls me Robby…that I know of."

"Really? Well, she's called three times this past week."

"Maybe she's trying to sell me something."

"Maybe she's trying to sell herself. Where do you go, anyway… those nights I wake up and you're not in bed?"

"The movies…I told you, Chris. I like the late shows at the Prospect—two-fifty and I get to escape from—"

"From me?"

"From myself, and you."

"Fuck you."

"Fuck you!" Rob always managed a louder "fuck you" than me when we argued.

I got off the couch, stormed out the apartment door, and walked the cold, short hallway to the stairs. I ran down the four flights to the street, unsure where I was going.

The corner of Beech and Bowne was dim in comparison to the lights along Kessina Boulevard. I drifted two blocks in their direction like a moth drawn to a lamp. The pink and blue neon street signs shouted in Korean, "*Kimchi gwa Mandu.*" Beneath them, smaller English letters whispered, "kimchee and dumplings."

I walked past the Prospect movie theater, toward the subway station on Roosevelt Avenue, where a hooker clucked her tongue at me as if I would be interested in anything she had to offer.

My night alone in Manhattan would piss Rob off for sure. Either he'd move out and take his dirty laundry back to his mother's house, or I'd tell him he had to leave. I paid three-quarters of the rent, and who needed his seventy-five dollars a month, anyway?

As I climbed down the subway stairs, the smells of alcohol-laced urine and the smoky essence of axle grease mingled with the September night's cool scents from above. I waited on the concrete platform next to mothers holding infants, Hispanic men in heated conversations, and couples speaking Korean. The train pulled up in front of me, tagged in big letters—STAY HIGH 420. In the car, I sat next to a sweet-faced black woman, her hair full of Afro-sheen. She smiled as she scooted over to give me more room. I opened my mouth to say thank you, but my words never formed in the greasy air. I stared across the car—the names "Jose" and "Emmanuel" leaped out at me from the twisting, twirling colors on the opposite wall.

When the Seven train screeched into Times Square station, I nodded to the Afro-sheen woman next to me as I got up first. She gave me a polite smile without a word, as if she understood my haste that night.

Above ground, Seventh Avenue shimmered in a light drizzle. But rather than take the subway, I walked the thirty short blocks to the Village just to blow off some steam.

As I moved south, to the place that used to be my home away from home, I thought about the night I met Rob in the Hamptons nearly six months ago.

***

An early spring crowd of tourists filled the Swamp that weekend. "Rusty, gimme another Cutty and soda," I shouted across the bar. I needed some Dutch courage to talk to the hot, mustachioed man standing next to me. But when the DJ spun Gloria Gaynor's national gay anthem—a song I'd hated since the first day it got airplay on Kiss97—I grabbed my drink and went outside. I smoked a cigarette on the patio and headed to the "old man's bar" behind the Swamp's disco.

A chorus of gray-haired men were singing "Drinking Again," sounding better than Sinatra or any other crooner who'd rendered that tired tune. As I walked in, more than one or two heads turned to look at me. It wasn't often that a swarthy, well-built twenty-something joined their crew. When I broke into the chorus, off-key as I was, the man next to me put a withered hand on my bottom. I whisked it away, like I would shoo a fly from my coffee, and went on singing about telling jokes to jokers and laughing at broken hearts.

A tap on my shoulder turned into a grip that forced me around. I looked into gunmetal-gray eyes, and something told me right then and there to run away. His eyes and sandy mustache would keep me captive if I let them. But I didn't run as I should have. Instead, I stood dumbfounded, like a pubescent boy who'd experienced his first wet dream. I was new to all of this—new to this chase and conquer. I had always been the outsider, a window-shopper never buying.

"You come over here to hide from me?"

I looked up from my drink and studied the long, lean man I'd stood next to at the disco bar just moments ago. I mumbled something about the music in the club being too loud and gulped my Scotch and soda.

He gave me a throaty laugh. "You older than you look?"

"I'm twenty-four," I said, spitting out my age within earshot of men who could have been my father. "Name's Chris—Chris Winter."

"Rob," he said, and motioned to the bartender. "Markey," he yelled. "Two Cutty and sodas."

"I got a full drink."

"Ah…you'll need another soon enough. You want lemon?"

I nodded, not sure I liked lemon in my Scotch.

"Twist or wedge?" Markey asked.

Rob turned to me.

"Don't matter," I said.

Markey pushed the drinks with lemon twists over to us. He held up his hand when Rob offered him a twenty. "On me," he said.

Rob tucked his money back into his billfold.

"You're friends with Markey?" I asked.

Rob shrugged. "He never makes me pay when I come into the old man's bar."

"You're a regular? Then how come I've never seen you here before?"

Rob picked up his glass and took a swig. "Only come out here once a month from Queens to check on my property."

"You got property out here on the East End?"

Rob took a long sip of his drink before he answered. "Not really. It's in Mastic Beach—I rent out my house there in the summer."

"Mistake Beach." I laughed at the nickname of that hamlet through my haze of Scotch.

"What's that supposed to mean?"

"It means what it sounds like—that town is a dump."

Rob lifted his glass and let out a throaty laugh. "That it is, but it makes me some good money from the couple of queers I rent it to—it's their cheap Fire Island."

The chords of "Skylark" rang out, and the gray-haired men singing dampened our attempt at idle conversation until our glasses were emptied, and Rob's lips were on mine.

Markey whistled from behind the bar when Rob took me into his embrace. It might have been my imagination, but the men around the piano gasped as Rob led me out the door to the patio.

That night, we didn't make it back into the disco. Instead, we headed straight to the back of my Pontiac. The leather seats were cold against my backside as Rob took off my pants. It was dawn when we were done, and Rob asked me to see him again. Maybe he could come to my apartment in Queens, or we could have dinner someplace on Northern Boulevard.

I nodded yes and kissed him. My first tryst with a man who looked like he'd stepped out of a Marlboro ad was better than I'd ever dreamt.

***

The rain on Seventh Avenue draped a veil over the memory of my first night with Rob. When it turned into a downpour, I ducked into the nearest bar on Christopher Street to avoid looking like a wet rat.

"Heart of Glass" played on the jukebox, but the din from the Friday night crowd drowned out Debbie Harry singing about love being "a pain in the ass."

I asked for a Scotch and soda—no brand names in Boots and Saddles. A man had to be butch in that place and not priss-it-up by ordering any fancy libations. Meanwhile, the conversation from two leather men standing next to me was something about choosing the right cornice for their windows that faced out on Twenty-Sixth Street.

Overhead, fat Christmas lights spun and twisted in flashing colors—strung up year-round, they were Boots' poor excuse for a disco ball the joint couldn't afford. I looked around at the scruffy men at the bar and asked myself what I was doing there.

I slugged back my Scotch and headed out to the street where I waited under the ragged awning for the rain to stop—September showers in Manhattan never lasted for more than an hour as they worked their way out to Long Island.

Once the downpour withered to a trickle, I turned and walked a half block west on Christopher toward Ty's. When I stopped under the rainbow flag to step inside, the smell of pizza caught my nose, and I decided I was more hungry than thirsty.

I crossed the street and waited in line outside Big Slice Pizza Parlor—the place was packed at nine-thirty on a Friday night. I studied the crowd inside, flaming queens and leather men sat together holding hands next to chic uptown couples all enjoying the biggest slices of pizza the city had to offer. In the corner, a man sat at a table with his back to me, his broad shoulders and sandy short-cropped hair caught my eye. He held the hand of a thin woman across from him. When she saw me staring, she nodded, and the sandy-haired man turned around. My heart skipped a beat.

Rob got up, ran out the door, and through the line. "What're you doing here?" he said.

"Getting pizza." I nearly spit the words in his face. "How'd *you* get here…and who's the fish?"

Rob's eyes darted to the blonde at the table inside. "That's my…sister."

"You always hold hands with your *sister* when you have dinner?"

Rob grabbed my arm. "C'mon in and meet her."

"Bullshit!" I pulled my arm from Rob's grip. "Is she the bitch who calls you 'Robby'?"

He forced a throaty laugh. "Could be," he said. "C'mon in and meet her, you might like her."

I bolted away from him and ran up Christopher across Seventh Avenue to the corner of Sixth. For the second time that night, I was running from the only man I'd ever invited into my life. I needed to get far away from the West Village, away from Rob and his "sister."

At the corner, I hailed a cab and asked the driver to take me to Stix Nightclub at the foot of the Queensboro Bridge. There, I would be halfway home, maybe see some friends I knew from high school on Long Island.

The yellow cab pulled to a stop in front of the gray, box-like building. Outside, the music throbbed as I paid the doorman five dollars to get inside.

I nodded with the beat of a song I'd never heard. Its lyrics were Caribbean, but its rhythms synchronized with the desperation of gay men living in early 1980s New York City.

I was in the middle of a head bob when a short, brown man came up behind me.

"You new here?" he asked in a heavy Spanish accent.

My head continued bobbing, ignoring his question.

"I'm Xavier," he said. "You like to make love?"

I turned to him and said, "*Vete pa' el carajo.*"

"Oh, you speak Spanish?"

"*Coño...claro,*" I said.

"You got a filthy mouth."

Then I kissed him. Kissed Xavier with a vengeance. Next thing I knew, we were making out on his couch someplace in Bed-Stuy, miles away from the Seven train. Miles away from Rob. Miles away from my moral sensibilities. Miles away from any decency.

"I have to go," I said before Xavier could get me into his bed.

"But why? You don't like me?"

I pulled on my shirt and buttoned up my jeans. "I'm faithful to one man."

On the street, I darted past shuttered Brooklyn buildings and down into the bowels of the nearest subway station. The fool in me had let a good-looking trick slip through my fingers. I zigzagged my way north to Queens, changing trains three times. Being born on Long Island had its privileges, but what city kids lacked in fresh air and green grass, they made up with street and subway smarts—two things I never had.

As I climbed the four flights up to my apartment on Beech, the sun shone through the transoms above the landings. Rob worked Saturday mornings, and I could sleep the day away. When he came home, dinner would be ready, and I'd serve him as if I were June Cleaver whether or not he deserved such pampering after the fight we'd had and my growing suspicions.

A stew pot simmered on the stove when Rob called from work on Saturday afternoon. Avoiding any talk of the previous night's argument, he told me how his boss at the electronics factory wanted him to take the train out to the Hamptons and stay overnight. It was the boss's wife's fiftieth birthday, and there would be fireworks. I could come out if I wanted to, but I'd have to get a hotel room—an impossible task on such short notice, even after tourist season.

I told him not to worry. I would put the stew in the fridge and get some take-in Chinese. He thanked me for my understanding before he hung up.

That bastard. I bet he's with his "sister."

Sunday morning, I woke up early, reached for Rob, and remembered what he'd said—he was at a birthday party and would be home later. After I flipped through the *Daily News*, I made a coffee, and watched Sam Champion's rainy weather report on Channel Seven.

When I heard the key turn the deadbolt in the door that dreary afternoon, Rob had that "I have something to tell you" look on his face—a look I'd come to hate in the months we'd lived together—it always meant he was hiding something.

"What?" I asked before he could speak.

He stared down at the floor, never glancing up at me. "I came home to change," he said, "but I have to go right away. My mom's making Sunday dinner."

"Sunday dinner," I echoed.

"Yeah, you know, sauerbraten and all the trimmings."

"I suppose..."

"C'mon, Chris." Rob's voice pleaded with me not to get mad at being left alone again.

"No, no," I said. "You go on to do what you have to do. I'll be here waiting. Your *sister* going to be there too?"

Rob shook his head and went into the bedroom to change clothes. He kissed me on the forehead before he went out the door. "See you later," he said.

I waited up that night as late as I could. At ten-thirty, I went to bed but kept one ear cocked to listen for the deadbolt to unlock.

It was after midnight when Rob climbed into bed next to me. I could smell the perfume on his neck—Chanel No. 5—the same fragrance my mother used to wear. I wondered if that were what his "sister" wore as well. I pushed the thought out of my head and slept until the alarm buzzed at six a.m. I made a coffee after I'd showered, shaved, and dressed. Another day at Queens College teaching punctuation lay ahead.

Before I left, I looked from the kitchen into the bedroom. Rob was still asleep on his day off. His sandy mustache fluttered with his snoring breath. He was the Marlboro Man I'd dreamt of finding, so if he had an occasional fling to satisfy his other needs, I could take that in stride.

***

When I got home from work, I thought it strange that the deadbolt to our apartment was unlocked. I pushed it open and called for Rob. The rustle of fabric from the bedroom first caught my attention, then the sight of Rob in his boxers greeted me.

"Wow, you're home early," he said.

"Half a day today. You know I only teach one class on Mondays."

Rob's face went red. "Oh, I forgot."

"Robby, what's going on?" a woman called from the bedroom.

"Nothing...sis," Rob said.

"Sis?" *the voice* asked.

I looked at my "Marlboro Man" with a jaundiced eye. "Your sister?" I bolted for the door.

He grabbed me by the shoulder. "It's not how it looks."

I shook myself free, hurried down the four flights to Beech Street, out to Kessina, and toward the subway station at the end of Main. Pink and blue lights flashed above me but, with my mind racing, I didn't recognize their words or their signs.

I drank my way from bar to bar, until the Manhattan evening turned to a blur of yellow cabs and sulfurous streetlights. I caught the last express train back to Queens and climbed four flights to face the man I thought I loved.

Rob was on the worn-out couch in the sitting area we called a living room. In the six months we'd spent together, we'd made love there more times than I could count.

He swirled the Scotch in his glass. "It's late," he said.

"Yeah, too late," I said. "Have to get up early tomorrow. I have two classes."

Rob nodded. "Let me explain."

"Explain what? That you used me to get out of your mother's house? Needed me to pay rent you couldn't afford? Wanted me to suck your cock?"

Rob stared out the window toward the brighter lights of Kessina Boulevard. "No, it's not that, it's—"

"It's that 'sister' of yours!"

Rob looked down into his Scotch and nodded. "Maybe," he said.

I blocked him out for the five minutes he droned on about orgies, bondage, water sports, and sex acts I'd never heard of nor understood. And imagined myself with my thumbs pushing in on his Adam's apple until he gasped for air. I would gaze into his gunmetal-gray eyes until they turned beet red, unclench my grip, and watch him fall dead to the floor.

"Did you hear me?" Rob asked.

I nodded, although I had no idea what he'd said.

"So if you want to find me, I'll be at the house in Mastic. Call me there when you decide what you want to do."

He went into the bedroom and pulled his suitcase from underneath the bed. Dresser drawers slammed closed with a hollow sound. The zip of his suitcase echoed through the sitting area, and wheels rolled out behind him to the front door.

I turned and stared out the window toward Kessina Boulevard. The suitcase rattled over the threshold and the door latch clicked.

"See ya," I shouted at the metal door once it closed.

***

After my breakup with Rob, I waited until mid-October to hit the bars again. On a warm, fall afternoon, I drove out to the East End. Sunday tea dance at the Swamp was what the old queens called "the fish fry," since it was the only day the club allowed in women and straight couples.

With the disco packed, I perched on the upstairs landing. From there, I could ogle the shirtless eye-candy moving on the dance floor. When a spot opened at the bar, I went down the stairs. "Rusty, a Cutty and soda," I hollered through the din.

Rusty held up a lemon wedge in his right hand and a twist in his left. I pointed to his left. He slid the icy glass to me, I left a five in its place, and took a seat with my back to the dance floor and the door.

It had been three weeks since I'd seen Rob. I didn't really miss him, although I did miss the sex. I swirled the ice with the Scotch in my glass, watched the lemon twist follow the cubes on the bottom, and remembered how I'd wanted to kill Rob the night he said he needed me *and* his "sister" to satisfy himself.

It's a good thing I wasn't drunk that night or I just might have done it. My picture would have been on the cover of the *Daily News* with a headline reading: "Homosexual Strangles Boyfriend in Fit of Jealous Rage." I imagined what my mother would have thought—worse than that, Father Jim at Saint Francis's Catholic Church. All the *Our Fathers* and *Hail Marys* in the world wouldn't have saved me from eternal damnation. Not to mention my subsequent confinement on Riker's Island.

The smell of cumin and musk exuding from somewhere at the bar distracted me from my daymare of Hell and prison life. I sniffed around to find out who it was that smelled so strange. Tight back muscles glistened on the shirtless man beside me. I pushed my barstool out to move a few feet away when the sweaty man turned to me.

"Chris!"

"Xavier?"

"You alone?"

I was in no mood to have a conversation with an almost-trick I met weeks ago at Stix, let alone put up with his heady scent. "What're you doing here on a Sunday afternoon, all the way from Brooklyn?" I asked as if I cared.

"Oh, a friend of mine from Mastic invited me to come out. So I took the train to Shirley."

"A friend from Mastic?"

"Yeah. He's out on the patio with his girlfriend, Linda. Come outside and meet them."

The patio seemed a more refreshing option than sitting next to Xavier indoors taking in his odor. I followed him into the bright light filtering through oaks ready to lose their golden autumn leaves.

On a bench, with their backs to me and Xavier, sat a man—his sandy-hair somehow familiar—and a blonde girl so slender she seemed made of matchsticks.

"Robby," Xavier called across the patio.

With the fall sun warming my back, I froze up inside. Rob turned and smiled when he saw me. I looked left, then right, wondering which would be the better escape option. The urge to wrap my hands around Rob's throat and murder him surged in me again. I swallowed that thought and my pride. "Hi," I said, as I studied the skinny girl next to him. "And this must be your sister." I extended my hand to the blonde.

She never reached for it. Instead, she turned to Rob and gave him a puzzled look.

He let out that throaty laugh of his, and I felt my stomach tie into a knot.

"No…not my sister. This is Linda," he said.

"Oh, I see," I lied as if I understood.

"I thought you knew each other?" Xavier asked.

"We used to," I said. "At least, I thought I knew *him*."

Linda looked from me, to Xavier, then at Rob as if she were watching a ping-pong ball bouncing off a table.

Rob patted the seat next to him. "Come sit," he said.

I sat on the wrought-iron stool. Its hummingbird and flower pattern pinched and pricked at my backside.

Xavier untied his shirt from his waist, buttoned it up over his bare chest, and took a spot across from the three of us.

I need a shot, a joint, a Valium…anything to get me through this farce.

"So, how've you been?" Rob said as if we were standing next to an office water cooler on a Monday morning after a long weekend.

"How have I been?" The words slithered through my teeth. "I've been in a 'fuck you' mood with everybody since you left."

Linda's eyes turned the size of muffins rising in an oven.

Rob laughed.

God damn it, I want to rip that laugh from you. I want to tear your vocal cords out.

"Why you so angry?" Xavier asked, as if he'd read my mind.

"I'm not angry," I said, mitigating my true feelings. "Hurt, I think is a better word. Hurt by a half year of lies."

"They were never lies," Rob said.

"Yeah, I should have surmised…"

Linda's eyes had sunk back into her head until that point, but bulged up again, like someone added too much baking powder to the muffin mix. She shifted on her stool. "Well, I don't mind it," she said.

"Don't mind what?" I asked.

Xavier nearly spit his drink across the space between us. "Boy, you dumb."

"I must be. Who are you, anyway?"

"Xavier's one of my summer tenants in Mastic," Rob said.

I glared at Xavier.

He grinned.

That laugh of Rob's sounded again, louder than before. "He knew who you were that night at Stix. I'd told him about you, showed him your picture, told him how good you were in bed, and he wanted to try you out for himself."

The urge to rip Rob's Adam's apple from his neck came over me again, but I checked my rage and stood up to leave.

Linda grabbed my arm. "Where're you going?" she asked. "I think an afternoon with three men like you would be much more fun than only two."

My eyes spun 180 degrees from Linda, to Xavier, and to Rob. I slammed my drink down on the low, wrought-iron table of hummingbirds and flowers next to me. "You all are into something I want no part of."

"Aw, live a little—take a walk on the wild side," Rob shouted as I stormed away. His throaty laugh carried down the path to my Pontiac in the parking lot. I kept the windows of the car rolled up and blasted the Police's "Wrapped Around Your Finger" through the stereo speakers. I must have rewound the cassette five times to that same track in the two hours it took me to drive home to Queens that evening.

NUMB NOVEMBER

THE CRISP NOVEMBER night invigorated my steps down Kessina Boulevard. From Roosevelt Avenue, I took the Seven train into Times Square, switched to the Seventh Avenue Local, and climbed out at the Christopher Street subway station. I cruised down the gleaming tar-covered, cobblestone street peering into plate-glass windows of bars along the way. Men in leather bomber jackets, their fur collars matching mine, looked back at me with lecherous eyes, but I ignored their stares. After my breakup with Rob, the last thing I needed was another cheap trick using me to satisfy his whims.

When I reached the Hudson River Drive at the far end of the West Village, I turned right. On my left, streetlights shone above the broken waterfront docks. I thought about the many men who'd fallen to their deaths at that spot, unreported by the *New York Times* or *The News at Six* on Channel Seven, their insipid lives unworthy—an everyday occurrence in 1980s New York City.

The wind picked up and I pulled my collar higher around my neck. I needed a drink, a stiff shot of Scotch, to keep me warm. The El running the length of the Drive broke the breeze somewhat, hanging derelict above the pavement like the skeleton of a dead elephant that a zookeeper neglected to remove from its cage. I scurried through its bones to a redbrick building. The black sign that marked my final destination creaked its name—"The Anvil." I pushed open the chalky-black door to a bar I'd never visited.

"Ten dollars," the pudgy doorman said.

I unzipped my jacket and reached for my wallet in the right inside pocket. As I thumbed through the money in my billfold, the doorman ran his hand over my pectorals bulging through my white T-shirt. I whisked his hand away as I gave him a ten.

He smiled at my reproach. "For you, I'll make it five tonight."

I didn't argue and switched the ten for a five. Whatever money I could save on a college teacher's salary would mean the difference between steak and tofu that week.

After my half-priced admission to what I was told was the hottest bar on the West Side, I tucked my wallet into my back pocket and checked my jacket at the door. I'd brave the drafty club in my T-shirt for the night. The cold air only added to my pectoral attraction, my nipples pointing hard through the cotton fabric. When I leaned up against the big, square bar and called for a drink, a muscle man next to me didn't hesitate to pinch my teat. I winced and stepped away. "Cutty, straight-up," I yelled to the bartender again.

He answered me with his middle finger and went back to mixing his regular customers' drinks. Undaunted by the barkeeper's gesture, I waited for my turn to be served.

I let my gaze drift around the bar while I waited. *Oh, no. Not Xavier...God, not that almost-trick from Stix. He's like a bad penny. Tell me it isn't so.* Next thing I knew, Xavier was waving to me across the thin early Friday evening crowd. *God, don't let him come over to talk to me.*

He picked up his drink and walked to my side of the bar, his cumin-laced, sweaty scent invading my privacy. "Hi," I said and feigned a smile.

He sucked the dregs of his drink from the bottom of his glass. "Haven't seen you since that afternoon in the Swamp when you ran away from Robby and me."

"I've been busy," I lied and looked away.

"With what?" he asked.

"With classes...and other things."

"Like tricks?"

"Like it's none of your Goddamn business," I said.

"You know, you are what we call *un esnob.*"

I nodded and thumbed my nose in the air.

Xavier threw his head back, gave me a defiant stare, and disappeared somewhere into a darkened corner of the club. The bartender slapped his hand in front of me.

"What'd you need?" he asked.

"Cutty straight—make it a double."

He poured a double shot of Scotch into a tumbler glass and held up a strip of lemon zest. "Twist okay?"

I nodded.

He pushed the glass to me. "Sorry about giving you the finger before, but—"

"You were busy."

He smiled and extended his hand across the bar. "Name's Samuel."

When I shook his hand, I was sure he could feel me trembling. "Chris Winter," I said.

Samuel patted my hand. "Call me if you need anything."

I cast an embarrassed grin down at the bar top and nodded into my full drink. Samuel's clear-blue eyes and bright-white smile certainly were something of an enticement, but deep down I recognized a gigolo when I saw one.

I took a walk around the club. The wood-plank flooring was standard for that kind of place in New York City and carried into the toilets. I cruised into the bathroom. The stained oak planks were covered in sawdust to absorb the urine and whatever other bodily fluids might fall on the filthy floor. Early as it was, the toilet action, that earned the Anvil its reputation, had yet to begin. At the trough, I relieved myself, just in case it got busy later and I'd be deprived of any personal space where I could pee.

I left the bathroom and headed to a far corner of the club. I leaned against the wall, hoping that Xavier wasn't somewhere lurking in the dark. By ten o'clock, the lights on a stage at the club's back wall lit up and began to twirl. Leather men and shirtless muscle boys bellied up to the stage. I moved to a seat at the bar and turned to face the show. I had no idea there would be live entertainment that night, but if my five dollars covered it, I was going to get my money's worth.

The swirling lights went out, and the entire club went pitch-black. A hand groped my ass. I grabbed it and pushed it away. The stage lights came back on and twirled again. In a spotlight's beam, Xavier stood naked on the stage, a tub of Crisco next to him. A barrel-chested man picked up a two-feet chain with three-inch links and greased it from end to end. Xavier bent over onto his hands and knees and moaned as the burly man shoved each link into his rectum until the chain completely disappeared.

I felt my Scotch climb into my esophagus and ran into the nearest toilet. Two men stood at the trough masturbating. Not wanting to throw up on the floor, I puked between them, breaking their momentum.

After my spontaneous vomiting, I made a beeline for the coat-check. I gave the boy behind the half-door a dollar, grabbed my jacket, and pushed my way past the pudgy doorman. Out on the street, the cold November air cleared my head somewhat. The wind blowing through the El whispered to my ignorance—*a night in a gleaming city is not as it seems.*

I crossed beneath the dilapidated El and headed to the Hudson River docks. The glow of streetlights cast my shadow across the rotted beams leading out into the river. With the collar of my jacket pulled up over my chin, wind-driven pins of ice stung my cheeks and ears. I let the breeze take my caution with it, and stepped onto the first treacherous beam. It creaked and groaned under my weight, the second splintered but held its shape. I took giant-steps over gaps between the plank logs until I came to a shipping container hanging precariously halfway in the water. The sulfurous light barely lit the inside of the rusted tin shack. I flicked my Zippo and lit a cigarette, its dull-red glow illuminated the space, its tilted metal floor strewn with used condoms and cigarette butts. I added my half-smoked Marlboro to the pile at the entrance of the container. But, with cold needles piercing my ears and nose, I decided I was wasting my time on a dark

November night. I turned and walked back through the skeleton of the El glowing yellow above the West Side's roadway.

By the time I'd crossed the pavement to the opposite side of Hudson River Drive, the wind had found its way underneath my jacket. With a shiver running up my spine, I pushed the chalky-black door of the Anvil open and waited in the short line that had gathered in front of the pudgy doorman. When it was my turn to get into the club, he looked me up and down. "You again," he said.

I nodded and brushed past him.

He grabbed me by the fur collar of my jacket. "Yo! You need to pay."

"What?"

"You didn't get stamped on the way out."

"But you know I was here less than an hour ago. You felt up my chest, and now you don't recognize me?"

Still gripping my collar, the doorman got off his stool, and dragged me to the door. The other patrons—all in leather jackets waiting to get inside—jeered as I went flying by.

I shook myself from the fat man's grip. "Wait a minute," I hollered. "I'll pay the ten dollars."

The doorman held his hand out and waited for my money. With a glint of victory in his eyes, he waved the bill I gave him in the air and bowed to the other men in line.

I hung my head as I walked past them, my face redder from embarrassment than from the cold wind outside. In the club, I kept my jacket on, albeit unzipped. I found Samuel at the bar and waved to him. "Cutty, double, straight up," I called. Rather than give me the finger, this time he smiled as he poured my order and handed it to me.

"You look like shit," he said.

"Gee, thanks."

"Where'd you go? I saw you run from the bathroom out the door."

"Out for some air."

Samuel laughed. "Any action in the air on the docks?"

I shook my head. "Too cold," I said and put a five on the bar. Samuel shoved it back.

"On me. I caught a glimpse of Tommy's little show with you at the door."

"Oh, that…"

Samuel grinned. "He loves to play that game with newbies. Don't let it bother you."

I shrugged. The guy next to me slammed his hand down on the bar top between Samuel and me. "You bitches done talking so I can get a drink?"

"Hold your horses, cunt, I'm getting to you next." Samuel gave me a wink. "See ya later, Chris," he said.

I stepped away from the bar to make room for the thirsty patron breathing down my neck. I walked around the club as it was filling up. The lights on the stage lit and swirled to signal the start of the eleven-thirty show. If it were going to be anything like the ten o'clock, I really didn't want to watch.

I found a nook that held a recessed door, its deadbolt locked tight. I nestled into the little cove. From my angle, I couldn't see the stage or the performance. A tall man with pockmarked skin found his way next to me in my secure resting spot. He pulled a joint from his pocket, lit it, took a hit, and offered me a toke. I took a swig of my Scotch, wiped my lips on my sleeve, and inhaled a deep drag of the harsh smoke. I nodded my thanks to the man when I handed the joint back to him. He took another hit and offered it to me again. I shook my head—one toke of pot with a tumbler full of straight Cutty was more than I needed to get me through the night.

Music thumped from the stage across the bar bouncing off the beams of the small nook I stood in. I leaned on the door behind me and let the vibrations run up my back. The alcohol and THC filtering through my brain let me float into a fantasy where I felt myself a part of the entire building, as if I were a structure anchored into the shallow bedrock of Lower Manhattan. Adrift in my euphoria, I heard someone shout, "Can you fucking move, dickhead?" Someone was pushing me aside. I spun around. The doorman stood next to me. He unlocked the recessed door that had been my support and switched on a light that lit a staircase to a basement.

"Jesus H. Christ, kid," Tommy said. "You have been one pain in my ass tonight."

I stepped aside and looked toward the man who'd let me share his joint.

He smiled and shrugged.

Tommy climbed down the stairs and the pockmarked man followed behind. I peered into the basement, wondering what was down there. When more men in leather jackets descended the stairs, I was piqued. I looked over to the bar and spotted Samuel. I had to ask him what went on downstairs before my curiosity got the better of me.

"Samuel, another Cutty, but with soda this time," I shouted above the thumping din. He handed me my drink. I got a five out to pay, but before Samuel took the bill, I grabbed his hand. "What's downstairs?" I asked.

"Just another bar—quieter than up here." He plucked the five from my fingers, and rushed over to the next man who shouted for a drink.

Quieter was what I needed after getting pushed and shoved around for the past two hours. I followed the narrow stairs down into the basement. The smoky air from the upstairs club mingled with the musty scents of damp concrete. The basement's walls were nothing more than rough-hewn stone, its floor a reddish sandstone worn smooth by what must have been two hundred years of steps. The man I'd met upstairs motioned for me to sit next to him. I pulled a stool over and moved closer to the bar. He took another joint from his pocket and offered me the first toke. I took a hit and drew the smoke deep into my lungs. "Thanks," I coughed, "but that's enough." He nodded, but looked at me blankly as if he didn't understand.

"Chris," I said and offered him my hand.

"I no English," he said as his grip tightened on mine. "Me Russian—Ivan."

Even though I could speak five languages other than English, Russian was not on my list. I smiled and nodded. "Nice to meet you," I said.

Ivan answered with a blank stare and took the last hit off his joint.

A hand slammed the bar top in front of me. Tommy's pudgy face was in mine. "Where'd you get that drink," he snarled.

"From Samuel upstairs," I said.

"Well, finish it quick, bitch. Down here, you buy your drinks from me."

"Why you so rude?" I yelled. The buzzing in my head forced my voice to ring across the small, rectangular bar.

Three leather men at the opposite side laughed. "That's the way Tommy shows he likes you," the middle one said.

Tommy put his hands on his hips and turned to face the three. "Don't be giving away my secrets, bitches," he lisped to the leather men.

"The new kid is cute," a man at the rectangle's corner hollered. "We'll see what he can do in the backroom later."

I downed the Scotch and soda in my glass and ordered a Cutty straight.

Tommy poured my drink and handed it to me. He grabbed my wrist before I could reach into my coat pocket to pay him. "On me, kiddo," he said. "Thanks for being a part of the show."

"Show?" I mumbled.

"It's all a show," Tommy whispered and turned to serve the new customers coming from upstairs.

I patted Ivan on the shoulder and got up to make room for the other men waiting for drinks at the bar. I knocked back my Scotch and walked away to explore the basement that was more cave-like than the quiet lounge I'd understood from Samuel's brief description. Tucked into its dim-lit corners were wooden benches and metal stools. In one small alcove, a rubber swing hung by chain links from the ceiling. I turned a corner and tripped into a passageway. A thick layer of fresh sawdust broke my fall and masked the smells of urine and semen that lingered in the air. I stood up and brushed myself off. I followed the narrow passage until I walked into a pitch-black wall. I took out my Zippo and flicked it to light my way lest I trip and fall again.

A hand reached out from the darkness and grabbed me by the nape of my neck. "You do that again, I'll rip your heart out and piss on it, you jackass."

It might have been the side effects of the Russian's pot, but I went into a panic. As I hurried away from the sinister grip, I risked flicking my Zippo again to get my bearings and ran toward the light of the downstairs bar. Before I made it out of the dim passageway, two hands grabbed me by my shoulders.

"Chris, where're you going?" I couldn't see the speaker's face, but his voice was somehow familiar.

Still in panic mode, my mind raced. *Who down here would know my name—fuck, not Xavier?* I reached into my pocket for my Zippo to light the face that spoke to me. But not wanting my heart ripped out and pissed on by a man I didn't know, I hesitated to strike it.

Then a kiss—warm and gentle—worked its way up from my neck to my ear. "It's me, Samuel," the voice whispered and pressed me against the rough-hewn wall. He held me in his embrace as we melded together in the sawdust on the sandstone floor.

CHRISTMAS CRISIS

On a mid-December Friday night, the wind whistled down Kessina Boulevard as I walked to the Roosevelt Station. Having taught two classes at Queens College that day, I was exhausted, but the end of the fall semester merited a night out in Manhattan. Besides, I hadn't been to a bar since that night at the Anvil back in November.

A light snow flurried down the subway steps, melting to a glisten on the treads leading to the Seven train's platform. I got out at Times Square station and strolled over to Broadway to check out the Christmas windows at Macy's. The crowd of onlookers blocked my view from the newest displays of boys riding in tandem on sleighs and reindeer leaping over skyscrapers—their hooves nearly touching towering roofs that mirrored the New York skyline. Rudolf led the sleigh above The Twin Towers—Santa's last drop-off point before he crossed the river to deliver gifts to the good boys and girls on the mainland.

I put aside my frustration at not being able to see more of the windows and stepped from the sidewalk into the street. Better to give the opportunity to children, so they could see what America was made of at Christmastime—materialism with a tinge of religious irreverence.

When I hit Thirty-Third Street, I made a right toward Seventh Avenue. In the middle of the block sat O'Sullivan's, a dive Irish Pub I'd visited the previous Christmas season. It still had a smoking section and was the only place not packed with tourists that time of year. Besides those two perks, O'Sullivan's oyster stew was the cheapest and the best tasting in the city.

A year later, the memory of the creamy concoction's pleasure made my mouth water in anticipation. When the waiter came to my table, he gave me a puzzled look. "You waiting for somebody else?"

"No, I'm alone."

He clucked his tongue. "Pity," he said as he took my order.

I nodded when he turned and walked away. Yeah, a pity that Rob and I couldn't last through the holidays, but as autumn froze into winter I didn't miss him, nor did I miss anyone else's company. After six months of waiting around for a man who only showed up when he felt like it, I enjoyed my solitude.

The stew arrived, and I devoured it along with a glass of sauternes. I scraped the last bits of creamy brine from the bottom of my bowl and called the waiter over for the check.

"Something else?" His crisp-blue eyes and blond hair made me long for dessert.

"No," I said, belying my inner thoughts.

"Very well, then." He turned to walk away.

"Wait a minute," I called. *What are you doing later?* my heart said, but my lips parted with the words, "An amaretto, straight up."

"Right away," the waiter said.

I bit my tongue with my foolish shyness. I should have asked him—I should have given up my stupid pride. What did I have to lose? The worst that could happen would be he'd tell me to go fuck off if he were straight. I lit a cigarette and waited for my drink.

"Anything else?" he asked when he delivered the amaretto to my table.

I shook my head, and he handed me the check. I slipped two twenties into the fold and held it in the air, but before he took it from me, I asked, "What's your name?"

"Joe."

"Chris." I shook his hand and let my brown eyes melt into his blue. "I'll be down on piano row later, if you're off."

Joe gazed around the nearly empty restaurant. "By the looks of it, we'll close by eleven. Where you gonna be?"

"I usually hang out at Marie's Crisis, provided it's not packed with tourists for the season."

"Might see you there." Joe patted me on the hand when he took the fold. "Any change?"

"No, that's for you."

***

When I left the restaurant, the wind howled from Thirty-Third down to Penn Station. I thought about taking a cab to the Village, but the queue for taxis stretched all the way to Thirty-Fourth Street. I figured by the time I got into the warm, smelly confines of a yellow cab, I could be halfway to my destination. I pulled the collar of my bomber jacket over my chin and braved the icy, winter chill.

In Chelsea, I stopped to study the mannequins in Barney's windows along Seventh Avenue—all male, dressed in festive reds and greens, their crotches pumped up, as if the winter weather had no effect on the size of their external genitalia. I crossed over Fourteenth Street and walked nine more blocks to Grove Street. The line I expected to find at Marie's was nil, but Rose's Turn was packed to the gills. With Momma Blake playing there that night, the crowd was clamoring to get inside.

I popped open the door of Marie's and went down the short, narrow stairs. Their balustrades were hung with silver and gold snowflakes that carried down the rails and back up again across the low ceiling in regular patterns. *Albert, the manager's work,* I thought—*it always takes a sissy to make something pretty.*

The piano player sat at the upright, arranging his songbooks for the night, as the sparse crowd milled about. Albert stood in front of a mirror in the small back coatroom adding the final touches to his makeup.

As I hung my jacket on a corner hook, John, the Quebecois bartender called to me, *"Salut, Chris, ça va?"*

"Bien, mon p'tit chou," I said.

"Cutty avec soda ce soir?" John asked.

"Oui," I hollered back. That summer I'd spent at the University of Laval perfecting my French came in handy if I ever needed a quick drink from any stray francophone I might meet.

At the bar, John kissed me on both cheeks and pushed my Scotch to me. "So how you been, *putain*?"

"Anything but," I laughed. "There ain't no whoring for a woman left lonely."

"I heard about that Rob you were seeing."

"What?" I shrieked loud enough to force Albert to turn away from his makeup mirror. "How'd you know about that mistake?"

"This is a small big town," John said, "and news travels fast from the Hamptons to Manhattan."

I threw my head back and clucked my tongue. *"P'tit monde."*

John nodded. *"Vraiment, mon ami.* I heard most of the story from that *putain,* Xavier."

"That fuck," I said. "Last time I saw him, he was getting a two-feet chain shoved up his ass at the Anvil."

"And Rob's not any better. He's got a reputation as a playboy, you know, but more than likely you didn't know *that* when you met him. *Dommage.* You had to find it out the hard way."

I looked down at the floor. "I let him fuck me over—"

"*C'etait pas ta faute.* You didn't know...but next time..."

I took the bartender's hand in mine and kissed his palm. "*Merci, mon cher.*"

***

Thirty years my elder, John L'Eauclaire was my gay Dutch-uncle. Right after I came out, Marie's Crisis was the first gay bar I visited in Manhattan. That night, John poured my drinks for free, as he explained the history of the mirror running the length of the wall behind him. With the words, *Liberté, Egalité, Fraternité* etched into its copper and silver finish, covered in protective Plexiglas, the mirror was said to be a gift from Lafayette himself to the original 1820s owners of the house on Grove Street.

After a long night of drinking, and an even longer history lesson from John, my head pounded the next morning. I swore I'd never go back to Marie's again, but the following Friday, I sat across from John drinking—only difference was, I went home with an empty wallet on that second visit.

***

The piano player's trill over the keyboard forced my memories of John to trickle away, as Albert let out a shrill vibrato, "La, la, la…" to get the early crowd's attention.

I moved from the bar and took a seat next to the piano.

"Well, boys, what'll it be to start the night?" the music maker asked.

Men on stools around him mumbled titles of different shows they may have done in high school—where they played a tree or a silent soldier, but never sang a note. While they searched for a title, I shouted, "Something from the *Fantasticks*."

The short, squat piano player smiled at me and pounded out the first major C chord of "I Can See It."

I didn't dare sing Matt's tenor part, I left that to a blond *ingénu* next to me. But when the time came, I belted out El Gallo's warnings of deception and big city despair. By the middle of the song, I was in a duet with the young blond at my side, but I got lost as the tempo picked up, and the piano player had to jump in to help my weak vocals through to the harmonic end. With all our flaws, the boy and I got a round of applause for attempting a difficult song to start the night.

When the couple next to me asked for a tune from *Bye Bye Birdie*, I got up and walked over to John.

"*Je pars,*" I said.

John scrunched his brow. "You're leaving so soon?"

"I need a smoke and some air, beside I hate this show."

He leaned over the bar and kissed me on both cheeks. "*A bientôt, mon ami.*"

"By the way," I said, "if a cute blue-eyed guy named Joe comes in asking for me, tell him I'm next door at Rose's."

"Joe?" John shouted over the rising chords of "Normal American Boy."

I nodded to him and waved to Albert through the silver and gold snowflakes on the stairs.

***

I lit a cigarette in front of Rose's Turn and got in the line that had shortened somewhat over the past hour. Either people had given up waiting in the cold or they were inside pressed shoulder to shoulder against the walls.

Nonetheless, Momma Blake was worth the wait. Rumor had it she was a great-niece of Eubie Blake, something she refused to confirm or deny. Her talent was certainly akin to the great Eubie's—what other singer would ever attempt to craft a blues rendition of Blondie's "Rapture"?

As I waited, the December wind found its way under my jacket, and I pulled it tighter around my waist. A young, uptown, straight couple in front of me gave up their spot and headed back to Seventh Avenue. I took two steps forward and waited for the doorman to check the IDs of five people ahead of me.

From behind, an arm wrapped around my shoulder. I turned and met face-to-face with two crisp, blue eyes.

Joe grimaced. "Ain't you cold?"

I feigned a deeper shiver than I really felt just to have him pull me closer into his embrace.

"What the fuck you out here for?" he said as he wrapped his other arm around me.

I pulled myself from his grip. "It's Momma Blake playing tonight—"

"Oh, fuck that," Joe said. "Come on down to Marie's…at least there's heat and plenty of room there."

I hesitated to give in to a man whose last name I didn't even know, but I nodded and followed him into Marie's where Albert held the door for us.

"So, bitch," Albert said when he saw me, "you've decided to come back and join the gay world."

I smirked at his dull wit and handed him a ten to cover the entrance for me and Joe. He pushed the bill back to me. "You were here just a half hour ago. Give the tip to the piano player, or better yet get a drink for yourself and your new beau."

I put my arm around Albert's thick waist and kissed him on his chubby cheek.

He pushed me away. "Now don't go messing up my makeup, bitch. Just go downstairs with your pretty blond and drink lots of drinks."

Joe flinched when Albert pinched his ass as he walked past. I grabbed Joe's hand, and we went over to John at the bar.

"Mon cher," John shouted. "Cutty and soda?"

I held my palm up and turned to Joe. "What do you want?" I asked.

"Scotch is fine."

I nodded to John. *"Deux."*

"La meme, deux fois?"

"Oui."

John looked over my shoulder, spotted Joe, and winked. When he reached for the bottle of Cutty sitting under the word *Fraternité,* he gave me a stealthy thumbs-up. *"Tu as de chance avec lui,"* John said as he pushed the drinks across the bar.

"Maybe," I whispered in John's ear and handed him the ten Albert had refused at the door. I passed the Cutty and soda to Joe. "John's a friend from way back."

Joe nodded. "I can tell. You two always speak French?"

I smiled. "It's our little game. It keeps the tourists guessing if John and I are really lovers…it's all a show."

"A show?" Joe put his lips to his glass and took a long sip. "Like you inviting me here tonight?"

I grasped his free hand and squeezed it in mine with the gentlest of grips. "No, there was nothing fake about asking you to join me here."

The chorus around the piano was singing a tune about a trip somewhere over the rainbow when I took Joe into my arms. I held him close and pressed my lips against his. Next thing I knew, his tongue was in my mouth and we were grinding against each other.

John slapped his hand on the bar, and Albert sang in my ear, "Break it up, young lovers, before you go too far, and I have to throw you both out of my bar."

Joe and I pushed away from one another and laughed at the musical interruption.

"These friends of yours are too much," he said.

I stared down at the floor and took another gulp of my drink. "Friends," I slurred from the effects of exhaustion, alcohol, and walking in the cold night air. "I really don't have any."

"I've lost most of mine," Joe mumbled.

"What?"

Joe shook his head. "Never mind."

We went over to the piano where I put a dollar in the tip cup along with a request for "Ol' Man River." When the piano player finally got to my song, I made a feeble attempt at Paul Robeson's version of the *Showboat* tune, but in my less than sober condition, my voice cracked like eggs falling to the floor.

Joe looked me up and down. "Are you drunk, Chris?"

I nodded, then shook my head. "More tired than drunk," I said. "The holidays…the cold…it all wears me down."

"Let's get out of here. I don't think you need anything more to drink. You want a coffee?"

I agreed and bid *adieu* to John and Albert. Joe held my hand through the silver and gold snowflakes on the stairs, out the door, and into the cold wind blowing across Grove Street.

We passed Rose's Turn and ducked into the New Moon Café—the favorite coffee shop of every gay man who'd drunk too much on a night out in the West Village. We grabbed two stools at the bar where Michael was both waiter and barista.

"Chris—Joe," he said. "What are you two doing here... together?"

I looked at Joe.

"We're not here like that...well, together...yes," Joe said, "but not like *together...*"

I scrunched my brow. "Well, maybe later," I blurted out.

Joe frowned and ordered two cappuccinos.

Michael nodded and went to the espresso machine to brew the early morning coffees.

I wobbled on my stool.

"Chris, my place is just over on Tenth. We can go there and—"

"And what?" I ran my hand down Joe's chest.

He stopped me before I could reach his waist. "And you can sober up on my—"

"Café, Signori!" Michael put two frothy cups in front of us interrupting Joe's thought.

I straightened my back and took a sip of the steamy drink, hoping its warm caffeine would sober me. I locked eyes with Joe's and ran my hand over the light stubble on his cheek. "Listen," I said. "I'm still on the rebound... I'm sure you don't want to hear about any of that, but my heart's still broken."

"Still broken?" Joe's mellow tone turned angry. "Whose heart's not been broken in this fucked-up world we're living in? My lover, Tim, died a year ago from the 'gay plague' that's going around. How do you think I feel? Not a single friend that Tim and I had wants anything to do with me—they're afraid they might catch it too. And who knows, they may be right. I might be the next to die from a disease that doesn't even have a name."

I wrapped my arms around Joe and pulled him close to my chest. "I know...I understand...I just broke up with my boyfriend after six months, so—"

Joe pushed me away. "Oh, bullshit," he shouted. "Don't even try to compare a six-month boyfriend with the five years I spent with my Tim. We were happy…now everything I had is gone."

I looked away, searching for words that would ease the bitterness raging in Joe's eyes.

He took one last sip of his coffee and got up.

"Don't go," I pleaded.

Joe shook his head. "No, it's time I leave. This ain't gonna work." He hurried out the door of the cafe. I followed after him, but the flurries from earlier that evening returned as a steady snowfall and blocked my view of Joe's direction.

Downy white muffled my footfalls along Grove Street. I stopped in the middle of the block and considered walking over to Tenth to search for Joe and at least give him my number. But instead, I turned back toward Seventh Avenue. On the corner of Sixth, I hailed a cab to Times Square station and caught the Seven train back to Queens. The snow along Kessina Boulevard covered my shoes as I walked home to my apartment building.

I curled up in my bed, and Joe's blue eyes filtered into my mind as I drifted off to sleep. In a half-dream, we rode a sleigh down a slope in Central Park. Joe's arms wrapped around my waist as I glided us to a stop on a flat, smooth stretch of packed snow.

"Thanks for the short ride," he said. "Too bad your sleigh won't fly."

NEW YEAR PROMISES

I WATCHED 1983 SLIP away on the TV screen with a bottle of Korbel Extra Dry at my side. Once the ball dropped over Times Square, I downed one last glass of champagne and clicked off the set. I stared out the window toward Kessina Boulevard, where revelers shouted and firecrackers burst under the pink and blue neon signs along the street. I lit a joint and took two long hits before I clipped the roach and let myself drift into a reverie of what 1984 might bring.

That Orwellian-numbered year was something I'd thought about since high school. Would Big Brother be watching over my shoulder as Reagan set fire to the Evil Empire? Could we survive another term of his senile rambling State of the Union addresses? Would the CDC deal with the epidemic sweeping the nation?

I lifted the champagne bottle to my lips and sucked the last drops of its dregs. A new year in which I'd turn twenty-five. Another year alone. I thought of Joe, and how his eyes filled with rage at the memory of his dead lover and the government's lack of concern. And how his anger kept us apart that night we'd spent in the Village. Did I blow my chances with another man because of my naivety?

I pulled the shades down in the bedroom and cuddled under my down comforter. Tomorrow would dawn a new day—a new year, where I could look Janus-faced and move in a different direction.

***

My first week back at Queens College started with a freshman class crammed with the usual shining faces—boys and girls just a few years younger than me. All eager to learn the difference between a period and a semi-colon. All longing to be the next Fitzgerald or Hemingway. I gave them my standard first assignment's writing cue: *My winter break was full of____*. Inevitably, a class clown in the back of the lecture hall called out, "Shit." And I had to give the obligatory eye-roll and cluck my tongue. "So, three hundred words," I said, feigning my re-composure. "That's one full page, double-spaced, written on a standard Remington or Royal typewriter."

In the back of the room, a handsome, dark-haired boy's hand shot up.

"Yes," I called on him from the lectern.

"What if it's more than three hundred?"

"More than the word limit and you will lose points, so be precise—tightness matters."

"Like those pants you're wearing," I heard a snide, blond jock whisper from the far end of the first row.

"What was that, sir?" I stared him down.

The boy, not more than nineteen, turned red with surprise at my keen hearing. I cleared my throat and continued explaining the assignment. "It's due by Monday, so go home and get to work. Try to surprise me, and you just may end up on the cover of the *Sunday Times*."

As fifty feet shuffled out of the lecture hall, I sat at the small desk next to the lectern and marked my plan book with what was ahead. Nothing more than reading some poorly written assignments and struggling to discover one or two that deserved to be copied and distributed among the class—essays that had either major flaws, or a rare gem to be polished for possible publication.

How many of those gems had I written myself when I was a teenager? All of them with inclusions, but none of them rare enough to be acquired by an agent or major magazine.

I threw my pencil down on my plan book and reflected on the three hundred words I would write about my winter break. A night wasted in the Village, a blue-eyed man who turned on me, a drunken spree on Kessina Boulevard where I drank sake and ate so much kimchee I puked for two days.

I stuffed my plan book into my leather satchel, headed to the lecture hall's doors, flicked out the fluorescent lights, and walked across campus to Jamaica Avenue. I took the Seven train up to Roosevelt and went back to my empty apartment on the corner of Beech and Bowne.

***

When I met my Monday freshman class the following week, I collected the papers on the cue I'd assigned. Each was clipped and double-spaced following the format I'd outlined on our first class meeting. After I had all twenty-five in my hands, I read the hook lines in their first paragraphs. I didn't read the names, just their first sentences.

"'It was a cold and snowy break, filled with icy wind,'" I read and looked out on the sea of shining juveniles. "Reactions?"

"Trite."

"It's been done before," another voice called.

"Ditto, trite," I said.

"Jane Austen–like," a girl from the back yelled.

"Nineteenth century indeed," I said.

I flipped through five more papers and began to read one that caught my attention.

"'I thought the night I met Rob would be full of love. I was in the Village at a club called the Eagle's Nest. It's a dark and mysterious place, where the men all dress the same, like they just walked off a stock movie set in Hollywood. Rob stood out in the crowd, his steel-gray eyes, light-brown hair, and…'" I stopped and held my breath. "Who wrote this?" I mumbled.

I looked around the lecture hall, pulled myself together, and called, "Reactions?"

"Brilliant."

"Uniquely original."

"Redundant phrasing," I said, "but true."

The dark-haired boy who'd asked about writing more than three hundred words sat in the back of the hall—his eyes downcast, his chin in his hands. "And you, sir?" I said pointing to him.

He picked his head up.

"What do you have to say?" I asked.

"A nearly true story," he called across the hall.

"Ladies and gentlemen, I give you case in point. A story from the heart is the essence of good writing."

A murmur went through the class.

"Today we adjourn with this. Next time we meet, I want you to read pages 119-230 of the Chicago Manual and be ready to apply it to an in-class practical. I will also have your papers back by next Monday. Good day, be good, and…smoke 'em if you got 'em." My last line got its usual laugh as my students emptied the hall.

When I came home that late afternoon, I pulled out the dark-haired boy's paper, whose name my class records indicated was Gonzalez, and put it on the top of my pile for review. Could it really be the same Rob of my six-month affair?

I re-read the lines I spoke in class earlier that day.

I thought the night I met Rob would be full of love. I was in the Village at a club called the Eagle's Nest. It's a dark and mysterious place, where the men all dress the same, like they just walked off a stock movie set in Hollywood. Rob stood out in the crowd, his steel-gray eyes, light-brown hair, and tight blue jeans certainly were an eye-catcher.

I tried to ignore the fact that he was the hottest thing in a bar filled with men who looked like they belonged on the cover of American Bear Magazine*.*

I walked away from the steel-eyed man. My heart still pounding when I went to order a Bud—hoping the bartender wouldn't ask for my ID again that had the five of 1965 altered to a two so I could get into the Eagle at eighteen. The hairy-armed barkeep didn't ask for my license and handed me a tepid Bud. I chugged it back and walked the perimeter of the square bar where men twice my age ogled me.

I ordered another beer and settled into a corner, when a hand crept down my pants and grabbed my rear. I whirled around, ready to smack whomever it was, but when I looked into the feeler's steely eyes, I melted straight away. Nonetheless, I raised my hand in a threat. He gave me a guttural laugh and grabbed my arm.

"You new to this place?" he asked.

I stared him down through the dim light. "Not really," I lied.

He laughed a deep, chesty laugh again. "Well, then, you should be used to getting felt up."

Not wanting to seem the outsider, I nodded, and gave him my name, "Georgy."

"Rob," the steel-eyed man said and pressed his lips to mine. "You want another Bud?" he asked when our lips parted.

"Sure," I said.

Rob called to the bartender, and the beer was next to me in a second. Next thing I knew, he forced me to chug another. After he pressed me to down a third, he told me to follow him into the toilet to take a piss. I suppose it was the alcohol that made me do what I did, but when I left the Eagle, my throat was burning from the effects of uric acid, and my clothes stank of stale urine.

On the subway ride home, I sat alone on a corner seat until my stop in the Bronx. I ran back to my apartment on Conduit Avenue, ripped off my shirt and blue jeans, and tossed them down the garbage chute.

A winter break full of piss was something I'd rather forget about.

My stomach retched when I read the last lines. That son of a bitch Rob. How could he do that to a boy nearly half his age? The amoral bastard.

I considered the comments I would make on Gonzalez's paper. He was over the limit by nearly one hundred words, but the realism of the story was worth the extra reading. Should I put a "see me," note on his paper? Should I pull the kid aside and tell him not to degrade himself again with anyone like Rob? No, I would leave the personal out of my critique and grade him as I would any other student.

He'd lose ten points for going over the word count and a point for every grammatical error—of which there were few that I noticed. Of course, my blind eye to the paper helped the total score. I would also take off another five points for the repetition of the trite use of "steel eyes"—although I knew it was an accurate description. How could I fail a student who'd been brave enough to put a bad experience into an essay and hand it to an English instructor he didn't know? In green ink, I gave the assignment a score of eighty.

I pushed aside Gonzalez's paper and went on to read a girl's account of a ski trip in the Adirondacks. Her father had paid for a stay at an exclusive lodge, and the snow was perfect—"so full of cold-white fun…"

I read to the middle of the page, gave her a green grade of ninety, and went to bed.

***

By week's end, I'd finished my Queens College tasks. All the assignments read, all the grades noted in my ledger, and the following week's classes planned out, so I decided to reward myself with a night out in Manhattan. I tugged on my 501 button-fly jeans and tucked the cuffs into my leather work boots. I pulled a sweatshirt over my white cotton T-shirt and grabbed my bomber jacket out of the narrow hallway closet.

As I rode the train into the city, I thought about Rob and mulled over various ways I'd exact revenge on him for what he'd done to me and how he'd used Gonzalez. Maybe a penknife into his back, or perhaps I could lure him to the docks along the Hudson. I would push him into the cold, swift-moving current, and he'd end up decomposing on a beach in the Bronx.

As the train made its last stop at the Hudson River Railroad Yards, I set aside my murderous thoughts and climbed the stairs up to Thirty-Fourth Street. From there, I walked along the river's edge to the Eagle's Nest. At ten o'clock, a long line of men waited to get inside—all looking to cop a feel someplace in a dark corner of the club, or maybe get pissed on in the backroom's oversized, porcelain bathtub.

The doorman waved me in. My good looks and city garb must have been to his liking. When I stepped inside, the place smelt of sweat, stale urine, and burnt hemp, mingled with a hint of patchouli air freshener. I bellied up to the dull-black bar and ordered a Scotch and soda. I wanted to be halfway sober if I were to run into Rob at his usual Friday night hunting grounds.

Although I'd visited the Eagle many times, I still found it the strangest bar in Manhattan. It had a DJ but no dancing was allowed. In a black booth on the back wall he spun tunes that never got any airplay, as men, all dressed in obligatory leather, walked in circles. Reminiscent of a scene from *Midnight Express*, they'd stare at each other with lustful eyes. One would stop to grope the other and move on to the next.

I made the rounds. Not seeing Rob, I parked myself at the bar. The keeper came over to me. "Another?" he asked.

"Cutty, but make it straight with a lemon twist," I said over the DJ's throbbing mix. I grabbed my drink and put a five on the bar. I got up to take another stroll around the busy club. And there he was, Rob, with his hands inside the pants of the man who'd served me dinner just a few weeks before Christmas. I took a slug of my drink and walked up behind the two of them.

"Copping a good feel?" I said over Rob's shoulder. "Or is he trying to mend your broken heart?" I snarled into Joe's ear.

They whirled around and glared at me. Joe stepped back from Rob and buttoned up his fly.

Rob adjusted himself in his jeans. "What're you doing here?"

"Not the same as the two of you." I locked eyes with Joe. "So, this is how you ease your pain of lost love and mourning?"

He diverted his gaze from me to Rob.

Rob let out that throaty laugh of his. "Always the intellectual. Can't you just suck a dick and forget about it?"

"Can't you ever think past your crotch?" The three of us made a triangle with me at its apex. I felt for the penknife in my pocket. If I were to do what I had thought about, I would surely be the loser—my three-inch blade wouldn't even make it through the outer lining of Rob's bomber jacket.

Rob shoved his face closer into mine. "Get lost, you little fuck. Why don't you go back to your Queens' apartment and read a book?"

My frustration at overload, I splashed my drink—Scotch, ice, and lemon twist—into Rob's gunmetal-gray eyes.

His face dripping, he lunged at me, but Joe held him back.

"Just go away," Joe said. "Just get out of our space."

"Fuck you," I shouted, "fuck the both of you." I stormed away and strode up to the bar. "Cutty, double, straight up," I hollered to the nearest bartender.

I grabbed the glass, hid it under my jacket, and hurried out the door. On the street, I lit a joint and smoked it until the roach burned my fingertips. I leaned against the Eagle's cold, brick outside wall and sipped my drink to cool my throat. The THC and alcohol eased my shivering from the rage boiling inside me.

With my head buzzing, I knocked back the dregs of my Scotch, smashed the glass on the pavement, and walked south along Hudson River Drive in the direction of the Anvil.

"Chris?" a voice called from somewhere under the El. Through the sulfurous light, I thought I recognized the man who'd made love to me two months ago in sawdust chips on a sandstone floor.

"Chris," he shouted again.

I focused on his face, not sure it was really him—his crow's feet made him look a little older—but when he kissed me, I recalled Samuel's gentle lips.

"Where're you going?" he asked.

"The Anvil," I slurred. "I'm looking for something… somebody."

"Like who?" Samuel gave me a puzzled stare. "You lose something?"

I shook my head.

"Look, I just got done with my six-to-eleven shift at the bar. I'm going to the Eagle. Come along."

"I was just there," I mumbled.

Samuel took me by the hand. "C'mon, we'll have a drink."

I followed him, not knowing if I could stand up much longer after too much Scotch and a whole joint.

Inside, Samuel ordered a beer and asked me what I wanted. "Coke with ice," I said and reached for my wallet. It dropped from my hand, but Samuel caught it in midair. I fumbled trying to get my money out and dropped it again. Samuel picked it up off the floor.

"You know what?" he said. "Let me hold on to this. You're in no condition…" He grabbed the drinks through the crowd that had built up at the bar. "You okay?"

I shook my head. "No, I'm not. My ex is here…up to his old tricks. He's like Big Brother…always watching." I gulped my Coke, hoping it would dilute the alcohol running through my brain. "It's like he knows…knows the men I've been with."

Samuel put his arm around my shoulder. "Chris, you know you're not making any sense?"

I nodded. "Maybe not, but…"

"C'mon, let me get you out of here."

Samuel grabbed my elbow. We walked to the street and got into the first yellow cab cruising down Hudson River Drive. I turned to him in the back seat and grinned. "Where're we going?"

"Back to Queens," he said. "To the address on your license—210 Beech Street. Is that right?"

I nodded and passed out.

My eyes slit open when the cab stopped on the corner in front of my apartment building. Samuel helped me out of the backseat. "You're home," he whispered. In the hallway, he put his hand in my pocket and fished out the deadbolt's key.

***

Saturday morning, the sun shone through my bedroom window. I must have forgotten to pull down the shades. I rolled over. A warm man snuggled next to me. I sat up with a start. "What the fuck!"

Samuel laughed. "How's your head?"

I put my hands to my temples and groaned.

"That good, eh?" he said.

"How did you…we…?"

"Taxi."

"What! How much did *that* cost?"

"Twenty-five dollars," Samuel said. "It was either that, or risk losing you in the gap on the subway platform, and that wouldn't have been fun. How'd you get so fucked up anyway?"

"Too much pot. Oh God…did we…?"

Samuel grinned. "Not with the condition you were in. Now lie down, and I'll get you a cold cloth for your head."

When he got out of bed, the tighty whities he wore accentuated his firm butt and V-shaped torso. He went into the bathroom, and I heard water running. Samuel came out with a wet washcloth in his hand. "You got ice?"

"Why, you thinking of making a drink?"

Samuel clucked his tongue. "No, stupid—for your head."

I pressed the wet cloth to my forehead and mustered a chuckle. "I know…in the freezer. I'm sure you'll find it with the size of this place."

"Your apartment's a palace compared to mine in Manhattan."

He came back into the bedroom with three ice cubes in his hand, took the cloth from my head, and wrapped them inside. "Better?" he asked.

I nodded and scrunched my brow. "Why are you doing this for me?"

Samuel ran his hand over my bare chest. "Because I like you… because I saw something in you that first night at my bar in the Anvil. Not only a pretty face, but you're not a jerk." He lay down next to me and pressed his lips to mine. The three ice cubes tumbled out of the washcloth and melted between us.

***

The late January sun had nearly set that Saturday when Samuel stepped out of the shower and dressed. "I got the six-to-eleven shift again tonight," he said as he walked out of the bedroom into the sitting area.

"Oh." I looked out the window toward the lights flickering to life over Kessina Boulevard.

Samuel grabbed my chin to force me to look at him. "But I'm off tomorrow."

"Really?"

"You know, Chris, 'really' is not what you're supposed to say. How about, 'would you like to get together?' or something like that? Well, I really would, so here's my number." He handed me a slip of paper.

I stood up and put my arms around him. "I'm sorry I'm such a dope. It's just that…I never thought a man like you would—"

"Would fall in love with you at first sight? Well, I did. Sometimes good shit happens when you least expect it." Samuel kissed me hard. "So what do you say we get together for dinner tomorrow night?"

"Dinner would be nice."

"Finally a correct answer." Samuel smiled. "Just come into Manhattan and ring the bell on the box next to the entrance at Ty's—apartment three is mine."

"What time?"

"Five okay?"

"Five it is, then." I threw my arms around Samuel's neck and kissed him. When he went out the door, I ran to the window and watched him fade away in the dim streetlight on the corner of Beech and Bowne.

VALENTINE VOWS

SUNDAY AFTERNOON, I took the subway into Times Square station and switched to a downtown train. As I climbed the stairs up to Christopher Street, my heart pounded. Would Samuel keep his promise? Would he answer the bell when I rang apartment number three?

A cold wind blew in my face, but I plodded down the block looking forward to a new adventure. My relationship with Rob was the first I'd ever had, if I were not to count locker room encounters with high school seniors when I was just a freshman. They'd let me suck them off after gym class and go back to tell the older boys that they'd found a queer slut in the school's basement. If I refused to do as they asked when they came downstairs, I'd end up with welts I couldn't explain away.

I suppose that's why I buried myself in books. I read *Catcher in the Rye* five times trying to figure out if Holden Caulfield were a latent homosexual—much to my chagrin, he turned out straight. And then there was Hemingway—why did he shoot himself? In my opinion, *The Big Two-Hearted River* revealed his sexual ambiguity through the use of Jungian archetypes. When I presented that idea to my eleventh grade English teacher, he scoffed at me. "Ernest Hemingway was a big game hunter—a man's man—and *you* think he was a homosexual?" The class laughed at me, and I was put to shame for the rest of that school year.

But in senior year when we read *In Cold Blood,* I wagered that Capote was homosexual. My teacher, Mr. Field, had a tendency to agree. "A man with Capote's turn of phrase," he said, "must see the world from a different angle." And there were many different angles that Mr. Field and I saw together—like the brother's habits in *The Glass Menagerie.* Where did Tom really go on those nights he said he was "at the movies"? All those memories flew through my head as my finger hovered over the buzzer to Samuel's apartment above Ty's.

After I overcame my initial hesitation, I pushed the button labeled "three."

"Chris?" Samuel's smooth voice sounded through the speaker.

"Yeah, it's me."

"I'll be right down," he said.

I folded my arms as I waited in the January chill blowing off the Hudson. Samuel bounced down the stairs like Tigger longing to greet Pooh Bear. I pushed him back when he planted a wet kiss on my mouth.

"Not here," I said, "in the middle of the street…in broad daylight."

Samuel pulled me in closer to his face. "Oh, fuck that!" He slipped his tongue into my mouth, stepped away, and laughed at my blush. "You wanna walk?" he asked.

"Are we going local?"

"Well, I was thinking Auntie Maude's up on Forty-Fourth."

"Are you nuts?" I scowled. "I'm not walking forty blocks in this cold."

"I could keep you warm along the way."

"No, that's okay, I'll pay for a cab."

We walked arm in arm along Christopher to Sixth Avenue and grabbed a taxi uptown. We got out on the corner of Forty-Second Street and hurried past the porno houses leading to the Theater District.

Auntie Maude's was nearly empty at six on Sunday evening. The theater crowd had gone to see their matinees, and the gay clientele was either napping or primping for the evening.

Samuel chose a table next to a small window that looked out on the street.

The waiter, most likely an off-off Broadway actor, brought us our menus. "Drinks, gentlemen?" he asked.

Samuel looked at me. "You drink wine?"

"Sometimes," I said.

"Well, would you share a bottle with me?"

"Yeah, okay."

"Red or white?"

"I think I might like white." I guessed at my preference.

Samuel looked up at the waiter. "A bottle of Mouton Cadet, Maine et Sèvre."

"Very good," the waiter said.

I squinted at Samuel. "Where'd you learn to pronounce French like that?"

"My mom was Belgian. I heard French around the house when I was a kid. I can still understand it, and I can fake it if I have to."

"I have a Master's in French," I mumbled.

"What?"

"I have a degree in French…not that it's done me any good."

"*Really.*"

The waiter brought the bottle of wine to the table, uncorked it, and poured two glasses. Samuel and I toasted to our first dinner together.

"What is it that you do, anyway?" Samuel asked to break the silent pause between us.

"I teach English to wannabe writers at Queens College."

"I'm impressed."

"You'd be *de*pressed if you knew what it's really like. I read bad English all day long and try to right the world with proper grammar."

"Sounds pretty boring, I have to say."

I took another sip of my wine. "And you?" I asked. "What do you do, besides tend bar?"

Samuel looked out the window. "That's what I do—tend bar."

"Can't be," I said. "How is it that you afford that apartment over Ty's? Even that place must cost a fortune in this city."

Samuel swirled the wine in his glass. "My parents were killed by a drunk driver ten years ago. I got a good settlement when I was eighteen. Since then, I've been a free spirit—was even engaged for a while."

I took a gulp of my wine. "To a woman?"

Samuel laughed. "Well, of course. I might as well be up front with you. I'm bi."

My mind raced back to that autumn afternoon with Rob, Linda, and Xavier. Suddenly the soft-leather seats in Auntie Maude's felt as uncomfortable as the hummingbird and flower metal stools on the Swamp's patio.

Samuel reached across the linen tablecloth and grasped my hand. "You okay?"

I shook my head, but when I looked into Samuel's eyes, I nodded. "It's just that…my first boyfriend was bi. At least, he was screwing his girlfriend and me at the same time."

Samuel squeezed my wrist. "Look, just because I can love both sexes doesn't mean I don't want to be monogamous. When I fall in love, it's with one person at a time. I loved the girl I was going to marry, but *she* fell out of love with me."

The waiter came to our table and interrupted Samuel's next thought. "Gentlemen, ready to order?"

I looked at Samuel. "I have no idea."

"Well, the steak is always good here." Samuel closed his menu. "I'll have the New York Strip, rare, with a side of fries."

"Very good," the waiter said.

I looked down at the menu that had turned into a blur. "You know what, let's keep it simple. I'll have the same."

"Coming right up."

We both stared out the window at the traffic and passersby on Forty-Forth Street, until my laughter broke the silence.

Samuel caught my eye. "What's so funny?"

"Well, I'm sure the waiter found that gauche."

"What?"

"Here we are drinking white wine and ordering steak."

"Fuck that. We drink what we like."

I picked up the bottle and filled our glasses.

Samuel took a long sip of wine and squeezed my hand in his. "So, you okay with what I just told you?"

"I'm fine. This is the first time I've enjoyed another man's company in a long time, especially the company of a man who looks like you."

Samuel raised his glass to clink with mine. "Well, that makes two of us."

When our steaks arrived, both perfectly done, we devoured them with voracious appetites. Samuel looked down at his plate and picked up a french fry. "You have to work tomorrow?" He popped the fry into his mouth.

"I have one class, but it doesn't meet till ten."

"In that case, you can come back to my apartment and…"

I lifted my glass to my lips. "You foolish schemer, I thought you'd never ask."

"Hey, chalk one up for Chris! You finally got an answer right."

"I only use my talents on men who appreciate them."

The waiter came back to our table. "Dessert, gentlemen?"

"No," I said. "I have all the sweetness I need in front of me."

***

We grabbed a cab on Seventh Avenue and rode south as January's twilight glinted off the lower Hudson. When we got out on the corner of Christopher, I hesitated. "You want to go to the Monster for a drink?"

Samuel shook his head and grinned. "I have something else in mind."

From the gleam in his eye, I understood his intent. I recalled what he told me at dinner and froze in the middle of the block.

He pulled me closer. "What's the matter?"

"I don't think I can…"

"Why? Don't you trust me?"

Rather than express my true consternation, I shook my head. "No it's not that…It's just that…I've never done anything like this before."

"You've never had dinner with a man and gone home to his apartment for a drink?"

I shook my head again.

Samuel stared directly into my eyes. "Look, Chris, I'm not forcing you. If you want to leave, we can make it another time."

I nodded that it was okay and took his hand in mine.

When we came to the doorbell panel in front of Ty's, Samuel entered a code and pressed the buzzer. I followed him up the narrow stairs to the third floor.

He unlocked the door and flicked on the entranceway light. "It's not much." He pointed to the sofa on the short wall. "Have a seat."

I sat down on the middle burlap cushion of his couch.

Samuel pressed his lips to mine and kissed me firm and hard. When he let go, he grinned his bright-white smile. "What do you want to drink?"

"You got Scotch?"

"Cutty okay?"

"My Scotch of choice…but I think you should remember that."

Samuel went into the corner kitchenette, and I heard the crack of an ice-cube tray. "Lemon?" he called.

"Don't bother," I said, "my lemon days are over."

"Oh, how poetic."

I laughed as he handed me the drink. "There's a story behind lemon in my Scotch."

"Do tell." Samuel set his glass on the small, round coffee table.

I took a swig of my drink. "You don't want to know, but someday I may write about it."

"Well, that'll give me something to look forward to—Chris, and the Story of Lemon in his Scotch: part one…or would it be part two?"

"Shut up!"

"Make me—"

I put down my drink and kissed Samuel's full, red lips, ran my hand through his thick, blond hair, and let my fingers work their way to his crotch.

He pulled me closer to him. "I want you inside me," he whispered. "I've wanted that since the first night we met."

I thought about our first time together in the backroom of the Anvil, and how I let Samuel take the lead—little did I know he would treat me as his equal.

He pulled off his pants as I unbuttoned my jeans. We pressed against each other, throbbing in desire. I licked his chest and he moaned in pleasure until my mouth found its way to his erection. I tasted his sweet saltiness, and he begged for more.

"Not yet," I said.

Samuel got up from the couch and turned out the lights. He held my hand and led me to his tiny sleeping area.

I eased him back onto the bed. With my erection already wet with pre-cum, I gently entered him. He gasped as we thrust together in perfect rhythm. I felt him quiver under me. I released myself, and we collapsed into each other's arms.

Samuel kissed me full on the mouth. "Don't go tonight," he said.

"Only tonight?" I whispered.

"Tonight…tomorrow…never."

I propped myself up on my elbow. "You know, I never believed in love at first sight—"

"Until now." Samuel cut off my thought.

"Until now," I echoed. My lips pressed against Samuel's warm, soft mouth, and we entwined again, until we lay in the sweat of a second orgasm better than the first.

***

The last week of January, I floated in a mist of emotional ecstasy. Samuel would spend his nights off in Queens with me, and when he worked his shift in the Anvil, I would watch TV in his apartment until he came home. From his window, I'd see men my age holding hands or arguing on the street and fill in their dialogue with words I couldn't hear. From time to time, I thought I saw Rob, Xavier, or Joe—all passing through the sulfurous light like phantoms that I let go once Samuel came into my life.

The second to last day of January, Samuel was off. I had no classes to teach the next day, so we went to 88 at the foot of the Manhattan Bridge for dim sum. The weeknight crowd was sparse, since winter had descended on the city, and we enjoyed half-priced sake and more small plates than we could count.

Samuel downed another shot of fortified rice wine. "I was thinking," he said.

"Uh-oh, this sounds like dangerous territory—you thinking."

"Oh, shut up."

"No, you shut up." I gave Samuel the sly smile that always followed our playful banter. "What?"

"My lease is up in two days."

"And?"

"And…are we in love?"

I downed my sake and locked eyes with Samuel's stare. I stretched my arm across the wooden table and took his hand in mine. "Well, if I told you that you make me dizzy when we have sex, does that count?"

Samuel nodded. "And if I told you that when I'm away from you my stomach is in knots until I see you again, does that count?"

I put my finger to my temple. "Let me see. Dizzying sex, plus knotting stomach, equals…I don't know?"

Samuel shook his head. "Oh, shut up."

"No, you shut up."

We laughed at our exchange.

"So when are you going to move in with me?" I asked.

"Wednesday?"

"That's in two days! You think you'll be able to pack by then?"

"Chris, what do you think I got in that tiny place—some underwear, T-shirts, jeans—"

"Dildos," I interrupted.

"Oh, shut up."

"No, you shut up."

"Make me," I said to end our little game.

I flagged down the waiter, and he pushed a fresh cart of dim sum plates over to our table. Samuel and I each took two different dumpling dishes and ordered another round of sake.

We clinked our shot glasses. "Welcome to life in Queens and the Seven train into Manhattan."

"L'Chaim," Samuel said.

"Salut," I replied.

***

It was a snowy Sunday two weeks after Valentine's Day. I was enjoying a coffee and the morning paper, when the photo of a handsome, sandy-haired, mustachioed man in the *Daily News* caught my eye. He stood next to a mousey blonde. The caption read:

> *The parents of Ms. Linda Messina and the parents of Mr. Robert (Robby) Faust are proud to announce the nuptial of their children. Wedding set for June 17, 1984.*

"Hey, Samuel," I called into the bedroom of our apartment, "get a load of this."

Samuel came into the sitting area in his tighty whities. "What?"

I showed him the grainy, black-and-white photo in the paper.

He scratched his head as he squinted at the page. "And?"

"And this is…" I stared at Samuel's broad shoulders and V-shaped waist. I took the newspaper from his hands and tossed in on the floor. "It doesn't matter," I said and pulled him into my embrace.

ABOUT PAUL IASEVOLI

Paul is a transplanted New Yorker who now lives on the Manatee River on the West Coast of Florida where he enjoys sunrises and sunsets over the Gulf of Mexico. He holds a Master's degree in Latin-American Literature. Writing has always been his passion. This work is dedicated to his late husband of thirty-four years—William J. Montagne.

SOCIAL MEDIA

Website: www.pauliasevoliwords.com

Facebook: www.facebook.com/paul.iasevoli

BY PAUL IASEVOLI

"A Night at Madame Beauseau's." Florida Writers Association Collection, vol. 9. *What a Character.* 2017. https://floridawriters.net/shop/9-what-a-character

"Forced into Freedom." Deep South Magazine. January, 2018. Winner Honorable Mention: *Race in Place.* http://deepsouthmag.com/2018/01/29/forced-into-freedom/

Coming October 2018. "The Manatee Sings." Florida Writers Association Collection, vol. 10. *Where is Your Muse.* 2018.

YEAR OF THE GUILTY SOUL

A.M. LEIBOWITZ

Antonia Moskowitz is caught in the middle, always having to pick a side. Whether it's between her family's two religions or in her relationships, she has choices to make. But learning who she is has a price, and every decision has consequences. Sometimes it's hard to choose between being good and being right. Four seasons. Four kisses. One year to figure out what her heart wants.

***

Genre: young adult LGBT fiction

Keywords: bisexual, genderqueer, literary YA, romantic elements, religious (Christianity & Judaism)

JANUARY

IT'S THE FIRST Sunday of the new year. I slouch into the upstairs room where all the teens meet for Sunday school. For over a year, I've been coming to church because of this girl I know from school. Gwen is nothing if not enthusiastic about her evangelism. I'm not the New Girl anymore—every few months, Gwen brings a recruit to the youth group. We get to be her best friend until the next person comes along. Most of us stay, always hopeful Gwen might turn her attention back to us even though she never does.

She's had a string of boys like this too. Gwen has a policy not to date boys who aren't Christians, so a lot of the ones who like her follow her to church. It always surprises me when they stay after Gwen uses her "not ready for a relationship" line on them. I'm sure some of them genuinely became Christians. The rest? Who knows. Maybe a few of them think they still have a chance.

Over the summer, she replaced the previous kid with a quiet girl named Cari: pronounced *Cah*-ree not *Care*-ee. Since Gwen's already moved on to the boyfriend of the month, Cari is left to the rest of us. Like me, she doesn't seem to fit anywhere. I know the look about her, a lost expression which speaks volumes about Gwen's motivation for inviting her in. Cari and I aren't Gwen's real friends now, and we weren't when she dragged us here. We were her pet projects, people she saw as being in dire need of a thorough churching. I'm never sure if it was the lesbian rumors at our school or my unfortunate history with the bullies which brought Gwen my way, but in either case, she saw her work as done once I was sucked in.

Cari isn't Gwen's usual type, and I wonder how it happened. Maybe someday Cari will tell me. That would probably be on the same day I explain to her why I stayed after Gwen moved on.

I try to look like I'm focused on the Student Bible and the yellow highlighter in my lap, but I'm stealing glances at Cari. She's like me in the way she stands out. Most of the other girls have this creepily similar Sunday aesthetic—modestly feminine dresses, light brown and blond hair pulled back with a clip or a scrunchy, delicate cross necklaces, and button earrings.

Instead of the standard church uniform, Cari is in all black. The skirt of her scoop-neck velvet dress touches the floor, but I can see her Renaissance boots peeking out from underneath. Her choker is a black ribbon with a chain down the back and a heart-shaped pendant. She wears large, dangling stars in her ears that catch the light when she moves. She's paler than I am, but her hair is darker. Where mine is a frizzy deep brown, she has thick, smooth hair that's almost as black as her clothes. I'm in awe of the cranberry-colored lipstick she has on and the way she's made her eyes pop with black liner and smoky shadow.

I'm the only girl wearing pants. Gray-green cargos with a pink fabric belt and a pale pink T-shirt. I own one dress, and I never feel like it looks right on me. Not only do I hate pantyhose, I also don't care for the way it emphasizes my stomach. At least with the shirt, I can cover everything up. Pink isn't my favorite color, but I'm making the effort to look somewhat more feminine as a way of dressing up for church.

The couch dips next to me, and I look away from Cari. It's Hannah, a bubbly girl one grade above me, and her brother, Noah, who is in tenth grade like me. I swallow. I have nothing against either of them. Like most of the group, we all go to the same school. We're not real close or anything, but they're the nearest I have to friends here now that Gwen's ditched me.

Their father is an elder, and their mother is on half the committees at church. It intimidates me, the authority their family has. Hannah is so outgoing, it's always overwhelming to be in her personal space. Noah is one of those guys who makes me sweat by being in the same building. My hands are clammy, and I have the urge to check if my deodorant is working.

Hannah glances at me and grins. Startled before I can work up to hyperventilating, I do the only sensible thing and squeak, "Hey."

"Morning," she says, her tone breezy. She leans in as though sharing an important secret. "They're starting hellfire school today."

That's not the real name for it, of course. We all got a letter to bring home to our parents letting them know we were going to watch a video series called *Hell's Bells*, all about the satanic influence of rock music. It's about two years old, but our teachers seem to feel it's highly relevant. As my parents are both agnostic, Dad rolled his eyes and asked if he and Mom should throw out all their old vinyl. Mom nearly forbade me to attend but gave in when I said all my friends would be there. That may have been a stretch. I don't have that many friends even at church.

"Should be fun," Noah adds. Something in his tone suggests he doesn't mean he thinks he might learn something.

I nod at them both, too surprised to reply. They've always struck me as the goody-goody types, and their faint mocking of the class causes me to see them in a different light.

Noah stretches, and when he brings his arms back down I notice his nail polish. It's lime green to match his shiny shorts. I can't decide if I'm more shocked at the color or the fact that it's snowing and his legs are bare. I look back up at his face, and he winks.

My cheeks go hot, and I turn away. Now is not the time for whatever games he's playing. I'm used to boys at school doing that kind of thing, flirting for the sake of mocking me, but Noah hasn't ever joined them in their sport. Annoyed, I face forward with my arms crossed, trying to ignore him. I imagine his eyes are still on me, but I'm careful not to sneak peeks at him.

At last our Sunday school teacher arrives, flanked by two of the other adult volunteers and a couple of the student leaders. One of them is Bonnie, a girl who makes a career out of being holier-than-thou. She's a senior, and she and her stuck-up boyfriend are the youth group popular couple. She wheels in the television and pops the tape into the VCR. I try to relax as our teacher introduces the video, but I can't. Out of the corner of my eye, I keep seeing Noah almost making a show of his disinterest in what's on the screen.

There's nowhere I can look that isn't a problem. I can't look at either Hannah or Noah, and I can't stare at Cari. So I focus on the television, where there's now a warning about sexual and occult material. For the next half hour, I listen to the mustached host and wonder how much truth there is to what he's saying. Does it apply to the collection of cassettes on the shelf in my bedroom? Or to the books? I'm too lost in my own thoughts to pay attention to the post-video discussion.

When class is over, I throw on my sweatshirt and head for the door as fast as I can without seeming rude. Noah stops me before I can leave. I don't want to talk to him. All I want is to get out of there, away from the images we've been subjected to on the screen.

"Hey, Toni. What did you think of the film?" he asks.

I can't tell if he really wants to know or if there's some other reason for this conversation. I shrug. "It was okay." No way am I going to tell him how rattled it has me, with the talk about us being fertile soil for Satan's seeds of deception. He'll think I'm stupid or crazy or both.

"Yeah," Noah agrees. He clears his throat.

"Is that what you wanted to ask me about?"

"Sort of."

There's a longish pause, and it's so uncomfortable that I blurt the first thing to pop into my head. "What's with the nail polish?"

"This?" He laughs, waggling his fingers. "I do it to piss my parents off. Also to keep them from knowing what else I'm doing. If they're jailing me for the nail polish, they don't ask about other shit."

I want to ask him more about that, but I don't. He's swearing, and it's thrown me off, right along with the blatant disregard for the whole "honor your father and mother" thing. He doesn't seem concerned that one of the adults will hear him and give him a lecture about keeping his words and thoughts pure.

He reaches out and toys with the cuff of my sweatshirt sleeve, surprising me for the second time in under a minute.

"Can I call you?" he asks. "I mean, maybe to talk. About…the stuff from Sunday school or something. You know."

I'm burning up despite the fact that it's chilly in the church. My face must be giving me away, but Noah doesn't say anything about it. He's gone a bit red too.

"Yeah, okay," I say.

He holds out his forearm and hands me his pen. When I finish, he winks at me again and walks away, leaving me stranded and a little confused outside the Sunday school room.

***

Mom calls me to help set the table. I'm still on edge, both from the video in class and from Noah's attention. He's good-looking in the sense of filling a spot on my list of top ten boys I'd like to kiss, but I've never thought of him seriously as someone I'd go out with. If I'm honest, I don't think about most boys that way. I'm not the kind of girl boys go for.

I sigh and rise from the couch, leaving my copy of *A Prayer for Owen Meany* on the coffee table. Dad bought it for my birthday a few months ago, and this is my second time reading it. Only now I wonder whether it's on the approved book list at church.

In the kitchen, Mom hands me a stack of plates and gives the silverware to my sister, Sofia. Wordlessly, we put out the place settings. Sunday afternoons are our big family meal. Sometimes Mom's parents, Gran and Gramps DiNapoli, join us. Other times, they drop me off after church and go visiting with other members. I think they're secretly pleased to think I picked their religion over my Bubbe and Zayde Moskowitz.

I should say something about my parents. They have this running joke that my mother was going to become a nun and my father a rabbi, but they met, had my oldest brother Dominic, got married—in that order—and the rest is history. It's not even true. Well, the part about having Dom is, and they are married, but not the rest. My mother's parents like to bring up the fact that she wanted to be a nun for about five minutes when she was eight, usually as a way of reminding her she chose poorly when she married Dad. Which doesn't even make sense because my grandparents are Baptists, not Catholics, and the only reason Mom wanted to be a nun was because her best friend at the time said *she* did.

Meanwhile, there is no possible way Dad ever wanted to follow in his uncle's footsteps. Needless to say, neither side of the family was thrilled when my parents got together. They still aren't. That's why there's such a big gap between Dom and Vincent, the second oldest. They waited a while to let the families cool off then had the next three of us pretty close together.

We sometimes share a Shabbat meal with Bubbe and Zayde on Friday nights, and they like to ask Mom really weird questions about her religion during dinner. They're a lot better than Gran and Gramps, though. Gran still tells Mom at least once a month that she's praying Dad will accept Jesus as his Messiah. That's not going to happen, seeing as both my parents are against organized religion, and in twenty-four years, he hasn't done it yet.

Vince is home, doing laundry before going back to Syracuse. He's eighteen, a freshman with a full scholarship to play soccer.

He still comes home weekends to eat all our food and take up the washing machine for hours. At least he's cleaning his clothes, right?

As he passes me on the way to the kitchen to steal something out of the pot on the stove, he says, "Hey, squirt," and messes up my hair. I'm long past the age when that's even a little bit funny or cute, so I glare at him. He smirks. I don't know why he never does any of this crap to Matteo or even Sofia.

I'm short one setting, leaving an empty place at the table. "Isn't Dom coming?" I ask Mom when I return to the kitchen.

"He has plans this week." There's an awkward pause before Mom adds, "With Levi."

Levi is Dom's boyfriend, but no one says so. It's one of those things everyone avoids talking about, like how Dad doesn't tell his parents I'm going to church with my other grandparents or how no one says anything when Matteo wears Sofia's outgrown dress-up clothes and gets into Mom's Avon drawer and pinches her tiny sample lipstick tubes. Gran and Gramps call Dom and Levi "roommates." I don't think my parents are against Dom being gay, but it's not open for discussion. I wonder sometimes if it's because they worry about him, not because they agree with my church or with Gran and Gramps.

Dom is nine years older than me, and he and Levi have been together for a while. Levi is really cool. He's the exact opposite of Dom. Both my brothers are sports freaks, but Levi works at Xerox doing some computer stuff. He looks like a complete nerd, if kind of a hot one—tall and skinny, thick glasses, the whole thing. He also plays the piano, dances like you wouldn't believe, and talks a lot with his hands. Aside from some of my DiNapoli relatives, I've never met anyone more expressive.

Unlike me, Dom chose Judaism. He had a bar mitzvah and everything. Of course, I don't remember it at all, seeing as I wasn't even in Kindergarten at the time. It's made him more or less Bubbe and Zayde's favorite. Vince is even more anti-religion than Mom and Dad. At college, he's picked up a bunch of stuff about how only the weak-minded need it.

When I started going to church, Sofia begged to come along. She's a lot more into it than I am, and she hasn't needed any help making friends there. Then again, Sofia hasn't needed help making friends anywhere she goes. Sofia is thirteen and beginning to be a pain in the butt. I don't think I was ever that cranky when I was her age, but I'm not sure. We get along all right, for the most part. We just don't have anything in common. We don't even steal clothes from each other like regular sisters do. That's probably because she's so skinny and I'm so…not skinny. We couldn't even fit in each other's jeans.

Sofia's one of those girls who if she weren't a nice person—relatively speaking—would be easy to hate. She's pretty and popular and good at stuff, like ballet. Meanwhile, I'm dumpy and have two left feet. To Sofia's credit, she doesn't really make fun of me, but some of her friends do.

While I'm busy laying silverware by the plates, Sofia twirls into the kitchen. Mom smiles at her and hands her the basket of rolls. She takes them gracefully and brings them to the table.

"How was Sunday school?" she asks. "Marcia's sister is in that class, and she won't tell us anything. She says we're too young."

It's not surprising that some of the older girls are acting like they're the adults and lording it over the middle schoolers. They'd probably be mad at me for saying anything, but this is the first time in ages Sofia's wanted to talk about stuff with me.

"It was okay. A little weird. I don't know what to think."

"It sounds creepy."

"If you want, I'll fill you in tonight after we go to bed," I offer.

"Okay."

She returns to the kitchen, and I go into the living room. Matteo is there, reading a book. He's dressed in ordinary jeans and a plain blue shirt. I suspect Mom made him change and wash his face because of Gran and Gramps. I see a faint smear on his lower lip where he didn't get all the lipstick. The color reminds me of Cari.

Matteo looks up at me and grins, wiggling his toes inside his gray wool socks. "Hi, Toni."

"Heya. Can I sit?" When he scoots over, I plop down on the couch next to him. "What're you reading?"

He holds up the book: *Castle in the Air.* Maybe too advanced for a seven-year-old, but Matteo is a smart kid. I check inside the cover. It's not a library book.

"When did you get that?"

"I went to Wegmans with Mom yesterday, and it was on the rack in the book section."

I can't help smiling. I remember when I used to go with Mom and Dad to "help" with the grocery shopping. I always ended up spending most of the time in the part of the store where they keep greeting cards, gifts, and books, browsing the racks for the latest Christopher Pike or Diana Wynne Jones novel. I suppose it's only right that Matteo is starting his journey now that I'm too old and Sofia's almost there.

Matteo was the "surprise baby" my parents had after they were sure they were all done. He's in second grade, and at the beginning of this school year, he developed an obsession with Disney's *The Little Mermaid.* He started asking us to call him Ariel sometimes. My parents are fairly understanding, but they drew the line there. I've been thinking a lot about it lately, and I'm all right with calling him that when we're alone. At least he didn't decide he wanted to be Tinker Bell or Duchess or Lady. I'm always afraid other kids are going to make fun of him if they find out about his name or the princess dress-up clothes and the lipsticks. I know how cruel kids can be.

He slides closer and curls into my side. I put my arm around him, and he opens the book again. I can hear Mom rinsing the salad vegetables and Sofia talking to Vince. Dad's probably downstairs in the family room, and Gran and Gramps aren't here yet. I close my eyes and enjoy the little bit of quiet with Matteo before the chaos of the family dinner.

***

I don't know what this thing is with Noah. He's called me a bunch of times, which made Sofia smirk and Mom do that thing parents do, treating phone calls from a boy like they're as important a milestone as walking or losing a first tooth or learning to ride a two-wheeler. I've apparently now properly grown into being a teenager because boys want to talk to me.

There's a phone on the wall in our kitchen, an old one with a rotary dial. The only other phone is in my parents' room. When I turned thirteen, I begged for a phone in the room I share with Sofia. That was the year I was hanging out with a couple of girls from school, and I was sure we were going to be just like the group from *The Against Taffy Sinclair Club* and that we'd be lifelong friends. This was before the rumors and the thing that happened with Philip Hanson after Homecoming.

The best friends group fizzled out, and my parents said no to the phone. The one in their room doesn't have a long enough cord to reach all the way down the hall, so I ask if I can go in there for some privacy. Mom's so excited that I'm not a failure of adolescent normalcy that she doesn't bug me about it. There's not much Noah and I talk about that I need to keep secret from anyone, but it's the principle of the thing.

I couldn't say what all we talk about, Noah and I. It's stupid stuff, nothing that matters. Mostly our conversations are about random things we like or which teachers are okay and which ones we could do without. Noah doesn't seem surprised when I tell him Ms. Lorring is my favorite. I have her for orchestra, and she's probably the best music teacher I've had. Unfortunately, she's been out sick for a couple of weeks. She used to go to our church too, but she hasn't been there, either.

Noah turns out to be a huge baseball fan. He talks about opening day the way most people act at Christmas or how movie fans get about the Oscars. Their family is originally from Ohio, so Noah's a Reds fan. I guess it was a big deal to him when they won the World Series last fall. I try to sound like I care when he goes on about it because it's obviously very important to him. I'll bet he feels the same way when I talk about music. Not the stuff we're supposed to avoid at church—we've never gotten around to discussing the videos. I mean when I try to explain why I like Vivaldi better than Bach or how Mozart sounds easy but really isn't.

The conversations never get deeper than that. He's not the kind of guy I want to pour my heart out to. Besides, what would I tell him? I'm sure he knows the snotty popular girls still call me lezzy behind my back, but he obviously doesn't believe them or he'd have said. I can't tell him about Philip Hanson, and the only other big secret I have is the books under my bed that I borrowed off Mom's shelf. Talking to Noah in my parents' room is a good cover for sneaking them back into place and taking new ones.

It's not that Mom would mind, probably. I doubt she'd tell anyone, either. She has this massive collection of romance novels, and no, I'm not reading them cover to cover. They aren't the best education, but it's not like my parents have been all that useful.

The next time we have a youth group meeting, Noah catches my sleeve and tells me he has something for me. I'm caught off guard because he usually pretends there's nothing going on between us while we're at church. Then he calls me and tells me how much he likes me. I wish I had some clue how I'm supposed to respond. Is this what it feels like to have a boyfriend?

Gwen showed us a picture of her latest guy. He's cute, with wavy dark hair and a lanky build. She's lucky to be able to get someone like him to notice her. I remind myself I'm lucky too, with Noah.

When I agree and follow him into one of the empty Sunday school rooms, he takes my hand and drops something into it. His class ring, on a long chain. I thought that was the sort of old-fashioned thing our parents did, like getting pinned and going steady. The ring itself is kind of ugly, but I don't comment.

"What does this mean, exactly?" I ask, slipping the chain over my head.

"Well, I guess that we're going out."

Before I can register what he's said, Noah's leaning in. My palms are sweaty, and my body can't decide if it wants to be too hot or too cold. Do I want to kiss Noah? I'm not sure. We haven't even been on a date yet. In about five seconds, I won't have the chance to back out before it can happen. I don't know why the first thought in my head is that I might as well get it over with.

Noah doesn't go for my mouth, though. He brushes against my cheek with his warm, dry lips. It's nice. He doesn't try to go any further. It's gentle and so sweet I'm almost embarrassed all over again. Noah could use a shave, and I feel the scratch of his barely-there stubble as he shifts away again. I have a wild urge to giggle, but something tells me that wouldn't be polite or fair.

"Was that okay?" Noah asks.

"Yeah." The word comes out shaky, and now I do laugh, high-pitched and nervous. "It was nice."

I don't know what I'm agreeing to or all the rules of whatever we are now. I don't want to be like Bonnie, already telling everyone how she and her boyfriend are going to the same college so they don't have to be apart. Or like Gwen, who talks all the time about being modest and pure but is always nearly in the lap of whichever boy she's currently dating.

We step out of the Sunday school room, and Noah takes my hand. It feels weird to be walking back toward the others like that. Everyone will see, and they'll know what's going on. I look over at him, and he's as red-faced as I feel. Suddenly it's okay; we're in this together, and Noah isn't any more brave or experienced than I am. I give his hand a squeeze, and he smiles at me.

The rest of the night is a blur. People keep sneaking glances at us, but it all seems to be low-key and casual. After youth group, we all pile into the upperclassmen's cars and ride to Denny's like usual. Noah slides into the booth first, then me, and I'm surprised when it's Cari who takes the last spot on the bench.

Her clothes are more subdued tonight, just ripped gray jeans and a black sweater. Her choker has an ornate silver cross, and her earrings look like long daggers with a blood-red stone in the middle. She has on the same cranberry-colored lipstick I like. I wish I could pull off that kind of makeup, but I'm afraid it would make me look ridiculous instead of pretty.

"You and Noah, huh?" she asks. There's neither judgment nor enthusiasm in her tone.

"Yeah, looks that way." I show her the ring.

"Interesting," she says. "I didn't know people still did that."

I giggle. "Me neither." I look sideways at Noah to see if he's heard, but he's not paying us any attention. He's laughing at some stupid joke the kid across from him made.

"I think it's cool," Cari says. "It's different."

The fact that Cari said it's cool makes me blush, though I'm not sure why. For some reason, I don't want to disappoint her. We're not much alike, and we haven't spent a lot of time together. But she fascinates me, and I don't want her to think I'm a hopeless dork. She smiles at me, and I finally relax.

I elbow Noah and ask if he wants to split an order of fries. He shrugs and says sure before going right back to whatever he and the other guys are talking about. Cari peers around me and gives him a bemused look. It feels strange and grown-up having a boyfriend, though I will never admit that to anyone because I already feel a million miles behind everyone else when it comes to dating. Still, it's nice to have someone to share my fries with.

***

This is the first Valentine's Day I've ever had an actual valentine. In fourth grade, back when we still exchanged cards in class, there was this boy who sat behind me. He gave me a giant one with a pink elephant on it that said, "How about a big kiss?" Needless to say, I did not kiss him. But it was the closest I ever came until now to going out with anyone.

We don't do anything right on Valentine's Day except talk on the phone because it's a school night. At this point, Noah and I have yet to go on a real date at all. He came over once, supposedly to do homework. Instead, he let Sofia and me paint his nails with her hot pink Wet n Wild polish while Mom was making dinner. We laughed so loud Mom came out twice to give us The Eye. Noah said he thought the polish looked great.

On Saturday, Noah takes me to see *White Fang* for our first official date. I don't know whether it's because he really wants to see it or because he thinks I do. Not that I would tell him this, but I'm perfectly fine with watching Ethan Hawke for an hour and a half. I'm sure the dog is great too.

Noah offers to get popcorn, but I'm always wary about eating in front of people, so I say no thanks. He seems relieved that he doesn't have to spend more money, and I let him think that's why I told him no. Inside the theater, we sit somewhere toward the middle. Noah tries to hold my hand, but after about two minutes, it's too sweaty and I take my hand back. He drapes his arm over the back of my seat, and all I can think is that I hope he doesn't try to move his hand anytime soon.

At fifteen, I shouldn't still be treating this date like we're seventh graders playing at being grown up. Sofia would probably be more mature on a date if our parents let her. I'm reminded again how backwards I feel compared to everyone else my age, while at the same time wondering if I shouldn't be waiting until I'm older.

I don't know what's wrong with me. I like Noah a lot. We've had fun talking on the phone and sitting together at Denny's when we go out after youth group. He's cute. Maybe not Ethan-Hawke-as-Todd-Anderson cute, but definitely Matthew-Broderick-as-Ferris-Bueller cute. Except he doesn't make my stomach flutter or my knees shake, and sometimes I wish we could go back to being just friends. Everything was less complicated then.

Noah's been pretty patient with me, but even he probably has his limits. Isn't that what everyone says, that boys have expectations? I'd say that's what happened with Philip, but it's not even close. His expectations didn't have anything to do with wanting me. At some point, I'm going to have to stop going back and forth on this and make a decision.

After about ten minutes of this internal fight with myself, I relax back against the seat. Noah's arm drops so it's resting on me, his left hand playing with my sleeve a little. It surprises me that I like it. He's nice, not trying to do anything else. Maybe I'm wrong about him. It makes it easy to settle in and enjoy the movie.

When the film is done, Noah takes me across the street to a diner where we order hot cocoa. He does that thing I like, where he fiddles with the cuff of my sweatshirt. It feels more intimate than having his arm around me in the theater.

The server interrupts my thoughts with the hot cocoas she sets down on the table. Noah picks up his spoon and immediately eats all the whipped cream off the top. I like to let mine melt so it changes the flavor of the cocoa.

"So," he says, pausing to lick a bit of whipped cream off his upper lip, "have you heard anything about what's going on with Ms. Lorring?"

Noah's not in orchestra; he's in band. But everyone sort of knows everyone else in the music classes. Ms. Lorring has been out for so long it's not really news anymore, but it is of interest because no one seems to have any idea why she's been absent.

"No. We've had a sub, and she's okay. She was the student teacher last year. I don't think she knows anything, or if she does, she's not saying."

"My dad thinks—" Noah cuts himself off.

"What?"

"He thinks it's serious. Like…cancer. Or…something."

I get the feeling there's more Noah's not telling me or more his dad hasn't told him. I stick my spoon in my cocoa. "Obviously it's serious. She's been out for a month already."

"Dad says there's stuff people don't know about her."

"Like what?"

Noah has the good sense to blush. "He won't say. Something about her 'lifestyle.' That could mean, like, a bunch of things."

He drops the subject after that, and I'm glad. It made me uncomfortable, like it was something we shouldn't be talking about. I look out the window to see both that it's snowing again and that Dad's pulled up outside the diner.

We drive Noah home, and I walk him to the door. I'm shivering, but I don't ask if I can come inside and Noah doesn't offer. Instead, he leans in. I surreptitiously peek over my shoulder to see if Dad's looking. He's not, so I lean in too. We meet a little too quickly, but Noah recovers and shifts so the kiss is nice and not painful. He tastes like cocoa, and I think this isn't half bad for a first time.

Noah ends the kiss, and I follow his gaze. Now Dad really is watching us, and my cheeks heat up despite the frosty air. Noah grins, squeezes my hand, and ducks inside his house. I retreat to the car.

I like that Dad doesn't make a big deal on the ride back to our house. He's good that way sometimes, letting a thing be unless I want to talk about it. Mom would use prompts that sound like she read them in *Redbook* magazine. Basically advice on how to grill your teenager without seeming like that's what you're doing.

How she hasn't figured out I read those magazines so I know what she's up to is beyond me.

Later that night, I'm up in the room I share with Sofia. After that Sunday school video series, I took my tapes off the shelf and put them in a box. I now have it on my bed, looking through them. It's pretty standard stuff. I'm not really into the kinds of hard rock they showed in those videos. Mostly these are mix tapes of stuff I recorded off the radio. The only one missing is a Metallica album my cousin gave me, which I unspooled just in case.

While I sort through the tapes, I think about my date with Noah. It was nice. I'm not sure how I feel about having a boyfriend. I still notice other guys, even when I'm with him. I also still read those novels I sneak out of Mom and Dad's room, but I don't replace the characters with visions of Noah and me. And I don't mention even to myself that it's not always boys I want to look at.

Sometimes I wonder if the people at church are right and I'm letting myself be too influenced by music or books. I didn't care much when the guy in the videos talked about violence or Satanism. I'm not that interested in either of those things. But the stuff about sex…I worry that it's not normal for girls to think about it so much. Boys, yeah. Everyone says we have to be careful because they're so easily tempted. But girls? No one talks about that.

Sofia eyes me from her bed. "Are you gonna put that away and turn out the lights?"

"Yeah, okay."

I slide the box back under my bed. Maybe tomorrow I'll get rid of the rest of those tapes. My hand brushes the book I've hidden. I should put it back and not take another one, get my thought life under control like they say.

I withdraw my hand and turn off the bedside lamp. Once I'm snuggled down under the covers, I wait and listen for the even breathing that tells me Sofia's asleep. If I'm going to start being good, especially now that I'm dating Noah, I can do it tomorrow. Tonight, I take one last opportunity to slide my hand under the waistband of my pajamas. As I close my eyes, it's not Noah's face I imagine while I touch myself.

APRIL

IT'S STILL CHILLY the second week of April. The big holidays have come and gone. Being from a multi-faith family means we half-heartedly celebrate all of them, which is always interesting. We don't normally keep kosher, but Dad does for Passover, which means beforehand Bubbe's always in our house, helping Mom get rid of everything we're not supposed to have. Fortunately, my parents avoided the whole issue of what candy we were allowed by not giving us any.

The pick-a-mix religious celebrations in our house never struck me as strange until I was in fourth grade or so. That was the point at which I found out most people only do one. I discovered most people then—as now—decide which one I am by different means. If they know we celebrate Christmas and Easter, they'll assume we're Christians. If they can correctly pronounce my last name, they'll assume we're Jewish. Inevitably, someone's bound to be disappointed.

It wasn't long after that when I read Judy Blume's *Are You There, God? It's Me, Margaret.* Everyone mocks it for being "the period book," which I guess it kind of is. That's not why I read it so often the cover fell off and half the pages were dog-eared. Margaret Simon is like me—her father is Jewish. Almost everyone I've ever met with one Jewish parent, it's their mom. This was the first time I ever saw myself in a character. I related a lot more to her search for faith than to her wish to be a grown-up. I didn't care much about periods or training bras, but I sure did want to know what I was supposed to be.

The problem with that is I've never been much of a believer. We hear in church all the time about how God wants to change our hearts or about being filled with the Holy Spirit. I don't have a clue what any of that involves. The only time I ever feel much of any kind of connection is with music or books. The hard part is finding anything on the official approved list.

Right now, I'm reading a different book, one that has nothing to do with religion. We still do small gifts for Easter, courtesy of Gran and Gramps. Mom and Dad made a no-chocolate rule because of the whole kosher for Passover thing. Gran made a fuss over it until Mom told her it was to keep us from getting cavities. Matteo's the only one still young enough for toys. Even Sofia got a bunch of new Bonne Bell lip glosses this year. I got a book: *The Firm*, by John Grisham. It's not bad.

I can't focus on it, though. We have youth group later, and that means seeing Noah. Having a boyfriend is pretty convenient at school, especially since it's put an end to all the whispering everyone does like they think I can't hear them. He and I don't have any classes together, though, or even the same lunch period. It's both good and bad.

Lately I've been wondering if I should break up with him and be done with it. Nothing much has happened in the almost three months we've been going out. I remind myself this is how it should be, all polite and chaste, hands to ourselves and all that. But I also think I should at least feel something when we're together, only I don't.

At church, they tell boys that they're going to be ruined for marriage if they keep looking at *Playboy* or late-night movies. The pastor's wife once got up in a rare moment of letting a woman talk and said it's like that for romance novels. Reading them gives women false ideas about what love is about. She doesn't say whether reading only the sex parts has the same effect as watching movies with a lot of boobs. Even so, I wonder if that's the real reason I don't have those feelings with Noah.

After dinner, Dad takes Sofia and me to the church. In the first hour, we all hang around and talk or play games. When the weather turns warm again, we'll go outside to play basketball or four square. Right now, most of the guys are in the social hall playing floor hockey. I'm upstairs with Hannah and Cari, and Cari is teaching us how to play some card game. We're trying to keep out of the way of the adults. Some of them are a little weird about cards. Last fall, Hannah's father got after us for playing Go Fish in the narthex after the service.

I still haven't figured out all the rules when Cari excuses herself to the bathroom. A few minutes later, she's back, and she leans down to whisper in my ear.

"Can I talk to you for a sec?" she says.

I follow her into the women's bathroom, which is the best place if you need to have alone time to discuss anything sensitive. There's this area outside where the stalls are that has plush chairs and a long counter with a mirror. Cari leans up against the counter, arms folded.

"What's up?" I ask.

She frowns. "You and Noah are still going out, right?"

I fiddle with the chain around my neck. "Yeah. Why?"

Cari cuts me off. "I feel really bad about this, but I thought someone should probably tell you."

"Tell me what?"

"When I came in here to use the bathroom, I passed by that spot under the stairs. Noah was there. With Gwen."

"And?"

Cari sighs, and she sounds somewhat exasperated. "They looked pretty cozy, with their faces mashed together."

"Oh."

"Just 'oh'?" Cari does the puzzled eyebrow thing better than anyone I've ever seen.

I'm not sure how to answer her. I might be a little mad that Noah is locking lips with Gwen instead of telling me he wanted to break up. He could've said he didn't like my slow pace and uncertainty. But I feel relieved more than anything.

"Can you come with me? I need to find him, and I'll need help distracting Gwen so I can talk to him."

Cari shrugs. "Okay." I'm guessing she thinks it's more like I want someone there so I don't punch either of them, but no one is in any danger from my fists.

We find them exactly where Cari said they were, but all they're doing is sitting with their fingers twined. Noah sees us first and hastily tries to hide it. Gwen inches a little away from him; I roll my eyes. They're not convincing anyone.

"I think Hannah wanted to show you something," Cari tells Gwen. Even I don't believe her, but Gwen gets up and follows her anyway, glancing back at us with a frown. I sit down next to Noah.

He won't look at me, so I put my hand on his. "I'm not mad," I tell him. "Okay, I'm a little mad. Gwen? Really?"

It's dim under the stairs, but I still see his blush. "Not my finest moment."

"You like her?"

"I don't know," he says. "Maybe. I like kissing her, anyway." He finally turns toward me. "Why aren't you pissed? Or more pissed."

I curl my fingers around his ring. "I liked it better when we were just friends."

"Me too," he says, and I feel a lot better.

"So that's it, then. We're breaking up?"

"Looks that way."

I give it some thought. He did cheat on me, even if I didn't really care. Gossip spreads pretty fast, so I imagine most of the others have heard by now. Cari wouldn't say anything—I don't think—but she can't have been the only witness, and Gwen's out there too.

"Do we give them a show?" I ask.

Noah laughs. "We might as well."

I follow him out from our hiding spot, and we find somewhere we know is in earshot of at least three other people. I make a production of giving him his ring back, and then it's done. When we become less interesting than the floor hockey game, I take a moment to give Noah a quick side hug. I catch a flash of his blue nails, and for the first time since Cari pulled me aside, I'm sad.

***

Rain is beating down sideways. The wind whips around me, blowing my hair into my eyes as I fumble in my bag for my key. The key I've apparently forgotten or lost because it's not in there in the inside zipper pouch. Frustrated, I stamp my foot and make a small screech. No one will be home for at least an hour.

I glance up and down the street, wondering which of our neighbors might be home. Most of them work. There's only one house with a car in the driveway—Mr. Sullivan's and Mr. Cohen's. I shiver again, and I decide I don't want to stay outside for the next hour, getting soaked and freezing my butt off. Gathering every ounce of nerve I have, I cross the street and go up two houses to the red one with the white trim.

Mr. Cohen and Mr. Sullivan lived there before we moved in when I was five. Mr. Cohen goes to the Synagogue with Bubbe and Zayde. I'm not sure what Mr. Cohen does for a living, but Mr. Sullivan used to be an editor for the local newspaper. When I was still in Girl Scouts, and still cute enough to make sales on my smile alone, they used to buy a dozen boxes from me—each. Mr. Cohen claimed it was because they didn't like the same kinds. I have no idea if Girl Scout cookies are even kosher; maybe Mr. Cohen gave them away to friends, or maybe Mr. Sullivan ate them all.

I dropped out of Scouts in seventh grade, so I don't go over there for that anymore. But in the nice weather, they're usually out on the porch or weeding in their front garden. They always have a friendly smile and a wave for me. I haven't seen much of them this winter, though I catch Mr. Cohen on occasion going out somewhere.

No one answers when I ring the doorbell. I press it again for good measure, and after another minute, I turn to go. Either they're not home after all, or they don't want to come to the door for some reason. Before I can step off the porch, though, the door opens a crack and Mr. Cohen puts his head out.

"Oh, Antonia, hello," he says. "It's a little early for Girl Scout cookies, isn't it?"

I giggle, but it makes my teeth chatter. "I'm not here to sell cookies, Mr. Cohen. I forgot my key, and there's no one home to let me in." I take a deep breath. "Can I stay here until my sister gets off the bus?"

Mr. Cohen glances over his shoulder. "I don't know…now isn't such a good time." There's a funny strain in his voice that confuses me. "Tommy…" He trails off and looks back into the house again. "He's not feeling so good."

Tommy is Mr. Sullivan. "I promise, I won't be a bother. I'll just sit quietly and do my homework, and you'll never even know I'm there."

"I don't think your parents would like it. Try Mrs. Pitkin up the street."

I don't understand. Why wouldn't my parents want me to go to the neighbors' house if I get locked out? That makes no sense. If anything, they'd be more mad at me if I didn't. Mom would lecture me about frostbite or something, even though it isn't really cold enough for that. Cold enough to make me shiver, though, which I do again.

"Mrs. Pitkin has a dog. I'm allergic." It's a lie, but Mr. Cohen doesn't need to know the real reason is that Mrs. Pitkin is always making remarks about my weight or my clothes or whatever she's decided this week is the matter with me.

Mr. Cohen's shoulders slump. He slides the chain on the door so he can open it all the way, and he nods as he sweeps his hand. I step inside, and I'm hit with a sort of medicinal smell. The room isn't dark, but it's not as bright as we keep ours. I take a look around, trying not to seem like that's what I'm doing. I don't think it fools Mr. Cohen.

When I finally see Mr. Sullivan, I'm shocked by how he looks. He's what my English teacher would call gaunt. So thin I could probably count every single rib if he had his shirt off. It looks like he's sleeping, sitting up in his chair. He's got oxygen tubes in his nose, like Grandpapa DiNapoli when he had lung cancer. But when I see the bluish-purple patches on Mr. Sullivan's skin, I know lung cancer isn't what's wrong with him.

I'm frozen in the entryway so long that Mr. Cohen finally says, "You can't catch it from him."

"I know," I whisper. That isn't what's on my mind. All I can think about suddenly is Dom and Levi. I turn to Mr. Cohen and say, "I'm really sorry."

"Me too," Mr. Cohen answers. He brushes past me, farther into the room.

I follow him and set my bag and my violin by the couch, trying not to peek at Mr. Sullivan out of the corner of my eye. I know why Mr. Cohen said my parents wouldn't like my being here. It's not because they think I'm going to be tainted somehow by being around a pair of middle-aged gay men, and it's not because they think I could get AIDS from them. It's because of Dom and Levi.

In the same way my parents don't talk about Levi as Dom's boyfriend, they don't talk about the relationship between Mr. Cohen and Mr. Sullivan. They're "the neighbors" or "the housemates across the way." By not saying what they mean, my parents have decided they don't have to think about the fact that men like them—men like my brother—have been dying in large numbers for years.

Ages ago, my mother watched some documentary on PBS, about a quilt. It has the names of people who died on it. She sat through it and sobbed when she thought no one knew. Somewhere in her, she thinks this is what's going to happen to Dom, and she knows there's nothing she can do about it.

It doesn't matter they've started telling us horror stories in health class about how everyone is at risk now and arguing over whether we should have free condoms in the nurse's office or vending machines in the bathrooms. My parents don't worry about whether Sofia and I are going to live to see our next birthdays. Matteo, though…

I'm taking out my biology textbook when I hear a faint cough from the other side of the room. I stop with my hand still inside my book bag and look up at Mr. Sullivan. His eyes are open now, focused on me.

"You play that thing?" He's pointing a skinny finger at my violin.

"Uh," I say. "Yeah. Yes, sir."

"Can you play something for me?"

I want to tell him the same thing I'm always saying to my family, that I don't take requests and I can't play on demand. Something in his voice makes me feel different.

"What do you want me to play?" I'm expecting him to say something like church hymns or something popular on the radio. That's not what comes out of his mouth.

"What do *you* want to play?"

It's a good question. I'm not bad; I've been taking lessons since second grade. That doesn't mean I have any idea what I should do for an impromptu concert in the home of a maybe dying man. I close my eyes to think. Right now, I'm working on learning "Autumn" from Vivaldi's *Four Seasons* for an audition next month. I'm not nearly good enough yet, but for some reason, I want to play it.

"Is Vivaldi okay?" I ask.

"I love Vivaldi," Mr. Sullivan replies. He looks to Mr. Cohen. "Don't I?"

Mr. Cohen's smile is somehow both sad and amused. "You do."

I pull the music out of my backpack then kneel on the floor to open my case. While I tighten and rosin my bow, I imagine the notes on the page. In my head, I can feel the motion of my fingers and the press of the strings as I play. I hum a few measures, focusing on how I want it to sound. "Autumn" is my favorite of Vivaldi's *Seasons*. The first movement is quick and upbeat, but there's a slight sadness underneath, even in the sweet, high notes. I could focus on the music for hours, losing track of everything else around me.

With my violin in my hand, I stand up and prop the music against a table lamp. Placing the instrument under my chin, I check my tuning. When I play the opening notes, I shift my gaze briefly from the page to meet Mr. Sullivan's. His smile is serene before he closes his eyes again to listen.

***

After serenading Mr. Sullivan in his living room, they asked me to stop by more often. I don't tell my parents. Since my bus is the first one, I visit them about once a week and then duck out before anyone else is home. I've played other stuff, but Mr. Sullivan always asks me to play the Vivaldi. They've been witness to my steady improvement and effort to memorize it. Mr. Cohen sometimes gives me pointers, but Mr. Sullivan only says, "Lovely. Just lovely."

It's finally audition day. I'm only a little nervous when I stand in the unfamiliar classroom and face the three adjudicators. I take a few deep breaths to slow my rapid pulse. I've done this plenty of times before, but I've never played such a difficult piece. Am I ready for this?

My accompanist raises her eyebrows, indicating she's waiting for my signal. The judge in the middle, a woman with curly, iron-gray hair, picks up her pen. Her gaze meets mine, and a small flicker of a reassuring smile passes across her lips. I relax enough to stop the trembling in my fingers.

The man to her left says, "Whenever you're ready."

I nod to my accompanist, and we begin. There's no introduction, no time to think, no time to allow any intrusive thoughts into my brain. There is only the music: the steady, cheerful opening, the double-stop harmonies, and then my fingers are flying up and down the fingerboard. I'm pulled into the music, the way it sways and bends like the autumn breeze it mimics. I draw out the long, sorrowful notes of the slow section, low and soft, while the piano takes the moving part. Then at last we end together with the same joy as the beginning, slowing in perfect sync.

The final note tapers, and I'm surprised to find I've had my eyes closed. I open them and look at the judges, breathing a little fast as I lower my instrument. Gray Hair is smiling for real now, and both of the men have open, warm expressions. They won't say much yet, but I know they're pleased.

The judge on the far left says, "Thank you. Are you ready for scales, or do you need a moment?"

"I'm ready any time," I tell him, and I am.

When it's over, Ms. Lorring meets me outside the classroom. Teachers aren't allowed in, so she's had to listen from the other side of the door.

"Beautiful," she tells me, beaming with pride.

"Thanks," I say. My limbs feel like jelly, and I'm ready to sit down.

Ms. Lorring seems to understand because she leads me back into the auditorium where other students are warming up and waiting their turn to play. We sit at the back. It'll take about a half hour for the judges to discuss my performance and write it up, and then we can go. Mom will be back for me soon, but for now, it's just Ms. Lorring and me.

"There's no doubt the judges will give you a good score," she says. "I'd like to recommend you for the town's community orchestra, and there's a string festival this summer you might enjoy. Workshops, sight reading, and a chance to play with people of all ages."

"Sounds fun," I say.

"It is. You'll be in the advanced orchestra next year at school, too. I'd like to suggest you sit principal second, if you're willing."

She clears her throat. "Of course, that'll be up to your new teacher."

"New teacher?" I'm more awake now, and I shift in my seat to look at her. "Where will you be?"

She sighs and looks away for a moment. "When I was out earlier this year... I had a series of mini strokes. Surely you've noticed I'm not in as good shape as I was before. I'm not coming back."

"But...you're here now," I argue. "Can't you do some kind of therapy or something?"

She shakes her head. "They can, and they've tried. But it's not enough. It's complicated. They found out it was caused by a blood disorder. There's no cure, only treatment."

I'm trying not to react too strongly here in an auditorium full of strangers, but it's hard. All I can do is nod, unsure what else to say. I think about what Noah said, how there are things we don't know about her, and I wonder again what he meant.

Ms. Lorring continues. "I wanted you to know how proud I am of you and all your hard work. I hope you keep on with your music." There's a catch in her voice at the end.

"Thanks," I whisper.

"Find your instrument's voice, Toni. You have it in you to be a great violinist."

It's time to go get my scores. We stand, and I hesitate for a moment. I'm long past the age where it's appropriate for a student to hug a teacher, but I do it anyway. I wrap my arms around her, and she squeezes back. It's the only response I can give to someone who has been my favorite teacher for the last two years.

The teacher at the scoring table hands me the sheet, and I take it with trembling fingers. I can hardly breathe as I look it over. Ms. Lorring is peering over my shoulder. I've gotten a ninety-eight, good enough to make the Tri-County orchestra in November, and more than enough for the community orchestra. When I look back at Ms. Lorring, there are tears in her eyes despite her wide smile. It's all I can do to hold it together while I accept her congratulations.

When Mom pulls up outside the school, I wave goodbye to Ms. Lorring and set my violin in the back seat. I settle into the front and buckle my seat belt then lean my head back. Mom glances at me out of the corner of her eye.

"How'd it go?"

"Good. I got a ninety-eight." I need to tell Mom about the orchestras, but I'm still feeling on edge. I close my eyes in an effort to keep from letting the tears fall.

"Are you okay?" she asks.

I crack one eye and turn my head toward her. "Yeah. Just exhausted."

"Well, lets get you home. Dinner's in the oven and should be ready when we get there."

She pulls away from the curb, and by the time we're on the main road, I'm drifting off to sleep.

***

Over Memorial Day weekend, there was a spring retreat about an hour and a half from home. The whole point of these things is to get away and spend time with God and each other. Mostly what I got out of it was a lesson in how to embarrass the boys. Someone had a copy of *Sassy*, and there was a tampon ad in it. A girl had written into one of those "Dear Abby" kinds of things to ask if she was still a virgin if she used tampons. Somehow, the boys got hold of the magazine.

I have never once in my life wondered if I was still a virgin after using tampons. Is that really a thing other girls think about? I'm a lot more worried that someone is going to find out I haven't given up reading Mom's romance novels, even though I've been through the entire shelf at this point. I also discovered her copy of *The Joy of Sex*. I'm not brave enough to steal it, but I did flip through it when I was in there on the phone with Hannah.

The end result of the weekend away is that Gwen's been hanging out with us a lot since then. She hasn't brought anyone new to youth group in a while, so she's taken us up as her makeshift hobby, I guess. Meanwhile, Hannah, Cari, and I have gotten closer too. It's not so bad having Gwen join us, even if she does talk endlessly about whichever boyfriend she's on.

The thing with Noah was over almost as fast as it started. I feel bad for him. I can tell he really likes her, but she's not as into him. She broke up with the dark-haired guy before moving on to Noah, and now she's with someone new. His name's Elliot, and even I have to admit how cute he is. He reminds me a little of Levi, but I can't figure out why. They look a bit alike, though Elliot's blond. Otherwise, they're not similar aside from both being bookish. Maybe that's what it is.

Elliot's family is new to our church. His parents are really strict, so he doesn't seem as interested in being publicly groped by Gwen as her previous guys. Instead, he hangs out with a couple of the wannabe youth leader guys, learning how to play guitar as taught by one of our actual leaders. These guys are the seriously spiritual sort and can quote long passages out of the Bible and happily explain it to anyone willing to pay attention for more than five minutes. Except for Elliot, they're all upperclassmen. Bonnie's boyfriend, Steve, is one of them.

Dad drops Sofia and me off at church on a Friday night the week after the retreat. There's a fundraiser yard sale for the youth group's senior mission trip to Mexico next spring, so we're here tonight to set up instead of tomorrow for our regular meeting. I've only been here on Friday a handful of times, so I wasn't aware of what else goes on during those hours. As I climb out of the car, I watch a curly-haired man who might be Dom's age heading up the front steps. He has a big, black Bible tucked under his arm, and he looks around before hunching his shoulders and slipping inside.

A few other men and one woman show up, and Sofia and I trail after them. They turn toward the staircase headed up to the classrooms, and Sofia heads the other direction down to the fellowship hall. When I go to follow her, the curly-haired man is angled so I can see his face. He and I lock eyes for a moment, and then he gives me a tiny, grim smile. I barely acknowledge it before I hurry to catch up to Sofia. I'm not sure what it's about, but it makes a shiver creep up my spine.

A number of the other kids are already in the social hall, talking in small groups while they arrange stuff on tables. I see Cari with Hannah, laughing and holding up the world's tiniest tie-dye T-shirt. She's wearing black jeans, a white shirt, and a leather jacket, even though it's warm out. I like the way she's drawn her hair up into a high, messy bun to show her dangling feather earrings.

As much as I want to go hang out with her and Hannah, I need to check in first. I cross the room to where Gwen is talking to Bonnie and a couple of the adults in charge. Bonnie turns to smile at me.

"Hi, Toni."

Gwen shakes out her blond hair. "Hey, Toni."

Once the leaders have marked my name on the list as present, I head for Hannah and Cari. Elliot is with Noah at the next table over, and they wave to me. I wave back, but I'm quickly swept up in peeling orange price stickers off the sheet and applying them to the junk on the tables.

Three hours later, the room is ready to go. Tomorrow, we'll all be back to take shifts at the register and rearranging items on the tables as people clear stuff out. It's an annual tradition and one of the few big things I look forward to.

Hannah, Cari, and I are outside on the main steps of the church, waiting for rides. A few feet away, Sofia is laughing with her friends. I used to feel jealous of how easily she connected with people, but now I realize I've found my group. Maybe one of these days I'll finally be able to tell them some of the things I've kept hidden.

Gwen comes up beside me. The four of us make small talk about the yard sale. We're interrupted by a couple of older men coming out of the church. They're elders, I think, and one of them teaches adult Sunday school classes. I know because Gran raves about his instruction. Seeing them reminds me of something.

"Hey, guys." Curiosity has gotten the best of me. "Do you have any idea what else meets here on Fridays? I saw a bunch of people coming in and going upstairs when Sofia and I got here. Is it an elders meeting?"

Gwen glances over her shoulder before leaning in and whispering, "No. It's a meeting for, you know, them. Homosexuals."

"Why?" I frown. Not that I'm up on the lives of gay men in my city, but Dom has never said he or Levi attend weekly meetings, certainly not at a church.

She rolls her eyes and huffs. "It's a prayer group."

"Why?" I ask again.

"So God can heal them. Because it's wrong, silly."

I know perfectly well that's what our church teaches. The few times the pastor has mentioned it in a sermon, he seemed pretty clear about his opinion. It's why I don't feel right telling the others about Dom and Levi. But a prayer group to heal them? I wonder if that's what Gran and Gramps think my brother should be doing. It's not a topic of conversation at the dinner table, that's for sure.

I'm about to ask if the prayer group is only for men, but I remember there was a woman there too. I've never met any other women like her, that I'm aware of, but I know it's why certain music isn't on the approved list. I have a couple of tapes in the box under the bed that might be disqualified on those grounds.

Before I can say anything, Gwen pulls her Bible out of her backpack. She flips through it and finds some things which she highlighted for who knows what reason. Probably so she could show people like me, who she thinks are completely ignorant about important rules. She seems suddenly energized, eager to educate me.

"See?" she says. "All of these show how God expects us to live. Those people at the meetings are trying to get right with God. Just between us, this is basically the worst kind of sin."

"Okay," I mumble. I'm sorry I asked.

"I think that's ridiculous," Cari says, startling me. "What makes it worse than anything else?"

Gwen huffs. "Because it's like what Paul says in the Bible. People burning with 'unnatural lusts.' Why do you think God is punishing them?"

"Punishing them? What?" Cari looks like she either wants to rage or laugh.

Leaning in, Gwen says, "Like God when he sent all the *plagues* on Egypt."

She emphasizes the word *plagues*, and I get her meaning. It's a word I've heard used sometimes, and I know it only gets applied to people like Dom and Levi. Or Mr. Sullivan. My eyes sting with unshed tears, but I stay silent.

Gwen shrugs and puts away the Bible. All I can think about is Dom and the men at church, how different they are. Dom is outspoken and politically active, but those men looked like they wanted to be anywhere else. The shiver I had earlier returns, this time accompanied by the low-level fear someone will find out about my family. There's no way I want to tell them now.

It doesn't matter anyway. Dad shows up, and I yell for Sofia. She races over to claim shotgun, and I climb in the back. I wave at the others as we pull away from the curb.

***

After the yard sale, I stay over at Hannah's house. I'll ride to church with her family in the morning. Her mom greets me with that forced politeness I sometimes get from adults who think my soul is in danger from living with so many non-believers. They don't know my family, so they won't let their kids go to my house in case they're exposed to ritual sacrifices of virgins or something. Despite everything else, my family is honestly pretty boring ninety-five percent of the time.

We hole up in Hannah's basement. She pulls out the sofa bed, and we sprawl across it. She puts her copy of *Princess Bride* in the VCR, even though we've both seen it a bunch of times already. We take turns reciting lines along with the movie.

When it's over, we flip through Hannah's magazines. They're all the same stuff most of the kids at church have—*CCM*, *Brio*, *Campus Life*. She opens a recent issue of *Campus Life* to "Love, Sex, and the Whole Person." This is secretly my favorite column, but no one else ever seems to talk about it. The only things we hear in church are what we're not supposed to be doing.

In this particular issue, someone's asked a question about masturbation. The writer doesn't call it that, but the advice columnist does. Just the word makes me cringe. It shouldn't. Even Matteo can say it with a straight face. My parents are a little funny about Dom and Levi's relationship, but they at least made sure we knew all the right terms for things.

They don't call it that at church, either. The only time it gets a mention at all is in this hushed, roundabout way when they're talking about boys getting hooked on looking at *Playboy*. I'm pretty sure it doesn't occur to them that this is a thing girls do, and I'm definitely not up for discussing it tonight.

Hannah is, though. She reads us the advice columnist's answer, which is surprisingly open-minded. There's another question in there—he always answers two or three—about whether or not petting is okay. The answer is something vague about that basically being a form of sex. When she's done reading, Hannah stretches and tosses the magazine aside.

"Do you think he's right?" she asks.

I shrug, trying to seem like I don't care. "About which part?"

"That it's okay to—" She wiggles her fingers.

"I don't know."

Hannah sits up. "My parents think it's wrong, but they think everything is wrong. They can't stand it that there's, like, two swears in *Princess Bride*."

At the same time, we both recite Inigo Montoya's last words before he kills the six-fingered man. We collapse into giggles before Hannah turns serious again.

"I mean it," she says. "It's why Noah's always doing stuff to get them mad."

I nod, wondering if I was one of those things. I have the impression Hannah's parents don't think highly of me, but I don't tell her that. Instead, I say, "I don't think my parents would care."

"Well, mine do. How do you think I got to be almost to the end of junior year and still haven't had a boyfriend?" Her cheeks turn deep pink. "I've never even kissed a boy. Meanwhile, Noah's always messing around. My parents yell at him over the nail polish and the music he listens to and his homework. They don't even know he's smoked weed or that he and Gwen—" She stops herself, pursing her lips.

"He and Gwen what?" I frown.

Hannah bites her lip. "He says Gwen let him finger her at the lock-in back in April."

I scoff. "Boys always say that stuff."

"I don't think he's making it up. He was pretty crushed when she dumped him. He wouldn't have messed around with her if he'd known they'd end up mad at each other after."

It wouldn't be a big deal anywhere but in our friend group. Plenty of kids at school have done a lot more. I want to ask if Hannah thinks it's wrong, what Noah and Gwen did, but I'm afraid she'll think it's because I still like him. I'm curious about what it felt like, but I definitely don't want Noah's hands anywhere on my body. He's a good friend, and that's all.

"Oh," is all I say.

Hannah scrunches her nose. "I'm sorry he was such a jerk to you, especially with Gwen."

"It's okay."

We don't talk about it any more than that, and I'm grateful. Hannah goes upstairs, and I hear her rummaging around. When she comes back down, she has a bag of Cheetos she tosses into the middle of the pullout bed. She stretches out next to me and reaches for the television remote control.

She turns on the TV and flips channels. "Would your parents be mad if you watch *Saturday Night Live*?"

"I doubt it."

"Mine would, but I'm sick of caring. They won't check on us, and I shut the door."

We lay on our stomachs and share the Cheetos straight out of the bag. I'm half watching the show, but I'm also keeping an eye on Hannah. I have a vague, squirmy feeling in my spine, something brought on by lying next to her in our pajamas.

It's not the first time. When I was twelve, there was this girl I used to hang out with sometimes before she moved away. We didn't have any classes together, but we had the same lunch. She was taller than me and had bigger boobs at the time. Back then, that was a big deal, who had boobs and who maybe used socks to fake it. She had stringy, dirty-blond hair and glasses, and she liked Star Wars and dragons.

She slept over at my house a few times, but I liked going to hers better because she was an only child. She had a television in her room and an Atari 2600, and we would try to beat each other's scores at Pac-Man. I never won. I liked watching her play, though, and something about her gave me the same prickly thrill I have now with Hannah.

I finish licking the orange cheese powder off my fingers. Hannah is giggling madly at a penis joke on the show like it's the first time she's ever heard one. Maybe it is, given what she said earlier. She rolls toward me and starts to ask what I think, but I'm too close, and she bashes her nose into my cheek. It only makes her laugh harder.

I'm laughing too, and then, out of the blue, she kisses me. Or I kiss her. It's hard to tell because I think we both went for it at the same time. It's sticky from the Cheetos, and neither of us knows what we're doing. We don't go any farther, which makes it awkward—we stop in the middle of it, and we both back away.

We don't say anything about it afterward. I want to tell Hannah that it doesn't mean anything, that I'm not like what some of the kids at school say about me. Except what if it does mean that? What if those feelings I had for my friend years ago meant more than liking her Pac-Man skills? I stare at the television, willing myself to focus on Dana Carvey. Except he's playing the Church Lady, and all I can think is that she sounds uncomfortably like the church elders.

Hannah coughs, bringing me back to my senses. She glances at me and says, "I'm not a lezzy, you know."

"I know," I say. "Me neither." *But what if I am?*

She doesn't seem to be able to read my thoughts, so I relax and go back to watching the show. But after it's over, it's a long time before I can quiet my brain enough to sleep.

JULY

This is my favorite time of year—high summer, far enough from either end of the school year to almost forget about it for a moment. There's a traveling carnival in Cari's part of town, and we all make plans to go for my birthday. It's only a few streets over from her house, so we walk there. Even Gwen comes along. She's seeing a new guy, Mark, and she brings him with her. He's older than we are, almost nineteen, and just back from his freshman year of college. I guess he used to go to our church, but I barely remember him. He was a senior when I was a freshman, and we didn't hang out much.

It's different between them than it usually is with Gwen. More serious. They're not all over each other the way she sometimes is with the boys she brings to church. They hold hands while we walk up the crowded street.

Noah doesn't say anything, but I can tell he doesn't like Mark. Aside from jealousy, there's no good reason for it. Mark's about the most polite person I've ever met—soft-spoken, not a harsh word about anything. He's the kind of guy I'd bring home to meet Gran and Gramps. A little old-fashioned, I guess, but the type adults praise for having good manners. Gran would call him a "fine young man." Come to think of it, he doesn't seem at all like Gwen's usual boyfriends.

Whatever it is, he rubs Noah the wrong way, and it's making our time at the carnival strained. I ignore Noah's pouting and concentrate my attention on Hannah, Cari, and Elliot. There are only a couple of tame rides, which we try out. The rest of the time, we browse the booths and watch people trying to win at the games.

There's a guy in one of the booths who yells out to us. He winks, making Cari scowl and Hannah giggle. He's pretty cute, and Hannah forces us to walk past him a bunch of times so she can stare at him. I don't know how I feel about the way he licks his lips and calls us babes.

The sky is darkening, and the carnival is going to close for the night soon. We stop at one of the food vans and buy french fries in cups, eating them on the way back to Cari's house and licking the salt and grease from our fingers.

Gwen says Mark's going to take her home, and they leave. The rest of us aren't ready for the night to be over yet. Hannah and Cari are both seventeen and legal to drive after ten, so Noah suggests we all go down to the beach. We pile into their two cars and hit the road with the windows down.

The main part of the beach closes at eleven in the summer, but that's not where we head. We go around to the more secluded side of the lake. There are signs posted saying, "No Lifeguards" and "Swim at Your Own Risk." It's quieter there, though a few scattered people have made fires. We don't have wood or matches, but we bring the blankets from Hannah's car and spread them on the sand.

The moon is up now, big and bright over the water. I lean back and watch as Hannah and Noah splash each other at the edge of the lake. It's peaceful here. Cari kicks off her shoes and wades out farther than the others. The moonlight shines on her hair, and I'm struck by how beautiful she looks like this. Unguarded.

The blanket shifts a little as Elliot settles beside me. "Hey."

"Hey," I reply, tearing my eyes away from Cari. I move over so he's not crowded onto the edge.

"This was nice." He pauses. "I don't really get to do this a lot."

"No?"

"My parents are a little protective. I've never been to a street carnival before. They only let me come because it's people from church."

There's a longish break in his speech, during which we listen to the lapping of the water against the sand and the faint laughter of the others. I wonder what it's like at his house. He's homeschooled, along with his brothers. We've only hung out a few times since they joined our church, mostly with the whole youth group. He and Noah have gotten to be friends since Gwen dumped them both, but I don't know him all that well. This summer is the first time he's gone anywhere with our smaller circle.

Eventually, Elliot continues. "They kind of think I'm into Hannah."

"Are you?"

"Not really."

We've rolled to face each other, and we're really close. It's hard to see his light blue eyes in the dark, especially with our noses almost touching. My heart thunders. Maybe it's wrong, but I really want to kiss him. We're not even dating, and what I'm feeling now isn't remotely pure or innocent. I remember what Hannah said about Noah and Gwen in the spring, and I wonder what it would feel like if Elliot touched me like that.

We move at the same time, and then our lips meet. It's not at all like the chaste, innocent kisses I had with Noah or the weird, random experiment with Hannah. It's intense right from the start. I don't hesitate when Elliot tries to slip his tongue into my mouth. Is this what other people feel? This spark, like someone's lit the top of my head on fire and it's blazing down my spine and out through my limbs?

I make an inadvertent noise, trying to figure out how to keep breathing. Somehow he's shifted so he's partially on top of me. His hand slides up my side until he's cupping my left breast through my T-shirt. My rapid pulse becomes erratic, and instead of Elliot's face, all I can think of is Philip Hanson's. I force myself to lift my hand, and it connects with a firm shoulder. I shove hard.

Elliot backs up. His face is unreadable, a kaleidoscope of shifting expressions I can't make any sense of.

"I—I'm sorry," he says, panting. He rolls onto his back, and I curl my arms around my stomach.

"It's okay," I tell him, even though it's not.

My heart knows Elliot wasn't trying to hurt me, but my brain has yet to catch up. He stopped when I pushed, and that's almost enough to edge Philip out of my thoughts. I rub my face and stare up at the stars until I'm calm enough to look at Elliot.

He says nothing, and there's a tear sliding from the corner of his eye down his temple and into his hair. I sit up.

"What's wrong?" I ask, even though I think he should be asking me that question.

"I'm sorry," he repeats. He wipes his eyes with the cuff of his plaid shirt and sits up too. "I can't do this." He buries his head in his arms.

"Do what?" I whisper, feeling the weight of some unknown force pressing down on us.

Elliot looks up. "Do you know why my parents really let me come tonight?"

"No." I frown. "I thought you said it was because it's church kids."

"It is and it isn't." He stares out at the water, watching the other three for a long time before he answers me. "I told them I thought I was gay. Last fall."

"Are you?"

"I don't know."

There are so many things going on in my head, but I can't process them and I don't try. There's no way I can find words to explain about Dom or the thing with Hannah or my confusing feelings about Cari and how I don't know what they mean. I can't tell Elliot how my grandparents won't acknowledge Levi or that my parents still don't know I kept visiting Mr. Cohen and Mr. Sullivan after the day I got locked out of the house. Instead I do the only thing that feels safe.

"But…isn't it…wrong?" I choke out the last word. "At least, that's what they say at church."

Elliot nods. "My parents wanted me to go to a camp this summer. To get help. It's why we left our last church. Dad was an elder there, and people found out and wanted him to step down. When I started hanging out with Noah after we joined your church, they got suspicious. I had to tell them I was only spending time with him to get close to Hannah."

"You…and Noah?" Now I'm more confused than ever.

Elliot shakes his head. "We're friends. That's all. But he knows. He was supposed to be keeping me accountable, but mostly we sit in his room and listen to the kind of music my parents think is sinful. Sometimes we sneak over to the park and smoke weed." He grabs my forearm. "Don't say anything, okay? I'm working on it, I swear."

"I won't," I promise.

"I really am sorry about…earlier. You know." He wipes his eyes again. "You're, um, not exactly like the other girls, so I thought… I don't know what I thought. Maybe that it wouldn't be so bad." His voice is down to a whisper. "More like what I want."

What else can I do but nod? So that's why he kissed me. I normally hate that, when boys say I'm not like other girls. Is that good or bad? Most of the time, I think it's bad—I'm their pal, not someone they see as a girlfriend. It's different with Elliot, and I can't put my finger on it.

It's almost the reverse of whatever reason Hannah had for testing me out. Or maybe it's almost the same, in a weird way. I don't know whether to be flattered or angry that so many people think I'm willing to be their experiment. Maybe this is the life I'm condemned to for my sins. I'm always going to be the one people mess around with but never the one they really want.

Another, more intrusive thought works its way in. What if I were who Elliot wanted? I think about it sometimes, what it would be like to be a boy. It never feels quite right, any more than wearing a dress and twirling my hair into a scrunchy-wrapped bun feels right. Boy and girl, at least the way our church defines them, both feel like ill-fitting costumes. But I still wonder what it would be like to be a boy kissing another boy in the same way I wonder how it would feel to kiss a girl for real, not in a messy, Cheeto-dust-covered trial run.

I've only seen Dom and Levi kiss each other once or twice when they thought no one was watching. Neither time was any more interesting to me than seeing my parents kiss. But here, on the beach in the moonlight with Elliot, the idea dances at the corners of my mind the way the lake water plays with the sandy shore.

There's a slight breeze, and I shiver, but it's not from the cold. I don't want to be sitting here with Elliot, having this conversation. I'm not sure what he wants from me, but whatever it is, I don't know if I can deliver it. I stand up and peer down at Elliot. He seems to have recovered and isn't trying to talk about it further.

"Come on," I say. "They look like they're having fun. Let's go over."

He lets me pull him to his feet, and we head for the water. As soon as we're in range, Hannah gets a mischievous look and splashes us both. I squeal, Elliot yelps, and our uncomfortable exchange is temporarily forgotten.

***

Somehow, after the night on the beach, I've become Elliot's cover. Everyone else is oblivious except Noah, but he's still smarting over Gwen going out with Mark and doesn't seem to care. It's mostly so Elliot's parents will let him hang out with us. They do the same awkward thing with me that Hannah's parents do but with the added bonus of gushing over me because at least Elliot's dating a girl.

Not everything is just for show. Elliot's got a car because he has a job at the public library. A couple of times, we've ended up making out in his back seat, and once, we shocked ourselves by grinding against each other until we were both panting and kind of a mess. It usually happens when I'm dressed more boyish, and he's never tried to grab my boobs again. I think Elliot and I are both pretending things, but I'm not sure where his fantasies end and mine begin.

Hannah's having our group over for a party in the middle of the week. She has an above ground pool. Even Gwen shows up. I haven't seen much of her since the carnival almost a month ago, which doesn't surprise me. She was all right with being part of our group until she started going out with Mark. I assume she was spending time with him. It's pretty much what I usually expect from her. She doesn't bring Mark to the party. Something about him going back to college soon and having too much to do.

When I look closer at her, though, something seems off. She's wearing makeup, but it doesn't fully cover the dark circles under her eyes. She's not acting unfriendly, but her smile seems frozen in place and forced. I wonder if she and Mark broke up. More than likely, she'll be on to the next guy by the time school starts again.

We spend most of a lazy afternoon splashing each other and trying to make a whirlpool by swim-walking around the outer edge. When we're sick of that, we pick black raspberries and turn our fingers and mouths purple. Only half of them make it into the basket.

We sit on the deck in our damp bathing suits, chowing down on the burgers Hannah's dad grills. All except for Elliot, whose family is vegetarian. He sticks lettuce, tomato, and Doritos in his bun instead. Hannah's mom made a dessert pizza, a giant sugar cookie with sliced fruit artfully arranged and decorated with whipped cream. She used some of the black raspberries in the center.

When we're fed and warm and dry, we sit downstairs in the finished basement. Noah puts *Willow* in the VCR. It's not because any of us want to watch it. We chose something from the parent-approved movie list so we could hang out without the adults checking on us every five minutes. They'd be asking us if they could get us anything, but really they'd be seeing what we're up to. If there's a movie going, they won't bother. No one wants to be interrupted during *Willow.*

Hannah throws a bunch of pillows on the floor, and we stretch out. I sit on the sofa. Elliot lies with his head in my lap, and I play with his hair. He smiles up at me then closes his eyes. Gwen's leaning on Noah, and he has his arm around her. That confirms my suspicion she broke up with Mark because I doubt he'd be happy about it. If there's one thing I've learned, it's that someone like Mark has pretty strict lines that don't get crossed.

Hannah's on her belly, propped on a pillow, and Cari has her back against the sofa beside my knee. We'd been planning to ignore the movie, but we're all so relaxed, and no one seems to mind the quiet. Even though I'm enjoying running my fingers through Elliot's bangs, my eyes are on Cari instead of the movie.

She has on ripped jeans and a black sleeveless shirt. Her usual black choker has a new pendant—a silver moon. It matches the earrings she has in, a cascade of thin silver chains, each ending with a moon or a star. She's done her nails in silver, and I wonder where she found the polish.

Cari must sense my eyes on her because she looks back and up at me and smiles. She tips her head at Elliot and does that cute eyebrow-quirk thing. I feel the blush spreading over my cheeks, but it's dim and I hope Cari hasn't noticed. She doesn't know the kind of relationship I have with Elliot, even though I've thought about telling her a dozen times. I don't know what I'm so afraid of. The others would probably judge us, but something tells me Cari wouldn't. Except half of it isn't my secret to tell, so I keep quiet even about my part.

After the movie is over, Noah and Elliot escape up to Noah's room. After what both Hannah and Elliot said about Noah, I figure they're going to listen to unapproved music and do whatever keeps Elliot from losing it once he's back home with his family. Hannah throws in a Twila Paris tape, and the four of us talk quietly.

I'm comparing upcoming school schedules with Cari when I overhear Hannah ask Gwen, "Did you and Mark break up?"

Cari and I both look over, waiting for her answer. Gwen shrugs. "He's going back to college. It wasn't going to last anyway."

"Well, that's fine, but Noah thinks he has a chance with you. Don't lead him on."

Gwen huffs and rolls her eyes. "It's not like that."

"No? Because it looked exactly like that to me while the movie was on."

"You mean because we were sitting together? So what? Toni and Elliot were all cuddly too, but no one's saying anything about them."

"That's different," Hannah counters. "They're going out."

Gwen scoffs. "Everyone knows what's really going on."

My blood runs cold. I haven't said a single word to anyone about Elliot. When we're at youth group, everything is as chaste and polite as it was with Noah, and no one else has any idea that I'm his cover or that we've been trying stuff out in private. I don't want to be drawn into the argument between Gwen and Hannah over Noah, and Elliot doesn't deserve it either.

"What's that supposed to mean?" I demand, trying to keep my voice from shaking.

"Oh, please. We all remember those rumors about you after homecoming freshman year. Are you using Elliot as a cover?"

I don't know whether to be relieved that's all she thinks is happening or angry that she has at least a partial truth. I hide my conflicted feelings behind a dig of my own. "Like you're any better. You're always talking about God hating sin, but you've messed around with every boy at church by now."

Gwen flips her hair over her shoulder and takes on that superior expression she gets. "You don't know anything."

"I know you said God punishes men like my brother with *plagues*." I spit out the word like it tastes bad. "You think that's what I deserve too, even if those rumors are all lies. But you let Noah stick his hands in your pants and then dumped him like yesterday's trash. Tell me again how that's supposedly more pleasing to God or whatever. Is that what you did to Mark?"

Cari stares at me with her mouth open. Hannah glares. I'll deal with her later. Breaking her confidence is worth it for the look on Gwen's face.

"How dare you," she hisses. "It wasn't like that at all. You think you're so smart, but you don't know anything. Not one single thing."

"No? How about this. I know my brother and his boyfriend are worth a thousand of your lying, self-righteous ass. You hook people with promises you don't keep and then drop us the second something more interesting turns up."

I stand. Gwen is outright crying now, but I don't care. She's always after everyone else for needing to be "saved," but she doesn't think all her rules apply to herself. I don't want to stay in this house with her a minute longer than I have to. I grab my backpack and head for the stairs.

We must've been louder than we thought because Noah and Elliot are in the kitchen, looking stricken. Noah's mom pokes her head in and asks if everything is all right. I compose myself long enough to tell her I need to go home. She offers a ride, but I tell her my dad's picking me up and I'm going to wait for him outside.

Once I've shut the door behind me, I start walking. There's a convenience store a couple of blocks away where I can use the pay phone. I hike my bag up on my shoulder.

"Toni, wait!" It's Cari. I stop walking, but I don't turn around. "You want a ride?"

"No, thanks."

"You can't walk all the way home."

I jingle the pocket of my cargo shorts. "I have a quarter. I'll call my parents."

Cari catches up to me and touches my arm. I finally face her. She says, "Let me drive you, okay?"

"Fine."

We walk back up the driveway to her car. Inside, I buckle up, but I don't say anything or look at Cari. She sighs, but I can't tell what she means by it. Is she annoyed? Worried?

"She was out of line, but so were you," Cari says.

I don't answer. She's probably right, and I definitely shouldn't have said what I did about Gwen and Noah. I'm not ready to admit it, though. Cari glances at me out of the corner of her eye, but she doesn't say another word as she turns the key in the ignition and backs out of the driveway.

***

Summer vacation is almost over. I haven't talked to Gwen at all since Hannah's party, and I've only spoken to Hannah briefly. She's still mad at me. I know I need to apologize, but I'm not ready to face them.

I also broke it off with Elliot. As much as I enjoyed what we were doing, we can't keep it up. He doesn't feel about me the way I might about him if we were a real couple. I really like him, but I want someone who is with me for myself and not because they're hiding from the truth. Even Cari doesn't know, though I think she's guessed at a good part of what really happened from the hints I've dropped. I would tell her everything, but I still don't want to rat Elliot out.

For the last few weeks of the summer, I keep busy spending time with Cari in between back-to-school shopping trips. Those never end well. Mom and Matteo had another fight the last time. It was about clothes, like always. He wanted to look in the girls' section, but Mom said no. He hasn't let up on asking us to call him Ariel, and he sobbed in his room for two hours after Mom said he couldn't have the pink *Little Mermaid* backpack.

I'm now hiding out in my room with Cari while they talk downstairs. Mom and Dad have had Matteo seeing a counselor for the last couple of months, but it doesn't seem to be helping. I don't know what to think. I wish Matteo could just wear whatever he wants, but I know how mean kids can be. It's only this year that I've stopped feeling everyone's eyes on me and hearing the whispers.

Currently, I'm turning this way and that, examining every angle in the full-length mirror on the back of the door. We hardly bought anything for me, partly because I haven't grown at all and partly because I hate shopping. Nothing ever looks right. About eighty percent of the time, I want to stop looking like…well, me, for one thing. My current fashion style can best be described as "depressed potato."

Cari peers at me over the top of this months' issue of *Seventeen*. Probably another thing on the Thou Shalt Not list, as Hannah calls it. It's not a Christian magazine, and there's always some stuff in there Pastor has words about.

She sets the magazine down and crosses her legs, tilting her head to the side. I flush under her scrutiny. At last she says, "Why do you want to look like them?"

I know who she means—the Stepford Teens. Those girls who look like they stepped out of a modesty fashion show. Or off the cover of *Seventeen*. And I do want to look like them, but not for the reasons Cari thinks.

"What do you care?" I mutter. It's easier than trying to explain the way my hair, my face, my body all feel like baggage.

She stands and comes up behind me, peering over my shoulder at my reflection. "You don't have to imitate all that boring, bland crap."

"I do if I want—" I take a deep breath and turn around. "If I want to blend in."

"And what if you don't want to?" She puts her hands on her hips. Cari's not exactly the blending-in type herself.

It might sound strange, but I've never thought about it. From the time I was nine, I've always tried to mold myself to what I thought would make other people happy. And then for almost two years, I've tried to be inconspicuous, to keep my head down and prevent anyone from noticing me.

"I don't know," I answer truthfully.

Cari pushes gently until I rotate again. She puts her hands on my shoulders and says, "What would you change right now if you could?"

"My hair," I say without hesitation. "I hate it. It's so thick and wavy I can barely comb it, and it looks awful whether I put it up with a scrunchy or hold the front back with a barrette."

"Hm. I could cut it for you, if you want."

My mouth drops open. "Right now?"

"Sure."

I peek out of my room to see if anyone is around. The house is silent, which means Mom and Matteo have finished their discussion. Or rather, Mom's lecture. I motion to Cari, and we sneak into the bathroom to do the deed. There's a pair of scissors in the drawer under the sink and towels on the shelf over the toilet.

It doesn't take long before what feels like an enormous weight has been lifted off my head. Cari's given me this really cute cut. It's messy and boyish and I love it. I can't stop staring at my reflection and wondering why I never thought to do this before.

We clean up and go back in my room. I'll worry about Mom's reaction later. She'll probably be more annoyed that I didn't tell her I wanted it done than that I had Cari do it. It's not like I got a tattoo or had my nipples pierced or something. I didn't even dye my hair purple.

I'm too busy looking at my hair again and wondering what sorts of clothes might work with that style to notice when Cari pulls my bin of tapes out from under the bed. I hear her giggle, and I whip around to see her holding Billy Joel in one hand and a mix labeled "Wymyn's Protest Music" in the other. I practically leap across the room to snatch them from her hands and throw them back in the box. I shove it under the bed with my foot.

Cari is gaping at me, but I'm too upset to do anything except sit on Sofia's bed with my knees drawn up. I know the tapes she found aren't the worst thing in the world, and she probably listens to some really out there stuff too. I don't know whether to be embarrassed because it doesn't fit the good church girl image or because she probably thinks it's stupid.

"Toni?" Cari's question is timid, like she's afraid of what I'll say when I respond.

"What."

"Why are you so upset about the tapes?"

I shrug. "You were laughing."

"Yeah, because I was remembering that stupid video series and how afterward, they didn't just tell us to get rid of our AC/DC albums. They wanted us to, like, unspool all our secular music tapes! I'm glad to know I'm not the only one who didn't."

I let out a breathy laugh and uncurl my legs. "I wasn't sure whether you thought I was stupid for hiding them or stupid because I like stuff that's kind of average. Well, maybe not the protest music, but the rest."

"Neither," Cari assures me. "We're gonna have to play some of that protest music later, though. And I definitely need the story of why you have it in the first place." She tilts her head again, and now I know it means she's assessing something she senses under the surface, like with my hair. "Why are you at that church, anyway?"

"Gwen," I say. "She invited me freshman year."

"But you're not really close with her." She doesn't just mean the random fight at the party.

"I was kind of her pet project, I guess." This is dangerously close to having to tell Cari what happened, so I deflect. "What about you? Weren't you one of her tag-alongs?"

Cari laughs again. "No way. My parents go there because of the people my dad works with. We moved here from Ontario for his job. I don't think they realized what kind of place it was."

"Can't they just go somewhere else?"

"I guess, but Mom says change happens slowly. They want to help make it better from the inside." She smiles, and it makes my stomach flip in a way I know I can't ever tell anyone. "So that's what I'm trying to do too."

"Do you—" I bite my lip. I've never asked anyone this, mostly because I made assumptions about everyone else. "Do you believe the stuff they say?"

"You mean, am I a Christian? Or do I believe all the crap they say about music and books and sex and gay people?"

"Both?"

"Then yes to the first, no to the second. Same for my parents." She's doing that piercing gaze thing again. "I'm guessing your answers are the exact opposite of mine."

I nod, relieved to be able to tell someone. "I don't even know what religion I am. Gran and Gramps think I'm a Christian. Bubbe and Zayde say I could be Jewish if I convert like my oldest brother did. I don't think I believe any of it, and maybe my parents are right after all. They're both basically agnostic. My other brother is an atheist and thinks we're all wrong. Not the little one," I add hastily at Cari's puzzled expression. "Vince, the one who's in college."

"And yet you think they're right about all the stuff God hates?" Cari wrinkles her nose.

"They aren't the only ones who hate all that stuff."

It's now or never. I stand and go to the bookshelf to pull off a large hardbound volume. I bring it over and sit on the bed next to Cari, opening the book as I settle in. I flip through the black-and-white photos until I locate the one I want.

"This is Philip Hanson," I say, pointing at his yearbook picture.

"Cute," she says.

"I thought so too at first, but he spent all of seventh and eighth grade tormenting me. He sat behind me in two of my classes. He used to throw stuff at me or poke me in the back to make me squirm. Twice, he spit on me."

"What a jerk."

"Yeah, but then we got to high school. He acted overnight like he'd changed." My hands shake, and Cari takes one. As soon as our skin touches, I feel calmer. "At homecoming, he asked me to dance. He got me into a corner by the bleachers, and he—" I swallow. "He grabbed my breasts and tried to get me to put my hand down his jeans. He wouldn't stop until I pushed on him and kicked him. I guess he got scared someone would hear us—no idea how, with the music so loud—so he let me go. He said I was lucky he tried it because that's the best I'll ever get. The next day, he and his friend poured milk inside my shirt in the cafeteria and called me a cow. They mooed at me for a month, and I'm pretty sure they're the ones who started the lesbian rumors."

The only way I managed the rest of that year was by coming to the church group. There, I wasn't Toni-the-lezzy-cow. I was just Toni. Some of the kids there knew what Philip did, but most didn't because they weren't in my grade or classes. It was the only place I didn't have to think about it. Did it matter whether I believed or not? If I could be good enough, follow the rules, do what was expected, then no one ever had to know all the secret things about me. All the things they'd have easily used to keep hurting me.

"That's horrible," Cari says, interrupting my thoughts.

I look at her out of the corner of my eye. Before today, I hadn't known there was a third option, to stay and be part of making changes. I don't know what that means for me, but it gives me hope.

"You know what?" I say.

"What?"

"I think you're right. I don't need to look like them. You want to come shopping with me for some new clothes?"

"Now you're talking. But first, let's hear that protest music tape," Cari says, and we both grin.

OCTOBER

IF LAST SCHOOL year was our church taking a stand against the dangers of music, this year it's all about sex. There's a not-so-subtle shift, leaving behind some of the fear we'll be tainted by satanic lyrics. Now they're in fear for our bodies, and maybe they're not entirely wrong. But the way they're keeping us safe is by scaring us.

I'm familiar with that tactic. They used it at school, too. Filmstrips with pictures of people messed up by drugs and diseases or videos of live births. A few years ago, they were all about how to keep us from getting pregnant. Now they want to keep us from dying. They won't call it sin in a public school, but it amounts to the same thing. Some part of me wants to cling to the safety provided by the church. Another part is disgusted with it.

I probably wouldn't have been able to see it if not for Cari. I was surprised to learn her parents, even though they're Christians, gave her a much better education even than I had from mine. Now I can't *un*see it. She and I are in a constant state of exchanging glances and biting the insides of our cheeks to keep from saying anything. Even so, it's irresistible to show up for every youth group meeting waiting to see what they'll tell us next.

The first week, it was a story: a man put poop in his kids' brownies to see if they were willing to tolerate a little bit of something gross. The next week, it was spitting into a glass of water and asking who would be willing to drink it. Week three, they gave us each a piece of gum and had us stick it together in one big wad. Then they offered us the chance to pull a piece off. They've been working their way up to something, but it's hard to tell exactly what.

We find out when we show up on Saturday night. Instead of our usual meeting, there's a guest speaker. They've done that before, but it's a bigger deal this time. He's a local musician and popular enough we've heard of him. He starts the night with a set of pop-style versions of the songs we're used to singing at youth group, stuff out of the YoungLife book.

At some point, he invites us to sing that stupid camp song where you go around giving everyone hugs or head pats or whatever silly thing they come up with. I hate it specifically because someone inevitably suggests wet willies or noogies. This guy doesn't do that, though. He works his way through the song until he tells us to get into it by shaking hands with as many people as we can during the verse. He has to repeat it a couple times because it's not just our youth group—which is about sixty kids already—but several other churches as well.

We're all out of breath by the time he wraps up the song and invites us to sit. He tells us to look at our hands, so I do. I'm covered in red glitter. All around the room, the others are doing the same thing, and we're all puzzled as to where it came from. I look at Cari on my right and Hannah on my left, and I see they're equally confused. Cari wrinkles her nose in disgust.

The speaker holds up his hands for silence. "Some of you have red glitter. Some of you don't. It started with just three people, and you can see how fast it spread to all of you."

This sounds like typical evangelism talk. They're forever telling us that just a few people can help spread the good news everywhere if they just tell one other person. I'm ready to roll my eyes, partly because I've never been all that enthusiastic about dragging anyone to church with me. But then the speaker continues.

"Every single one of you with red glitter—congratulations, you now have HIV."

It's like the air has been sucked out of the room all at once, leaving me gasping. I stare at the glitter covering my palms. The speaker's voice sounds like the adults in a Charlie Brown cartoon. Every now and again I catch enough of it to piece together that this guy is telling us his own story of how he got it. Somewhere in there, he's explaining the importance of saving ourselves for marriage because emotionally and physically, we're apparently having sex with every single other person our partners have been with.

I can't listen anymore. He's giving the kinder, gentler version of telling us this is God's punishment for the immorality of a generation. He doesn't use the word *plague*, but I know he means it. He's not saying it's just gay men—they've mostly stopped doing that everywhere already anyway now that so many people have died—but it's implied in some of what he says. It's obvious he still thinks God is punishing men like Mr. Sullivan and everyone else is collateral damage. He's saying something about how it's led to "the new feminism," women who reject men to "burn with unnatural lust for each other." I don't want to hear the rest.

I fight my way past Cari's knees and take off for the exit. Once I'm through the doors at the back of the sanctuary, I race for the bathroom. I can barely open the door because I'm trying not to cover the handle in glitter. At last I manage a crack to wedge my foot in and kick it so the gap is wide enough to squeeze through.

At the sink, I turn on the taps and stick my glittery hands under the running water. Some of it comes off, but getting it wet only seems to be making the mess worse. I let loose crying, tears pouring down my cheeks as the water sluices over my fingers. By the time I've been at it for a few minutes, I'm a mess and there's glitter everywhere, including in my hair.

A hand on my shoulder makes me jump, and I whirl to face Cari, leaving the tap running. She takes a step back.

"Sorry!" Her expression relaxes. "Are you okay?"

At least Cari hasn't guessed what's on my mind. I'm not even sure myself anymore. All my thoughts have become jumbled, mixed up with the red glitter experiment and the things the guest speaker was saying. Cari reaches around and shuts off the water while I think about how to answer her.

"I—"

It must've been a while since I left the other room because I hear the bathroom door open and a voice says, "Toni?" It's Hannah, and Gwen is right behind her. I shrink back against the sink. Gwen and I still haven't made peace, and I'm not sure I want her seeing me like this.

"Y-yeah," I reply. "In here."

"You okay?" Hannah repeats what Cari asked. "You looked for a sec like you'd seen a ghost, and then you took off."

"It was hot in there, that's all." The others look at me expectantly, and I know they don't believe a word of what I'm saying. "I'm having kind of a rough night."

Hannah nods. "Because of your brother?"

I want to pretend I have no idea what she's talking about, but instead I shake my head. "Not exactly."

Cari squeezes my arm. "Not everyone thinks the same as that guy does. You know I don't."

"But a lot do." I glance at Gwen, whose gaze is on her toes. She's biting her lip.

"I used to," Hannah agrees. "But not anymore."

"Wh-what changed your mind?"

"A lot of things," she replies. "Do you want to talk about it?"

I close my eyes for a moment. When I open them, I peek at Gwen, but she's looking at me expectantly like the others. "Not just my brother. That too, but it's the whole thing."

I start by telling them about Mr. Sullivan and how I've been spending time with him. And about what Elliot and I were up to over the summer and Philip Hanson and Dom and how I'm not sure about myself, the confusing feelings I have with girls. I stop short of confessing that I sometimes feel stuck between being a tomboy and a girlish guy. It's too much for me to wrap my own head around, let alone explain it to someone else.

Turning to Gwen, I say, "I'm sorry for how I acted over the summer. I was hiding all this stuff, and I took it out on you."

"I get it," she says. "I was sort of doing the same thing."

"What do you mean?"

"Mark," she says. Tears shimmer in her eyes.

"What really happened?" Hannah asks.

"Did you know he was my first boyfriend? Back when I was in eighth grade." A tear slides down her cheek. "He made me put my mouth on him. A week later, he was going out with someone else." She shrugs. "When he came home from college, he apologized. Said he'd learned his lesson. But then..."

She's outright crying now, and she doesn't have to tell us what Mark did. We can all guess. Hannah puts her arms around Gwen, and Cari and I move in as well. We're no longer worried about getting glitter all over each other.

Eventually, we manage to pull ourselves together. We make a sad attempt at cleaning up all the glitter, which only results in more mess. It breaks the tension, and we're laughing by the time the door opens again.

Hannah shrieks, and Gwen whirls around to yell, "What are you doing in here?"

It's Noah and Elliot, looking sheepish after being hollered at. Cari giggles, and I flick water at the boys. "This is the girls' room," I say, like they couldn't figure that out.

"Yeah, we know," Noah says. "But you were gone forever, so we came to look."

"Are you all okay?" Elliot asks.

"We are now," Gwen tells him, and she reaches over to squeeze my hand.

"I don't know about you guys, but I'm sick of listening to Reverend Hate out there. Wanna go somewhere else and hang out?" Noah asks.

"My house this time?" Cari offers. "My parents won't care that we skipped out."

"Sounds good to me," I say, and without another look back, we're heading out of the ladies' room and to the parking lot.

***

Mr. Sullivan dies on a Tuesday. It both is and isn't a surprise. He's been too sick in the last couple weeks for me to play for him anymore. By then, I think I was going over more for Mr. Cohen than for Mr. Sullivan. Every time I went, Mr. Cohen would say, "Today isn't such a good day. Maybe next time." He always looked like he wanted to let me in anyway, but he never did.

A couple days later, I'm at Bubbe and Zayde's, and Bubbe is teaching me how to braid the challah. She's making a shiva basket for Mr. Cohen, which I'll take to him when I go home. The basket already has apples, Bubbe's homemade preserves, and black and white cookies. I can't stand those, but maybe Mr. Cohen has a different sentiment.

Tante Gisela is there too. She isn't really my aunt, but I call her that because she's Bubbe's oldest friend. Tante Gisela came from Germany after Dachau was liberated in 1945. I can't think of a single person my age with Jewish family who doesn't know at least one survivor. Tante Gisela doesn't talk about what they did to her there the way some people do.

For as long as I can recall, at least once a year, Bubbe gives us what I call "the talk." It's this thing where older family members pass on their wisdom to younger ones about what we'll do if *it* ever happens again. They mean the Holocaust, but no one uses the word, like they won't say Dom is gay. Whenever I'm with Tante Gisela, this is all I can think about.

She's an eccentric woman. The way she pierces me with her gaze always makes me think she knows things she's not letting on about. Tante Gisela can speak in heavily accented English, and occasionally does, but she mostly communicates in German or Yiddish. She never married. For a while, she lived with Bubbe and Zayde until she moved into her own apartment. She doesn't drive, so they pick her up every week to go to synagogue. On occasion, she's with Bubbe when I go to visit.

Today, they're talking mainly in Yiddish. Bubbe told me she learned it by listening to her parents and practicing with her sisters at night. In her generation, she says, parents sometimes kept their children from learning Yiddish so they could talk about grown-up things without them understanding. She was determined to learn, and she'd hoped my father would too. He wasn't so interested, especially as Zayde doesn't speak it much.

I try to pick up what they're saying from context, but I can only understand a word or two here and there. I know some good slang, mostly from Levi, and a handful of common words. I should ask Bubbe to teach me. I continue to work on my loaf, which isn't coming out half as tidy as Bubbe's.

She looks bemused by my braid when she slides the pans into the oven, but she doesn't say anything. When we're seated at the table, she takes my hand.

"We were talking of our Mr. Cohen," she tells me. "We must care for him. Mr. Sullivan's family is making trouble."

She explains that even though Mr. Sullivan had a will, they're contesting it with the claim he wasn't of sound mind. One of their friends from Beth Israel is a lawyer, and she's helping Mr. Cohen for free. Mr. Sullivan's care was expensive, and the money he left was supposed to pay for some of it. Now his family wants to take that and more from Mr. Cohen.

I hate that it's like this. Mr. Cohen should have whatever Mr. Sullivan wanted him to. But the law says they weren't technically each other's next of kin, so it doesn't matter what I think.

When the basket is ready, Bubbe makes it look pretty. Dad's waiting in the driveway, and I'm about to pick up the basket when Tante Gisela grabs my wrist. She says something to me in Yiddish, and I shake my head. The only thing I understood was *Dom aun Levi*.

Bubbe translates for her. "She says we have to take care of your brother too because they've come for men like him and Levi again."

I nod, and Tante Gisela lets go of me. I give Bubbe a hug and then, after a pause, I offer one to Tante Gisela. She kisses me on the cheek before I grab the basket and dash out to Dad's car.

When I deliver the basket, Mr. Cohen wraps me in his arms. He's sobbing, and it feels weird. Aside from the sometimes showy emotions of the pastor at church, I've rarely seen a grown man cry. Mr. Cohen thanks me, and I head home.

About two minutes after I walk in the door, the phone rings. It's Cari. "Hey," I say. "What's up?"

"My dad just got home. He says—" She sniffles. "Ms. Lorring passed away this morning."

"What?" I stretch the phone cord so I can sit in one of the kitchen chairs.

"He works with her...girlfriend. Her partner, and she was out today because of it."

I'm stunned into silence. Ms. Lorring, the one teacher I adored, is gone. And she was, at least in some way, like me. I wish I'd known. My head is full of these complicated things, and I forget I've left Cari hanging on the other end of the line.

"Toni?"

"Yeah. I'm sorry. I—"

"I'm coming over, okay? We'll talk."

She hangs up, and I sit there. When Mom comes into the room, I tell her what happened. Words come out of my mouth, but they feel dry and impersonal. I remember to tell her Cari is coming over and to ask if I can go for a drive with her. She says yes.

I hear the car in the driveway an indeterminate amount of time later. When I stand, Mom pulls me into a hug, and I shiver against her for a few minutes. She smooths my hair, kisses my forehead, and lets me go.

Cari and I drive up to the beach. Not the secluded spot we went to over the summer but the other side, where the pier and the lighthouse are. The weather's begun to change, but it's not cold yet. My jacket is plenty despite the crisp air and chilly breeze.

We walk through the park toward the lake. It doesn't close until ten, but there's no one around. The only sounds are the last of the leaves rustling in the wind and the water slapping against the sand. Cari and I are quiet too. She understands I'm not ready to talk, so she takes my hand as we make our way to the pier.

About halfway along the pier, we stop. I look out into the dark water, and suddenly all I want to do is yell. At God, at the universe, I don't know.

I must've said something out loud because Cari says, "Go ahead."

For a moment, I stare at her. Then I turn back to the water, open my mouth, and yell, "Screw you!" as loud as I can. I'm not sure who or what the target is for my rage, but it feels good to let it out, hearing it echo back.

I let my anger and grief seep out as I slide down to sit on the cold concrete. Cari sits too and takes my hand again. Her fingers are warm against my chilly palm.

"I'm sorry," she says.

"Did you know?" I ask. "That she had a girlfriend. Before today, I mean."

"Yeah. Her girlfriend works with my dad. When I came out to my parents, they told me to talk to her. For a while, I had lunch with her once a week."

I don't know why this surprises me. Cari's never said anything about it. "Are you…like me?" I ask.

She smiles. "No one is like you, Toni. But if you're asking if I'm bisexual, nope. I only like girls."

"Oh. Oh! Is that the right word for me?"

"Sure, if you like boys too. Didn't you know that?"

"I guess not. My parents don't know, and it's not like I talk about it with my brother."

I wonder about Ms. Lorring. There's so much I didn't know about her. It's possible that if she'd said, I wouldn't have felt so confused that whole time. It's not something teachers talk about with us, but maybe they should.

"This might not be the right time to tell you this," Cari says, interrupting my thoughts, "but I've had a massive crush on you all year." She sighs. "It's okay if you don't feel the same. Been there and done that before."

My thoughts run back over the last ten months. Cari's fascinated me ever since the day she showed up at church. I remember how beautiful I thought she was the day we started watching that awful video series. Maybe she's right, and this isn't a good time. Or maybe, after all the hopeless sorrow of the last few days, this is exactly what makes sense. I'll never know unless I confess to her how much I like her.

"And what if I do feel the same way?" I ask.

"Then would it be okay if I kiss you?"

I nod, and she shifts so we're angled toward each other. When our mouths meet, everything else fades into the distance. Her lips are soft and cool, and it tastes like she uses some kind of lip balm. It's nice—fruity. I don't have time to think about it because she's unlinked our fingers and moved her hand to run it through my short, wavy hair. Soft and slow, like our kiss.

It's different from the others. Not hesitant and innocent, like with Noah, or rushed and experimental like with Hannah. There's no eager tongue or wandering hands like with Elliot. Only sweetness and warmth and moonlight and joy, all the things I will forever associate with Cari.

At last we part, and she smiles. I lean my head on her shoulder, and together we brave the grief and hope that are bound up in this moment. I don't know what tomorrow or the next day will bring, but right now, we have each other, and it's enough.

***

It's Halloween. Matteo is eight today, exactly half my age. He's supposed to have a party at school. Mom made him chocolate cupcakes, frosted in every color of the rainbow. I think this was to appease him because she said no to the all-pink ones, but Matteo seemed happy this morning before school.

I know something is wrong the minute I walk in the door. Mom's home, which she shouldn't be. Either she should still be at work, or she should be at Matteo's school to take the cupcakes and help out with the party. She used to do it every year for all of us until we got too old.

The scent of baking is still in the air, but Mom's banging around in the kitchen again anyway. Aside from the birthday treats, Mom only ever bakes when she's stressed. Something must've happened, but I can't fathom what. I don't want to disturb her right now, so I sneak up the stairs to drop off my bag in my room. I'll come back later to see if I can figure out what's going on.

On the way past Matteo's door, I hear muffled sniffling. Dumping my bag on the floor in the hallway, I knock. The sniffling stops, and then I hear a wavering, "Come in."

Matteo's on his bed, and I have to hold in my shock so I don't upset him. His face is a mess, both from the crying and from the dark bruise forming around his left eye. Someone at school got in a good punch. I have a sudden urge both to grab Matteo and hold on forever and to run back downstairs and join Mom in the dish-slamming.

I don't do either of those. I cross the room and sit on Matteo's bed with him. "What happened?"

"Tanner Hanson."

Oh, God. Philip's younger brother. I can't say I'm surprised. Obviously being a jerkface runs in the family. I pull Matteo close, and he leans on me.

"Bullies suck." I would love to tell Matteo how much I want to rip that kid's throat out, but it won't help, so I keep quiet.

"He called me a name." Matteo leans up and whispers it in my ear. I've heard people call Dom that before, and it makes me bristle. Matteo continues, "Because of my mermaid costume. So I grabbed him, and he punched me. We both got suspended. We never even got to eat my cupcakes, and I missed the dressing-up part." Fresh tears streak down his cheeks.

So that's why Mom's mad. The suspension, not the uneaten cupcakes. Matteo's behavior might've been out of line, but Tanner shouldn't have said anything to him, and he definitely shouldn't have given Matteo a black eye over it.

"It's not your fault," I say.

Matteo's face screws up in anger, and he shoves himself away from me. "Yes, it is! Mom says it. Dad says it. Even Dom kind of thinks it. I can tell."

He might be right. Dom never had much of a problem with bullies. He was cool and popular and didn't go around wearing unicorns and rainbows on his shirts or carrying a pink backpack. I kind of think Levi might have, but I obviously didn't know him then. Dom was into sports and stuff, and he didn't tell anyone he was gay until he was out of high school. Matteo… I don't know. Something is different, and it isn't only the clothes.

"Toni?"

"Yeah?"

"I'm sorry I yelled at you."

"It's okay." He slides in close again. "I don't think it's your fault." I look down at him. "Can I ask you something?"

"What?"

"Do you think— Are— are you a girl?" When he doesn't answer right away, I stammer on. "B-because I sometimes don't quite feel like one, and… I might be like Dom. I kissed a girl, even. Twice. And two boys. And…"

I look at him, but his eyes aren't on me. His gaze is trained on his doorway, where Sofia has appeared. I wonder how much she's heard. Matteo looks back and forth between us, and the silence is tense.

At last Sofia crosses the room and sits on Matteo's other side. "It's okay," she says, and I'm not sure if she's saying it to me or to Matteo.

"What is?" I ask.

"All of it," she answers.

"Oh." I blink. "I wasn't sure if you believed the stuff they say at church."

She shrugs one shoulder gracefully, like the dancer she is. "I don't really care what they say. Did you know even some of our youth leaders don't believe half of it? I asked one time because I wanted to know if I was supposed to try to fix Dom."

I hadn't realized she was feeling that way too. I also hadn't known she'd told anyone about Dom. And here I was, trying to keep it a secret. "What about the things the pastor says? Or what we learn in Sunday school?"

Sofia sticks out her tongue. "A lot of it is stupid, like how they want us to try to get Mom and Dad to come to church. They don't know them very well, obviously."

I laugh, and Matteo giggles too. He quickly turns serious again and looks up at me then Sofia then back to me. "Yes," he says.

"Yes?"

"What you asked me. I'm a girl. Or I want to be. It's what I keep telling Dr. Saliers, and she hasn't said I have to stop saying that." His shoulders slump. "But I can't be one at school, or else Tanner's going to keep beating me up."

I understand. I'm not sure I'd want to tell everyone at school about any of my stuff, and I'm in high school and most people wouldn't know by looking, not really. It's a lot worse right now for Matteo.

"So you really do want us to call you Ariel?" I ask.

He—she—shakes her head. "It's silly. Maybe when I'm bigger, I won't like that name anymore." Her cheeks turn pink. "I still like mermaids, though."

I think for a minute and then snap my fingers. "Remember that old movie?" I ask. "The one about the mermaid. Um… *Splash*."

"Yes!" Sofia says. "I used to love that one. We should watch it again sometime."

"Her name was Madison," I tell Matteo. "We could call you Maddie for short. It's almost like Matty."

"It's like a secret code," Sofia says. "Other people wouldn't know, but we would."

"And Mom and Dad won't get so upset while they're getting used to the idea," I add.

While we wait for Matteo to think it over, I wonder if we're doing the right thing. I don't know anyone else like her except in books. There's a trans woman in *The World According to Garp*, and I've heard of a few really famous ones. What do people do when they're still little kids? And how do I keep the Tanner Hansons of the world from beating her up?

"I like it," Matteo—Maddie—says. "For now."

It's settled, at least temporarily. Sofia is watching me, and I can tell something's on her mind. I ask, "What?"

"Did you really kiss a girl?"

"Yeah." I hold up two fingers.

"So you're really a lesbian?" Sofia's probably thinking about the rumors at school.

"I don't think so. I mean, I've never heard of lesbians who also like boys." Is that something a person can be? Somewhere between girl and boy, between liking girls and liking boys.

"No, I guess not," Sofia agrees. "Are you gonna tell me who it was?"

"Not one of them," I say. "I think she wants it to stay private. The other is Cari." My face is warm just thinking about her.

"Is she your girlfriend, then?"

"Yeah. She is." I smile, and Sofia grins back.

"Good. I like her. What about Mom and Dad?"

"One thing at a time." I laugh.

That seems to be all there is to say about it right now. We sit quietly for a few moments before I ask, "Should we see if Mom needs help?"

"No way," Sofia replies. "I would definitely not go down there yet."

I turn to Maddie. "You want to play a board game?"

"Guess Who?" she asks.

"Sure. You get it set up."

Maddie slides off the bed and goes to the shelf where she keeps them. I don't know what's going to happen tomorrow, but today, I'm going to play games with my sisters.

***

The Tri-County Orchestra is about to play. We're in the dressing rooms backstage at one of the largest theaters in the area. I've never played on a stage this big. My violin case sits on the long table in between a flute and a viola. I stand at the mirrored counter, examining myself and fussing with the lapels on my jacket.

Mom took me shopping last weekend for concert clothes, and Cari came along. I told them I didn't want to wear a dress. Mom brought me to this store where they sell women's suits. Even though I sometimes imagine how I'd look if I wore a tux, this is good too. We bought one that's lightweight enough it doesn't pull uncomfortably when I play.

I finally told my family everything, including about Cari and me. I shouldn't have worried. Dad's always pretty cool about stuff, and Mom reacted almost exactly the same way she did last winter with Noah. That is, she fussed over us and made a big deal out of my having a girlfriend like I'd won some kind of award.

After rehearsal yesterday, Cari picked me up and we had Shabbat meal with Dom and Levi. Before we left, Levi pinned a new button on my jean jacket. It has pink and blue eyeglasses with different pairings of male and female symbols, and underneath it says, "Bi-Focal." Levi said a queer friend of his makes them to sell at rallies and stuff. When he used the word "queer," it sounded like power and not a slur. As in, *We're here. We're queer. Get used to it.* I guess now I'm part of that too.

Sofia did my nails last night after I got home. She picked out a color called Silver Lilac. It's a somewhat neutral shade somewhere between pink and brown with a slight shimmer. It's not one of Sofia's—I think she pilfered it from Mom's drawer. Mom hasn't worn nail polish in years, so I doubt she noticed.

Cari taught me how to do the kind of makeup that will look flattering when I'm on stage but won't make me look too feminine. I think I've managed it successfully by myself. The girl next to me glances over, pausing in applying her lipstick to give me an approving smile. I breathe out a sigh of relief before tearing myself away from the mirror to retrieve my instrument.

Even though I've cleaned it already, I take out the soft cloth and wipe it down again. The motion calms my nerves. I know once I start playing, I'll be fine, caught up in the flow of the notes and the blending of my sound with the other strings.

I've thought more about what Cari said. She's a Christian, and she has a deep faith that I don't quite understand. I'm not on the same level as Vince, who makes a hobby out of arguing with religious people. I'm not like Sofia, who takes comfort in Bible verses about the Lord always being with us and having a plan for our lives. She's the most tidy, organized kid I've ever met, so it makes some sense. And I'm not like Dom, who enjoys wrestling with deep questions and poring over holy texts to study them.

I never have those feelings about anything religious. I wanted to—I hoped being in a church would give me those feelings, especially if I could follow the rules well enough. It never happened. The only time I ever feel anything like what they describe is when I play.

Having gotten lost in my own thoughts, I almost miss it when everyone begins to file out. I follow them onto the stage and take my spot, setting my music on the stand as I sit. I warm up by playing a bit of the first piece. We're opening with the overture to Mozart's *The Magic Flute*. The rest of the program is good too—Tchaikovsky's *Marche Slave*, followed by Howard Hanson's *Symphony No. 2*, and closing with "Berceuse and Finale" from Stravinsky's *Firebird*.

The lights flicker, and the audience hushes. The chairperson of the school music association introduces the program. I tune him out and look around. I'm on the outside, third chair—that's the second stand—of the first violins, so I can see out into the audience. I choke up when I see a full row of people and Mom's tiny wave. I lift my hand back and manage a smile.

Mom and Dad are in the center. To Mom's right, Maddie sits between her and Dom, who is holding the program and pointing something out to her—maybe my name. Mom won't let Maddie dress up for school, but at home and on special occasions, she's allowed to wear Sofia's outgrown clothes. Today, she has on a pink satin Easter dress. She's got barrettes in her hair, the kind with ribbon streamers. Her curls are still pretty short, but because she has DiNapoli hair, it's thick enough to keep the barrettes in place anyway. No makeup—Mom says eight is still too young. But she did her nails with us last night, so she and I match.

Levi is leaning in and talking to Bubbe and Zayde. Vince is on Dad's other side, and he's brought his girlfriend. I've never met her, but I guess she's coming out to dinner with us after. Then there's Sofia, followed by all of my group of friends. Cari and Hannah are looking at the program together, and Noah has his arm around Gwen. Elliot's brought his boyfriend with him because my family are some of the only people he can safely be himself around.

Gran and Gramps chose not to come because they are very angry with us right now. They're scared, which I understand, but they also believe that people like Dom and Maddie and me are gripped by Satan and in danger of losing our souls to the fires of hell.

I think about that too, how some people are connected to the people who raised them while others, like Mr. Sullivan or Elliot, have to make their own families. I remember what Levi said last night at dinner, how one of the things he and Dom are fighting for is their right to get married. He says that will stop things from happening like with Mr. Cohen or Ms. Lorring's girlfriend after their partners died.

My mind wanders, and I can picture it now, Dom and Levi getting married. They'll both look handsome and happy in their matching tuxes. Maybe they'll even let me play my violin at their wedding. It makes me feel proud to have family like them and sad that not everyone is so lucky.

The chairperson has stopped speaking, and the concertmaster walks out to the audience's polite clapping. We tune, and there's a brief pause. I love this moment because it's full of anticipation, an almost electric energy I can feel in the tips of my fingers. I'm itching to play.

Our conductor walks out on stage to enthusiastic applause. She shakes hands with the concertmaster, bows to the audience, and turns to step up on the podium. When she lifts her arms, I raise my violin and place it under my chin. On her downbeat, we play the dramatic opening chords of the Mozart, and I am swept up in the piece, transported by the music to another time and another place.

###

ABOUT A.M. LEIBOWITZ

A.M. Leibowitz is a queer spouse, parent, feminist, and book-lover falling somewhere on the Geek-Nerd Spectrum. They keep warm through the long, cold western New York winters by writing about life, relationships, hope, and happy-for-now endings. Their published fiction includes several novels as well as a number of short works, and their stories have been included in anthologies from Supposed Crimes, Witty Bard, and Mischief Corner Books. In between noveling and editing, they blog coffee-fueled, quirky commentary on faith, culture, writing, books, and their family.

FIND A.M. LEIBOWITZ ONLINE:

Facebook: https://www.facebook.com/amymitchell29

Facebook Author Page: https://www.facebook.com/UnchainedFaith/

Twitter: https://twitter.com/amyunchained

Pinterest: https://pinterest.com/amyunchained

Website: http://amleibowitz.com

Goodreads: https://www.goodreads.com/author/show/8544236.A_M_Leibowitz

BY A.M. LEIBOWITZ

Fifteen Minutes
Electricity
Finders Keepers
The One That I Want
Chemical Reaction
Imperfections: An Anthology
The Law of Radical Expressions: An Anthology
Christmas at Mary's
The Royal Family of Hell
(S)no(w) Angels
Pink in the Mirror
An Act of Devotion
Lower Education
Ashes and Alms (in Never Too Late)
Passing on Faith
Walking by Faith
Leaps of Faith
Keeping the Faith
Anthem (Notes from Boston #1)
Nightsong (Notes from Boston #2)
Drumbeat (Notes from Boston #3 - expected 2018)
Year of the Guilty Soul (Seasons of Love)

THE GREAT VILLAGE BUN FIGHT

DEBBIE MCGOWAN

All's fair in love and war. But not in baking.

***

Genre: contemporary fiction, humour

Keywords: LGBTQ+, humour, British, rockin' reverend, village politics, love

Advisory: There is some coarse language in the first chapter, as appropriate to the context, after which there are only a few mild swear words.

ACKNOWLEDGEMENTS

Many thanks to Reverend John Bennett, Vicar of Spalding, St Mary and St Nicolas, for permitting me to include his suggested prayers and blessing for same-sex couples, and for re-instilling some of my lost faith in Church of England clergy.

As always, thank you to the amazing Beaten Track team—special thanks to Jor for a) proofreading every story I throw your way, often at very short notice, and b) making requests I can successfully and gladly fulfil.

***

Church of England Prayer for Same-Sex Marriage taken from http://www.stmaryandstnicolas.org.uk/prayerssame.html

The Bible Societies (1976) *Good News Bible: Today's English Edition*, 1 Corinthians, 13: verses 1–13, pp. 216–7.

BEGAT HENRY, RECURRING

IN 1874, UPON the birth of his son—and to the chagrin of his father and grandfather, both stonemasons—Henry Jones the Third established *Henry Jones and Son, Baker,* in his home village of Banton, population: 123, all of whom, prior to Henry's entrepreneurial escapades, baked their own bread.

John Porter, Butcher, came soon after, followed by *Albert Thorndike, Tailor and Haberdasher, Edith Forsythe, Grocer,* and countless others who would not stand the rigours and trials of time but nonetheless played their part in putting Banton High Street on the map.

So it came to pass that Henry Jones the Fourth, having inherited both his father's name and business acumen, commenced his apprenticeship in 1889. By 1895, his creations—not least the infamous Banton Bun made to the Joneses' secret family recipe—took pride of place on the bakery shelves. In 1899, he married Josephine the farmer's daughter; a year later, they welcomed Henry the Fifth into the world, who (later) begat Henry, who (much later) begat Henry, who… Well, you get the idea, I'm sure.

Now, successful and influential as the Henry Joneses were, they saw their fair share of strife. Young Henry the Fifth was still wet behind the ears when his father died on a WWI battlefield and, in a cruel repeat of history, failed himself to return from WWII, leaving the bakery in the safe but bellicose hands of newlywed Henry the Sixth, who worked until he dropped dead, right there in front of his own ovens, at the age of fifty.

To the good fortune of all concerned—a staff of no less than a baker's dozen—Henry the Seventh proved a much more placid boss than his father. That is, until it came to his retirement.

As one would expect, Henry begat Henry, but he begat Jennifer and Susan first, and Jennifer and Susan were children of the sixties. Generation X. Riding the second wave

and

Henry Jones

and *Son*

got right

up

their noses.

Not least because said *son*—Henry the Eighth, lest we have forgotten—lost his head. Couldn't happen to a nicer person, you might think, but no. We're talking figuratively, as opposed to some kind of four-centuries-later karmic biting him on the bum just for happening to be the poor begatted bugger who landed that particular incarnation of the family name.

Henry Jones the Eighth. What an idiot, although whether he's more so than his father is the subject of ongoing debate…

***

"Naughty, naughty…"

"Very naughty."

A horn blared, long and loud.

"Shit, them strobes, mate."

"Very naughty… Yeah, don't think we're at the rave no more, Jonesy."

"What's them lights, then—oh, fuck!"

Tripping on the kerb, still tripping in general, they rough-and-tumbled to safety, laughing and crying and serious and crying and laughing and up on their feet, and off they went again.

"Got any matches on you, Mick?"

"Er, yeah." Pat, pat, pockets, chest, pockets. "Somewhere." Matches found. "Here."

"Ta."

"What for?"

"Wanker what just nearly run us over." Parked outside the kebab shop. "Gonna have him." Across the road, to the wanker's car. "His own fault..." Window down. "Should look where he's fucking going."

"Jonesy, what the hell, man?"

Discarded newspaper on the passenger seat. *Strike.*

"Jonesy, don't—"

Whoosh!

"There. That'll teach him."

"What the fuck have you—"

"Run! Fucking run!"

***

Yes, they ran, not very far and not very fast, because... dragons. Big red dragons chasing eighteen-year-old ravers up Banton High Street. Of course, they weren't really dragons, but that's what Henry 'Jonesy' Jones the Eighth will tell you to this day. *We didn't know it was a fucking fire engine, did we? Aceeeeed! Ha-ha. Naughty, that. Good night, though.*

Arson, a five-year-prison sentence...oh, and the conception of Henry the Ninth. A good night, indeed.

To be fair to Henry's father (fairer than he deserves), those darker-crust days brought the comedians out in force—*Is your lad out, then? No? Oh, so it was* you *who burnt the bread*—and the jokes continued right up to his retirement, making a misery of the last ten years of his working life. There was nothing else for it.

"Let us take over, Dad," Jennifer beseeched.

"Then it won't be Henry Jones *and Son*, will it?"

"So change the name," Susan told him. Again.

"No. Can't be doing that. Your great-great—"

"Here we go."

"Dad, we know."

"—great-grandfather would turn in his grave if…"

To cut to the chase: upon his retirement—and to the chagrin of his daughters—Henry Jones the Seventh shut the doors on *Henry Jones and Son, Baker*, leaving the burgeoning village of Banton, population: 900, for the first time in 131 years, without their daily bread.

FIRESTARTER

13 Years Later...
Guy Fawkes Night

Like every Guy Fawkes Night since time immemorial, the village green was crammed full of revellers as Bantonions young and old, and all those in between, gathered for fun, fireworks and far too much food. There were fairground games and kiddies' rides, ice cream kiosks and catering vans, all vying for custom with their joyous racket of music, bells, shouts and squeals. The air was crisp, the breeze brisk and sweet with toffee apples, candy floss, roasted chestnuts, potatoes, burgers, hot dogs… The tantalising aroma of caramelised onions set Henry's stomach off in a loud, hungry growl.

Daniel glanced sideways at him and grinned. "Do you want to get something to eat?"

Henry shook his head. "You could get cavities just from breathing tonight."

"Not if you breathe through your nose," Daniel pointed out, to which Henry gave a sad, snotty sniff. "Sorry. I keep forgetting you're sick. Look, we can go home if you want."

Henry rolled his eyes. "Don't be daft. I've only got a cold, and anyway, it's better out than in."

Daniel's grin returned, full force. "I bet you say that to all the boys."

"You'll never know…" Henry tormented in a spooky vibrato that became a shrill "Ouch!" when Daniel squeezed his fingers. A woman walking past frowned at the noise, not looking their way, the frown quickly morphing into a smile when she saw who had made it.

"Evening, you two," she greeted.

"Hi, Ness," both answered, and Henry asked, "How you doing, cuz?"

"Great!" she said through a gritted-teeth smile, the reason for which soon after became apparent.

"Mummy, *please* can I have a toffee appley?"

"I want candy foss!"

Nessa's two kids tugged at her sleeves—one on each.

"We've only just had tea. Let's wait a bit, shall we?"

"But—"

"No."

"I want one *now!*"

"I said no, Kira."

Nessa's five-year-old went into an immediate sulk but didn't argue. Nessa sighed. "Kids," she said.

"Glad I never was one," Henry quipped.

"Yeah. Tell me about it."

Daniel coughed, failing to cover his laughter, but there was no need. Henry's mum was brilliant, but she'd had a hard time looking after him when she was on her own and so young herself, and he'd always tried to be good, not give her any trouble. More than that, he wanted to prove he wasn't like his dad. He wasn't a criminal. He was a responsible graduate with a decent job and a long-term boyfriend. Next year, they would have saved enough for a deposit on a house, and they had big plans. It was why they'd come to Guy Fawkes Night, or partly why. The other part was that Daniel loved fireworks.

"Ness, Ness! I haven't told you, have I?" She'd started to move away from him but stopped and turned back.

"Told me what?"

Henry's cheeks tingled with the onset of a blush. "Danny and I are…um…we're getting married."

"You're…" Nessa's mouth fell open. "Oh wow! That's awesome!" She threw her arms around them both, squashing them together until they could hardly breathe. Nessa was a big lass and strong. Really, *really* strong.

"Lemme go!" Henry squeaked while Daniel merely looked afraid for his life.

With one final, rib-cracking squeeze, Nessa released them. "I'm so happy for you! Congratulations!"

Henry beamed. "Thanks, Ness."

"If you need me to help with anything…"

"I'm sure there'll be loads of things, but it's sixteen months away yet, and we're still figuring out the logistics, like where to have the ceremony and reception, and…the cake."

***

Freeze-frame.

OK…remember all that *Henry begat Henry begat Henry* that ended when Henry the Eighth set fire to a car outside the kebab shop and was thereby disinherited? Right, well, the good people of Banton still needed their daily bread, and let's just say Henry the Third wasn't the only entrepreneur to ever grace that fine village.

Enter Margaret Sharpe (nee Thatcher, believe it or not), the great-great-granddaughter of Edith Forsythe, our olden-days greengrocer. And she is a sharp one, our Margaret, rightly sharing the name *and* heritage of Britain's first female prime minister.

Just weeks after Henry Jones the Seventh turned his 'Closed' sign for the final time, Margaret Sharpe had *The Village Bakery & Grocery* up and running faster than you can say 'I'll have a small batch and a couple of floury baps'.

More on that later…

***

"Ah," Nessa said knowingly. All their family weddings so far, their grandad had made the cakes, but at seventy-seven, he was a bit forgetful and not in the best health, and Henry and Daniel didn't want to be a bother to him.

"Yeah, so," Henry continued, "we're going to ask Margaret."

"Uh-huh?"

Henry nodded. And waited. When Nessa said nothing further, he prompted, "Bad idea?"

"No. Well…she can only say no."

"That's what worries me."

All three glanced over to the food vans, parked in a line, at the end of which was a gazebo adorned with a façade transforming it into a miniature Houses of Parliament—guaranteed by history to be the one thing left standing at the end of the night should the carnival atmosphere get out of hand.

"We could go and see her now, while it's quiet," Daniel suggested.

"Good idea," Henry agreed—out loud. He was still hoping for a medical miracle to restore his grandad's youthful vigour, but he said *au revoir* to his cousin and let Daniel lead him by the hand over to Lady Margaret's grand stall. Unnoticed by the proprietor, they watched her ice a smiley face and scarf onto a gingerbread man, and then another, and another… They could be there a while.

"Those look delicious," Daniel gushed to alert her to their presence. She startled and lynched a gingerbread man by his sugar scarf.

"Good heavens! What a fright you gave me, boys!" Casting her icing bag aside, she wiped her hands on a tea towel, nose crinkled in a grimace as she tugged the terry fabric to unstick it from her palm. "What would you like? I've some lovely moist parkin—" she pointed to a tray containing a slab of very dark brown cake "—as good as your grandfather's, I dare say…" In lieu of raising an eyebrow, she part-closed one eye, head wobbling with her boast. "Or perhaps some coconut ice? How about this delicious creamy vanilla fudge made with fresh dairy cream. Or—"

"A gingerbread man for me, please." Daniel cut off her inventory recital.

"I also have gingerbread ladies," Margaret singsonged. To prove it, she delicately lifted a beskirted ginger person from the tray and held it aloft, wafting her free hand in illustration of her craft.

"Either works for me," Daniel replied so solemnly Henry turned away to battle the guffaw set to explode from him with at least the velocity of the rockets set to imminently decorate the skies.

"A lady for you, Henry dear?" Margaret prompted. She wasn't selling confectionery; she was selling brides. That was when he knew for sure theirs was a lost cause, but they'd come this far.

"Too much biscuit," he muttered out of the side of his mouth, followed by a louder, firmer, "That would be lovely, thanks, Mrs. Sharpe." He even managed a controlled smile to go with it. "Actually…" He focused on the discarded icing bag as he spoke. "We came to ask you…" *Big breath.* "Something."

"Did you now?" She handed Daniel his biscuit but kept Henry's hostage.

"Yes, um… We wondered if… Well, see, we're getting married, and—"

***

So, here's the thing. That comparison of our Margaret to the formidable Mrs. Thatcher? It wasn't accidental. Margaret is…for the sake of politeness, let's call her 'traditional'. Family values, individual liberty, the free market—Conservative with a capital C—and yes, she *was* responsible for organising the Banton street party to celebrate Mrs. T's election win in 1979, amongst other things, but that was her shining moment. She even took home the Union Jack bunting and insisted Mr. Sharpe hang it around the garden. These days, it's a tad faded and frayed around the pointy ends, but there it will stay until they commit Margaret's mortal remains to the earth, because you can bet your sweet bippy she'll be taking it with her.

While most Bantonions have moved with the times, sadly our Margaret isn't one of them. This lady is most certainly not for turning. Turnovers? You might be in with a chance.

You can probably figure out where this is going…

***

"—we wondered if you'd make our wedding cake."

Silence.

Above the houses at the back of the green, a rocket launched optimistically, sprayed the sky with a spatter of green, and *pff*'d out of existence.

Slowly, and with great dread, Henry shifted his eyes left and up, up, up, meeting the judgemental glare first of the gingerbread woman, which was bad enough, and then of Margaret, except her expression was less judgement than disappointment.

In the near distance, a Catherine Wheel whizz-whizz-whizzed in a frenzy. Sparklers popped and crackled, and Postman Pat completed another revolution of the kids' merry-go-round.

At last, Margaret broke her silence with a heavy sigh. "Oh dear." She handed over Henry's gingerbread woman and waved away Daniel's offer of payment. "How old are you now, boys? Twenty-two?"

"Yes," Daniel confirmed. He was getting annoyed, Henry could tell from the weary, talking-to-an-idiot tone he'd developed since they'd returned from university to their home village only to hear the same thing over and over again—

Haven't you put that nonsense behind you?

It's about time you both grew up.

You just need to meet the right girls, settle down…

—no matter that they'd been together since they were sixteen.

"No," Margaret said. "I'm sorry. The day God allows you to marry in His church—"

"Reverend Osbourne has given us his blessing," Daniel argued.

Margaret laughed, all high-pitched and ridiculous. "He is not *God*."

"He's a man of God, though, and if the Church would let him, he'd marry us."

"Hmm." She tilted her head back so she was looking down her nose at them.

"Come on." Henry grabbed Daniel by the arm and pulled him away, too angry to stay and fight. There was no point, and he didn't want her rotten cake anyway.

Of course, she still had to say her piece, loudly calling after them, "I love you boys dearly, but I cannot condone your choices."

Henry took a vicious bite and decapitated his gingerbread woman.

"I'll say a prayer for you on Sunday," Margaret offered.

"Yeah, don't," Daniel muttered and thrust his biscuit at Nessa, who intercepted them halfway across the green.

"I was coming to rescue you," she said.

Henry shook his head. He didn't want to dissect their conversation with Margaret, such as it could be called that.

In silence, the three of them walked over to the area cordoned off with fluorescent orange rope, beyond which half a dozen men were lining up the first of the fireworks. "What have you done with the kids?" Henry asked.

"On the teacups." She thumbed behind her. "With Grandad."

"Oh! He's here?"

"Obviously."

"Isn't it a bit chilly for him to be out? And he's on a fairground ride? He could fall off or anything!"

Nessa sighed in exasperation. "It's a kids' ride, Henry, and he's really not that frail. You know—"

"Don't, Ness."

"Don't what?"

"Don't say it."

She took a bite of gingerbread and crunched noisily, which was as good as saying it. *Ask Grandad to make your cake.* It was bad enough that *that woman* had stolen his grandad's business... well, she hadn't. If Henry's dad hadn't been such a let-down, or if his grandad had been less stubborn...because, in a way, he was no better than Margaret when it came to 'respecting tradition'. The world wouldn't have ended if *Henry Jones and Son* had become *Henry Jones and Daughter* or just *Henry Jones, Baker...*

"Looks like we're ready for lift-off," Daniel said.

"He's on his way over," Nessa said.

"Can I have a toffee appley now, Mummy?" Kira said.

Henry only vaguely heard them. Only vaguely noticed his grandad come to stand next to him. Only vaguely saw the fireworks.

Don't make problems, create solutions. That's what his boss said, pretty much every day. Cheesy, yes, but Henry liked his job. It paid well, and he'd already had one promotion.

"Dan?"

The crowd *oooooohed.*

"Mmm?"

And the crowd *aaaahed.*

"I want to go self-employed."

"Doing?"

"*Henry Jones, Baker, est. 1874.*"

A rocket spluttered and launched, and Henry and Daniel watched it shoot high into the sky.

"She's really upset you, hasn't she?"

"Yep, and maybe it's a stupid idea. I mean, I don't know anything about baking."

Above them, the rocket loudly exploded in a shower of red sparks.

"But you know a man who does," Daniel said, peering past Henry and then right at him as he sought out his hand and gave it an encouraging squeeze. "Go for it."

Henry nodded, grateful for Daniel's support. Drawing a long, shaky breath, he pivoted to face the man on his other side. "Grandad?"

"Aye, lad?"

"Are you busy?"

A deep, bushy-browed frown was his answer.

Henry chuckled, suddenly full of nerves, and crossed his fingers. "I've got a favour to ask. Well, two, actually…"

TRICYCLE, ICYCLE

The Following Winter... Christmas Eve

D*O WHAT YOU do best.*

So said Henry's grandad a year ago to the day as he handed Henry a small, red-foil-wrapped box that gave a metallic rattle when he shook it. Inside: a large bunch of mismatched keys held together by a ring the size of a bangle.

The keys to the bakery.

Henry's bakery.

No going back. Definitely not after Margaret changed the sign on her shop so it read:

THE Village Bakery & Grocery
Home of the Banton Bun

Not THE Banton Bun, mind you—Margaret doesn't have the Joneses' secret family recipe—but a reasonable approximation.

As for Henry doing what he does best... Henry Jones the Ninth is no baker, that's for sure. He wouldn't even know how to assemble a Banton Bun, let alone bake one. But he *does* know his way around computers, accounts, managing staff and stock inventory. And he rides a mean tricycle.

You might wonder how that could be a good thing. Read on, and all will be revealed.

***

"Have you seen?"

Henry slapped his hand down on the paperwork to anchor it against the icy gust that rushed into the bakery—along with a pink, panting Nessa—and set the Christmas tree bead strings into a wave of tsunami proportions. Nessa whipped her umbrella shut, javelined it into the stand and frivolously kicked the door with her heel. The force wasn't quite enough to shut it—luckily.

Mrs. Broughton was a step behind her and whinnied, pulled up short by the obstruction between her and her weekly egg—*free range, of course*—custard tart. Nessa didn't appear to notice and scurried around the end of the counter, unfastening and pulling off her coat on her way past Henry.

"Have I seen wh—"

"*Not now!*" she hissed, disappearing out back then reappearing a second later, still pink and panting, with her *Henry Jones, Baker, est. 1874* apron dangling from her neck, hands labouring at her back and a big, false smile for their customer. "Good morning, Mrs. B. How are you today?" She side-eyed a further warning for Henry to keep his mouth shut until they were on their own.

"Oh, you know how it is." Mrs. Broughton wearily rubbed her left wrist and then her right with gnarled old fingers sporting freshly manicured, glittery red nails. Evidently, the bakery wasn't her first stop of the morning.

"Your arthritis giving you trouble, is it?" Nessa simpered. No time to waste on small talk when she had gossip to impart, she tugged a brown paper—*recycled, it goes without saying*—bag free of the hemp string and flicked it open.

"It is, love," Mrs. Broughton lamented. "Still, it's to be expected with the damp and the cold." She glowered in disapproval.

Henry peered out the front window at the drizzly gloom. "Snow's on its way," he mused aloud.

"Don't say that!" Mrs. Broughton chastised, aghast.

"According to the—ouch!" Nessa stamped on his toes. "BBC," he finished obstinately.

"Aye, well, what do they know about the weather?"

"The Met Office too—ow!" Henry inhaled sharply at the stamp on his other foot and shut up for good this time. Not his snowflakes, not his blizzard.

Nessa raised the serving tongs and crocodile-snapped the air. "One or two-tart day today, Mrs. B.?"

"Two, please. I have to entertain the Reverend Osbourne this afternoon." She patted her hair and honked out a heavy sigh. "I could do without the rigmarole on Christmas Eve, I must confess."

Nessa muted a snort and got to transferring two egg custards from glass cabinet to bag. Henry cleared his throat and faked concentrating on his paperwork. Better Mrs. Broughton think them rude than realise they were laughing, although not at her, or not *just* at her. Most of the older village folk thought their young vicar, with his long hair and love of rock music, was a lout. If only they took the time to get to know him, they'd realise what a lovely guy he was. Well, Henry thought so. Nessa just wanted to get into his pants.

Mrs. Broughton had a soft spot for him too, regardless of her 'could do without the rigmarole' of the manicure and, Henry observed, new hairdo. She was the long-standing, completely unbudgeable and somewhat dictatorial leader of the Parish Council, of which Margaret Sharpe had been secretary until a few months ago. Suffice to say, she now knew why Mrs. Broughton—and other members—had stopped buying cakes from THE Village Bakery, and it had nothing to do with calorie-counting or diabetes.

Nessa twisted the corners of the paper bag and set it on the counter. "Anything else, Mrs. B.?"

"No, that's it, love. How much do I owe you?" She clicked open her purse and tinkled the loose change inside.

"Two pounds twenty, please."

"Have they gone up again?" They hadn't, as well Mrs. Broughton knew, but she had to say it. Every week. "Eeeeee, I don't know how they expect us to live on a pittance of a pension, cost of living being what it is and all. Here, love. I can't get hold of the little so-and-sos with these nails."

Without warning, she upended her purse. Nessa swooped in with a well-aimed palm and caught most of the coins before they hit the glass top of the cake cabinet. A two-pence piece bounced off and rolled across the floor, coming to a stop next to Henry's bruised toes. He retrieved it and rose to return it to their customer.

"Stick it in the Sally Army tin, love," Mrs. Broughton ordained, clicking her purse shut and zipping her coat right up under her chin, creating a dimple in her crinkles, but at least she'd be warm. She gathered her wares. "I'll be off, then. A Merry Christmas to you."

"And to you," Henry called.

"Yeah, and you, Mrs. B." Nessa wide-eye-watched her all the way to the door, which she fought with a fierce determination when the wind flung it open and refused to relinquish its hold. Nessa dashed over to help and, between them, they managed to put wood back in t'hole before Mrs. Broughton set off at a fair old speed.

Nessa gave a conspiratorial glance up and down the high street before she returned to the counter. "Soooo…" she said, eyebrows arched to embellish the suspense.

Henry nonchalantly dropped the tuppence into the Shelter—not Salvation Army—collection tin and straightened the paper bags. "So?"

"You haven't seen it?"

"Depends."

"On?"

"What you're talking about."

"The notice."

He shrugged. "Outside the camping shop?"

Now is the winter
Of our discount tents

Henry thought it was hilarious.

"Not *that* one," Nessa said. "On the noticeboard?"

"Good place for it," Henry quipped. Nessa folded her arms and glared. Henry grinned. "No, I haven't seen *the notice*. Not that I know of."

"Well!" Nessa unfolded her arms again and rubbed her hands in glee, back on track with the juicy gossip. She went over to the coffee jug. "Is this fresh?" she asked, already pouring a cup.

"Made just before you got here," Henry confirmed.

She turned to face him, sipped coffee, smacked her lips. Either she was building up to something big or was worried about his reaction. Still he refused to prompt her further and instead reached for his paperwork, his fingers grazing the top sheet as she finally relented.

"Hold that," she said and thrust her cup at him so she could get her phone from her pocket. "I took a photo of it on my way out."

"Out of where?"

"The village hall."

"Is playschool on today?"

"If it's not, Marky'll be sitting on his lonesome for the morning." She unlocked the screen, and they did a quick, awkward swap of items.

She'd taken one of those pictures that refused to stay upright, and Henry had to hold the phone at a jaunty angle, with his head tipped to the side, to read the notice. He didn't even make it past the headline before his stomach did a somersault. "No way." He shoved Nessa's phone back at her. "No. Way!"

"We'll easily win," she goaded.

"We won't, because we're not entering."

"Why not?"

"Are you kidding me?"

"Friendly competition…"

"Friendly? Remember the Easter Bonnets? I told you it was too soon."

"We were more than ready to take her on."

"I don't *want* to take her on!" Henry snapped.

“Really?” Nessa questioned. “Because that’s not how it looks. OK, I know we’re *artisan* and *catering for a different demographic*—” he couldn’t believe she’d air-quoted at him—twice! “—but *you* re-opened the bakery.”

“Yep, and have you noticed she’s gone all ‘free range, organic’ la-de-dah? She doesn’t give a hoot about ethical sourcing or hens’ well-being. She’s just an out-and-out copycat.” Henry picked up his pile of papers, tapped them to straighten them, put them down again and propped his hand on his hip.

Beside him, Nessa took a breath and paused, as if she were considering saying more, but merely huffed a, “Fine, whatever,” and stormed out the back.

That was where she stayed for the next three hours, only emerging to help in the busy periods. Henry was surprised so many villagers had braved the increasingly bleak weather to pick up a Christmas Eve treat—weather which, sooner rather than later, he was going to have to brave himself. He still needed to get out with the deliveries.

By twelve-thirty, when he could stand the dramatic thumps and bangs no more, he prepared a peace offering of leek and potato—*vegan, locally sourced*—soup plus a couple of sourdough—*baked in-house*—rolls and tentatively approached the kitchen, loitering in the doorway to watch his cousin’s purposeful march back and forth with sundry items, all destined for the delivery trailer. She slotted three French batons into a corner and made brief eye contact, her scowl still firmly in place.

“I’ve brought lunch,” he said, holding it up as evidence.

“Thanks.” She marched off to the storeroom—*bang, clatter, grunt*—and returned with four jars of cranberry jelly. Into the trailer they went.

“Will I be in your way if—”

“No.”

He was in the way simply by being there. To avoid upsetting her further, he dodged around the centre island to the microwave and stayed with it while the soup warmed, pretending to look around the room when he was watching Nessa, yet over those few moments, his focus shifted and he started thinking about the kitchen instead. He'd felt more welcome there as a mischievous kid getting in his grandad's way than he did now, and not just because of Nessa's mood, which was still icier than the chilly December afternoon.

He missed the baking. It wasn't like it didn't happen, but it didn't happen while he was on the premises. By eight a.m., when Henry arrived, the baker was done, leaving only dozens of loaves lined up on the racks and the residual heat of the ovens. At this time of year, he appreciated the warmth, especially first thing; come spring and summer, it was…well, like an oven.

For all that Henry's name was above the door, it wasn't his bakery, and not because—secretly—he and Nessa were equal partners. Henry could manage staff, do the accounts, cash up, clean up, take care of the deliveries, but when it came to the real work—baking bread and serving customers—he was clueless. It hadn't troubled him until today.

Until Nessa showed him that notice.

"I'm done," she mumbled and flopped sulkily onto a stool. "What soup is it?"

"Leek and potato." The microwave pinged and he removed the bowl, shoving it in front of her. "Here." He edged past and out of the kitchen.

"Are you not having any?" she called.

"Nope." Yanking his coat from the hook, he struggled into it on his way back. "Not hungry. I'm gonna get the deliveries out before it gets any colder." *Hat on, gloves…*

"Where's your helmet?"

…delivery chits… "Can't wear it with a hat."

"Henry—" The rumble of the rising bay door cut off her warning.

Henry lugged the trailer out into the yard, calling, "See you later," through the slowly diminishing gap as the door rolled shut.

***

All right, let's take stock here. We've got a loaded trailer, a Henry agitated to the point of recklessness, icy roads and a tricycle. That, folks, is what we call an accident waiting to happen. And the thing is, Henry's not really angry with Nessa. If she hadn't told him about the contest, someone else would've done. Indeed, by the time he's done with this fateful Christmas Eve (that's fateful, *not* fatal—one wedding and no funerals, I promise), almost everyone in Banton will have asked him if *Henry Jones, Baker, est. 1874* is doing it.

'Doing what?' you may ask. Well.

The clue's in the title, innit?

OK. Christmas Eve tricycling on ice. Are you sitting comfortably? Good, because Henry most definitely is not.

***

For the first hour or so—in spite of a slightly deflated back-left tyre and arm-ache from compensating for the subsequent veer gutterwards—Henry made good progress, fuelled by the systematic renewal of his annoyance each time he heard 'Have you seen the poster? Are you going to enter?' On the plus side, he got a pleasant surprise around the halfway point when he discovered the next address on the list was his own. Daniel had been watching through the front window and came out to help.

"Don't say it," Henry warned.

Daniel took the bags from him. "I wasn't going to say anything."

"We're not entering."

"We are talking about the Cake-Off, aren't we?"

Henry grunted and took off his hat to scratch his hot head. Tricycling with a fully loaded trailer was hard work. "You know whose idea that is, don't you?"

"It wasn't Margaret's," Daniel said.

"Pshure."

"Honestly. It's the talk of the village."

"Yeah, I noticed," Henry grumbled. "I can't wait to get finished today." He eyed the remaining six deliveries in his trailer. "So, who came up with that brilliance?"

"The vicar."

Henry was horrified. "You'd think he'd be encouraging his parishioners to get along, not forcing us to compete with each other."

"Did you actually read the poster, Hen?"

"Yes. Well…no. It was on Ness's phone—too small—but whatever. I saw enough. I'm not going up against Margaret Sharpe." With more force than was necessary, Henry pulled his hat on, scowling under the pressure both of the woollen band half-covering his eyes and Daniel's continued surveillance. "What?" he snapped and shoved the hat up his forehead.

"You wouldn't be going up *against* Margaret."

"That's exactly what I just said! No way are we entering that competition. Absolutely n— Wait. What did you say?"

"You're not going up against Margaret."

"Why not?"

"Because, my sweet, lovely, totally unflustered and entirely reasonable darling, it's an inter-village contest. Judging is at the County Fair on May Day."

"The County… An inter…" Henry's indignation diminished to soundless lip-flapping.

***

If he wasn't horrified before, he certainly is now. What's worse than competing against THE Village Bakery? Competing *with* them. Of course, he could just say no, but that wouldn't be much of a story, would it?

***

"No." Henry hurried into his gloves, and out of them again to get the requisite fingers in the requisite…fingers.

"Hen…" Daniel beseeched.

"Got to finish these deliveries." He planted a quick kiss on Daniel's chilled lips—"Home by five, love you"—straddled the trike and set off at a pace for his next drop.

Black ice.

Up ahead.

He didn't see it in time to avoid it, naturally. That's why it's called *black* ice. And if there's a positive to come out of this, the trike's brakes were as responsive as one could possibly hope for. Pity they didn't come with ABS.

Slam on, jackknifed trailer, headfirst over the handlebars...

Henry crumpled to the ground amid a grisly mess of French batons and cranberry jelly.

> *"Like severed limbs all over the road, it were," an eyewitness told the Banton Gazette.*
>
> *First on scene, Mrs. Margaret Sharpe [proprietor of THE Village Bakery] whose home is adjacent to the site of the accident, tended to the injured Mr. Jones and ~~smothered~~ wrapped him in blankets to keep him warm while awaiting the ambulance.*
>
> *Mr. Jones was later discharged by the hospital, into his fiancé's care, with cuts and bruises and a slight concussion. He [begrudgingly] expresses his gratitude to Mrs. Sharpe for ensuring he didn't get hypothermia and lived to celebrate another Christmas.*

FLIPPING OUT

Early Spring... Shrove Tuesday

"YOU'RE GETTING MARRIED *in four hours... Ding dong, the bells are gonna chime...*" Aunty Jen sang and sashayed into the bakery kitchen with another empty tray.

Henry covered his ears and grimaced. Jen nudged him with her hip, knocking his pencil out of his hand and onto the floor. Still humming her ditty, she picked up the pencil and returned it to him before repeating the same two tuneless lines as she filled the sink with scalding-hot water.

"Four more hours and you'll never have to listen to her dying-cat routine again," Nessa muttered as she passed Henry on her way to the pantry. "And we're nearly out of crêpes." She disappeared from view, reappearing less than thirty seconds later, clutching a cellophane-wrapped tray. "This is the last dozen."

"It's not even lunchtime," Henry pointed out, already mentally running through the options. Yes, he and Daniel were getting married today—the anniversary of the day they came out, together, to their families, which, *coincidentally*, had fallen on Shrove Tuesday and did *not*, in any way, symbolise their enduring mutual love of pancakes—but not for another four, pancake-less hours. "What are we going to do?"

"We'll just have to send people to Margaret's," Nessa suggested, quickly retreating to the shop.

Henry didn't want to do that. He didn't suppose Nessa did either, but what choice did they have? Henry's last attempt at pancakes was basically scrambled eggs, Nessa didn't have time in between serving customers, and there was no point even asking Aunty Jen. She'd only come to collect serving dishes—she'd sworn she'd never set foot in the bakery again—but instead was helping out and intermittently torturing Henry through the medium of song.

She turned towards him, drying the tray. "Are you going home soon?"

"How can I? We sold out of Scotch pancakes by ten o'clock this morning. Now we're nearly out of crêpes. It's a disaster! The pancake apocalypse!"

Aunty Jen laughed. "Well, at least you'll know for next year."

"If we're still in business. *She's* going to steal all our customers, and win the Cake-Off, and probably get an OBE for her contribution to the industry. *And* I let her have exclusive selling rights on the Banton Bun. It's so unfair."

"Oh, Henry." Aunty Jen's laughter had gone full-belly. "I think you might be making a bit of a mountain out of a molehill, but you know, it's not too late to join forces."

"With that…that *cutthroat*? After what she did last Easter? Never!"

***

The previous year…

Easter Saturday: a grand day for an opening! Spring had sprung spectacularly. The sun shone, birds sang, and Henry and Nessa had everything they needed for their Easter Bonnet competition. Or *not really* a competition. There were prizes for *all* the children, a free taster buffet with wine for the adults…

…and the proprietor of THE Village Bakery was livid. LIVID, I tells ya. Oh, she'd heard the gossip; she only had to step out of her premises to see the preparations taking place a few yards along the high street. But she'd refused to believe it, even when Henry told her to her face—

"I'm re-opening my grandad's business. Artisan bread and pastries, organic, free-range ingredients sourced from local producers. Rest assured, Mrs. Sharpe, I have no intention of competing with you."

—until the day came when she could deny it no longer.

On Easter Saturday, to Margaret Sharpe's tremendous chagrin, Henry Jones the Ninth opened the doors on *Henry Jones, Baker, est. 1874*, providing the commuter-belt village of Banton, population: 1,500, for the first time ever, with a choice of where to buy their daily bread.

Villagers flocked from far and wide (OK, not very far and not very wide, it's not *that* big a village) to taste Henry the Hipster's fantastic new baked goods while a mardy-faced Margaret watched on from the doorway of her deserted shop. There was nothing else for it.

She bustled back inside and got straight on the phone to Mr. Sharpe, putting him immediately to work on the new signage, but the icing on the cake—a poor pun in the circumstances, I appreciate—was her answer to Henry and Nessa's Easter Bonnet and Buffet.

Complimentary chocolate egg
with every Easter Saturday purchase
if accompanied by child

"It's a free market," Margaret later defended to Henry's Aunty Jen (who, incidentally, has a Master's degree in economics and is also a bit nifty with a frying pan and a gallon of pancake batter—relevant but problematic, as we shall see).

"Free market, my arse," said Jen, eloquently, like the scholar she is.

"Simple supply and demand, *Ms. Jones*. The invisible hand ensures resources are allocated efficiently. Banton is too small to sustain two bakeries—"

"Just as well, *Mrs. Sharpe*, because my visible hands are going to wring your visible bloody neck."

***

"What d'you think you're doing?"

The bakery back door swung wide open. Henry and Aunty Jen stopped talking and stared at their visitor like headlight-illuminated wildlife.

Tick, tock, tick, tock,
Just a lil ol' clock,
I'm here all the time,
But these seconds are mine.
Tick, tock, TICK, TOCK!

"I, um…" Henry fidgeted and almost toppled off his stool. "Hello, Grandad."

"Never mind that. Why are you here?"

"Why wouldn't I be?"

Grandad raised his arm with slow deliberation, squinted at his watch and nodded. "Tuesday. Thought so."

Henry chuckled nervously. His grandad was a sarcastic sod when the mood took.

"Get yourself off home, lad. Even I took us wedding day off."

Aunty Jen's mouth fell open. "You lying swine!"

"What do *you* know? You weren't there."

"Don't believe a word of it," Jen said to Henry. "He told your gran she could set any date she liked as long as it was a Wednesday."

Grandad shoved his hands in his trouser pockets and gave a little shrug. "Aye. Half-day closing. No point wasting it."

"See?" Henry grinned smugly.

"Oh, I see, all right," Jen said. "Two stubborn buggers called Henry."

Nessa reappeared with the tray she'd taken through not two minutes ago, now empty. "Comes with the name, I reckon."

"Listen," Henry interjected as firmly as he dared. "I can't go anywhere till we've figured out what to do about the crêpes."

"Crêpes?"

"Pancakes, Grandad."

"I'm well aware, lad. What about 'em?"

"We've run out," Nessa said.

"So make some more."

"Ah. Well." Henry cleared his throat. "I don't know how."

"What kind of baker doesn't know how to make a pancake?" Before Henry could answer—and 'you don't bake pancakes, you fry them' would have done him no favours anyway—Grandad nodded at Aunty Jen. "She knows how."

"Who's she? The cat's mother?" Aunty Jen muttered and shook her head. "Sorry, Hen, I'm not making them—" she glowered at her dad "—on *principle*."

Grandad grunted. "For goodness' sake. That again? It's not as if he's asking you to run the place."

"He wouldn't bloody dare, would he? Not with you sticking your oar in every five minutes."

"Oy! Watch your tone with me, young lady..."

Henry shrank as small as could be on his stool, but it was nowhere near small enough when not there at all would have been his ideal.

"Watch my tone?!" Jen yelled back, advancing on her father. "You're damn lucky I still talk to you at all. Our Susan had the right idea."

Nessa edged along the wall like a burglar and jerked her head to get Henry's attention, rolling her eyes meaningfully towards the back door. He nodded his understanding and made a run for it.

"This has been brewing for years," she said, once they were safely out in the courtyard where the argument was just as loud but with enough distance that neither could be dragged into it.

Henry sighed. "I know. But couldn't they have left it till *after* the wedding?"

"Maybe it'll clear the air a bit," Nessa placated, which was optimistic at best. And maybe it would—between Grandad and Aunty Jen, but not with Aunty Susan, who hadn't spoken to her dad in thirteen years. Then, of course, there was Henry's dad…

***

By now, it will come as no surprise when I tell you that Banton has always prided itself on being a traditional, tranquil little hamlet, a homogeneous, harmonious community of ordinary folk going about their ordinary lives. Henry Jones the Eighth hasn't been welcomed there since the Night of Fire and Dragons that brought shame upon his once well-respected family and resulted in the biggest upheaval in village history.

But take a fingernail to that veneer and scratch just a little beneath the surface, and what've we got?

Henry and Daniel—two young men in love whose families, supportive as they are, advised them to set up home in Anywhere But Banton.

Margaret—OK, her politics might be a bit skewed and her beliefs need a damn good shake-up, but let's give some credit where it's due. She's the *only* female proprietor on Banton High Street, fighting tooth and claw to keep her livelihood.

As for Henry's dad? Well, he wasn't the first Bantonion to go off the rails and he most likely won't be the last. Can we really lay the blame for all of this at his feet?

Idiot that he is, he's still had the good sense to keep his distance. So far…

***

"D'you think they've killed each other?" Henry whispered.

"Possible." Nessa cocked her ear. The fighting had stopped some time ago, and all was quiet. She hopped down from the back of the retired trike—still with buckled wheels—and crept towards the building, pausing at the kitchen door to listen. "I'm going in," she said.

"I'll cover you," Henry said.

"No, you won't. You need to go home and get ready."

"But the bakery—"

Nessa spun on the spot and bumped noses with him. She didn't back off, and neither did he. "My mum's right, you're as bad as Grandad."

"That's not very nice."

"It's the truth," Nessa contended.

Henry blinked and turned away, hurt by her words. He loved his grandad, looked up to him, but he wasn't blind to his faults, like his stupid sexism that led him to shut down the family business rather than hand it over to his daughters—the same sexism that had Henry and Nessa lying to the entire family. He was fed up with it—the lies, the constant battles with Margaret, all of it, and today of all days, the stress was too much.

Frustrated, upset, Henry couldn't help it; he started to cry. "I wish we hadn't bothered."

"With the pancakes?"

"Everything," he sniffled angrily.

Nessa appeared in front of him. "Ohh…Hen." Her expression softened, and she lugged him in for a hug. "I'm so sorry. I didn't mean to upset you."

"It's OK, it wasn't you," Henry wheezed within the squeeze. "I should've stood up to him, told him what we'd planned from the beginning. You're right. I am as bad as him."

"*Stubborn* as him," Nessa corrected.

"Not what you said."

"'s what I meant." She hugged him harder, sniffling a little herself. Henry was sure he was turning blue.

"Ness?"

"Yes, Hen?"

"Can't breathe."

She laugh-cried and released him, straightening his shirt front out of habit. He wiped his eyes on his sleeve and attempted a smile. She kissed his cheek. "It's not all bad, Hen. Really. Just an emotional day. When you get back from your honeymoon, we should have a business meeting, work out what we're going to do, yes?"

"Yes," Henry said.

"In the meantime, I can handle this—them—so *please* go and get ready for your wedding."

"Fine. I'll go…just as soon as I know everything's OK here."

"I swear to God…" Nessa hissed but didn't stop him from following her in, though they barely made it through the door before both tumbled to a halt in time to watch their grandad give a sharp flick of the wrist, send a pancake several feet into the air and then effortlessly catch it in the pan.

Returning it to the stove, he acknowledged Henry and Nessa with a nod. "All right, you two?"

"You made all those while we were outside?" Henry asked, indicating the tray next to the stove. It held at least a dozen pancakes.

"Aye, lad."

"Where's Mum?" Nessa asked.

"Out front, manning the counter." Grandad slid the cooked pancake onto the tray and poured more batter into the pan. "Womanning the counter," he corrected. "I heard you, by the way. What you were talking about in the yard."

Henry and Nessa both mouthed an *oh* and dipped their heads.

"It's hard for you young'uns to understand, but I did what I had to—what I thought was right. As you know, my dad took over this place after the war. He was the same age as you, near as damn it—" he glanced at Henry, paused to flip the pancake, and continued "—and he didn't want it. He'd not long married my mother, and they'd planned to emigrate, but his mother and aunt insisted, said they hadn't kept the bakery going during the war just for him to sell up and ship out. So he did as he was told, and made sure the world knew how bloody miserable he was into the bargain."

Another pancake made, more batter into the pan.

"It was the same for me when he died. Hobson's Choice. I was happy enough, though, fulfilling my obligations, but I didn't want to put that same pressure on my son. I let him do his own thing." The pancake flip was less enthusiastic this time, lifting only enough to turn it over. "At eighteen, I was in bed by seven, in here by three in the morning, six days a week." Grandad sighed, deep and wistful. "I should've brought him in, got him working. It'd have kept him on the straight and narrow."

"You don't know that," Henry said. "Not for sure."

"No, I suppose not." Grandad slid the pancake onto the tray with the rest. "Here, lad. Your turn."

"Oh! Um…" Henry looked to Nessa in panic and could've thumped her when she just nodded in encouragement. "But I'm getting married in…eek! Two hours!"

With that, Henry dashed from the bakery, not even stopping to gather his belongings. As the door shut behind him, he heard Nessa say, "Nice one, Grandad. I thought he was never going to leave!"

***

While Henry races home to prepare for his suddenly impending nuptials, let's review, briefly, the Jones' family dynamic, because there are an awful lot of hesitant Henrys in there. Indeed, it would seem that Henry incumbent is the first to have willingly taken the oven gloves—so to speak—since the original *Henry Jones and Son, Baker.*

One might expect, given young Henry's sense of displacement and minor feelings of baking-related inadequacy, he'd have leapt at the opportunity to pick up a few tricks of the trade from his grandad, as opposed to legging it—a snap decision he's regretting already and he's only just turned off the high street.

As for Nessa…well, she's certainly got her head screwed on, hasn't she? I suspect it comes from being the eldest of the four cousins and a single mum to boot. No real drama there—just one of those 'wasn't meant to be' situations—which is as well when the Joneses as a whole could benefit from a few group sessions with their local therapist (great guy, incidentally, though he wouldn't thank me for the recommendation).

Now, up to this point, Nessa's stayed out of family politics. Sure, she takes after her mother, and doesn't shy away from saying it like it is, but she's more peacekeeper than warrior, which is why she agreed to keep quiet about the bakery joint venture…

…until after the wedding.

Yep. In a few hours, it'll all be over bar the shouting, but even waiting that long is getting to be a stretch. Nessa's old enough to remember the fallout between her mum, Aunty Susan and Grandad. Crucially, she's old enough to remember the party her grandparents threw to celebrate Uncle Henry's release from prison…and their disappointment when he showed no signs of remorse or reform. Never mind that both daughters graduated with honours, successfully pursued careers, set up homes and are caring, responsible parents. If there had been any expectations made of them, they would surely have surpassed every last one.

Sadly, the only thing that ever mattered was handing down the bakery from father to son, father to son, even though Henry Jones the Eighth is still an idiot who never accepts responsibility for his actions and makes promises he can't possibly keep, like, for instance, saying he won't cause trouble at his son's wedding when his mere presence will provoke a kick-off of epic proportions.

Poor young Henry. His mind has been in turmoil since he fled the bakery, his steps becoming slower the closer he gets to home. He wants to get married. He really does, but…

***

"I wish we'd eloped." Henry pushed the front door shut with his bottom and sighed so heavily his back crackled like popcorn.

Daniel appeared, fastening his shirt cuffs, at the top of the stairs. "What did you say?"

"Why didn't we elope? Or better still, never move back here in the first place?"

"Ah." Daniel nodded knowingly. "Are you coming up or shall I come down?"

Henry shook his head and pushed away from the door, using the momentum to climb the stairs. He stopped in front of his husband-to-be and attempted a smile. "You look very handsome."

"Thank you. As do you, Mr. Bun the Baker, but we went to the trouble of buying these suits, so…" Daniel gestured grandly towards their bedroom. "This way, sir. I have something for you."

"Danny…" Henry groaned. He wasn't in the mood, but Daniel just laughed and grabbed his hand, pulling him along, straight past the bedroom to the bathroom. "Oh my…" Henry stared at the bath, then at Daniel, then back at the bath—not the scratched-enamel antiquity that had been there when he'd left for work that morning. "Where…? How…?"

"My wedding gift to you."

Henry smirked. "Just for me?"

Daniel tilted his head from side to side. "OK. For us. Later. I'll leave you to it." Delivering a quick kiss to Henry's cheek, he departed.

"I won't be long," Henry called after him, already tugging his shirt over his head and stamping his way out of his trousers, eager to submerge himself in the ocean-blue, decadently scented water. He oohed and hissed—it was a little on the warm side—as he settled against the back rest, experimentally poking at the closest button on the control panel and getting it right first time. The water erupted all around him in tickly bubbles that made him giggle. He heard an answering laugh from Daniel and closed his eyes, smiling as his earlier worries washed away.

ONE WEDDING (AS PROMISED)

Also Shrove Tuesday

Reverend Osbourne wasn't a dog collar, blazer and slacks kind of vicar. Black jeans were more his thing, accompanied by Converse boots and T-shirts that looked like heavy metal band merch until you got close enough to read the gothic text depicting the Word of the Lord. He was, legit, one of Jesus's biggest fans, and slowly but surely, he was winning over his parishioners... even if some of the older folk were still affronted by his rockin' style.

He wore the dog collar for services, of course, and when he was on official business. That he was wearing it to Henry and Daniel's wedding meant the world, but the twitch he'd developed from fighting the urge to tug it away from his neck had the two grooms on the brink of nervous giggles. At least, Henry was on the brink, and if he went, he'd take Daniel with him. So it had always been.

With the civil (in all meanings of the word, astonishingly) part of the ceremony done, the registrar stepped aside, and Reverend Osbourne moved forward to speak. Henry used the change-around to glance over his shoulder, quickly scanning the rows of guests. Emma—Daniel's twin sister—had been in charge of seating and had put literally months into coming up with the 'least combustible' arrangement.

To that end, Daniel's family—normal, sensible, got along famously—were all seated together, front-left, with his friends and select work colleagues behind, while Henry's clan—like a busload of E-number-high six-year-olds on a school trip—were dotted all over the show with the bakery staff and other friends forming sturdy people barriers between. His mum and Grandma Parker were at one end of the front row; Gran and Grandad Jones were at the other. Two rows behind them was Aunty Jen, along with Nessa's littluns; back another two rows were Aunty Susan, Uncle John and Henry's other cousins.

As for Henry's dad…

He was there, all right, and he'd put himself at the back of the room, though Henry wished more than anything his dad had forgotten or bottled out or whatever stopped him showing up to every previous event to which Henry had invited him. His suit was creased, he wore no tie, and he looked drunk. He always looked drunk, irrespective of whether he was.

A subtle nudge from Daniel reminded Henry where he was and why, and he turned to face front, focusing on Reverend Osbourne's patient smile and doing his best to ignore his almost (they had yet to sign the register) husband's frown.

"Daniel, Henry…" The reverend's smile broadened as he peered down on them for several seconds, then up and over them, at their guests. "Family and friends, it is my privilege to join you on this very special day."

As he did on Sunday mornings, the reverend spoke with clarity and slow deliberation, emphasising certain words—*privilege… special…*

"When Daniel and Henry first came to discuss their wedding with me, I'd been in Banton less than three months. They were the fifth couple with whom I'd met. Alas, they were the first I had to turn away.

"The Church is prevented by law from conducting weddings for people of the same sex, nor do the Bishops permit me to conduct a service of blessing for this wonderful union. But who would doubt the love these two young men share?"

Henry turned to Daniel, quite certain they had matching pink cheeks and silly wide grins.

Reverend Osbourne chuckled and held out his hands. "Love speaks for itself, does it not?"

Murmurs of agreement rumbled around the room like a distant, departing storm. The reverend waited for them to dissipate before he spoke again.

"Daniel and Henry have declared before you that they will live together, bonded by their love. They have made promises to each other and exchanged solemn vows. In a short while, they will formalise their commitment under English law. They have also chosen to mark their commitment to each other with prayer."

Henry and Daniel, still with hands clasped, bowed their heads, and an incredible silence filled the room. Not a whisper was heard, not even from the children.

"Loving and gracious God, who made us in your image and sent your son Jesus Christ to welcome us home; protect us in love and empower us for service. Through the power of the Holy Spirit, may Daniel and Henry become living signs of his love, and may we uphold them in the promises that each make this day, through Jesus Christ our Lord. Amen."

"Amen."

"Jesus told us to 'Love the Lord your God with all your heart, with all your soul, with all your strength and with all your mind' and 'love your neighbour as yourself'. For the love that we receive and give let us all thank God, saying together…

"Almighty God, source of all being, we thank you for your love, which creates and sustains us. We thank you for the physical and emotional expression of that love; and for the blessings of companionship and friendship. We pray that we may use your gifts so that we can ever grow into a deeper understanding of love and of your purpose for us, through Jesus Christ, our Lord. Amen."

"A reading from 1 Corinthians 13, verses one to thirteen:

"I may be able to speak the languages of human beings and even of angels, but if I have no love, my speech is no more than a noisy gong or a clanging bell. I may have the gift of inspired preaching; I may have all knowledge and understand all secrets; I may have all the faith needed to move mountains—but if I have no love, I am nothing. I may give away everything I have, and even give up my body to be burnt—but if I have no love, this does me no good.

"Love is patient and kind; it is not jealous or conceited or proud; love is not ill-mannered or selfish or irritable; love does not keep a record of wrongs; love is not happy with evil, but is happy with the truth. Love never gives up; and its faith, hope, and patience never fail.

"Love is eternal. There are inspired messages, but they are temporary; there are gifts of speaking in strange tongues, but they will cease; there is knowledge, but it will pass. For our gifts of knowledge and of inspired messages are only partial; but when what is perfect comes, then what is partial will disappear.

"When I was a child, my speech, feelings, and thinking were all those of a child; now that I have grown up, I have no more use for childish ways. What we see now is like a dim image in a mirror; then we shall see face to face. What I know now is only partial; then it will be complete—as complete as God's knowledge of me.

"Meanwhile these three remain: faith, hope, and love; and the greatest of these is love.

"This is the word of the Lord."

"Thanks be to God."

"Daniel and Henry…"

Henry was immediately attentive and returned Daniel's earlier nudge accompanied by a knowing smile. The Scriptures always transported Daniel to some other place, a different level of consciousness. He blinked several times, as if waking from a nap, and mouthed an apology at Henry and the reverend. Henry thought his heart might burst from how much he loved this man.

"Daniel and Henry," Reverend Osbourne repeated, finally securing the attention of both. "Will you be to each other a companion in joy and a comfort in times of trouble, and will you give each other opportunity for love to deepen?"

"We will, with God's help."

"Will you, Daniel, give yourself to Henry, sharing your love and your life, your wholeness and your brokenness, your success and your failure?

"I will."

"Will you, Henry, give yourself to Daniel, sharing your love and your life, your wholeness and your brokenness, your success and your failure?"

"I will."

"Jesus, our brother, inspire Daniel and Henry in their lives together, that they may come to live for one another and serve each other in true humility and kindness. Through their lives may they welcome each other in times of need and in their hearts may they celebrate together in their times of joy, for your name's sake. Amen."

"Amen."

"Let us say together…Our Father, *who art in Heaven…*"

The mass of voices swelled and merged like the balls of dough Henry's grandad used to leave to prove, the resulting bread rolls often bearing tiny dents where naughty Henry had poked his finger. He'd been a little monster, far worse than Nessa's two. But today, he wasn't the poker; he was one of Reverend Osbourne's bread rolls, squishing into Daniel, and when they were baked, nothing would ever tear them apart.

That was marriage. That was baking. That was Henry, daydreaming his way through The Lord's Prayer.

"…the power and the glory, for ever and ever, Amen."

"Spirit of God, you teach us through the example of Jesus that love is the fulfilment of the Law. Help Daniel and Henry to persevere in love, to grow in mutual understanding, and to deepen their trust in each other; that in wisdom, patience and courage, their life together may be a source of happiness to all with whom they share it; and the blessing of God Almighty, Creator, Redeemer and Sustainer be upon you to guide and protect you and all those you love, today and always. Amen."

"Amen."

"Heavenly Father, we are your children, made in your image. Hear our prayer that fathers and mothers, sons and daughters, may find together the perfect love that casts out fear, walk together in the way that leads to eternal life, and grow up together into the full humanity of your Son, Jesus Christ our Lord. Amen."

"Amen."

***

"No apology needed! Thanks so much for coming." Daniel embraced his departing colleague side on. The small fractious baby in her arms screamed louder still.

"Thank you for inviting me. The ceremony was lovely, as was the reception, apart from…" The woman smiled apologetically and rubbed her child's back. "He's colicky."

"Aww, poor mite," Daniel cooed. He liked babies and flat-out *adored* Nessa's kids. They'd have their own someday.

"Now, if the gift's wrong…" the woman began.

"I'm sure it's perfect!"

"I have the receipt if it's not. See you in two weeks."

Henry and Daniel waved as she departed, and Henry rubbed his ear. "That baby could be the next town crier," he said.

Daniel nodded and laughed. A couple of other guests were getting ready to go, but Henry's attention was on Nessa. He'd spotted her at the bar a while ago, and she kept glancing to see if they were free. They were, so she was on her way over. "Hey, cuz," Henry greeted.

"Hey. You two OK for drinks?"

They both nodded and reached for their glasses at the same time. Nessa rolled her eyes.

"Soooo…did you see her?"

"Who?"

"Margaret."

"Where?" Henry made a quick, panicked search of the room.

"Not now, you nutter. After the service. In the foyer?"

"Really? What's she even doing here?"

Nessa shrugged. "There's a Chamber of Commerce meeting this evening. Maybe she's here for that."

"Or she was trying to sneak a peek at our wedding cake..." Henry was ever suspicious of Margaret Sharpe's intentions. He looked over to the top tables, where his mum and grandma were *still* admiring the three-tier white and silver cake, although he'd been as bad. On this occasion, he resisted the temptation to take photos...more photos...of it. They'd only start on him again if he went anywhere near.

***

Henry can dilly-dally all he likes, but at some point soon, he and Daniel will have to make that inaugural cut. After all, what's the point in having their cake and *not* eating it? His reluctance is understandable, though, for it is a stunning creation. True, the icing is patchy in places, and some of those swirls are a bit on the wobbly side, but from a distance, no-one would know. Or no-one but Henry.

Yes, he's stubborn and fussy and often gets worked up over little things he can do nothing about, but he knows his grandad struggled this time, even if he's doing a sterling job of hiding it. And he knows Nessa is worried what will happen to the bakery after Grandad's gone—what if he's left the building to Henry's dad? (It would be disastrous, that's what, but he's not popping his clogs on my watch, so we can safely forget about it for now...or can we?)

Henry also knows this is probably the last wedding cake his grandad will make.

Which is sad.

So sad.

Still, if nothing else, it's something for the village annals:

> *The last 'Henry Jones' wedding cake was made by Henry the Seventh on the occasion of his grandson's marriage to Daniel Miller, which was also Banton's first same-sex marriage.*

***

"You know what? I hope she did see our cake—in fact, I'm going to take her a piece." Henry finished his champagne in one big gulp and handed his glass to Daniel.

"What…you're doing that now?" Nessa's horror was clear to see, but no, he didn't mean right now.

"You can take it round there tomorrow if you like. Come on." Without further ado, Henry marched off, expecting Nessa to follow. She didn't.

"What are you doing?" she called after him, then asked Daniel, "What's he doing?"

"Not sure."

Henry sighed and went back.

Daniel grimaced. "Uh-oh. I know that look."

"She's brought this on herself," Henry said. "Are you coming?" This time, he hooked his arm around Nessa's, and she could easily have pulled away but instead went willingly, more or less.

"You're not going to do something silly, are you?"

"I don't plan to. I had an idea."

"OK?"

"Wedding cakes."

"Whoa." Nessa tugged on his arm, effectively putting on the brakes. "I'm sure we already discussed this. We can't afford to employ another baker."

"But we could if we took on an apprentice."

Nessa's brow creased, but the frown was gone before it fully formed. She was considering it. "Who'll train them? Our bakers are bread specialists—"

Henry nodded slowly, leaving her to figure it out in her own time.

"—and none of us know the first thing about cake decorating. Even if we managed to talk my mum into helping us out more, she can't do fancy cakes. We'd need an artist like Granda…doh."

Henry beamed. "Yes!"

"No, Hen. We'd have to tell him about…" She wiggled her finger between them.

"I know. It's time, Ness."

"Are you insane? It's your wedding day!"

"You were going to tell him after the wedding anyway. I'm actually surprised you haven't told him already."

Nessa shook her head in denial, but she couldn't fool Henry. He'd felt her bristling when Grandad was narrating the bakery's history, like they hadn't heard it a dozen times before, and it always ended the same way—Grandad's guilt for how Henry's dad turned out, with absolutely no acknowledgement of his brilliant daughters, who had succeeded in spite of him.

It wasn't Henry's dad he'd failed, it was Aunty Jen and Aunty Susan, and the only way Henry and Nessa could make him see sense was to prove to him how successful *their* bakery was. So successful, in fact, they'd sold two gross pancakes in under four hours, and that wasn't a one-off. But, of course, Nessa had been set on getting Henry to go home and get ready for his wedding, so she'd let the opportunity pass.

"It's been such a lovely day, Hen. Don't ruin it now."

No need for her to worry on that score.

"Oh, no." Henry closed his eyes, counted to five, and opened them again, whispering to Nessa, "I thought he'd left after the ceremony."

"Apparently not."

(Henry's dad at two o'clock—directionally. Chronologically, it's closer to seven.)

Henry's dad halted but kept his distance.

"Hello, Henry," he said.

"Dad," Henry said.

Awkward shoe-gazing and feet-shuffling ensued, and neither spoke for several seconds. Indeed, their entire relationship may well have ended in goodbyes right then and there, were it not for Nessa's intervention.

"How are you, Uncle Henry? You're looking well."

Henry the younger peeped through his eyelashes and had to agree. Aside from the crumpled suit, his dad seemed healthier—and happier—than ever.

"Yeah?" Henry's dad's smile was so genuine it were as if he'd never smiled before. "Thanks, Vanessa."

"Just Nessa," she corrected. "Or Ness."

"Sorry. I…" He stuffed his hands in his pockets and shrugged, so much like Grandad. "I'm sorry if I offended you."

"You didn't," she assured him, which was a blatant lie. Even when they were arguing, Henry wouldn't dare call her Vanessa. She hated it.

"So…um…Henry?"

Henry nodded and looked up, at once captured by blue eyes too familiar, in his peripheral vision the same brown hair, pointy ears, squodgy noses—his reflection eighteen years into the future.

"Have you enjoyed your day?"

Henry nodded again and found his tongue. "Yes, I have. The happiest of my life."

There was that smile again. "I'm glad. You deserve it."

"Thanks, Dad. I…um…didn't realise you were still here."

"Your sister-in-law's been taking care of me." He glanced around him, a bit shifty-like.

"You escaped, didn't you?" Nessa said with a chuckle.

Henry's dad grimaced and turned pink. "I told her I needed a slash. I mean, I do, and I'll get going soon, but I couldn't leave without speaking to my son." He met Henry's gaze again. "I'd like to meet Daniel at some point, if it's all right with you."

Decision time.

Henry looked over at Daniel—watching them, expression pensive—and then at his grandad—also watching them, pretending he wasn't—and finally at Nessa.

"I'll talk to Grandad," she said.

Henry sighed, part relief, part nervousness, and kissed her cheek. "Thanks, cuz."

She waved him away and strode off, full of confidence and purpose; Henry watched to make sure she safely made it to Grandad (because a hotel function room is a terribly treacherous terrain to traverse) and beckoned to his dad, leading the way back to Daniel, who immediately straightened and fixed a smile over his mild surprise.

"Mr. Jones," he said and extended his hand.

"Mr. Jones?" said Henry's dad, accepting the handshake. "That's my dad. And my dad's dad, and his dad…" He laughed and gave Henry a sideways glance, as anxious as Henry was himself. "My mates call me Jonesy. Would that be weird?"

"Yes," Daniel said. "Yes, it would."

"Right." Henry's dad sucked his teeth and shrugged. "Mr. Jones it is, then. Good to meet you, son-in-law." He put his arm around Henry's shoulders and grinned. "You landed a good'un here, lad. A right chip off the old block."

Daniel eyed Henry in alarm. Somewhere out of line of sight, Aunty Susan muttered—quite loudly, "Chip off the old block? Is he having a laugh?"

Henry's dad's grin drooped, along with his arm. "So, Daniel, what do you do?"

"Job, you mean? I'm a teacher."

"Yeah?"

"Yes…primary school…" Daniel's eyes strayed past Henry and his dad to what was going on behind them. (Short version: The War of The Joneses.) "The local primary school. How about you, Mr. Jones? What do you do?"

"Maintenance technician at the Clayworks."

"Oh, wow." Daniel raised his voice to be heard over the din. "I bet that's interesting." He was just making it up as he went along. "And hard work."

"It can be. I'm on the nightshift—that's the only time the kilns aren't operating, but they're still bloody hot…" Henry's dad fell silent—one of his acid flashbacks, perhaps—while the racket behind them escalated to the point of being impossible to ignore.

With much dread and a fair idea of the sight that would greet him, Henry turned around.

"…just waltzes in here like he didn't destroy this family while you—" Aunty Susan pointed at Grandad accusingly "—welcome him like the prodigal bloody son."

"Sue," Aunty Jen calmly beseeched, but Aunty Susan wasn't done.

"And you're still stuck on it, Dad. After all these years, you still think he's going to change. Be the son you always wanted him to be. Well, I've got news for you…"

"I'll go," Henry's dad said.

"No, Dad."

"I'm sorry, son. I shouldn't have come." With a quick hug for Henry and another handshake for Daniel, Henry's dad dodged out of the nearest exit, unseen by the rest of the family.

"Come on, Sue," Jen tried again, still keeping her cool. "This isn't the place for it."

"Isn't it, Jen? Isn't it? One word from that…jackass brother of ours, and *he*—" another vicious jab of the finger at Grandad "—will snatch the bakery right out of Ness and Henry's hands."

"Sue, that's enough!" Jen bellowed. "Come on! We're going for some fresh air." Gripping Susan firmly by the hand, Jen steered her towards and out of the door. It was several seconds later before their argument could no longer be heard.

"Oh God," Henry whispered, not in blasphemy, and buried his face in his hands.

"Well, that was exciting," Daniel said far too gleefully.

"Exciting?"

"Hen, Hen, I'm so sorry."

Henry peered at Nessa through his fingers. "It's OK. It wasn't your fault…was it?"

"No, but…" She sighed so heavily her breath reached Henry's partly shielded eyeballs. "I didn't tell him. I was going to, but he heard your dad and got all uppity."

Henry let his hands drop. "I thought you were the brave one, Ness."

"I am!" she protested, and she was. Growing up in their family, under the benevolent but misguided rule of a patriarch, she'd had to be. She was also thoroughly disappointed with herself.

"Look on the bright side," Henry said, "Aunty Susan's just done the hard bit for us."

"I suppose so," Ness accepted. "And by the time you're back from your honeymoon, he'll be over the shock. Then you can hit him with your wedding cake idea. On which note..."

Henry's mouth fell open, but before he could respond, Nessa whipped her hand from behind her back, dazzling both men with the flash of ten inches of tempered, sharpened steel.

"Gosh, is that a massive knife in your hand, Nessa?" Daniel said.

She grinned. "Nah. I'm always pleased to see you. Shall we?" With a dangerous flourish, she directed them towards their cake, and they went willingly. More or less.

A BUN IN THE OVEN

March

ENGLISH BAKERS HAVE something of a penchant for concocting sweet treats with, if not a distinctive local flavour, names which ensure there can never be any doubt as to the origin of said treat.

The Eccles Cake, for instance, hails from the Greater Manchester town of Eccles, and its slightly older oval cousin, the Banbury Cake, from Banbury, Oxford. Both consist of flaky pastry stuffed (and I do mean stuffed) with currants and generously sprinkled with demerara sugar. They're best eaten cold, really, as they're a bit of a fire risk with all that sugar.

Not dissimilar is the Chorley Cake, except it's flatter, made with shortcrust pastry and no added sugar. Apparently, currants are sweet enough for Chorley folk, hardened Lancastrians that they are.

Then there's the Bakewell Tart—a shortcrust base upon which are layered jam and frangipane topped with flaked almonds or sometimes icing—and the Gloucester Tart, which is made with ground rice rather than frangipane.

It would be terribly remiss of me not to mention the dessert that could be found in every British school canteen in the 1970s and 80s: the Manchester Tart. A pastry base (or cardboard, possibly), a scraping of jam and a slab of custard (vibrant yellow, back in the day) with desiccated coconut just kind of free-floating on top. Honestly, it was delicious—there was nothing quite so magnificent as arriving at the canteen at lunchtime to discover it was a Manchester Tart day.

Lastly, but by no means leastly, I present for your delight and delectation the Banton Bun, which is neither cake nor tart but something between a scone and a bread roll, which may or may not have had something to do with its creator, one Henry Jones the Fourth, falling asleep one morning while the dough was rising. It rose, and it rose…and it rose some more. And then…

It collapsed.

Poor Henry. He worked so hard. The bakery was bigger, more successful than he or his father could ever have imagined, but it would all be for nothing if, even for a day, the villagers had to do without bread. He was exhausted and could no longer cope on his own; he needed an assistant.

But first, he needed to rescue the dough.

In a heroic effort to 'waste not, want not', he added a cupful of soda to the gloopy mess, gave it a quick knead, put it in the oven and hoped for the best.

Later that morning, Josephine, daughter of farmer Edward Thatcher (yes, indeed) was passing the bakery on her way to the grocery with the milk and butter when her horse spooked, almost toppling the cart and knocking Josephine to the ground.

Upon hearing the commotion, Henry immediately—and fatefully—raced to the aid of the young damsel in distress, and the rest, as we say, is history. And *her*story, of course. After all, were it not for Josephine taking a knife to one of Henry's insubstantial buns (sounds way more gruesome than it was) and sprucing it up with a generous dollop of cherry preserve and whisked cream, the Banton Bun may never have seen the light of day.

"It's not quite there," Henry said, taking another bite of their brand-new creation.

"I think it's delicious," Josephine murmured, licking cream from her lips. Henry blushed as red as the cherry preserve. Josephine shuffled along the bakery bench, closer to Henry. Closer still. Closer… "You know what it needs?" Josephine's lips brushed Henry's cheek. He dumbly shook his head. "It needs…"

She whispered in his ear.

He smiled. He nodded. "Yes!"

And so it was.

One final point: Josephine is Margaret's great-great-great-great-aunt, so yes; she and Henry are distantly related, and she probably has a rightful claim to the Joneses' secret family recipe.

But I'm not going to tell her that. Are you?

***

Henry could wait no longer. Not even long enough to flip the sign to 'closed', although it was late morning—their quiet period, hence it was when Nessa had booked her doctor's appointment—and Henry wouldn't be away more than a couple of minutes.

Typically, the shop bell tinkled the second he'd started to.

"Tough luck," he muttered and got on with it. There were no thieves in Banton. Well, there were, but they tended not to steal from their own, and in any case the few quid in the till wouldn't get them very far. No, whoever it was would wait, and if they couldn't, there was always THE Village Bakery…

With that thought, Henry squeezed, trying to pee faster and cursing that third cup of coffee. "Stick at two in future," he admonished himself as he shook off, zipped, flushed, washed his hands, ignored his panda-face reflection in the tiny mirror over the basin, hurried back to the shop…and stopped like a sheet of glass had slammed down in front of him when he saw who was there.

"Oh! It's you."

Margaret Sharpe. In his bakery. Unattended.

Henry edged along the counter and slid open the cabinet door, smiling like a madman.

"Henry, *what* are you doing?"

Surreptitiously checking for signs of sabotage. "Ensuring I'm ready to serve you, Mrs. Sharpe. What will it be? A slice of lemon drizzle cake? Jam tart, perhaps? I'd offer you a Banton Bun, but, you know…"

"Hmm." She raised her chin, all haughty, but it lasted only a second or two, ending in a sigh, followed by, "How was the wedding?"

"The…w-w-what?"

"I haven't seen you to ask. Did it go well?"

"Yes…thank you…for asking." Henry straightened the paper bags in bewilderment.

"Good, good." Margaret nodded, quite a lot. "And your wedding cake? Was it everything you hoped for?"

"Um…yes, it was." Henry cut to the chase. "Look, Margaret, I appreciate your interest, and I'm not trying to cause a fight, but… did you really come here to ask about our wedding?"

Henry's question wiped the big fake grin from her face, but what replaced it was far worse: a rueful smile. Margaret Sharpe did *not* wear rueful well.

"Ah, Henry, you always were such a perceptive boy."

Man, he corrected in his head but let it slide.

"I popped in to give you this." Margaret unclipped her handbag and pulled out a white envelope. "I had hoped to give it to you on the day." She reached forward, offering it to Henry. "After what passed, it would have seemed disingenuous, so I felt it best to wait."

Perplexed, Henry took the envelope and studied the front, on which was written 'Henry and Daniel'.

"I was uncertain whose surname to use. Traditionally, it would be the husband's, but, well, you understand my dilemma, I'm sure."

"I do," Henry uttered, by now having extracted the card from the envelope and not quite believing his eyes. It was just a generic 'Congratulations on Your Marriage' card, signed with a neutral 'Best wishes, Margaret and Peter Sharpe', but still. It was a wedding card from Margaret Sharpe. "Thank you. This is… lovely."

"My pleasure." She fussed with her coat buttons. "Well, I must—"

"Would you like to see the cake?"

"I'd be delighted!"

***

Approximately fifteen minutes from now, when Nessa returns from her doctor's appointment to find Henry and Margaret enthusing over the *one hundred and twenty-six* photos Henry took of his wedding cake, she'll wonder if gluten intolerance can cause hallucinations. Probably not, but now you know why she's been to the doctor (the gluten intolerance, not the hallucinations—we'll leave those to Henry's dad), and it's going to set the bakery on an entirely new course, but that won't happen until long after we've said goodbye to the lovely people of Banton.

As for what Margaret's up to—the wedding card, the well wishes—yes, it's all a wee bit suspicious. But her intentions are good. *Mostly* good. Bear in mind she wasn't always a baker, although really, who makes their own wedding cake? OK, some people do, but my point is, Margaret didn't. Henry's grandad made it, and it was beautiful. One of his best, without a doubt. Was it *the* best? Margaret likes to think so, and she's only interested in seeing Henry's photos to reassure herself whilst unaware that Henry is sharing them with her for the exact same reason. Who knows, maybe they're both right in their own way.

But that's only a part of the story. The rest has a lot to do with a meeting at the village hall this coming Wednesday, along with a few pointers from Reverend Osbourne on how Margaret might begin to heal the rift with Henry and Daniel. She might never approve of their marriage—the card was the reverend's idea—but she knows better than most that times change, and attitudes change with them. She also knows beyond doubt that Henry and Daniel's love is true, faithful and strong. How could she not when, as a young woman working in her parents' shop, she cooed over those baby boys as if they were her own.

Perhaps this lady is for turning after all.

***

"Jones," Henry said. "We're Henry and Daniel Jones because of..." He circled his finger in the air to indicate the bakery.

“A logical decision,” Margaret concurred, “although Daniel’s family has excellent standing in the community.”

Henry pursed his lips. It was the usual jab at his dad and the shame he’d brought on the Joneses. It wasn’t as if Margaret was the only villager who held that view—they all did—but Henry was proud of his family. He refused to deny his heritage.

“And did you have—oh, yes. Look at that.” Margaret shifted her glasses down her nose to inspect the photo more closely. “Two little grooms.”

“Yes,” Henry confirmed, his thoughts spinning ahead to the sourcing of suitable cake toppers for their wedding cakes, assuming there would be wedding cakes, seeing as Grandad was still ‘thinking about it’. Henry was in half a mind to ask where Margaret got hers, but Nessa arrived before the other half of his mind caught up.

“Hey, Hen, guess….wh… Margaret?” She stumbled to a stop before she reached the counter.

“Good morning, Nessa, dear. How are you?”

“I’m…fine? I think?” Her eyes shifted from Margaret to Henry, to the wedding photos, and back to Henry.

“Margaret popped in with a card,” he explained.

“O…K. I, um…” Nessa shook her head rapidly and blinked a few times. Henry stifled a laugh. She was right to be confused. He was feeling that way himself. “I’m gonna go…do something,” she said, scooting past them to the kitchen, and there she stayed until Margaret left the premises.

“You two were getting on surprisingly well,” were Nessa’s first words upon her return. It sounded like an accusation, and Henry was fairly sure it was.

“I was just showing her the wedding cake.”

“Uh-huh? I hope you didn’t leave her unattended.”

“Er, well…” Henry shut one eye in a grimace. “Not exactly. But she didn’t poke her nose anywhere she shouldn’t.”

“Hen…”

"I know, I'm sorry! I drank too much coffee this morning, and—"

"Lock the door next time."

"Yes, sorry. I will." He dodged into his seat and hid behind his computer. If he couldn't see her…

Nessa grunted. "Did she tell you about the environmental health?"

"No?"

"Oooooh…gossip time!" She perched on Henry's desk, her disgruntlement forgotten. "Someone told the council they found mouse droppings in their seeded batch."

"Now that's what you call an eye for detail," Henry joked, though he was terrified of mice, especially if they were only three doors down the high street. "So that's why she was here—she's been shut down?"

"Nope. The environmental health inspector found no evidence of mice, but the word on the street is Margaret's confidence has taken a beating."

"The word on the street? Did you turn gangsta while I was on my honeymoon, cuz?"

Nessa ignored his mockery. "You know what this means? Someone's trying to stop Banton taking part in the County Cake-Off."

"Don't be ridiculous, Ness. It's only a stupid baking contest."

"It's a big deal, Hen. Cash prizes, loads of publicity, kudos—there's a whisper one of the TV networks is interested in it."

"Pshure. As if they're gonna bother with a few Victoria sponge cakes at the county fair."

"Reality TV's all the rage, Hen. Sooooo, anyway…" Nessa unhooked a mug from the tree, filled it with coffee and offered it to Henry. He waved it away. "Are you coming to the meeting on Wednesday?"

"Meeting?"

"To figure out what we're doing for the Cake-Off."

"Why are you even asking me that?"

"Just checking you hadn't changed your mind."
"Not a chance."

***

Wednesday evening

"That's it, I'm done." Daniel slapped his planner shut and shoved it back in his bag. "I can't concentrate with all your fussing and fidgeting."

"Sorry." Henry's phone vibrated across the table. He unlocked it and fake-sobbed as he read the message onscreen.

"What does she want this time?"

"Who?"

"Nessa?" Daniel moved over to the sofa and switched on the TV. "It *is* Nessa, isn't it?"

"Yeah." Henry went to join him. He didn't even get his bottom on the seat before his phone vibrated again.

"Just turn it off," Daniel advised.

"I can't."

"Why not?"

"Because..." He trailed off as he read the message.

> *Please Hen. The hot Rev. Ozzy says we need something spectacular. Suggestions?*

"Because?" Daniel repeated.

Henry sighed. "Because I can't."

***

There it is again, that familiar obstinate streak. Chop any Henry Jones in half—hypothetically speaking—and he'd have lettering running right through him like a stick of rock:

One Stubborn Bugger

Herein lies the problem. Since Nessa told him about the notice in the village hall, Henry's stuck to his guns. He's not doing the Cake-Off. Absolutely not. No way, José.

Except
he really,
really,
really,
wants to do
the Cake-Off.

***

He called her back.

"Is Margaret there?"

"What kind of question is that?"

Henry got up and started pacing. "Put her on, Ness."

"Wh—"

"I've got an idea. Quick!"

"OK, OK, hold on."

After a half-minute of muffled scuffling, Margaret's (not surprisingly) surprised voice sounded at the other end. "Hello?"

"Margaret, it's Henry. What's the biggest Banton Bun you've ever made?"

"Hmm…about eight inches. Why?"

"Could you make bigger?"

"Of course."

"How much bigger?"

"How big are you thinking?"

"The size of a Mini."

"The size of a Mini?" Margaret squeaked. "Why would you… oh! Yes, well, that would be rather spectacular, wouldn't it?"

"Yes." Henry was nodding along and grinning, and Daniel was shaking his head at him like he was completely bonkers. Daniel flapped his hand, and Henry moved out of the way of the TV. "Could we do it?" he asked Margaret.

"Theoretically, if we had a large enough oven."

"Would ours be large enough?" Theirs was the oven Henry's grandad had installed, back when the bakery employed thirteen members of staff.

"We'd get the dough in," Margaret confirmed. "But once it starts to rise…"

Henry smacked his forehead at his oversight. Rubbish baker that he was, he still knew dough doubled its size. "OK, how big does this oven need to be?"

"Well, big enough to fit a Mini inside. Or half a Mini, at least—we'd have to bake the two halves separately."

"That's a bit more manageable." Who was he kidding? "What about a pizza oven? The pizza restaurant in town might help us out."

"I doubt theirs is any bigger than yours."

"OK…" Henry clutched wildly at straws. "Could we barbecue it?"

Daniel snorted at something on TV, or Henry thought that was what he was snorting at until he realised the news was on—not even an 'And finally…' witty ditty. Daniel was laughing at him.

Henry glared, and Daniel attempted to straighten his face, but a residual smirk of amusement remained.

"Never mind, Henry," Margaret consoled. "I'm sure we'll come up with something just as spectacular but…possible. Perhaps aim for quantity? If we use both kitchens, we could bake an awful lot of normal-sized Banton Buns in seventy-two hours."

"OK, Margaret," Henry agreed tightly. "Whatever you think is best." With a huff, he hung up on her and stared, unseeing, at the TV. "I hate admitting defeat."

"I know you do," Daniel said.

"This is why I tried not to get involved. I mean, it's just a stupid baking contest."

"Yes."

"It's not important."

"No."

Henry re-joined Daniel on the sofa and tuned in to the newsreader's drone. He heard about three words before his mind took off again, imagining trestle tables lined with hundreds of Banton Buns. Impressive, yes, but was it spectacular?

"There's got to be a way," he mused aloud.

"There is," Daniel said without taking his eyes off the TV.

Henry swivelled to face him. "There is?"

"Your dad."

"My dad?" Henry scoffed. "He's got even less clue about baking than I have, unless we're planning to get the judges stoned on hash cakes."

"That wasn't what I meant, Hen. He works the nightshift at the Clayworks."

"How's that supposed to...ohhhhh." The penny dropped. "He works the nightshift at the Clayworks."

"Yep"

"And kilns are *massive* ovens." Henry grabbed Daniel's head with both hands and planted a sloppy kiss somewhere in the face region. "You're a genius," he said. He jumped up from the sofa and sprinted from the room. "I'll call him on the way."

"Way where?"

"The village hall. Don't wait up!"

MAY DAY, MAY DAY

Not Quite May Day

County Show Cake-Off
Rules of Entry:

1. One entry per village.
2. All those involved must reside in said village at the time of the contest.
3. Entries must be prepared a maximum of seventy-two hours before judging takes place and must be entirely edible.
4. All entries and entrants will present to the County Fair main marquee at twelve noon on May Day.
5. Any entrants breaking the rules above will be immediately disqualified from the contest.

***

"The oven is all well and good," said Margaret, "but where on earth will we get an oven tray to fit it?"

All eyes were on Henry, and he racked his brains, searching out solutions. Short of growing a magic beanstalk…

"I ask my boss man," said Igor—the scary-looking trucker who lived in his cab and parked up at the back of the church in between jobs, with Reverend Osbourne's permission. "He gets things done."

Henry doubted, but the reverend's faith overruled.

"Thank you, Igor. Keep me posted."

The gigantic trucker gave a singular nod, and the meeting moved on.

Don't make problems, create solutions. It seemed to be Reverend Osbourne's philosophy too, and Henry was in awe. By the end of the evening, everyone was on board—

"I'm delighted you've joined us, Henry," the reverend said as they stacked away the chairs. "We couldn't do this without you."

—yes, even Henry.

***

You will need:

- Forklift truck
- Heavy goods vehicle
- Cement mixer
- Teflon-coated aluminium pallet (custom-made)
- Industrial kiln

- 450 lbs strong white flour
- 9 lbs salt
- 8 lbs yeast
- 4 lbs bicarbonate of soda
- 53 gallons buttermilk
- 50 lbs cherry preserve
- 5 gallons cream, whipped
- [redacted]

"What have you got there?" Margaret glanced up from her bucket of yeast and eyed the plain white drum in Henry's arms.

"Oh, just…um…"

"None of your beeswax." Nessa stepped in front of him, blocking Margaret's view.

"Have it your way, dears," Margaret said blithely. "I have *no* interest in your family's *silly* secret ingredient. However, we *are* all in this together. What would Reverend Osbourne have to say?"

"We don't care," Henry muttered as he and Nessa side-stepped together out of the kitchen into the yard—

"I care," Nessa said.

—where the cement mixer merrily churned away under Grandad's supervision.

"You could always invite him round for dinner sometime," Henry suggested. He set the drum on the ground in front of the mixer and levered off the lid. "How much, Grandad?"

"A pound and a half to fifty pounds of flour."

"So...thirteen and a half pounds, but this is only a fifth of the mix." Henry calculated the necessary proportion and added it to the mixer. Maths, he could do. "OK. Nessa, can you stick this back in the safe for now, please."

"Righteo." She scooped up the drum and paused. "Do you think I should? Invite Reverend Osbourne round?"

"Why not? It works for Mrs. Broughton." Henry grinned.

Nessa flicked his ear and marched off with the drum, back through the kitchen whence Henry heard Margaret exclaim to herself, "They keep it in the safe? Honest to goodness!" He ignored her and inspected his checklist.

"OK, where are we up to? Dough...in progress." He'd left that to Grandad and Margaret—the experts. "Transport...jet-washed and ready to go." Courtesy of Igor the Horrible. "Preserve..." He took out his phone. "Aunty Jen, it's Henry. How's the jam coming along?"

"Cooling as I speak."

"Great work!" *Tick.*

That was the other thing Henry could do. He might be a rubbish baker, but when it came to organising people and coordinating who needed to do what and when, he was pretty darn good at it, even if he did think so himself.

Nessa came back out and stood next to him. "Time check."

"Quarter past four." Still sixty-eight hours left. Forty-eight would have sufficed, but the saboteurs hadn't stopped at reporting THE Bakery to the council; they'd done the same to Henry and Nessa, and the environmental health officer was sympathetic, but she had a job to do. Thankfully, like Margaret's, their bakery was given a clean bill of health. Then, the following morning, Henry arrived to find the egg delivery was nothing more than an enormous raw omelette running into the gutter.

That wasn't the end of it. The stopcock on the mains water supply for the entire high street mysteriously turned itself off, Margaret's alarm developed a fault, and then someone threw a firework into the yard. It was at that point Henry called the police, and of course they initially assumed his dad was the culprit. Once Henry and Margaret had given full statements—and Reverend Osbourne had put in a good word for Henry's dad—they released him.

For whatever reason, the vandals hadn't come back after that, but the Banton competitors were taking no chances. At six p.m., accompanied by Henry and Margaret, Igor would transport the dough to the Clayworks, where it was warmer and—Henry was reliably informed—it would speed up the rise. By midnight, the kiln should've cooled to around 150 Celsius, and the baking would commence—under the constant supervision of one of their twenty-strong team.

The Banton Bunnies.

Daniel's contribution. Not a bad one.

And tomorrow, they'd do it all over again with the other half.

***

And the day after that, too, as it turns out.

"But you can't have three halves," I hear you say.

No, indeed you cannot.

***

Seven o'clock, Saturday morning

The door to the foreman's booth opened, startling Henry, who was alert and attentive but entirely focused on the view of the kiln through the grotty heat-retardant window.

"Morning, Margaret." He stretched his arms in the air and stifled a yawn.

She sniffed.

"What's up?"

And sniffed again. "Can you smell that?"

Henry shook his head. "I can't smell anything." Nor could he feel his bottom. The foreman's chair had been comfy two hours ago; now, not so much, but no matter. Margaret was here to take over, and the first half of the bun should be more or less done.

She pointed to the monitor screen on the desk. "Does that work?"

"Yeah. I switched it to standby."

"Henry! You're supposed to be watching our bun."

"Half a bun," he corrected. "And I'm not, I'm watching the oven to make sure no-one tampers with it. What's the point in me watching the bun when I have no idea if it's cooked?" He got up and switched the monitor on, taking the opportunity for a proper stretch. *Home, quick shower, maybe a nap, and back to the bakery—*

Margaret gasped. "Henry! It's burning!" She flapped her hands around in panic.

"Oh heck!"

The two of them dashed from the booth and down the rattly metal stairs to ground level where Henry caught a whiff of burnt toast.

Not burnt toast.

"Open the door," Margaret ordered. "Quick!"

"I'm quicking!" Henry ran over and heaved on the lever, releasing the door lock. "I'll fetch my dad." He dashed off before Margaret got a look at the oven's contents.

A minute later, he was back with his dad and the forklift truck. While Henry senior manoeuvred into position, Henry junior tried to console a devastated Margaret.

"Vehicle reversing, stand clear," the forklift informed them.

Henry steered Margaret out of the way, and the forklift, complete with a five-foot half-sphere of steaming baked produce, emerged from the kiln.

"Well, it's not *burnt* burnt," Henry said, which was true. The half a bun had risen beautifully, but it had a seriously dark crust.

"I…I don't understand," Margaret whimpered. "The temperature is exactly right, the ingredients, the mixing…I've made hundreds…*thousands* of Banton Buns. I did everything exactly the same as always!"

Except…

"Oh…crêpes!" Henry slumped. "I think…this might be…um…our fault."

"What do you mean? Whose fault?" She turned and glared at him. He shrank a little. "What did you do?" she accused.

"OK, well…um…see. I mean, I might be wrong, but—"

"It's your secret ingredient, isn't it?"

Henry pursed his lips.

"What is it?" Margaret demanded.

"I can't tell you."

"So help me. The contest is in two days and we've got to start from scratch! You have to tell me!"

"Please, Margaret, don't make me—"

"Now, Henry!"

"Vanilla sugar," he blurted and clapped his hand over his mouth.

"Sugar?" Margaret screeched. "You added sugar to my recipe?"

"*Your* recipe? Since when?"

"I've been making the Banton Bun for thirteen years!"

"So? My family made it for over a hundred!"

"Henry Jones *and Son*, Baker. Sugar…"

"I didn't think it would matter."

"It's sugar. You add sugar, of course it'll burn, you stupid boy!"

"Excuse me." Henry's dad raised his hand, but they argued over him.

"I'm not a boy, Margaret. I'm twenty-four years old."

"But you accept you're stupid."

"Yes, I'm stupid," Henry snapped. "For ever thinking we could do this together, you…you horrible old bag!"

"Excuse me, folks," Henry's dad tried again. Still no joy.

"That's right, call me names. I came to make peace with you, remember?"

"No, you didn't! You came snooping for the secret ingredient to the *real* Banton Bun!"

"And it's cost us our chance of victory in the County—"

A shrill whistle cut Margaret off mid-flow. Both she and Henry turned and glowered at the source.

Henry's dad laughed in disbelief. "And people say I'm off my bonce? Thank God I went off the rails is all I can say. What do you want me to do with this bread boulder?"

"Chuck it in the skip," Henry said and stormed off up the stairs. He was hot and tired, and sick of everything to do with the Cake-Off. He just wanted to go home.

"Vehicle reversing, stand clear. Vehicle reversing, stand clear…"

"No!" Margaret yelled. "Wait, wait!"

The forklift warning stopped. Curious, Henry stopped too.

"Only the outside is burnt. The inside will still be edible. It would be a terrible waste to throw it away. Couldn't we give it to The Poor?"

Henry about-turned and strolled, hands in pockets, back down the stairs. "You know it's 2018, don't you, Margaret?"

"There are still poor people in 2018, Henry."

"But we don't call them 'The Poor'—"

"What about the soup kitchen in town?" Henry's dad interjected. "They usually only accept non-perishables, but it's got to be worth a shot."

Henry shrugged. Margaret nodded.

"Great. I'll borrow one of the vans and take it down there when I get off shift. For now, I'll stick it in the storeroom." He climbed back onto the forklift.

"Thanks, Dad." Granted, it was an afterthought, but Henry meant it.

"Yes, thank you, Mr. Jones," Margaret added.

Henry's dad gave them a nod, finished reversing his truck and trundled away.

"I'm sorry, Margaret."

"I'm sorry too, Henry."

"What are we going to do?"

"Fix it, dear Henry."

He managed a laugh at that. "How?"

"Pool our resources. Empty our pantries, beg, steal and borrow if we have to…"

***

And that was precisely what they did, apart from the stealing; there was no need. Villagers flocked to the bakery with grocery bags full of flour and salt mined from their pantries. Henry and Nessa traipsed around the farms, buying all the buttermilk available; Grandad made up the shortfall with milk and lemon juice, and Margaret recalculated the cooking time, taking into account the vanilla sugar.

Saturday evening, Igor transported the second enormous ball of dough to the Clayworks to rise; at ten p.m., Henry's dad transferred it to the kiln. Meanwhile, Henry and Nessa were entrusted with mixing the dough for the second half—their first real attempt at baking—so it would be ready to go in the oven at three a.m., by which time the first half should be cooked. If it wasn't, they'd have to leave the second half until Sunday night, and it wouldn't cool in time for the contest. They were flying on a wing and a prayer, and they were exhausted. But they were determined.

Three a.m. Sunday morning, Margaret arrived at the Clayworks with a fencing foil and laughed off the jokes about how rough the village was these days.

"Mr. Jones, when you're ready."

Henry's dad dutifully lifted their creation from the kiln. No burnt-toast smell this time; it was plump, round and golden-brown, and it smelled utterly divine.

"The moment of truth," Margaret said, advancing, foil at the ready. Delicately piercing the soft crust, she plunged the foil deep into the five-foot-wide half-bun, waited a few seconds…and withdrew it. Cheers echoed off the Clayworks' old brick walls when the foil came away clean.

***

By Sunday evening, the two halves were safely stowed in the bakery kitchen where they could slowly cool to room temperature, and the Banton Bunnies gathered in the yard to celebrate with a barbecue and a few drinks.

Henry tapped the barbecue tongs against his beer bottle, garnering everyone's attention. "Reverend Osbourne would like to say a few words."

"Thanks, Henry." The reverend moved so everyone could see him and gave them a moment to read his T-shirt: *And know that I am with you always; yes, to the end of time.* "Well, folks, you really rose to the challenge." That earned him a communal groan. "I'll keep this short because all I want to say is I never doubted for a second we'd succeed, and we have. Whether we win tomorrow is of no consequence, although…it would be nice, wouldn't it?"

"Yes!" came the resounding reply.

"Many, many thanks to all of you for your incredible hard work. Eat, drink, be merry, and get a good night's rest."

ALL'S FAIR...

Actual May Day (or the bank holiday created in its likeness)

"WOW!" DANIEL WALKED the circumference of the assembled Banton Bun—twice—and said it again. "Wow!"

"Is that a good wow or a bad wow?" Henry fished. He was a nervous wreck, and Margaret—on the far side of the bun and jabbering at Mr. Sharpe—was in much the same state.

Daniel rolled his eyes, exasperated yet patient; being a primary school teacher had a lot to do with that. "A good wow. It's brilliant, Henry, as are you."

"There's no I in team," Henry blustered and blushed, although it was true he couldn't have done it alone. Well, he couldn't have done it at all, but he was going to change that…just as soon as this contest was out of the way. He sneaked another harried peek at Hillview village's entry on the table next to theirs: shortbread dominoes arranged to depict the village's coat of arms, which was innovative and clever but taking an age to set up when the tiniest jolt from an unsteady hand felled the entire display. Of course, that was what it was supposed to do, but not until the judges were there to see it.

"We should take a look around the fair before it gets too hot," Daniel suggested.

"Can't." Henry stubbornly crossed his arms. "And it's already too hot." He shuddered at the mental image of the judges tucking into their bun, all joyous in their anticipation, and then spitting out the sour cream in disgust.

"But it's cooler outside. Come on, Hen… No-one's going to chance getting up to shenanigans today."

"Better safe than— Oops!"

There went the shortbread dominoes again.

"Pssst, Henry," Margaret whispered, although she was so loud as to make the whispering pointless. She beckoned then changed her mind and came to him, leaning close and cupping her hand around her mouth. "It's her," she said.

Shifting eyes only, Henry looked around their fellow competitors, or those present; of the five villages that had entered the Cake-Off, three had turned up so far, but it was only ten in the morning.

"Who?" he asked.

Margaret shuffled sideways and tapped her shoulder to indicate. "Her."

Henry watched the woman in question apologising to the Hillview competitors for 'accidentally' knocking their table. He didn't recognise her. "Who is she?"

"I don't know, but I'm almost certain she came into the shop the day before the—" Margaret mouthed the words "—mouse droppings incident."

"Guess I was wrong, then." Daniel sighed despondently. "I'll see if I can find us a cup of tea somewhere and come back, OK?"

"There's no point in us all staying," Henry said. "Why don't you go and find Ness? She'll be over by the funfair."

"Why don't you *both* go?" Margaret suggested. "We're fine here, aren't we, Peter?" Mr. Sharpe gave a thumbs up. "I'd rather hoped to watch the dog agility at eleven, but our bun is more important."

"Then we'll be back for eleven," Henry confirmed.

"If you're sure…"

"It's only fair."

Margaret laughed ruefully. "There is nothing fair about this contest. Now, off you go, boys. Have fun." She shooed them away.

Daniel was right; it was cooler outside, and they wandered through the crowds, at various points being intercepted by children from Daniel's class, excited and surprised to see their teacher.

"We live in the stock cupboards, don't you know," he joked to Henry after one little girl asked if he'd get in trouble for being out of school.

Henry laughed half-heartedly, struggling to get into the spirit of the day in spite of the fun going on all around the park—the rhythmic tinkle of the morris dancers' bells, children singing as they skipped and weaved around the maypole, collies yapping as they warmed up on the agility course—none of it could shake his bad feeling about the Cake-Off.

"Your dad's over there."

"Where?" Henry shielded his eyes from the low morning sun and looked where Daniel was pointing. "Is that woman juggling…"

"Fire, yes," Daniel confirmed, and Henry's dad was at the front of the crowd gathered around the juggler. Indeed, he was standing so close, he'd be lucky to escape unscorched. "Maybe it's as well he didn't take on the bakery, huh?"

"Yes, just as well," Henry agreed. His dad had an unhealthy interest in fire—not exactly a secret—although, after three days of baking, Henry was starting to understand the fascination, not with fire as such; with its magical ability to transform matter. "I think it must run in the family."

Daniel raised an eyebrow but didn't get as far as passing comment, distracted by Nessa, who was waving frantically at them from the top of the Ferris wheel, which she wasn't riding alone. "Well, well, well!"

"Have you seen today's T-shirt?" Henry asked.

"No? What does it say?"

"I am the bread of life."

"Ah, a nice bit of subliminal messaging. Way to go, Rev! He must have loads of T-shirts."

"Yeah. I don't think I've ever seen him wearing the same one twice."

They continued their chatter as they walked around the stalls, indulging in doughnuts and ice cream because it was the done thing. While Henry welcomed the distraction, eleven o'clock couldn't come soon enough, not that he doubted Margaret's valour when it came to protecting their pride and joy.

When they returned to the marquee to take their turn, Henry wasn't in the least surprised to discover the two other competitors still hadn't arrived, and by quarter to twelve it was clear they weren't coming. Whoever had gone after the Banton Bunnies had also frightened off the others, which left just two suspects: Hillview with their shortbread dominoes, and Westleigh with their…Henry had no idea what it was.

"What actually is that?"

"A cupcake replica of Westleigh."

"Right." Henry nodded. It was very colourful and pretty, but it looked nothing like Westleigh village. To Henry's mind, the contest was a two-horse race between Banton and Hillview, and he honestly didn't care who won as long as it wasn't Westleigh because by now he was almost certain they were the saboteurs.

"All competitors please vacate the marquee. Judging will commence in five minutes." The order was issued by a stout, red-faced man in a tweed blazer to which was pinned a rosette bearing the words 'chief judge'.

With one last check that all was well with their bun, Henry and Daniel left and went to watch the rest of the dog agility display with Margaret and Mr. Sharpe. Now they just had to wait.

***

"Disqualified?" Margaret marched over and yanked out the cardboard sign skewered to their bun. "For what reason?"

"I'm afraid, madam, you broke the rules."

"We did not! We followed them to the letter."

"Mrs. Sharpe…it is Mrs. Sharpe, isn't it?"

"Yes."

"Mrs. Sharpe, is this a cake?"

"Of course it's not, you silly man! It's a Banton Bun."

"Which is a kind of bread, is it not?"

"It's a dessert."

"As that may be, it states clearly in the rules that exhibits must be cake-based."

"Where?" Henry asked. He stepped forward to stand at Margaret's side. "Where in the rules does it say that?"

The chief judge cleared his throat. "Mrs. Tomkins? Would you be so kind…" He held out his hand expectantly, and a timid-looking woman scurried over with a clipboard. "Thank you. Right, let's see…" The man dabbed a handkerchief at his suddenly sweaty neck. "Ah, yes, here we are. Types of desserts to be entered: cakes, biscuits and cookies, brownies and pies. Strictly no breads or products requiring refrigeration."

"Rubbish!" Henry said. "That wasn't in the rules. I'd have seen it if it was."

"And you are?"

"Henry Jones."

"Ah, the famous Henry Jones and Son, Baker, inventor of the Banton Bun—which is not a cake. Now, if you'll excuse me—"

"I will make a formal complaint," Margaret warned. "That rule was added after we entered the contest."

The judge tried to stare her down. "Prove it," he challenged.

Without a word, Henry took out his phone and loaded the PDF of the rules he'd downloaded the night of the meeting at the village hall. "There," he said and thrust it at the obnoxious judge, who barely looked at it.

"Well, it's obvious what's happened here."

"Yes," Henry said. "It's called *cheating*."

The judge laughed, but he'd been caught out and he knew it. "Clearly, you doctored those rules so you could make this… monstrosity. I've made my decision." He turned his back on them.

"Monstrosity?" Margaret repeated, her voice rising in both pitch and volume. In spite of the urge to flee, Henry stayed put. They were a team, after all.

"Mrs. Sharpe, please be quiet or I'll have you removed—"

"*Monstrosity?!*"

"*Mrs. Sharpe!*"

"*How dare you!* Taking bribes from those people with their ridiculous cupcake village. It's an absolute disgrace!"

There was nothing Henry could've done to stop what happened next. Margaret scooped a handful of cream from the middle of their bun and launched it at the judge. Stunned, the man stood still as a statue as whipped cream slid down his face and plopped from his glasses and chin onto his blazer.

Margaret was only just getting started, and she had an impressive aim. Four handfuls fired in quick succession found the woman from Westleigh and her three teammates, while the rest of the Banton Bunnies watched on, astounded, amused, amazed. As Margaret loaded up to take another shot, Henry finally snapped out of his trance.

"Stop!" he yelled and leapt between her and her target, with predictable consequence. The cream thudded against Henry's chest, splattering his face. "Margaret, what are you—"

"Out of my way, Henry!" She re-armed.

"No!" He ducked and blindly grabbed for her, but she broke free and flung the cream with an overarm shot. This time, she missed, or perhaps she didn't, because she got Henry's grandad who'd only come to see what all the commotion was about. Henry stared at his grandad in horror. He had no idea how everything had got out of hand so quickly.

"Agh! I'm hit!" Margaret cried.

Beyond bewildered, Henry spun on the spot and gasped at the sight. A cupcake was stuck to Margaret's cheek, her face twisted in a disgusted sneer as she peeled the cake from her skin, leaving behind a swirly mess of pink and blue glittery buttercream.

Thwack! Something hit Henry on the back of the head, and he stumbled forward into Margaret, who made helicopter arms as she lost her balance and toppled helplessly into the bun. The top half skated eighteen inches backwards, leaving her sitting on a ledge of cream and jam.

"H-hen-ry?" She was shaking with rage.

"Yes, Margaret?" he asked as if steeling himself to hear her dying wish.

"This. Is. War!" On those words, she struggled and wriggled but couldn't quite get traction and made a wild grab for Henry, who momentarily froze. Margaret was furious beyond the capacity for reason, and while Henry wanted revenge as much as the next Bantonion, he was thinking it might be safer to leave her where she was…until Daniel took a cupcake to the chest.

"My favourite shirt!" he cried and crumpled against the marquee's flimsy canvas wall.

That was it. Henry saw red.

Red velvet.

And it was going to stain something chronic.

"I'm with you, Margaret—bakers in arms!"

Determination renewed, Henry grasped her hand and pulled her clear of the bun. Nessa and Reverend Osbourne upended the top half to use as a shield, and every Banton Bunny loaded up with ammunition.

"Aim…" Margaret commanded.

All raised their arms.

"Fire!" Henry and Margaret yelled in unison, and handfuls of whipped cream flew through the air, some finding their targets, most not. Accuracy was difficult under a bombardment of multicoloured cupcakes.

"We're almost out of ammo!" Nessa cried, scraping through to the cherry preserve. It would make a ghastly mess of the marquee, although it was far too late to worry about that.

"Henry, look! He's escaping!" Margaret pointed at the chief judge, who was attempting to crawl, unseen, under the tables.

Henry broke away from the frontline and tore a chunk from the bun. A cupcake whistled past his ear and detonated on impact with Nessa's shield. With Banton Bunnies taking hits all around and buttercream in his hair, Henry bravely struggled on, using the bread to scoop up all that was left of the cream and jam. He turned back to Margaret. "You'll need to cut him off at the overpass," he said.

She nodded her understanding and took the bread, dodging behind their demolished fortress before she went undertable. Cupcake fire was sporadic, the enemy also having depleted their stockpile and caught unawares by shortbread snipers.

In the final throes of battle, everything rested on their last stand, but Margaret was nowhere to be seen, and the chief judge had made it to the end of the marquee. Everything went slow-mo as the man struggled to his feet, and Henry prepared to surrender. Then, as the judge made a run for the door, out of nowhere, Margaret leapt in front of him and smushed the creamy, jammy, soft-with-delicate-hints-of-vanilla bread in his face.

"THAT'S IT!" he roared. "BANTON IS PERMANENTLY BANNED FROM ENTERING THE COUNTY CAKE-OFF!"

"And Westleigh?" Henry demanded. "You're banning them too, yes?"

The judge snorted on each inhale and for a moment looked like he was going to explode (as if things weren't messy enough already). He clenched his fists, his flared nostrils in amid all that cream looking awfully like weeholes in the snow, and gritted out, "The county council *will* hear about this. And you *will* be invoiced for the damage." With that, he marched out of the marquee without looking back.

The Westleigh competitors huddled and jumped up and down, singing, "We are the champions…"

"Oh, poo to you," Henry muttered, turning to his fellow Bantonions. "Who cares about a stupid Cake-Off anyway? We took part. That's what matters."

"On the contrary, dear boy," Margaret said, making it back to them and looking ever so pleased with herself if not a little sullied by assorted confectionery. "Winning is what matters." Anticipating Henry's protest, she raised her voice and went on, "To wit, the Guinness Book of Records will be in touch to arrange a visit."

Henry groaned. "Does that mean we've got to do it all over again?"

"Yes, but it will be bigger, better..."

"Strong and stable," Nessa added. The Banton Bunnies fell about laughing.

"What was that, dear?" Margaret asked, but no-one was listening to her; they were listening to the tannoy announcement:

"The winner of this year's Cake-Off is Westleigh village!"

The Westleigh team cheered loudly and trooped out of the marquee to go and collect their prize.

"So much for TV networks," Nessa grunted. "I can't believe we're banned and *they're* not."

The Hillview team members were nodding in agreement. "If it's any consolation," one of the women said, "we won't be entering next year. Not after all that's gone on. And for the record, we think you should've won. Your Banton Bun was fantastic." She smiled and came over a little dreamy. "I haven't had one in years. My mum used to pick them up whenever she went over to Banton. But the last one I had...I don't know... Nothing tastes quite as good as you remember, does it?"

Henry and Margaret exchanged a knowing glance, and Henry's tummy did a flip. The Joneses didn't yet know he'd let their secret slip.

"Mum's the word," Margaret whispered and tapped the side of her nose.

HALF-DAY CLOSING

The Following Wednesday

THE SHOP BELL tinkled, and Henry glanced up. "Hello, you!" he greeted Daniel with a smile and a modicum of surprise. "What are you doing out of school? You'll get a detention."

Daniel laughed. "I've got a permission slip." He came around to Henry's side of the counter. "Reverend Osbourne took assembly this morning and I gave him a lift back to the church."

"Just so you could steal our profit margin?"

"Not *just* for that reason, although I am a bit peckish." He opened the cake cabinet. "Mmm…what do I fancy?"

"Ahem," Henry said and gestured to himself.

Daniel grinned. "Goes without—whoa!" He did a double-take. "Those are Banton Buns."

"Yep." Henry chuckled at Daniel's confused frown. "I'll explain when I get home. On which note, I might be a bit late. I need to finish this business plan."

"OK. I'll make a start on dinner, then." Daniel picked out a bun and took a bite, pondering as he chewed. "Where's Ness?"

"Out back, overseeing a delivery. D'you need to speak to her?"

"I will at some point, but that wasn't why I asked."

"Oh?"

"I think you might get a visit from the reverend this morning."

"He's coming to see Ness?"

"Uh-huh. Anyway, I'd better get back. Morning playtime's nearly over." Daniel moved to leave, but Henry blocked his exit.

"Hold on, you said you didn't come *just* to steal my buns."

Daniel's grin returned, and it was a bit wicked, but he relented at Henry's huff. "OK, you know how, when we were on our honeymoon, you were stressed out about your dad and the Cake-Off and whatnot?"

"Hmm?"

"And you know how teachers get all that time off in the summer?"

"Yes?" Henry folded his arms. The build-up was suspicious.

"Well, Moira the teaching assistant has a villa in Italy."

"Right?"

"And it's available for two weeks in August."

"OK?"

"Hen, are you really going to make me spell this out?"

"You're suggesting we go on holiday."

"I am," Daniel confirmed.

"A summer holiday."

"Correct."

"Hmm." Henry rubbed his chin in a pretence of consideration just long enough to secure a glimpse of Daniel's best puppy-dog-pleading face before he said, "Yes. I'd love to."

"Fantastic!" Daniel hugged him, planted a quick, jam-and-creamy kiss almost on his lips—"See you at home"—and verily danced, whistling 'Summer Holiday', all the way across the shop.

"Bye," Henry called after him in bemusement. The bell tinkled as the door clicked shut.

Smiling to himself, Henry gave his face a quick wipe with a paper towel and went back to his business plan.

***

"Morning, Reverend."

"Good morning, Henry."

He saved his progress, took a quick gulp of coffee and spurted it straight back out again when he saw Reverend Osbourne's latest T-shirt.

Let he who is without sin cast the first cupcake.

The reverend grinned. "Like it?"

"Love it! What can I get you this fine morning?"

"Me," Nessa said right next to Henry's ear, making him jump. "Sorry, cuz." She didn't look it.

"I thought you were out in the yard."

"I came in when I heard the bell," she said.

"Did you now." Henry eyed her suspiciously. You couldn't hear the bell from the yard.

"Yep." Nessa nodded. "Soooo…can you manage without me for a bit?"

"Why? Where are you… Oh! You, um…" Henry blushed, a bit slow on the uptake with his brain full of calculations. "Yes. Absolutely. You go. We close in an hour anyway."

"Great!" Nessa dodged around the counter, a little breathless, and smiled coyly at Reverend Osbourne.

"Thanks for this, Henry," he said.

"Anytime, Reverend." He stifled a chuckle as his ultra-confident cousin and their calm and collected vicar awkwardly negotiated their exit from the premises.

Henry Jones, Baker, est. 1874

A good, solid name, but times change, and sometimes people change with them. Even the Margaret Sharpes of this world.

Yes, the village was big enough to sustain two bakeries, but why compete when they could cooperate? The proof was in the pud…Banton Bun.

Henry refilled his coffee mug and returned once more to his business plan—*their* business plan:

Banton Bakery and Tea Rooms
Opening in 2019
(to the delight of everyone)

…guaranteeing the welcoming village of Banton, population: all kinds of folks…would always have their daily bread.

And buns.

And cakes.

For all.

The End

ABOUT DEBBIE MCGOWAN

Debbie McGowan is an author and publisher based in a semi-rural corner of Lancashire, England. She writes character-driven, realist fiction, celebrating life, love and relationships. A working class girl, she 'ran away' to London at seventeen, was homeless, unemployed and then homeless again, interspersed with animal rights activism (all legal, honest ;)) and volunteer work as a mental health advocate. At twenty-five, she went back to college to study social science—tough with two toddlers, but they had a stay-at-home dad, so it worked itself out. These days, the toddlers are young women, and Debbie teaches undergraduate students, writes novels and runs an independent publishing company, occasionally grabbing an hour of sleep where she can.

SOCIAL MEDIA LINKS

Website: debbiemcgowan.co.uk
Newsletter Signup: eepurl.com/b8emHL
Blog: deb248211.blogspot.com
Facebook: facebook.com/DebbieMcGowanAuthor and facebook.com/beatentrackpublishing
Twitter: @writerdebmcg
YouTube: youtube.com/deb248211
Instagram: instagram/writerdebmcg
Google+: plus.google.com/+DebbieMcGowan
Tumblr: writerdebmcg.tumblr.com
LinkedIn: uk.linkedin.com/in/writerdebmcg
Goodreads: goodreads.com/DebbieMcGowan

BY DEBBIE MCGOWAN

Checking Him Out Series

Checking Him Out (Book One)
Checking Him Out For the Holidays (Novella)
Hiding Out (Novella – Noah and Matty – HBTC Crossover)
Taking Him On (Book Two – Noah and Matty)
Checking In (Book Three)
The Making of Us (Book Four – Jesse and Leigh)

Seeds of Tyrone Series

~ co-written with Raine O'Tierney
Leaving Flowers (Book One)
Where the Grass is Greener (Book Two)
Christmas Craic and Mistletoe (Book Three)

Hiding Behind The Couch Series

The ongoing story of 'The Circle'…
Nine friends from high school;
Nine friends for life.

The Story So Far…
in chronological order:
novellas and short novels are 'stand-alone' stories, but tie in with the series. Think Middle Earth—well, more Middle England, but with a social conscience!

Beginnings (Novella)
Ruminations (Novel)
Class-A (Short Story)
Hiding Behind The Couch (Season One)
No Time Like The Present (Season Two)

The Harder They Fall (Season Three)
Crying in the Rain (Novel)
First Christmas (Novella)
In The Stars Part I: Capricorn–Gemini (Season Four)
Breaking Waves (Novella)
In The Stars Part II: Cancer–Sagittarius (Season Five)
A Midnight Clear (Novella)
Red Hot Christmas (Novella)
Two By Two (Season Six)
Hiding Out (Novella – CHO Crossover)
Breakfast at Cordelia's Aquarium (Short Story)
Chain of Secrets (Novella)
Those Jeffries Boys (Novel)
The WAG and The Scoundrel (Gray Fisher #1)
Reunions (Season Seven)
To Be Sure (Novella)
Tabula Rasa (Gray Fisher #2)
What A Scorcher! (Short Story)
Goth of Christmas Past (Novel)

Stand-Alone Stories

Champagne (LGBT Historical Novel)
'Time to Go' in *Story Salon Big Book of Stories (Contemporary Short Story)*
And The Walls Came Tumbling Down (Sci-fi Novel)
No Dice (Sci-fi Novel)
Double Six (Sci-fi Novel)
Sugar and Sawdust (M/M Romance Short Story)
Cherry Pop Valentine (M/M Romance Short Story)
Coming Up ~ co-written with Al Stewart (LGBT Short Story)
Of the Bauble (LGBT Fantasy Romance Novella)
So Long, Little Black Diamonds (Short (True) Story)
The Pastor's Last Drop (Historical Novel (Ongoing) – Wattpad)
When Skies Have Fallen (LGBT Historical Romance Novel)
A Snowy Ball (When Skies Have Fallen #1.5)
The Great Village Bun Fight (Contemporary Novella)

www.hidingbehindthecouch.com
www.debbiemcgowan.co.uk

A SPRINGFUL OF WINTERS

DAWN SISTER

Kit is a bit socially awkward. In fact, the rules of social encounters are mostly a bit of a mystery to him, but he gets by, with lots of lists and contingency plans. He doesn't have any plans in place for when he first meets Stephan, however, and he keeps bumping into the man in the most embarrassing situations. The trouble is, Stephan keeps turning up in unexpected places, arousing suspicion that this gorgeous man might just have some contingency plans of his own where Kit is concerned.

***

Genre: LGBT romance, humour

Keywords: gay, autistic MC, humour, dogs with jobs, love, romance, humour

ACKNOWLEDGEMENTS

As always, there are people to thank. People who work tirelessly behind the scenes to make my scribblings into a professionally published book. People who answer my questions at three a.m. in the morning when I forget that they need sleep. People who sit and listen to me ranting about a difficult plot point I just can't work through. People who put up with my absent-mindedness and forgetfulness when my brain is focused on the story and not on real life.

To those people: thank you. Too numerous to mention, but all there for me when I need them.

A special mention must go to the person who designed the cover of this book. Steve, your doodles are epic.

CHAPTER ONE

It Shouldn't Snow in Spring
or
My Dog Isn't Trained Not to Crash Weddings

SNOW? ON THE first day of spring. It goes against all the rules of nature, Yenta." I huff as I look out the window of the bookshop where I work.

"Oh, come now, Kit," Yenta says in a soothing tone. "Even if it is the first day of spring, you have to admit, the snow looks beautiful. It's like Christmas again, or how Christmases used to be when I was a child."

"Christmas?" I exclaim, giving her a startled, disgusted look. "But it's nearly Easter. It's been winter for three flipping months. That was ample time to give us some snow, but nooooo, first day of spring and boom, it's bloody Snowmageddon out there. What the hell is going on?"

"In Russia, where I grew up, Lapushka, the snow would last well past Easter."

"Hmpf. That doesn't make me feel any happier. It's just wrong for it to be snowing when there should be sunshine and flowers. How will the daffodils grow now? I like daffodils. They can't grow if the ground is covered in snow. What if they don't come? What if the snow never goes? What if it stays winter forever, like Narnia when the White Witch made it forever winter and never Christmas? Or what if the winter lasts for decades like in Game of Thrones? It's the end of the world, Armageddon." I throw up my hands in despair, pacing back and forth as I speak, watching my reflection in the glass.

I get distracted by the fact that I may not have brushed my hair this morning and it's falling in messy waves over my shoulder. I'm surprised Yenta didn't remind me. My eyes stand out, bright against the dark glass. I rarely look at myself in the mirror, so I am always surprised by how green they are. I stick out my tongue and then stop when I realise people passing by outside might wonder what I'm doing, a grown man staring at his reflection in the window and making faces.

"Lapushka." Yenta chuckles. "I think you may be overreacting. It is a late snowfall, and heavy, yes, but it is not the end of the world, I assure you. Come and have some tea. It is time to close the shop, anyway."

With a heavy sigh, I turn away from the front window and move to the door. I flip the closed sign over and push the bolt home. The bookshop has not been very busy today, mostly because of the snow.

I join Yenta on the comfy chairs in the window where our customers often sit and read. She pours the tea for us both.

Yenta is my boss and my landlady, since she owns the bookshop and the flat above, which is where I live. Most of all, though, she is my closest friend. She calls me *Lapushka*, even though my name is Kit. I don't mind her calling me that, because, apparently, in Russian it's some kind of term of endearment.

As always, there are cakes to go with the tea. Yenta likes to bake as well as own a bookshop, although I technically manage the shop, so she does have lots of time for baking. My stomach isn't complaining, anyway.

"The cakes are delicious, Yenta. As always."

"Thank you, Lapushka." She smiles as she takes a bite of hers.

This is our routine every weekday. Routines are good. Routines are safe. They make sense.

This routine is a way of winding down after work, and Yenta's way of thanking me even though I get paid—which is thanks enough—for being here and working for her. She is eighty. A spritely eighty, but she always says she could never have kept this shop going if it wasn't for me. I am just grateful that she gave me this chance after it seemed I would never get a job. No one wanted to employ me, even though I have two degrees, and I was in danger of becoming homeless and jobless when she stepped in and saved the day. A familiar sick feeling washes over me when I remember how close I was to losing everything. Including my mind. Two years and it's still difficult to even think about it.

Bessie, my beagle, slinks in, hoping for her walk to start early. She stays upstairs during the day but must have heard me throw the bolt home. She pushes her head up against my palm in greeting. It's her way of telling me she senses I'm upset about something, and she's there to ground me. I give her a grateful scratch behind her ears, and her tail thumps steadily on the floor as she accepts the attention.

I do overreact sometimes. Especially when things happen that I'm not expecting. I don't like change and I don't like when my routine gets interrupted. Snow certainly interrupts everyone's routine, especially when it is unexpected. So, to put it mildly, I'm not having a very good day.

"It was supposed to be sunny today. The weather app said it was going to be sunny. I'm never trusting that app again. The trouble is, I'm running out of weather apps to try. None of them seem to be one hundred percent accurate."

"Weather forecasting is not an exact science. The meteorologists do get it wrong sometimes."

"Hmpf."

To say I'm grumpy would be an understatement. "Why can't things just stay the same? It's the first day of spring, and this time last year, we had a glorious day…sunshine, warmth, lots of daffodils. This year, it's all gone to hell. And I have to walk Bessie in this."

"She will love it," Yenta tells me.

I shrug and sigh. "Yes, you're probably right. Judging by her behaviour this morning. She went absolutely crazy when I let her out in the yard. I've never seen dogs do the things she did. She rolled in snow, dug in it, buried herself in it. She ate it, Yenta. She ate the snow. At least it wasn't yellow." I grimace and shudder. "Or rather, it wasn't until she'd done her business."

Yenta is laughing, holding her sides. "Oh, I wish I could have seen that. She is a funny dog."

"She's a crazy dog." I chuckle. "She always does as she's told, though. I'm quite lucky in that respect."

"You will be all right walking her tonight?" Yenta asks. "You are not worried about the snow? You must wrap up very warm, of course."

"I've seen snow before, Yenta, just never at this time of year. I can cope with it, even if I have spent most of the day complaining about it."

She gives me a slightly admonishing look that says she's noticed I've spent all day complaining but really doesn't mind.

"It will most likely be gone tomorrow," she assures me. "And spring can begin in earnest."

"Hopefully." I'm not convinced.

"Where will you be going on your walk this evening?"

"It's Wednesday," I explain. "On Wednesdays, I walk Bessie in the woods."

"The track may be blocked."

"If it is, then I'll turn back and come back through the park."

"That sounds like a good plan, Lapushka."

With the plan settled, I take Bessie out for her walk.

I listen to Yenta's advice and put on warm layers. I've even put on a hat even though I hate wearing hats because they make my hair itch.

Most people don't get itchy hair. I do. I wish I didn't. It's a little difficult to explain how my hair can itch when strands of hair don't actually have any nerve endings. It's not my head that itches, though; it's definitely my hair. For the same reason, I don't get my hair cut very often. The last time I got it cut was two years ago. Yenta says it doesn't matter, that I suit long hair. That's just as well because if I could, I wouldn't ever get my hair cut again. The only reason I got it cut before was my mum made me, and after she died, it was my boyfriend, Harry. Then he left, so I didn't have to do what they said anymore. I miss my mum because she did more than just tell me what to do. I don't miss Harry because that's all he ever did.

Bessie behaves herself for the time it takes us to get to the woods and the track we usually take. This is mostly because the snow has been flattened down and frozen and she can't roll in it or dig it up. Once we reach the track, the snow is deeper, with even deeper drifts, and she goes completely bonkers again.

Like I told Yenta, I've never seen a dog do the things she's doing. Once I let her off the lead, she loses it. She jumps in the stuff, dives at it, like it's something alive for her to hunt. She's rolled in it so many times within the first five minutes, it's hard to tell if she's still a real dog or a snow dog. Her tail is wagging so fast there's a real chance she'll wag it off. She's utterly ridiculous about the entire thing and I don't think I've laughed so much in my life. I'm afraid I'm going to do myself an injury.

This continues throughout the woodland portion of our walk. The harder I laugh, the more outrageous she becomes. She is so wound up that when I call her to heel, for the first time since I got her, she doesn't come.

Thinking it was all part of our 'snow game', she waits until I get close enough to put the lead back on her collar, but before I manage to do it, she runs off again. She does this three times before I stop laughing. Things are beginning to get out of hand, and I start to panic.

"Bessie. Come here." I try to sound firm, commanding her the way I was taught at dog obedience classes, but it doesn't work. What am I going to do if she doesn't come? I can't leave her here, but I have to get home soon because Yenta is cooking dinner and she will worry if I'm not back.

I chase Bessie along the track as she runs from side to side chasing imaginary rabbits. I eventually catch up with her as she rolls enthusiastically in a patch of snow that does not look particularly white. In fact, it's not snow at all, because it is brown.

"Oh god, Bessie, I hope that's just mud."

My hopes are dashed when my nostrils are attacked by the familiar and most unwanted scent of fox excrement. This is a beagle trait, built into their genes by generations of her breed being used for fox hunting. Bessie is not a fox hunter, but she still rolls in fox poop whenever she finds it. I'm sure the bloody foxes leave it by the side of the track just for her…and to annoy me.

"Bessie!" I exclaim. "There is no way you are ever going to get anywhere near a fox, so why the hell do you roll in their crap?" I click my tongue as I fumble with the clip of her lead, trying, with frozen fingers, to attach it to her collar. "Now I'll have to bath you, and because you're such a mad dog, that means bathing me as well. Yenta won't have you anywhere near her house when you smell like this. Gah! You stink."

I'm getting increasingly worked up, cold, wet, and fucking annoyed, quite frankly.

Bessie decides that she needs to up her game because I haven't laughed for the last five minutes. So, instead of letting me clip the lead to her collar, she finds a hole in a fence that runs alongside this part of the track and disappears through it.

"Crap crappy crap crap!" I curse as I watch her squeeze her slightly puppy-plump body through the hole.

Beyond the fence is private land—belonging to a hotel, I think. I have no choice but to follow her, so we will both technically be trespassing. I hope the owner is understanding.

I can't fit through the hole Bessie wiggled through. I'm slim, but with four layers of warm clothes, there's no way I'm getting through there. I have to scale the fence.

I'm just glad there's no one around to see me fall on my face in the snow drift on the other side.

I get up and brush myself down just in time to see my wonderfully smelly dog disappear across the back lawn of the large mansion house hotel and in through an open door that's lit up like a beacon of welcome to a sociable beagle like Bessie.

I vent my utter frustration with a growled, "Fuuuuuuuck," before I set off in pursuit.

Judging by the flashing strobe lights and the noise emanating from the propped open fire door, there is a party going on in that very swank hotel. A party that has just been crashed by an overly friendly beagle covered in snow and fox poop.

I reach the door, out of breath and feeling the effort of running in my snow boots through freshly fallen, foot-deep snow. Peering inside, I gasp and feel the need to go off and hide somewhere on another planet—in another universe, maybe.

There is a woman…not just a woman. A bride, in a meringue-style white dress, except it's no longer white because there are two very obvious brown paw prints on the hem. She is holding a champagne flute, shouting and gesticulating wildly with her other hand and glaring in the direction that I assume Bessie has gone.

Shit, I hope she's already had her wedding photos taken because I am pretty sure that wedding insurance doesn't cover attacks from wild, shit-covered beagles.

I sneak in through the door, not really wanting to draw attention to the fact that I am responsible for this unfortunate mishap. I feel sick with panic now. When I make a plan, I like to try and include everything that might go wrong and list all the things I can do, or say, if those things do go wrong, but there's no way I could ever have predicted this would happen.

For a moment, I am frozen in indecision. Everyone is too busy consoling the hysterical bride so they didn't really notice me, which is just as well, because I'd rather have the floor open up and swallow me than have to talk to anyone right now. And right now, the possibility of the floor opening up is just as likely as the actual turn of events.

From my vantage point at the back of the room, I see Bessie weaving her way around the perimeter in stealth mode, heading towards the buffet. This is just getting worse and worse. I have to get to her before she gets to the food.

I can't go across the dance floor. I would attract too much attention, and I don't really want to face the wrath of an angry wedding party with an upset bride. I don't do interactions with people at the best of times, but angry people, I just can't deal with. Most of the time I don't even know what they're angry about, although it wouldn't take a degree in rocket science to work out the source of their anger tonight.

I edge around the room and exit via a side door. Surely there's a corridor running alongside this room. I can see other doors that lead off to somewhere. I can probably get to Bessie quicker going along the corridor than feeding through the party. My assumption is right, and once out in the corridor, I run.

I just get to the nearest door to the buffet section of the room when I am accosted by a member of staff—at least, I assume he is because he is wearing a waiter's uniform and carrying a bottle of champagne in an ice bucket.

"Can I help you? You look a bit lost." He's obviously taking in my appearance and realising I don't exactly fit the dress code for the night. I'm at a loss to think of a place I would fit in right now. I'm in such a state I must look like a wild man. "You can't be here, it's the staff access corridor. Are you invited to the party?"

He approaches me, and I feel my heart start to pump wildly. Words escape me, and I simply stare. That might have something to do with the fact that I am still out of breath after my run through the deep snow across the hotel lawn. It also has a lot to do with the fact that talking to people is not really one of my strong points, especially when I'm stressed. But my tongue-tied state might also be due to the fact that he is *fucking gorgeous.*

My eyes meet his perfect azure blue ones. It might still be winter outside, but it is definitely spring in here, because his eyes are like a clear spring morning. I don't usually notice people's eyes.

I avoid looking at them altogether because meeting someone's gaze is just too intimate, and overwhelming. It's like looking into someone's soul, and you can't do that when you first meet them. Eye contact is for close friends and family and something that happens after you get to know them very well, and I want to get to know this man. It's never going to happen, though, because he looks angry.

This tall, blonde Adonis in a crisp white shirt and black dress pants is hot as hell as he storms up to me, his blue eyes taking in my appearance and making judgements I don't want him to make, but in this situation, what else could possibly happen?

"What are you doing here?" he demands and I manage to hoarsely answer.

"M-my dog." I squeak. "She's in there." I grimace. "S-sorry!" He takes one startled look at me and then looks through the door, propped open with my foot.

"Holy shit! What's her name?" he asks, turning back to me.

"B-Bessie," I tell him.

"Stay there, I'll get her."

"Careful, she's covered in...oh." I'm too late to warn him about the fox poop because he's already through the door.

I try to shout the warning to him but the music is too loud and swallows my words, and it is already too late anyway. The Adonis that looks like spring has found Bessie and scooped her up in his arms. I see he has begun to realise the folly of his actions by the expression of disgust on his perfect face. His nose is wrinkled because there is no way he can ignore that smell.

I jump away from the doorway as he pushes backwards through it, turning his head from side to side to try to avoid Bessie's insistently friendly tongue.

"Here," he hisses urgently. "Take her and go, quick, before anyone sees you." He hands her over and I hesitate. Surely that can't be it. Surely I have to stay and face some sort of retribution for my part in this disaster.

"B-but the bride," I stutter. "Her dress. I should—"

“Her insurance will pay for it to be cleaned.” Mr. Spring turns me and pushes me towards the main entrance. “You really don’t want to go in there and try to explain. She’s fucking bridezilla, and her family are all bonkers. They’ll kill you. Literally. Go, before they come out here looking for you.” His eyes sparkle, and I’m not sure if it’s with mirth, or concern, or something else. I can never tell in the best of circumstances.

I do as he says. I really don’t feel like getting murdered today, or any day. I don’t dare look to see how dirty his shirt is. I don’t even think I say thank you, the ungrateful sod that I am.

I get home without any more trouble and Bessie firmly on the lead. She looks as if she has had the best walk ever; I feel like I’ve been hit by a forty-ton truck.

After I’ve cleaned Bessie up as best I can, I go over to Yenta’s house. She lives just across the back lane from her shop and flat. I tell her what happened over hot cocoa and crumpets, and I don’t think I have seen her laugh so much. I’m glad my embarrassment has been such a good source of amusement.

Well, all right, thinking back it was kind of funny, but not while it was happening, and that waiter… I fancy my chances of ever seeing him again are pretty slim to non-existent, at least not unless I’m dreaming. I’m sure he will feature in my dreams tonight.

I know I should go over there and apologise, but I’m just a great big cowardly shithead when it comes to things like that, so yeah, not gonna happen.

CHAPTER TWO

Finally Some Spring Weather
or
People Should Really Look Before They Open Their Car Doors

THE SNOW LASTED two days. The worst two days of my life. Yenta has suffered more than me, however. Not only has she been stuck inside because she is eighty, and eighty-year-olds don't do well in icy conditions, even sprightly ones like her, but she has been stuck inside with me: an extremely grumpy twenty-four-year-old who hates having his routine disrupted by anything.

I like to keep fit. I go to the gym, and I cycle. I haven't been able to do either because the weather stopped me.

The weather has also prevented me from going over to apologise to that lovely waiter at the hotel. Apologise and perhaps check he didn't lose his job. Well, I'm using the weather as an excuse. I could have gone over, but I'm a coward, and things like this take time to plan. I can't just go over there and improvise. I have to think about what I'm going to say, write it all down, practise it all in front of the mirror, practise in front of Yenta. I know she's ready to throttle me because I've obsessed about this so much.

It's what I do when something is playing on my mind, and I won't get over it until I get it over with. He might turn out to be really nice and we can—urgh! I don't know—be friends maybe?

I am such a hopeless case. Who am I kidding? Even if I do pluck up the courage to go over there, he's going to see me at my most awkward and at best, accept my apology and send me packing. At worst, he'll call me something unpleasant and tell me to fuck off. People like him never want to get involved with people like me.

To take my mind off things, I go out on a bike ride. The shop closes half-day on a Saturday and the weather, though still cold, is dry with little trace of snow left anywhere.

Yenta takes Bessie home with her when we close the shop; I can't take a boisterous beagle on a bike ride, and she keeps Yenta company when I'm not around. I then get ready for my ride.

I always wear the same clothes. My cycling shorts are a little worn, but they're comfortable and familiar. I hate having to buy new things, and I'm fussy about what I wear, so when I find something I'm happy to wear, I tend to wear it out.

I always take the same route. I don't really mind riding different routes, but if I take the same one every time, I don't have to think about it. It means I can think of other things.

Other things like a good-looking waiter that I have nicknamed Mr. Spring because he has eyes like a clear blue spring sky.

It is because my mind is on 'other things' that I don't notice the car door open in front of my bike until it is almost too late.

With a cry, I slam on my breaks, stopping as my front wheel hits the open door. The bike overbalances and I fall sideways, straight into the lap of the driver of the car. Thank god for my helmet, otherwise my head would be in direct contact with this guy's, erm, helmet.

"Holy shit, are you all right?" the guy exclaims. "I didn't see you. I'm so sorry. Oh god…it's you."

"Bloody hell," I gasp, scrambling to get out of this guy's lap, except I'm wedged between the car, his lap and my bike. "Hasn't anyone ever told you to look before you open your door into oncoming traffic? I could've bloody broken my bloody neck." I don't really register his words until I utter the last 'bloody'. The situation is embarrassing enough without the lap belonging to

Mr. bloody Spring. “Hoooo, shit.” I give a half-sob, half-laugh of sheer embarrassment as I scramble unsuccessfully to stand up.

This is worse than Bessiegate. Far worse. I wish I had broken my neck now. Then at least I’d only have to face eternal damnation. A better option by far than facing him, like this.

“Hello again.” Mr. Spring sounds as cheerful as his nickname suggests, and his eyes… Oh my god, they’d melt a frozen tundra.

“Um, hi?” I try to sound as casual as I can as I stop struggling, but it’s not easy with my head in his lap and him acting as if we’ve just bumped into each other on the street.

“Hi.” His smile gets broader, showing two rows of perfect teeth. “I was hoping I’d run into you again.” He rolls his eyes and gives a low chuckle. “Well, not quite like this, obviously. Are you okay?”

“Er, what?” That eye-roll distracted me and his words kind of echo somewhere in the distance, drowned out by the bells I can hear. Is someone ringing bells? Maybe I hit my head and I have concussion. Did he just say he was hoping to run into me? Didn’t I just run into him? “I’m not sure if I am all right, actually.” When I’m embarrassed I get snippy and edgy and a little confrontational, all in an attempt to deflect from my utter humiliation. “Maybe that has something to do with the fact that someone who shall remain nameless thought it was a good idea to open their bloody car door without checking behind them first.”

“Oh, well, sorry.” He snorts. “I think I did apologise straight away but it bears saying again. Of course, while we’re here laying blame, let’s not forget one of the first things they tell you when you’re doing your bikability at school is to watch out for arseholes who might open their car doors without looking behind them.” He says this all with a smirk firmly in place, waiting for me to join in the joke. Well, if he thinks I’ll let him off the hook that easily, he can think again, and also it gives me a perfect excuse to be angry with him and hide the fact that his smile, his eyes, his voice, his entire being melts me from the inside out.

He begins to help me to stand, pushing and lifting me from his lap. I bat away his hands in irritation.

"Thank you, I can manage," I hiss, pulling myself to my feet with as much dignity as a beached whale.

I smooth down my cycling shorts. Thank goodness they've managed to come out of this unscathed. I straighten and instantly regret standing so abruptly as a dizzy spell threatens to send me back into his lap.

I grab the open door as he jumps forward from his seat to support me, his hands on my hips, his head level with my crotch.

For a moment, time freezes and his eyes widen as he glances up at me through thick, blonde lashes. I find myself swallowing hard at the multitude of possibilities that are running through my head as I gaze into those spring-light eyes. Too much information, too much. I should look away but I don't want to. I don't think I've ever wanted anyone more than I have at this moment.

There must be some giveaway in my expression because his eyes widen even more and he pushes me gently away before letting go of my hips slowly, as if he is unsure of what he should do next.

Just when I thought this could not get any more embarrassing, my face heats to the boiling point of something metallic. If he was any closer I'd be in danger of melting his gold eyebrow stud.

"Erm, yes, well, sorry that I crashed into your car door," I stutter as I back off rapidly.

Without taking my eyes off him, I bend down to retrieve my bike and hear a telltale ripping sound as my threadbare bike shorts pick that moment to finally give up the ghost.

Oh my god, I'm going to die. The chain of my bike is jammed, and there's no way I can stop to fix it because my head is whirling. I now face a very awkward hike home with a broken bike and ripped shorts. When Mr. Spring opens his mouth—to point this out, I'm sure—I hold up my hand to stop him.

"Please don't," I say, not able to look him at him. "Don't look at me or even think about offering to help. I can manage."

"B-but your bike. And your shorts…" His breath hitches and I look up, startled.

"Are you laughing at me?" I glare angrily and he backs off, his hands up in defence, shaking his head.

"N-no. I wouldn't dream of it." He sounds a little less than genuine, and when my eyes narrow, he continues, his hands in a pleading position, "Truly, I'm not laughing at you. This is a terrible situation to be in, and some of it was my fault."

"Some of it?" I squeak, desperately trying to hold my ruined shorts together at the back.

"Well, all of it, because your shorts might not have, you know, if I hadn't, you know… At least let me offer you a lift home." He gestures towards the relative items as he speaks and he looks genuinely apologetic, but this is more than my low embarrassment threshold can take. I have to get out of here before my life starts flashing before my eyes and I expire from heat exposure.

"Look, thanks for the offer, but I don't think it's a good idea. I only live around the corner anyway." That's not true, but accepting a lift from a relative stranger was never part of my plan for today, nor was running into his car door. Things are beginning to get out of control, and I might have a bit of a hike to get home, but at least it will be along a route I know. Plus, the time it takes will give me the opportunity to reflect on how crazily embarrassing this has been.

"I'm sorry about the dog thing, you know? The other day. I hope you didn't lose your job or anything drastic like that." God, I sound like a right twat, but I have to get out of here, and because I doubt I am ever going to get another opportunity, I guess this is the best time to throw an apology at him and hope it sticks.

"Okay, that's no problem, mate." He frowns as he replies, obviously remembering how I'd just scarpered to let him take all the blame. "And I didn't lose my job, so no worries there either," he adds, still frowning as if he can't quite fathom me out.

He tips his head to one side, his blue eyes narrowed slightly and his brow furrowed so deeply I have the sudden urge to lick it.

Good god! I have to leave now.

"Oh, good, well, I'll be seeing you."

I'll be seeing you? I'll be bloody seeing you? Now I definitely sound like a twat. Why the hell would he ever want to see me again?

I turn and start to walk away as rapidly as I can with a buckled wheel and a bruised ego, not to mention torn shorts of which he now has an unobstructed view.

I turn with a gasp and start backing away, giving him a helpless pleading, pathetic look as I make another attempt to hold my ruined shorts together and retain the thin thread of dignity I have left. Dignity that has faded into myth.

Please stop watching me! Please get in your car and drive away. There's nothing to see here but a twat in ripped cycling shorts about to die of embarrassment.

He's biting his lip in an attempt not to laugh. I can see the laughter in his eyes, though, and I can't bear it. I don't care if he sees my arse, I need to leave now. I don't even stop when I hear him call out to me. I can't. I just can't deal with any more humiliation.

CHAPTER THREE

Yenta Helps Me Make a Plan
or
Reading over People's Shoulders Is Quite Rude Actually

When I eventually get home and manage to shower away some of the tension, I find a message from Yenta in her usual beautifully scripted handwriting:

> *Come over for dinner, Lapushka. I'm having roast chicken and I can't eat an entire bird on my own.*

I smile. She doesn't have to cook an entire chicken. She buys too much food because she knows I won't refuse to go and help her eat it.

I get ready and join her about half an hour later.

"You look tired, Lapushka," she comments as I kiss her forehead. She grabs my face and gives me an intense searching look.

"I've just had a five-mile hike with a buckled bike wheel," I admit. Knowing that she will demand no less than a full explanation and will know if I've left anything out, I tell her everything, from the car door opening to my less than dignified escape with ripped shorts.

When she finally stops laughing and wipes the tears from her eyes, she directs an admonishing look my way. "Oh, Lapushka.

You should perhaps have accepted his help. It would have saved you such a long walk home. Would it have been so bad?"

"Yenta!" I gasp. "Didn't you hear anything I've just said? I couldn't accept a lift from him. I mean, I abandoned him like a coward the first time we met and then never went back to apologise for mine, or Bessie's behaviour. Then I land in his lap and get all angry like it was entirely his fault when I'm really the one who should have been looking where I was going. Why would he even want to help me after such atrocious behaviour? He only offered out of politeness."

"And a wish to get to know you, perhaps, Lapushka?"

"To know me? What's there to know? I'm a grumpy grotbags and a coward to boot. He's probably back at home now, wherever that is, thanking his lucky stars I didn't accept."

"Nonsense, Lapushka. Sometimes I want to knock your head against something hard. Really." Yenta sounds angry. "You tell me that you wish to meet someone, but when you do, you do everything you can to push them away."

"I didn't meet him, Yenta. Bessie covered him in fox shit and almost cost him his job the first time. The second time, I landed in his lap and tried to blame the entire incident on him. Poor guy probably thinks I'm mad or that he's been run over by a steamroller. In fact, he might prefer that fate to ever getting to know me."

"You put yourself down so much. I don't understand. Anyone would be glad to know you, Lapushka."

I don't reply. I simply heave a sigh, blowing air out through my nose in a sort of derisive snort. Yenta says these things that I find very hard to accept. I think she sees a different me when she looks. I don't have any idea why because she's seen me at my very worst, when I get so anxious I can't even remember my own name. But she was there to help me when no one else was. She stayed when everyone else disappeared into the woodwork, never to reappear, including my boyfriend at the time. She's allowed to think what she wants and say what she wants, and there is nothing I wouldn't do for her, including this idea she has that I need to get out there and meet new people.

I mean, it's not as if I don't ever want to have friends, or perhaps a boyfriend eventually. It's just that, for me, it takes a little more planning and a little more effort on the part of potential friends or partners. Sometimes it is easier to just be by myself, but that isn't always possible and just a little bit lonely, to be honest.

"You should apologise to him," she suggests, and I sense she is about to make this an order that she knows I will never refuse.

"I did that already," I remind her.

"I don't mean something you just threw at him while you were running away." She waves her finger at me. "I mean a proper apology, with flowers."

"Flowers? Yenta, flowers are for funerals."

"Okay, beer, then, or whatever you think a man would want as an apology from another man who likes him."

"Likes him?" I choke.

"Kit Winters." Yenta rarely calls me anything but Lapushka, and even more rarely uses my full name. I am in real trouble now. "Are you a man or a parrot?"

I want to say I'm a parrot, because then I could fly off and hide in a tree. Instead, I lower my eyes and shuffle my feet as I reply.

"I'm a man." I try not to sound like a sullen teenager, but I fail miserably. Yenta has this way of making me feel so much younger than I am. Sometimes it's irritating, but most of the time I'm happy to let her get on with it, grateful that someone still wants to mother me, even when I'm such a grumpy grotbags.

Okay, maybe I do need to stop calling myself names. I don't like it when anyone else does.

"So, now we've established you're a man…" Yenta continues, a thoughtful expression on her face. It's the look she gets when she's planning my next move, because I am obviously incapable of doing this, especially where Mr. Spring is concerned. "What you need to do and what you should have done two days ago, but couldn't because of the weather, is to go over to that hotel and apologise to him properly." She steps up to me and tips her head back to examine my face. She's quite a bit smaller than me, but she can still boss me about, like a—well, like a boss. "Brush this lovely dark hair," she tells me, pretending to smooth her hand over the messy waves. "And flutter those mysterious green eyes and see what happens next."

I ignore her flattery, not because I don't have all of those things she described, but because I don't believe they are as beautiful as she says.

"But I don't even know his name," I counter. "How can I go and ask for him if I don't know his name?"

"You know what he looks like."

"Like spring." I sigh, gasping when I realise I've said this out loud.

Yenta's eyes dance as her grin broadens. "What was that you were saying about not liking him?"

"Okay, okay, so yes, I like him. Or rather, I'm attracted to him… You know, Yenta, I'm not really comfortable discussing this with…with you."

"Why? Because I'm a woman? Because I'm old? Because I grew up in a generation where men loving men was considered not only wrong, but illegal?"

"Maybe all of those things?" I grimace because she's asked me too many questions at once. I can't process them all. Her eyes stop dancing and she fixes me with a steely gaze. Uh-oh, what did I say to make her look like that? "Er, I mean, you're not old. I've known people half your age that were old and doddery. You're not like that at all." I won't make the mistake of calling her spritely to her face. I did that once and regretted it, even though it is a true description. "And I don't really think of you as a woman."

"Really?" She raises her eyebrows as she folds her arms across her chest.

"Okay, that was probably the wrong thing to say." I grimace again and she sighs, shaking her head but resigned to my awkward apology. "You see, I'm no good at anything like this, Yenta. He'll think I'm an arse if he doesn't already. He already thinks I'm a twat."

"So what do you have to lose?"

I regard her helplessly. Does she have to have an answer for every objection I put forward? And why does she have to sound so reasonable, and by default make me sound so unreasonable?

"I notice that you do not deny I am a twat."

"Oh, stop it." She hushes me. "I'm not being unreasonable here, Lapushka. Go over there and apologise to him. If he kicks you to the kerb, at least you'll have tried."

"Oh god, do you think he might really kick me? He didn't look the violent type, but I'm not a very good judge."

"Lapushka, stop worrying and start planning your next move."

"Okay." I hiss, my hands over my ears as I begin to pace. "But I need to find out his name first. I-I can't just go in there and ask for him by description. What if they say they've never heard of him? Or tell me to get lost?"

"So find out his name beforehand. It won't be that hard to do."

"How?"

"I can't believe I have to even say this to someone of your generation." She huffs. "Ever heard of Google?"

"I can't just google him by description," I say in disgust. Yenta might be more knowledgeable than most eighty-year-olds, but she doesn't know everything, apparently. "The internet and Siri are not omnipotent, Yenta."

"No, but you can google the hotel where he works. Sometimes these websites have staff photos. Sometimes they have lists of employee names and job titles. Try that."

I sigh. I'm not going to get out of this. Yenta will not rest until I've exhausted every avenue trying to find this man and apologise to him. If she has to, she will personally drag me by the ear into that hotel foyer and make me stand there while they parade every member of staff in front of me until I find my guy. Not *my* guy, obviously, but…urgh…I pinch the bridge of my nose.

"Okay. I'll search on Google tomorrow in my lunch break," I promise her.

"Got all your contingency plans in place?" she asks me before I leave for the night.

"Yes, Yenta." I smile as I reply. She always makes sure to remind me that I have plans in place for almost every possible outcome in a given situation. Well, all possible outcomes except Bessie crashing weddings or me landing in beautiful men's laps.

I suppose you might call them risk assessments, my contingency plans. They tell me what I can do if something doesn't go to plan. In any given situation, I have contingency plans covering expected and unexpected events, or as many as I can think of. They help to calm my anxiety and let me know what I can do if something goes wrong.

Because of a burglary a few months ago, I do not have a laptop right now and my phone is just a basic standby for the same reason. I could use the computer in the shop. Yenta wouldn't mind at all, but I wouldn't feel right using it for personal stuff, even if it was her idea to use Google.

The next day, I finish off my morning tasks, leave Yenta in charge of the shop and make my way to the library. The library is one of the few places I feel comfortable besides the shop or my own flat. No one expects you to talk in a library; no one tries to strike up unnecessary conversations. Small talk, Yenta calls it. I never could get the hang of it, so I avoid it as much as I can. For situations when I can't avoid it, I have a contingency plan that usually involves steering the conversation towards one of my safe subjects.

"Hello, Kit," the librarian—I can't remember her name—greets me cheerfully. I should know her name, I mean, we talk all the time about books. We're in the same business, almost, so we always talk shop, which suits me fine. It's a safe subject. She knows my name. I just never got around to asking hers. Or maybe I did and I've just forgotten. I'm not very good with names. Does she think I'm a twat as well? She never seems to be thinking that when I'm speaking to her, but then, I'm not that good at reading expressions unless they're really obvious ones.

"Er, hello, erm…" I smile, because Yenta says my smile always hides any awkwardness I might be feeling. The librarian smiles back. A good start. "I need to use the internet," I tell her, suddenly remembering to look at her name badge. Ah, there it is. "Angela, please."

Well, that was bloody awkward, but never mind. She continues to smile. I can't tell if it's a genuine one or a fixed one. All smiles look the same to me. But she gives me an internet log-on code and directs me to a free computer.

Computers are easier than people. They're pretty predictable and usually do what you want them to, and if they aren't doing what you want, there's usually an easy solution to the problem. They're pretty black and white, with no variables to worry about.

The Google screen loads up, I type in the name of Mr. Spring's hotel, The Cosy Casala, and wait. Nothing comes up with that name—well, nothing that is local anyway. Most of the suggestions want to direct me to timeshare properties in Spain. That can't be right. I frown at the screen. Maybe I spelled it wrong.

"There's two 'S's and two 'L's in Cassalla," a voice from behind me offers.

"Oh, thank you," I reply automatically as I type in the correct spelling. The image of the correct hotel appears at the top of the list. Humming with satisfaction, I lean back in my seat.

"You're welcome," the voice behind me says.

I frown. Is someone reading over my shoulder? That's a bit rude. I turn to give the nosey git a piece of my mind and swallow the words as my eyes meet Mr. Spring's. I jump out of my seat in shock.

"Hello again." He grins, his spring-light eyes dancing in the bright lights of the library.

I glance at the computer screen which still shows the evidence of my search. There is no way he is going to think I was looking up the name of his hotel for any other reason than to stalk him.

What other reason could I possibly have? I could splutter out a million excuses, but he'd know I was lying because people can usually tell when I am. Now what do I do? I don't have a plan for this.

I can almost hear Yenta saying, *Ask him his name, Lapushka. He's standing right in front of you.*

However, the part of my brain that is able to think rationally is frozen to a standstill because him turning up and reading over my shoulder was never a part of the plan I had made with Yenta. We didn't factor for this, therefore I have no idea what I'm supposed to say or do. If I could just phone Yenta and ask her, but how stupid is that going to look and sound?

Hello, Yenta, it's me. That guy I like, the one I've been obsessing over for the last three days, has just caught me stalking him online. Please could you tell me what to say and do now so that he doesn't think I'm a complete and utter creep? Preferably with pictures, because my brain is seizing up.

"Hey, are you okay?" Mr. Spring frowns. Is he angry? Concerned? Worried that I'm going to beat him to death with the computer keyboard? Not that I would, but I can never tell what people are thinking just by looking at their faces. Sometimes there's just too much information to process. Sometimes there isn't enough. Plus, when I'm anxious, I do things that most people find quite strange, like wringing my hands together, rocking back and forth from my heels to my toes and other things that help me to calm down. Some people find that intimidating and upsetting. I try not to do it, but sometimes I can't help it, like now, I'm flicking my fingers and biting my bottom lip.

Come on, Kit, this isn't that difficult. People speak to other people all the time. Just open your mouth and make words come out of it.

"You're not supposed to be here," I manage to blurt out, directing my words at the floor by his feet rather than at him. It is the completely wrong thing to say, obviously.

"What?" he asks. "This is a public library, mate. I thought anyone was allowed to come in here."

I chance a quick peek at his face. He's confused, I think, which is better than angry, but not by much. Maybe I can explain a bit better?

"No, no, I mean, I didn't have a contingency plan because I didn't expect you to be here while I was searching for you online."

"Eh?" He looks even more confused. "Why were you searching for me online?"

I want to look at his eyes, because they're the thing I noticed first about him, so I glance at them quickly before staring at the floor again. His bright-blue eyes are now clouded and narrowed, and his top lip is curled in disgust, or maybe just bewilderment?

Oh god, what do I do now? I think I need to explain myself a little better. I take some deep breaths and make a conscious effort to stop flicking my fingers like some crazed lunatic.

"I'm not a stalker," I say so quickly that the words all meld into one.

"No? I, er, didn't think..." He seems a bit lost for words, and I think I might have messed this up very badly. If only I'd had a contingency plan for this, but it hadn't even crossed my mind that he might show up here.

I do have a plan for getting out of awkward, stressful situations though: run, run, and don't stop until you get home. So I follow that.

I back away from him. Unfortunately, I back into one of those trolleys the librarians use to return books to the shelves. The trolley moves, taking me by surprise, then it gets stuck against the side of a row of shelves, turns and slides away from me so I do a sort of pirouette before falling sideways like a dying swan, pulling several books from the nearest shelf as I do. They fall to the floor around me with resounding, ominous thuds, and I wince as each one hits the floor. Now, not only Mr. Spring is regarding me as if I'm an alien, the entire population of the library is also looking.

I scramble to my feet and scarper before anyone can start accusing me of destroying books. Oh god, I'm never going to be able to come back in here ever again.

"Hey, wait!" Mr. Spring calls to me, but I pretend I haven't heard and pick up my pace. I do that sort of quick walk that people do when they cross the road and realise there's a car coming so they speed up but don't quite make it into a run. They always look ridiculous, so I must look a right prat too.

When I get out of the door I do start to run, hoping he hasn't followed me. I don't stop until I get back to the shop, only to realise that I left my backpack behind at the library.

Oh god. Everything I need is in that backpack: my notebooks with all my contingency plans, my special shaped pen, my phone, my wallet, my collection of shells, my cards.

"Yenta?" I call as I burst through the shop door. "Yenta, I did it again." I wheeze, beginning to hyperventilate.

"Lapushka?" Yenta is worried, and I don't want her to be, but I don't know how to stop her feeling that way when I'm feeling so out of control.

"M-my backpack." I gasp. "Mr. Spring," I manage to stutter out. "Stalker."

I start pacing, rubbing my hands together. I haven't felt this anxious in such a long time, but that's because everything has been so settled and normal, with no surprises or any stress. Yenta's seen me like this, but she shouldn't have to cope with it. She's not my mum. She's not Harry. Harry never used to be able to calm me down either. Mum always knew what to do, but she never told anyone else how and she never wrote it down, so when she died, I couldn't explain to anyone how they could help me. Many people just stare at me, avoid me, or leave me on my own. Sometimes they get frustrated and angry.

Is Yenta going to do that? Will this be the time she eventually says enough is enough and tells me she needs someone more stable to run her bookstore?

Oh god, I'm going to lose my job, all because I wanted to find out more about some guy who probably doesn't even want anything to do with me. He definitely won't want anything to do with me now.

"Sit down and take some deep breaths," Yenta urges me, although she doesn't touch me. She knows I can't bear to be touched when I'm in this state. Every sense is heightened—touch, hearing, taste, sight. Touching hurts. Listening hurts. Every bloody thing hurts. "Lapushka, please."

"That isn't my name." I sob, holding my hands over my face.

"I know, I'm sorry. Kit, please. Sit down. Tell me what happened. Let me help if I can." She points to a seat as she tries to calm me.

She shouldn't have to say she's sorry. She calls me Lapushka because she loves me, not because she doesn't know my name. I don't mind her calling me that. In fact, I like it. But when I'm like this, I snap and say things I don't mean.

"I'm Kit," I say, sitting in the seat she pointed at and rocking as I hug myself tightly. Sometimes I feel like I'll float away if something doesn't hold me down. Yenta knows this. She gets my blanket and wraps it around my shoulders. I pull it over my head and rock. Bessie appears from somewhere and pokes her head beneath the blanket to get as close to me as possible. "I'm Kit," I repeat. "But I don't mind you calling me Lapushka. I'm sorry I snapped at you, Yenta."

My voice is muffled but I know she can hear me.

"It's quite all right, Lapushka. Settle now. Bessie's here. I'll make us some tea and then, when you are calm, we can go back to the library for your backpack."

"No!" I lift my head and the blanket falls away so I can see her. "I can't go back there, not ever. I fell over and pulled some books off the shelf. Mr. Spring thinks I'm stalking him, and everyone was staring at me as if I'd done it on purpose. I didn't do it on purpose, I swear, Yenta."

"Of course you didn't," Yenta assures me. "And the librarians will know that, Lapushka. They know you and they know you wouldn't damage a book on purpose."

"No, no, never. But I'm still not going back."

"What about your backpack?"

I grimace. If I don't go back for my backpack, what will happen to it, to all my things? I can't start all over again. Some of those shells were collected when I was on holidays with Mum. I can't do that over again, and they wouldn't be the same shells anyway.

"Can't you go for it, Yenta?"

I know her answer even before she's taken a breath to reply. She looks after me, but at the same time, she makes sure I know how to look after myself. That includes doing things that I hate doing but have to do anyway. What this means is that at some point today, after discussing the contingency plan, I will be going back to collect my backpack.

This fact both thrills me and fills me with dread. I want my stuff, but I don't want to go back to the place where I was embarrassed and embarrassing.

Yenta leaves to tend to a customer in the shop. I take the opportunity to go over what has happened and reassure myself that everything will work out, eventually, I hope.

I left my backpack in the library. This is okay. I can go back and get it. I just have to write down all the things I need to do and say, and try and predict what others will say or do in response, so there's no big surprises.

As for what happened with Mr. Spring…I doubt I will have to do anything about that, because if he didn't think I was a complete loony before, he does now and I doubt I'll be seeing him anymore.

"Kit?" Yenta's gentle tone makes me jump. "Oops, sorry. Kit, there's someone here to see you. They have your backpack. I think it's the young man you told me about, judging by your description."

"Oh god!" I gasp, actually flapping my hands in front of my face like some maiden in a Jane Austin novel. "What's he doing here? How did he find out where I work, live, work?"

"Perhaps he followed you?"

"No, no." I shake my head. "I ran too fast. Left him in the library. He couldn't have..."

"Maybe he looked you up on Google?" she offers. "The way you were trying to do to find out about him."

"There's nothing about me to look up." I frown. How could he look something up if he didn't know anything about me?

"Perhaps he asked the librarians?"

"They don't know where I live," I say in confusion. "I've never told them."

"No, but you wrote down your address on your library card application," Yenta reminds me.

"Oh, of course." Why didn't I think of that?

"Come and meet him, Lapushka. He's waiting, and his name is Stephan, by the way."

"His name is Stephan, by the way," I repeat.

Yenta's eyebrows rise, and I bite my lip. "Sorry," I say, because repeating what people have said to me is something else I do when I'm anxious. I hope I don't do this when I finally speak to... Oh god, I've forgotten already. I'm so used to calling him Mr. Spring. "What's his name again?"

"Honestly, Kit. I just told you, it's Stephan, Stephan, Stephan. Write it down then you won't forget."

I immediately reach for my backpack, then stop. "I can't," I wail. "I left my bag at the library."

"And Stephan brought it back for you."

"Oh." Sometimes my brain doesn't think in linear; it thinks in circles and wobbly lines that criss-cross and get entangled with each other. It means I often remember the ending, or the beginning of something, but the middle part gets lost somewhere in the ether. It's why I have to do things in a certain order because if I forget a step or miss it out, I'm screwed. And new situations, like this one, where I haven't even begun to think about the order of events, have me in a complete and utter flap.

"Get out there and say hello to him. You know how to do that."

"Of course I do." I know how to greet someone. So I should be able to go out and speak to Mr. Spring without any problems.

I stand up and walk to the opening that leads into the shop. It has a curtain rather than a door. I slowly lift one edge away from the wooden frame and peer through.

There he is, Mr. Spring, as large as life standing in Yenta's shop, holding my backpack.

"Oh dear." I step back, breathing hard. "I can't do this. He saw me lose it in the library, and I don't just mean my backpack." I turn back to face her. "Don't make me, please, Yenta."

She turns me around. "He would not have made the effort to bring your backpack here if he did not want to meet you." She gives me a gentle push to encourage me through the curtain as I try to remember my 'hello' protocol.

"Hello again," Mr. Spring says as I enter the shop.

"Oh, I'm supposed to say that first." I scowl, then realise this is not what I should have said and immediately turn to leave again, except Yenta is standing in the doorway, her face stern, as she holds Bessie's collar with one hand and points in the direction of Mr. Spring with the other. All my exits are barred until I've spoken to him.

I turn to face him, surprised that he's stayed actually. First sign of any oddness from me and people don't usually hesitate to leave.

"You know I don't mind if you want to start again," Mr. Spring tells me. I suddenly feel much better. If he wants to start again, that's fine. We can start from the proper beginning.

"Okay, thanks," I say and disappear behind the curtain, much to Yenta's annoyance.

"Get back out there, Kit Winters," she hisses. "He came to see you, not to stand in the middle of a bookshop and be completely ignored."

"He wasn't completely ignored. You spoke to him." I know I shouldn't point out the obvious, but sometimes the words are out of my mouth before my brain can stop them.

"Oh, goodness me, get out there before I blow a fuse," Yenta tells me.

I've never really understood what this means, because humans don't have fuses like plugs do. I know it means to lose your temper. Why can't people just say that instead of inventing all these verbal images that have nothing to do with what is being said?

I don't want to think about that right now, so I put into place one of my first contingency plans I ever wrote: 'saying hello'.

"First, you say hello," I whisper. "Hello," I say out loud to the rather startled looking Mr. Spring. "Then you put out your hand to shake theirs."

I'm forced to look up to see why my hand isn't being shaken by his. I haven't put up my hand, that's why. I immediately rectify this, and then, as he shakes my hand, I make a conscious effort to smile and do my best not to make it seem false or sardonic. Sometimes people think I'm making fun of them when actually I'm just trying my best to fit in and I have an unfortunate tone of voice, or expression on my face, like right now.

"Am I doing this right?" I ask out loud. "I think I forgot to tell you my name."

"Would it help if I told you mine?" Mr. Spring asks, one eyebrow quirked.

"M-maybe." My voice shakes with anxiety. This is very close to going wrong again.

"My name's Stephan," Stephan tells me without any hint of irritation, a smile on his face that is making the spring light in his eyes dance about like fire fairies.

"I'm, er, Kit," I tell him. "Kit Winters, and I'm sorry for running away, sorry for stalking you online, sorry for being an arse when I rode into your car door, and most of all, I'm sorry that Bessie covered you in fox crap." I grimace. "I probably shouldn't have said crap, maybe poop would have been better. Of course, I could have said shit, but that's probably worse than crap. Excrement, is the correct term for it, but that sounds a bit formal and scientific when you're just making an apology."

"Yes, it does." Stephan is staring at me, his eyes wide and his mouth twitching. I'm not sure what he's thinking, but at least he doesn't look annoyed. Things seem to have got a bit awkward until he speaks again and doesn't look uncomfortable at all. "I brought your backpack."

He holds it up for me, and I take it, trying my best not to stare at the floor but finding it difficult to look at him, because then I'd get distracted by his eyes. I could lose myself in those eyes.

"Th-thank you. I shouldn't have left it. I shouldn't have run off. I'm sorry."

"Yes, you said that already. You have nothing to be sorry for, Kit. In fact, I really should have looked before I opened my car door yesterday. But I suppose if I had, then I wouldn't have met you again and I really did want to."

"You did?" I look up now, his words distracting me from my awkwardness. He looks like he's telling the truth. "But why would you want to meet me again after the things Bessie did at your hotel?"

At the sound of her name, Bessie eventually bursts through the curtain, having been restrained by Yenta too long. Stephan gives a cry of alarm and then laughs as Bessie makes a beeline for him and covers him with doggy kisses.

He crouches down to make a fuss of her.

"Careful, she'll try to sit on your…" My warning comes just a little too late, as Bessie does her usual trick of trying to sit on someone's knee regardless of the position they are sitting in. She's not a big dog, but she's heavy, and she and Stephan end up in a heap on the floor as Stephan overbalances and she takes this as an invitation to sit on his stomach instead.

"Oh god." I grab her collar. "She's usually so well behaved. Bessie, heel," I command. She immediately stops smothering

Stephan and comes to my side, pushing her head up against my palm.

"Wow." Stephan sits up, regarding me with what looks like respect. "She's well trained."

"Oh, yes." I shrug. "Except I didn't really train her. We got her from an agency that trains support dogs. She's my erm…" I grimace. I really didn't want to tell him anything like this in our first conversation. It could be our first and our last, so I want him to go away thinking positive things about me, not wondering at how much of a basket case I am.

"We went to obedience classes so I could learn how to look after her properly," I explain. "She is usually very good at staying by my side. She was over-excited about the snow, and our evening walk is when she can let off some steam and burn some energy. Unfortunately, all of that combined the other night, and you and that poor bride got the brunt of it. Was she very angry?"

"No." Stephan dismisses my worries, and then makes a face. "Well, okay, she was angry—livid, actually, and so were her family—but believe me, the things with your dog were not the worst things that happened that night. She was a bridezilla, you know what I mean? She already had two of the waitresses in tears over some trivial thing to do with a smudge on a glass. And the rest of her family weren't much better. I caught two of the bridesmaids having sex in the men's toilets. And a bloke had to be escorted off the premises for making a pass at the barman. The evening ended up with the entire wedding party having a free-for-all brawl in the car park. We had to call the police."

"Oh dear." I'm trying to keep up with everything he's telling me. "Sounds like you had a horrible night."

He nods. "Yes, and your dog here provided a much-needed bit of light relief." When I still don't smile, he continues, "You have to admit, it was kind of funny."

"Not for the bride. She probably spent a fortune on that dress."

"Oh, she did. Apparently, it was designer, and she'd already told just about everyone who would listen how much she'd spent before Bessie here decided to add her own design. We offered to get it cleaned for her, but she refused. Said she had insurance. Anyway, that's not the best part of the story." Stephan waits for me to catch up, or perhaps he's waiting for me to ask him what the best part is. I hope I don't leave it too long to respond. I'm not good at knowing when it's my turn to speak.

"Oh?" I ask.

"No." He snorts, shaking his head. "The next day, after they'd all left, we discovered the wedding dress had been left behind. When I called her to ask if she wanted it delivered to her house, because I really didn't want her or any of her family back in the hotel, she told me to just put it in the bin."

"Her dress?" I ask in shock.

"Yes. She said just put it in the bin. It's ruined. I'm getting another one."

"Another one, but it's a wedding dress. Why would she need another one? You only need to wear it once."

"I know." Stephan holds up his hands in a gesture that I interpret as him being completely baffled by the entire incident. "Don't even ask. I don't know. One of our domestics, his partner runs a dry-cleaning agency. They've taken the dress to be professionally cleaned, and then we're doing what we do with all lost property—we donate it to a charity that deals with LGBTQ homelessness."

"Oh, that's a good idea." I regard him with curiosity. "Do you get a lot of lost property, then?"

"Tons. Mostly things people have left behind by mistake and they call us and we send them on to them. But sometimes it's stuff that the owner either didn't need, wanted to get rid of, or just plain forgot they owned. I've had people deny they left valuable jewellery before, when we know it could only have been them." He shrugs. "Whatever they leave is the charity's gain in the end. It just isn't worth arguing with some people."

"I used to volunteer in a charity shop," I offer, because this is one of my safe subjects. "That's where I met Yenta. She owned the shop, see, and allowed the charity to use it rent free."

"And now you work here?" Stephan looks about, nodding. "Sweet. At least, I'm assuming you work here, although..." He frowns. "This is the address that the librarians gave. Maybe they didn't want to give out your home address."

"Oh, I live here too. Above the shop."

"That's handy." His smile is a little wider than I might expect, like I've said something really amazing, instead of just offered a boring fact about myself.

"Yes, it is, but no snow days when the weather is bad." I scowl. "Which I hated, because it snowed on the first day of spring. I mean, I hated the snow, not the fact that I didn't get a snow day. I wouldn't have wanted a snow day. I love working here. I'm not just saying that because Yenta is listening at the curtain, because she probably is." I bite my lip when I see his expression go blank. I've said too much again. "What I'm trying to say is, I don't like the snow interrupting spring. It's wrong."

"Forecast is for snow again tomorrow," Stephan offers, his voice sounding a little strained, as if he's emotional about something. His news makes me gasp.

"Oh no, not again."

"Long-term forecast looks like this spring is going to be full of mini winters. A springful of winters. Ha, that's funny."

"You know springful isn't a real word," I point out.

He grins, showing a row of white teeth against his pink lips. He's so colourful, all golden, sky-blue, white and pink. There is something going on in my stomach that I really don't understand, and I wish I could leave and ask Yenta, but I know that would be rude, and the sensation isn't unpleasant, just strange.

"Good on you for making the most of the good weather by going out on your bike yesterday."

Exercise is a safe subject for me.

"I like to stay fit. Yenta says we should all do as much exercise as we can to stay healthy. She's eighty and still really fit, so I suppose she's right. She also says we should all eat well. She likes to make sure I eat well." I stop, because I'm oversharing again. "You probably didn't need to know that."

"Have dinner with me." Stephan is staring at me with an unreadable expression on his face. "That's why I was hoping to bump into you again. I would have asked you out yesterday when you crashed into my car, but you left. And just now, at the library, when I saw you at the computer station, I couldn't believe my luck. Have dinner with me, Kit, please?"

I feel a little overwhelmed, and if it wasn't for Bessie pushing her head against my palm and grounding me, I'd have left by now.

"I-I don't know…"

"I know you don't know anything about me. I can tell you, but I don't want to overload you. You can ask me anything you want over dinner. You choose the place."

I bite my lip. "It's not that I don't want to accept, because I do. It's just that I need a bit of time to plan, er, I mean, think about it." I wait for him to laugh, but he doesn't. Instead he smiles again, bombarding my brain with all that colour once more.

Stephan's smile is wide, and his eyes shine with the light of a thousand spring mornings. He looks like one of those footballers that's just scored the best goal of his career and is about to start running about with his shirt pulled over his face. Oh dear, I hope he doesn't actually do that. There's not a lot of room for running in the shop and Yenta might not like that there's a torso on display in her bookshop. Apart from the ones on the covers of the books, that is.

"That's okay." He continues to smile, as if the thing is a permanent feature now and he will keep on smiling even when he's left the shop. "I don't mind waiting."

"You don't?" I ask in surprise. "I mean most people, they just want an answer straight away, and I can't always give one."

"You get asked out to dinner a lot then, do you?" His smile has turned into a smirk.

"No-no, that's not what I meant. I mean, I need time to answer any question I'm asked." *Way to make yourself sound like a special case, Kit.*

"That's fine. I said I can wait." Stephan heads me off, saving me the effort of another long explanation. "How about I give you my number and then you can call me." I look up in alarm. He bites his lip. "Okay, text me, then. Text me when you've made a decision, and Kit?"

"Yes, Stephan?"

"Will you let me know either way?"

"Either way?" I ask in confusion.

"If you want to go to dinner, or if you don't, let me know. Please don't leave me hanging."

"I-I'll text you either way," I repeat for him.

This seems to satisfy him and he stands, holding out his hand to shake mine, this time in a goodbye gesture. I shake it, trying to give him eye contact but worrying too much about it and ending up staring at his hands, which are lovely, but not as lovely as his eyes.

"It was nice to finally meet you properly, Kit." Stephan says, shocking me into leaving go of his hand which I think I've held for longer than I should.

"Nice to finally meet you properly." I grimace, because I've just done that parrot thing, almost. "Er, too." I add to make it seem like I'm using my own words and not his. "I mean, it's nice to finally meet you too."

Now he needs to go before things get more awkward. Not that they ever got past the first stages of awkward to begin with, but there's still time yet. Up until the moment he disappears out the door, I hold my breath, just to stop myself from saying anything stupid or repeating what he's said again.

I turn away from the door to go back and speak to Yenta when the door opens again and he returns, breathless. It's unexpected and completely throws me.

"What?" I snap, sounding rather ungracious. He looks taken aback, and I shake my head. "No, no, I mean, sorry. You startled me. Did you forget something?"

"Y-yes, I forgot to give you my number."

"Oh." I sigh. Thank goodness it's something I can help him with rather than him asking me something I won't be able to answer. "Here, I have some paper."

"I could just put it in your phone," he suggests.

"No, I need it written down. I won't remember if it's put straight into my phone, but if you write it in my contingency—er, I mean my notebook, then I'll remember I have to call you."

"Okay." He takes my contingency plan notebook from me, and too late I realise the title of this particular notebook is fully on display.

–Contingency plans for meeting people and making friends–

"Oh god." I pull it back and fold the front cover back so he can't see. "Sorry." I hope he didn't read it. His expression is indecipherable as he writes his number and his name on the blank page I present to him.

As he hands it back to me, he smiles, and his hand brushes mine, not softly, because that would make me jump. The touch is firm, and I realise he is closing his fingers around my hand to hold it.

"Call me—I mean, text me, please?" He meets my gaze and holds it.

I can't reply because it's all too much: his eyes, his hand on mine, the strange fluttering sensation in my stomach. It's sensory overload. I nod, swallowing hard and sweating with the effort to not do anything that might make me look odd. He gives my hand a firm squeeze before letting it go and running out of the shop.

CHAPTER FOUR

Jogging Accidents Need First-Aiders
or
Bessie Likes Fishing for Phones

SO, STEPHAN SEEMS like a nice young man." Yenta is trying to get me to talk about him. I know this only because she hasn't been very subtle about it at all.

She's already asked me sixteen direct questions relating to what Stephan and I talked about after The Library Fiasco two days ago. I know for a fact she was listening at the curtain and heard every word, so I haven't told her anything she doesn't already know.

"So, are you going to call him?" she asks.

"I told you, I need to think about it," I tell her, not turning around as I place a book up on a high shelf.

"Yes, well, don't think too long, Lapushka." She huffs as she ticks off items on an invoice whilst unpacking our latest delivery.

"He said I could take all the time I needed." I climb down from the ladder and stand in front of her.

"People say that, yes." She regards me over the top of her tiny glasses. "But what they actually mean is they would like you to call them at least the next day."

"I texted him as soon as he left the shop."

"A text to tell him you have his number, something he already knew, does not count." She picks up a pile of books and hands them to me.

"Then someone's rewriting the rules." I scowl, balancing the books on both arms and huffing and puffing as I take them to the next shelf along, moving the wheeled stepladder with my foot. "Why didn't he tell me how long he was willing to wait?"

"Because to him, that would have seemed like he was pushing you, and some people, they don't like to be pushy." Yenta shrugs. "He wants you to make the decision by yourself."

"Yes, and I will. And if he isn't willing to wait however long it takes me, then he isn't the one for me. And if he had a deadline in mind, then he should have said so."

Yenta comes to stand below the ladder as I climb it.

"Not everyone understands how your brain works, Lapushka."

"Huh, tell me about it." I read the title of the first book on my pile and place it in the correct spot on the shelf. I wave the next one at Yenta. "Sometimes I wish I could just write a manual and get everyone to read it. Like this Haynes manual except for me instead of a car."

"I would help you." She nods, strands of her grey hair falling across her face. "And I would buy ten copies, then I would translate it into Russian and German."

I laugh. "Of course you would, and you would hand out copies to everyone that passed by the shop and I wouldn't make any money from it."

"Would making money be your first priority, Lapushka? Really?"

"No." I watch her as she bends over the box of newly delivered books. "Having people understand me, and therefore, by happy chance, understand everyone else like me, that would be my goal."

"There is no one in the world like you, Kit. You are unique." Yenta directs her gaze at me, and for once I don't look away. I just roll my eyes.

"You know what I mean," I tell her, and she grins.

"Yes, yes, I do." She heaves a sigh, as if she is thinking some heavy thoughts. "Are you going to tell Stephan?"

I blow out my cheeks and watch her via her reflection in the window as I think.

"I know I should," I muse. "I mean, it would make things easier, for him, to understand I mean, but it always seems like I'm making a confession, and I haven't done anything wrong. I don't want him to think he has to do anything differently, but at the same time, I need him to understand that he might have to, you know, do some things differently. He probably does need to know that I'm a bit of an oddbod who occasionally goes off the rails quite spectacularly."

"You are not an oddbod. and you do not go 'off the rails'. You just get upset if something goes wrong with your contingency plans."

"Yes, yes, I know that, and you know that, but no one else does. Some people are just not willing to adjust the way they do things to accommodate. And it's not as if I'm asking for any special treatment, because I'm not. I just need more time to do some things."

"Stephan seemed to know that you needed to start over again, and he didn't mind."

For once, I can read her unsaid words as if I'm reading a book. "Yes, yes, I'll text him today after work. That doesn't mean that I'll be going on a date with him. People don't usually think a fast food outlet is the most appropriate setting for a first date."

"Tsh," Yenta hisses. "You do eat other foods, Lapushka."

"I know, I know, just not at restaurants. Too many people, too many smells."

"Maybe he will suggest something different."

"He said it was my choice, though."

"Yes, but perhaps he has made a contingency plan of his own."

"Why would he even do that?"

"Because he likes you? Perhaps you did not notice, but I saw the way he smiled at you, Lapushka. As if you were the world."

"As if I was the what? That's just nonsense, Yenta. Almost as nonsense as some of the stories in these books." I wave a hand in a wide arc to incorporate all of the romance section.

Yenta narrows her eyes and leans forward, poking a bony index finger at me. "The same nonsense that I see you reading every day, Lapushka, so don't pretend you don't know anything about romance."

"I read it. Doesn't mean I understand it," I mutter, feeling petulant that she's called me out on my 'nonsense'. "It's time for me to walk Bessie. Do you want me to get you anything on the way home?"

"No, no. You go. I will shut the shop and see you tomorrow, Lapushka. Have a nice evening."

A nice evening. It's spent all day snowing again. I can't believe we've just got rid of one lot of snow then another lot comes along. *A springful of winters*, was the way Stephan described it. And when I pointed out that 'springful' was not a real word, he laughed, but not in an unkind way. It was different, but not in a way I can describe yet.

I need more time to think. Yenta is right, though, I shouldn't keep him waiting. I want to call him, but I have trouble understanding when it's my turn to speak when I'm talking to someone face-to-face. I have absolutely no hope when it's just a voice on the other end of a phone connection.

I worry at my lip ring as Bessie and I walk towards the woodland track. It has been an entire week since Bessiegate. I have set routes that I walk with her. I would take her the same way every day, but Yenta says Bessie might get bored, so I have several routes in my dog-walking contingency plan. Today it is woodland day. Tomorrow we will go to the park.

The woodland track is slushy in some places and frozen in others. I don't like the disruption of snow when it's supposed to be springtime, but I still quite enjoy the phenomenon. I like the sound of ice cracking beneath my boots, and the way everything is muffled and echoey at the same time.

I like the feel of the cold on my cheeks, and when my ears get cold, I press my fingernails against them because it feels cool and soothing.

No one else understands why I do things like that. Stephan isn't going to either, yet…

The world, Yenta said.

The part of my brain that interprets everything literally wants to scream out that I look nothing like the world. The other part, the part that enjoys reading romance novels and dreaming of happy endings wants to curl up in his lap and let him shower me with silly metaphors like that, forever.

I should just call him. Right now. Without thinking about it. I mean, without thinking about it any more, because I have done nothing but think about what he asked for two whole days. I have already come up with a plan that may be acceptable to him as well as me. I don't like eating out, but I can cook. I don't like going to new places, but he already knows where I live. My plan is to ask him to my flat so I can make pizza. I haven't talked it over with Yenta yet, but it could work, couldn't it?

Okay, I need to stop and act before I overthink the whole thing.

I get out my phone, in the middle of the wood as Bessie runs back and forth across the path in search of whatever scent she can pick up. She's happy for a little bit while I stay in one place to use the phone.

You should never walk and talk on the phone, it's dangerous. Driving and talking on the phone is dangerous too. I always get funny looks for pointing this out, but people need to know how dangerous it is. I'm doing them a favour. They shouldn't be so bloody annoyed about it. They should thank me for trying to help.

I saved Stephan's number as soon as he gave it to me. I don't know his last name, though, and when you save a phone number there's a space for a last name. I don't like to leave blanks, so I put his last name as 'Spring'. I find that funny, since my last name is Winters and if his was really Spring, we would kind of go together. We did meet in the snow, he was a bit of warm sunshine on that icy cold, embarrassing day. I suppose he'd rather forget the entire incident. I would too, except I'd have to forget the first time I saw his beautiful, spring morning eyes.

Oh, well. I sort out in my head what I'm going to say. I quickly jotted down some notes before I came out. I hold my phone in one hand and the notes in the other, including a list of possible replies he might make. Here goes. I press connect.

"Er, hello?" he answers on the first ring.

"Hello, Stephan? This is Kit Winters. I don't know if you remember—"

"Oh god, yes, yes, I remember." He sounds out of breath. "How could I forget? Kit, hello."

"Erm, oh, Hello. Stephan. You said I should think about where I'd like to go and eat, and I've thought about it. I hope I haven't taken too long. I mean, I hope you haven't decided to do something else instead… What I'm saying is, yes, I'd like to go on a date with you… Hello?"

There's a sort of crashing sound and a shout. I wonder what I've interrupted. I listen for a moment. Is he still there? I'm about to ask when he speaks again.

"Look, Kit." His voice sounds a bit high-pitched and crackly. "I'm really sorry, but something's come up. This isn't really a good time."

I'm not very good at understanding different tones of voice, but he still sounds out of breath and now a bit stressed. There's some background noise, water by the sounds of it. Oh dear. Have I called him while he was taking a bath, or walking somewhere, or worse, driving?

"Oh, no, I'm sorry, Stephan. I should call back. When would be a good time?" I should have asked that at the beginning and then he could have told me straight away. I feel bad now. Everything is going wrong. I knew I should have texted. Oh god.

"Don't apologise, Kit. You couldn't know. I'm sorry, after you've taken all this time to… Anyway, could you call me back in like twenty minutes, do you think? I do want to talk to you. Please? I'm really sorry—ah—that I can't talk right—ouch—now."

"Are you all right?" I ask, because now it sounds like he's in pain.

"No, no, sorry, yes, yes, I'm—fucking hell, that's bloody cold—yes, I'm fine. Don't worry. I'll speak to you in about twenty minutes, Kit, I promise."

"O-okay." The call disconnects and I frown at my phone, as if it might give me some answers. I know I could ask the phone, but whilst Siri sometimes knows the answers to my questions, she most likely won't know what is wrong with Stephan and why he couldn't talk right now.

Well, that was confusing and a bit of a disaster. There are so many things I could have done better. The call only lasted forty-five seconds. This is why I don't do friends and relationships or even casual acquaintances when a forty-five-second conversation on the phone ends up a confusing mess. Still, he wants me to call him back. Maybe the second time will be a bit more organised.

Now I have a little time to think about everything that was said. Why did he sound like he was in pain? Was he in pain? What was it he said about something being cold? It's all very puzzling.

"Bessie?" I call, because whilst I was on the phone she's disappeared up the track. She doesn't usually stray too far from my side, unless there's exciting new snow to drive her batty, or she's found a really interesting smell.

Oh dear, I hope she doesn't roll in it, whatever it is she's found. I can hear her barking, so she hasn't gone that far.

"Bessie?"

She barks in response but doesn't appear on the track. Where the hell is she? I haven't got a plan in place for if she runs off again. I was just hoping she wouldn't do it after that first time. Why won't she come?

"Bessie?" I call, feeling a little more panicked as I shine my head torch about, trying to see where she might be hiding. I clench my fists, digging my nails into my palms. I have gloves on, though, so I can't feel it. "B-Bessie?"

"She's here." A voice calls out at the same time as Bessie begins to bark continuously.

There's too much noise. I can't process it. Someone is shouting and Bessie is barking. I put my hands over my ears and freeze. Bessie needs to stop, but I can't see her and she's too far away. I can't shout because that would just add to the noise.

"Kit?" the voice calls again, and I hear it clearly above Bessie's barking because it's my name, and I suddenly realise I recognise the owner of the voice.

"Stephan?" I shout out. "Where are you?"

"Yes, through here, in the trees at the side of the track. Bessie, go and find Kit. Find Kit, girl. Good girl."

Bessie appears, bounding towards me from further up the track, and my limbs are suddenly free of their paralysis.

"Oh, thank god," I greet her as she jumps up at me. I don't even tell her off because I'm so relieved to see her. Then I remember what else is going on. "Where's Stephan, Bessie? Take me to Stephan."

I'm not really sure if she understands me, but her retriever instinct, crossed with her beagle sense of smell, seems to comprehend what I want her to do. She takes off down the track, stopping a few paces ahead to make sure I'm following before running off again, with me in careful pursuit because the track is really quite icy and slippery.

Around a bend in the track, I stop. Before me is a sight I just didn't expect, so it takes me a little while to make sense of it.

Alongside this part of the track there is a drainage ditch. It is usually filled with water, or varying degrees of mud. Today, it is filled with a combination of icy water, slush, mud…and Stephan.

"Stephan?" I exclaim.

"Hello, Kit." He smiles, but it doesn't have his usual spring morning brilliance.

"What are you, er, doing here?"

"I'm sitting in a frozen, slushy pool," he tells me, as if this is something I haven't already worked out.

"Er, why?"

"For the fun of it, Kit," he snaps, sounding a bit angry as he splashes the water around him with the palms of his hands.

"Oh, I see." I frown. What he said doesn't match the expression on his face. "You don't look like you're having fun."

He heaves a deep sigh and pinches the bridge of his nose, grimacing as water drips down from his fingers and over his lips and chin. "That's because I'm not. I was being sarcastic, I'm sorry." He says all this through gritted teeth.

"Oh, I see." I'm still a bit confused. "How did you get there?"

"I fell, Kit. I was running, and I slipped and fell."

"Oh no, are you hurt? Do you need help? I know first aid. I did a course at the library last year. It lasted six weeks, one hour a week, on Tuesdays." I stop when his expression changes from annoyed to something else I can't interpret. "I'm sorry, you probably didn't need to know that. Do you want me to help you out of that ditch?"

"Yes, please." Stephan is smiling again. I think he's relieved I've stopped talking.

I get as close to the edge of the ditch as possible and extend my hand for him to grab hold of. Bessie is trying to help too, but she thinks it's a game. I don't need to write down any plan for this, because it's pretty easy to predict what could happen. Stephan is taller than me, so probably heavier. Bessie is not really helping, as she jumps into the ditch and starts splashing about, trying to lick

Stephan's face, or any part of him she can get to. With a startled cry, I end up in the ditch with Stephan, sitting on his lap, in fact.

I gasp as the icy water seeps through my layers of clothes. For a moment, time stands still as Stephan's arms wrap firmly around me and hold me in position to stop me struggling.

"Steady on. You're all right. I've got you," he says in a soothing tone much like the one Yenta uses to help me calm down.

It does the job and I stop thrashing about and sit still in his lap. The water is cold, but I somehow don't notice it so much as I do the warmth of his arms around me and the look on his face as I fix my gaze on the spring light sparkling in his eyes.

"That's the second time you've ended up in my lap, Kit. We have to stop meeting like this." He smiles.

"Huh." I try to smile in response to his smile, but my teeth are chattering with the cold. "I have to stand up."

I wish I could have said something different. Something a little more appropriate. I recognise the way he spoke, because it sounded like a line from a movie, when the two main characters are flirting. I want to be able to flirt back, but I can never think of anything to say in the time allowed. Now it's too late, because he's already pushing me off his lap and letting me pull myself to my feet using the long, thick marsh grass that grows along this side of the track.

Once I'm up, I turn and extend my hand to him again. "Second try," I say, trying to smile and make it sound light-hearted. The truth is I'm worried that the same thing will happen again if I don't call Bessie to heel, but if I stop to do that, then Stephan will be left longer in that pool of freezing water, and I can't help noticing that he's wearing a lot less than I am. He's in danger of getting hypothermia. I know that because of the first-aid course I did.

There are too many thoughts in my head now. I need to organise them into a list. My hands cover my ears as I try to sort it all into a workable order, then I click my fingers as I mutter to myself.

"Bessie first, then Stephan, then think about first aid." Finally having everything sorted in the order I need to do it, I say, "Bessie. Heel." I keep my tone firm. She does as she is told. I can now concentrate on Stephan. "Sorry. I'll help you up now. Did you say if you were hurt?"

"I can't tell, I'm so bloody frozen," he replies through teeth that are chattering more than mine.

"Oh dear." I grab his hand and pull.

He scrambles up the side of the ditch with my help and ends up on the track, on his knees, breathing hard and looking rather pale. Muddy water drips off his hair and down his arms. I look him over and see he has lost a shoe. He's wearing running gear. Something is connecting in my brain. Was he running when I phoned him? Was that why he sounded out of breath? Did he fall when he was speaking to me?

"Oh god, was this my fault?" I ask him in shock. "Did you fall because I phoned you?"

He looks up at me, his expression one of surprise.

"No!" He gasps. "How could this have been your fault? It was my own stupid fault for answering the phone. I shouldn't have, but I've been, you know, waiting for this important phone call for days now."

I grimace. "And instead you got me. Oh god, Stephan, I'm sorry."

His expression has changed again. Good lord, I can't keep up with all the emotions he's feeling. He looks like he wants to say something, then thinks better of it. Instead, he heaves another sigh, then holds out his hand.

"Help me up, will you?"

I pull him to his feet, and he takes a step then immediately collapses to the ground with a loud cry. I understand the expression on his face now as he grabs his right ankle and begins to massage it. He's in agony.

"You *are* hurt." I fall to my knees beside him but don't touch him in case he doesn't want me to.

"Yes, I must have twisted my bloody ankle." He hisses through his teeth. "I'll need some help to get home, Kit. Will you help me?"

"Of course I will, although—" Oh dear. Now I'm in a pickle. "I don't have a plan for this. "I was going to make a plan for getting to your house once I'd asked where you live, but I haven't asked yet, and I haven't asked if it's okay for Bessie to come along as well, since she's here and I can't leave her. So, yes, I'll help you, but I don't know where you live."

Stephan smiles, and snorts a small laugh through his nose, his eyes twinkling, reflecting the sparkle of my torchlight. "Oh my god, you are so..." He chuckles. "That's okay, lovely boy. I know where I live. I'll tell you. You can even put it into Google maps so you can see where it is."

"Oh, that's okay. That's okay. Thank you." I smile and nod as I get out my phone. "But I'm not a boy, just so you know. I'm twenty-four."

I'm just opening the map app when he makes another noise that sounds like frustration. I put my phone away quickly, but he stops me with a hand on my wrist.

"It's okay, I'm not angry with you. I just realised, I dropped my phone in that stupid ditch."

"Oh, that's okay. Bessie will find it. That's what she's trained to do. Bessie." I call her over from the position I made her stay just a few minutes before. "Find Stephan's phone." I tell her. "His phone, Bessie. Find the phone."

Bessie regards me with her head tipped to one side and her tongue lolling out, in her 'thinking pose', before jumping feet first into the icy, muddy ditch. There's a fair bit of scrabbling about, whining, grunting and yelping and Stephan laughs out loud as he shuffles to get a better view. After about a minute of searching Bessie jumps back out of the ditch with something in her mouth. She shakes herself dry, showering both of us in great globs of freezing mud and slush before dropping Stephan's shoe at my feet. She immediately turns, jumps back into the ditch and repeats the process, this time dropping the retrieved phone at my feet and sitting back waiting for her reward.

"Bloody hell," Stephan exclaims and I can't help smiling. "She's found it. That's my phone and my shoe. She's a beaut. What a star, owned by a star."

I never know how to respond to praise without sounding either bad-tempered or awkward. Instead I make a fuss of my lovely dog, because she is the true star, even though she is covered in mud and worse. I fish in my pocket for a treat, give it to her, and then hand Stephan his phone and shoe.

"I'm afraid your phone is a bit wet and probably knackered," I say with a note of regret and sympathy.

He shrugs. "I can put it in rice when I get home. Heard that does the trick. And if it doesn't...shit happens, I suppose." He shrugs again and puts the phone in a holder he's wearing around his arm. "Now, how about getting me home, because I'm bloody freezing. Important parts of my anatomy are going to start falling off if I don't get warm soon."

"Oh no!" I gasp. "Here, you can have my coat." I unfasten it and hand it to him. "It's wet as well, but not quite so soaked as you are, since it's waterproof and kept some of the water out."

"I can't take your coat, then you'll be cold."

"No I won't. I've still got two jumpers on, a T-shirt and a vest. Yenta always says I should wear layers to keep warm when I'm walking Bessie in the winter. Although, technically this is now spring, but with winter weather. That's very confusing."

"It is, yes." Stephan is looking at me in a funny way, and it makes me feel a bit awkward. I don't really know what he's feeling now, but he accepts my coat, so that's okay. Now I don't need to worry about him getting cold. I just need to worry about how I'm going to help him home because he's quite a bit taller than me and I'm not very strong.

Turns out he doesn't live far. At the hotel, in fact.

"You live in the hotel?" I ask in surprise after he tells me. "Like, where you work? Just like me, living above Yenta's shop."

"Yes. That's something we have in common." His voice sounds strained, and he's gritting his teeth, probably because he's in pain. I wish I could take it away, or somehow take it into myself. I always feel so helpless in situations like this. That's why I did that first-aid course. But it still can't help him when he's in pain. I hate to think he's in this situation because I picked that precise moment to phone him. Especially when he was waiting for another phone call, which he won't get now because his phone is waterlogged.

"I'm sorry you won't get your important phone call now, Stephan. Did the person have your landline? Maybe they'll call you on that."

"That's okay, Kit. I already got the phone call I was waiting for."

I give him a puzzled look. "You said you answered the phone because you were waiting for an important call but instead you got me."

"No, not instead. Yours was the call I was waiting for, Kit."

"Oh. I—er—okay." I can't think why my call would be so important, since it was just to ask him if it was okay if we either went to eat at Subway or ate pizza at my flat for our date. Of course, he doesn't know this, because he fell into the ditch before I got the chance to ask him. "Why didn't you tell me you'd fallen into a ditch? I would have come to help. I wasn't far away."

"Yeah, but I didn't know that at the time, Kit, and it was kind of embarrassing."

"No more embarrassing than the things I've done. You caught me googling you in the library."

"Ooer, it's terrible when someone googles you in the library." He giggles.

"Yes, I know, and I already apologised for that, but I didn't know your name."

"I was joking, Kit, and I know you apologised. Now you know my name, and I know yours." He grunts as we stumble over a bump in the track. "Jesus, that hurt. Could you g-give me a minute?"

He looks very pale, and I'm afraid he might pass out. Fortunately, I remember how to help because of that first-aid course.

"If you pass out, I know what to do," I reassure him. "I know what to do if you suffer a heart attack, a fit, bleeding, vomiting, lacerations, fainting, going into medical shock, migraine, nosebleed—"

"Kit, I get the idea, but I've just hurt my ankle, mate. I don't think I'm going to die."

"I don't think you are either. At least I hope you're not. I don't even know your last name yet. I can't keep calling you Mr. Spring."

"Mr. what?" He gapes at me. Oh god, he thinks I'm a freak. "My last name is Cassillis," he adds, thankfully not asking about the Spring thing.

"Oh good. I can put that in my phone now. Stephan Cassillis. It sounds nice."

"Not as nice as Kit Winters. And I like that you called me Spring. Winter and Spring go together quite nicely."

"I was just thinking that, yes, they do, if one lets the other in. This spring has been full of winters."

"Yes, and I wish this Spring was full of Winters too." Stephan mutters beneath his breath, words I don't think I'm supposed to have heard. He coughs, clearing his throat and smiling as if to hide the fact he's said something wrong. "I'm good to go now," he says, still smiling. "And while we're walking, why don't you tell me all about that first-aid course?"

"Really?" I ask, wondering if he's serious. "Because I can, but you know, if you're being funny, or sarcastic, I can't always tell."

"I'm not being sarcastic. Talk to me, Kit. You could read me the Shipping Forecast and I'd be mesmerised. You've got the loveliest voice, and I want to know everything about you."

So, with Bessie bounding around our feet like she's trying to herd us and me trying very hard to make sure Stephan doesn't put much weight on his injured ankle, we make our way to Stephan's hotel and I tell him all about first aid.

CHAPTER FIVE

Bessie Is Almost a YouTube Sensation
or
I Don't like Wearing Other People's Clothes

And that doesn't actually work, you know. Rice doesn't absorb the water fast enough for it not to do any damage. What you need is a desiccant. I've got some in my flat. I collect all those little packets you get in shoe boxes because I once dropped my phone down the toilet and had to get a new one, and it took me ages to decide what to get because they'd stopped making the model I dropped. Now I know how to dry it out properly so I don't have to go through all the rigmarole of finding a new phone."

Stephan is still listening avidly to everything I say as we finally hobble into the foyer of his hotel. I'd finished talking about first aid, and when he told me to talk about something else, anything, I started talking about drying phones out, because that seemed relevant.

"Steph." A voice startles me into silence, as a large, tall man, with grey eyes and wearing a smart suit strides quickly across the foyer to join us. "What happened, son?"

"Dad, I'm okay. I fell when I was out running. Kit rescued me. This is Kit." He smiles as he waves his free hand at me. I'm still standing with Stephan's other arm over my shoulder.

The man regards me with narrowed eyes. "Oh, so you're Kit," he says in an ominous way that makes me want to hide, and my hands are full of Stephan, so I can't shake this man's hand, not that he offers his to shake, but that means I can't say hello properly. He's turned away before I can do anything about it.

"It's okay," Stephan whispers in my ear, the sensation sending shivers down my spine that aren't unpleasant. "You can say hello properly when he's heard what happened to me. He won't mind that it's all in the wrong order. He's my dad, by the way. George. George Cassillis."

I nod, feeling a little disconcerted that he knew to even say that to me. How did he know? Is he psychic? I mean, I know that's not a real thing, but Stephan seems to have some sort of magic all of his own. It's almost as if he has a contingency plan just for dealing with me and all my quirks before he even knows what any of those quirks are.

"Right, Kit, take him into the lounge, while I get him some decent clothes to wear." He looks Stephan up and down and snorts. "What the hell are you wearing anyway? Running shorts? Steph, you've never gone running in your life."

Stephan looks a little embarrassed as I help him towards the large, well-lit room his dad has indicated.

"Oh god, Dad. There's a first time for everything, y'know. And Kit got a bit wet as well. He might need a change of clothes."

"Oh, no, thank you. I'm not… I mean, I don't want to seem ungrateful, and thank you for the offer, but I don't like…" I grimace. How can I tell Stephan that I don't like to wear other people's clothes without seeming like a bit of a snob?

"That's okay, lovely boy. I understand," Stephan whispers, saving me the job of explaining. What does he understand, though? I didn't explain anything. "Bessie here will probably need a rub down with a towel or something," Stephan continues, pointing at my very wet, muddy dog.

"Good god, it's the bloody Beast of Bodmin that crashed the wedding the other night," Stephan's dad exclaims.

I grimace, waiting for the inevitable fallout that I have managed to avoid for an entire week now. I prepare to deliver the apology of the century, but am surprised to find that Stephan and his dad are laughing.

"Oh my god, Kit." Stephan's dad directs his smile at me. "I have watched the footage of your dog having a blast at that wedding party on CCTV so many times in the last week. If I could, I'd upload it to YouTube. It would go viral for sure. The wedding party was a bit of a disaster from beginning to end, however, ending in a massive bust-up in the car park."

"Yes, Stephan told me." I glance at Stephan for reassurance and he nods encouragement.

He's settled in a comfy sofa now, with a footstool to elevate his injured ankle.

"Right." Stephan's dad chuckles. "I'll be with you in a sec with a towel and some clean clothes for the wounded soldier, and then we can decide whether he needs an amputation, or just a stiff drink."

I try to make sense of what he's saying as I take a seat next to Stephan, trying to keep Bessie from making a mess of anywhere by jumping up onto the sofa with us.

"There aren't any soldiers here, Stephan," I whisper as Stephan's dad disappears from the room. I know what he really means, of course, but things like this, they play over and over in my mind when I'm a little stressed and I have to talk them out or they drive me crazy. "And he's not really going to cut your foot off, is he? I mean, I'm not a doctor, but I think it's only sprained. And even if it was broken, that doesn't warrant an amputation, not in the twenty-first century, anyway. Maybe if we were living in the eighteen hundreds, as pirates, then you'd probably end up with a wooden leg. That would be pretty cool. I mean, to be a pirate, obviously, not to lose your leg."

"Oh, god, Kit, you're so bloody adorable, I could eat you in a sandwich," Stephan says in response to my anxious mumblings, his forehead leaning very close to mine.

I lean back a little and give him a startled look. He smiles.

"Not literally, obviously," he clarifies. "I don't really want to make you into a sandwich and eat you, it's just a way of saying that I…" He doesn't finish the sentence because we are interrupted by another man entering the room.

"All right, sport?" He has a bit of an accent, a smirk on his face, and he's wearing a chef's hat and an apron. "What the fuck happened to you, then?" He looks Stephan up and down and snorts. "And what the hell are you wearing? Are they running shorts?"

"Yes, Guy, they are. What of it?" Stephan asks, sounding just a little unhappy. Maybe because it is the second time he's been asked this. Why would it be so surprising? People wear running shorts all the time.

Guy just snorts again in response but says nothing more about Stephan's clothes. Another person joins us, a woman, possibly my age. She bypasses me and goes straight to Stephan's side.

"Steph, what happened?"

"Lisa." Stephan smiles. "I fell. Kit here rescued me. Oh, and Bessie." He adds. At the sound of her name, Bessie jumps up to try and lick his face.

I grab her collar and draw her away. "Bessie, heel!" I gasp, shocked by her behaviour and worried that we'll be sent away if she doesn't behave. I'm not sure if dogs are even allowed in hotels. I'm sure Stephan's dad would have said something if that were the case, but I'm also sure that, considering Bessie's track record at this particular hotel, we'll be thrown out for sure if she does anything else outrageous.

Stephan laughs at her antics. "It's okay, Kit. She's just glad to be somewhere warm and dry." He turns back to the woman he called Lisa. "Lis, will you do me a favour and take my shoe off? Loosen the laces as much as you can, would you?"

The woman purses her lips and doesn't look very happy but does as she is asked whilst the other man, still laughing, sits beside Stephan in my place. It does feel like he's taken my place, but I suppose I did move and I don't really have any claim to sit closer to Stephan than anyone else.

I should have helped Stephan with his shoe, but I didn't think about it. Now he has someone else to help. I watch, trying not to stare because I know how uncomfortable people get when I do. The woman manages to get Stephan's trainer off, with poor Stephan looking very unhappy and pale. She's about to start with his sock when I step forward.

"No, leave the sock on," I say, rather too loudly, shocking her into turning to me and leaving go of Stephan's foot. He cries out as she drops it, and I grimace because that was partly my fault, but if she tries to take his sock off now… "You need to leave the sock on until some of the swelling has gone down. It'll be easier to get it off then, and it won't hurt as much." I risk meeting Stephan's gaze.

"Best listen to Kit there, Lisa. He knows his stuff." He smiles at me and winks.

Oh! That was a little unexpected. I'm never really sure what a wink means, but in this case I assume it means he's happy with what I've said. The woman, however, looks a little cross.

"Kit, this is Lisa, my sister."

I smile and hold out my hand. "Hello, Lisa, I'm Kit."

She stands, but doesn't take my hand, staring at it as if it's got spikes or something. "Er, yes. Stephan just said," she says through pursed lips.

Oh no. Somehow I've managed to mess this up. I know that look she's directing at me. I've seen it too many times before.

"Y-yes, of course he did. I-I'm sorry," I mumble as I take a step back.

"Lisa, I'd love a cuppa," Stephan interrupts before I can make the conversation any more awkward. "Do you think you could make me one, and something for Kit? He did rescue me after all." Stephan's request distracts his sister, and she directs her gaze at him instead of me.

"I'm not your slave," she snaps. "Get Guy to do it. He's quite happily sitting on his backside. You might have hurt yourself and I sympathise, but you're still an arse for going out jogging in the first place when you've never jogged in your entire life, and all in the hope you might meet some bloke you've been crushing on who hasn't even had the decency to call you back yet."

"Holy crap, Lisa," Stephan hisses at her, his head doing a funny twitch in my direction, his face stuck in some sort of tight grimace. "Could you have said that any louder? Open your mouth a bit more and you'll fit the other foot in as well."

"Oh god, is that him?" she whispers, turning her back on me so I can't see her expression. I might not be very good at picking up social cues but I'm pretty sure they're talking about me. I can't quite work out why, though.

Stephan answers his sister, but I don't listen. Yenta says it's wrong to eavesdrop, even when she does it all the time. Instead, I back away, until my heels hit a wall. I don't listen, but I do watch. Stephan hisses a few more words and Lisa leaves, directing an angry glare my way.

Half my problem is that I never know what I've done to make people angry. I must have done something to make her react that way, but I have no idea what. I am well out of my comfort zone here: an unfamiliar place, with no contingency plan, and unfamiliar people whom I haven't had a chance to meet properly. The guy sitting next to Stephan keeps giving me weird looks. I should leave before I'm overwhelmed, but I don't want to until I'm sure Stephan is okay, and he doesn't look okay. He still looks pale, and I wish I could do something for him, but I can't, and that makes me feel even worse.

"Got some ice." Stephan's dad returns at that moment with a bag of ice and lays it on Stephan's foot as gently as he can. "Now, tell me how this happened, Steph? Were you really out running?"

Stephan starts to tell his story, and the two men draw closer to listen. Stephan's sister returns, but by that time, I'm too stressed to notice if she's staring at me or not. There are too many people in the room. Too many voices all at once. My brain can't process any of it. I'm going to lose it in front of Stephan and his entire family and there isn't a thing I can do about it.

I'm drowning in a sea of words, with no way of sorting it all out into some sort of order.

I can feel myself floating free and out of control. I clench my fists, digging my nails in as hard as I can to get the sensation of pain rather than feel the chaos threatening to overwhelm me.

Bessie pushes her nose against my hand and forces me to open it so I can pat her head. I feel calmer almost immediately.

When someone asks me what Bessie actually does, I'm never sure what to tell them because I can't adequately describe it. She isn't there to find stuff, or warn me, or guide me, like other assistance dogs, although she has been trained to retrieve, but that's just in her nature. I don't need assistance. I can look after myself. What she does do is provide an anchor. Her job is to be with me without expecting anything from me in return, and that simple action of pushing her head into my hand calms me and grounds me like nothing else ever has.

I'm still in a very stressful situation, but she's there and she isn't leaving me, not even when someone offers her a bowl of water at Stephan's request. She'll be thirsty, but she won't leave my side until I'm ready.

"Kit?" Stephan's voice sounds distant, echoey, and usually nothing can get through the fog in my brain once it has taken hold. Somehow, his voice finds an opening. I force myself to look at him. He's alone now. Everyone else is gone. "Okay?" He looks concerned, but not in a bad way.

"Yes." I nod. "I just needed some, erm, space, I'm sorry."

"No need to apologise, mate. Take all the time you need."

"Maybe I should go." I still feel wobbly, on edge, but it's not as bad as I thought it was going to be. I still might flip, though, and I can't let Stephan see me like that.

"Only when you're ready," Stephan says. "I sent everyone else away. It's just you and me, and I'll shut up until you're ready to talk."

I nod, swallowing hard and feeling my mouth getting very dry which reminds me that Bessie needs a drink of water. "Drink, Bessie. It's okay now."

She goes to the bowl that was set out for her and drinks noisily. I focus on that sound and take some deep breaths to push the last of the panic away. When I'm sure it's all gone, I look up and find Stephan's eyes watching me, a soft smile on his lips. He waits.

"How do you know?" I ask him, frowning.

He tips his head to one side. "Know what?"

"What to do. That I need you to wait? Did Yenta tell you?"

"No." He shakes his head. "I just felt like that was the right thing to do."

"And you sent everyone else away because of me. Were they angry?"

"Not because of you. They were doing my head in as well, mate. My family can be loud and they swear. A lot. It's embarrassing sometimes, the way they fuss. And you don't need to go repeating that to them either, because I know I should be grateful I've got such attentive relatives."

I find myself smiling. "I won't. I promise."

"I trust you." He smirks. "Come and sit over here, only if you want, obviously. If you need to go, then go. I can speak to you another time."

"Another time?"

"If you want, that is, since I assume you called me because you wanted to either make a date for dinner or tell me to go to hell."

"I would never tell you that." I feel horrified that he would think that. "Jesus, Stephan."

"I'm sorry." He lowers his gaze.

"How's your ankle?" I ask. It's easier for me to change the subject than to try and think of something to say in response to his apology. I walk over to take a look at his ankle now that I can.

"The swelling is still pretty bad. There's bruising too." I point at some rather alarming discolouration along the side of his foot.

"I know." He makes a face. "Dad wants to take me to A and E."

"Oh. Then I should probably go." I make a move towards the door, but he catches my hand, the touch so unexpected I jump.

"I'm sorry." He pulls his hand away quickly. "I didn't mean—I just wanted to make sure you didn't run away and disappear from my life completely, because I do want to see you again, Kit." He looks up at me. "At least consider that dinner date, please?"

"I don't like restaurants," I tell him.

He nods, and pats the sofa beside him, giving no indication that he thinks the way I just blurted out that fact is weird. I sit, straight-backed as I try to order my thoughts enough to tell him what I originally wanted to say on the phone.

"I'm a bit of a fussy eater, I mean, I'm not fussy in a fussy way. I don't like it when other smells interfere."

"Smells?"

"Yes, restaurants, they smell. Too many different dishes, everyone ordering different things, and it stops me from tasting what I'm eating because of all the other smells. Also, people get dressed up to go to restaurants. They wear perfume and aftershave, and my food ends up tasting of that as well."

"Where do you prefer to eat then?" he asks, watching me carefully.

I bite my lip. "You won't think I'm weird?"

"Why would I think that? What you've just said makes perfect sense to me."

"Oh. Well, I like Subway. All Subways smell the same, because everyone is ordering the same things. I mean, you can smell Subway from the other end of the high street, even before you see the sign."

"This is true." Stephan laughs in surprise as if he's only just realised this himself.

"Anyway, at Subway, you can order the exact same thing every time. The people there remember my order now, and they do it the same way. They even made a list to give to new members of staff."

"That was good of them."

"Yes." I nod. "I mean, If I'm just ordering for myself I don't even have to speak to anyone. They just get my order ready for me. Of course, sometimes I have to order for Yenta as well, and she orders something different each time. Actually, I'm convinced she does it to force me to, you know, be sociable." I grimace, because I know that everything I've just told him is making it clearer and clearer that I'm more than different, I'm pretty damn weird.

Quirky, my mum used to say to me. *"You're not weird, Kit, you're quirky. Just because you do and say and think a little differently to everyone else does not make you any less than them."*

"Kit, are you saying that you'd be happy if we went to eat at Subway?" Stephan asks.

Oh dear. I knew this was a mistake. Subway was never going to be an acceptable location for a first date. I should have told him about the pizza straight away.

Yenta always says I should have a plan B, and I did have something all worked out—in case Stephan hates Subway—but now, with everything else that's happened, I can't get it all sorted in my head. I need to read what I've written down, but doing that will just highlight more of my oddness.

Besides, I still don't know why he even wants to spend time with me. "Why?"

"Why what, mate?" He frowns. I know I have difficulty keeping up with what people are saying to me, but I also know that what I say can be pretty difficult to decipher as well.

"Why do you want to, you know, go on a date with me?"

"Why do you want to go on a date with me?" he counters.

"I asked you first."

He chuckles. "You did indeed." He twists his lips as he thinks. "Well, apart from the fact that I could just sit and listen to you talking all night, I think you're really kind of cute and I'd like to get to know you better. Much better."

"Oh, okay, well, same, really. I-I mean, I'd like to get to know you. I don't have many friends. I'm a bit too much all at once sometimes."

"I can't get enough of you, Kit." Stephan's confession takes me a bit by surprise, and I can't really think of anything to say in response. "Kit?" He speaks instead.

"Yes?" I'm staring down at my hands, and am slightly startled when his hand appears and covers both of mine.

His skin is warm and rough and firm against mine.

"You know these contingency plans you have?"

"Y-yes," I stutter, surprised that he's remembered about them at all.

"Do you have a contingency plan for when someone wants to kiss you?"

"I, er, wrote one a while ago, but I've never used it, because no one ever wants to kiss me. Not that I've tried going out and finding someone to kiss. I did once, but it was a bit of a disaster. The guy didn't want to do any kissing, he just wanted to…" I bite my lip to stop oversharing. "You probably don't want to know about that."

"Not right now, no," he agrees. "Maybe some other time, when I'm not trying to kiss you."

"Kiss me?" I squeak as I finally meet his spring-light gaze. "You want to kiss me?" It's all very intense, and I can see everything reflected in that sky blue.

"Yes, Kit, I do. May I?"

"Y-yes, because I really want to kiss you. I have since I first saw you."

"Oh, Kit, me too." He leans closer, and I hesitate, just a fraction of a second, but long enough for him to stop. "Okay?" he asks, waiting.

I take a little time to sort it all out, the kissing thing, in my head, and then I nod.

"Yes." And I press my lips to his.

They're drier than I expected, and warm, and soft, and they move against mine so gently I can barely feel them. That's no good, because I want to feel him kissing me.

I reach up and lace my fingers through his hair, pulling him closer and opening my mouth just a little. I'm rewarded with a feathery touch of his tongue against my bottom lip.

With a soft moan, I press further, my tongue seeking his, tasting him and finding that I like the taste very much. It's different, but not bad. I guess he hasn't eaten recently as I can't taste any food. He doesn't wear strong aftershave, but I knew that about him already. All I can smell is some sort of mild-smelling shower gel, and sweat, because he was running, but it's not overpowering. I can also smell mud and grass and snow. I quite like the smell of snow.

Correction: I quite like the smell of snow on Stephan.

I never know when kisses are supposed to end, and this one ends a bit awkwardly, with me pulling away while he's still trying to lick my bottom lip.

"S-sorry." I watch as he slowly opens his eyes and smiles at me.

"What are you sorry for?" he asks, drawing a finger down my cheek and making my entire face tingle in a good way. I catch my breath and return his smile.

"I-I don't know, I just thought that was a bit…"

"Awesome," he finishes the sentence for me, and everything about the way he said the word, and the way he's looking at me, and the way he's touching me, is just that. Awesome, and I've got this warm feeling in my stomach, and in other places too, that I haven't felt for such a long time, because I haven't met anyone that I've wanted to feel that way with, until now.

Oh, I know if I tell him all of this right now, I'll probably send him running for his life, even with a sprained ankle, so I keep my mouth shut. I'll get the chance to tell him eventually, I hope. Right now though, I think I need to go.

Out of the corner of my eye I can see Stephan's dad hovering in the doorway, and it's pretty obvious, even to me, that he's waiting to take Stephan to the hospital to get his ankle looked at.

"I have to go." I start to gather my stuff: backpack, coat, Bessie's lead. Stephan catches my hand in his and pulls it to his lips to kiss the back of it.

"Thank you," he whispers.

"What for?" I ask with wide eyes.

"For everything. For rescuing me. For being so bloody adorable, even though you don't know that you are, but that just makes you even more so."

"Bollocks." I chuckle. "I think those painkillers your dad gave you are starting to kick in."

He grins. "Maybe, maybe not." He looks up at me as I stand, releasing my hand as I do. "Should I call you to let you know how my ankle is?"

"Yes, er, could you text me instead, please?"

"Of course." He nods. "But how will I get to hear your voice again if I can only text you?"

"I could come and visit tomorrow," I suggest, not finding it at all difficult to think of this contingency plan. "I know the way here now, but is it okay if Bessie comes too? I don't know why, but she does seem to get a bit over-excited around you."

"I know the feeling." Stephan tells me, his smile broadening. "Of course she can come. I'll see you tomorrow then, Kit."

"Okay." I nod and then turn to leave, clicking my fingers to get Bessie's attention. She follows obediently.

At the door, I stop and look back. Stephan is watching me, that smile still on his face. I put that smile there. Me. I find that quite incredible, that such an awkward kiss could have such a positive effect. Anyway, I might get a chance to try that again tomorrow, unless he decides it wasn't so awesome after all. At least if he doesn't want to do anything more, I think I'll have made a friend.

I pass Stephan's dad as I leave. He smiles and nods.

"Goodbye, Kit."

I'm a little fazed, because I haven't really said hello to him properly yet, but then I remember Stephan telling me that his dad won't mind if we do things the wrong way around, so I smile and nod back at him.

"Bye, Mr., erm, Stephan's dad."

He walks into the lounge and I can hear him talking to Stephan as I fasten Bessie's lead to her collar.

"He's a bit of an oddbod, isn't he, Steph?"

I freeze, my heart suddenly pounding in my ears and the air roaring as I gulp in shallow breaths. Is he talking about me? Describing me the way almost everyone in the world sees me.

"Dad, don't say that," Stephan corrects him, and I can suddenly breathe a little easier. "I think he's perfect."

I leave through the main door as quickly as I can so that no one can think I might have been eavesdropping.

All the way home, Stephan's words play over and over in my head—*I think he's perfect. I think he's perfect*—until I end up saying them out loud like a chant.

How can he think that? But then, I've never been able to fathom the way others think, or what they mean when they say things like that about me.

I'm not perfect, but if Stephan wants to think that, who am I to argue?

CHAPTER SIX

Planning Dates
or
Water Does Not Taste the Same from Other People's Taps

MORNING BREAK IN the bookshop is for catching up on news. Yenta likes to hear about the things I've been doing when not at work, so today, I tell her everything that happened with Stephan the night before. Well, almost everything. I leave out the bit about kissing because I'm still processing that.

"His ankle is only sprained," I explain. "He texted me last night and I replied with a smiley face emoji, followed by a sad-faced one just in case he thought I was smiling at his misfortune and not just the fact that his ankle isn't actually broken."

"You could have called and spoken to him, Lapushka," Yenta chides gently.

I purse my lips then blow out my cheeks. "Yenta, you know I don't understand the rules of talking on the phone. I mean, I don't want Stephan to think I'm stupid."

"He won't think that, he likes you."

"Yes, I know." I nod, thinking a little more about our kiss and smiling. "He wants me to visit him today. He said so in his text and asked me last night. I replied with a thumbs up emoji."

Yenta sighs and shakes her head. "You should take him some flowers," she suggests as we finish our tea and get back to work.

"Flowers?" I ask in disgust. "Yenta, you know how I feel about flowers. I mean they're technically dead as soon as you pick them.

And they stink, and the smell only gets worse as they sit there in the vase slowly decaying before your very eyes. Why anyone thought cutting the heads off living things and presenting them as a—"

"Most people think it's romantic, Kit," She stops me in mid-rant. "And it's a traditional gift when visiting someone who is ill."

"But Stephan isn't ill. It's not as if he's going to die or anything. He hurt his ankle."

"Or when they're injured," she adds. I can see her rolling her eyes. She isn't going to convince me. "Chocolates, then." She suggests as an alternative.

"Chocolates would be better." I give the matter some thought. "But which brand? I can't just give him any old chocolates and hope he likes them. Maybe I should ask him." I get out my phone, glad of an excuse to send him a text that is more than a simple picture expressing emotion.

"Kit, you can't ask him what he likes, that would spoil the surprise," Yenta exclaims with a degree of frustration in her tone that even I can hear.

I put away my phone with a sigh. "Okay, but I still need to think about what brand he would like."

"Go to the chocolatier's along the high street and pick out some special ones."

"But Yenta, it's Wednesday!" I gasp. "You know I don't go shopping on a Wednesday."

"Not even for a special occasion?"

I scowl. She's right of course, but I hate to change my routine. Oh, I know I'm older now and have developed strategies to cope when my routine changes, but that doesn't stop me resisting any unnecessary deviations.

"Perhaps I could make him a cake," I suggest, mostly to myself, but Yenta hears and shakes her head.

"He lives in a hotel, Kit. He probably has cakes coming out of his ears."

"Out of his ears?" I repeat, and then it dawns on me that she doesn't literally mean the cakes are coming out of his ears. Still, the mental image the phrase conjures up makes me smile.

"What are you smiling at?" Yenta asks, smiling in return.

I smirk. "Just a mental image of Stephan."

"Oh, I probably don't even want to know, then." Yenta raises her eyebrows and returns her attention to her clipboard. I feel myself blushing.

"Oh no, nothing rude, Yenta. I promise."

"And why not?" she asks, her eyes twinkling and her eyebrows flicking up and down. "He's a good-looking boy."

"Yenta!" I exclaim in shock, laughing when she grins like a wicked witch. "He's hardly a boy, and neither am I, for that matter." I frown, thinking about the kiss we shared the night before.

I stare down at my feet, my cheeks burning. I've never felt comfortable discussing these things with anyone, but for some reason, Yenta seems a lot more accepting than anyone else I have ever met. Even my mum had difficulty understanding my attraction to men and not women. She never understood why I didn't want to follow the rules when it came to relationships and I never understood why she thought her set of rules were the only ones to follow.

And Yenta's take on the whole relationship thing?

"We make our own rules, Lapushka."

Of course, this makes no sense to me at all, because, if we all make our own rules, how am I supposed to know if my rules are compatible with someone else's? It's all very confusing, and then there's Stephan, who asked my permission before he kissed me. No one has done that before.

Apparently, Stephan has a set of rules that are completely unique, and I'm intrigued to say the least.

"He asked to kiss me, Yenta," I confess, still staring at my feet.

"Oh, did he indeed?" She leans a little closer. "And did you allow it?"

"Yes." My cheeks are flaming now.

"And, it was good, yes?"

"Yes, but that's not the point. I mean, it is the point, because the point was the kiss, that's why he asked, but it was the way he asked, like he understood. Just like everything else he does, it's like he understands me. I don't know how he can. We've only met five times. I know I said I wanted to write a manual about me, but it's as if he's already read it."

"I told you, it was obvious to me that he likes you a lot." She nods, pushing her glasses up her nose and stretching out her back muscles after being stooped over the box of books for too long. "When someone feels that way, they are willing to make an effort to learn all they can about the object of their affections."

"Affections?" I gasp. "But how can I be the object of his affections after such a short time?"

"Perhaps it is even love at first sight." She has a far-off look in her eyes, one that I recognise because she has it when she's discussing romance with some of her bookshop friends. I snort.

"Huh, don't be silly. That sort of thing only happens in stories and movies. Not in real life."

"It happened for me, Lapushka, when I met my Samuel. We knew the very first time we met."

"Knew what?" I ask, stepping down from the stool I was using to reach the top shelf.

I want to focus fully on what she's saying. When she talks about her husband, she always has such a gleam in her eyes, and when she should be sad because Samuel is dead and has been for fifteen years, she always seems so happy. The memories are still so vivid for her. It makes me wonder if I could ever have something like that with someone special. Should I even allow myself to hope that Stephan might be that someone special?

"I knew I would spend the rest of my life with that man." Yenta sighs with a dreamy look before shrugging and picking up her clip board again. "Oh, well, he got to spend the rest of his life with me, at least."

"I thought I'd found that with Harry, but he wanted something different." I feel the familiar panic whenever I think of my ex-boyfriend. "I didn't know until he left. He never told me. Left it for me to guess and I just can't guess things like that, but he didn't understand that. He thought I was just being deliberately stupid. And now I've met Stephan, I wonder if what I felt for Harry was anything like love at all. Not that I'm saying I love Stephan. I don't really know him, but everything feels different with him. I now understand what people mean when they say they have butterflies in their stomach. It does feel like there's something fluttering around in there."

Yenta steps up to me and smooths down the front of my T-shirt before flicking away a piece of fluff from my sleeve. "Love is different for everyone, Lapushka, and different every time."

That doesn't help me at all!

"So how am I supposed to know, if it's always different? How can I make any kind of contingency plan for that? It would take up reams and reams of note paper and probably take a lifetime to write."

"You understand more than you think you do, sometimes, Lapushka. Give yourself some credit." She reaches up and plants a kiss on my cheek. "And contingency plans aren't always appropriate. Sometimes you have to just go with the flow. In fact..." She smiles, tipping her head to one side. "Why don't you make that your contingency plan?"

"What? Going with the flow?" I gape at her. "I mean, I understand what you're trying to say, but there are far too many variables to just go with the flow, Yenta. Far too many."

Although, with Stephan, there's only him, and no one else. I suppose I could just listen to what the rest of my senses are telling me instead of planning it all in advance. He does seem very patient. I suppose I could do that with the chocolates as well, but this is assuming that whoever is serving in the chocolate shop today is going to be equally as patient.

"Yenta, I might just have a plan that isn't really a plan."

"Now that doesn't make any sense at all, whilst it makes every sense in the world. Tell me."

I frown as I try to sort out the order I will be doing things. "I'm going to go to the chocolate shop and ask the person behind the counter to choose the chocolates. That way, they won't ask me a million and one questions that I won't be able to answer. And then I'm going to take them to Stephan, sit beside him and wait to see what happens next."

"No contingency plans for making conversation?"

"Nope." I smile. "He always seems to have so much to say I probably won't need to speak, and when I do, he listens. He told me I could read the Shipping Forecast and he'd be mesmerised."

Yenta laughs. "You're not actually going to do that, are you?"

"Well, no, I hadn't planned on doing it." I regard her with one eye closed. "Do you think I should?"

"No! Goodness me, no." She grasps my shoulders and turns me towards the door. "Now go and get those chocolates for this man of yours, and while you're out there, get us some sandwiches for lunch. You have a contingency plan for that, don't you?"

"Yes, Yenta." I tell her automatically, but I'm smiling as I leave the shop.

***

After the bookshop closes I walk over to Stephan's hotel. Well, I know it isn't technically his, but it is where he works and lives so, it is his in a way. I bring Bessie, because I'm always better when she is nearby, especially when I'm going into new situations. I just hope yesterday wasn't a one-off and she'll still be welcome.

I haven't made a plan. In the foyer of the hotel, I realise my mistake. Until Bessiegate, I'd never been inside a hotel. I have no idea how this works.

Do I walk up to the reception and ask for him? He isn't staying here, he lives here. Does that mean there is a different set of rules? I could phone him to tell him I'm here, but he can't come out and meet me because he can't walk. What do I do now?

Bessie whines softly by my side, doing her best to calm me down, whilst I am stuck in an indecision feedback loop, fully aware that I am rocking backwards and forwards from my heels to my toes and trying not to wring my hands. A voice startles me.

"Kit?"

I whirl around to see Stephan's dad standing behind me. I look quickly at his face to check it is him, and then I look away. I'm already beginning to feel stressed. Looking will overwhelm me with information I don't really need. I'm pretty sure what his expression will be anyway. It will be the same as Stephan's sister's yesterday, when she just kept frowning at me as if I was some sort of alien.

"Hello, Mr., erm…" I am very bad at remembering names. I have forgotten his. "Mr., erm, Stephan's dad." I smile, glancing quickly at his face again. The smile seems to do the trick, because he smiles back, and if there was any sort of confused look on his face, it is gone now.

"You can call me George," Stephan's dad tells me. "I really don't mind." He crouches down to make a fuss of Bessie. "And you brought Bessie with you. Hello, girl."

"George, of course," I exclaim, clicking my fingers whilst his attention is on my dog and not me. "I remember now. Hello, George. I'm Kit." I hold out my hand for him to shake. When he gives me a startled look I grimace and tuck my hand behind my back. "I'm sorry. I mean, you know that already, but we weren't introduced properly yesterday, and I like to do things like that properly, and Stephan said you wouldn't mind if we did it the wrong way around, plus, I'm really bad at remembering names unless I've done things the right way around. Sorry, that didn't make any sense at all."

"It made perfect sense, Kit. And I might add that you don't seem to have any trouble remembering Stephan's name," George muses as he leads me towards a doorway.

"Oh, well, Stephan is different." I hope he won't ask for an explanation because I haven't got one. Instead, I open my mouth, and complete and utter rubbish comes out of it. "Of course, I didn't know his name at first so I had to keep calling him Mr. Spring."

"Mr. what?" George stops to look at me.

I grimace again. Oh god, why did I tell him that?

"I mean, sorry, it was just a silly nickname I gave him until I knew his real name, and it kind of matched mine, you know: Spring, Winter. It just fits." I stop because I know I've said too much by the glassy look in George's eyes. I'm glad I didn't blurt out the real reason I called Stephan 'Spring'. That would have really made me sound odd.

George narrows his eyes and then shakes his head. He looks as if he is smiling and trying not to laugh.

"Come on, I'll take you to where Stephan has set up his throne room."

"Throne room? Does he think he's a king?"

"Ha, he wishes." George laughs. "No, but he's acting like one, ordering us all about and having us pander to his every whim because he has to stay off his feet for a few days. He's driving me batty, I can tell you. I'm glad you're finally here so I don't have to listen to his bellyaching for a few hours."

"Does he have a bellyache too?" I'm worried now that he might really be ill as well as broken.

"No." George gives me a sideways look, stretching the word out. "But he will if he keeps on stuffing himself with cakes. Guy made him a get-well-soon selection."

"Oh, I knew that would happen. I almost baked him a cake, but I decided not to because I knew he'd already have some."

"Yes, he does. So many they're coming out of his ears."

This is so close to the mental image Yenta conjured up earlier, I laugh out loud, a noise that startles George, making him jump, but then smile and laugh as well.

He stretches out a hand towards the nearest door and I think he wants me to walk through first. This door looks like an exit, rather than a door into another room, however. I hesitate.

"W-why are we going outside?" I ask in a sudden panic. Is this when he finally tells me that dogs aren't allowed in his hotel? I knew I should have asked. I knew I should have…

"It's okay, Kit." George steps forward and tries to meet my gaze. "Stephan told me I should explain and I forgot. I'm sorry. We have to go this way to get to the private family apartment at the back of the hotel. The only other way is through the kitchens, and Stephan says you don't like the smells."

"That's right. I don't." I follow George through the door feeling a little more relaxed, but I keep a tight hold of Bessie's lead just the same.

I'm completely astounded that Stephan even gave this any thought. Most people dismiss my sensitivity to smells because they just don't understand how it can affect me in such an adverse way. I told Stephan about this only yesterday and he's made a whole plan about the route I'd need to take to get to him without passing through my worst nightmare: a commercial kitchen.

I follow George through a garden area, around the back of the hotel and into a conservatory which is currently very pleasantly warm because the sun is finally shining after a week of adverse winter weather.

The place has a domestic feel, like it is lived in, as opposed to the hotel foyer, which felt very clinical and intimidating. The fact that Stephan is here also helps the feelings of comfort.

"Hello, Kit." He smiles at me from a large, comfy sofa, his spring-light eyes setting those pretend butterflies fluttering about in my stomach again.

What is the matter with me? I only saw him yesterday. I'm acting like I haven't seen him in weeks and even then, I don't usually get this worked up about meeting someone.

"Come and sit down, mate." Stephan indicates the space next to him on the sofa.

Bessie pulls free of my hold and bounds over to greet him. With a gasp, I grab her and pull her back, only just stopping her from jumping into Stephan's lap.

"I'm sorry. She's excited to see you," I apologise in confusion. "She isn't usually this badly behaved. I wouldn't have brought her if I'd known she would be all over you."

"That's okay." Stephan grins at me. "It must be my magnetic personality, and I know you're more relaxed when she's around. I would never have asked you to leave her behind."

"Oh, okay." I nod, not looking at him, still confused by Bessie's unusually flighty behaviour and by my reaction to being this close to Stephan again. I mean, we only kissed once, but I suddenly have the urge to jump into his lap as well, so I understand Bessie's eagerness.

I take a seat at the other end of the sofa, not too far away from where he said, but not so close as to be invading his personal space. I deposit my backpack beside me on the floor and then direct my gaze at my hands to check they aren't doing something odd, like wringing in my lap, or that my fingers aren't flicking and flexing.

"Hello, Stephan." I smile, but I know I've made a mess of this. "I mean, I probably should have said that straightaway, before I sat down."

"That's all right. You know I don't mind doing things in the wrong order."

"Yes, yes, I knew that, yes." When I eventually look up, he's smiling at me. So, okay, maybe I haven't messed up that badly—yet.

"There's a bowl of water for Bessie over there." He indicates a bowl on the floor in the corner of the conservatory.

"Thank you." I smile at him, then show Bessie, watching as she drinks the same way she does everything else: with enthusiasm.

"Would you like something to drink?" Stephan asks. "Tea, coffee? I don't know what you like."

"I-I, erm..." His question takes me by surprise. I can't process it quickly enough. "I don't drink..." Well, that sounds stupid, because everyone drinks. For want of a better way to explain, I pull out a water bottle from the side pocket of my backpack and show it to him. "I brought my own water."

"Oh, water from our taps not good enough, then?" George mutters from his position to the side of the sofa.

I jump, startled because I'd forgotten he was still there. Oh god, has he just watched all that awkwardness? What must he be thinking? I can't look. Instead, I fix my gaze on Stephan.

Stephan's eyes flicker to his dad, and they narrow. "Dad!" He jerks his head to one side. George rolls his eyes and huffs.

"I'll leave you to it, then," he says, sounding unhappy. "Seems I've had my marching orders. Nice meeting you, Kit. Enjoy your water."

"Er, I erm…" I stop, because he's gone before I can form a suitable reply.

I watch him disappear through the door and wince when it slams shut. I turn to face Stephan again.

"Was your dad angry with me for bringing my own water? I mean, I drink tea at home, and with Yenta, but anywhere else, I only drink water. I usually bring my own because water tastes different from other people's taps."

I wring my hands in my lap, waiting for him to laugh, or tell me that's a stupid thing to say, because water tastes the same wherever you are, it's just water. Unless you're me, of course. But he doesn't say anything, not until I look up at him.

"Don't worry about it, Kit. My dad's just a grumpy old sod."

"Some people say that about me," I admit. "I mean, not the old bit, because I'm not, old that is. Not that your dad is old either, because he's not. Yenta is eighty, and I still don't think of her as old, really. I'm rambling, sorry."

"Ramble away, mate. I love it. Anyway, You've got reasons to be grumpy." Stephan's eyes sparkle as he smiles. "My dad doesn't need an excuse. He frequently wakes up grumpy and stays that way all day."

"But I do that," I say, worrying now, that he might not know me as well as he seems to.

"Perhaps," Stephan agrees, as he shuffles closer to me on the sofa. "I think I could live with your sort of grumpy. At least it makes sense."

"To who?" I ask, puzzled. "Because it often doesn't even make sense to me."

Stephan chuckles and reaches out to touch my cheek. I lean back a little, out of reach, regarding his fingers before I look up at his eyes again. Instead of stopping him from touching me at all, I grab his hand and hold it. That way, at least the touch isn't so light and I have a bit more control over it.

"You don't like being touched?" Stephan asks, and not in an annoyed way because I've just prevented him from doing something he wanted to do. He sounds curious.

"It's not that. I do like being touched, but light touch—it hurts my skin. You probably think that's a stupid thing to say."

"I don't think that at all. I don't like being tickled," he confesses. "Everyone tells me I should like it, that it should make me laugh, but it just makes my skin crawl, and it's an invasion of my space, and I always want to go and take a long hot shower after someone's done it."

I gasp. "That's exactly how I feel! Except it hurts as well, really stings, like a cut, or as if someone's scratching my skin with razor sharp nails."

"Ouch." Stephan grimaces, looking sympathetic.

And that's it, I've run out of things to say because I came here without a list or a plan. If I open my mouth again, I'm afraid something else even more odd will come out of it. Everything I've said to this man so far has emphasised just how different I am, and I know he seems to be okay with it all, but there's a limit, and I've decided that three odd things is enough, so now I have nothing more to say.

Instead, I stare at my hands, clenched tightly in my lap.

"Kit, are you nervous?" Stephan asks me.

I take a deep breath, understanding why he might think that.

"I am a little, but not because I'm nervous of you or anything like that, because I'm not. I'm holding my hands like this because if I don't, I'm afraid they'll do something inappropriate."

Stephan snorts, and when I look at him, startled by his reaction, I see his eyes are sparkling and he's smirking. What did I say to make him react like that?

"Oh." I shake my head when I realise why he thinks my explanation was funny. "I don't mean that sort of inappropriate. I mean, you know, like clenching my fists, or flexing my fingers. I do that sort of thing without thinking. It's just that some people think it's a bit odd."

"You go ahead and do what you want, mate," Stephan urges me. "I won't think it's odd at all. And if it starts getting inappropriate, all the better."

I frown for a moment, processing what he's said, before laughing and meeting his gaze.

He laughs too. "I think that's the first time I've heard you laugh." He grins. "You always seem so serious."

"That's because I'm always concentrating on what I'm supposed to be doing next. It's a difficult job being me."

"I would have thought it harder to try and be something you're not, Kit. Personally, I wouldn't want you to be anything but yourself."

"Sometimes being myself can be difficult for other people."

"Sod other people," Stephan exclaims. "I think you're perfect just the way you are."

I look up at him, feeling the honesty of his statement as if it is a solid thing I can hold in my hand. I recall when I'd heard him say this same thing to his dad the night before and just how amazing it had made me feel. I want to say something to him, to make him feel the same, but I know nothing I say will ever sound as good.

Instead, I blurt out the first thing I think of. It's the first thing I always think of when I think of him.

"I think you have lovely eyes," I say, grimacing when those lovely eyes widen in surprise. "I mean, I don't usually notice anyone's eyes. There's people I've known for years and I couldn't tell you what colour eyes they have, but I noticed yours. They're like a clear blue sky on a spring morning."

"Oh." Stephan looks a little stunned, and I look away, embarrassed.

"I know that sounds daft, because how can your eyes be the sky? But that's how I felt when we first met, and when I didn't know your name I called you Mr. Spring." I chuckle nervously, staring back down at my hands. "Yeah, silly, isn't it?"

"No," Stephan breathes, his hands closing firmly over mine. "Not at all. I think…" His voice cracks, and he clears his throat, swallowing hard as if he's struggling to speak. "Kit, that's the most romantic thing anyone's ever said to me."

I snort. "Bollocks. I don't have a romantic bone in my body."

"I'm telling the truth." Stephan's grip tightens. "No one has ever said anything like that to me before."

"Oh, well, okay. So you don't think it's silly?" I ask, just to make sure.

"No. I think it's wonderful. I think you're wonderful, in fact, I think I need to kiss you."

"O-okay, you know, you don't have to ask my permission every time."

"No, but I love the look on your face when I do. Kiss me," he demands, so I do.

The kiss tastes of spaghetti Bolognese and not in a bad way, not like a shop-bought sauce. It's more like the homemade kind. He's obviously had some for lunch and living in a hotel it was probably homemade. I can taste fresh basil with an underlying hint of toothpaste, since he must have cleaned his teeth before I got here.

His fingers are laced with mine, and it feels nice. His hand is warm and firm and somehow safe. I don't understand how that can be. We don't know each other well enough to feel this secure.

"Stephan." I stare at our joined hands after the kiss has ended, because if I look at his face, I will forget what I want to say, or get it all muddled up and end up blurting out something strange. "Are we friends? Because I can't always tell if someone wants to be friends with me."

"You can't tell even when they kiss you?" he asks, his tone gentle, patient, unconditional.

"Friends don't kiss." I gasp, looking up and finding that he's watching me intently. I knew he would be and I knew it would affect me this way. My breathing quickens and my heart pounds in my ears. "Oh. You don't want to be friends with me, do you?"

"Of course I do." Stephan looks a little confused. "Kit, why do you think I asked you out, and kissed you and put up with your dog licking my feet?"

"Oh, god, Bessie, stop doing that." I shove Bessie away from him, embarrassed that she's been doing that and I hadn't noticed, but Stephan just laughs.

"Define friends to me," he says, as he scratches Bessie behind her ears. "Just so we're on the same wavelength here."

I hesitate, because what is it that he's asking me to do? Talk about friendship, or talk about radio stations?

"I mean, tell me what you think we are to each other," Stephan clarifies helpfully. "And then I'll tell you what I think."

"You kissed me, and you asked me out." I twist my mouth a little as I ponder his question. "I think you want to be my boyfriend?" I make the statement into a question. "Or a hookup."

"A hookup?" Stephan exclaims. "No, Jesus, Kit, what the hell?"

"O-okay, sorry. I think I've messed this up and I haven't even given you the chocolates." I move away from him, but he doesn't let me leave go of his hand.

"Wait, you brought me chocolates?"

"Well, yes." I nod. "Yenta wanted me to bring you flowers because she thinks it's romantic, but flowers are technically dead as soon as you pick them, and giving someone something that's dead, when you really want them to get better, doesn't make any sense to me. So I went to the chocolatier's along the high street, even though it's not a day I usually go shopping, and asked the lady to pick some for you. Sorry if there are some you don't like. I wanted to call you to ask you which kind were your favourite but Yenta said that it would spoil the surprise."

As I speak, I take the wrapped box of chocolates from my bag and hand it to him, waiting for him to turn away, or to continue talking about what I said to upset him, but instead, he no longer looks angry. He looks, well, as if he's going to cry.

"You went shopping for chocolates, at a chocolate shop—even though you hate shopping and hate places like that because they smell—just for me?"

"Yes." I nod. "I mean, I don't hate shopping. It's just difficult." I grimace, worried that I'm oversharing again. "I only had to leave the shop twice while I was there. I explained to the lady that I might have to, and she was okay with it. She just chose a selection of her favourites. I hope you like them. Maybe we could talk about something else other than that boyfriend stuff because I think I made you angry, sorry."

"I'm not angry with you, Kit," Stephan tells me, still staring at the box of chocolates as if it is a thing of wonder. "I was just surprised that you might think I only wanted to hook up with you."

"So you don't?"

"No. I want to go out on dates with you. I want to get to know you. I want to spend time with you because I think you're lovely. And I do eventually want to be your boyfriend—if that's what you want."

"I think I want those things too." I nod, frowning as I concentrate. "There are some things we need to talk about."

"Can we talk about them over dinner? At Subway if that's where you really want to go."

"I—" I bite my lip, wondering if now is a good time to mention my alternative plan. The one I had meant to talk to him about yesterday when I found him in a ditch with a sprained ankle and it all went out of my head until I got home.

"Kit." Stephan grabs both of my hands and holds them tight, in that safe, secure way that has me breathless again. "If this dinner malarkey is too much for you, then we can do something else. Anything. I just want to spend time with you. I don't mind what we do."

"I—okay. I think I need more time to think." I don't, but I'm in danger of doing or saying something stupid and making a fool of myself. "You did say I could take all the time I needed. Did you mean that, or did you really mean you wanted me to give you an answer straightaway?"

"I meant it, Kit. Take all the time you need."

I nod, watching his face for what, I don't know, because I won't be able to guess what he's thinking anyway.

"I think I need to go now," I tell him. "I'll come back when I've thought."

"Of course." He smiles, squeezing my hand before letting it go. There is no hint that he is disappointed in any way, and it's not as if I've said no, because I haven't.

I stand up and he follows me with his eyes as I get ready to leave. Those eyes have me tied in knots, quite literally: my legs and arms refuse to move the way I want them to. Instead, in an impulsive move that is completely out of character, I reach out and touch his face with my fingertips. He gasps as I deliberately meet his gaze.

"Spring light," I whisper, before leaning in to kiss him. "I'll see you soon, Mr. Spring."

"I'll be waiting," Stephan whispers against my lips after laughing at the silly nickname.

I call to Bessie and she comes, following me out of the conservatory door and into the garden. I don't look back because I'm already thinking about my alternative plan for this date. I mean, I've already thought about it long enough. Why couldn't I talk to him about it just then? Why can't I go back right now? Will he think I'm odd?

Who am I kidding? He already thinks I'm odd. In fact, his entire family thinks I'm odd, and it doesn't seem to matter to them, or to him. I surely don't have anything to lose.

I look down at Bessie. "What do you think, Bessie? Should I go back now, just walk in there and tell him my plan?"

Bessie tips her head to one side, her ears twitching and her eyebrows flicking up and down.

"Urgh, you're no help. I wish you could speak."

I bite at my lip, flicking my thumbnails as I make my decision and burst back into the conservatory before I lose my nerve.

"I've thought about it," I blurt out a little louder than I'd intended.

Stephan looks pretty startled at my sudden reappearance.

"Bloody hell, mate, that was quick." The smirk that never quite leaves his mouth is firmly in place as he waits for me to continue.

"Yeah, sorry." I grimace. "I already had a plan, and I was going to tell you last night, but then I found you in a ditch, which was a bit unexpected, and then, today, I mean, just now, you had me all flustered, you know—" I wave my hands about in the general direction of my face "—the kissing stuff, and spaghetti Bolognese and toothpaste, and relationship statuses. It doesn't take much to get me flustered. I'm a bit of a dork when it comes to, you know, interacting with people."

Stephan is just looking at me with this massive smirk on his face. "Mate, you have got to be the most adorable dork I've ever met. I think you might just be practically perfect in every way."

"Oh, like Mary Poppins." I laugh then frown. "Except I'm not a nanny, and you're not a chimney sweep."

He chuckles. "Why don't you come back over here and tell me your plan? And while you're at it, explain the spaghetti Bolognese thing as well."

He pats the sofa beside him, and I do as he asks, sitting closer this time, so he doesn't have to shuffle over in order to hold my hand.

I take a deep breath and tell him my pizza plan.

CHAPTER SEVEN

Shopping for Pizzas
or
Why Do People Not Follow the Rules?

TODAY, I AM shopping specifically for pizza ingredients for my date with Stephan. After I told him all about it, he agreed it was an awesome plan. I suspect he would have said that even if I'd suggested we go on a tour of the city sewers. That is something I'd quite like to do, actually. I'll have to write that down.

I want everything to be perfect tonight, so I have this shopping trip planned out meticulously. I really do like this man and want to make a positive impression after all the disastrous meetings over the last week and a half. He's already made a lasting impression on me. I know I will find it hard if he decides going out with me is too much of an effort.

I'm not hard work, just hard to fathom out. Stephan seems to have fathomed me out quite well so far. I just need tonight to go well and maybe there'll be some more kissing, perhaps something more than that, although that would indeed take a bit more planning and some understanding on his part.

Perhaps we'll talk about that some other time—if tonight goes okay, that is.

I live on the high street, right next to most of the shops I need to visit, but when any trip outside is fraught with the unpredictable, it's a good idea to have contingency plans in place for everything that could, or might happen. I packed the ones I need today in my backpack, just in case.

At the crossing, I wait patiently for the lights to change. Beside me is a woman with a baby in a pram. Beside her is a man smoking a cigarette. The smoke is blowing in the baby's face and the woman looks annoyed. It is rather rude of him, to say the least, and he doesn't seem aware that he is doing anything wrong. I find it very difficult not to point out these things when I come across them. Sometimes I wish I could just keep my mouth shut, but I really cannot help myself this time.

"You know, you shouldn't be doing that," I say, leaning a little over the pram so the smoking man knows I'm talking to him.

"Doing what, mate?" he asks, his voice gruff and gravelly enough to match his rough, tattooed arms.

"Smoking," I reply concisely.

"It's not illegal outside." He curls his lip and flicks the ash from his cigarette carelessly onto the ground. "Unless they changed the law when I wasn't lookin'."

"You're right, it's not illegal," I agree with him on that count, but still cannot let it go. "It's just that you're blowing your smoke in the baby's face and that's what I don't think you should be doing."

"Why don't you mind your own fucking business?" the man growls at me.

"Oh, that's a bit rude," I say, taking a step back. I don't think he'll do anything, because there's a pram in the way. Most people are a bit more accepting of my quirkiness, but this guy seems angry, which means he is actually very angry if even I can pick this up from his expression.

"He's telling the truth," the woman with the baby adds on my behalf, distracting the guy for a moment. "I really don't want your smoke in my baby's face."

The man gives her a long look, his lip curled in a sneer before looking back at me and stepping out onto the road. "Why don't you both just fuck off, eh?"

"Oh." I reach out to him as he steps out. "Wait, you shouldn't cross yet. It's not safe. The lights haven't changed."

"I can cross when I like, fucking weirdo," he growls back at me.

He takes a few more steps just as a car comes hurtling around the corner, horn honking as a warning. The guy jumps in shock and then makes a run for it, narrowly missing getting run over.

"Oh god," I gasp as I watch him turn and shake his fist at me and make obscene gestures at the driver of the car that just missed him. "He shouldn't have done that. He didn't follow the rules. Why don't people follow the rules?"

I'm not really asking anybody, but the woman beside me is laughing.

"He got his just desserts. That was rather funny, you have to admit."

"No, it was awful. He could have been killed." I feel a bit weak at the knees just thinking about it, and the fact that, because I know first aid, I might have had to do something about it if he had been hit, and after he was so horrible as well.

The lights change, but I freeze, because, although there are shops on both sides of the high street, the shops I want to go to are all on the other side and I don't much feel like crossing the road right now. Not when that horrible man is standing on the other side glaring at me like his mishap was all my fault.

I don't know what to do, because tonight can't happen if I don't get everything I need this afternoon.

"Are you all right?" the woman with the baby asks me. "Do you want me to call someone?"

Because of course she would come to that conclusion. I am rocking back and forth from my heels to my toes and flicking my fingers, muttering to myself like some sort of head case.

"No, no one thanks, I'm fine. I just need to…" I look around me for inspiration, a visual clue as to what I might have put in my contingency plan for getting out of situations like this.

– *Move away.*

That's a good plan. Move somewhere less—peopley.

I point ahead of me, towards a narrow alley between the shop buildings. Without looking in her direction I say, "I just need to go over there. Thank you for asking. Goodbye."

I make a rush for the alley. I don't look to see if she's watching me. I don't want to know.

Here, the sounds of the street are muffled. Today is not a particularly busy day, but even one person is one too many when I'm this close to losing my shit.

I lean back against the wall and take a moment to breathe. I can't cross the road. This is okay. I can just look at my contingency plan to see what my alternatives are.

I take my backpack off and swing it around to open it and get out my notebook. I wish Bessie was with me, but she isn't. I left her in the shop with Yenta for such a short, relatively simple shopping trip. It's easier than having to explain to every shopkeeper why she should be allowed into the shop with me. Most of them know she is my support dog, but some are funny about it. Besides, today I thought I'd be okay. How wrong was I about that?

Things would have been fine if that man had just followed the rules and not been so bloody angry about it when he almost got knocked over.

"Where's my bloody notebook?" I grumble as I rummage about in my bag.

Suddenly the bag is ripped from my hand, and I cry out as someone grabs my wrist and I'm pushed back against the wall.

"Think that was funny, did ya? What happened on the road back there?" It's the guy from the crossing. "Have a good laugh at my expense? Ya fucking weirdo."

I don't think he really wants answers to his questions. I struggle to get free, croaking out an apology that is so garbled it sounds like gibberish. I try to reach for my backpack, but he kicks it away and pushes me roughly up against the wall. I watch in despair as the contents of my bag are strewn across the lane.

"That's all my stuff." I gasp. "P-please let me go."

"God, you're such a spazz." The guy sneers. "I watched you pacing about like a loon. Leave yer carer at home, did ya? People like you shouldn't be allowed out in public. And where do you get off telling me what to do?"

"I've got as much right as you to be out anywhere I want," I croak at him, finally finding my voice because I'm angry now. He has no right to say those things to me. "I don't need a bloody carer, and I wasn't telling you what to do. I was reminding you of the rules."

"Yeah? Well, next time..." He leans in close, and his breath stinks. I turn my head but I can still smell it. He has bad teeth, but I don't think he'll appreciate me telling him about dental hygiene right now. I think he's already angry enough to hurt me. "Next time, keep your mouth shut and your thoughts to yourself. In fact—" his free hand grabs the front of my coat and twists the fabric until it tightens around my neck and nips the skin "—stay away from this part of the high street altogether, then you won't be bothering anyone. Understand?"

I nod as I pull at his hand to no avail. I've never been very strong even though I use the gym and stay fit. I feel panic start to set in, as it begins to get harder to breathe.

"Hey!" a voice calls from the end of the lane, and my attacker's grip loosens just a little bit. "Hey, what are you doing to him? Leave him alone, you bastard."

Oh god, it's Stephan. I don't want him to be hurt by this guy as well.

"What's it to you?" The guy lets me go and turns to face Stephan as he rushes into the alley. They meet chest-to-chest, their expressions dark and angry, and I'm afraid there'll be a fight.

Despite my throat burning and my shoulder feeling bruised where the guy had squeezed, I push between them, facing Stephan and looking up into his spring-light eyes that now look like a summer storm, flashing with thunder and lightning.

"Stephan, I'm fine. You can stop now. I'm not hurt. C-can we just go? P-please?" I want to run and not stop running until I get back to Yenta's shop, but I won't leave without him.

He's still glaring at the guy, his stormy eyes filled with anger and hatred.

"We're not the ones who should move on, Kit. He is." He leans past me and snarls at the guy. "Go on, get out of here before I do something you'll regret."

"You and who's army, then, pretty boy?" the guy hisses back.

Stephan smiles. I don't really think there's any reason to smile. No one said anything funny. I don't think it's a friendly smile, either. He holds up a clenched fist.

"I don't need an army," he growls. "I'm a Cassillis, and you'd better scoot before this connects with your face. You don't want to mess with me, mate, and you definitely don't want to mess with my boyfriend either."

The guy takes a step back, now looking unhappy rather than angry, and actually a little scared.

"Oh my god, a weirdo and a shirt lifter? I'm off, it might be catching."

Stephan takes another step forward, growling a warning, and the guy is gone before either of us can take another breath.

For a moment, Stephan stands very still, his fist clenched tight, before relaxing, his shoulders slumping.

"Jesus," he breathes as he turns to me and grabs me by the shoulders. His freckles are darker against his pale face. "Jesus, Kit, are you all right?" He takes a shaky breath. "When I saw that bloke with his hand on your throat, I saw red. What the hell was going on?"

"He was angry with me." I duck away from his hold and drop to the ground to retrieve my backpack and contents. He drops to his knees beside me, helping me to push things back into my bag but he's doing it in the wrong order. "Stephan, stop, let me do it myself."

"O-okay, I'm sorry." He moves back, but doesn't stand until I do, reaching out to support me when my legs threaten to give way. "Steady on, I've got you."

Again, I duck away from his touch. I can't process any of it right now. I need to find some way of calming down, but Bessie isn't here and my hands are shaking. I dig my fingernails into my palms, feeling the fog descend. I start to pace.

"I said something to him that I shouldn't have, except it wasn't bad. He wasn't following the rules. Why do people not follow the rules?" I'm gasping for breath now. "And now I want to go home, but I haven't finished my shopping, and I was shopping for stuff for tonight because I wanted it all to be perfect for you, and now it won't be."

"Kit, it's okay, mate. We can do the shopping together if you want, but I think you should sit down first, you're shaking like a leaf."

"Like a leaf. Like a leaf," I repeat his words like a mad parrot, jumping from one foot to the other as if I am a bird sitting on a perch. "No, no. I'm not a leaf and I can't sit, I mean, not here. I can't stay here. I need—I need—"

The words are stuck now as the world begins closing in around me. It feels like someone has put a sack over my head to stop me breathing. Things have got beyond the point where I can stop the panic. If I don't go home right now, I'm going to have a full-blown meltdown right here in the street, right in front of Stephan, and he won't want to be my boyfriend anymore and I only just found out that's what he thinks he is. Now he'll think the same as everyone else does: that I'm weird and I shouldn't be allowed out in public.

God.

"Kit." Stephan holds my shoulders again, trying to meet my gaze. His voice cuts through the fog like a beacon from a lighthouse, but it's too much, his touch, his concern, his kindness. I can't process it all. "Tell me what you need me to do," he says, and I know he wants to help, but I can't think about what I need when he's so close.

"Stop touching me," I yell, and his hands lift away from my shoulders as if they've been stung.

"I'm sorry, babe. I'm sorry. I won't touch you, but I'm not leaving. I'm not going anywhere. Tell me what else you need."

"I need…" I sob, trying to breathe and speak at the same time. "I need to go home. I need Bessie. I need…"

"Home. I can take you home. I can make sure you get there safely. Bessie will be there waiting for you, right?"

"She's always there for me. It's what she does." I'm clenching my fists so hard now I can feel my nails cutting into the flesh of my palms.

"Kit, you need to stop doing that, sweetheart. You're hurting yourself. Why don't you hold my hands instead?"

"I don't want to hurt you. I'm sorry I shouted at you, Stephan. You shouldn't be hurt. That man nearly hurt you, because of me. That shouldn't happen."

"No, that man hurt you because he's an arse. None of that was your fault, Kit, and if he'd hurt me, that wouldn't have been your fault either. Come on, let's get you home. Hold on to my hands, or anything, but please, stop clenching your fists. Your nails are cutting the skin."

I try to take some deep breaths. Through the fog, I hear Stephan's voice, soothing and pleading, and trying to make sense of what is going on. I have two choices right now: to carry on like this, getting more and more worked up, or let him help. I opt for the second choice. I hold onto his hands and let him guide me from the alley and across the street.

I don't look to see if people are staring. I close my eyes. Far from not wanting him to touch me, I find it is easier to tuck myself tight against his side, using him the same way I would use one of my blankets. I hope he doesn't mind. He wraps his arm around my shoulders and becomes a barrier between me and the rest of the world.

He keeps me safe until we reach the door of the bookshop.

"Oh my goodness, Lapushka!" Yenta gasps as we enter the shop.

I let Stephan explain what just happened. He does it quicker and more concisely than I ever would.

"Some guy attacked Kit in an alley, had his hands around his throat. If I hadn't turned up, I don't know what would have happened, Yenta."

"Oh no!" she cries, her hands on her cheeks. "Lapushka, are you hurt?"

Bessie is there, her head pushing up against my hands, letting me stroke her and calm myself down. As she does her thing, Stephan releases his hold on me but does not leave my side. Yenta steps to the other side and urges me to move.

"Come, let us get you upstairs. Stephan, will you take him up while I close the shop?"

Stephan guides me upstairs to my flat. This isn't how I'd planned for him to see my flat for the first time, but I'm now too tired to protest. I stumble to the sofa, grab a blanket and pull it over myself and Bessie, creating a safe, warm cave where the sounds of the outside world are muffled and distant.

"We should call the police," Stephan says from close by. Right now, it's like he's still a blanket, making the cave safer.

"No police," I mutter. "If the police come, I'll have to talk to them. I don't want to talk to anyone." I'm so drained I can't even lift my head. I rest it against Bessie and close my eyes, feeling her soft fur, breathing in her warm, spicy scent and loving her unconditional presence.

She's not the only unconditional presence, though, because I sense Stephan sitting close enough to touch, but keeping to himself. Waiting, always waiting.

How does he just know?

I peek from beneath the blanket. One of his hands is resting on the sofa beside me. Slowly, I reach out and place my hand alongside, my little finger tracing over his. The touch is gentle, but it doesn't hurt, not the way soft touch usually does. Without a word or even a glance in my direction, Stephan's little finger links with mine, and I feel a warmth travel up my hand and arm and fill my entire being.

Is this what it feels like? When you want to be with someone? It never felt like this with Harry. He never just sat beside me, waiting. Yenta is right, this feels different. But is it real? Will it last? Right now, he's here because he's worried, but once he knows I'm okay, will he leave?

Stephan and Yenta talk a little longer, in soft, quiet tones. I hear but I don't listen. It is probably about me, but it doesn't matter. All that matters right now, is that Bessie is doing her job and so is Stephan's presence. I am feeling more and more calm as the minutes pass.

"He usually sleeps after something like this happens," I hear Yenta say as the fog finally lifts and I can let myself listen again.

She has made tea. A peek from beneath my blanket cave tells me there's a cup waiting for me. I usually drink it cold anyway. I look to the side and see that Stephan is drinking his with his free hand, his other still occupied with mine, our little fingers still linked.

"Does it happen often?" Stephan sounds worried. "I mean, him getting attacked?"

"There have been incidents where people have lost their patience with him, raised their voice, called him names. He has never been physically attacked. This is awful, but a meltdown, he usually has one every two or three months. This was a bad one, but then, I think most people would react badly to being attacked like that."

"I'm sure. I sent the guy packing, but Kit should really report it to the police."

"Good luck persuading him to do that." Yenta's tone is now frustration. I recognise it because she gets frustrated with me quite a lot. "You might have noticed, but he finds it difficult speaking to people he's known for years. Think how he'll be when the police start asking him questions, and if he ever had to give evidence in a court? The prosecution would tear him apart."

"God, that's awful." Stephan sounds unhappy. "My dad's cousin does some things in a similar way to Kit. He's very different in other ways, though. He couldn't live on his own the way Kit does."

"Kit is his own person, Stephan. Autism affects everyone differently," Yenta tells him. "He likely has similar issues to your dad's cousin, yes, but he'll also be very different."

"Right."

I can't interpret Stephan's tone. He sounds unhappy, or maybe he's disgusted.

Well, that's it, I suppose. I never got to the stage where I had to tell him the reasons I do things the way I do. He knows now, and he's probably trying to think of an excuse to leave.

"I think he's amazing," Stephan whispers softly.

The words take a while to sink in, mostly because, at the same time, he moves his hand so that not only our little fingers are linked, but all our fingers are entwined. It feels like our entire beings have become joined and my hand is somehow part of him now. When his words finally register, they settle in my chest like something physical. My heart is beating so hard I'm certain he'll be able to hear it.

Some people talk about wanting to burst with excitement. I never really understood that until now, when I feel my heart will burst from my chest. I'd always thought it would be a horrible feeling, but it isn't. It's actually quite nice.

I suddenly want Yenta to leave because I want to be alone with Stephan. I want so much that it's all a bit scary.

As if he's somehow sensed what I'm thinking, Stephan urges Yenta to go back down into the shop, saying he will stay with me as long as I want him to. He does realise that could possibly be forever, doesn't he?

He sits back down beside me after letting Yenta out of the flat. He doesn't speak, as if he knows he has to wait for me to speak first.

I don't look up, my face still buried in Bessie's fur. "Did you push the top bolt right across the door?" I ask.

"Yes. Yenta showed me how to do it."

"I usually do that. It's always been me. I've never been here with anyone else except Bessie and Yenta."

"You can go and check if you want," Stephan says, his tone soft. "I won't be offended."

"That's okay. If Yenta showed you, then you'll have done it right." There's a moment of silence, and with Stephan, I know I don't have to fill it with chitchat. He just waits, like always. "You don't have to stay," I whisper, giving him the option to leave.

"I know I don't." He makes no attempt to touch me when I really want to be holding his hand again, melding our bodies into one. "But I will, unless you really, really want me to leave."

"I don't really, really want you to go anywhere," I confess. "But I know that some people find me hard to handle. Harry left because he couldn't cope."

"Well, Harry, whoever he is, is an arse."

"He was my boyfriend."

"Was he, indeed?" There's an edge to Stephan's voice that puzzles me enough to look up. I tip the blanket off my head to get a better look at his face.

Bessie takes that as an opportunity to leave me, her job done, and go and make a fuss of Stephan.

As he pets her and praises her for being a good dog, I study his face. Why did he sound so angry when I mentioned Harry? Was he jealous? I've never understood jealousy because I've never met anyone who felt it, nor have I felt it myself. I've read about it, but that's not enough to understand it.

"Are...are you jealous?" I ask him. "Why would you be jealous?"

He sighs as he continues to pet Bessie. "Don't worry, Kit, I'm not jealous, not really, just a bit envious that someone else got to call you his boyfriend, and we've never had any time to talk about us."

"But you are my boyfriend! You said so, to that guy, and you asked me if that was what I wanted to be the other night and I said yes."

Stephan smiles as his spring light eyes search my face.

"God, Kit, how could anyone ever want to hurt you? You're just—" His breath hitches, and I get the feeling that, if I let him, he would pull me into his lap and hold me in a tight embrace forever. "—perfect," he finishes.

"I don't know what you mean." I frown, looking away and staring at the floor. I want him to hold me, I do, but not just yet, it's too soon, and my body wants… It wouldn't just stop at a hug and Stephan doesn't want that, not yet. There are some things you have to do in the right order and I'm afraid I've got things terribly wrong. "I messed up our date. I didn't get everything I needed to make pizzas so now we can't eat together like you wanted."

"It's not always about what we want, Kit. What do you need to do right now?"

"Right now, I need to sleep," I say because I just want to hide away and shut out the world, especially if Stephan wants to leave.

"Okay." He nods slowly. "Why don't you go and have a sleep? Give me your shopping list and I'll get the rest of your shopping for you."

"Why would you do that?" I ask in shock. "I mean, I know I should say thank you."

"You're welcome, mate." Stephan smirks. He looks happy. I don't know why because now he's ended up doing the things I'm supposed to be doing. "I'm going to do your shopping so we can still have pizzas. Is that okay?"

"Yes."

"And is it still okay for me to come back and help you make them?"

"Yes. That too." I nod, still not really understanding why he even wants to do any of this.

"Where's your list?" he asks.

I produce it, pulling it from my backpack. I smooth it out before handing it to him. "S-sorry it got a bit crushed."

He stares at it, looking bewildered. "Gosh, I don't think I've ever seen such a detailed list."

"The actual list isn't that long," I explain. "The detail is there to remind me that it's okay if I can't get something specific and then I've sub-listed all the alternatives. It also has notes in the margins reminding me what to ask for and what to say to whoever is serving me and what they might say back. So I can, you know, have a normal conversation with them."

"Right." He's still studying the list like it's some sort of unfathomable user manual. I suppose it is in a way.

"If you ever wanted to understand exactly how I work, reading one of my lists will certainly help."

"You're not kidding." He chuckles. "When I get back, I think I might like to read some more of these lists of yours."

"I call them contingency plans. Do you really want to read them? Harry never did. He thought they were stupid."

"Harry is the one that was stupid if he didn't see these lists were as beautiful as the person who made them." He smiles at me before standing up and pressing a kiss to my forehead. "I really do want to read them," he assures me. "Now you go and have a sleep, mate, and I'll let myself out."

I think for a moment, getting it all sorted in my head. He waits for me to reply.

"Go out the back door, then I won't have to come down and push the bolt home. Get Yenta to let you back in, just in case I'm still asleep when you come back."

"Sure thing, if that's all okay with you." He seems a little unsure. I nod, smiling, not really needing to say anything more except I do. I need to check.

"You can just walk away, you know. You don't need to help me, or spend time with me or do anything with me. You've seen what I can be like. That wasn't an isolated incident, Stephan. It doesn't happen a lot, but I can't tell you it'll never happen again."

"Kit, I knew from the first moment I set eyes on you that no matter what, I wanted to get to know you. You should know that I don't scare easily and I'm not going anywhere."

"Yes, you are. You're going to the shops. You just said so."

He leans his forehead against mine, his hand on the back of my head giving just enough pressure for the touch to be pleasant.

"Oh, Kit." He sighs, kissing me quickly and leaving before I have even opened my eyes. "See you tonight, mate," he calls as he walks out of the room.

CHAPTER EIGHT

Pizzas Are Better When Shared
or
Grumpy Wake-up Calls Make For Great Bedtime Reading

I SIT UP AND rub my eyes, disorientated because I don't usually sleep in the afternoon, or in my clothes.

I freeze as I hear a noise that seems to be coming from my kitchen. I glance down at the floor where Bessie usually sleeps. Yes, she's there, so whoever is in my kitchen is obviously not a burglar or an axe murderer. It could be Yenta, although she rarely comes into the flat. I doubt it is Stephan. He's long gone. I'm not expecting to see him again after this afternoon. I know he said he would do the rest of the shopping for our date, but he's surely had time to think things over and decide that being with me is too much like hard work.

There's another noise from the kitchen. Bessie doesn't even stir. She obviously doesn't see whoever it is as a threat, but for that to happen they'd only have to give her a dog chew, and not even an expensive, posh one. Just one of those twenty-for-a-pound ones that look like they've been made from compressed paper pulp. She's a cheap date.

"Bessie, who's here, then?" I ask like she's going to answer. She does lift her head, twitch her ears towards me, whine a little and then goes back to sleep. "Some guard dog you are." I huff, swinging my legs off the bed and standing, stretching out my muscles and yawning loudly.

"Kit, are you awake?" Stephan's voice calls from the kitchen, startling me and also giving me a warm feeling. This man continues to surprise me, in a good way.

I frown as I walk to my bedroom door and look through the living room to the kitchen beyond. Even though he's surprised me in a good way I still need time to readjust.

"What are you doing?" I ask after yawning again.

"Hello to you too." Stephan smiles at me as he leans against the kitchen doorframe, rubbing his hands on a tea towel he has tucked into his jeans pocket. Was he washing my dishes?

I scowl. I'm not at my best when I wake up. Especially when things aren't as they should be. I shouldn't be waking up now, because I shouldn't have been asleep. Stephan shouldn't be here for our date yet. He shouldn't be washing my dishes. All my plans have gone awry.

"You're here early." I scowl, grimacing when he just stares at me.

"I'm at a bit of a loss as to how to answer that, mate. You knew I was coming back as soon as I'd finished the shopping, right?"

"Yes, yes." I pinch my nose, nodding but still scowling. "I'm sorry. I mean, I felt the need to point it out, even though I know the reason why." I run my hands through my hair, which has become all tangled while I was asleep. I hate brushing my hair anyway, but having to do it twice in one day is just annoying. I get a bit caught up with the task of using my fingers instead of a hairbrush, scowling at a particularly stubborn knot at the end of a clump of hair. I tease it apart and click my tongue.

Stephan chuckles and I look up, still scowling, this time at him.

"Are you always this bloody adorable when you first wake up?" Stephan says, not making any attempt to approach me.

"If by adorable, you really mean grumpy and bad-tempered, then yes." I huff.

"I think I already told you I think your kind of grumpy is pretty damn adorable," he reminds me. "Is there anything you want me to do to make things a little easier? Go out and start again, maybe, or just disappear until you've sorted yourself out and got your plans in place?"

"No! I don't want you to disappear." I make a frustrated noise, giving him a sideways look. "You didn't mean that literally, did you?"

"No, mate, I'm not a magician." He grins. "You did say it was okay to ask Yenta to let me in while you were still asleep."

"I know, I remember now. Yes. I'm sorry for being a grump. I get like that when something is happening that I haven't planned for. Mostly, I just need time to readjust. Sometimes, rarely now, it ends in a meltdown like earlier. I'm sorry that you saw that."

"Kit, I was just glad I was there to help." He doesn't sound as if he's angry about it, or irritated. When I glance at him quickly, he's smiling. "I got everything on your list, just as you wrote it out. It's all here, ready for when you are." He waves his hands over in the direction of the kitchen bench where I can see pizza ingredients all set out and ready to go.

"Did you get the readymade bases?" I ask as I approach the kitchen. I can feel things falling into place now, getting back to where they are supposed to be in the order I had planned them.

He steps aside to allow me access to the bench. "Yes. The vacuum-packed thin crust ones from the deli, as you requested, m'lord." He executes an elegant bow and I narrow my eyes, liking the way he smirks at me but not ready to admit it yet because I'm still a bit grumpy.

Okay, not so much grumpy as disconcerted. I should be really bothered that he is in my kitchen moving my stuff around and basically making himself at home—I note the half-empty coffee cup—but it doesn't feel wrong. There's a rightness I can't explain and a warm feeling that I just don't understand. Well, I do, but this is a first date, so it's too soon to be feeling things like that, except, I felt them when he kissed me those two times at his hotel…and all the other times he's just managed to do and say everything right.

Instead of thinking about it too much, I choose to inspect the gathered ingredients. Not because I'm looking for flaws but because I need a distraction to stop me from pushing him up against the kitchen bench and having him right there and then like some sort of wanton hussy. There's an order to these things, and he makes me want to do it all in the wrong order.

He really has got everything on my list, exactly what I had written down. I feel my grumpiness dissipating like oil in water when you add a drop of soap.

"Okay, you've passed," I tell him. "Thank you."

"Aw, you didn't tell me this was a test." He pouts. "If I'd known, I would have studied harder."

His statement makes me laugh out loud, and he tips his head to one side as I lean back against the kitchen bench, feeling a little more at ease but not completely relaxed. Not yet. There are some things that need to be said. I push away from the bench, aware I've begun wringing my hands and deliberately not looking at him as I try, unsuccessfully, not to rock backwards and forwards on my feet.

"You probably have some questions. Yenta said you might have some questions."

"No more than I would normally have on a first date," Stephan replies.

That makes me look up, in surprise. "But our date hasn't started yet. The date shouldn't start until seven o'clock and it's only six-thirty."

"Well, then." Stephan is still smiling, and I can't tell if this is because he's happy, or amused, but at least he doesn't look annoyed or frustrated because of my pedantics over timing. "Maybe I should wait until seven before I ask any questions."

I frown, not really wanting to pursue the subject of this afternoon, but I think it might be better to get those questions out of the way before we talk about anything else.

"You don't want to talk about what happened earlier?" I ask, still not looking at him. I see from the corner of my eye that he is shrugging.

"Not unless you do," he says, surprising me again.

I regard him with my head tipped to one side, perplexed and disconcerted.

"I think I do. Need to talk. I mean. I think there are some things you should know about me. Things that might make or break this date."

"Kit." Stephan sounds shocked. "Mate, there is nothing you can say that will make me want to break this date. Understand?"

"Er, yes, I-I think so." I still can't look at him.

"I knew from the very first time we met that I wanted to get to know you better, and then, even after everything that's happened and especially after what happened this afternoon, I am willing to do anything I need to do to be part of your life."

"I don't need a carer," I blurt out, before he gets any ideas, or makes assumptions after what he witnessed.

"I-I'm not offering to be anyone's carer," he says, his expression serious as I watch him from behind a veil I've made of my hair, because looking at him directly will overload me with information.

"Right. Because I don't need a protector either. That's Bessie's job." I turn away, to look over all the pizza ingredients, rearranging them in the order they are supposed to be. "I can look after myself."

"I know you can." His tone is quiet and gentle.

"I don't need anyone to come and tell me that the things I do are wrong, or odd, or that I should be doing things I'm not."

"I would never do that."

"Because I had that. I made the mistake of allowing someone to take over, and—" I take a shaky breath "—it didn't end well. I mean, for me. I have no idea how it ended for him. I never saw him again."

"You're talking about Harry, aren't you?"

There's an edge to Stephan's voice that I don't understand. "Are you angry that I mentioned Harry, or angry that Harry hurt me?"

"That he hurt you, Kit, definitely. Not the other. Never the other."

"You will probably get angry with me at some point. I mean, people do get angry with each other, don't they? But they do with me in particular. It's just, if you are angry or upset with me, or with something I've said or done, or even something that I haven't said or done, you have to tell me. I'm not good at picking up on these things if you don't tell me. That was Harry's problem. He thought I should have been able to work out what I'd done wrong. He never did tell me why he left, in the end. He just—did."

"That's awful." Stephan's voice is very quiet, and I don't know if he's upset or shocked now. I think he might be both, because when I chance a direct look at his face, his eyes look a little red and his cheeks are pale.

"I don't want you to think that you have to stay out of some sort of obligation," I tell him.

"That's not why I'm here."

"Okay, so you need to tell me exactly why you're here, so that I will know for future reference."

Stephan nods, smiling and looking pretty calm, to be honest. He definitely doesn't look like someone who doesn't want to be here. I can at least hope he'll stay for the pizza. Maybe he'll even stay for me.

Stephan takes a deep breath and speaks. "I'm here because I think you are an amazing, brave, determined man and I hope that some of that determination might rub off on me, because I've never had to fight for anything in my life until I met you. And by god, Kit Winters, I'll fight for you to my last breath."

I let out a surprised huff of air and look up, fully meeting his gaze. "I-I don't want you to fight anything or anyone. I don't want you to be hurt."

"It's not that kind of fighting I'm talking about, Kit. What I mean is, I'm willing to put in the time and effort to learn what I need to."

I lean back against the kitchen bench as I watch him very carefully, my eyes narrowed.

"I think you already studied," I tell him. "You studied so well you should go to the top of the class, even though there's only one of you in the class and there isn't really a class or a teacher."

"Well…" He smirks as he takes a step closer to me. "I'm really flattered to be given such an accolade, but I really didn't study anything yet, Kit."

I click my tongue. He doesn't know everything he needs to, or maybe he does and he just skipped over some parts. Oh well, if he's willing to learn…

"Say my name first," I tell him, meeting his gaze for longer than I have since I met him.

"Eh?" He takes another step closer.

"I know it's inconvenient to try to learn a different way to speak to someone," I explain. "But when you say my name right at the end of a sentence, I tend to focus on that and not what you've said. If you say my name first, then you will have my undivided attention."

"Oh, I see." He smirks as he takes one more step, which brings him close enough to almost touch me.

I can feel his presence prickling across my skin, like silvery tingles of blue static. Any closer without pressing firmly against me and it will hurt, but he knows this. I know he does, and when he closes the gap, he doesn't caress me, he places his arms either side of the bench and crowds me, pushing me back with his body, firm and warm and hard against mine.

I look up at him, lost in those spring-light eyes, wanting to be lost forever, because he's beautiful.

He leans in close and whispers into my ear, "Kit."

"Yes, Stephan?" I whisper back, sliding my arms around his waist and pressing my hands over the muscles of his back.

"I think you are incredible and gorgeous."

"And now you have my undivided attention." I grin. "Although I still don't see how you can think that. I'm not the one that's gorgeous."

"Oh, shush." He chuckles. "You said my eyes were like spring."

"That's right." I nod, my breath quickening as his words send a rush of hot air across my earlobe and a pool of heat to my groin.

"If I'm spring, then you're summer. Your eyes are as green as a summer meadow."

"Oh." I really can't think of anything to say in reply, since no one has ever described me this way before. "I want to say I can't be summer, because my name's Winters, but I know that's just my pedantic brain working overtime."

"Kit Winters, I think your pedantic brain is a thing of wonder, just like the rest of you."

"And now I really do want to kiss you," I tell him. "I mean, not that I didn't before, but it was all happening out of order. But now, suddenly, it doesn't seem to matter because you make it all seem so safe."

"Oh, Kit." His cheeks are flushed pink as he turns his head just a little in order to kiss me, lips pressed firmly on mine.

With a moan, I push my tongue against his. He tastes warm, and right somehow. Everything about him is right. His smell, his taste, the way he just knows what to do and say.

When I pull away from the kiss, liking the way his warm breath feathers across my face, I keep my focus on his eyes. The eyes are the window to everything and often give me too much information so I feel overwhelmed and have to look away. Not this time. I want to be overwhelmed by him. I want to see.

"God." He breathes out the word as a soft sigh as the kiss ends. "Kit, you've got my insides tied in knots. Have done since the first moment I set eyes on you. I could fall hard for you, keep falling and never stop."

"Oh dear! You've already fallen into a ditch this week. I wouldn't want you to hurt yourself again," I say, trying to sound serious, but his mouth curls in a delighted smirk.

"You know I don't mean that literally, don't you?"

I grin. "Maybe."

"Definitely." He leans back in for another kiss and I go with the flow, because that's how this kind of thing works. If I think about it too much, I'll get swamped in the organisation, when really, my body knows exactly what it's doing and what it wants.

Right now, it wants Stephan Cassillis very much.

Stephan Cassillis's body, however, wants food, because his stomach picks this very moment to rumble very loudly.

"Oh dear." I pull back a little to regard his stomach before looking up into his eyes again. "I think maybe we should eat."

"Hey, good idea, and sorry." He grimaces. "That kind of killed the moment."

"Oh, don't worry about it." I pat his shoulder. "Makes a refreshing change for it not to be me."

"Kit, you don't kill the moments, mate, you make them."

***

Later, after we have made and eaten our pizzas, we sit together on the sofa. I'd quite like to do some more kissing, but before I can suggest it Bessie joins us from the bedroom and attempts to sit on Stephan's knee.

"I'll have to walk her soon." I comment, as Stephan manages to fend her off by scratching her ears.

"I can come with you if you want," he offers.

"Okay, as long as your ankle isn't hurting too much. I realise this is the first time I've mentioned it, and I know it's been a few days but hardly long enough for it to be fully better. I feel a bit bad about that."

"My ankle's fine, Kit. Light exercise is good, and don't worry about not mentioning it. You had other things on your mind."

"Okay."

We fall into a comfortable silence for a little while, and Stephan slides his arm around my shoulders as we sit. I shuffle a little closer, enjoying his warmth and the way he just knows how much pressure to use when he's holding me.

"As far as first dates go, this one has been quite nice," Stephan states.

I shrug. "I wouldn't know. This is the first first date I've ever been on."

"Really?" He turns a little so he can face me. "But you and Harry...?"

"We never dated." I shrug. "Harry moved in because he thought I needed him to, and I told you, I just let him take over."

"Oh." He returns to the relaxed position he was sitting in before he spoke, with Bessie sitting on the floor at his feet, her head resting on his knee.

He scratches her ear, a thoughtful expression on his face.

Would now be a good time to talk about the rest of the night? I've resisted so far because, well, when I talk about how much I've planned something, it can sometimes kill the moment, except, Stephan thinks I make the moments. Perhaps now is a good time.

"Stephan, can I ask you something?"

"I think you just did, mate." He smirks.

I click my tongue and shake my head. "Then can I ask you something after this?"

"Of course you can. You don't have to ask to ask."

"Oh, stop confusing me, doofus." I hit him with a cushion and he curls up in self-defence.

Bessie gets in on the act, finally seeing her chance to jump up onto Stephan's knee.

"Bessie, get down. You're ten tons of solid dog," Stephan complains, still trying to defend himself from my cushion assault as well as her tongue. "Okay, I yield."

"I yield?" I laugh, but stop hitting him. "Who says things like that anymore?"

"I do." He huffs, smoothing his dishevelled hair. "Right." He turns to smile at me. "What did you want to ask?"

"Are you planning on staying the night?"

His lips part, as if he is half in the act of saying something but he doesn't quite know what to say.

"Bloody hell, Kit. That was a bit direct and to the point."

"I'm sorry." I grimace. "I don't know any other way to be. I mean, I don't do subtle, and I don't do spontaneous. I mean, I need to have these things planned out. I don't like uncertainty.

It stresses me to the point, of, well, you saw what happened this afternoon."

"That was a pretty stressful situation. Anyone might have reacted the same way you did."

"I doubt that." I look away. How can he always manage to make even my worst behaviours seem so acceptable? "But are you? Staying the night, I mean?"

Stephan sits up a little straighter, clasping his hands in his lap as if he is nervous now.

"You don't have to," I tell him, trying to make him not nervous. "It's just, I need to know, so I can, you know, put all my plans into place for, you know…" I grimace as I wave my hands in the vague direction of the bedroom.

"You have contingency plans for sex?" Stephan gapes at me, and I hang my head, knowing I've gone too far this time. I mean, who the hell has contingency plans for sex? And worse still, who the hell tells their potential partner they have already planned out their first bedtime activities to the last letter? He'll be running for the door, screaming that I'm a loony…

"Mate, that is awesome." His smile is broad, and his eyes, when I chance a look, are dancing with spring-light.

Once again he has managed to surprise me. I stare at him in surprise as his smile broadens once more.

"Kit, I think I need to see those contingency plans, because I really would like to stay the night at some point, if that's what you want, but only if I'm absolutely sure I know enough not to mess this up, because I don't want to, you know, mess this up."

"Do you really want to see my contingency plans?" I regard him dubiously. "I mean, I think I already told you that Harry never wanted to. He thought they were stupid, especially the ones for bed."

"But the bedtime ones are the most important ones to get right." Stephan frowns. "How did he know what you liked if he didn't read them? Did you tell him?"

"I would try to, but it never worked out the same way. Sometimes I'd get in a bit of a muddle, and he would just get impatient with me and we would end up doing everything he wanted and very little of what I did. I mean most of the time it was fine, because it felt good but at the same time, it all felt a bit out of control. Not that I'm a control freak, because I'm not. That's not the reason I need to know what's happening next."

"Oh god." Stephan sounds a little upset now, and he looks a bit pale as he falls back into the sofa cushions, his hand across his mouth.

"Are you all right?" I could remind him about my first-aid training, but I don't think this is an appropriate time.

He recovers quickly, his smile returning as he gazes at me. "I'm fine, mate. Never better."

His words make me laugh and he tips his head to one side, smiling. "What's funny?" he asks.

"I like the way you say mate, that's all, and I like that it has several meanings, one of which, has…"

"Sexual connotations." He nods in understanding. "I get it. It also means friend."

"We're not friends, though, are we? We're boyfriends. At least, that's what you said. If you want to change that after tonight then that's fine, I don't mind. Eating pizza with a friend is still better than eating on my own."

"Kit." His hand presses down firmly on my leg. He always uses just the right amount of pressure. He is so good at remembering. "I still do want to be your boyfriend, but boyfriends can be friends too. In fact, it's much better if they are."

"Do you think so?"

"I know so, mate." He smiles at me, taking my hand in his and twining our fingers together. "Now, why don't you go and get those contingency plans and we'll read them together. I'm not saying we need to do anything with them just yet, because I'm in no hurry. I just want to make sure I get everything right when we do."

"I don't think you could possibly get anything wrong, Stephan. You've been on a roll since we first met."

He laughs and is still laughing when I return from my bedroom with my backpack full of notebooks and other important stuff.

"Ah, the infamous backpack." He chuckles.

"Infamous? It isn't the villain in a movie. It's just a backpack."

"Maybe, but it is important. And if it hadn't been for that backpack, I might not have followed you home that day at the library or learned your name or asked you out on a date."

"No. I suppose you're right." I stare down at the unassuming black bag. It doesn't seem possible for something so nondescript to have been so integral to Stephan and I getting together. "It wasn't just the backpack, of course. If Bessie hadn't crashed that wedding…" I leave the sentence hanging.

"Oh god, yes." Stephan chuckles. "I don't think anyone there that night will ever forget. My dad plays that CCTV footage over and over on a loop. He's still laughing about it."

"Oh dear. Now I feel I'm infamous, or Bessie."

"Not infamous, mate, just famous, amongst my family, anyway. Are these the contingency plans?" he asks as I hand him a stack of three books.

"Yes." I nod. "Well, these are the most important ones. I don't carry all of them around with me. There are rather a lot, and some of them are quite detailed."

"Yes, I remember your shopping list," Stephan muses as he studies the intricately decorated front cover of the first book. He runs his fingers over the designs. "Did you draw these? They're beautiful."

"They're just scribbles," I tell him, surprised he could think they were anything else. "Sometimes I doodle when I'm thinking."

"You could sell these designs. People would love them."

"Bollocks." I laugh out loud. "Surely no one would want to pay money for my scribbles."

"I think they would." Stephan shrugs. His hand hesitates before he opens the first book and he looks up at me. "May I?"

He's about to delve deeper into my world than anyone, even Yenta, has gone. She sometimes helps me write the contingency plans, but she has never read one herself. With a little trepidation,

I nod. He said he was willing to do anything to be part of my life, and these plans are a big part of who I am and how I make sense of the world.

I watch as he reads, first one book then the next. The ones about shopping and walking Bessie; about having conversations and waiting for others to have their say. The ones about friendships, and how not to be an arse when someone is trying to be nice to me. I still need to do a bit of work on that one. And finally, he reads the one about being intimate. I try not to squirm.

"I haven't quite finished that one," I explain. "It all got a bit too graphic and I had to take a break."

"You're not kidding," Stephan whispers as he closes the book and holds it in his lap, his eyes wide and his cheeks a little flushed. "I can see why you had to take a break, mate."

For a moment, he just sits there, staring at nothing, probably deep in thought. It's a lot to take in all at once. When he does eventually speak, his voice is quiet, subdued even.

"What would your contingency plan be if someone told you that they love you?" he asks, not meeting my eye, staring down at the notebook in his hand, his finger tracing slowly over the designs I have drawn on the cover.

I think for a little while and I get the sense that Stephan is holding his breath.

"Love is a big word," I begin, still thinking. "I mean, technically, it's a small word, only four letters, but it takes up a big space in your head." I take a shaky breath. "And your heart." This is getting into territory I didn't really want to cross right now. Love is not a subject I feel I can speak of with any confidence. I don't understand emotions at the best of times, but when they are expressed and not meant… "No one should ever say it," I whisper, "unless they really, really mean it."

"Is that your rule?" Stephan looks up from the book but he does not leave go of it, holding it tight as if his life depended on it.

"Not just mine. It should be everyone's rule. But I…" I take a deep breath and sigh. Why are we talking about this? Would it be appropriate to try and change the subject? I don't want to get all flustered and upset in front of him, but if he pursues this, I will.

"Someone said it to you," he states before I can think of anything to say as a diversion. "And didn't mean it?"

I nod. "Yes."

"Was it Harry?"

"Yes," I say, my voice getting quieter with each question.

"Tell me," he urges, his voice gentle and caring.

"He said he loved me, and then he said I wasn't what he wanted. But if I wasn't, why would he say he loved me? When you say something like that, it means you'll stay forever, so he can't have meant it, because he left. I don't always understand how other people feel. I mean, I'm not very good at guessing how they feel, but I'm not an emotionless android. I can relate if the person talks to me and explains how they're feeling. If he was unhappy, he should have said, but he never did, and when he left…" I take another deep breath, because this is where it gets most difficult and where I have to explain a little more about myself than I really wanted to share right at this moment… "I find it hard enough to deal with small changes. Big changes are even harder to accept. When he left, it was one change too many?"

"Too many? What do you mean?"

"Six weeks before he left, my mum died."

"Oh god." Stephan's face goes very pale. "That's awful."

"I don't remember a great deal about those weeks. I know Harry found it very hard to deal with the fact that I was really not dealing with anything at all. So he left me to not-deal with it all by myself. If it hadn't been for Yenta, I might have ended up homeless on the streets—in hospital, even. I think I was very close to being committed."

"Really? You seem pretty sane to me."

"Perhaps now. But then…" I wiggle my hand "…not so much."

"And Harry, he never came back?"

"No. He did try to call me, but I never could hold a decent conversation on the phone. He took that to mean I didn't want to speak to him and that I hadn't actually felt anything for him at all in the two years we'd been together. You probably guessed that there's a lot of things I'm not very good at. And it's not from lack of trying. It's just the way my brain works."

"But there's an equal amount of things you are very good at, Kit. In some cases, you're an expert, judging by the content of these books." He points to the one in his hand and gives me a rather candid look, flicking his eyebrows. "I think I need a lot more practice at some of these things, with an expert as my tutor."

"Oh, you mean first aid, obviously," I say with a slight smirk because I know he really means sex. He snorts.

"Er, no, not quite, but there are healing qualities to the other activities."

He's quiet for a little while and then he speaks again.

"I think we touched on a very heavy subject just now."

"Weight has nothing to do with it, but yes, it is a difficult thing to talk about. Harry said he loved me, and I thought I loved him, but perhaps I didn't, because I didn't really miss him, once I'd got over the initial shock and the antidepressants started to work. I miss my mum, but not him. Perhaps that's just me, not understanding any of it. Perhaps I'm not even capable of feeling the same as other people."

"Kit, your feelings are no less relevant just because you experience them in a different way. Besides, this Harry was the emotional numpty. I've said this before, but it bears saying again: Harry is an arse."

"Right." I don't really want to talk about Harry anymore, so I change the subject and hope he doesn't mind. "Going back to your original question, about contingency plans. Do you think I might need one?"

"I think you might need one very soon," he says, the spring-light hovering in his eyes as he meets my gaze.

"Oh," I whisper, swallowing hard. "I don't really know what to say now, because I don't think I'm ready to say it back. It's the wrong time, and the wrong order. There are things we need to do before either of us says anything like that."

"I know." He nods. "I understand now that I've read these." He pats the books on his knee before turning to face me so he's sitting sideways on the sofa. "Kit, I'm going to make you a deal."

"I… Okay. Deals are things I understand really well since I have a degree in business studies."

"Bloody hell, really?" His mouth opens wide in shock.

"Don't sound so surprised."

"I'm not surprised because you have a degree, Kit. That's brilliant, but you and I are going to have to work on our information sharing, you know, so you don't drop any more bombshells when I'm trying to focus on something else entirely."

"You're the one who mentioned some sort of deal," I remind him. "So my statement was relevant."

"Okay, okay." He chuckles, holding his hands up in surrender.

I wait, but I'm not as patient as Stephan, so I speak before he's ready. "Well, come on, then, what's this deal?"

He regards me with narrowed eyes before taking a breath to speak.

"I won't say that big-little word until I'm sure that you've got a contingency plan ready, and definitely not until I am absolutely certain, without a doubt, that I will never ever leave."

"Right." There he goes again, knowing just exactly what to say and telling me he'll wait without him ever being told he has to. But how long is he willing to wait this time? "What if it takes me forever to make my plan?"

"Then I'll wait forever, Kit. I'm not planning on doing anything else, or going anywhere. I'll be right here waiting."

"And what if it takes until the next time we have a springful of winters? That could be decades."

"Then that's how long I'll wait, my lovely, lovely boy." He holds out his arms for me to decide whether or not I want to be held. I do this time. Perhaps I will every time with him, because he makes it all so unconditional.

"Not a boy, remember?" I remind him, as I snuggle into his side, feeling safer there than I ever did anywhere else. Stephan's arms wrap tightly around me, holding me in his warm, safe cocoon. "But thank you, Stephan. I think you're lovely too, and I think I shall enjoy this forever business."

"Oh Kit, me too."

The End

Well, not really the end; it's actually just the beginning. I mean, sometimes people write 'the end' and they don't mean that it's the end of the story, just the end of what they're willing to write.

"Kit, mate, come to bed." Stephan calls from the bedroom, sounding uncharacteristically impatient.

"Okay Stephan, don't have a cow."

I don't mean that literally. I don't think he's really going to have a cow if I don't come to bed right now.

"Mate, who are you talking to?"

"No one, Stephan, just my contingency plan notebook for dealing with boyfriends who snore."

"I do not snore."

"You don't have to listen to it. Believe me, you snore."

Really The End or I do actually believe Stephan will have a cow.

AUTHOR'S NOTE

Kit has Asperger syndrome, which is an autism spectrum disorder. Autistic people experience the world in a very different way to other people. They have specific difficulties with social interaction and communication. They can also have some sensory processing difficulties, which means they could have higher sensitivities to smells, tastes, touch, light and noise.

There are currently around 700,000 autistic people in the UK. That is more than 1 in 100. The condition does tend to affect men more than women, although we are slowly beginning to understand that women's autism presents in far more subtle ways than men's.

Kit's wish, if you will remember, was to write a manual to help people to understand him and be a little more accepting of his differences. It is the wish of most who are affected by autism that the wider world becomes more aware of the difficulties that they face every day. A little more knowledge and understanding equals a lot more acceptance.

For those of you who would like to know more about autism, or have in some way been affected by the issues explored in this book, here are some links that might be helpful.

https://www.autism.org.uk

https://community.autism.org.uk/f/adults-on-the-autistic-spectrum

https://www.autism-society.org

http://www.autismeurope.org

Autism charities around the world:
https://www.autism.org.uk/services/helplines/outside-uk/round-world.aspx

Autism Network International:
https://www.autismnetworkinternational.org

Assistance dogs:
http://www.assistancedogs.org.uk

YouTube currently has a wealth of information on autism, with many people sharing their own experiences with Asperger syndrome and autism spectrum disorders through video blogs. One such 'vlog' is Aspie World, which, along with others, was one I watched quite a lot while writing this story, and that, along with my own experiences, both professionally and personally, helped me a great deal when trying to put myself in Kit's shoes (even though I don't think they would actually fit me).

https://www.youtube.com/user/AspieWorld1

ABOUT DAWN SISTER

Dawn is from the North East of England. Her life is spent juggling. The juggling balls are: children, husband, work (occasionally), voluntary work, professional knitting (notice she doesn't class this as work), and writing. When she has time she actually sleeps.

The whole point of writing for Dawn is just to get it all off her chest and out of her head. If she doesn't write it down then she ends up having long conversations with the characters out loud and her husband thinks she's crazy.

CONTACT & MEDIA

Twitter: www.twitter.com/dawnsister1

Tumblr: dawnsister.tumblr.com

Facebook: www.facebook.com/DawnSister

Goodreads: www.goodreads.com/DawnSister

Beaten Track: www.beatentrackpublishing.com/dawnsister

BY DAWN SISTER

Dazzled By The Light

The Halloween Incident

See You Smile (Love's Landscapes)

*Merry F***cking Christmas*

Eagle Man and Mr Hawk (Love is an Open Road)

Not a Word (Love is an Open Road)

Locked in the Moment (Love Unlocked)

A Springful of Winters (Seasons of Love)

OUT OF SEASON

BOB STONE

It's the old, old story. Demon meets girl, demon falls for girl, demon creates a perfect summer's day in the middle of winter. What could possibly go wrong?

***

Genre: fantasy fiction

Keywords: demons, unrequited love, time, literary

DEDICATION

For Wendy, my love every season.

1.

REMICK HAD WALKED the worlds for millennia, keeping only his own company. Time belonged to him, and he was content to go where and when he pleased or was needed, his life solitary and unending. The possibility that he might be lonely had never occurred to him until the day he saw the woman in the coffee shop. He had been called many things in his time. He and his kind had been called demons, the Old Ones, even gods, but never anything as mundane as lonely.

His day had, up until that point, been fairly routine. He had secured the temporal bonds between two worlds which had become frayed and brittle. There had been a small amount of leakage, but the only witness had been a teenage girl who became convinced she had seen a ghost. She was, however, prone to telling her friends tall stories and realised that if she mentioned the old woman who had drifted into her room and out through the wall, nobody would believe her, so she said nothing.

Once the temporal bonds had been secured, Remick moved on to quell an uprising in a time that had yet to happen. Because he still had a great deal to do, he found that the best way was to remove the leader of the uprising from the time-stream altogether. With their leader gone, his followers found they no longer had any interest in the uprising and went home. The morning's work done, Remick had an irresistible urge for a double-shot hazelnut latte. What he actually wanted was a beer, but it was too early in most of his days for beer, so a latte would have to do.

He was doing his best to enjoy his drink, even though the barista had used rather too much syrup, making the latte overly sweet. At least there was one of those little biscuits with the coffee, and he did enjoy those. Outside, grey rain was steadily pouring down, as it had been doing for days. Winter had just started, and spring was a long way away, but the coffee was warm.

While Remick was drinking, his attention was caught by a man and a woman at a nearby table. The woman was quite simply the most breathtakingly, heartbreakingly beautiful person he had ever seen. He had seen, admired—and sometimes acted upon—beauty in many women and men in his travels, but never had he encountered anyone quite as fascinating as this.

It was not her hair, though it was black as carbon just before it starts to become diamond. She had been wearing a woollen hat when she arrived, but her hair, once free of it, cascaded over her shoulders, providing a stark contrast to her red coat.

It was not her skin, which had a texture that he felt he could never tire of touching, even though it was only the skin of her lovely face that was visible. It was not her eyes, which were as dark as midnight and sparkled with constellations of mischief. It was none of these things and yet all of them.

What was most striking was that he could not read her future timeline. She was an enigma, her destiny unknowable. The man with her was taking no notice of her astonishing beauty, just talking about himself and occasionally looking at his phone. The woman was a rare and priceless treasure; the man was a priceless idiot.

Remick continued to stare at the woman. She was talking to the man, telling him a charming story about something that had happened to a someone named Helen in the department store where she worked. She made the story entertaining, imitating several different voices, but still the man paid her only perfunctory attention, giving the occasional grunt or *mmm* to give the impression he was listening, when anyone could see he was not.

Remick found the woman's persistence in trying to gain her companion's interest at once delightful, because she was trying so hard, and upsetting because it was not working. He knew that he could listen to her stories and look at her face as she was telling them for a very long time indeed without ever tiring, and if there was something about which Remick knew a great deal, it was long times. It was at that moment, that one, glorious moment that stretched out for what felt like hours, that Remick knew he was lonely, and his loneliness could only be remedied by having this woman in his life. Remick carried on watching until the woman finished her tale, and the man said something about having to get back to the office.

As he drained his now cooling coffee, Remick watched the couple get up and leave. They seemed to be together, and yet there was little connection between them. The man opened the door but was oblivious to whether the woman had even followed him out. They rushed past the coffee shop window through the rain and out of sight, and there and then, Remick made a decision. He would have another latte and come up with a plan.

2.

THE PLAN WAS a fairly straightforward one, and the opportunity to put it into action arose three days later. During those three frustrating days, Remick had spent so much time in the coffee shop he had been given a loyalty card and had almost acquired enough stamps to get a free cup of coffee.

For the first two days, he watched and he waited, but neither of the pair came in. It was tedious, but at least it gave Remick shelter from the rain, which was showing no sign of letting up and was now accompanied by a fierce, chilly wind. On the afternoon of the third day, his patience was rewarded when the man came in and ordered a large Americano with no milk and a raisin Danish. He went and sat at a table by the window and became immersed in something on his phone. He did not appear to be expecting company.

Remick had known the man would be there, of course. His timeline had been transparent and predictable. It was the unreadable woman who had made Remick return to the coffee shop every day and consume too many lattes. It was not because he wanted to see her, though he most certainly did; it was that he wanted to catch the man on his own.

Remick, confident that he had not been observed, bought himself yet another latte and went over to the table where the man sat, typing something into his phone and smiling in the way of someone greatly amused by their own humour. Remick indicated a chair at the other side of the table and enquired, "Is anyone sitting here?"

The man looked up from his phone, looked at Remick, looked at the chair, and finally looked around at all the other vacant chairs in the coffee shop. He was obviously unwilling to be seen sharing a table with this stranger, with his unkempt beard and long hair which could do with a wash. And a cut.

"There are loads of free chairs," he said.

"I know," Remick replied. "But I like the look of this one."

The man sighed and waved a hand vaguely at the chair. Then he turned his body towards the window and away from Remick. *Sit there if you want,* the gesture said, *but don't expect me to talk to you.* Remick found it incredibly rude, and it made him even more determined to carry out his plan.

"Have you got the time?" he asked.

The man glanced at his watch. "Ten to," he said, then went back to his texting.

"No, you misunderstand me. I know what time it is. I always know what the time is. It's a gift. And it's actually eight minutes to. I meant have you got the time? I was wondering if you have got the time left in your life to waste it with someone who does not interest you in the slightest."

The man looked up and stared at Remick, his face a mixture of confusion and irritation. "Look, I don't know who you think you are, but—"

"I don't *think* I'm anyone," Remick replied, interrupting him. "I know who I am. I know who you are, too. It *is* Brian, isn't it? Brian Norris?"

"Who are you?" the man demanded. "Are you from the VAT, because—"

"No, Brian. I'm not from the VAT. They won't be visiting you unexpectedly until next Thursday, I believe. How you fiddle your VAT returns is of absolutely no concern to me. It also may not be relevant to you, but that depends on what you do with the suggestion I am about to make."

Norris stood up, making a great show of finishing his coffee.

"Look, I don't know what you want, but I'm really busy. I've got a business to run, so I suggest you sod off and go and bother someone else."

"Sit down, Brian," Remick said pleasantly. When Norris remained on his feet, he said it again, and this time it could not be described as pleasant. "Sit *down*!"

Norris glared at Remick, but mutely sat back down.

"That's better." Remick smiled again. "It's always best to keep things polite."

"What do you want?" Norris hissed, glancing around in case there was anyone else in the coffee shop who might know him.

"It's really very simple. The woman you were with in here the other day. I want you to end things with her."

"Which woman? I don't know what—"

"Oh don't be ridiculous, Brian. You know very well who I mean. I don't really think that a man like you would have many women. She's very beautiful, and you are completely unworthy of her, so you will end it. Today."

This incensed Norris, and he leaned forward in his chair, pushing his face up close to Remick's. He smelled of cheap aftershave and cheaper cigarettes.

"Now you listen," he snarled, his mouth a thin, angry line. "She's got nothing to do with you. I'm not used to being threatened, so either you back off right now, or…well, let's just say I know people."

"You know people?" Remick laughed. "What a curious expression. Of course you know people. Most people know other people. The thing is, most of the people you know dislike you. They think you are a self-obsessed, arrogant idiot. And of course, they're right. You are."

Norris did not seem to have a ready reply to this. He sat back in his chair, folded his arms across his chest and stared at Remick.

"So," Remick continued, "here's my offer to you. If you end your relationship, such as it is, with that woman today, by, say, five o'clock, I will leave you alone. You will never see me again and you will continue with your rather miserable existence. Your life will carry on exactly as it is now. You will run your business badly until your creditors catch up with you in about two years time and force you to sell up. You will go on thinking you are happier than you actually are and die reasonably peacefully in your bed in twenty-eight years time. If you don't, however..."

"What? What if I don't?"

"Then your life will end twenty-eight years earlier than it was supposed to, and it won't be very peaceful, I'm afraid."

Norris stood up again, shoving his chair back so violently it almost toppled over.

"That's it!" he declared. "I've had enough. You can't come here and threaten me like this!"

"Five o'clock," Remick said with a slight smile because he now knew what he would be doing at that time.

He watched Norris storm out of the coffee shop and then went and ordered himself another latte. Because he was in a good mood, he treated himself to a slice of lemon drizzle cake to go with it.

3.

AT FIVE O'CLOCK, Remick was waiting outside the office block where Brian Norris rented a suite of rooms for his web design business. He sat on a bench on a small patch of grass at the front of the office block. The rain had stopped for a while, but the wind was still strong, whipping old newspapers and takeaway coffee cups around his feet. The bench was surrounded by discarded cigarette butts, despite the very clear notice next to the bench politely requesting smokers use the bin nearby. There were times, Remick thought, when the human race did not deserve the world that had been provided for them.

Remick was dressed innocuously in a long, black leather coat and jeans, his normal attire for walking in this world. Although he had made frequent studies of the clothing and habits of the people in every time period he visited, he had not chosen his outfit out of any desire to fit in. He just liked the way it looked. He sat pretending to be interested in a copy of the local newspaper which he had found on the bench and was several days out of date. He was not really reading the news; he knew only too well what today's news was and tomorrow's as well, and the wind made it hard to keep the paper still. He waited until his internal clock ticked round to five o'clock and watched as Brian Norris emerged from the building.

Norris was worried about something, if the frown etched into his brow was any indication. He walked hurriedly, looking all around him with anxious eyes, the collar of his coat turned up, ostensibly against the wind but really intended to obscure his face, as if that would make any difference. Because he was looking around, he very nearly walked straight into Remick, who had risen from the bench as Norris approached and stood right in front of him.

"Hello, Brian," he said. "Don't try and run. You won't be able to."

Norris was not used to being told what to do, Remick could tell. He watched in amusement as the human stubbornly tried to move but found that his legs would not cooperate. All around him, people passed by, rushing home from work and oblivious to his plight. It was almost as if they were not there at all. The air was still, and he could no longer feel the wind. He wanted to ask Remick what was about to happen to him but found that his mouth did not work any better than his legs.

"You had a chance to do the right thing, Brian," Remick said. "One chance. It wasn't even as if it was a difficult thing to do, but I knew you wouldn't do it. Your sort never do. So here's what I have done. I've taken you out of time. But because you're not really a bad person, just vain and arrogant, you're not going to die. I could end your existence without thinking about it and without regret, but instead, I'm just going to leave you here. It will give you plenty of time to have a good old think about how you could have done things differently."

As he spoke, Remick's eyes flashed red with a fire that burned into Norris's mind and soul, and then suddenly Remick and the familiar background of the world he knew were gone, leaving Norris alone and cold and screaming in a vast, empty, timeless void.

People carried on with their lives, scurrying along to catch trains or buses, phones clamped to their ears, having meaningless conversations that could easily have waited until they got home. The wind continued to blow litter in circles like small animals playing chase. The world could, and would, continue to thrive without Brian Norris and his web-design business. Remick grinned. That was the easy part of his plan completed.

4.

THE NEXT PART of Remick's plan required him to be patient again. He knew it would be fruitless to return to the coffee shop immediately, so busied himself with other things. A girl had been born on all the worlds, and Remick knew that, like her brother, one of her would one day be important. Remick spent a little time investigating, and once he was satisfied he knew which version of the girl was the important one, he returned to the world with the coffee shop and the woman.

The rain had also returned. The skies were heavy and the colour of old slate. Remick waited across the road from the coffee shop, pretending to look in a shop window. When he saw the woman approach, it should have been like a small patch of spring had arrived, but in her dark-grey coat and the hat she had been wearing when Remick first saw her, she looked as downcast as the weather. Remick felt a little sad for her, but it was all part of his plan, and he fully expected her mood would change soon. He waited until he was sure she had entered the coffee shop and gave her time to order her drink, then crossed the road and followed her.

The coffee shop windows had misted up, so it was not until he had gone inside that he spotted her. She was sitting on her own in a corner booth, her gloveless hands wrapped around a steaming mug to warm them. Enchanted by her long, slender, ringless fingers, Remick forced his gaze to the phone beside her at which she kept casting glances, as if she could not quite believe there had been no messages since the last time she looked—mere seconds ago.

Remick ordered himself a latte—no syrup this time, he was starting to find the taste cloying—and sat at the nearest free table. From his coat pocket, he pulled a battered paperback copy of Proust's *A La Recherche de Temps Perdue* in the original French and opened it at a random page. He was not reading it—he found Proust's prose stodgy, the language over-elaborate—but he had carefully selected the paperback from the shelves of a charity shop because it seemed appropriate and he wanted to convey an air of wistful intelligence and safety.

In her booth, the woman sipped her drink and waited for a message that would never come. Remick wished she would take her hat off so that he could admire her hair again, but it was clearly not that sort of a day. He contented himself with stealing glimpses of her face, each one imprinted onto his mind like a snapshot. Even in sadness her face was exquisite. Her mouth, devoid of make-up and turned down at the corners with misery, had full lips over which Remick longed to run his index finger. Her eyes glistened, not with the mischief that he had seen before, but with tears. Remick could bear her sadness no longer; closing his book, he picked up his coffee and went over to her booth.

"Excuse me. Would you mind if I join you?"

She shrugged and turned away, staring at the rivulets of condensation trickling down the window.

"It's a horrible day," Remick observed, doing the *let's talk about the weather* thing everyone seemed to do.

"Nice for ducks," the woman replied, not looking at him.

"I think the ducks are getting a bit fed up now." Remick took a sip of his latte, waiting for a response. When none came, he tried again. "They do a great latte here, I'll say that."

"I don't drink coffee," she said. "Green tea."

Remick sighed. This was not going to be quite as easy as he'd thought. He opened his book at another random location and began to read, watching the woman in his peripheral vision. He turned several pages before she paid him any heed.

"You read Proust?" she asked.

"Now and again, when the mood strikes me."

"In French?"

"That's how he wrote it. It seems rude not to."

"I tried reading it once." She shrugged dismissively. "I couldn't get into it. Maybe it's because I read it in English."

Remick put the book down. "It's a bit too sad for today anyway. It's miserable enough out there." He studied the watch he always wore on his wrist, even though it never told the correct time. "Is it that time already? I'm sorry, I've got to go. Lovely meeting you."

Then, in a move that had been carefully planned, he stood up and hurried out of the coffee shop without waiting for a reply, leaving the book on the table. Protruding from the pages was a business card—one of a box of a hundred Remick had ordered from a local printers—on which was the fictional name 'R. Thompson' and the number of a mobile phone he had bought especially for this purpose. He wondered if she would find the card and ring the number. He very much hoped that she would.

5.

THE PHONE RANG an hour and seventeen minutes later. Remick was sitting in another coffee shop two streets away from where he had left her. He was not keen on this coffee shop; the latte was distinctly substandard. Whereas the latte in the other place was thick and smooth with the partly sweet, partly bitter tang of good Ethiopian coffee, the one he was drinking at the moment was just warm and wet with hardly any flavour at all.

He watched, fascinated, as the display on the phone lit up and a merry electronic tune announced that a call was coming in. In all his time in this world, Remick had never owned one of the devices that held everyone captive, and he let it ring so long that it stopped. Remick was uncharacteristically unsure what to do next, but then a message popped up on the screen telling him that he had *one new voicemail.*

Remick had never had a voicemail before and was very intrigued by this new word, a word which when you broke it down actually made no sense. You either used your voice, or you used the mail, but not both. He picked the phone up and studied it and after a few moments of fumbling, found out how to access the recorded message. It thrilled him rather more than he had expected to hear a familiar voice emanating from the phone.

"Er…hello?" the voice said uncertainly. "I don't know if I've got the right number. Is this Mr. Thompson? Well, no, I know it's Mr. Thompson because that's the name on the card. If you're the man I just spoke to in the coffee shop, you left your book behind. Call me back if you want and I'll get the book to you." There was a pause, while she tried to decide what to say next. "If it's not you, I'm sorry to bother you. Anyway, my name is Angie and my number is…" She recited a number, which Remick did not need to write down. He had an exceptional memory. He put the phone down on the table and smiled. *Angie*.

Remick resisted the urge to call her back. He resisted it for exactly fourteen minutes, during which he wondered if she might call again. Then he decided to save her the cost of another call and, feeling strangely nervous, dialled the number he had memorised. She answered on the third ring.

"Hello?"

"Oh, yes, hello. Is this…er…Angie?"

"Yes it is. Who…? Oh. Thank you for calling back."

"Not at all. Thank *you* for taking the trouble to ring me. You found my book, I believe."

"Yes, I did. You left it on the table. By the time I realised, you'd gone. I wasn't sure if the card was yours."

"I like to use it as a bookmark. I hate people turning the corners of pages."

"Oh God, so do I! It ruins a book. I always use a bookmark."

"I'm very pleased to hear it. I'm also a bit forgetful, so it's useful for people to be able to contact me when I leave books in coffee shops."

He heard her laugh on the other end of the line and decided that he loved her laugh. It was a throaty, genuine laugh and he wanted to hear it more.

"So how can I get your book back to you?" she asked.

"Well I'm often in the coffee shop around that time. Maybe if you're passing sometime…?"

"I could drop it in tomorrow," she suggested.

"That would be…oh no, wait. I'm busy tomorrow. Would Thursday be any good to you?"

"Thursday's fine. About one? I'm on my lunch then."

"Perfect. Thank you so much. It's only a cheap paperback, but it does have sentimental value. I'll buy you a green tea for your trouble."

"Deal. Oh, look, I have to go. I've got a customer. I'll see you on Thursday, Mr. Thompson."

"You can call me Remick."

"Remy? Okay, Remy. See you Thursday."

He did not see fit to correct her. She called him Remy, so Remy he would be. It was just one lie in a call full of them. He had never left a book in a coffee shop before, the book had no sentimental value—although it might just acquire some now—and he was not particularly busy tomorrow. He did not want to appear too keen and risk unsettling her. In any case, time meant little to him. He could make it Thursday right now if he wished. So he did.

6.

Remick was so used to living his life in a non-linear way that he felt sorry for anyone who did not. How frustrating it must be for them to have to wait for things. In seconds, he had stepped out of Tuesday into Thursday and was walking the short distance from one coffee shop to another. He only hoped that the woman—Angie—did not judge him harshly for not changing his clothes. He knew these things could sometimes be important.

Thursday was raining again. Judging by the pools of water which had accumulated in the gutters and spread across parts of the road as the drains were unable to cope, Wednesday had seen it fair share of rainfall too. Remick had to jump over one large puddle but managed to do it without getting his boots wet. Not that it mattered; these boots had seen far worse than a bit of water. He had chosen to arrive in Thursday at six minutes past one. He could, if he wanted, be there at precisely one to the second, but not everybody had the same regard for time he did, and she had said 'about one', after all.

He shook some of the rainwater off his coat sleeves as he stepped into the coffee shop, where Angie was sitting in the same booth as last time. She smiled when she saw him and did a kind of half-wave. He returned it and, noticing she did not yet have a drink, gestured to the counter. She nodded and smiled again. It was a magnificent smile.

Remick bought a latte and a green tea, and carried them carefully over to the booth. He did not yet know whether she felt as strongly as he did about drink slopped into the saucer, nor did he want to find out. He placed the cups on the table and sat down.

"Hi," she said, still with a smile that warmed Remick more than any latte could. "You came."

"Well, of course I did. You've got my book."

Confusion momentarily crossed her face, but Remick grinned to show he was joking, and she relaxed.

"And I owe you a green tea," he added. "I don't know if you want anything to eat..."

"No, I'm fine, thanks. I had a sandwich back at the shop."

Remick allowed himself a moment to look at her. Today, she was dressed not in grey, but in the red coat she had been wearing when he first saw her, complemented by a russet-coloured scarf decorated with an intricate and delicate design in black. No hat, her ebony hair hung loose.

He must have let his gaze linger for too long, because she frowned and asked, "What?"

"I...er... I like your scarf," he replied, cursing himself inwardly.

"Do you? Yes, so do I. I got it from the market. There's a stall that sells hundreds of them, but this one just caught my eye." She took a sip of her tea, then reached into a tan leather bag at her side. "Your book," she said, putting it on the table and pushing it towards him.

"Thank you, but you didn't have to go to this trouble."

"It's no trouble. Really. So...Remy. Is that French? It's just with the Proust and everything..."

"Yes, it is," he confirmed, even though he had not really thought about it until now. "A couple of generations back. My... er...grandfather. Came over after the war."

"Do you go there much? France, I mean."

"Funnily enough, I've never been there." He'd been just about everywhere. "I will one day. And Angie. Is that short for...?"

"Evangeline." She laughed. "Yes, I know. Sounds like I've come from the Bayou." She said this with a Southern American accent which did something to Remick that he liked. "My grandparents were from Jamaica, though." She switched her accent to Jamaican. "But I've never been there either."

"How do you do that?" Remick asked. "The accents. They're perfect."

"You think?" She beamed. "I should be an actress. Good ear, I guess. But when my grandma talks like that alllll the time..."

"So, what do you do? You said something about a shop?"

"I manage a concession in Doyle's. You know, the department store on Parker Street? I've got the china concession. Yes, I know. It's a job. It's not forever. What about you? What do you do? Your card didn't really say."

Remick was suddenly aware that he should have prepared a bit better for this. He was not used to human contact and certainly not used to conversation. He said the first thing that came into his head. "I repair clocks. And watches."

"Really?" Her eyes went wide. "Wow. I'd never have said that. I thought you were a musician or something. Wow. That's amazing."

"Not really." He feigned modesty. "My father taught me."

"Look, this is going to sound really cheeky..." She pushed her coat sleeve up and unbuckled a watch from her wrist. "Could you take a look at this for me? It's always slow. I guess that's why I'm always late. It's okay, say no if you want." She passed the watch over to him.

"Of course I will," he agreed without the slightest idea how he was going to do it. He examined the watch, trying to look like an expert. It was quite a plain piece: a steel case and a worn black leather strap. The black Roman numerals on the dial were slightly faded with age, and Remick could see at a glance that the second hand was running fractionally slower than it should. It was four minutes and twenty-seven seconds slow.

"It's a lovely watch," he said.

"My grandma gave it to me for my twenty-first," Angie explained. "My grandpa gave it to her. It means a lot."

Remick ran his fingers over the watch, and in his mind's eye, he saw a young man, uncomfortable in the first new suit he had ever owned, handing over money in a shop in exchange for this watch, brand-new and gleaming in a black velvet-lined gift box. Remick felt the pride and love with which this watch had been purchased and it tugged at his heart.

"It was the first thing he bought her," he said, barely aware he was speaking.

Angie gasped, astounded. "Yes, it was! He bought it with his first wages. How did you know?"

"Just a guess," Remick answered. "Yes, of course I'll fix it for you. I'd be honoured. I'll call you when it's ready."

"I'll pay," Angie offered. "Doesn't matter what it costs. I'd love it to be working properly."

"Don't be silly. I'll do it as a gift. No charge."

"No, that's not right," she protested. "You hardly know me. And you've got to make a living."

"All right," Remick conceded. "The price is one latte when I bring your watch back."

"You're mad!" She laughed. "But okay. One latte."

Yes, Remick thought. Yes, he must be mad for offering to fix the watch without any idea how to accomplish it. But it was a very pleasant madness and one he was prepared to embrace.

She left shortly afterwards, apologising for having to get back to work, but she thanked him once again and touched him on his arm as she departed.

Remick stayed the coffee shop for a long time after that, staring at the second hand of the watch as it ticked around, feeling that touch on his arm and for once unsure about what to do next.

7.

Remick spent some time in the room he used as lodgings, staring at the watch and wondering what to do. He could simply visit the time and place where it had been bought and buy another one that was the same. Seeing as he knew the exact time and place, nothing would have been easier. However, there were problems with this plan, the first and most obvious being that the shop might only have had one watch like it, and Remick couldn't just buy one that was similar. Even if he found the same brand and model, what if it had a serial number or something and Angie recognised the one she had now was different? He did not yet know enough about her to be able to tell how closely she had studied the watch.

But the real problem was that this—even if it worked—was an untidy solution. Of course, there would be other worlds on which he could have bought the self-same watch before Angie's grandfather did, but that would mean depriving the Angies of those worlds of the pleasure of receiving and owning the watch. In any case, Remick had promised to repair the watch, not replace it with a similar one. If he were to have any kind of relationship with Angie, it could not start with a broken promise. It would have to be done the hard way.

So Remick took himself to a different time and place and, after some searching, located an elderly watchmaker for whom the work was getting too much. For a financial consideration, which Remick was only too happy to provide, the watchmaker agreed to take him under his wing and train him.

Remick spent what amounted to several years with the watchmaker, working and training and learning and listening to the old man's stories. Only then was he confident enough to take the back off Angie's watch and look inside. He was nervous about stripping the watch down and cleaning and oiling the component parts, and the first time he did it, he was almost happy. The watch was now only losing a small amount of time, but it was still losing, and Remick wanted it to be perfect, so he did it again.

This time, the watch was as near completely accurate as any device made by man could be, and by the time he had polished the case and carefully cleaned the surface of the dial, he was satisfied that the watch had been restored to a very good state, one that belied its age. He was reluctant, in a way, to take his leave of the old watchmaker but was pleased that he had been able to provide him with some companionship in the last years of his life.

Remick took the watch and returned to Angie's world and time but still waited for several days, checking and rechecking the timekeeping of the watch before he turned on his mobile phone and called her to tell her it was ready. Three years had passed for Remick. A week had passed for her.

8.

THEY MET IN the coffee shop once again. Remick had wondered whether the time was right yet to try meeting somewhere else, but decided that, for now, the coffee shop was safe and familiar. The day was another wet one, just as four out of the seven days since they last met had been. There was talk that it could turn out to be one of the wettest spells on record. Rural areas were beset by flooding as rivers swelled and overflowed their banks. Here in the city, it was just very wet.

When Remick arrived at the coffee shop, Angie was already there, sitting expectantly in the corner booth with drinks on the table.

"I bought you a latte," she said as Remick wiped the rain from his face with a napkin. "Is that okay? If you'd rather have something else…"

Remick found the concern in Angie's lovely face touching and surprising. She wanted to please him; it was not something he experienced often.

"No, no, that's perfect," he replied, sitting down. He sampled the coffee and made exaggerated *mmm* noises of approval. "But you didn't have to."

"Of course I did. You've fixed my watch for me. A deal's a deal. You *have* fixed it, haven't you?" Her face shone with such a childlike eagerness that Remick could wait no longer. He reached into his inside pocket and with a flourish produced the watch. She took it from him and compared the time with the time displayed on her phone.

"It's spot on! Pretty much to the second! That's wonderful. And you've cleaned the dial and everything. I've never seen it look like this. Thank you, Remy. Thank you so much."

"It's my pleasure," Remick replied and meant it. "It's a good watch. It deserves to be looked after. May I?"

He reached over and, taking the watch from her, fastened it securely on her wrist. She held her hand away from her to admire how it looked.

"Are you sure I don't owe you anything? I feel bad about not paying. All the time you've put in…"

If only you knew, Remick thought, but instead said, "It didn't take that long, really. It's a gift, Angie. A gift to brighten up a miserable day."

"It's done that, all right," Angie told him. "Thank you. Nobody has ever done anything like this for me."

"What, nobody? I can't believe that. Surely you have a boyfriend or someone to do nice things for you?"

"I did have…" Angie cloud passed over her face. "He wasn't really that much of a boyfriend, but he was…*someone*, I suppose. And no, he didn't do many nice things for me."

"What happened?" Remick asked, putting on an expression of concern.

"I don't know. He just stopped calling me. He didn't call me that often, anyway—only when he was bored or lonely and wanted to see me. But he just stopped completely, and when I tried calling him…it was like he had just vanished. I even went to his office, and the people in the other offices said he'd just up and left."

"That seems like a strange thing to do. You must have been very worried."

"I thought about telling the police or someone, but he's a grown man. What can they do? I knew his business was in trouble. While I was with him, he kept getting calls from people he owed money to. He tried not to let me hear, but I did. I think he just ran away from it all. And from me."

Remick risked reaching across the table to take her hand. She let him, and he marvelled at how warm and smooth her hand was in his.

"Now, you listen to me," he said. "He obviously wasn't worth it. If he could just walk away from you, he can't have cared enough about you. The man was a fool to leave you. I know I couldn't have done it."

Angie squeezed his hand and smiled. Even though the smile was tempered with regret, there was warmth in it.

"That's sweet," she said. "I thought I'd done something for a bit, but now I just think sod it. It's his loss."

"It is indeed," Remick agreed. "Very much so."

"Thank you. I suppose I needed to hear that. Look, Remy, would you like to have dinner with me one night?" Remick must have looked shocked, because Angie let go of his hand. "Sorry! I just blurted that out. I'm such an idiot. You could be married or anything for all I know. I'm sorry, I just say things sometimes without thinking!"

"Angie…" Remick took her hand again. "Angie. It's okay. I'm not married. Or anything. I would love to have dinner with you. I was just a bit surprised that someone like you would even think about it."

"Someone like me?" Angie laughed. "I'm not all that, Remy. Not when you get to know me. You haven't seen me at my worst."

"I'd like to," Remick said and in all his years had never meant anything more. "I'd like to get to know you at your worst and your best. But I definitely think we should start with dinner."

And that settled it. They arranged to meet two nights later at a restaurant they both knew. Then they talked of other insignificant things until it was time for Angie to return to work. Remick walked with her through the rain, which no longer touched him, and left her outside the store. She waved briefly as she went through the revolving door and then was gone. Remick felt her absence immediately and stood outside for a long time.

9.

REMICK STOOD IN front of the mirror in the room he used and studied his reflection. He was not accustomed to looking in mirrors as a general rule. He saw no purpose in vanity and seldom did anything without a purpose. But he was aware that the rest of the race among whom he walked were often very concerned about the way they looked and, although Angie had not seemed overly bothered by his appearance so far, he wanted to make a good impression. This seemed to be very much a time of firsts. So, to that end, he studied himself in the mirror and tried to see himself through her eyes.

It was not especially easy; he was still only learning bit by bit what her eyes saw. The look he currently wore was not, he supposed, a bad one by the standards of this time and on this world. That was partly why he had chosen it. He did not carry excessive weight, he had reasonably good bone structure, and all his features were more or less where they were intended to be. If one looked closely at his eyes, one might imagine they were they eyes of someone who had seen a great deal in their time, and he would have to be careful to curb their occasional tendency to flare up with crimson fire, but otherwise he was fairly confident that he was relatively pleasing to look at.

His beard could perhaps do with a trim, and he did wonder about whether he should find something with which to tie his hair back, but then, he decided, that was not really him and he wanted Angie to know *him*, or at least, as much of him as he could reveal without making her run away screaming. Instead, he found a comb in one of his pockets—without the slightest idea how it had got there—and ran it with some difficulty through his hair.

The only other change he made was to put on a new dark-blue shirt he had procured. Then he was ready to arrive at the restaurant at seven: the time they had arranged. He had booked the table for seven-thirty, so they would have time for a drink beforehand. There had been no reservations available for that time initially, so Remick had had to go back a few days and find a day before anyone else had booked. It took a few tries, but he managed it eventually. It had not occurred to him that the restaurant might be so popular.

He was waiting outside at three minutes to seven. They might have agreed on seven, but Remick knew enough to understand that when ordinary people specified a time, there was usually a significant margin for error. As a result, when seven o'clock arrived and Angie had not, Remick was not really surprised. It did not even matter that there had been no let up in the rain because the restaurant had an awning outside, so he could wait without getting his new shirt wet.

When first five past and then ten past came with no sign of Angie, he was initially irritated, then increasingly worried that she might not be coming. Maybe she had changed her mind. Remick had not been able to read her well enough to know if this was the sort of thing she might do. It came as a considerable relief, then, when at thirteen minutes past seven he saw her hurrying around the corner.

"Sorry," she said as she approached. "Half the buses seemed to have been cancelled, and then the one I did get took forever. I don't know if it's the weather or what." She paused and then startled him by kissing him quickly on the cheek. "Hello. Sorry. Have you been waiting long?"

"No," he lied. "I've just got here myself."

"And there's me with a newly fixed watch and everything. Come on, then, let's go in before they give our table to someone else. We should still be able to grab a drink. Am I talking too much? I do that sometimes when I'm nervous. I don't know why I'm nervous. *Am* I talking too much?"

"No, you're not," Remick reassured her, holding open the restaurant door. "I like to hear you talk. And there's nothing to be nervous about. It's just dinner."

The restaurant was warm inside, and the air was fragrant with cooking. A dinner-suited waiter carefully checked their reservation, trying very hard to disguise his contempt for Remick's appearance with a veneer of perfect manners. He offered to take Angie's coat, which she declined, but he stopped short of wanting to handle Remick's and then showed them to their table. By the time they sat down, it was obvious that Angie was struggling to contain her amusement. The waiter oozed off to get some menus, and as soon as he had gone, Angie burst out laughing.

"Oh my god! What a knob!" she said as she shrugged off her coat. "I'm sorry, but he is." Then she stopped, catching the serious expression on Remick's face. "I haven't offended you, have I? I just say things sometimes."

"Of course not," Remick said with a grin. "You're right. He *is* a knob. No, I was just about to say how beautiful you look."

"Shut up! Do I?"

Remick thought it was possible he had never seen anyone more beautiful. She was wearing a simple black dress with a high neckline, and her only jewellery was a pair of small pearl stud earrings. Her hair was loosely plaited and hung over one shoulder and was tied at the end with a black ribbon. Remick was no expert on make-up, but she appeared to be wearing hardly any at all. He was aware he was staring but found he was unable to look away.

"Yes," he said. "You do."

"Well, thank you, Remy," she replied, smiled, then changed the subject. "The watch is keeping great time, by the way. Did I say that?"

"You did, but it's still good to hear."

They were interrupted by a discreet cough from the waiter, who handed them leather-bound menus and then withdrew.

"Wow, look at this!" Angie exclaimed, opening her menu. "Real leather and everything. Have you eaten here before?"

"Not recently, no. It's supposed to be very good."

"Look at the prices! Remy, it's really expensive."

"It's fine. Don't worry, really."

Angie raised an eyebrow. "You must have repaired a lot of watches recently. And charged for them. You don't get to eat here if you do them all for nothing like you did with mine."

Remick had to think fast. He never really gave money much consideration, as he had many ways of acquiring it. He had never met anyone who'd questioned it.

"I don't rely on the watch repairs," was the best he could come up with. "That's more a sort of hobby. I've got—shall we say—other sources of income."

"Say no more," Angie said. "I won't ask. As long as you're sure. I was going to suggest going halves."

"It's fine, really. Have whatever you want."

Angie frowned briefly, then tilted her head in a *whatever you say* gesture. "I just hope it's worth it. I'd hate to see you paying all that for a smear of sauce and a piece of lettuce on a slate."

When the waiter returned with his pad, Remick waited until Angie ordered and then ordered the same and passed it off as a remarkable coincidence. In truth, he didn't actually need food, so it meant little to him, but he thought that at least pretending to have the same tastes as Angie would give them some common ground. As long as it was nothing too rich in iron, it would not give him any problems. He ordered a bottle of what looked like a good wine and the waiter disappeared off through a set of double doors at the back of the restaurant.

While they waited for their food, Remick and Angie made small talk, something he had never found easy before. His mind was usually on higher things, but they were not things he could chat about now, if ever. Instead, he let Angie tell him all about her day at work and some of the amusing or even irritating customers she had served, and he surprised himself by finding her conversation interesting and entertaining. It helped that she told the stories so well, making full use of the talent for mimicry he had seen in her before, but more than that, he just felt as though he could listen to her forever. He decided then and there that was exactly what he would like to do.

The food arrived, and, for Angie's sake, he was relieved that it was considerably more substantial than the smear and lettuce she had described. Angie ate with obvious enjoyment, and Remick found pleasure in her pleasure. He ate his food too. Even though it tasted of nothing to him, he found himself agreeing with her enthusiastic remarks about the flavouring of the sauce and the expert cooking of the lamb. He enjoyed the wine rather more but took care to sip it and make it last.

All too soon, they had finished their meal, even though Remick did his best to prolong it by insisting first on desserts and then on coffee.

As she drank her coffee, Angie leaned back in her chair and sighed happily. "That was gorgeous," she said. "I'll have to fast for days, but it was worth it. I feel absolutely stuffed. Thank you, Remy."

"My pleasure. We must do this again."

"I'd love to. But maybe not somewhere quite as expensive as this. Do you know what I'd like? I'd really like to go for a picnic. Somewhere by a river or something. Looks like I'll have to wait for a bit, though. I don't think we're going to see summer anytime soon."

"Funny you should say that, but I've heard next weekend is going to be perfect for picnics," Remick told her impulsively.

"That's not the forecast I heard."

"They always get it wrong. No, trust me, Saturday is going to be perfect. What do you think? Shall we?"

"I can't Remy. I'm in work on Saturday."

"Take the day off."

"I can't just do that. It isn't fair."

"When was the last day you took off?"

"Ages ago, but… No, you're right. Helen can cope for one day without me. She's done it before."

"That's settled, then."

"Well, if you're sure…"

"I am."

"And as long as you're not getting fed up with me…"

"That won't happen either. I promise."

"Well, okay, then. But if we get drenched, it's all your fault."

They agreed a time that Remick fully expected Angie would not keep to, and he paid the bill, leaving the waiter a reasonably generous tip. Outside, it was still raining, and Angie put up an umbrella she had been concealing in her bag. So that Remick could share the umbrella, she linked her arm through his as they walked. When they reached her bus stop, she turned to face him, standing so close he could smell the delicate perfume she was wearing.

"Thank you for a lovely evening, Remy. I won't invite you back, if you don't mind. Not this time. I'm just a bit tired."

Then she leaned in close and kissed him briefly and softly on the mouth.

"Goodnight, Remy," she said, as her bus arrived. She climbed aboard, leaving Remick looking at the rain-soaked street and wondering just how he was going to make a summer's day out of winter.

10.

Whenever he encountered a problem which appeared insoluble, Remick was inclined to take himself off to the place where he found it easiest to think. He went back to the beginning, when the worlds were new, a time when life had not begun and problems were yet to occur. The landscape was harsh and uninviting, but Remick was able to sit on a rock he had sculpted into the rough shape of a seat and gaze out onto an arena filled with almost infinite possibilities. The fact that he knew how many of those possibilities would develop did not stop him from contemplating the wonder of it all and allowed him to think with a clarity he could not find elsewhere.

In theory, the answer to his current problem seemed obvious. He could either wait for a summer's day to occur or take Angie to a summer's day that had already existed. Both options had their drawbacks; the first was out of the question because Remick just did not want to wait. If he had been able to see further along Angie's timeline, he could have checked whether her feelings remained the same or even became stronger, but as her future was a blank to him, he was not prepared to take the risk.

The second option was better, but he was not yet prepared to reveal his true nature to Angie and was not sure he ever would. She believed him to be human, and he thought, quite correctly, it might be a bit too early in their relationship to demonstrate to her that he was not. If he could not take her to another time—nor wait for that time to happen—he would have to bring another time to her.

That was where the problems really arose. Remick could not just take a day of time from one place and put it somewhere else because it would be noticed. Somewhere down the line, it would be apparent that the order of things had been disturbed, and even if Remick were able to put the day back, it would have been changed by his and Angie's presence. The changes might only be small but would inevitably lead to bigger ones. Remick had made enough mistakes in his many years of existence to know that time had to be handled carefully, or there could be dire consequences. Even if he felt inclined to try, there were rules preventing him from doing so and the rules were made by forces whose power he dared not think about.

Remick was left with just one option: he would have to build a summer's day, minute by minute, with time stolen from as many other days as he could find and hope no-one noticed.

That beautiful, warm day when a grey cloud suddenly crosses the sun and you think it might rain, but then the cloud is gone and the day is perfect again? That was Remick stealing a couple of minutes and replacing it with a couple of minutes from a day that was not so fine. That time when you are sitting outside in the sun and an unexpected cool breeze raises goosebumps on your skin? That was Remick too.

Little by little, piece by piece, Remick dismantled Saturday and replaced it with the most glorious Saturday he could build. It was long, painstaking and exhausting work, taking moments out of time and then moving them back into a different place. It was a colossal juggling act, the like of which Remick had seldom attempted before, but when he had finished, there was a perfect Saturday just waiting for Angie, and the best part of all? It was sealed in a capsule of its own time so that she could enjoy it and explore it over and over for as long as her heart desired. She would never have to put up with the rain again.

There was only one thing left to do, and it was the easy part. Remick would buy the best ingredients he could find to make the most delicious, sumptuous picnic Angie had ever seen.

11.

On Saturday morning, while Angie was waking up early to find the rain had ceased and sunlight was streaming through her window, and while Remick tried to remember how to drive the car he had just acquired, a man named Derek Benson was arriving at the newsagent's shop he owned to start sorting through the morning's newspapers. He was quite surprised to find an unexpected addition to his delivery this particular Saturday. There was a body lying outside his shop.

He was only quite surprised, rather than very surprised, because this was a Saturday, after all, and sometimes strange things went on in this neighbourhood on Friday nights. He often had to step over uneaten takeaway meals, half-empty pint glasses, vomit, and, on one notable occasion, various items of ladies' underclothing on the pavement outside his shop. Up until now, however, he had never before found a body.

It appeared to be that of a man in maybe his early thirties. It was hard to tell because he was partially concealed by the bales of plastic-wrapped newspapers. Reaching for his phone, Derek approached cautiously and stopped. He was sure he'd seen the man's leg twitch, but he still kept his finger poised to dial the emergency services. The man might not be dead, but he'd probably need an ambulance, or Derek might need the police. He continued to approach with caution.

As he drew near, the man suddenly sat bolt upright, startling Derek so much that he dropped his phone—something he would later discover caused a crack in the screen that would cost nearly half a day's takings to fix.

"Are you okay, mate?" Derek asked. "Are you hurt?"

The man just stared, looking around, disorientated, which Derek put down to drink or drugs or more likely both. He was even more convinced of this when the man said, "I'm back!"

"Yes you are," Derek humoured him. "You're okay now. Just take it easy?"

"Take it easy?" Brian Norris echoed. "Take it easy? He's got to be stopped, don't you see? He's the Devil! He's got to be stopped!"

Then he slumped back against the bales of newspapers, and Derek decided it was time to call an ambulance. The papers were going to be slightly delayed today.

12.

THERE WAS A moment, just as Remick halted the car outside Angie's building, when he had a horrible feeling he had forgotten something. Warm sunlight streamed through the car windscreen, and the half wound-down window was letting in just the right amount of breeze to make the temperature bearable. There was hardly a cloud in the sky, and the rain seemed a very long way away.

All around, people were starting their day and leaving their houses, surprised by the weather. Everyone had been expecting more rain, and Remick saw several people dash back into their houses to leave coats behind. One or two still carried umbrellas, though. It was as well to be safe.

The Saturday Remick had created was perfect, but there was something wrong, something he had missed. As the door opened and Angie emerged, Remick sensed it. The man, Norris. He was somewhere here. Somehow, as Remick had taken his stolen moments out of time and brought them back into their new place, Norris had come back with one of them. Remick cursed himself briefly, but he had dealt with Norris before and could do so again. Then he saw Angie and every other thought went out of his head.

He saw her before she saw him, and he had the opportunity to observe her delight as she shut the door behind her and stood on the step, looking up to the sky and basking in the sun's rays as they warmed her face. She was wearing a pale-blue dress decorated with a subtle floral print, and her hair was tied casually back with a silk scarf in a matching colour. A brown suede bag was slung over her shoulder. The dress left her arms bare, and Remick could almost feel her pleasure as she felt the sun on her skin. He smiled with quiet amusement to see that, just like everyone else who did not quite trust the sudden good weather, she had a coat over her arm. Then she spotted him, and her smile almost eclipsed the sun. She ran over to the car and threw open the passenger door.

"You did it! Look at the weather! It's a beautiful day! How did you know? This wasn't forecast!"

"Lucky guess," Remick replied. "Jump in. I know the perfect place for a picnic."

Angie climbed in and tossed her coat onto the back seat. "I don't think I'll be needing that."

"I'm absolutely sure you won't. It's going to be like this all day."

"And look at you! You've even left your coat behind. I've never seen you without it. You look…different. In a good way."

She stopped talking and leaned over to kiss him on the cheek. As she did so, he inhaled her perfume, a tang of citrus.

"Thank you for this," she said. "I think it's going to be just what I need. Come on! Let's go!"

Remick allowed himself to be swept away by her enthusiasm and started the car.

"Where are we going?" she asked. "Or is it a surprise?"

"Not really. I thought we might go to the beach."

"Really? I haven't had a picnic on the beach for… God, *years*! Not since I was a kid. What a brilliant idea. Pity I haven't got a bucket and spade."

Remick drove out of the city and past the docks with their container ships and scrap metal yards. In the sunlight, the grey streets were transformed and the ships were magnificent. Angie foraged in her bag and pulled out a pair of sunglasses and put them on.

"I almost couldn't find these, it's been that long."

As they drove, Angie kept up an excited monologue, mostly about the weather and how jealous anyone would be who was in work on a day like this. She said she felt a bit bad for her assistant, Helen, who would be stuck in the shop while Angie swanned off on picnics, but, hey, Helen had phoned in with hangovers before now, so she'd have to get on with it just this once. Remick listened, added the occasional reply, but mainly concentrated on driving. This was not the day to crash a car.

After half an hour or so, they had driven through deprived, shuttered suburbs and more affluent, tree-lined ones and parked the car in a designated—and expensive—car park, which, even at this time of the day, was filling up as everyone had the same idea.

"Everywhere's dried up really quickly," Angie observed as they got out of the car. "You'd think it would be soaking after all the rain we've had."

"Must be the sand," Remick replied, guessing at something that might sound plausible. "It'll just absorb the water."

"I hope the beach is dry. I don't want to sit on damp sand."

Remick opened the boot of the car and took out a picnic basket and a folded plaid blanket.

"Well, just in case…"

"You've thought of everything, haven't you?"

"I hope so," Remick said. "I've tried."

As they walked from the car to the beach, he carried the picnic basket in one hand and the blanket under his arm, leaving the hand nearest Angie free. As he had hoped, she slipped her hand into his, throwing him a glance as if to say *you don't mind, do you?* He smiled reassurance back but said nothing, fearing that if he did, it would break the spell and she might pull away. Her hand felt warm and comfortable in his and he did not want to let go, but when they reached the ideal spot on the beach, a good flat patch of clean sand slightly sheltered by dunes, he had to let go to spread the blanket out. They sat down side by side, and this time, when their fingers touched and intertwined, there was no need to let go.

They sat in silence for a while, watching dogs tear around the beach, enjoying a freedom they had not had for months.

"So tell me about yourself," Angie said. "I know you're a part-time watchmaker, a pretty damn good weather forecaster and brilliant at organising picnics, but other than that… Who are you, Remy? I feel like I've known you ages yet hardly know you at all."

"I'm no-one special," Remick replied. "I've been around a bit, done some things. Nothing really interesting."

"You're too modest. I think you're a very nice man, that's what I think. Can I guess? I think…I think your parents are rich, but maybe they've made their money in something you don't like? You've rebelled by growing your hair and pretending to be someone ordinary. Am I close?"

"Close enough."

"But you're not ordinary, are you? There's something extraordinary about you. I don't know what it is, but I'll find out."

"No, really, I'm not that exciting. I'd rather talk about you. Tell me all about Evangeline."

"Not much to tell there, either," Angie said, looking out to sea. "All very typical. Parents came here looking for a better life for themselves and for me and worked damn hard to get it. Sent me off to school and told me to study and be the best I could be. And I tried. I really tried. But, I don't know, the teachers seemed to be more interested in the kids who were, well, whiter than me, and I sort of stopped trying. I left school as soon as I could—which broke my mum's heart, I can tell you—and tried to get a job. My dad had a heart attack when I was sixteen and couldn't work, so someone had to bring some money in. My mum was working all the hours she could, but it wasn't enough. Then my dad died, and it just got harder."

A solitary tear trickled down Angie's cheek. Remick reached out and brushed it away with one finger. She rewarded him with a weak smile.

"I shouldn't be getting into all the sad stuff. This is supposed to be a lovely, happy day out."

"I'm with you and getting to know you. It *is* a happy day."

"That's sweet of you. Looks like I was right about you being a nice man."

"Tell me more. You were looking for a job...?"

"Same story. Plenty of jobs out there if your face fits—or rather if the *colour* of your face fits. Or if you want to work in a burger place. I really, really didn't want to work in a burger place."

"I don't understand this thing about skin colour," Remick said. "I don't see why it bothers people. Take the skin off and everyone looks the same."

"You are definitely a rare one," Angie replied. "Luckily, the owners of Doyle's think like that too. They gave me a job in the underwear department of all places and I took it. That means I have really nice underwear, by the way. Just saying."

This flirtatious candour caught Remick by surprise and he found he did not have a good answer. Instead, he said, "But you're not on—er—*that* department now."

"No. I did two years on it, though, which I didn't expect. Then the assistant manager on the china department left, and I was asked, actually asked, to go for the job. I got it, too, and I really didn't expect that. Then the manager retired last year, and they didn't even advertise the job. They just gave it to me. They've been so good to me there, Remy, and I love it. I love being around beautiful things."

"You should be surrounded by beauty," Remick told her. "It suits you."

"Annnyway!" Angie laughed, all tears forgotten. "Enough about me. All the time we've been talking, I've been thinking about one thing. What's in that hamper you brought? Come on, Remy, get it open!"

Remick opened the hamper, and it did not disappoint. It was filled with freshly baked breads, cooked meats and the finest cheeses he had been able to get. Angie ate ravenously, savouring every mouthful and remarking on everything she sampled. Remick ate too and found that Angie's appetite and clear enjoyment of the food made it taste better to him. Eventually, Angie stopped eating and sat back on the blanket.

"That was so good," she said. "Thank you. I'd better stop now or I'll be the size of a house."

"That isn't possible," Remick answered. "You're perfect as you are."

Angie wiped some crumbs from her lips with the back of her hand, and then snaked an arm around Remick's shoulders, drawing him close. When she leaned in and kissed him, it nearly took his breath away. Then she pulled him down onto the blanket, and time stopped altogether.

13.

I WISH THIS DAY could go on forever," Angie said, lying with her head on Remick's chest. They were in her bed and had just made love for the second time. The first time had been rushed and urgent, starting the instant they had crossed the threshold of her flat. The second time had been slower, more tender and longer-lasting. Now Angie drowsed in Remick's arms.

"It will be back tomorrow," Remick replied, stroking her hair. "Tomorrow's Sunday."

But it wasn't. Tomorrow was Saturday again.

14.

ON THE SECOND Saturday, Remick loaded the hamper in the car and drove to Angie's building. She answered the door to him with a faintly disappointed look on her face. She had, she explained, hoped he would be there when she woke up, but he had gone with no note, no message, nothing. Remick showed her the picnic hamper in the car and told her to be ready to leave in ten minutes. Understanding that he had only left her to go and prepare today's treat, Angie had brightened immediately and scampered back upstairs to her flat.

Remick sat in the car and waited. Refilling the picnic hamper was not the only thing he had done since he had left Angie sleeping in her bed. He had also done some searching and located Brian Norris. He had been considerably reassured to discover that Norris was currently in hospital, having been found lying in the street, and was receiving psychiatric care because he was raving about being kidnapped by the Devil. This amused Remick greatly. There was no Devil, of course, but some of the upper hierarchy of his kind would not have been impressed that Remick had been mistaken for one of them. But while there was little chance that anyone would take Norris seriously, it was reasonably safe to leave him where he was.

On this second Saturday, Remick had decided to venture a little further and planned to take Angie to a charming little waterfall he knew of in Snowdonia. Somewhere remote suited him well, partly because he wanted to spend time with Angie alone and not share her with other people, but also because the further away from the city they were, the less chance there was of Angie spotting that this was not Sunday as she thought, but Saturday once again. He could only sustain the stolen Saturday for Angie, though; everyone else in the city would have to get their coats and umbrellas out again because more rain was due for their day. This was not something he felt like explaining to Angie just yet.

She emerged from her building, dressed in the same pale-blue floral print dress, and once she was in the car, they set off.

"You did it!" she said excitedly. "Look at the weather! It's a beautiful day! How did you know? This wasn't forecast!"

As soon as she said it, she stopped and frowned.

"Are you all right?" Remick asked. "Have you forgotten something?"

"No, it's the weirdest thing. I'm sure I've said that before."

"Déjà vu," Remick remarked. "Or it could just because you said it yesterday."

"Did I? Really? How did I forget that?"

"You've had other things on your mind."

"And elsewhere," Angie said with a giggle. "Speaking of which, thank you for last night.

Remick smiled a *you're welcome* and tried to drive on in silence for a while, but Angie had other ideas.

"It was okay, wasn't it? I mean, I'm a bit out of practice. Brian was more a vanilla sort of guy, if you know what I mean. I think I might have got a bit carried away."

"It was perfect, Angie, honestly." Remick tried to keep the irritation he felt at the mention of Norris's name out of his voice. "Don't worry. I'm not him."

"No," Angie agreed. "You're certainly not."

Remick took the compliment at face value but still did not welcome any comparison to Norris. Remick had lived a life and had abilities that a protoplasm like Norris could not even dream about, but he had spent time with Angie, slept with her, even meant something to her, and this gave rise to feelings in Remick he had not encountered before.

He imagined it could be called jealousy, and he had never had cause to be jealous of humans with their brief, petty lives. He should have erased the man from this timeline altogether while he had the chance. But then he looked over at Angie, who was watching the world shoot past through the half-open car window, a smile on her lips that he was not meant to see, a smile that was just for her, and he knew he was making her happy in a way Norris never had. For a while, that was sufficient.

They spoke very little throughout the journey, but Remick had now understood Angie intimately enough to know she talked a great deal when she was nervous. If she was content to be silent, then it meant she was relaxed and comfortable and he did not want to spoil that with unnecessary conversation. So he drove and she watched out of the window as the grey of town and motorway was replaced by the green of the countryside.

The road he had chosen wound around the base of the mountains of Snowdonia, through villages whose names had too many consonants, and began to climb upwards.

Angie let the window down the rest of the way and breathed in deeply, tasting the clean country air. "I know why dogs do this now."

"Dogs do lots of things. There aren't many of those I'd do, though."

Angie tried to bark but could not manage it for laughing. She was still laughing when Remick pulled the car into a lay-by and announced that they had arrived.

"Is this it?" Angie asked. "I mean, it's nice and everything..."

"I hope you've got sensible shoes on. There's a bit of a walk yet. This is as close as I can get the car."

Angie looked down at her feet. She was wearing a pair of shoes which looked to Remick to be constructed of several strips of blue leather and a lot of not much else. She shrugged.

"They'll have to do. If you'd told me in advance... You might end up having to carry me."

"I can't do that *and* carry the hamper. I'll just have to leave you and have the picnic on my own."

"Don't you dare!" She slapped him on the arm playfully, but hard enough. "Come on, then. Which way?"

Remick got the hamper and blanket out of the car and led Angie through a gate to a rough footpath. The path took them first across a rock-strewn field, then through a copse of trees with moss-lined trunks where the air was cool and moist. They paused there for a moment, and as they did, the sound of running water drifted through the trees.

"Is that a river?" Angie wanted to know.

"Better than that. Come and see."

They emerged from the copse onto the banks of a stream, which had carved its way through lichen covered rocks, but the sound of running water was coming from a waterfall which cascaded down the mountainside and fed the stream. Angie gazed at the waterfall, shielding her eyes against the sun to try and spot its source high up the mountain.

"Will this be all right?" Remick asked.

"For the picnic? It's perfect!"

He smiled, and shook the blanket out onto the ground.

"How did you find it?" Angie asked him. "How would you even know it was here?"

"I get about. I just came across it one day and thought it might make a good place to bring a beautiful woman for a picnic sometime."

"Have you brought many beautiful women here?"

"I haven't brought anyone, beautiful or otherwise. I haven't wanted to. Not until now."

"And I'm beautiful, am I?"

"You are the most beautiful woman I have ever seen. Now that's enough compliments. Let's eat."

"Oh I don't know," Angie said as she sat down on the blanket. "I don't think I could ever get enough compliments from you."

"You'll get them too, but for now, eat!"

Remick opened the hamper and took out a fresh selection of delicacies, all chosen to be as tempting as those he had brought the last time but with enough variety to stop Angie thinking he lacked imagination. Once again, she tucked in with relish.

After they had eaten, they lay back on the blanket side by side, hands touching, warming themselves and dozing in the sun, or at least, Angie dozed. Remick was not the dozing kind. Instead he lay there, enjoying the feel of Angie's hand and listening to her breathe.

Humans, he thought. They rarely appreciated the simple functions, the eating, the breathing. They took them for granted. But the pleasure with which Angie ate, the blissful smile on her face as she dozed and breathed, all made her feel so *alive* to him. It was a feeling he never wanted to let go and, lucky him, he had the ability to ensure he never had to. There were one or two things she would have to get used to, but she seemed an adaptable sort of person. She would, he hoped, understand the benefit of it in the end. Who wouldn't want to live forever?

Angie had been dozing for nearly an hour when she rolled onto her side and said, "You know what I want to do?"

"What's that?" Remick raised himself on one elbow to look at her.

"I want to get under that waterfall."

"You'll get your clothes wet."

"I won't be wearing any clothes. What do you think? You want to?"

So they did. Leaving their clothes on the blanket, they ran hand in hand to the waterfall. Angie shrieked as the cold mountain water hit her shoulders, but she would not come out. They stood in each other's arms as the torrent battered them and kissed as the water formed a seal between their bodies. Remick could almost believe the water made him feel cleansed.

Afterwards, they huddled together, still naked, with the blanket wrapped round them. Angie kissed him again, long and sweet, and he knew without question what she wanted.

"What if someone comes?" he asked.

"I'm counting on it."

Remick did not leave her that night, not exactly. When she invited him to stay, he readily agreed. Unbeknownst to her, he left her for a while as she slept to make his preparations for the following day, but he closed time around him so she never knew he was gone. There were things he had to do because as far as Angie knew, she was going to wake up on Monday, and Remick could not allow the day to end.

15.

BRIAN NORRIS LAY in the hospital bed, staring at the ceiling. Around him in the half-light which the hospital called night, machines attached to other patients bleeped and pinged. The nighttime meds they had tried to make him take had been concealed under his tongue and were now sticking his pillows together in a saliva-coated mass. He knew his clothes were in a locker beside his bed—he had checked several times. He just needed the opportunity.

It came when the basket-case in the bed at the end of the ward woke up from a nightmare screaming. The night staff hurried over to calm him down before he disturbed everybody, and as they did, Brian climbed out of bed on wobbly legs. One of the nurses spotted him and asked where he was going.

"Toilet," he replied, and the nurse, apparently satisfied, turned her attention back to Mr. Screamer. Brian quickly opened the locker, grabbed the carrier bag containing his clothes, and hurried to the patients' toilet at the end of the ward. By the time the other patient had been sedated and settled down, Brian was gone.

16.

IT WAS FAIRLY easy for Remick to make Angie believe she did not need to go into work the next day. Although he could still not see forwards in her timeline, he could see back and, after some searching, located the last time she had arranged some time off. It was a little more difficult than he had expected; for some reason, she rarely took holidays, but once he had located the memory, he was able to adapt it subtly and plant it back in her sleeping mind. He did not take the decision lightly. Normally, using his abilities in this way would not have given him any second thoughts at all, but he found himself reluctant to trick Angie. It was, however, necessary if he was to make this perfect summer last for her. He knew it had worked when she woke up and remarked that it was another beautiful day.

"Aren't you glad you booked the week off?" he asked.

"I know! Wasn't that lucky? Mind you, this time of year it can't last."

"We'll see," Remick said, knowing it could.

That day, they went to an outdoor cinema to see a film Remick thought she would like and spent the whole film kissing like teenagers. That evening, he cooked for her. It was the first meal he had ever cooked for anyone, but fortunately, he had been able to spend some time while Angie slept the previous night practising and perfecting a meal in the style of a chef whom he had found, while in Angie's memories, to be one of her favourites.

As they lay in bed that night, they made plans to visit a nearby stately home and have yet another picnic in its grounds. It surprised Remick that Angie wanted to go there, but she simply replied, “I like old things.” That, Remick thought, was very lucky indeed.

The whole day was so perfect Remick never considered Brian Norris once. That was probably the biggest mistake that he had ever made in the whole of his long, long life.

17.

ON THE FOURTH day of summer, Brian Norris found them. It had not been hard. He knew perfectly well where Angie lived. Even though whenever they had spent the night together it had always been at his flat, he had dropped her off at her building many times. He preferred his flat to hers; his was bigger, more expensive and furnished in the latest, minimalist style. Hers was full of stuff, things scattered about at random, and if there was one thing Brian Norris hated, it was mess.

After leaving the hospital, he had gone back to his flat, which he was relieved to find was still there, just as he had left it. He showered, changed and drove to Angie's street. He had sat in his car, peering through the rain as it hammered down on his windscreen, and waited for the morning, hoping to catch Angie on her way to work. He badly needed to talk to her, to try to explain what had happened to him. He was horrified when the door to Angie's building opened and she came out dressed bizarrely in a summer dress, accompanied by *him*, that creature, whatever he was, the one who had done all this.

Before Brian could do anything, they had got into a car and driven off. Angie had been laughing at something, clinging to that monster's arm, walking through the rain to the car as if she didn't feel the downpour at all. Brian watched the car turn a corner and knew that his shocked indecision had cost him the chance to follow. He had no idea where they were going, but dressed like that, she certainly wasn't being given a lift to work.

He wondered at first whether to go to the police. But to say what? They had not believed him in the hospital, and Angie hardly seemed to be being held against her will. He resolved instead to wait. He was used to sorting out his own problems, and this would be no exception. He made a mental note of the make and registration number of the car the Devil was driving and sat in his own car all day with the rain pouring down the windows, awaiting its return.

It was early evening before the car came back. By then, Brian was cold, tired and hungry and all the more determined to let Angie know exactly who she was getting involved with, but when he saw the car draw up and Angie and the man who was not really a man get out, something happened which stopped him from acting. He suddenly felt, with a chilling clarity, the cold emptiness of the place this creature had sent him and remained frozen in his seat. He watched as Angie and that…*thing*, whatever it was…got out of the car and walked arm in arm to her building, looking like the rain did not touch them. He watched them go through the door and into the building, then waited some more to see if he/it would come out again. *This time*, Brian thought. This time he would get out of the car and put things right. But the door to the building did not open and remained closed all night.

He sat hunched over the steering wheel, fuming. Angie had clearly wasted no time. It had only been days since that bastard did whatever he had done. As the night dragged on, Brian thought more and more about what had happened to him. He was a rational man and did not believe in ghosts, UFOs or the Loch Ness Monster. He was not even sure he believed in God, and yet he had been prepared to believe that he had been attacked by the Devil.

He was now trying to come up with a rational explanation for what had happened, and all he could think of was that maybe his coffee had been drugged while he wasn't looking. Maybe that was why he had reacted so badly. That empty place was surely just a trick of some kind or a hallucination, and nobody's eyes burned like that…did they? But as soon as he was out of the way, Angie had obviously jumped straight into bed with the man. Or maybe she hadn't waited at all. Maybe it had been going on for a while, and what had happened to Brian was all part of it. Perhaps they were working together against him, Either way, as soon as they showed themselves in the morning, he intended to end it.

Brian assumed he'd fallen asleep at some point. One minute, he was squinting through the darkness and the driving rain at Angie's building, and the next, the sky was a murky, lighter grey and Brian was wiping a sticky tendril of drool from his chin. He briefly considered driving to the nearest McDonald's to grab some breakfast but thought better of it. It would be just his luck if he was delayed and could not get a parking space when he got back. The clock on his dashboard told him it was just gone six, so, assuming Angie was going to work, he would not have long to wait.

He must have dozed off again, because when the door to the building opened, the dashboard clock was showing eight-fifty. From what he knew of Angie's routine, it meant she was either running late, or not going into work at all.

She came out of the building wearing a summer dress again and sunglasses. *He* was in a T-shirt and jeans. They were dressed like it was the middle of the summer, and yet the rain which had been threatening for the last few hours had just started to fall. Neither of them seemed to notice. They kissed on the steps of the building and walked hand in hand to a nearby car. That was more than enough for Brian. He got out of his car and slammed the door shut.

18.

IT WAS THE slamming of the car door that alerted Remick. He looked over to see the source of the noise, and there was Brian Norris crossing the road towards them. Remick was incensed. *How dare he?* He let go of Angie's hand and stepped in front of her. He felt heat building up behind his eyes and did not want her to see.

"Good morning," he said, keeping his voice as light and controlled as he could. "Can I help?"

"You bastard," Brian spat. "What the hell did you do to me?"

"I don't know what you mean. Do to you? I haven't done anything to you. I'm sorry, but I don't even know who you are."

"You know damn well what you did. What was it? Acid? Roofies?" He turned to Angie. "Your boyfriend drugged me. He couldn't get you any other way, so he drugged me."

"I did nothing of the kind. We've never met before. Come on, Angie, let's go."

"Don't do it, Angie," Brian warned. "Don't go with him. You can't trust him."

"Look..." Remick tried to sound reasonable. "You and Angie clearly have some kind of history, but she's with me now. I suggest you let it go and leave us alone." He tried to turn his back on Brian, but the other man was not prepared to leave it there.

"He's lying, Angie. He knows damn well who I am. He followed me and drugged me and made me see things."

"Wait a minute," Angie said, speaking for the first time. "Stop it, both of you! I'm not going to have you arguing over me in the street like this. Let's talk about it like grown-ups, shall we?" Both men were shocked into silence. They looked at their feet, at the sky, anywhere but at each other or Angie, who had not finished yet. "When's Remy supposed to have done this, Brian? You can't just go round accusing people—"

"Couple of days ago. He turned up in that coffee shop and warned me off you. Told me to finish with you. When I wouldn't, he did…well, he did *something.* He put me in bloody hospital."

"That explains it," Remick said. "If you've just come out of hospital, that says it all. And it was a psychiatric ward, wasn't it, Brian?"

There was a long, stunned silence. Then Angie said, "Hang on. A psychiatric ward? Remy, how do you know that?" and Remick knew he had made a grave mistake.

19.

ANGIE HAD NO idea what was going on, but she did not like any of it. She had woken up that morning feeling great. Another gorgeous sunny day, and Remy had stayed with her, holding her all night. Then, suddenly, instead of taking her to the stately home he had promised, Remy was standing in the middle of the road arguing with her ex. What was worse, much worse, was that they sounded like they knew each other and Remy had lied.

"Remy," she asked again, "what the hell's going on?"

"Nothing's going on. I had a quick word with Brian here and suggested that he left you alone, that's all. All this stuff about drugs is nonsense."

"When?"

"When what?"

"When did you speak to him?"

Brian started to answer, but Angie held a hand up to caution him.

"*When*, Remy?"

"I'm not sure. I…"

"Let's see if we can narrow it down then. Was it before or after we started to go out?"

"I can't think. Does it matter? He's just trying to cause trouble. I think we should go."

"It matters to me. Was it before or after? And please don't lie to me."

Remy delayed long enough for Angie to know that the next thing that came out of his mouth might well not be the truth.

"Before."

"Right. I see." Angie turned away, her head reeling. This was obviously the truth, and it was all a bit too much to take in. "Look, sorry. I can't do this right now."

"I can explain..." Remy began.

"I don't want explanations. I don't know if I can trust them. You've already lied to me once. You pretended you didn't know Brian, and all the time, *all the time* we've been together, you knew what you'd done. I don't know if you did drug him or what, but you did *something*. I can't deal with this. Sort it out between you, but leave me out of it."

As she started up the steps, she heard Brian speak.

"Say what you like about me, but I never lied to her. I didn't have to trick her into bed..." Then his voice was cut off and he made a peculiar choking sound.

Angie looked back and her new boyfriend had her ex-boyfriend by the throat and had lifted him one-handed off his feet. For some reason, it was raining.

20.

THE ANGER WHICH had been building in Remick burst like a dam breaking. This pathetic mortal who had no more significance than an insect dared to challenge him? He felt the fire burning in his eyes and the glamour which kept him in his ridiculous human form began to slip, but he did not care. Angie was *his*. All he had done to win her, all the time and planning and love he had given to her and one stupid, short-lived gnat was going to ruin it for him.

His hand closed around Norris's throat. It would just take one squeeze and he could end it. No second chances, no taking him out of time, just the end of his tiny existence. Rain hissed and turned to steam as it hit him, and he flexed his muscles, ready for that one last, terminal squeeze.

But then Angie screamed, "NO! Remy, leave him!" and then, "Jesus Christ, what *are* you?" and that was that.

Summer was over.

21.

IN THE END, Remick could only do one thing. Instead of killing Norris—something he surely deserved—he erased all memory of the last few days from his mind and set a few fail-safes in there that would wipe his mind altogether should he try to remember. Then, as a last gift, he placed his hand on Angie's beautiful cheek even though she tried to shrink away from him.

He wiped her memories too, but without the fail-safes; that would be too cruel. As he did so, he knew why he had not been able to read her future. It was a future he would have no part of and did not want to see. He had hidden it from his own sight.

He looked at Angie for one last time, and then he walked away, leaving the two mortals standing bewildered in the rain outside Angie's building.

22.

HE NEVER TRIED to check on her, not in this world or any other. The thought that she might have returned to Norris or that she might just be getting on with her life without him was too much to bear. For a brief moment, Remick had known what it felt to love with all its joy and all its pain. He did not know how mortals went through their short, flickering lives doing it all the time. He just knew he never wanted to do it again. He was better off alone and would remain that way.

He took himself to a beach, but not the one he had been to with Angie. This was one guarded by a hundred iron statues who stood in the sand gazing blankly out to sea. It was a place Remick never visited because of the physical pain the element they were made of caused him. But it was a pain he wanted now, a pain he welcomed. All his powers had not been able to help him, and he wanted to be free of them. He trudged across the sand to the nearest of the iron men and placed both his hands on its head. He felt a wrench, like a million hooks tearing at his soul, and it was all he could do not to scream as his power, his very being, poured out into the metal. Then he slumped, spent, onto the sand and stayed there for a very long time.

It was night before Remick was able to heave himself to his feet. Unsteadily, he got up and started to walk back to the room he used, where he would stay for a very long time, drinking and dreaming of one perfect summer's day in winter which, like a flower growing out of season, bloomed gloriously and briefly but could never last.

ABOUT BOB STONE

Liverpool born Bob Stone is an author and bookshop owner. He has been writing for as long as he could hold a pen and some would say his handwriting has never improved. He is the author of two self-published children's books, *A Bushy Tale* and *A Bushy Tale: The Brush Off*. *Missing Beat*, the first in a trilogy for Young Adults, is his first full-length novel.

Bob still lives in Liverpool with his wife and cat and sees no reason to change any of that.

BY BOB STONE

A Bushy Tale

A Bushy Tale: The Brush Off

Missing Beat

Out of Season

SEASHELL VOICES

ALEXIS WOODS

Once upon a time, a merboy spied a human child. The merboy, who longed to walk the sandy shore, spent his days watching the human boy grow to become a man who loved the sea. A man he's admired from afar. The one he wishes he could be.

But how can a merman express his greatest wish when he has no voice with which to speak?

***

Genre: young adult MM fantasy romance

Keywords: merman, love, romance, LGBT, gay

SEASHELL VOICES

I FIRST SAW HIM when he was only knee high, hand clamped tightly by his mother. He did not see me as I hid beneath the waves. I envied his chubby human legs even as he stumbled on the uneven sand of the beach. He kicked at the surf, squeals of infectious laughter carried away by the brisk breeze. Pudgy toes and rolls of fat, curls of the fairest hair danced in the wind, and the brightest smile, full of joy.

I longed for what he had: a mother, a life of happiness and ease. These eluded me. Orphaned while still a tadpole, I'd been fostered in the Royal Orphanage, raised to serve King and Court, until they turned me loose at sixteen to make my own way.

Odd jobs kept me in the good graces of my kind, but I yearned for greater freedom, to go wherever and whenever. Not only to swim to the depths of the oceans, ride the wild waves in a storm or bask in the shallows, but to venture farther ashore. This I could not do, for I did not have what that human child had.

Often, I would return to my secret hiding spot, observing the child as he grew. Always his mother hovered, at first hand in hand. Seasons passed and she began to give him leeway, allowing him to wander a few feet ahead of her. When he reached her in height, she stayed behind, but continued to keep a watchful eye on him.

One day, when he was still young, I saw Mother hold a seashell to his ear and whisper the secrets of my home. She told him if he listened carefully, he'd hear his father speaking to him, or perhaps another of the merfolk telling whimsical tales of life beneath the sea. Her stories held a mixture of truth and fantasy, so I worried not that she knew I existed. I did wonder about her telling him his father was one of us though.

I was jealous of the boy who had a mother's love, how fiercely protective she was of his safety. No one ever asked how I fared on any particular day. No one inquired as to my whereabouts or why I'd been absent of late. No one questioned my life or hoped I was well.

Despondent, I stayed longer and longer in my secret place, came more often, watching the boy sprout taller, all arms and legs, hair shaggy then short. He broadened across his shoulders and curls of hair appeared on his chest, bristles on his chin and cheeks. Not always, but more frequently as time passed.

My boy had often gone away for weeks at a time, but now it was months, whole seasons passing before I'd see him again. Mother continued to walk the dark sand, sometimes alone, sometimes with others. When she had company, I would raise my head above the water to hear her words, listen to her recount stories of the boy's youth or made mention of his current doings.

Hope blossomed whenever she would say he was coming to visit. Those times, I would linger if only to catch a glimpse of him farther up the sand.

Humans came with their loud machines. I went away for they made too much noise, and the vibrations through the currents scared both the fish and me. When I returned, I saw they had added sand to the shoreline. Huge rocks were piled and joined into long jetties that jutted into my territory. My secret place was gone, covered by boulders too heavy for me to move, and in my despair, I missed the net which tangled my hair and fins and limbs. Twisting and turning only made matters worse. I was good and stuck.

Since the net held me, I gave over to its embrace, floating and thinking of irony. Above me, the sky darkened to black and I slept. A slap upon the water and a shake of the ropes woke me as dawn lightened the sky.

Belatedly, I realized I was being hauled towards shore, towards the human world where our secret would be revealed. Thrashing, I managed to turn and gain some inches back out to sea, but I could not fight the incessant drag of the net nor the current pushing me towards the beach.

My heart pounded with fright. My people told horrific tales of what humans would do to us if we were ever caught. They'd cut us up to look inside. They'd put us in cages and display us to others. They'd make us learn skills and tricks and keep us far away from our homes and our families.

But I had no home. I had no family. There was only Boy and Mother. A human boy, and his human mother. The human boy with eyes of the deepest blue who stared at me in shocked silence, with his mouth gaping and hands frozen in the act of dragging in his net.

We had never been this close though I'd thought about it too many times to count. I'd fought with myself whenever he'd swim out beyond the breakers. Always I'd accompany him at a distance, fearing for his safety as he was so far from Mother, so far from land. I'd wanted to swim up to him, to touch his scaleless skin, to feel the texture of the hair on his face, to hold his hand. Once, I almost did, but he chose that moment to return to land, where I could not follow.

He reached for me, for the net entangling my arms. Carefully, he freed me, not touching, but curious and wanting. Daring, I held out my hand to him, palm up, and he slid a finger along my skin. It tickled, making me shudder and smile.

"Who are you?" he asked, but I could not answer. While I could understand him, my voice could not duplicate theirs. I could chirp and trill, make a variety of sounds to communicate with my own kin and the sea life around me, but not his.

I touched my throat and my lips, opened and shut my mouth.

"You can't speak."

I shook my head.

"But you understand me?"

I nodded and grinned.

"Amazing." He laughed. "I can't believe I caught a merman. All I thought I'd catch is a few crabs to study before returning them to the sea. No one is ever going to believe me… But you can't stay here. You best be getting back into the water."

Go back? His words surprised me. I was certain he would keep me. Truthfully, I wanted him to, sure he alone, of all the humans, would protect me. But he didn't know how I felt about him. This boy was my whole world. I grabbed his hand and pointed towards the house I knew to be his.

"That's where I live." He looked down at me, a frown pulling his corners of his mouth. "How did you know?" Concerned? Angry? His voice strained as he asked, "Have you been spying on me?"

I nodded again. I pointed to him and then leveled my hand a foot off the ground. Pointed at him and leveled my hand higher, another point and another indication of him growing. His eyes got wider and bigger with each added mark of height.

"You've been watching me since I was a baby?"

Yes, I nodded.

"Why?"

But I could not answer. I could not tell him how I wished I was him, craved what he had. How could I explain I longed to see life beyond the ocean's edge? Again, I pointed at his house, at myself and my eyes, back to his house.

"You want to see where I live?"

Yes, I nodded eagerly, gave him a brilliant smile. Many had told me I had a nice smile, I hoped it was true and he liked it too. I assumed he did when he responded in kind.

"But don't you need to be in the water? Won't your tail dry out?"

I shrugged. I didn't care. Maybe later I would, but right now, with a wish within my grasp, I cared little for myself, only for the adventure. Possibly a once-in-a-lifetime experience.

"If you're sure… I guess I can carry you. You're a tiny thing."

I raised my arms in silent plea, allowed him to scoop me up and carry me across the sand. He had one arm along my back and the other under my tail, while I held on to his neck and shoulder. I took the opportunity to touch him, to finally feel the skin that I thought to be soft, to brush my fingertips against his sand-colored hair. I strengthened my grip on his shoulder to feel the muscle barely straining with my weight. My tail hung over his arm, but not far. I was small compared to him; maybe if I stood on my tail, the top of my head would fit under his chin. And my body was slim compared to his broad chest and thick arms.

When we arrived at the door, it opened to reveal Mother. She stared as he had stared.

"Let us by, Mom," he said, and she opened the door wider, sliding out of the way for him to enter.

"You should take him back," she said, even as she shut the door. The loud thud startled me, a strong shiver shook me.

His arms tightened around me. "I tried, but he insisted on seeing the house, and I could not deny his request."

Her forehead crinkled in long wavy lines, and I liked the way she pushed the errant silver strands of her hair behind her ear. I did not have ears like they did, and so I touched his, wiggled the outer casing and delighted in the softness of the bottom floppy piece.

He smiled at me. "What are you doing?"

I tilted my head and tapped my own small ear holes in answer. My schooling had been limited, so even if I could I wouldn't have been able to tell them how our ears worked both above and below the waves.

"Tiny ears to go along with the rest of tiny you."

I frowned at his choice of words. I did not want to be tiny, though I knew I was. Even compared to my fellow merpeople, I was stunted. *The runt.* A nickname that stuck. Another reason to want to escape my life.

I slapped his chest and poked him, then sized him up, stretching my arms wide and tall.

"I'm a giant," he laughed, carrying me through a sunny room of shiny silver boxes and into another dimmer area of muted blues and greens. He dropped onto a soft, dark blue receptacle covered in a red flora pressed flat onto its surface. I landed in his lap, and he pulled me closer to his body, continuing to support my back. The arm that had been under my tail he moved to lay across the top, but he stopped at the last second.

"May I?" he asked, spreading his hand wide.

I took hold of his wrist and guided his hand to slide along my scales from waist down towards my fin. It was uncomfortable to have one's scales stroked upwards. His fingertips glided along slowly, gentle in their exploration.

"Your tail is lovely," he remarked quietly after a few minutes.

"It is," Mother agreed from her spot across the room. I beckoned to her, offering my tail for her to touch. She advanced cautiously, so I held still to ease her fear. Her touch was as soft as his, like a sea anemone's waving arms, a tickle more than a press. After a few passes she stepped away, saying, "I'll make breakfast."

I wondered if I would like what Boy and Mother ate. On the beach, humans always seemed to be stuffing their mouths with odd-shaped food. It was tiresome to always eat the same kelp and seaweed. Some merpeople ate fish and shrimp, but I could not stomach the killing of those dear creatures who swam alongside me, my only friends, even though we could not communicate. Once I tried to befriend a dolphin, but he was flighty and leapt away; he only came around to visit when he wanted to play. The seals threw back their heads and laughed at me whenever I tried to join their games. I gave up after a while.

"Are you all right?" he asked. "You look sad."

I nodded and laid my head against his chest and shoulder. He carded his fingers through my drying hair, working the tangles out, in lieu of speech.

It was a quiet sort of introspection, both of us silently exploring each other's facets. He let me touch his chest, the stubbly hair on his chin, the plumpness of his lips. His thumb stroked the skin just above my tail; he seemed fascinated by the webbing between my fingers.

Mother brought water in a clear glass and handed it to me. "Drink. You need to stay hydrated." Her logic was without fault, so I drank it all and asked for more, intrigued by its lack of texture without the salt of my ocean.

"Andrew," she said quietly, and he looked up from my tail to Mother, continuing his slow caress of my scales while giving me the support of his body.

Andrew.

She called him "my son" when he was barely walking, "Andy" when he learned to swim, "Drew" with a roll of her eyes. Another name, but still him. As he had called her "Mommy" when he was small, "Mom" when he grew tall, "Mother" when he was mad.

All I had was Runt. Perhaps he could give me a new name. But how to tell him.

I poked him and patted his chest.

"What?" His eyebrows looked funny slanted in towards his nose. I smoothed them out until he smiled at me, a big one I returned in force.

Again, I poked and patted, pointed at Mother, and then patted him once more.

"Your name?" Mother queried, and I nodded vigorously.

"Don't you know it?" he asked. "You told me you've been watching me for a long time."

I did the same motions as on the beach, but in between, I patted him in different places on his body.

"I think he's saying that you've had different nicknames as you've grown up. Andy and Drew, but—"

"But now I go by Andrew, the name Mom gave me when I was born." He looked into my eyes, his forehead wrinkling. "Do you have a name?"

Sadly, I shook my head, dropping my chin. I gave motion to an idea, touching his head, then his mouth before pointing at myself.

"You want me to think of a name for you?"

Yes, I nodded.

"Hm. It should be a good sea name. How about Caspian?"

I reared back, not liking the sound of it.

"No, huh. Okay. Davy?"

No.

"Jack?"

No.

"River?"

NO! I frowned deeply at that choice.

"Kip?"

I opened my eyes wide and grinned.

"I think he likes that one," Mother said, rising from her chair. "I should check on—"

A shrill buzz sent a wave of panic through me. I nearly slid off Andrew's lap, but he hauled me back into place.

"Guess I don't need to check. Breakfast is ready."

"Are you hungry, Kip?" Andrew asked.

Yes, I nodded, watching Mother hurry away.

He stood easily, his legs bunching beneath my tail as he leaned forward and pushed upwards. I weighed nothing to him as he carried me back into the room of silver boxes. Mother pulled out a chair for Andrew to sit, and he kept me on his lap as he sat. I placed my hands on the big slab of wood, ran my fingertips over its smooth surface, traced the swirls of grain. It was a beautiful table. Under the sea, we used stone, its weight securing it to the ocean floor. Occasionally, a strong storm would cause a surge and disrupt our homes, but I had no home, nor anything to be disrupted.

All I had was my secret. *Him.*

Mother placed a white circle on the table. On the circle was a tan lumpy block, dotted with blue specks. I slid Andrew a questioning sidelong glance as I pointed to it.

"Blueberry baked French toast. It's delicious, especially with syrup."

Mother placed another piece in front of me along with a glass of translucent mud-colored liquid. Andrew picked up the glass and poured the liquid over the toast on his circle, and then he added a small amount to the side of the piece cut for me. He gestured for me to dip my finger in the liquid so I could taste it.

The flavor exploded in my mouth. Previously, I had dared to taste some of the human food carried off by the waves cleaning the sand. None had tasted as wondrous as this sweet liquid. I dipped my finger again and again, until Andrew stopped me. He picked up a strange stick of pointed metal, broke off a piece of the toast, and rolled it in the liquid before offering the dripping bite to me. I wrapped my hand around his to keep him steady as I opened my mouth to accept the food. Good was not accurate; amazing fell short. Extraordinary, incredible… I could not pick a single word to describe how remarkable the human toast was.

"You like it?"

Yes.

Andrew fed me another bite, and another, until both our circles were empty. Mother gave me another glass of water, and as I rubbed my full belly, I noticed how dry my tail had become. Once noticed, it began to itch and become uncomfortable.

A knock on the door Andrew had carried me through startled all of us. Mother rushed into the other room and came back with a blanket, draping it over my tail before hurrying to the door.

She opened it a little and said, "Hello?" I could not make out what the visitor said, but it didn't matter when she opened the door all the way and invited whomever in.

Although he walked on two human legs and wore human clothing, there was no way I could deny knowing him. *Triton.* His long, wavy, sun-bleached hair hung around his shoulders, his clear sea-blue eyes piercing me with their anger. I clung to Andrew, fearing I'd be ripped away, never to see him again.

"Runt," Triton spat. "You know the law."

I held Andrew tighter, buried my face in his neck. If this was my last moment with him, I wanted to remember it always.

"His name is Kip," Andrew growled, not knowing the Prince of the Sea graced his home. Prince Triton, son of King Neptune. *Royalty.* Only they had the power to change their bodies, to morph tail to legs, to speak with words and not trills and chirps. The power to not only hurt me, but Andrew as well. My arms locked in his embrace, my fear for his life all-consuming.

"Kip!" Triton laughed. "Did you name him? Like a pet?" Triton sobered at Andrew's lack of response and, in turn, stared intently at him. "He is Runt. An orphan who knows not his place and will pay dearly for it. Give him to me so that I may bring him to my father to deal with."

"And who might your father be?" Mother asked from across the room, as far from Triton as she could get, having edged her way there while he spewed his cruel vitriol.

"King Neptune," Triton answered, pinning her in place with a sharp look. "And I am Prince Triton."

"Your Highness," Mother quickly responded with a deep curtsy. "I apologize, but you must realize we cannot give Kip to you."

Shock rippled across his features, quickly smoothed. "And why is that?"

"Because your father has already spoken on his behalf."

"What?" was repeated twice over, plus a squeak from me. I clapped a hand over my mouth in embarrassment.

Andrew looked down at me sweetly. He pulled my hand away from my face and guided it to my lap, where he covered it with his own. His hand squeezed mine for a long moment before he turned to Mother.

"I think you'd better explain yourself."

Triton harrumphed, crossing his arms over his wide chest. The shorts he wore sat low on his hips, and I supposed, if I didn't have eyes only for Andrew, I would have said Triton was a handsome merman. However, I had made it one of my life's missions to avoid bullies and overly dominant merfolk who thought they could order me around, and Triton had never been kind to any of the orphans.

"Many years ago, about the time you started college, Andrew," Mother began, "I had a visitor. He was quite the silver fox, tall and muscular, with long flowing hair. His bronze skin shimmered in the sunlight, which is what tipped me off to him being more than a simple man. We had walked on the beach a ways before I asked him why he'd come. He told me the most fantastical tale of a young merboy who appeared to be infatuated with my son. He thought nothing would come of it—the merboy would grow older and eventually find another of their kind who would interest him.

"I asked him what if the merboy did not give up? What should I do if they one day meet?

"He said he would be watching and would keep me aware of the situation. It was the best he could do for the moment. It had happened before, but each case was different. He would decide the course of action if and only if my son and the merboy should meet.

"He took his leave and strode out into the ocean, giving me a flickering view of his tail to lend credence to his words."

"My father, King Neptune, came to visit you?" Triton sneered. He waggled an accusatory finger at Mother. "I don't believe you. You're making this up."

A cross between a trill and a growl rose from my chest. Andrew's legs shifted under my tail, and his grip on me tightened.

"How dare you call my mother a liar!" Andrew roared, the resounding echo deafening near my ear, scaring me. I wanted to escape, to return to the soft sounds of my home and, in doing so, twisted and fell from his lap. Hands and tail slapped to the hard blue-squared floor.

Mother yelled, adding to the chaos. A flip of my tail and a push with my arms propelled me forward, the blanket beneath me helping me slide.

"Kip!" Andrew reached for me.

"Runt!" Triton sneered, moving forward, seeking to block my path.

"Hold!" bellowed a new voice, thunderous with the command.

Everyone froze. Andrew returned to his seat. Mother drooped to lean against the table. I trembled until my arms refused to hold my weight any longer, sagging to lie on the cool floor. I lay there a moment to regain some energy, and a semblance of calm, before rolling to my back, sitting up and tucking my tail out of the way. Triton stood behind and to the left of Neptune, smirking at me around his father's arm. I glared back.

A snap of King Neptune's fingers broke our stare-down. "I'm disappointed in you, Triton," he admonished his son, without even looking at him.

Triton's smirk fell away, his shoulders slumped and head hung. "Sorry, Father."

A roll of Neptune's eyes had me covering my mouth to stifle a smile, but I couldn't stop the sharp intake of breath I took in amazement when Neptune knelt down on one knee in front of me. "Kip—that's a good name, by the way. I like it. Kip, you understood Mother's story?"

I nodded. Andrew and I had met, and now Neptune had to do *something.* It was the something that had me nervous, feeling like a school of guppies had taken residence in my stomach. Would he…? My thoughts went in wild directions, quickly tamped when Neptune cupped my chin, raising my head so he could look me in the eyes.

"The decision is yours, but it's also Andrew's and Mother's."

"Why do you call me Mother?" she interrupted.

Neptune smiled at her. "It is how Kip named you. Andrew's name went through a cycle of changes and so, in not knowing the true one, to Kip he was always 'Him' or 'Boy', until you gave voice to his birth name, but you… You were always, *his* mother."

Mother's eyes filled with tears and she pressed her fingers to her mouth. "Oh… That is simply the dearest thing I've ever heard." Andrew extended a hand to her and she grasped it, coming around the table to stand next to him. "But I must insist, if we three are involved in the decision, then we should make it together."

"I agree." Andrew said.

I slapped the floor in agreement and raised my arms to Andrew. He came and lifted me up, returning to his chair and placing me once more in his lap.

"All right, sir," Andrew said, but I stopped him right there, waving him silent. I fashioned a circle with my fingers and mimicked putting it on my head. Andrew's eyes widened. "Really?" He looked up at Neptune. "Your Majesty."

Neptune nodded.

"Wait a sec." Andrew twisted to look at Mother. "Let me make sure I have this right. King Neptune came to visit you, and Triton is his son, and everyone is a merman."

"Except me," Mother said.

Andrew's lips pursed. "Except you… Then what am I?"

"You, my dear sweet Andrew," Mother stroked the back of two fingers down his cheek, "are the son of a human and a merman."

I giggled at how even bigger Andrew's eyes got. Leaning over, with one hand holding tight to Andrew's shirt, I ran my other hand down Andrew's leg. Straightening, I peered at Mother and shook my head.

"It's true," Neptune confirmed. "Andrew, your father fell madly in love with your mother and begged me to change him. I did, but the call of the sea is hard to resist for some. After you were conceived, and Mother insisted she could and would raise you to love the ocean, he returned home."

Neptune took Mother's hands in his. "He would like to see you, Melinda. Would you meet with him?"

"Does he want to meet Andrew?"

"I believe so."

"If he will meet us both, then yes. A son should know his father."

Her simple statement struck me deeply. A weak keen escaped, my throat choking on nothing, stifling needed air. I had no one left to meet. No one to whom I could introduce Andrew.

Andrew's arms tightened around me. He pulled me close, hugging me to his chest, his chin resting heavily on top of my head. It was a weight I bore with ease, especially when he murmured, "You're mine, and he shall meet all three of us or none at all."

Neptune knelt once more, to the side of the chair, where he could look at me directly. "Kip, Andrew, you've found your mate. The one being who completes you. It was fate that drew you to each other. It's why, Kip, you've continued to come to this shore and watch Andrew grow up, and why you, Andrew, have always loved the ocean and all its creatures. Why your fascination led you to a life of studying the sea with the hopes of protecting its resources, its creatures big and small.

"When I first learned of Kip's continued journeys to this particular shore, I followed him. Watching Andrew, as he grew older, was a harmless infatuation, but as the years progressed, I realized that Kip had fallen in love with you, and I could no longer stay silent. It wasn't until I met you, Melinda, that I made the connection to Huron, for I had never sought out the woman he impregnated. I never told you my name, but you knew, didn't you?"

"I didn't know you were a king," Mother said, "but I knew you were someone of importance. That you wielded considerable power if you were able to make such life-altering decisions."

"That I can, and so you must decide. Andrew, because you carry within you the ability to become a merman, you can join Kip below the waves, but if that is the path you seek, your human legs will be no more. You'll never walk the sands again, nor see more than what you may with your head above water."

Andrew's arms tightened, and I turned to look at him. His eyes were wide and his mouth parted, and I knew he'd say "Yes."

"Wait," Neptune said, holding up a hand to forestall Andrew. "This is not the only choice. Kip, you may decide to become human, gaining legs but losing your tail."

Neptune directed a penetrating stare into my eyes. "You'll never again be able to swim to the deep recesses, play with the schools of fish, tangle with the dolphins and seals. However, if this is the path you choose, you will also never have the ability to speak. Only your outward appearance changes."

"And what is my choice?" Mother asked.

"Your choice, Melinda, is to either lose a son or gain one."

"Well, for me," she said, "the choice is easy. I would choose to have both of them."

"I'm sure you would, but in doing so, Kip will never be able to share his world, the one that Andrew also loves, even without ever seeing more than what humankind has reached. Although Andrew would also lose the chance to show Kip his world, the one Kip has longed to explore his whole life."

I twisted in Andrew's lap, gripped his shirt in white-knuckled fistfuls. He gazed down at me. "It would be nice to see with my own eyes what I've only seen pictures of."

Oh, no. Panic seized me, I gasped for breath. Shaking my head vehemently, I gestured my desire to walk, pointing to myself and miming legs with my fingers.

"You wish to stay?"

Yes.

"But you'll never speak…"

I shrugged. I touched my lips and then wiggled my fingers.

"True, we have been doing okay." Andrew smiled warmly, but after a moment, his mouth reversed. "Won't someone miss you?"

No.

"Kip was orphaned at a young age," Neptune explained. "He lived in the castle, serving once he grew old enough, but we must insist that all orphans leave the nursery at some point to make room for the new ones."

Mother drew in a sharp breath. "Are there many?" A single tear glistened below her right eye.

"Unfortunately, yes, we shelter and care for many. Larger and larger fishing boats and transport ships have caused great detriment to not only my merfolk, but all those who dwell under the water. I've been forced to put some areas of our ocean off limits. Decades ago, we had no need to worry about huge trawling nets or gigantic engines. Now, we teach safety and awareness to the younglings as soon as they are old enough to wander off."

"That's one of my potential end goals," Andrew said. "I've been trying to decide if I want to go the science root and study more, or take a job inspecting ships. Or maybe go into training mariners in safety. So many roles where I could be useful…"

As he trailed off, his words furthered my resolve. He was needed here on land. Under the sea, we could live simply, we could swim off to secluded shores and never worry about life on land, but he would miss Mother. As would I. On land, he could make a difference, and I could help him with my knowledge of the water's secrets.

Trilling softly and gaining Andrew's attention, I motioned once more that I wanted to stay and walk with him. This time, I slipped my hand into his and gave it a squeeze.

"But—"

I pressed my fingers against his mouth, stopping his objection. I wanted this. I'd wished for it for so long, and now, King Neptune would grant me my heart's desire.

"Andrew." Mother laid her hand on his shoulder, and he turned his head to look up at her. "Did you ever once wish you could live under the sea? And I don't mean fancifully, I mean wished with your whole heart that you'd never leave the water."

Andrew shook his head just once.

"I believe Kip has that wish, that single desire to be what we are, to only return to the water to swim. He understands what he is giving up, and also—" Mother's gaze softened "—what he will gain."

Yes! I reached for Mother, the taste of tears heavy on my tongue, and she stepped forward, allowing me to hug her tightly.

Neptune cleared his throat, the loud rattle breaking our emotional moment. "Andrew, the decision must be unanimous."

"This is foolishness, Father," Triton exclaimed. "How can you let him go? He's one of us. Runt doesn't belong here. He's..."

"He's what?" Neptune's narrowed glare directed at his son lessened the hurt of hearing Triton call me that name.

Triton spluttered, "He's too small. He won't survive. He doesn't even know how humans live."

"He's perfect, and I'll teach him," Andrew threw at Triton. "His name is Kip. He's mine, and I say he stays."

My heart leapt at hearing Andrew's declaration. Happiness coursed through my blood, along my nerves, lighting them afire. But it wasn't just emotion; I felt it, a fire between my fingers, the sides of my head and neck, all along the length of my tail. Hotter and hotter. I gripped Andrew hard, gritted my teeth, a low wail of pain radiating from my chest. My spine arched, straightening and curving my body in a vain attempt to escape the agony.

"Kip... Kip! Mom, he's burning up. His tail!"

I compelled my body to curl, forcing my eyes open so I could see what was happening to me. My scales flaked and fell, the chalky dermis beneath beginning to show. Larger and larger those scaleless patches grew, the milky skin beneath dull and itchy. My attempts to scratch were held back by Andrew's arms wrapping around me. I thrashed my tail, pumped my hips, anything to try to soothe the ache within.

And then I was free. Sort of. A violent kick caused my tail to tear and—Toes. Toes appeared and a foot attached to them. Wiggled. Wait... I wiggled them. I gave an experimental bend and a knee broke through. My knee, my leg, my foot, my toes. A good shake and my tail fell away, leaving me with two very pale appendages.

I lifted one leg to touch my new skin. Soft and smooth, harder near the bones. Andrew's hand hovered beside mine, which is when I noticed the webbing between my fingers was gone. I brought my hand closer to inspect it.

"Ears," Andrew whispered into mine. I grabbed for them, feeling the new growth of skin and silky bottom flaps just like his. Lowering my hands, I touched my neck, feeling for the usual slits, but found none. "Your gills are gone, too."

A trill of delight rippled from my throat. Joy manifested itself with me throwing my arms around his neck and pressing my lips to his. He took hold of my hips and held me still. Though the quick flash of fire was gone from my blood, a new heat arose from deep within, and when I tried to pull away, Andrew cupped the back of my head and deepened the kiss.

I tried to follow his movements, to give to him as much pleasure as he gave me. I could only hope he liked it for I'd never kissed anyone before. As we came apart, he gazed at me, and my heart overflowed with love for him. I swore I could see his desire for me returned within the depths of his deep blue eyes. even though we'd just met.

His possession of me was as strong and fierce as my possession of him. *Mates.*

"It's time for us to go. I'll send word as to when and where Huron will meet you." Neptune turned to leave, but Triton blocked his path. "What is it?"

Triton leaned close to Neptune's ear and spoke too quietly for us to hear. The prince's eyes appeared red-rimmed and swollen, and I had the fleeting thought he'd been moved by Andrew's words and my subsequent transformation. *No,* I mused. Triton thinks of no one but himself.

"Do what you think is best, my son," King Neptune said, patting Triton's shoulder before leaving the house.

We three stared at Triton, waiting for him to speak. He lifted his head and stopped to gaze at each of us individually.

"It seems I was wrong, and for that I apologize. Kip, you are very brave to have made this life-altering decision. It will not be easy, and so I wish to bestow a gift to you. It won't be perfect, but hopefully it will make your transition a little easier." Triton stepped across the room of silver boxes and reached towards the small shelf below the window above the washbasin. He chose a colorful flat scallop shell and laid it on one palm, covering it with the other. His hands began to glow, a bright light emitting from small gaps between his fingers. The light faded and he held out a necklace to me.

I slipped it over my head, wondering what it would do. Andrew and Mother made simultaneous noises of surprise.

What?

"I can hear your thoughts," Andrew said, cautiously touching the shell, and running a fingertip over its bumpy exterior.

"I can, too," Mother added.

"Only you two will be able to hear Kip. No one else." Triton kneeled beside me and whispered, "I suggest you remove it before any kissing or whatnot happens."

Kissing? Oh!

Andrew and Mother laughed, my melodic trill joining and echoing around the room. The sound would become a sweet memory of a day I'd always remember… the day I became human.

The End

ABOUT ALEXIS WOODS

Me? Well, I do a bit of everything. Read and beta top the list, writing a close third. I'm a licensed drug pusher by day, and a homework checker by night to three—getting older (and taller) every year—children. If I'm lucky, my husband lays off the gaming soon enough in the evening to crawl into bed and snuggle up for back rubs. I recreate the medieval ages with the Society of Creative Anachronism and guide young ladies on their path to become leaders with the Girl Scouts.

It's been an incredible few years since I wrote Opening Day, the first M/M story I ever penned. And the most amazing part of all this: the friends I've made around the world. South Africa, Romania, Australia, Sweden, Germany, Great Britain. Plus those far across the United States: from my home in southern New Jersey clear to the North, South, and West with many in between. A true four corners, full of color and life.

On Goodreads at: www.goodreads.com/AlexisWoods

By Email: alexiswoods553@gmail.com

On Google+: https://www.google.com/+AlexisWoodsAuthor

Twitter: @alexiswoods553

Facebook: https://www.facebook.com/profile.php?id=100008026278147&fref=ts

BY ALEXIS WOODS

Lion's Hero – Chosen Angels I
Hammer's Thief – Chosen Angels II

Opening Day – Southern Jersey Shores – Book 1
Evading Exodus – Southern Jersey Shores – Book 2
Ultimate Summer – Southern Jersey Shores – Book 3
Spin Play – Southern Jersey Shores – Book 4
Cue the Music – Southern Jersey Shores – Book 5
Say You Will – Southern Jersey Shores – Book 6

Cupid's Arrows – Divine Connections

Moondrake – Free read available through Goodreads
**** *Revised and expanded story coming late 2018/early 2019* ****

Metamorphic Heart (w/ KC Faelan) – Free read available through Goodreads
**** *Revised edition coming to retailers late 2018/early 2019* ****

Seashell Voices

COURTING LIGHT

A. ZUKOWSKI

Our days were numbered but precious.

Courting Light is the story of Josie, an eighteen-year-old about to leave home to start university in London. She volunteers at a summer camp for disabled children. When Josie is paired with the autistic teenager Lucian, she faces intense experiences that are truly eye-opening. To her surprise, Lucian is not the only one who captures her attention. Over the weeks, Josie develops powerful desires evoked by the camp's enigmatic young leader with a shaved head and tattoo on her skull.

***

Genre: LGBTQ+, young adult contemporary, lesbian lit

Keywords: lesbian, coming-of-age, disability, teens, young adult, friendship, romance

ACKNOWLEDGEMENTS

To the boy who likes to draw lights.

Hey, Jason, you remember Hebden Bridge and the fly that committed suicide by diving into your drink?

Ellie, sing me the song in your perfect pitch. Pretty please.

Thank you, A.M. Leibowitz and Andrea Harding, for your careful beta-reading.

Sometimes we have stories that we need to tell but are afraid to. Perhaps they are too personal, or they are simply too emotionally demanding to write. So, we put them aside, forgotten like dreams in the morning. When I saw the call for this anthology, I remembered one of those stories. I was reluctant, both because I knew it'd be a difficult one to write and because I write slow. Writing to deadline isn't my forte. Somehow I found it in me to get my arse in gear to complete this novella. Thank you, Debbie McGowan, for your wonderfulness, and for including this story in the collection. I look forward to reading all the other diverse stories.

In the short time since I 'joined' Beaten Track, writing has become a less lonely pursuit. Thank you for your encouragement, my fellow Beaten Trackers.

COURTING LIGHT

It was the summer before I started college. I was eighteen and didn't feel particularly clever even though I was on my way to become a university student in September.

DAY 1

"ARE YOU ONE of the volunteers? Get your arse in here," a young woman bellowed, her voice bold and impatient. I couldn't see her face since she stayed in the front cab of the van. When I caught her profile in the side mirror, a pair of Jackie-O sunglasses obscured her face. "Come on, jump in and shut the door behind you."

I learned later that 'come on' was a favourite phrase of hers.

I did as I was told and climbed onto the back of the transit van, struggling to slide the heavy metal door behind me. It shut with a loud clang. I turned to face the dozen or so people who were already seated. Searching around for an empty space, I could see that my fellow volunteers were mostly young and in their twenties. I'd probably be one of the youngest since they only allowed over-eighteens as helpers.

They were mostly women but I found two guys among us. Clad in T-shirts, casual jeans and trainers, the dozen or so faces were fresh and eager. I felt apprehensive and cursed myself for thinking this working holiday was a great idea. One of the guys stood up and let me climb over the crowded bench to sit by the window. He smiled. I noticed the freckles on his face and the rosy cheeks, as if he hadn't quite grown out of his baby fat.

I stared out, then, and saw about twenty adults of varying ages and sizes waving to the other van that was idling a few parking spaces down. Some of the kids' faces pressed against the glass. I knew they were under eighteen, but they seemed to represent a wide range from about six to big kids, teenagers who were in fact not much younger than me.

What was I doing? The guilt surfaced alongside nerves. Did I qualify as a carer only because they had some kind of disability? Was it purely selfish to do something I was clearly untrained for just to gain some experience? For my benefit? For my curriculum vitae?

Several of their parents linked hands, as if their offspring were being taken to meet their fate with the Gestapo, not a summer camp. Worry lines spread across their foreheads. I saw a woman in her thirties dab her eyes with a handkerchief, trying to wipe away her tears. That did nothing to ease my nerves. *What if I accidentally hurt* her *child?* The responsibility weighed me down. I wished they had rejected my application.

I turned back to survey my fellow helpers instead. I wondered if they were seasoned carers who knew what they were doing. Fear was probably obvious on my face. My seat mate nodded as if hearing my inner voice.

"My name's Tim." He held his hand out and I shook it. "They're worried about their kids. That's all."

"Josie." I should have offered further information but my brain froze. My reticence didn't seem to bother him. He carried on with the serendipitous induction. I obviously looked like I needed it.

"You're doing them a big favour. Believe me. It's not easy being a carer twenty-four seven. For some of the parents, these two weeks once a year are a life-saver."

"Some of them don't look very happy." I thought of the crying mother.

"They never get a break looking after their children, but they're also terrified of leaving them in our hands for two weeks. Some of the kids are quite severely disabled. You'll see," Tim explained patiently.

No shit. I would *not* want to leave a child in my hands.

My mum had a good job as a hairdresser. She'd been working in the same salon for twenty years. We didn't have money problems, but I never had the kind of relationship with her like other daughters seemed to have with their mothers. I didn't care about my hair, make-up or looking pretty while those things were her livelihood. Mum was emotionally distant, especially so after my parents divorced when I was ten. She had boyfriends, dudes who came and went, but she never remarried. I had a hunch that she resented having two kids—I also had a know-it-all older brother—as we made her less eligible in the dating market, but she didn't have much of a choice. That was why she'd left me mostly to my own devices. Dad was absent. He took up with another woman. We knew where to find him if we needed to, but that was about it.

After the holidays, I was going to study sociology at a university in London. I had the vague idea that I wanted to know about 'society'. Having read a few key texts during my A' Levels, I had impulsively put it down as my first choice for a degree. I would leave my home town and start a new life. For that was how I'd imagined being at university—behaving like an adult, living independently and making new friends.

So, I gathered that it was my first summer as an adult, and I needed to get out there, to be part of *the* society. I wanted to volunteer for the summer camp because I'd lived such a sheltered life that I didn't believe I was remotely qualified to study the subject. Of course, much later on, I realised that sociology was as removed from the way we lived as it could be. I would spend hours arguing about structure and agency, and theorising capital and labour. Then, I decided that I'd like to see how care workers dealt with kids. I thought I'd be helpful and contribute something for once. Besides, the information for volunteers said 'no prior experience necessary'. They accepted my application and put me through police checks.

Here I was, completely clueless but with a healthy will to learn, sitting among all the other young volunteers and waiting to be told what to do for the next fourteen days. *What have I signed up to?*

As Tim and I talked, the van shook and came to life. Our driver must have started the engine.

"Take it you've done this before," I ventured, glancing at him briefly. The van moved off the city centre car park and merged into the traffic. It would probably take over an hour to reach the Peak District where the outdoor centre we were staying in was located.

Tim grinned, showing much pride. "Yeah, this is my third summer. What about you? Are you staying for one or two weeks?"

My worries surfaced again. It'd probably be useful to talk to someone more experienced, though. "My first time, I'm afraid. I'm staying for the full fortnight camp, but I have absolutely no clue how to look after kids, let alone those with disabilities. Let's hope I don't accidentally hurt them."

Our transportation left the city centre streets behind. Tim focused back on my face again. He opened his mouth a couple of times but couldn't form the words. Finally, he smiled. "You'll be fine. I don't think physically harming them is that common."

What was left unsaid? How else could the kids be easily hurt? Crikey. Bile threatened to come up my throat.

"Anyway, Sam will sort you out," Tim concluded with conviction.

Sam. It was the first time I heard the name. I wondered who that was, but didn't want to appear ignorant or too eager. Tim sounded sure of this person's leadership. I returned to gazing out the window; I appeared like a ghost on the pane of glass: reddish-brown hair, pale eyes and a button nose. Short strands fell untidily around my oval face. I dug out my beanie and put it on to keep them under control.

The bus rolled along, taking too long to reach the hills away from the city. Even the air was thinner up there. My eyelids threatened to close as green scenery passed by. The Dark Peak was rugged and wild in parts, like a hardworking man without sentimentality. Apprehension still sat in my gut, though, as if the journey was further than the Peak District, and the hills were harbouring the unknown. I imagined the purple heather might be hiding the cloudy dreams I had as a kid when I was growing up and I'd been afraid of the strange monsters in my sleep. Now, it was waiting for me up in the hills.

The van eventually pulled into a narrow lane. Light shot through the thicket and streamed through the windows. After a mile or so, we stopped in an opening with enough space for only a few vehicles, and I saw the outdoor centre that was going to be our home for the next two weeks: a one-storey wooden structure that spread out like a resting bird; windows lined its wings that might contain the bedrooms.

Once the doors to the van opened, one by one, the helpers climbed down. I was almost the last to emerge, carrying my heavy backpack. I stood on the edge of the group, waiting to be told what was to come. Tim was deep in conversation with another young female volunteer.

The driver and her companion jumped down from the van. The first thing I noticed was the driver's legs—long and tan, strong and lean muscles stretched beneath her sports shorts. Lumberjack boots and thick socks reached her lower calves. She wore a sleeveless black T-shirt, even though it was not that hot. This was July in England, not the Mediterranean. But I found myself ogling her lithe and firm arms and thought about how the taut skin might feel if I glided my fingers along it. I had to shake my head discreetly to stop that line of thought because it was strange and as frightening as the prospect of facing the kids for the next two weeks.

The woman's head was shaved with short sides showing a tattoo just above her left ear. I was too far away to see what the tattoo was on that first day. Heat surged inside me as though I was in a hotter climate. My heart skipped a beat. I liked how she looked. A lot. I'd never had a boyfriend or girlfriend. Some of my secondary school mates were already dating. My best friend Jason was gay, so I'd gone out with him to gay clubs a few times. We'd even tracked down the only gay bookshop for miles around. We had to take a train and ride the bus to get there. But, so far, I'd thought of myself merely as an observer of Jason's world.

I'd honestly assumed I was straight. Why wouldn't I be?

"My name's Sam," the obvious leader announced. "And I'm the manager of the camp."

She related something about safety. I should've been listening to her instructions but I heard nothing but a buzz in my head.

An older guy stood by her side and introduced himself as Grant, Sam's assistant. "So, at all times, either Sam or I will be at base camp. We have two senior volunteers, Rose and Beth, who are coming with the kids in the other van. They both work in childcare, so they know their stuff. If you're in any doubt, come to one of us."

I found myself focusing on Sam. Her round face, light tan and bright brown eyes. Shit. *Pay some attention to what's being said, Josie.* I shifted in my stance to recoup. But instead of listening to Grant, I could hear birds chirp, and when I glanced to my right, I saw a squirrel running away to a clump of trees. *Deep breath.*

When I returned my attention to the two managers, I saw Sam assessing us one by one with her sharp eyes. I wasn't sure if she realised that my gaze had been following her. Her scrutiny reached me eventually, and she gave me a slight lilt of her mouth as if to wonder out loud, *who have I got here?*

I smiled back, without the same kind of confidence. We held each other's gaze for a moment. I decided then I would like her attention. No matter what. It was a far less noble motive than why I'd become a helper at a summer camp for disabled children.

Sam and Grant led us to the dormitory block. I walked side by side with Tim. The dorm was basic but clean. The scent of pine filled my nostrils as the two organisers came to a stop in the corridor flanked by several rooms. She turned to face us.

Indicating the group of dormitories, she smiled. "These are for you. You'll be sharing with another host. Ten minutes. Grant and I will be waiting for you in the hall."

Come on. She might as well have said that. Tim and I looked at each other and nodded. The others were talking, seeking out partners and inspecting the bedrooms. We grabbed the one closest to us since they were identical anyway. It was sparsely decorated, as I'd expected: two single beds, a wardrobe, a desk and chair each. Reading lamps for the occupiers. It was more than adequate for a short break. Another door led to a small bathroom with a shower stall. We dumped our bags. No time for the 'which bed would you prefer' conversation.

Tim smiled. "It ain't much but it's home for the next two weeks. Do you want to freshen up first?"

"Oh, yes. We only have ten minutes. She doesn't joke around, does she?"

"Nuh-uh. Sam runs a tight ship. Go ahead." Tim opened his backpack and pulled out some clothes to put in his wardrobe.

We had a quick wash and returned to the hall where Sam and her assistant explained that we'd ease the kids in this evening. Sam clapped her hands to draw our attention. A dozen eager faces gazed at her and her apparent leadership. Grant produced a couple of sheets of labels and some felt-tip pens.

"Everyone, pass the name tags around and write your names in big letters, so the older children can read them. Please," he instructed us.

We spent the next few minutes putting our names on the labels. As we did so, Sam added, "Of course, some of the children don't know how to read and write, but—"

She was interrupted when a timid hand was raised among the volunteers. Sam tilted her head. "Yes?"

"Do you have a list of who we're paired with?" asked a young woman with black-framed glasses and a dark short bob, and looked to be in need of summer supervision herself.

Sam read her name tag. "No, Susanna. When they arrive—" she glanced at her watch "—in a few minutes, you will simply choose one another. The children will have one-to-one supervision by their hosts at all times. It's perfectly fine, though, if you or your guest want to change during your stay, except maybe in a couple of cases because the kids can't deal with instability. Whatever it is, Grant and I will be at hand to sort things out, okay?"

With a small frown on her forehead, she looked to Grant as if to get an agreement, and he nodded.

"Some of these children have never been away from home like this. They might be emotionally challenging, as well as having physical needs. Once you've found your match, I'll have a chat with each of you individually. If you find yourself in situations you can't deal with, whatever they are, come straight to me or Grant. Understood? Any questions?" Her voice was authoritative enough that I found myself trusting her straightaway.

Grant smiled at us reassuringly. "And here's a map of the site and a list of the kids and their allocated rooms." He waved more sheets of paper and started to pass them round.

The same bespectacled young woman piped up, "What disabilities have the kids got? I don't have any experience of working with disabled children."

That made at least the two of us. I looked around, noticing several of the other volunteers nodding.

"Well, they have a wide range of disabilities, some physical, some are learning disabilities. Most of them have a mixture of both. As I said, once you've found your buddy, Grant or I will have a chat with you about individual requirements. But we don't have rigid rules here. If your guest or you feel that it's not working out, we'll try to swap you. I ask for your patience, though. Sometimes it's hard for these kids to trust people, so try to stick with them as much as possible during their stay. It *will* be fun but hard work."

At this point, I was hoping for just survival.

I squinted to see her as clearly as I could. I could see a stud in her right ear and another in her nose. The large brown eyes were deep and perfectly balanced on her face. They sparkled with enthusiasm. I was absorbed and encouraged by her unbound energy and tried to convince myself that I'd cope with whatever came my way.

Sam's phone chirped and she scanned the screen before answering. "Right. Come on in. We're ready for the guests."

I shifted my feet, still feeling nervous.

Pushing one of the kids in a wheelchair, an older woman led the group of noisy guests. I assumed she was one of the senior volunteers. Some of them were already chatting away to each other far too loudly. At first glance, they really were very different. The dozen children were of different sizes, ages and genders.

The guests, too, had name labels on their lapels but I was too distant to read them. After all the kids had entered the hall, a woman about Sam's age brought up the rear. Sam introduced them; Rose was the older woman, and the younger senior helper was Beth. I was reassured since, according to Sam, they were both trained in caring for disabled children.

I surveyed the kids. My eyes were drawn to a couple of boys who stood awkwardly to one end of the group. They were both taller than me. One of them might have been a teenager but he already had an adult's body, and yet, one side of him drooped. His right arm and leg were bent and his pale face blank. He stared at us, the helpers. Saliva drooled from the corner of his mouth.

With a mop of messy curly brown hair, the boy standing at the very end of the group was probably a little younger than his neighbour, but he also appeared tall for his age. He didn't seem physically disabled, unlike the teenager next to him. He shifted slightly backwards, as if he wanted to get away from the line-up, and glanced up momentarily. His eyes were so large and deep, clear blue like two pools of tarn. He caught my gaze and quickly directed his eyes down, away from my scrutiny. I felt bad, as though I was staring too much. Later, he'd teach me that most people over-compensated all the time. They deliberately looked away from physical disability or behaviour that seemed out of the ordinary. He would catch on anyway when they did that. For him, over-compensation was a sign that 'the real people'—his words for the able-bodied—were scared.

I'm scared of them, but not as much as they are frightened of us freaks.

And I would ask him not to use that word to describe himself. He smiled at that with a slight upturn of his mouth. Then, standing awkwardly in that hall, I had no clue what I was doing, and wondered why the boy had come to the camp because he didn't look like the rest of the gang of kids.

For now, he avoided eye contact and leaned uncomfortably, one hand holding onto his bag so tightly that I saw his white knuckles from ten feet away. All I could remember was the parent dabbing her eyes, trying to will away her worries. She might be his mum, and now he wanted to show her he was a big independent boy who was not scared to death.

I was not alone in feeling nervous. I took comfort in that thought.

"Come on, why don't our hosts pair up with the guests? One-to-one. My lovely helpers, you may show them where their bunks are. All the allocations are shown on the plan we gave you." Sam, as ever, sounded excited and enthusiastic and stopped my wandering train of thought.

The other volunteers went up and started to 'claim' their companions. The hosts and guests eagerly greeted each other, some striking up conversations right away. Tim went to the tall teenager whose twisted leg dragged along as Tim made his introductions and led him to the dormitories.

The remaining boy flapped his hands and moved away even more, as if he was making for the door he'd just come through to escape. He shook his head and muttered something to no one in particular. While he waited in absolute agony and I hesitated, all the other children and volunteers had made their acquaintances and, one by one, the pairs disappeared.

Rose and Beth had left with them to offer assistance. Sam wasn't in the room anymore. Only Grant hovered, ready to lend a hand.

I moved towards the last boy standing. He still held onto his bag tightly with his eyes downcast, avoiding my gaze.

"I'm Josie. What's your name?"

I extended my hand to shake his while I tried to read his name label and saw that he'd written his name in rather small letters in the left-hand corner of the white rectangle. The handwriting was neat and controlled, but I couldn't read it. Except the 'L'.

My offered hand remained untouched.

"What's your name?" he replied without meeting my eyes or returning my handshake. His speech was clear. Words pronounced in imitation of my accent.

I hesitantly moved closer and was now near enough to see his name: Lucian. The letters were drawn in a tight script that broke the white surface.

I didn't know what might be considered wrong about him by society, but my instinct told me we'd be fine. That we'd make this work. "Would you like to pair up with me, Lucian?"

I smiled because at that time I still believed if I did that enough I would gain people's trust. Except, Lucian was exceptional. He failed to look up to meet my smile and he didn't respond.

I was at a loss as to how to act in front of the teenager. Nothing in my eighteen years of experience prepared me for understanding differences. I considered him again. He appeared like any other boy of his age and yet in that simple rejection betrayed an innate distinction.

As I pondered upon his disability, he flapped his hand once more and pointed to the sheet of names and room arrangement, still without meeting my gaze. I held it up and read through the list of names and in which room he was allocated.

I'd already withdrawn my hand since it had become quite clear he was not going to touch me. I offered instead, "Okay, Lucian. Shall I take you to your room?"

I realised that he'd have known that I held the information in my hand. He would have deduced that fact because of his ability to observe and remember the minutiae.

He risked a glance at my face, his blue eyes glistening. He nodded and started for the door. Instead of being the host, I had to follow his long legs and head towards the corridor where the children's rooms were found.

We marched past the room he was to share with two other guests.

"Hey, this one. Here." I puffed, holding onto the map.

Lucian's bunk sat empty in one corner. The other volunteers and children were chatting away. Lucian approached his space. Immediately, he took his possessions from his bag and arranged them in the small wardrobe and on the desk. His colouring pencils were neatly ordered in the rainbow colours they came in, and I could see he'd sharpened them to equal length. I watched him carefully claiming his personal space with fascination.

"How old are you, Lucian?"

"How old are you?" he countered, without directly addressing me. "Why don't you look at your sheet?"

I found him on my list. *Lucian Charles. Fifteen.*

Damn it. He was making me feel like an idiot, which was precisely his plan. Lucian had probably been treated like one his entire life. Now he was taking me for a fool. Perfect.

What I could deduce after my first evening with Lucian: he didn't like crowds. He liked to stick to a schedule. Minimum eye contact when he interacted with others. He put everything in order, including food.

By my own bedtime, I was exhausted from trying to be on form all day.

DAY 2

Lucian knew exactly what he wanted from the breakfast bar. He'd arranged the egg cup in the very centre of his plate. The beans sat to the left, a single sausage next to the tomato sauce. A small plate held the piece of toast to the right. Still not speaking to me, he was happy enough with the meal, finishing everything meticulously. I wondered if someone made a mistake to let Lucian onto this camp since he appeared capable enough. For a start, he didn't need feeding like some of the other kids.

Lucian took a sip of the orange juice and stuck his tongue out. "Disgusting." He pushed the drink as far away from him as possible, as though it might contaminate the rest of the meal. If that was his only complaint, I thought we were doing great.

Sam caught up with me when Lucian had nearly finished breakfast. "Rose could sit with Lucian for the moment. Would you like to come with me to the office? We'll have a chat."

Oh, the honeyed tone. It went with the brown eyes. Sam wore a plain black T-shirt and a pair of cutoff shorts. Her body was harder and leaner than most women I knew. I stared, as if hypnotised, and I stood up and followed her into the office. The small room was sparsely furnished. It wasn't somewhere that was used constantly. Sam sat behind the narrow desk and I took the seat opposite. The two feet of wood between us added to my anxiety.

She launched into it without pleasantry as preparation. "How's it going with Lucian?"

Feeling oddly tongue-tied, I mumbled, "Fine, I think."

Sam arched an eyebrow, which might have betrayed how she felt uncertain about my ability. Did I seem like a useless kid who needed guidance? I wished I had more confidence about the whole situation.

"Fine? How do you find him?" Impatience permeated her question.

"He…he is intense. Kind of quiet. It's too early yet." *Lucian is odd, intriguing, not particularly communicative.* I couldn't say any of it. It'd seem too much like I was complaining about the disabled kid whom I was supposed to be taking care of.

"Lucian has autism spectrum disorder," she advised me.

I racked my brains to see whether I knew anything about autism. Sam's dark gaze made me give up. "What do you mean? What should I expect?"

Sam waited moments as if she was measuring out the words. "It's hard to tell. From my experience, every autistic kid's quite unique. I don't know where he is on the spectrum. Some of them can be 'highly functional'." She made the quotation marks in the air. "I don't like the term. It makes them sound like flipping robots. Some call the condition Asperger's syndrome. As you've seen, they can be anxious in social situations. They need familiar routine and order. I've worked with Lucian before. He's pretty good at looking after himself."

"He just seems a bit peculiar," I ventured. After only brief encounters with Lucian last night and this morning, I'd only say he wasn't particularly 'dysfunctional'. Perhaps that was why Tim went for the other boy whose name was Eric and who was certainly much higher maintenance.

"It's your first time at these camps, right? Lucian's probably not a bad guest to be teamed with."

Sam was distracting me. Under the tight T-shirt, her small breasts and the shape of her nipples were barely visible. My mind had instantly deserted me.

"He seems particularly anxious, which is not surprising. His mum seldom lets him out of her sight, I think. He's been here the last couple of years," Sam continued. Lucian was nervous, but perhaps no more than I was. "He doesn't relate well to the other kids and the helpers. He's a stickler for routine. No doubt you'll find out for yourself. Some involuntary hand and head gestures, and repetitive speech pattern. It's called echolalia."

I was staring, mesmerised by Sam's voice, but the list of Lucian's 'symptoms' washed over me because they sounded like a biology lesson.

As though she could hear my thoughts, she added, "But other than that, Lucian's a great kid. You'll probably get on. I have a feeling."

Once more, I asked myself what I was doing there, but Sam's laughter broke through the tension. After a minute, she was still chuckling. "You are staring with your mouth open. Lucian wouldn't look you in the eyes. You will make a great pair."

I felt like a fool, again, pretending that I could look after someone not much younger than me. Someone who had special needs, which I must provide for. I must have blushed.

Sam gave me one more wide beam. "Humour. Above all, you need some of that. Otherwise, he's going to run rings around you, my love. And working with these kids is hard work. It can be emotionally draining."

I was serious. I'd been told many times about that particular personality trait, and Sam's pep talk had not eased my apprehension one bit. I still felt the warmth on my cheeks.

She clapped her hands to signal the end of the conversation. "The kids are doing the great escape this morning. Ha, it's only the second day and they're trying to get away already. Come on. Let's go see." She stood, came round to my side of the desk and offered me her hand. Her long, slender fingers touched mine, and the next thing I knew I was standing, our palms together.

Sam dropped my hand, then, winked and ran ahead. I thought if I stared at her any more my eyes would pop out. Instead, I followed her and found the others out the back of the camp where the adventure playground was.

Complex climbing frames and rope structures dominated the middle of the field. A zip wire and balance beam stood to the side. Most of the kids were crawling inside the rope tube. Two of the centre staff were shouting instructions to them, while the volunteers and children who were waiting for their turns cheered on those currently in action.

I scanned the area looking for Lucian and found him, squeezed into a corner as far away from the others as possible.

Under the natural shade of a bush, he sat cross-legged, his baseball cap low, and he was reading.

I sat next to him. The novel in his hands was dog-eared and tatty. After a few minutes, he took off his hat, and re-focused on the page, frowning with a deep V in his forehead as he read.

"Why aren't you doing the activity?" I instinctively knew the reason but I wanted to engage him in conversation.

His attention didn't shift from the words. "I am too big to get through the nets. And. It's my reading time."

I wondered. He was lanky for his age. Would he prefer to be doing something else, going on holiday somewhere more exotic? Most boys of his age might be out with their friends. It was the summer after all.

Instead of asking about that, I ventured, "What are you reading? Do you like it?"

He showed me a Philip K. Dick novel, then in his most deadpanned way, he answered, "No. I hate reading and I hate the books I read."

No laughter. Not quite irony. *I need a fucking sense of humour.* It would certainly seem odd to most people if they didn't know Lucian because he wasn't smiling and showing that this was a joke.

"I watch films I hate again and again, too." I could see a slight lilt of Lucian's mouth, just for a fleeting moment before he went back to his book and ignored me.

I remained on the damp grass, keeping Lucian company, and watched the kids having fun, letting their hair down. I remembered the guidance from the brochure, and Sam and Grant: the holiday camp was for the children, not the volunteers. So, it wasn't up to me to force Lucian to try anything.

Eric and Tim were playing in the nearby playground. Coordinating his movements for the ropes would have been too much for Eric, and, like Lucian, he was too big for some of the equipment. Lucian didn't once talk to me again. By the time the activity finished, he had read half of the thin paperback. I thought the fact that we'd shared comfortable silence meant that I'd penetrated his hard shell. Sam suggested that Lucian wasn't difficult to deal with.

I couldn't be more wrong.

At lunch, I led Lucian to the restaurant. The noise hit us first as we entered the dining room. We were the last to arrive. The volunteers and the kids talked animatedly. The senior helpers and the cook were bringing out the food. Sounds vibrated and echoed between the wood floor and the slatted ceiling.

A few steps into the lunch hall, Lucian stopped and stared at the scene in front of him. His feet refused to move, and his right hand flapped. Always the right hand.

"Hey, it's okay. We can sit in the corner." I talked softly as though I was compensating for the noises.

I could tell Lucian had to stop himself from bolting. We walked over to the corner, even though there was still little privacy. Lucian waited until all the others had got their lunch before asking for a plate of chips and sweetcorn. I went up to the serving hatch and conveyed his order, asking for the same and a bowl of green salad for myself.

As we ate, I tried to start a conversation with him. "So, Sam told me you came to the camp last year as well. You must like it."

His hand stilled and he frowned. "My mum needed a break."

No, I don't love it here. I can't stand you all, and please don't pretend to be friendly.

I, somehow, understood all of that except how to deal with it. So, we lapsed into silence once more and ate our lunch.

He concentrated on the food and refused to make eye contact. The scowl on his face never left, though. I must have reminded him that he missed home. *Shit.*

It was hard to tell how he was feeling.

Lucian arranged the chips in rows, pushed to the top left of the plate. The sweetcorn proved a challenge. They were not behaving and staying in the bottom right corner. He struggled a little with the fork and the chips, then he reached out to the bowl of salad, which meant crossing in front of me.

I made a fatal mistake in my attempt to 'help' Lucian. I grabbed his hand. Mine was too cold, but against his slim digits, it felt like burning.

"It's okay. Let me put some on your plate."

But he didn't stop. He desperately tried to reach the leaves; our joined hands hovered above the bowl.

"Let me help you. You want some salad, right?"

"Salad, right."

I took it as a cue to take the fork from his hand. Leaning too close, I tightened on his hand with the fork. "Let me, it's okay."

But he didn't let go of my hand. Instead, he jerked away, switched the fork to his other hand. A sharp pain cut through the back of mine and travelled up my arm. He'd stabbed me with the fork, momentarily pinning my hand to the table. A couple of drops of blood oozed out of the back of my hand. I stared at the wound, unsure how long I was still like that. I must have whimpered. I didn't scream because it'd looked worse than it was. I couldn't feel much pain.

I looked up, and Lucian was watching my hand.

The unruly sweetcorn escaped from the plate and scattered on the floor.

I was aware of Lucian but nothing else, as though we were in a bubble. It was almost peaceful. I couldn't sense the other people in the dining hall at all. Lucian shook his head violently.

I gradually came back to reality, as I could hear rather than see the commotion around us. One of the young girls at the next table, Anna, saw what had happened and she was now screaming. Lucian covered his ears. He stood up, pushing his chair back and trying to shield himself from the distress call by hiding under the table and behind the chair.

Tim and Sam immediately came forward. They stood there while I felt hopeless. I turned around and realised that the other children were horrified and staring. Anna's host hurriedly led her out of the dining room. Sam asked the other pairs to go back to the children's bedrooms, too, so they could take a nap before the afternoon's activities. The kids were curious and some remained focused on us as they departed from the room.

Tim took my hand and inspected the wound. I had little flesh there, so Lucian had only managed to prick the surface of the skin. Even though Anna's scream had ceased, Lucian stayed behind the chair and he started to mumble to himself.

Sam held out her arms as though she was trying to surrender. "Lucian, it's okay. Would you like to go back to your room? Let Tim take you, okay?"

He peered out from under the table. He clutched his chest, and inhaled and exhaled, as if he was hyperventilating, but he managed to stop himself after several minutes. Sam used her eyes to plead for help. Tim came forward and gestured for Lucian to follow.

Sam knelt down. "It's okay. Come on out."

Lucian climbed out slowly and followed Tim. For the first time, he held my gaze, and I could tell he was trying to say sorry. His quickened exhales were beginning to ease. Finally he dropped his head and exited the dining room behind Tim.

Sam smiled calmly, and for the second time in two days, she took my hand—the good one. The back of the other was a little raised and swollen. She led me down the quiet corridor to the small medical room.

It was stuffy in the room, and I was conscious of our close proximity as she sat me on the patient's chair and leaned over me to inspect the back of my hand. Her warm arm touched mine, our hands linked.

I flinched not because of the touch, but the tingling I felt in my groin. My hand should be feeling, not anywhere else in my body. She bent down further to have a look at my wound. I closed my eyes and smelled her: the faint sweat and a grassy kind of scent. I loved that it was earthy rather than feminine. And I found myself inhaling, trying to remember her that way. When I opened my eyes, I saw her brown irises looking right back at me, assessing my face rather than the small stab wound.

I might have noticed the lust in her gaze but my self-doubt asked if I was misinterpreting. My wishful thinking. Perhaps my sweat could be translated as a natural reaction to the non-existent heat of a British summer.

"He hit the bone. Does it hurt?" She dropped my hand to look for the first-aid kit, removing her body heat. *No, come back. Never mind the first-aid kit.*

"Not really." It throbbed a little at first but I'd been thoroughly distracted.

Sam approached me again, and opened the first-aid box and wiped my wound—the reddened flesh—with saline lotion. Her head bowed in front of my chest. Her faint scent filled my nostrils once again.

Then I remembered a similar scene when I fell over during sports day at school and my good friend Ginnie had come with me to the medical room. She even cried with worry. We were close, and I'd marvelled at her beautiful round brown eyes, fat teardrops and freckles, and my insides swelled. Ginnie had smelt of something sweet and fragrant. We were eleven. I had not thought of Ginnie after she moved away to Australia. But as Sam was patching up my hand, the memory came back to me.

Sam seemed to know what she was doing with the sterilising and she finished with a plaster. "If you feel anything unusual. It starts hurting bad, anything like that. You need to tell me right away. I'll take you to A and E."

I nodded. It didn't hurt, and even if it did, I couldn't blame Lucian.

"Will Lucian be okay?" I whispered. I didn't want him to be sent home.

Sam lifted her eyes to meet mine. "Of course. You?"

"Yes. I'm fine. Lucian would love to go home, though. Sorry, I fucked up."

She shook her head. "I'm not sure if his mum will be okay with that. And, you haven't messed up. Believe me."

I'd only been there a day. I'd already failed the boy I was supposed to care for, and my insides were still trembling as Sam held onto my hand. The dull pain was long forgotten. Instead, I was embarrassed and aroused in a mess of warring emotions.

I avoided her eyes. It was easier that way. There was so much I wanted to ask her, needed to ask her, but I didn't. I'd do nothing and wait for the two weeks to be over. I'd tell myself that it was a silly crush and nothing more. We all had our lives outside of this, and hers would certainly exclude me. Yet, I knew she would impart the wisdom that I was to be convinced of, and I wanted to hear it.

Becoming eighteen was supposed to be a sign of childhood passing, but what I'd learn about myself in fourteen days would somehow turn all previous years of socialisation upside down, as though I had been stripped of my adult status, and rebuilt.

As if Sam knew that already, she pulled away and ruffled my hair as though I were a child. I wore it short. The red strands hung over us. I could never grow it out. Instead of looking like a pre-Raphaelite beauty, I usually ended up as if I had a giant orange over my head.

"Remember, if anything changes, you need to come to me right away." She looked the most serious I'd seen her yet.

"All right."

"You're okay to carry on tomorrow? Tim can swap with you, if you want?" she asked tentatively.

No, I wasn't going to regret being Lucian's helper. I was even more determined to get it right.

"I'm staying with Lucian if he'll let me." I smiled.

DAY 3

I WOKE EVERY DAY as if I was waiting for a date, needing to get up, see to my charge, and impress the hell out of Sam. I found myself trying to catch her attention. I didn't even know if she liked girls, let alone a young inexperienced one like me. She often caught me watching her when she was speaking to another volunteer or organising the activities, and she would smile at me. Her grin lit up her face and made my heart flutter.

I couldn't stop myself from thinking about her. From that point of view, it was going to be two very long weeks.

Lucian was a good distraction. He was, in fact, the perfect partner in crime, making me use all my senses differently and forget about my Sam obsession.

After breakfast on our third day, Lucian ran back into his room and sat on his bunk, burying his head in his hands. "No! No! That wasn't in the timetable you showed me."

All the activities were planned in advance. Lucian had already seen the timetable and decided whether he would participate or not. He also had his own schedule.

Sam and I followed him but kept our distance away from his bed. Sam tried to placate him. "We have to change the schedule because it's raining, darling."

Sam and Grant had decided to change the planned outdoor activity due to the weather. Big drops of rain were hitting the wood structure, like a few bars of staccato. The air felt damp. I stared at the water-soaked windows.

Lucian lifted his eyes and gazed at us for a moment, his irises large with indignation but his words steady as always, showing conviction in his stubbornness. "I won't go to an indoor play centre."

They were driving the kids away from camp so they could use the indoor frames, slides and ball pools. I had to agree that it was not really an appropriate option for him because he was too tall and too old, though Eric was going to come with us anyway and he'd probably have a drink and lunch while the younger kids played. I could do that with Lucian, but I also understood why he was reluctant. I imagined that a confined space full of screaming and running kids was not Lucian's thing. Sam and I looked at each other. She arched an eyebrow like a question mark.

"I… I could stay with Lucian," I offered despite what had happened last night. Lucian might not want me to, though.

Sam hesitated. "Lucian?"

He flapped his hand and averted his eyes after stealing a glance at me. No objection from Lucian was as good as a 'yes' since he wasn't usually shy about his demands.

Sam considered me for long moments and nodded. "Okay. Grant can stay behind, too, if you need him. I'll take Rose and Beth." She gazed intently at Lucian again. "Lucian, you'll be good, yeah?"

He stared at his feet with the same blankness and did not reply. Sam tilted her head, so I followed her out.

Once we were away from Lucian's room and his earshot, we stopped and Sam turned to speak to me. "To be honest, a play centre would overwhelm him. Are you happy with this? Honestly. I'm sure Grant can deal with him, and you can come with us to Tumbleweed."

I nodded. "Come on! I'm getting used to him. Even another fork incident wouldn't be that bad." I smiled, amused by my mockery.

Sam grinned at my little joke. "Ha! Come on. Don't you get another injury. I have to write a stupid report every time something like that happens."

I was oddly confident about my ability to cope with Lucian. I didn't know why. It was as though Lucian stabbing me with a fork meant his heart was open to me now. I couldn't care less that he'd hurt me. I touched my chin with that same hand; I'd put a fresh plaster on the spot this morning.

"Well, good luck with it. Don't hesitate to get Grant to call me," Sam said at the end. She turned abruptly. I watched her strong back as she left, and exhaled.

When I returned to Lucian's room, he was reading his book.

I sat on the chair by his bed. "What would you like to do today, Lucian?"

He didn't look up from his book. "It's Tuesday. I draw in the morning."

"Okay. Let's get your art materials out, then."

He put his book down and carefully slotted a bookmark.

I took his bag from under the bunk, but he snatched it back without meeting my eyes. He brought out colour pencils, a pencil case, a pad of paper and placed them in a neat arrangement on the narrow desk. The pencils lined up tidily in their rainbow colour range, and the paper sat squarely on the flat surface. He used a ruler and the pencils to draw sixteen rectangles—two rows with eight each. He took out a yellow pencil and filled in the boxes except one. The room was quiet except for our breaths and the sharpened colour pencil tips that danced across the paper, making a scratchy sound.

"What are they?" I was curious.

Lucian raised his eyes and, as if he'd seen me for the first time, his pupils dilated. "Lights."

"Lights?"

"You're repeating what I said, and yes." He breathed out, as if exasperated by my ignorance.

"Lights, yes." Repetition felt good. It really did.

"The lights in the main hall. Two columns and eight shades in each."

I scrutinised his picture again. It was meticulously drawn. If I stopped thinking about the rectangles as shapes, I could see them from Lucian's perspective. I had never thought to look up, to see what kinds of lights there were. I closed my eyes and tried to remember the warm glow from them.

When I opened my eyes again, the afterglow of the yellow had imprinted in my mind's eye. I pointed to the blank one. "Why is that one different from the others?"

Lucian's head covered the drawing as he concentrated. "It broke. On the day we arrived, it flickered. Then it stopped working. It should be fixed." The grave tone in his voice said it was an important issue.

Imperfection. It made sense. None of us would have noticed something so small, but it was beautiful. If it was important to him, then it was not trivial.

"What else do you like looking at? Do you count anything else?"

"Lots of things need fixing. The loudspeakers there. They are not balanced. The one on the right-hand side hangs sideways, so it sounds wrong. No one cared when they played the movie last night." He delivered this piece of information with authority, his voice steady.

When he finished the first drawing, he tore out another blank sheet and drew the lights again, slowly, moving the ruler and the angle of the sheet systematically. After he finished the rectangles, he filled them out with the yellow again, making sure that it stayed within the lines.

Before meeting Lucian, I'd thought I was impulsive and sometimes too twitchy, but he taught me patience, to sit for hours, working in repetition. I would spend some of those hours writing stories or reading books. I read my tales later and found them unbearably childish, but they reminded me of Lucian and that summer. My heart would ache for the innocence.

"Tell me more about the lights." I couldn't help it. He'd made me care about them as much as he did.

He never broke his concentration but continued to draw and colour. "I like them."

At some point, I looked up from my book to catch Lucian with his eyes closed and his head tilted.

"You okay?" I asked.

Lucian didn't answer for a while but his eyelids fluttered. Finally, he asked me a question instead. "What can you hear?"

I copied him and closed my eyes. It was quiet since all the kids and volunteers had gone. Grant was probably in the office. At first, I only heard our breaths, but I persevered. The rain pattered on the window and the wood of the building. The sounds were different, more vibrant than any rainfall I'd heard before. At intervals, they were muted. Lucian hadn't said a word.

I thought Lucian was pulling my leg, one of his quirky things, but then something changed. My consciousness took me away. It was as if I was transposed outside in the damp. Birds were chattering despite the rain. Tree branches swayed in the breeze. The rain and wind increased their velocity like a crescendo before they retreated again. When the wind pelted the raindrops hard against the windows, the sounds were like small hammers on a dulcimer.

When the rain eased for a few moments, I'd hear a distant bark. The gust picked up once more, howling through the structure of the centre. I couldn't tell how long Lucian and I had been listening to the symphony of nature.

I didn't open my eyes until Lucian spoke. "You heard them, then?"

I nodded.

Lucian's pencils glided across the drawing. When he did glance at me, it was as if he saw through me. "Most people can't. All they hear is the noise they make themselves."

I was mesmerised by that idea, and his ordered picture.

"What do your schoolmates think about the stuff you draw?"

He stopped to sharpen the yellow pencil. "I don't go to school."

Two days with Lucian and I'd almost forgotten that we were in a camp for disabled children. Lucian had abilities that were not exactly valued by most people. And most schools wanted to teach kids who were cardboard cutouts. Kids were often little tyrants who would taunt anyone who didn't belong, and pick on those weaker than them. I must have stared at him. 'Sorry' nearly escaped my mouth but I kept mum because it seemed like the wrong word.

"My mum home-schools me." Something else clicked into my information bank about Lucian. I imagined his mother working hard to teach him at home, protecting him from harm. It probably explained why she needed a break and how Lucian felt abandoned being sent to a summer camp and forced to be befriended by a bunch of strangers.

I wondered why he was home-schooled; perhaps I'd asked him out loud.

"When I was eleven, some boys thought it was funny to laugh at me." He raised his right hand and tilted his head towards the window and the sky beyond, his fingers drawing in the air. "My mum was late collecting me one day, and they hurt me."

His hand stalled and it started to shake. I wanted to hug him, but this time I knew better.

Instead, I asked quietly, "What happened?"

His eyelids fluttered once more. Still half-facing the clouds outside, he mumbled, hardly audibly, "They hit me and took my trousers down and…"

"Did they hurt you?" I wasn't sure if I should ask him what they tried to do when they took his pants down. I had no right to ask him to re-live something bad for my benefit, but I was too concerned to stop myself from asking the question.

For a few seconds, I wasn't sure if he'd answer, but he did.

"I beat them up. This boy Simon."

I was worried about him. I wouldn't expect that he was the one who hurt the bullies. *Was he quick to respond, to stand up for himself? Like he did last night?*

"I broke his teeth and I hurt him pretty bad. They had to take him to the hospital. After that, they said I had to go to a special school and Mum didn't want me to go, so she looks after me at home." As he explained it to me, he started drawing another picture of the lights.

I could visualise the scene. He wasn't small in stature and he'd be strong when provoked. The indignation of the bully. The school put in an impossible position. His mum's protectiveness. I stared at the teenager for long moments. *How do you feel about it all, Lucian?*

That night I flopped onto my bed exhausted. I observed Tim reading under the weak lamp.

"I'm so knackered." A big yawn escaped despite myself.

He gazed over the top edge of his paperback. "Yeah, well. Coping with the emotional engagement is hard. At least you don't have the physical stuff to deal with." He was referring to Eric.

I agreed. I'd come into this rather blind, so the reality shocked me.

Tim put a bookmark in his novel. "Did you say you're the youngest in the family?"

"Yeah. I've got an older brother." He was a couple of years older than me, but we didn't exactly get on. Just like my mum, he left me alone unless he had something smartass to say to me. I mostly kept myself to myself at home.

His intelligent eyes assessed me. "Then, you don't even have experience of looking after younger siblings."

"No. But, I'm not surprised that the kids' parents need some time off." I thought of the woman who cried at the beginning of the camp, tearing up when she saw her child going off without her. "Caring for Lucian is tiring, but I feel guilty for thinking it."

"Don't be. It's only natural."

I smiled. "Thanks."

"It's definitely more working than holiday. Do you like it, though? Think you'll come back next year?"

"Hmm. Ask me again after this ends, or a few months down the line." It was a life-changing experience, but I didn't know if I'd repeat it next year. My future was wide open.

Tim laughed, his shoulders shaking with amusement. "Yeah. I was absolutely horrified at first, and swore I'd never do this again. Here I am three years later, happily wiping Eric's bottom."

I chuckled, too, a little impishly. I'd seen Tim clean Eric up because he had to wear incontinence pads. I was uncomfortable about it at first, but after a couple of days here, I'd begun to get used to the kids. I no longer thought of them as strange and vulnerable.

"You okay?" Tim asked.

"Yeah, why?"

He winced. "I've seen Lucian during previous years' camps. He has a foul temper, for sure. I know it's part of his condition, but none of his helpers before were able to deal with it, or stay with him. Sam had to keep changing his partners. But, you seem happy. You get on with Lucian and…"

I chuckled. "What? Even with the fork incident?"

Tim laughed. "It's just a meltdown. Believe me, I've seen him in a much worse state. He's more grown up this year. You're doing great."

The compliment was ego boosting, but I was still wary of a repeat of Lucian's meltdown. "It's early days. I don't want to jinx it."

"No, you don't."

"Why have you volunteered?" *And kept at it.*

Tim cocked his head as if deciding whether he'd tell me. "I like working with children. I'm doing my teacher training, and this is extra experience." He paused for moments. I waited for him to continue.

"My mum died when I was thirteen."

"I'm sorry," I offered.

Tim raised his hand to accept my very belated condolence. "It's ten years ago. I'm an only child. My dad seems to have decided not to date or remarry. We had help, though, from relatives, friends, good teachers. That's what made me believe it's important to give to children as much as we can, in whichever capacity we can."

I nodded. It made sense.

Tim continued, "I'm gay. So, I reckon I'm not going to have kids in the traditional way. I love helping them grow. I want to work with them, and volunteer in my spare time." The sparkle in his eyes filled me with joy. If all our teachers felt the same, we'd have a nation of happy kids.

I smiled. "That's so cool. I wish I had as much conviction as you."

Tim chuckled. "You're here. You're doing a good thing." He raised his hand again, this time to high-five me. I obliged.

"Maybe you can adopt?" I suggested.

Tim smiled. "Yeah. I think I'll find a good partner first. You know how much work raising kids is now."

He went back to his book for a few minutes while I wrote in my diary. I wondered whether I should ask him. I was intrigued and he obviously knew the working of these camps well.

"What do you think of Sam?" I tried to sound as casual as I could.

He hesitated, putting down his book yet again. There was something he wasn't saying. Tim was only a few years older than me, but he'd finished university, was training to be a teacher and had volunteered with Sam before. Eventually, he breathed out. "Sam. She's enigmatic, for sure."

He uttered those words like a warning. I hated the feeling of being too young and innocent to comprehend caution, but I was already far too infatuated.

I had glimpses of evidence that I ignored. Sam talking on the mobile to someone, standing away from the crowd, listening and speaking in a hushed voice. Her face seemed serious, different from how she was with the kids and how she talked to me.

DAY 4

It seemed that every day was a struggle against Lucian's sensibility.

After an hour in the pool, the kids were going to tackle the maze, but Lucian declared he had to do writing. *It's in my schedule.* He felt unable to join in many of the activities, but most of the time it was because the other kids were too noisy. They were far too much stimulation for Lucian.

I managed to persuade him to take his notebook and write outside, so at least we were sitting near the group. The sun had returned and we were set to have great weather for the rest of the time. I sat next to him, watching the kids get lost in the maze through the tint of my sunglasses, with the warm sun touching my bare skin.

Lucian hunched over and wrote in small controlled letters. His writing was extremely neat, but he liked to confine himself to the corner of the page, no matter how big the white space was. This morning, he was filling up the pages of a bound notebook.

"What are you writing?"

"My diary." He didn't look up. "My mum will read it. I'm telling her what we've been doing here."

I knew better than to remind him that he wasn't at home, so I avoided talking about how she might have missed him. "What've you written so far?"

He took so long to answer, I thought he wasn't going to. His head bowed low, he quietly responded at the end, "I told her I had one meltdown, and I hurt this lady. I won't do it again."

His apology. I didn't expect one but it was good to hear it. Tears pricked the back of my eyes. I could only whisper, "Thank you."

Lucian continued to scribble, but I saw him glance at my injured hand. So I suggested, "Do you want to touch it?"

He waited a few beats. "Okay." His fingers reached out and they ghosted my hand. Our skin connected, and the touch magnified in importance. All around us, laughter of the children drifted and filled the air with a renewed optimism.

But life for Lucian did seem a long string of challenges. The kitchen made a fatal mistake by changing the lunch menu because they ran out of one ingredient or another. He stared at the gooey beef stew and a lasagne.

"Only pizza, chips, sweetcorn and macaroni cheese, tomato sauce with no bits, mash, Quorn sausages. I put them on my form." Lucian's arms were crossed in front of his chest, protecting and protesting. He wore his trademark frown. I gazed at Rose and Beth who were helping to dish up the food, but we all felt hopeless in the situation.

Sam came forward. "Lucian, we have spaghetti and meatballs tonight. I promise we will have one of those things for you tomorrow."

"The tomato sauce has green bits in it." His face was pinched. This was a serious problem.

"It's basil," Beth offered meekly.

"I don't eat that."

I intervened, my protective host persona taking over. "Would you like some bread? Tomorrow, I'll make sure they cook something you'll eat." I glanced at Sam, appealing for her help. *Whatever you do, sort him out.*

Lucian shifted his feet. He behaved as though he was sulking, and yet his facial expression was rather bland except the V between his eyebrows. He was more perplexed and frustrated than angry. It was difficult for him to accept what a disorder the world was in. I recognised his traits now. Many of the other kids had stopped eating and stared at him, wondering if they should have a complaint, too.

Eventually, he uttered, "Okay."

I put the bread and butter on his plate. He walked over to his corner and sat down, while I tried to hide a sigh.

Sam smiled at me and whispered in my ear, "I'll personally drive to the village store and cook him the damn meals if it causes such disruption." She then strolled off.

I grinned at her departing form. During those days, I seemed to be obsessed with nothing but parts of her: the dark eyes, tan and taut skin, the boldness of her speech. My heart sang when she was around, and my eyes automatically searched for her whenever I entered a room. It was a crush or something incurable.

For the rest of the time, alongside Lucian, I had to be grown up and responsible. Hell, the kids' parents had to be desperate enough to let us look after them at the camp. But no judgement. I'd never know what permanently living with a teenager like Lucian would be like. If I were his mother or maybe big sister, I'd love him so much and want to be there no matter what. And it'd hurt seeing how he struggled to fit in.

He ate his bread quickly and drank the milk, stealing glances at me or some part of me anyway as he always avoided people's faces. I was getting used to Lucian and all his quirks as though I'd known him for some time.

The guests tended to go to bed early. By nine, they'd have all disappeared to their bunks. Lucian would go to his room and read.

The evenings were time for ourselves, time to relax and unwind.

It was close to midnight. Sometimes the children used it during the day, but at this time of the night the swimming pool was usually quiet. Tonight, I'd come particularly late, having impulsively decided to have a late swim. I came out of the changing room, gripping my towel, and trotted along while my flip-flops made a plop-plop noise. The chlorine smelt strong. The fluorescent tubes were too bright, bathing the cavernous room with blues and greens.

The splashing of water caught my attention first. A lone figure was there gliding through the lanes.

Sam wore a black one piece that showed off her shapely body. She was swimming freestyle; her movements were powerful even though she wasn't perfect in her strokes. Water parted around her as she came up for breaths. Her body stretched and glided along in between the waves. I stared, mesmerised, forgetting that I'd been motionless by the steps.

Drops of water turned sparkly, clinging to her golden skin as if they were jewels. I was paralysed from the potency of the image. When I realised I'd been gazing at her for too long, I gingerly moved to enter the pool. She glanced up, taking her goggles off and soaking up my physique in return. Instead of feeling self-conscious, it felt as though this was natural, that our bodies should announce themselves to each other.

I smiled and let my skin acclimatise to the slight chill of the pool water.

Sam grinned at me. "It's one of the best things about this camp. You're the first person who's come to swim this late at night, though. I normally have the whole place to myself."

"Sorry to disturb your peace."

"Nah. I'm nearly finished. Go ahead." She turned, secured her goggles and was off again. I followed.

Sam left after completing a couple more lengths. I'd forgotten about the strokes because all I could think about was her lithe body like a big fish, possessing the water. I nearly choked and came up for air, just in time to see her pushing open the door into the showers.

DAY 5

I climbed onto the driver's seat of the van. The plaster on the back of my hand was a reminder of what Lucian had done. No doubt Sam had taken me along for the ride to give me a break from caring for him, from the intensity of being there for someone this way. I felt like I'd known the boy for five years not four days, and yet, he was as opaque to me as the black shade on the window. Something had been changing, though, between Lucian and me. His body language said so. We didn't always need to talk, touch or make eye contact. There were other means of communication and he was teaching me his ways. I closed my eyes and listened, tuning into the cacophony of sounds, some noisier, some no more than whispers.

When I opened them again, I watched Sam glance sidelong and smile, her dimples deepening. Hesitating only for a moment, she turned back to watch the road.

I stared at the passing green lanes. If I watched Sam, I would do something crazy like touch her. At least this way, all I could see was a blurred shadow of her in reflection.

We had to drive fifteen miles to the nearest town or about seven to the village shop, so the latter was where we went. The dusty little emporium doubled up as a post office. It was how these places were before the post office branches all closed down. Sam casually parked the van outside, jumped down and stormed around in her desert boots. I hung back.

The bell announced our arrival as we pushed the door open. The proprietor—an elderly gent—barely looked up. Sam held the shopping list of supplies, including ingredients that would fulfil Lucian's meal requests. He'd won, as always. Sam grabbed the food efficiently and I helped her load the bags in the van. I thought we were heading straight back to the camp, but she sat down on a bench in the village green outside of the shop. Her flat chest and strong muscle stretched the tank top.

She extended her long legs and waved me over. "Come on, take a break."

I sat down with a stomach full of butterflies. I wanted to be with her, but I was also afraid of betraying my attraction to her. She lit a cigarette, inhaled the smoke and blew it out slowly, savouring the taste.

"Want one?" She held out the pack. I shook my head. I couldn't help but enjoy sitting next to her, sharing the brief break, despite my apprehension.

"What was it like at college?" I asked when Sam finished her cigarette. I'd probably subconsciously wanted a safe subject.

Leaning across the back of the bench, she propped her head up with her hand and looked intently at me. "I had a good time. I belonged to all kinds of clubs. There were so many activities. So much to discover and so little time. I used to run a lesbian film club once a month."

I swallowed. My guess was correct, and now I didn't know what I'd do with that knowledge.

She sat up again, crossing her legs, and took a swig from her water bottle. As if she was reading my mind, she added, "I realised I was into girls when I was maybe eleven."

Avoiding her gaze, I focused on a stray lint in my T-shirt, pretending that the heat inside of me didn't exist.

Sam stood up abruptly as though she was startled by a revelation. "Come on. We'd better drive back."

We got in the van, and Sam pulled away from the village. I wondered how she had begun working with children with disabilities. Did she study the subject at college?

I might have asked the question aloud, or, she kept guessing what I was thinking. Uncanny.

"I went to Oxford and majored in Physics. So, nothing to do with disabilities and children."

I half turned, while trying to keep my eyes on the road. Physics sounded so clever. None of my classmates made it to Oxbridge. I'd gone to the local college for my A' levels and my acceptance by the London university was already an exceptional result.

I wanted to listen to her talk forever. "Any advice for me?"

"You're going after the summer, yeah? Well, I'd say live your life. There's so much beyond the walls of our universities, outside of book learning." She gazed out of the windshield, her right elbow resting on the open window, while she kept her left hand on the wheel. Casually, not a care in the world.

"Shouldn't you be solving mathematical problems or something? What made you work with these kids?"

She shrugged. "I wanted to do something real, to actually make a difference, have a direct impact on someone's life. Oxford was fun but it was too privileged. All my classmates' parents had villas in Europe."

I wondered if she really believed that or if she was telling me because I was clearly a local lass who was not particularly well off. The point about making an impact, too, was inspiring.

"I'm going to be the first in my family to go to university," I mused. My dad was an electrician before he had an affair and left, and my mum was a hairdresser. I was basically a working-class girl without a hint of sophistication.

Sam asked me what I was about to study and why. When I told her that I was 'interested in people', she laughed.

She tried to stop herself, causing the van to swerve. Luckily there was no traffic on these country lanes. "Sorry. It's honourable. Really. I'm sorry to be such a cynic. I don't think university equips us to face the real world, though, whether you study physics or sociology."

Later, when I too was out there 'in the real world', I thought of Sam and how she might have planted that seed in me about how to live my life, that I should make a difference. At that time, speaking with someone ten years older than me was revelatory. It was as though Sam was speaking a new language structured by the grammar of life.

As we drove on, I thought about wanting to be like her, and then immediately chided myself for sounding like a child. *What do you want to be when you grow up?* I wanted to be like Sam. I knew by instinct that I would be a different person by the end of the working holiday. It was exhilarating and frightening at the same time.

School, which broke up only some weeks before, already seemed so far away. That was the old me, and this boy Jerome had liked that me. Tall, broad, muscular and dreadlocked. He was lots of girls' wet dream. Last year, he'd asked me out to the movies one Saturday night. It was supposed to be an instant cult film that Jerome had sworn was the next big thing. We ate subs for dinner and tried to converse.

I like hip-hop.

Oh, no. Left field for me.

Football.

Hmm, swimming.

Pizza. Fried chicken.

We'd found that we had absolutely nothing in common. We chuckled.

Opposites could attract.

Yeah, you're great but I don't really think it's happening.

We'd laughed some more. He bought way too much popcorn, and the cult film was too obscure for either of us to understand. *But there's cool music in the score.* Still, it was a good first date, and we'd kissed. It was more a sweet peck than a passionate tongue twist. I wondered what the athletic Jerome was doing now.

"Did you say you're going to study sociology at uni?" Sam jolted me out of my musings.

I repeated my non-existent résumé and why I'd chosen the subject.

She nodded, as if she understood. I supposed ten years were enough to make someone realise what one should have done and what could have happened. Should. Could. Would. All the words that meant little to the youthful me. So, I did the only thing that I felt like doing and watched her from the passenger seat and smiled. She glanced back at me when she could and returned with a grin, showing off the two subtle dimples that graced the edges of her mouth. What if my feelings were entirely one-sided? It'd be embarrassing, and I'd have to live through the humiliation for the next week.

DAY 6

THE WALK TOOK in a pine forest and stream. Most of the kids came despite varying degrees of disability. Eric seemed excited alongside Tim, his hands flapping. He smiled wide, saliva dripping down his chin. Tim wiped it away.

It was only a few kilometres, but the hike was a challenge to someone like Eric and the younger ones. Lucian had no problem physically, but he didn't seem able to get his head around the following-in-a-line part. It was making my job that much harder, but I was also amused by his ability to make the walk so much more exciting. I'd learned over the last few days that unless he was drawing or writing, he found it hard to stay still.

"Lucian, where are you going?" He'd already run off to an invisible target. I wasn't sure if he could hear me, so I ran after him down a shaded side track. He knelt down and touched the thorns of some brambles, lost in a world of his own.

"Be careful of the sharp needles." I sank down to his level.

He withdrew his hands but continued to look at the varied vegetation.

"This one." Lucian pointed to some long stems of tiny leaves. "They close up when you touch them. See." He demonstrated. I remembered being fascinated by those, too, when I was young.

He picked up a small grit stone that was mostly white. "This is quartz. It's not so common in the Dark Peak. The Dark Peak has sedimentary rock."

I considered him. "Where did you read about this?"

He palmed the quartz. "On the internet. May I keep this?"

"Of course." He would go on to collect quite a few keepsakes from our trips out.

I'd have liked him to do whatever he wanted but we needed to follow the group. "Come on." I had to herd him along to keep up with the others, and borrowing a leaf from Sam's command book was as good as any.

He reluctantly stood up, and we walked side by side back to the main path. "I don't like this," he muttered. And again and again he told me how he disliked hiking. We soldiered on regardless.

Our steps were sometimes soft on the soil ground, and sometimes hard on the crunchy leaves and branches. When we were shrouded in the thicket, I used my body to open a path, disturbing the brambles, while Lucian followed. As we walked close to each other, I became more aware that he was taller and broader than me even though he was three years younger. Sometimes I'd forget his age because his facial expression was blander than his peers, so I couldn't employ the same communication tools that I'd use with other teenagers, like the younger pupils at my school. At those moments, I felt bad for treating him like a child. But I was learning fast. Every day, I discovered Lucian's quirks and understood them better.

He was challenging himself. I knew that. Trips were unpredictable, but he was forewarned and he'd forced himself to participate as much as he could. Whenever we joined in an activity, he'd stare and then followed my lead stoically. His growing trust in me had started from the fork incident.

I glanced back over my shoulder to see that he'd picked up a bit of speed. My urge was to hold his hand, but he wouldn't appreciate it.

"All right?"

He nodded.

A few minutes later. "Josie, shall we go down that path?" He pointed to another track that promised greater adventures.

I discovered on this walk that paths were star attractions to him. Lucian wanted to explore all of them. He was a walking contradiction. He liked order and couldn't stand anything unscheduled, but he was also fascinated by nature, which was unpredictable.

I saw the next pair of host and guest about six feet in front of us. "No, Lucian. We're staying on the main trail, remember? If we explore every side track, we will never reach the top."

Lucian's arms flopped to his sides but reluctantly he continued.

We'd been walking in dusk under the layer of trees, the morning light only filtering through the gaps in the woods occasionally. We'd come to an opening because I could feel the warmth of the sun on my face and exposed arms. Instead of quickening our steps, we stopped because Lucian had. He closed his eyes and tilted his head to face the sun. I stood next to him.

I wasn't going to ask what he was doing; I simply copied his gesture. When I closed my eyes and faced the rays, I saw the afterglow that was brighter than ever. The colours lingered long.

He taught me when I tried to see without my eyes, the vision was all the more vivid. I'd learned over those days that if I only focused on one sense, it would become more vivid, like that day we listened to the rain. Lucian reached out and touched my little finger, the tiniest gesture sent a thrill through me. I knew the enormity even though his touch was feathery. An earthy scent engulfed us. I was so emotional from sharing this moment that the warm sun on my skin, the fragrance of summer, our light breaths came together like a hypnotist's chant.

This was the moment when I knew I'd courted the light. In the middle of the forest, as the stream flowed closely by. When I turned, I saw Lucian gazing at me, a rare smile on his face. He was beautiful like that.

We wanted to capture that instant and never let go, but after long minutes, I grudgingly urged us on. "Come on. We have to catch up."

We came to a small rock platform overlooking the moor. Only six of the pairs had made it up, and most of them looked tired from exertion. Eric hugged Tim, who scratched his head, embarrassed by the physical contact. The teenager hopped around a bit, delighted by his own achievement.

A breeze grazed my face as I tilted my head to catch the rays, and when I opened my eyes Sam was standing next to me, replicating my gesture. Early heather carpeted the field in front of us. I wondered if she, too, had courted the light that afternoon, whether she'd opened her heart to the spell of summer.

DAY 7

"This morning I have two hours of drawing from ten a.m." Lucian clutched his drawing pad, pencil case and colour pencils, waiting for me by his door.

I could almost hear a 'come on'. It seemed that was all we used in order to command. Sam was too impatient. I'd tried to coax Lucian into joining in the group activities, and he wanted his way.

He read the time on his watch and his lips thinned into a line of displeasure. "O nine fifty-eight."

I smiled because he sounded like he was in the military or some other regimented environment. I guess in a way he was in his own strict regime.

We went to the day room. Some of the other kids were running around outside, using the adventure playground. Lucian had decided he'd grown too big for most of the outdoor facilities here, though I gathered he didn't feel comfortable with too many stimulants around.

We found two seats close to the window. He laid the pencils out neatly and started drawing. Yellow dots in neat rows and columns within a circle. Petals delicately graced the edge of the sphere. I read a book while letting him create. Peace and calm claimed me.

After filling the paper completely with exquisite yellow flowers, he took out a fine black pen and added thin strands.

"Sunflowers?" I asked. We'd looked at them yesterday in the grounds of the activity centre. Lucian had tilted his head and squinted in the sun and observed, and memorised. His flowers were absolutely stunning and life-like. They were shining and proudly present under the sun.

"Hmm," he answered. I was glad he'd found new subjects to draw while on this trip.

When he finished the first drawing, he carefully tore it from the pad and started immediately on the next one. A frown formed on his forehead as he concentrated.

"Lucian, what do you do with your drawings?" I imagined his room at home full of neat piles of these acutely observed pictures.

"Mum helps me put them in files."

As I thought. They'd never see the light of day but lay happily, recording his mind.

I took up the first drawing. "Do you ever give them to anyone? Or show them off? I mean, I'd love to have this as a reminder of the camp, if it's okay with you." I felt as though I was exploiting him, to even ask for his creation like this.

He looked up from the piece of paper and stared at me for a brief moment. "You mean…you think they're good?"

"Yes, absolutely. More than good. Has no one told you so?" I felt bad for him if that was the case.

Lucian shook his head slowly. "Usually, only my mum sees them really. She loves them. I have categories, and she helps me put my drawings away." He went back to his art, and didn't give the drawing to me. I didn't press.

Sam and I took the bikes out to the village store when the kids were having their afternoon nap. It was as if Sam made excuses about things we needed, because the holiday complex was well stocked. Sam's strong legs pedalling became an enduring image, while I struggled to keep up, changing gears a little too late on the undulating country paths.

"Come on!" she shouted over her shoulder as we rode the few miles out to the shop.

The hot sun had come out during those July weeks. I was soon sweating with the exertion, but it was exhilarating at the same time as the wind blew in my face.

The dusty small post office and general store was the nearest spot of civilisation to the camp. Sam stealthily brought out her packet of cigarettes. She couldn't smoke around the kids, so she'd have one when we were away from the group. She grinned like a naughty child because we were taking a breather from work, bunking off during the guests' afternoon rest. A cigarette in her mouth, she leaned against the stone cottage that housed the shop, her slender frame perfectly moulding to the mossy grey.

"Come on," she whispered when she finished the ciggie. I followed, inhaling the lingering scent of cigarette smoke as we entered the shop. A bell rang over our heads, announcing our arrival to the proprietor.

Sam took too long pouring over relic merchandise, pointing some out so we could giggle under our breaths. Pairs of flesh-coloured tights with packaging that might have dated back to the 1980s, teddy bears still in wrappers but which appeared to have seen better days. Sun-bleached pale labels. We drifted over to the food section, which fared no better.

I chuckled at the two kinds of limp white bread, tins of beans and carrots. I dreaded reading their sell-by dates.

Sam eyed the small chest freezer. "What about an ice lolly? Would you like one, Josephine?" She was working hard to suppress her glee.

I pouted. "I'm not twelve."

Opening the heavy glass door of the small freezer, she pulled out a multicoloured tube. "I want one."

I stopped her hand that was closing the cold door. "Me too." The warmth of our joined hands contrasted with the temperature of the ice stick.

She paid the owner and we walked out. Cycling several miles to the nearest store and eating ice lollies… It was the kind of extravagance that one could only indulge in during the summer holidays. We stood by the side wall of the squat building and tore open the wrappers. Between licking and biting into the ice, we grinned at each other.

All around us, as if transformed by childish magic, the mossy summer air chimed. Birds chirped overhead. The smiles on our faces never left.

I was so close to Sam, I smelled a faint scent of something lightly flowery. Jasmine, perhaps. I'd always associate that fragrance with the heady sensation of attraction to a hot-blooded woman. The tattoo on her skull fascinated me. A no-entry sign peeked out from under the short stubble. Did she know my desire for her, and would she decide to spend the next week fighting it and taunting me, ignoring whatever was hanging in the air until it was time to go home?

She leaned in and licked my lolly. Mine was lime and lemon and tangy to taste. I shook my head at her childlike behaviour. While she wasn't looking at me, I returned the favour. She had some kind of multicoloured fruit stick that tasted like berries. That earned me a laugh from her.

We clicked our lollies together as though we were toasting. To what, I wasn't sure, but as our faces neared each other, I was captured by the warmth, by an imagination of togetherness. It felt as though the world had become only the two of us, and I didn't want to have to return home. I didn't want to think about university. Perhaps stolen moments were the most precious. They were fleeting; they kept us on edge. *Is this the day when we'll take the van out for a short chat down a country lane? Will we cycle to the village and get an ice cream or lolly again?* Most days we were far too busy looking after the kids to do anything. The actions that were not repeated only became imprinted in my mind as the best representations of the summer.

In my room, I found a postcard that I'd packed with me to write home. On the small rectangle, I drew the cartoon of a girl eating an ice lolly. She had short hair and freckles, as the sun bore down on her. It made me think of Lucian's drawings, though, which were so controlled and detailed. I couldn't draw like that. Mine was free and childlike. I never sent the postcard home.

Later, Tim had gone out with a couple of the other workers. Their mission was to find the nearest pub and have a drink. I could understand it. Some of the volunteers were leaving tomorrow and their replacements would arrive. The constant demands of our guests were driving some of us insane. Caring for Lucian was hard work and exhausting, but I was glad that he didn't have to get used to another helper. I was learning new things every day. I sensed Lucian's trust in me developing, manifested in small things like his furtive glances at me. Minor victories felt like triumphs.

But tonight, I'd stayed behind, craving solitude. I liked Tim and I got on with all the other volunteers, but it was also a rare opportunity to be silent. I went to see the willow tree that I'd discovered next to a stream, and walked a few miles on my own, meeting no one on the way.

Then I read in bed and wrote in my journal. The moon was bright enough to cast light into the room while I worked under the desk lamp. I'd written about Sam, and put the diary carefully in the locker in case anyone should read about my infatuation. My eyes drooped eventually but I couldn't get to sleep.

The night chill had little effect on my imagined heat. I changed the sheet, so it was crisp and fresh against my bare skin. I lifted my vest but the cool surface of the cotton couldn't calm the emotions that surged through me. I took the vest off and tossed it to the wall side. I needed to be discreet in case Tim came back early. My knickers were next to be shed. I hid my hands under the cover and they found my naked body. My breast met the bed sheet and the pillow pressed to my cheek as a substitute caress. Soon, my rubbing hands were not enough.

A faceless body pushing into me. I sought more friction. Gradually my senses heightened when I could in my mind's eye see the body that defined pleasure. I gasped but I still suppressed any noises I was issuing. She had gentle curves and hard lines. Beautiful amber eyes and firm muscles pressed against me. I gripped her head, threading my fingertips through the short stubble, and clenched my jaw as the two contrasting shades of our bodies collided. I thrust harder and harder until white spots like melting snow appeared in front of my eyes.

Her image crystallised, seeped into my consciousness, my dreams, and my world turned upside down.

DAY 8

OVER THE FIRST week, we'd settled into a routine, which was great for Lucian's sensibility. He still stared at his timetable every day and frowned if there was a slight variation. I hated to break it to him, but Sam was a pragmatist, which meant Lucian might have to force himself to be just that little bit flexible. Otherwise, I let him win the small battles.

"Would you like some orange juice?" I filled a jug for our lunch.

"Would you like some orange juice?" Lucian stared at the glass with his big eyes.

All of a sudden, I saw through the clear blue. There was so much intelligence inside of him, bursting to be let out, but it wasn't something most people could understand. He had a differently brilliant mind that we 'real people' couldn't fathom.

"Quit it!" I bounced back. "Just drink the juice. Don't you play up your disability just to make me cross." I smiled to show that I was joking and poured him a small glass of orange juice.

Lucian sipped from his glass and grimaced. He confronted me again. "Oh, you are angry. You'll have to consult your instructions. How to deal with an autistic child one-o-one." He picked up his sandwich—ham and cheese, no extras—and took a bite.

I feigned annoyance. "Ha-ha. Very funny. Just finish your lunch."

"Good job I'm eating a sandwich. We won't have another fork incident, will we?"

I narrowed my eyes at his cheek, but I secretly enjoyed the teasing. "I think I much prefer the rigid Lucian. I thought I'd never get a laugh from you."

"I am still special needs Lucian." He bit into the sandwich with glee.

I hated that he was teased. "Don't call yourself that."

"Just special Lucian, then." He finished the juice and made another face.

I'd grown to see him that way too. "That's better."

His hand flapped once, as if it was betraying how Lucian was pleased with the nickname. He looked away.

The one pastime I had during the camp was completely Sam related. Spotting her whenever I went into group activities was fun. She would have stood out, of course, even if she was not the tallest. The two male volunteers were at least her height. In turn, I wanted her to pay attention to me while I worried that I was being too obvious to the other volunteers. I'd found out that I was the youngest of the helpers, and they would more than likely think I was being an easily impressionable kid.

I needed to find myself a nook in the extensive grounds of the camp to have a breather, to think about my newfound infatuation. The massive weeping willow tree by the stream became my sanctuary. I took breaks under it whenever I could, seeking shelter among its long hairy branches and imagining no one could see me. Inhaling the grassy scent and seeking respite from the summer heat, I'd close my eyes and have imaginary conversations with my friendly listener.

I'm sure she's interested in me.

If you say so.

She watched me yesterday when I helped Lucian with the navigation activity.

He gave me an eye-roll. She's supposed to look after everyone. Why wouldn't she be checking up on you?

Great. What should I do now? I've no one to talk to about this.

He laughed. I'd hear him.

What do you want to do?

The internal dialogue was cruel and it never went anywhere. I always took hold of the swaying willow and rested a branch against my cheek to feel the softness, as though I was holding her warm face against mine.

Do you think she has a girlfriend? What does she look like having sex?

How I blushed when I asked my willow friend, who chuckled some more because of my idiocy. Just ask her.

Thanks. What was the point of speaking to him if he only told me what I already knew?

Apart from our secret trips out to the village, nighttime presented opportunities for us to get to know each other. The British summer would last until ten at night. The volunteers usually gathered after the guests had gone to bed. Rose or Beth would make us hot chocolate or coffee.

I took my cup of cocoa to find Tim, who was speaking to Sam. Feeling nervous, I forced myself to sit down on the bench, next to Tim and facing Sam, and tried to appear as natural as possible.

The two of them were already deep in conversation. Sam waved her arms about.

"I'm vegan." She frowned. "Killing animals is unnecessary and unethical."

Tim countered, "Okay. But you don't actually kill chickens to collect their eggs. You use milk to make cheese."

"Battery hens. Dairy cows. Farm practices are dreadful, so you may as well be killing the animals." She touched her almost bald head, ran her big hand down it. The hair was growing back a little after a week.

I quietly observed the argument. As Sam was talking, she waved her hands and the smooth tan skin stretched beautifully in the setting sun. She had this small furrow on her forehead when she made a particularly important point. She'd then hang back a little to hear what Tim said in reply. Watching her like that made me want to grab her and put my lips against her cheek or perhaps the plump lips.

Tim proffered some more facts about free-range farming.

"Oh, come on! So you're going to fatten the chicken and be very nice to lucky lickin' only to slaughter it later when you feel like a bit of free-range breast meat. That's bullshit and you know it."

Come on. There were so many possible meanings to the phrase: keep up, no time to waste, discover something new.

She may consider the recipient of the imperative foolish. Or, it could be a sexual remark. *Coming on to you.*

Tim put a piece of chicken sandwich, his nighttime snack, into his mouth.

"I'm not going to bother explaining anymore," she concluded with a sulk.

I loved her conviction, and I bought what she was arguing easily. I was silently following, discovering, finding myself ignorant. Conscious or not, her bold remarks made me notice her more. I was stunned by my wanting a girl for her sex for the first time. How her breast protruded proudly. What her nipples might taste like and how she might react to my tongue running down her arm.

Sam was persuasive, and now I felt guilty at the thought of dead meat in my mouth. I stared at my cup of hot drink. "I think I'll try being a vegetarian, too."

Sam beamed at me. Tim's eyes went from me to her face but he didn't comment.

The weather changed again, and it was torrid for three days as though it reflected my mood. I lay there at night remembering her flushed face when she was excited. Tim snored faintly, rhythmically. My hand meandered down my body. I turned and hid under the thin cover, face down. Suppressing any sounds I might make, I lifted my T-shirt and rubbed myself against the soft pad underneath. My mind drifted to her, to the silky skin and strong bony limbs. I wrapped myself around her.

No, the light was not broken, but in the darkness it had a different kind of radiance. If I seek it, I'll find it.

Life at the summer camp was intense. During the day, we didn't have time to think about much else. Minor crises were always around the corner. I knew my time there was running out, but I'd pushed it to the back of my mind, to block out the 'real life' that I'd soon return to. I couldn't envisage what it was before this, before knowing Lucian and Sam. All the days took on a vibrancy that couldn't be possible. In my mind, it was given an importance that even the three years at university wouldn't rival.

In years to come, my memory of those hazy days morphed into imagined scenes where I'd spent time in her room and we'd talked and laughed and she'd touched me. My memory told me it was all true or at least that those scenes were based on some kind of experience.

When I told my girlfriend, she laughed and pretended to be jealous. Because Sam *had* asked for me, and we'd kissed in the tiny box room that served as her temporary domicile, she made every other bed I'd sleep in take on less significance, and all other arms and legs I'd touch intimately different from hers insofar as they had come *after.*

After that year.

DAY 9

"YOU LOOK AT her all the time."

"Who?" I knew who Lucian was referring to, but I thought I'd get away with pleading ignorance. The thing was, Lucian was observant. He remembered everything and was direct about it all.

"The leader."

Lucian didn't do eye-rolling, but I could see it. He was mocking me, and I enjoyed his sense of humour. So unexpected and hidden, as though I was only allowed in through a secret door that opened infrequently.

"You make this sound like one of your futuristic dystopian sci-fis." It was his preferred genre, and he'd read the same book again and again. All his books were dog-eared and well-used. Philip K. Dick. Huxley. *The Time Machine.* Classic science fiction in paperback. I wondered what he made of it. The perpetual allegory of our present day, just like the summer camp being a concentrated form of socialisation for me, and we were controlled and manipulated by the great leader. The invisible eyes were everywhere, affecting us, as if this was a panopticon.

I wondered if there was some truth in Lucian's vision. Maybe we were only constrained by the limits of our own imagination. Were we all trapped by superimposed norms and unable to break out? He was the one who was looking at that conventional world and laughing at the 'real people'.

He stared at the table next to me for long moments. He wasn't smiling but there was a rare inflection of his lips. "I saw you and her, and the way you always follow her with your eyes. You two are like these people on television. My mum said they're love stories."

Oh, gosh. "What do they do on telly?" I shouldn't have asked one of the kids, but strangely, I felt at ease with Lucian who oscillated between childhood innocence and an all-seeing sage.

"They fall in love and stuff." *They.* I stopped for a second. Lucian knew. The one person who people probably did not expect to comprehend emotions understood my attraction to Sam perfectly. And he hadn't shown any strong reaction. He was as matter-of-fact about it as he was about how he wanted his boiled egg in the morning.

Fall in love. I blinked several times and felt wetness around my eyes.

Lucian carried on drawing his grassy field picture while talking to me. He didn't see the tears fighting to surge. Perhaps he was the last person I should be speaking to about this. About how a woman with a shaved head and a tattoo on her skull was drawing my attention.

I pretended to look at his pictures. After the lights that he kept drawing last week, we'd seen so much more this week: the moors, heather, forest leaves. Trip after trip had expanded all our horizons. The last few days, he'd been doing these intricate drawings of grass with minuscule green stems as well as the sunflowers.

"Well, what are you going to do?" He carefully put back his green pencil.

"What do you mean?" I frowned because I wasn't expecting Lucian to be interested in my personal life. But I was confused as to what he had asked me.

"About the leader." He brought a pen out of his case and added black lines on the picture. It was as if the strands of grass had come alive and they were swaying in the wind.

I gazed at his face and thought about what he might experience as love. As if he heard my thoughts, he shrugged. "Yeah, I've thought about the people on telly. I've used my right hand."

Ouch. Too much information. I coughed. But Sam said something about not being able to get social cues, though. "You're not supposed to notice these things."

"I can see the way you look at each other." He'd taught me the restriction of those assumptions. Of course, Lucian would know about love and probably crave it as much as any other boy.

"I'm sorry to assume you don't think about love."

His head remained inclined towards the drawing. Detailed strands of grass punctuated by black streaks now, separating light from dark. The blank among the colours accentuated the brightness.

"Why are you sorry? You don't know what I think about." His face was almost buried in the drawing; his hands delicately danced across the sheet of cartridge paper.

"So, what do you suggest I should do about the leader?" I found myself asking Lucian for advice. Chuckles threatened to bubble up my throat due to the irony.

Lucian stared at the spot next to my face. "I guess you can try telling her." He'd put it in such a starkly plain way, as if my willow friend had come alive.

It's simple, really.

The campfire nights were the highlights of the week. We could roast marshmallow and nuts, sit around and sing songs. The children adored it, especially the melted gluey sweets. Sam played the guitar. She had a good voice and was not afraid to launch into a song whenever it took her fancy. She was usually joined by some of the volunteers and the kids.

But the fire scared Lucian, so this was the first time he'd come out.

"Oh no. No." Lucian backed away.

"It's okay." I asked, "May I hold your hand? We can walk closer. I promise you won't burn."

Lucian stood there, his gaze fixed on the scene, considering the possibility. He held his hand out tentatively and I took it. He half wanted to try and half wanted to escape back to his room.

It wouldn't matter if he didn't join in, but I wished he could experience the campfire, something that he was unlikely to have at home.

Linking hands, we approached slowly, advancing a few inches at a time. At some point, his fingers tightened around mine. I squeezed his hand as a reassurance.

We sat five feet away where the fire didn't reach but we'd still see the glow of the flames on the others' faces and hear the songs. That was good enough for me. Lucian faced the side but the orange and yellow lit his cheeks up. He covered his ears for a while. I brought him some syrupy nuts and a hot chocolate, which he took. His hands didn't go back to protecting him afterwards.

I waited impatiently until the others had drifted to bed one by one. Lucian wanted to go and read by nine o'clock, so I took him back to his bedroom. When Tim eventually bid his good night, I was elated and uncomfortable at the same time. Sam and I were alone. I stared at the flames until my eyes hurt, but I refrained from looking at her. I understood the benefits of avoiding eye contact now. My rational self told me to return to my room and get out while I was still head above water.

She was strumming a song that I didn't recognise. Her voice wasn't traditionally trained, but it had a certain appeal—sultry, honeyed and, at this time of the night, alluring.

When Sam glanced up from playing, she caught me looking at her. So intensely. Warmth rose in my face but I hoped she wouldn't realise what it was and would put it down to the red heat from the campfire.

The light flickered over Sam's skin. Rouge. Orange. Glow. Blue streaks appeared among the flames every so often. I gave in to my urge to touch her exposed arm, tracing the light that danced on her warm flesh, and she let me. It had to be the worst cliché to imagine myself the moth flying towards the light, but the image consumed me and I couldn't turn away. My hands were clammy and I couldn't decide where to put them. I felt ridiculous all of a sudden but couldn't stop myself.

We sat so close that our knees touched.

She stopped strumming. I saw her swallow with the vague ripple of her throat. After long moments, Sam put the guitar down gently on the floor and stood. She ran back to the house and brought out two opened bottles of beer. I wasn't used to drinking and was already a little light-headed. She took a generous gulp, so I followed. I felt drunk and dizzy. When I was eighteen, I'd be tipsy after a couple of beers. I was a complete lightweight.

After swallowing a mouthful of lager, I burped.

"You're drunk!" Sam sounded amused.

I hiccupped as well, proving that she was absolutely right. Then I laughed alongside her. "I don't drink much."

"You'll have plenty of opportunities when you get to uni." She squinted at the flames that were flickering in her eyes. "The first proper drinking session I had when I was a freshman, I puked a mixture of cider and vodka. It was disgusting. I did it right at the feet of the Jacqueline du Pré statue."

"Who's Jack... Dupré?"

Sam laughed some more. "Jacqueline. I think she was a famous cellist. The music department at St Hilda—my college—was named after her. Anyway, I've not touched cider since."

She picked up the guitar again, and started to pluck the strings and hum a song. I didn't know what the song was called then, but it'd made an impression on me. So, I found it afterwards. *Perfect. It's got to be perfect.* I wondered if she'd sung it because she'd considered those moments perfect or she was lamenting about relationships in general. Perhaps she was in a perfect love affair. Or, she was warning me that I should wait for the perfect person. There was no telling.

We are forever double guessing when it comes to matters of the heart. When we are young, we may believe in perfection, but we won't know how to find it or cherish it even if there is such a thing. When we get older, after too many failures, we regret not waiting for our soul mates and no longer believe in happily-ever-afters.

In front of the campfire, I thought I was as close to perfection as possible.

The fire was crackling now while the red, yellow and orange mingled, struggling to give out more warmth. We'd waited until we could be alone, as if we had a secret pact to spend some stolen moments together. We were both overstaying, willing each other to want company.

I had been staring at her ear stud long enough. I reached out and touched it. "What does the black triangle mean?"

Sam's face turned serious for a second. "The Nazis persecuted gays and lesbians, as well as Jews. They made them wear emblems: yellow stars for Jews, pink triangles for gays and black triangles for lesbians. Well, we believe they did. It was for the asocial or *arbeitsscheu*—work-shy."

I was stunned. I learned history at school, but I hadn't a clue that they imprisoned and killed more than Jews. I thought of Jason, my gay school friend, but Sam was the first lesbian I'd met properly. Wearing the black triangle on her small shapely ear was a kind of interpellation. *Come on, I'm a dyke and I'm proud of it.* I'd never even thought that anyone should hide their sexuality but it made sense. It was defiance.

Years later I'd start doing the same: joining the Pride parade and waving the rainbow flag. At that age, I was too sheltered to know. I was bright and I'd got into a good secondary school where the few working class kids like me were the exceptions. Even so, I lacked experience or friends who were different. It made sense why I was naturally drawn to Jason.

I came back from my reflections to meet her curious eyes, light dancing in her pale-brown irises. Her face coloured golden.

"I like you like this." I couldn't work out where that came from. Speaking my thoughts was dangerous. It left me wide open but I was too drunk to think straight. I wasn't exactly socially awkward, nothing compared to what Lucian had to deal with in any case, but I was mostly quiet and reserved. I usually waited until everyone else had had a say before I piped up. That's just the way I was.

Sam smiled, the tenderness incompatible with the tough façade. She ruffled my short fluffy hair with one hand. *I like you too.* I licked my lips but refused to accept that a kiss could be negotiated. Instead, I closed my eyes, but the bright fire was already imprinted in my mind and it refused to leave.

The afterglow made me think of Lucian's drawings. "There are sixteen lights arranged in rows of eight and two columns."

She laughed. "Now you sound like Lucian."

"Yeah." Because he saw light in a beautiful way, courting it, caressing it. I didn't realise my fingertips skated across her arm up to her long neck.

She caught my hand and our linked digits were electric, as if the fire was nearer and stronger than it actually was. When she caressed the back of my hand, I gazed at the outdoor light back at the centre that was shedding an orange glow over us. A couple of moths raced towards the brightness, flapping their wings to their destiny, just like the vision I'd had earlier. I wondered if we were all animals like that, unable to control our own emotions and wanting so desperately to reach the glow in our hearts only to realise that we'd get burned and die a little in the process.

"Can I come to you tonight?"

"No, not tonight, or any night." Sam's lips thinned but her eyes sparkled. The deep amber drew me in. "You're not so much older than Lucian and Eric. I work with teenagers."

"But they let me come as a volunteer." I reasoned, "Isn't it arbitrary that they're considered disabled and need looking after, and I'm not? There must be something I'm terrible at, like I find the violin impossible to learn. Am I musically disabled?"

I smiled. I was pretty good with languages but completely lousy with sciences at school, too.

Sam returned the grin but she shook her head. "It's society's expectation that we should all be independent. Can Eric ever live by himself? Sadly, it's unlikely. Lucian, I don't know. He seems to function quite well. So, he can probably learn one day."

"Do you know much about Lucian?"

Sam shook her head. "Probably no more than you. Last year, I had a brief conversation with his mum at the end of the holiday. She was ever so grateful for the respite care. His dad left them claiming he couldn't cope with Lucian's disability. She said he was having affairs while she struggled to care for her son and was mostly housebound."

"Bastard." *Does Lucian know all that?*

Sam nodded in agreement. Her hand on mine stopped stroking. As though she needed to disconnect from me, she removed her hand. She fumbled in her pocket, drew out a cigarette, and lit it. Her gaze was drawn back to mine, though.

She sucked on her cigarette as smoke snaked up and obscured her face. After long moments, when I thought she wouldn't say anything, she uttered, "You don't lose that pure heart now."

And you could have my heart. I hated myself for wanting to get her attention that way, and braced for disappointment.

"Are you…" I hesitated. "…interested in my heart?" There, I'd confessed, and what she did with it was no longer my responsibility.

For a long moment, I thought she wasn't going to reply. She blew more smoke clouds towards the sky. After an age, and after I'd given up knowing the answer, she casually drawled, "I have this theory. If something won't be remembered after a few months, no matter how important it seems today, it's still a frivolity."

A frivolity. I wondered. Was it me, my heart or her own sanity?

Sam sighed. "You and I. We belong to that category."

I think that day, shrouded in the hazy glow of the fire that was dimming, Sam believed that. She thought I'd forget about her after the camp, like soap bubbles that were destined to evaporate. But it did mean she thought there was a 'you and I'. And if so, wasn't that important even if it was short-lived?

"I can never do anything I'd like to do with you, y'know?" Sam stubbed out the cigarette end, rubbing her trainer over it a little too forcefully.

"Why not?" She was damn clever to throw me too many balls to juggle at once. The more pertinent question here was what she'd like to do with me, but I was too distracted by her refusal.

Her face flushed, but she wasn't going to elaborate.

"You really think it's because I'm too young?" I hated how I sounded; maybe I was proving that was exactly the case.

A few days ago, I didn't even know I was into girls. And now, I was propositioning the most enigmatic woman I'd met and bracing myself for rejection. Would it matter indeed? Would I remember this in a few months, in years to come? I gazed at Sam's face intently. I couldn't tell her how shocked I was by wanting her, by finding myself needing her. And yet, it all made sense. How I'd felt like an alien in a straight world, and hadn't realised that was the case until then.

I thought about how my family might respond. I hardly saw my dad after he'd left and set up home with a younger woman. My older brother always thought I did and said things just to be different. I bet he would declare that this was the beginning of a phase. *Just a phase.* Did I wish it was only that? Would it have made things easier for me? I had no hindsight that summer. Everything was forward. Going in one direction, towards the light.

My parents and brother didn't have to live my life. I did.

Sam's sigh was almost inaudible. "You should never look down on yourself because of your youth. I'd have liked to be in your place."

"But you did imply I was too young for you."

Her warm palm moved to the small of my back, and it stayed there, with all the excitement and expectation that it brought. I'd understand later that as we age, we lose a lot along the way. People say we gain wisdom or something similar, but it never replaces what we've left behind. It's not a balance sheet.

The city, the heather, that perpetual warm sunshine in July were once experienced and then reappeared only in my dreams.

My home town would feel different after all this, too, as though the city was even more vibrant. I'd spend much of my youth roaming the canal-side bars and the rundown area with its warehouses and curry cafes whenever I was home. And I have tried to cling onto all of that.

She patted my neck a couple of times, affectionately, and then she stood up. "Time for bed, I think. The kids get up too fucking early. Come on."

She lent me her hand, this time just to pull me up.

DAY 10

Sam asked me to help her with the shopping in town. We were quiet on the drive there and in the store. She followed her shopping list efficiently and I helped. We were avoiding the awkward day-after conversation. And yet everything was still up in the air. Nothing resolved. Too many possibilities.

On the way back, she put on a local radio station. The passing sunlight through the slightly smeared window nearly lured me to an afternoon nap, but I recognised the detour. On an unfamiliar country path a few miles away from our activity centre, Sam stopped the van. A bend created a serendipitous parking space. She reversed the van with its back to the yellow field in front of it.

"Come on, a little rest?" She winked.

I was still staring at the clear blue sky when Sam hopped down from the van with boundless energy. She opened the boot up and laid out a couple of blankets in the hollow space, adding our backpacks as pillows. I was amused by what she was planning.

She lay down and patted the space next to her. "What do you think of this?" She gestured to the field and the sky, a horizon that seemed to stretch for miles.

I shook my head but joined her anyway, lying flat with my back on the blanket. It was a perfect position under the opened boot to watch the clouds flying by like white cotton. From that perspective, it was only the blue sky and our trainers floating in the air. Instead of gazing at the sun, I shifted my scrutiny to the two pairs of legs stretched out pointing to the horizon. Sam wore dark-coloured chinos. Mine were washed jeans. Our pumps in white, blue and yellow against the backdrop of the summer clouds. It was picture perfect: her dark, heavy trousers and my ripped jeans against the fields of yellow grass. We didn't speak for a long time. The idyllic scene, the colours, Sam's closeness, her golden skin would become forever etched in my memory as the summer's riches.

My willow friend was right. I wanted to ask her so many things and I should, but I didn't. I tacitly understood that it would have been a hopeless pursuit. I was off to London. She was ten years older, I guessed, and working in the North of England. We hardly exchanged much personal information. What people might ask if they were interested in each other. *How old are you? Where do you live? What's your favourite food? Would you like to go out on a date?* I wanted to keep her in a little box in my imagination, cocooned and preserved for that summer only. I didn't want to care that she had a life outside of this, whatever this was.

I loved the residual light that I'd see after staring at a bright spot for too long. *Chiaroscuro.* Light and shadow play off each other and become one.

Sam moved her leg so the toe of her left foot touched my right, our chores long forgotten. This was a hell of a detour.

We conversed intermittently about the camp.

"I don't think I'm any better than these people who look down on the disabled. At first, I was so frightened by Eric and even Lucian. I mean, he doesn't look different, but…" I admitted.

Sam turned her oval face to my side. The more I watched her, the more I realised how very symmetrical her features were.

"It's okay to be imperfect. For me, imperfection may be about doing my job badly or getting frustrated or impatient with the kids. For someone like Lucian, I don't know. He doesn't care for things that people assume we should have."

"Like what?"

Sam touched her head. "I don't know. For a teenager, maybe he should care about being popular, winning sports competitions, a first girlfriend."

"Maybe he wants those things." I thought about his drawings, his books, and the way he flapped about and couldn't concentrate except when he was drawing or reading.

"Yeah, probably." Sam sat up a little and grabbed her water bottle for a sip. "My brother Matt has Asperger's."

I also propped myself up on my elbow so I was facing her. "Is that why you've chosen to work with disabled kids?"

"I suppose. Partly. Growing up with Matt and living with his condition make me see having a disability as the norm, y'know."

I could imagine. "What's your brother like?"

"I think Matt has all the classic Asperger difficulties. He's socially awkward, can't make friends easily because he doesn't know how to empathise with others. Clumsy. Matt breaks things all the time. Direct. He was home-schooled as well." Sam inhaled. "But you know what? He has the most brilliant mind, almost like a cliché. He taught himself Japanese in three months."

How I wished I had that kind of linguistic ability. "Did he go to university?"

Sam nodded. "Matt tried for a while. He was there for a year and a half but doing the coursework and exams was too much. He just wasn't wired that way. He dropped out and went travelling. My parents were so worried about him."

"But, was he okay?"

Sam nodded. She fished a cigarette out of her bag and lit it. "Yeah, he didn't tell us much about what he'd done, but he travelled through China and Japan and learned the languages quickly. He's amazing."

I gazed at her profile, loving how her long lashes left a shadow on her cheeks. I wanted to reach out, to touch the smooth skin. But instead, I continued my enquiries in a bid to understand autism. "What does he do now?"

"Hmm. Not much. He helps my dad out with his company. It's a kind of part-time job." She shrugged and took a long drag of her cigarette.

"Lucian's just differently wired, or something like that," I mused. "I find him fascinating."

Sam smiled. "That's what I think of my brother. He's not 'disabled' so much as simply neuro-atypical. Does it make sense?"

"That's the right way to describe it. It feels like Lucian sees and interprets the world in a different way. His drawings are absolutely stunning."

She watched me for a second and took my hand into hers. I stared at our joined hands and wondered what I should do about it.

"You're doing a great job with him. It's hard to be with someone in such an intense way." *And thinking about intimacy when you know so little about someone.*

I managed to respond. "I've been really enjoying the camp even though it can be difficult at times."

From day one, I'd been dying to ask her about her tattoo: the symbol for stop. A slanted line in a circle. I touched it, and the short stubble pricked my fingertip, arousing my fascination.

Sam laughed, sounding like bells. "It says: No one should brainwash me. *Ich denke Ich bin.* All thoughts are my own. I possess my own mind. Josie, you will too. Don't let the buggers tell you what to think. Even at uni. Especially at uni." Her lips thinned into a serious long dash. A sudden determination to be this independent spirit flooded my brain.

"Do you think Lucian possesses his thoughts?"

She sighed. "Of course I do. I think it's criminal that people like Lucian are considered incapable."

I nodded in agreement.

The perfect British summer was often only a few days a year, but in that remote field we had it. Light breeze blew the thick mountain of clouds along. I felt like sleeping, imagining sheep jumping over the white fluffy cumulus.

Before I did fall asleep, she squeezed my hand once more, then released it.

"Come on. We need to head back before the kids run riot and Grant gets in a flap."

Sam stood. I looked up and beamed at her. The sun was behind her, so she appeared like a mirage. A silhouette. Black against yellow. Another icon of that summer.

DAY 11

Tim told me it was a yearly tradition when the lights in the hall were dimmed, and all the chairs were pushed back. It reminded me of school disco.

The dance hits piped out of the not-so-great music system, as Lucian had already pointed out. I was standing near the entrance waiting for him to show up, when Sam came out of nowhere and stood next to me. She refused to look at my face, though. We observed the kids, instead.

"Where did you get this muzak from?" I grinned and leaned in so she'd hear me. "It's so last year."

Sam's face-splitting laugh echoed in my head. "Look around. The kids are loving it."

The lighting wasn't like a standard club since the strobe effects were inappropriate, but there were soft-coloured lights and bubbles from a machine, and some of the kids and carers were dancing alone or with each other and smiling. Most of them were wriggling along to the ghetto blaster, currently hooked up to the loudspeakers. Even the two guests in wheelchairs manoeuvred the chairs around a bit trying to keep up with the rhythm. Their carers came along and helped them. Eric and Tim were gyrating to Abba's 'Dancing Queen', cancelling out any tics and unwanted gestures that Eric normally displayed.

My eyes shifted to search for Lucian and I saw him hovering by the far wall away from the reach of sounds and colours. I hadn't noticed him arriving. The noisy crowd would have been too much for him, but at least he was here.

I shouted into Sam's ear, "I'm going to talk to Lucian for a minute. Okay?"

She nodded and smiled, flashing her small dimples.

When I reached Lucian's side, he had his eyes closed. He looked as though he was in pain. His hands were balled into fists as if he was trying to stop them from moving.

"Hey." I had to talk quite loud for him to hear me but I was also afraid to startle him because he was standing in a way that told me he was trying to shut himself off from the rest of the room. He clearly found the noise and a hall full of dancing kids too much.

"Do you want to go back to your room?"

His eyes snapped open to reveal something unknown from a faraway place, and yet he seemed all seeing in that confined mental space. Slowly, he uttered, "I can stay. I want to try."

I nodded in agreement, grateful for his bravery. "Come on," I urged, "let us dance."

Lucian's lips lilted from his effort to smile. "I don't dance."

"Let's go through to the middle a little bit. You can keep your eyes closed and stand still. You don't have to dance. We can just listen to the music. Can I hold your hand?"

He held it out to reach for mine. His palm was clammy from worry. We headed towards the centre but kept a distance and stayed outside the edge of the main group. It wasn't the kind of music I liked dancing to either but I tried to gyrate to it. Lucian closed his eyes, as I'd suggested. I watched him as he started to subtly sway to the music. Over his shoulder I could see Sam's gaze and her faint grin. We let the moment sink in. The camp had been a place where the challenges of the outside world could not penetrate. It seemed that Lucian felt safe enough to participate.

Rebecca, a girl with Down's syndrome, walked up to Lucian and tapped on his arm. Lucian opened his eyes and squinted even though the lights were not so bright. She asked if he would like to dance with her, and he nodded; his head and right hand jerked. I created space for them and returned to the side.

I watched Rebecca and Lucian face each other and move to the sounds of nineties pop. She pasted a wide grin on her face and hopped wildly. Lucian, not looking at Rebecca directly, held his arms and fists up as if getting ready for a boxing match, but then he shifted his body, trying to keep up with his dancing companion. I smiled, wondering if he would have done this ten days ago.

I stayed as the kids started to drift off to bed. Sam had been watching the dancers with an amused smile as she leaned against the wall with arms across her front. My eyes were on her, though I tried to be as discreet as I could. Our gaze met infrequently.

Even so, her appearance next to me startled me.

"Wanna get out of here? It's not a chat-up line." I'd been the victim of her audaciousness all through the camp. How could I resist her non-chat-up?

Impulsively, I decided to take her to the stream, so my willow friend could meet her in person. After all, with three more days to go, I needed to make the most of my time with my imaginary friend.

The night walk was peaceful. The only sounds we heard were little animals and the light breeze.

"This is my spot." I waved my hand as if to introduce her to my den. The willow flowed softly. I'd come here a few times after the kids' bedtime and rested until it was time for sleep. I could stay out until nearly ten at night, taking advantage of the long summer day. After that, I'd have to use my torch.

Sam swirled three hundred and sixty degrees. She stopped and held my gaze. "Hmm. You've found an oasis." She took my hand. I closed my eyes so I could focus on the sensation of her palm.

I felt intoxicated. It was too late to worry, so I reached over and touched my lips to hers. When she didn't resist, I advanced. More, needing the return of the wet tongue.

She tasted of berries and vanilla, more feminine than her looks. The soft and lush lips pressed onto mine. I was inexperienced, though I'd kissed a boy before. I should've been thinking *am I doing this right?* But I couldn't. I needed to give the kiss all my heart and hope for the best.

My hand sought her out, resting on her neck that felt silken. How could anyone not understand the power of the connection? When two people breathe into each other seeking out what has become vital to their existence, it's no longer a simple kiss. But we always have to come apart to take a breath of air, as though we are swimming. Raise the face out of the water and catch a breath. Otherwise we drown.

Long lashes fell over her flushed cheeks. She took my breath away. Sam gasped like she needed more air.

"I won't forget this." She pulled me closer.

I thought the willow was swaying with his approval.

DAY 12

THE COMMOTION HAD escalated quickly. I ran down the corridor, through the throng of volunteers and some of the children to the wailing of Lucian that sounded like a keening animal. I found Tim among the crowd and stood next to him, paralysed as to what I could do to help.

Lucian shook his head and shouted but he wasn't making sense. He'd become a cornered creature, his territory violated by those differently reared. I could see the red rim of his eyes and the waves of his arms. The sounds he was making in between screams cut through the air like a siren.

"Damn. What happened?" I turned to Tim.

He sighed. "I think Charlotte might have used his colouring pencils without asking him. It was something small for sure."

It's not trivial. I'd been warned of this. Lucian's meltdown. Deep down, I'd been expecting and waiting for another.

A cacophony of noises was enough to unsettle anyone and certainly not helping to calm Lucian any. The kids were shouting back, all having an opinion about what had happened. The helpers offered to do *something*. Lucian had his ears covered now.

I gazed at him again; he was shaking with rage. I felt his pain. His pale cheeks were a shade of pink from the frustration and anger. He held onto his case of colour pencils tightly. It might have been a small thing for Charlotte or another kid, but it'd affected him deeply. He couldn't cope with something like that. Those pens and the personal boundary were important to him.

Sam was talking to Lucian to try to calm him down. She looked harassed since she couldn't physically constrain him. It was the first time I'd seen her appear out of control.

Lucian howled. He raised his arms over his head once more, and when he jumped with two feet and landed on the floor, the thud was strong enough to sound like a wild beast had fallen among us. He threw the case down and it fell open, the pencils scattering on the floor.

When he shakily stood back up, he grabbed his stomach with both hands as though he was in agony.

"Could we please clear the area? Now." Sam regained her composure at some point, as the kids and volunteers started to leave the corridor, going back to the day room or the bunks. At least Lucian wouldn't feel overwhelmed. I didn't leave. Couldn't.

"Sam, let me. Let me try." I stepped up next to her.

She half-turned and nodded. "You're the one he trusts."

"Lucian, buddy. Could you close your eyes for a minute for me?" I pleaded, "Please."

He looked away, unconvinced. At least he was distracted from his outburst. He momentarily stopped screaming and moving, but continued to breathe heavily, his chest heaving. Slowly, he did what I'd asked.

"How many lights? How many are there in this corridor?" I found myself closing my eyes too and trying to imagine the space.

Lucian breathed out. "Six rooms on each side. Lights between two rooms. Five on the left. Five on the right. Ten all together."

I didn't open my eyes but I could see them.

"What is the colour on the wall called?" We had looked at the colour wheel and he told me he'd memorised the numbers.

"Y11. Approximately."

After moments, I instructed him, "Now, open your eyes slowly, and breathe."

Spit had gathered at the corner of Lucian's mouth. He was still shaking with rage, with uncontrollable emotions. But he heaved and breathed out shallowly. Sam and I waited. We could see Lucian was trying hard to control himself. After minutes, he was calm enough to chance a look at me. I nodded, encouraging him.

I knelt and picked up the pencils and put them in the case, but I knew Lucian wouldn't like the disorder.

"Come on. Shall we go back to your room, Lucian?" Sam asked.

Sam and I led him back into his room. His sharers were still outside. I pulled two chairs out for him and me to sit. Sam stood against the door frame.

Lucian sat rigidly. His hands in between his thighs.

"It's okay," I whispered. He'd managed to soothe himself. I'd come to accept that meltdowns were part of him.

He slurred. "Not."

I wasn't going to argue, but instead a distraction was in order. "It's movie night. Would you like to join the others? Lucian?"

He glared at me. "No. Forty-five hours. I'll be home."

I wished he hadn't felt so bad that he was counting down the hours to go home. I wished we were enough for him. I thought he might have at least enjoyed himself a little. I felt like I'd failed him again. I blinked a couple of times; perhaps I could stop the tears prickling at the back of my eyes.

"This is a sentence. A two-week sentence and you're nothing but wardens. I hate you all." His voice wasn't accusatory. It was flat, delivered as resignation. His fists tensed. White knuckles nested on his thighs.

I exhaled. "Lucian, could I have done better?" I was still a novice at this; I'd tried to be as caring as possible. I wanted him to trust me. So as not to startle him, I gently held on to his wrists and pulled his fists away. He let me this time.

He huffed. "Don't care. It's my stupid head!" He jabbed at the side of his head and tore at a couple of the dark curls.

My heart felt the pain in those words. "You. Your head. You are not stupid."

"This." He waved his hands down the sides of his body. "This here is useless. I wish I could burst open and let everything out. Like you real people." His shoulders shook, but no tears came. He hiccupped from the earlier exertion and stared at the middle distance.

I feather-touched his shoulder with my right hand remembering how it all went wrong when I didn't respect his space. Today, he'd accepted my physical contact.

"You're not useless, Lucian."

He looked up, tears swam in his eyes but he didn't jerk away. A teardrop did fall down his cheek. "Then, why did my mum put me here? Why?" His voice shook, wavering with self-doubt.

"Your mum loves you. That's why she needs help from time to time." I was certain of that, just as I was sure of my own love and protectiveness towards Lucian. He'd have found it difficult to make the connection.

The teardrops froze on his long lashes.

He opened and shut his fists to try and relax. "My dad left because of me."

So, he heard.

Slowly, I shared my thoughts. "You know what? My dad left and it was nothing to do with me. He wanted to be with another woman." I let my tears fall, too. "I must have been hurt by his action, but now I'm glad that he's not with us. He didn't love us enough to stay, so he wouldn't have been any good if he did."

Lucian blinked.

Sam stepped up next to us. She knelt down to our level. "Lucian, I don't know your father, but sometimes people need an excuse to leave. Sometimes people are selfish. Your mum is not selfish for wanting you to be cared for by someone else for two weeks. She loves you. That much I know."

Lucian's body was finally under some degree of control. "She tells me she loves me, too." He turned in my direction. "I didn't hurt anyone this time. I tried to control myself."

I wiped my tears away and squeezed his hand gently. "Yes. That's good. You're doing great. I'm glad you can be home soon." I was proud of Lucian who'd participated as much as he could, who'd tried to overcome his disability with sheer will and determination.

I pointed to his colour pencils. "Why don't I help you arrange the colours?"

Lucian nodded and opened the case.

DAY 13

We were completing another long trek. Only seven of the kids came along, including Eric and Lucian. Seven miles across relatively undulating terrain because of Eric's leg. Tim pretty much carried him the last couple of miles. It was hard graft, a test of our resolve.

We stopped for lunch by a reservoir. Lucian sat on a rock and stretched his legs out. He carefully peeled back the wrapped sandwich before eating it. I was really going to miss him.

I closed my eyes again, and all my senses were heightened: the sun on my button nose, the sounds of birds, the herby scents. When I re-opened my eyes, I saw Lucian glancing at me sidelong.

"You got it, Josie."

I smiled back even though he wasn't meeting my gaze. Even if I could never imagine what it felt like for Lucian, I loved the way he'd taught me how to tune in to my senses. "Yes, I do now. Thanks to you. Thank you for this lovely holiday."

He flapped his hand but said nothing for a while. "I don't hate you, Josie." He turned to face the other way.

I grinned. "I know you don't."

I became acutely aware that our time was running out.

***

Sam found me while I was communicating to my willow friend for the last time. The air was damp and grassy. The weather was changing as we prepared for our impending departure from the camp.

"I'm glad I took a detour." Sam's white teeth shone in the moonlight.

Sam had one of the two single rooms. Grant had the other. I wondered what her bedroom at home was like, and thought about my small box room that I'd soon be leaving behind. It had too many unnecessary girly possessions anyway. It was time to ditch them, and other emotions that might have come with being an ordinary, inexperienced young woman who hadn't seen enough of the world.

I sat on the edge of Sam's bed and rubbed her feet. A seven-mile walk wasn't normally a problem for her or for me, but having to help out some of the kids at the same time added a level of challenge. She grinned at me. Sam smelled of sun lotion—a mixture of coconut and lemon—a culinary impossibility but I'd forever associate summer with those scents.

Nights like this reminded me of a holiday in the Far East a long time ago, where my grandmother came from. It was a few years before my father left, so I was maybe six or seven. The air was always sultry and full of the synchronic sounds of the cicadas. They were like musicians in a symphony orchestra, all playing together and the tunes rose and fell as if coordinated. In the British summer time, we could hear the sizzling chaotic noises of bugs but no cicadas. I sometimes missed the East even though my memory of it was hazy, lying dormant only in my DNA. I told Sam about that and she smiled.

My eyes were drawn to a small discoloured mark on her leg. It was perhaps a faint birthmark. It stretched two inches from her knee. My fingers danced across it.

"It was a burn. My first holiday in Tehran, and on the first night I ran into the kitchen of my grandparents' house because they told me they'd bought me sweets. I tipped the pot of hot water on my leg." Sam considered her scar. "It served me right to expose my leg."

"You were young, weren't you?"

She covered my hand with her bigger one. "Yeah, I was too young to need covering up. I still haven't done that for any religious reasons."

I couldn't imagine her doing that either. A burn, a subversive act that had left a mark.

Even though we'd walked back from the stream without verbalising an arrangement, I was still unsure if she wanted me to be there. My head was lowered so I couldn't see her face and she wouldn't realise my warring emotions, between needing to know what it felt like and not wanting rejection. But, she didn't tell me it was impossible this time. We were returning home tomorrow. To our separate lives.

Lucian to his home. A cocoon that protected him.

Sam to her work in the city.

I realised I still knew next to nothing about her personal life. I'd avoided asking questions. *Do you have a girlfriend? Will I see you again?* I'd known the answers and didn't want them. When my rational brain took over and my heart lost the battle, it'd hurt. Though not then, not when the idea of being with each other was possible.

I'd move forward with my future. When I was eighteen, it had felt like forever. I had all the silly visions: we'd keep in touch, she'd come to visit me in London and we'd hold hands and walk down the city streets and through the royal parks; she'd wait for me to finish college. I knew damn well they were all futile dreams. Our days were numbered but precious.

Sam closed the distance and wound her strong arm around my shoulders, drawing me close. "Professional misconduct. I really shouldn't," she whispered, though I heard a lack of conviction in her own words.

Well, I was a volunteer. I didn't work for her as such, and I'd wanted her. *Informed consent.* Something that an eighteen-year-old should be able to give. Except I wasn't exactly informed or experienced. I found myself chuckling and all I could say was "Come on." She giggled in return.

The bed is so small. I found myself wondering what could happen in that narrow space.

Images of sex came into my mind, but they were always between men and women. I tried to think whether I'd seen anything that suggested otherwise. A young woman coy, waiting for the man to come and undress her. I decided that this was different. It had to be, and so I wasn't going to let Sam initiate it even if she seemed more experienced. For all I knew, she might have done this with a thousand girls before me. It didn't matter at that moment because when we touched each other's bare skin, all rational thoughts vanished.

A tear escaped the corner of my eye and Sam kissed it away. She kissed me all over, and her warm, strong hands were surprisingly soft and gentle on my body. I rubbed against her, and she pushed back. We were like creatures caught up in a tide, happy to be persuaded by the waves. We let the sensations take over, knowing full well it might be the only time we'd truly be free.

As if it was hard for her to admit doubt, she swallowed hard. "I probably shouldn't have done it."

I didn't want to hear the guilt in her voice, as if she'd violated me, which was untrue. I felt elated even though my performance seemed forced, as if I was merely playing a role. Hindsight was a powerful thing that twisted our perception. For a brief moment, fear flooded into my brain. Was I only one of many conquests? Sam was one of those women who wouldn't give a shit, and I was ripe for picking. I must have shaken my head. I wanted this. My mouth on her and hers on me kissing and arousing me once more.

I wanted to avoid the whole conversation about it being my first time. That reminder of my inexperience wouldn't do. It thrilled me to see Sam fall apart and come, her face inches away from mine, her eyes half-closed. The golden brown grew in depth.

I wondered how I appeared to her. I knew my face was flushed because of the heat and the sweat, making the air in the room muggy as a swamp.

Instead, I closed my eyes and smiled. “I want to get pregnant by you.”

Sam laughed even though she tried to be quiet so no one would hear us. “That’s the cutest thing I’ve heard in a long time.” She kissed my cheek and brushed a strand of stray hair away from my forehead. “Anyway, you’re too fucking young.”

Yes, we were back to the age difference. Ten years. Later, when I’d had other partners, travelled, worked, I’d think back to that heady summer; twenty-eight would soon come to me, too. Then, I thought I loved her. I was in love. Innocent and passionate. I felt an intensity that I would never experience again.

I didn’t recognise her vulnerability, because she was the leader, and leaders didn’t falter. But she scratched her skull and sighed. “I hope it was okay. For you, I mean.”

“Why wouldn’t it be?”

“First time is important. I fear you’ve done it with the wrong person.” Her voice was a whisper.

I closed my eyes against the light from her desk lamp. It was strong, bright beyond the dusk in the room. “I’m happy. I’m glad we did it, Sam,” was my answer.

She stood, pulled on a vest and lit a cigarette out of the window. The smoke was pungent and swirly. I joined her, sticking my head out of the window into the chilled air of the night. She gazed at me intently, as if she was seeing a different person.

“Is it really Samantha? Your name, I mean.” I’d been wanting to ask that question all week.

She chuckled. “It’s Samira, actually. My mum’s Iranian.” I was reminded of her story about the family trip to Tehran.

“And I’m Jo to most people,” I replied. I liked names like that. Short, androgynous. “My gran was half-Chinese. Can you tell? I don’t have Asian facial features.”

Sam smiled. “No, I couldn’t tell, but you’re beautiful.”

I stared at the tattoo, half hidden under her short hair that had grown back a little over the past two weeks. I’d tried to remember how she looked. I couldn’t bear the acid that was building as the night wore on; I was already suffering from the impending forced separation from her.

I couldn’t stay all night. She walked me back to my room—the whole fifty yards that could well have been universes between us.

DAY 14

IN MY WILDEST fantasy, something grand—deus ex machina—would happen on the final day of the camp. But our routine seemed to continue like all previous mornings. We had breakfast. Lucian still couldn't quite stand the 'disgusting' orange juice, and he put his egg, toast and beans in exactly the same order. I helped him pack, even though everything was in neat piles already. He had a few extra stones and leaves that he'd collected, so I found a small box from the kitchen for him to put them in. The kids would leave first, mid-morning. He avoided my gaze. I wanted to tell him that he had wonderful clear blue eyes.

We stood outside the squat building. The pairs of hosts and guests said goodbye to each other. I wished I could have avoided this, while wanting to share one more moment with Lucian. He wrung his hands and shifted to the far end of the group, again.

"You'll miss me." It was a statement.

"Yes." Definitely. I'd always remember Lucian, the boy who showed me how to see with my mind's eye. "You're hard to forget, Lucian."

"And you'll remember the leader."

I didn't reply. He'd always known. Lucian was intuitive that way.

I took off my leather bracelet. I'd bought it during a music festival the year before. It had a small silver heart. I held it out. "For you. Would you like me to put it on?"

Lucian avoided looking at my face but he'd see the bracelet. "Okay." He stretched out his arm so I could put the thin strap on.

"Thank you." Lucian fingered the leather and was deep in thought for moments. He looked into his art bag and withdrew his drawing pad. He flipped through the pages and found one leaf. It was one of the beautiful sunflower drawings—the one I'd asked to keep. He pulled the sheet out carefully and handed it to me.

"For me?" My eyes widened. Tears threatened to surge.

He nodded.

I took his drawing. I wanted to tell him how much our time together meant to me. "Thank you. I'll cherish it. I'm glad to be here. Thank you for spending time with me." I probed, "You must be looking forward to going home."

Lucian blinked. "My mum needed a break. It's okay. I'm not upset now."

I stared at him and had the most urgent need to touch him. "May…may I hug you? I promise I won't crush you or anything."

He stiffened, then let his arms hang next to his sides. "Okay."

I went forward to him and encircled his tall, slender body. He tried to hug me back. His hands barely skated across my back, but it was enough.

When I let him go a few beats later, he smiled. "No meltdown."

"No meltdown." I grinned back.

"Goodbye, Josie." He picked up his holdall and turned to join the others in the waiting bus. I watched his strong back, his frame larger than his age suggested. He disappeared up the short flight of steps onto the bus.

I returned to my room and packed my bag, my mind blank. I'd been expecting this, but now a heavy load weighed on me. I took my large backpack and climbed the back of the van, refusing to search for her. Tim saved a seat for me again. I watched the landscape fly by. The sky had clouded over. The miraculous summer had come to an end.

The sky was threatening rain by the time we arrived back in the city. We stood where the van stopped, in the middle of an ugly car park on the back of Oxford Road, near the university.

Standing in the dreary concrete car park, it felt like death. Final and permanent. I didn't want us to end there. It was completely incongruent with whatever fleeting thing we had.

In my heart, I'd already begun to heal the hurt, to convince myself that this way was better, for whatever reason that only older adults would understand. It'd have been no use to explain it to my eighteen-year-old self. No use at all.

It wasn't easy to think about losing someone unless she had a name, a status. But Sam was beyond a label. And I understood too well she'd be gone forever, out of my life, after these goodbyes. I wished I could care less.

Sam kissed my cheek briefly. It was so light that a feather would seem like weight compared to it. She stood back, then, as if embarrassed. "You take care of yourself, okay?" she whispered. "Because I see your future. It's so radiant that I find it hard to watch. You keep going with that bright heart inside of you."

Tears stung the backs of my eyes. I wanted to say goodbye but the words wouldn't come, as though I knew whatever I said would seal our fate. We'd never see each other again, and by not bidding each other goodbye, we were preserving what we had. Nonetheless, sadness filled me. Deeply, overwhelmingly. I wished I could close my eyes and never see again if this was the last moment I laid my eyes on Sam.

I forced myself to open them. I was a grown-up, and grown-ups faced whatever life threw at them. I might as well start here.

Her girlfriend waited patiently in the car. Sam gazed over to her and back at me.

"Lucian means man of light. It's Latin," Sam uttered.

I managed to nod. I knew that. I also wanted us to kiss again, not a peck, but one that would have let me taste her again. Sam could see that in my face but she looked away.

"Why didn't you tell me?" I asked.

She bit her lip. "I wanted you, and you me. I think you did. Didn't you?"

Yes, I wouldn't have cared. I wouldn't have asked for a different outcome. I must have spoken aloud.

"I'm the one who's lost something. I'll miss out." She touched my arm. "I'm sorry."

"I'm not." I blinked back my tears. "And you don't get to tell me it's a silly holiday romance."

"Never." Her voice was so small but I heard it. I forced myself to grin, to show defiance.

She smiled, then, and ran over to the waiting vehicle, got in without looking back. I never asked for her number because I knew I wouldn't use it.

I tilted my head to see that the sun managed to shine through a gap in the rain clouds, and the glory hurt my eyes. I closed them and all I could see was the light imprinted in my mind. When I opened them again, their car had gone, and the tears crowded my eyes, shutting out the light. The white amidst Lucian's yellow. Since everyone from the camp had left, I let my tears fall. Yet I regretted nothing. I was crying from a grief for my childhood. But I was also happy in a way.

I'd found out that sometimes it only took fourteen days to change a life or two. I often wondered how three such disparate people should be brought together, serendipitously, randomly, and yet, our crossed lines exploded with lasting effects. It was as beautiful and exhilarating as fireworks.

My home town. It had started to drizzle. Instead of going home, I wandered around the area where Victorian warehouses had been turned into trendy shops and eateries, and apartments for young professionals. I stared at the pedestrians and felt angry. *How dare they go about their daily business as if nothing has happened.* I scanned their faces as I walked from the university through to the city's transport interchange. I knew I was close to the Gay Village. I'd been there numerous times with Jason, but I seemed to automatically dial up my gaydar. No, it was not about finding out that I was a lesbian. It was my first love. The first time

I'd given my heart to someone who couldn't reciprocate in the same way.

That became my modus operandi for many years, through college and afterwards. Sure, there were Sam-like girlfriends, wonderful companions in their own right, but no one could be the same as the first. No one could compare to her because she broke my fragile heart and brought so much wisdom to me. These women came close, but were never good enough. I'd learned to measure out my love, to rationalise, to hold back. I argued and broke up with them for no good reason. I wonder if Sam knew the effects she had on me.

I went back to volunteer for the camp the next year. *More accolade for my CV.* I recalled how I justified it. Tim was there, but I'd known in my heart that Sam and Lucian would be absent. Tim had smiled at me in the same open and kind way. *Sam's travelling the world. I've seen her photos from sunny climes. Lucky woman. She wanted to do it before she turned thirty.* Lucian and his mum had moved to Southampton where she came from. I wondered how Lucian would cope with such a big move. Not great, I assumed.

Eric could no longer come. *No, it's only for under-eighteens.* Oh, everyone grew old even though Lucian would always stay the same overgrown teenage boy in my memory. This reminded me that perhaps Lucian, too, was much taller and wiser. *Would he remember me?*

We talked for minutes about them. The camp kept us busy so there was no more time to dwell on our absent friends. One night, I sat with Tim by the campfire. Tears came suddenly. I pretended that my eyes were stung by the hot flame, but Tim guessed the real reason.

"Would you like her email?" He didn't need to name her.

I dried my face with the back of my hand. Sam was on the other side of the world, perhaps wondering what I was doing, whether I'd returned to the Peak District that summer. She might imagine my life as a young student in London, how I would date other people. Or, she might have completely forgotten about me. That would have killed me. I didn't want to write to her, pour my heart out for her not to bother replying. I couldn't bear it. Or if she replied and told me all about her adventures with another girl and pretended that our time didn't exist. No, that wouldn't do either.

"No, thank you."

"She's travelling alone." Tim cocked his head. "Are you sure?"

I understood what he was implying, but I wouldn't have changed my mind, and I didn't want to explain to Tim why not. It was better this way. Sam who took so much of me without realising. I couldn't explain to all my lovers why it was hard to love them with all my heart. I never told any of them about the true nature of that summer. Instead, I recited the way I'd come out. No, it wasn't a definitive moment. How had I known? It'd taken two weeks in the summer. Perhaps that wasn't the case. It was deeply seeded in me. Sam was only the water, and Lucian the light that helped me sprout.

For a while, I had photos of Sam on my mobile phone, but those images were grossly inadequate to represent my memory of what happened between us. Even years after I'd deleted those photos, I'd pick up a fork and remember Lucian and the way Sam's face was close to mine when she tended to the small stab wound. I'd smile and think of the teenager when I had pizza or spaghetti. In time, I'd lose the sharp edges of the visual images but something stayed with me.

A spark of light.

Pure as innocence.

~ The End ~

ABOUT A. ZUKOWSKI

I am a London-based British writer who grew up in the gay village and red light district of Manchester, UK.

I was trained in screenwriting at the University of the Arts, London; National Film & Television School and Script Factory, UK, followed by a series of misadventures as a film journalist, writer and producer of short films. My stories are based on personal and emotional experiences, and feature strong LGBTQ-identified characters.

CONNECT WITH THE AUTHOR

Blog: http://azukowskiblog.wordpress.com

Goodreads: http://www.goodreads.com/author/show/16509569.A_Zukowski

FB: http://www.facebook.com/aleksander.zukowski.353

Twitter: http://twitter.com/saszazukowski

Tumblr: http://azukowski.tumblr.com

BY A. ZUKOWSKI

The Boy Who Fell to Earth (#1 London Stories)

Liam For Hire (#2 London Stories)

BEATEN TRACK ANTHOLOGIES

BOUGHS OF EVERGREEN

A two-volume collection of short stories celebrating the holiday season in all its diversity.

SUMMER BIGGER THAN OTHERS

Fourteen short summer reads filled with friendship, romance and enough heat to make your ice lolly dribble.

LOVE UNLOCKED

A collection of seven unique LGBTQ+ short stories and novellas inspired by the Love Lock Bridge.

TAKE A CHANCE

Twelve tales of young/new adult gay romantic fiction exploring the courage needed to take a chance on love.

NEVER TOO LATE

A collection of nine stories featuring LGBTQ+ characters over the age of fifty.

SEASONS OF LOVE

A diverse collection of ten stories that prove love is as universal and as varied as the seasons.